"[A] NEAR-FUTURE SCI-FI THRILLER . . . AN EXCITING DEBUT . . . IMAGINATIVE, SNAPPY, AND INCIDENT-PACKED."
—*Kirkus Reviews* (starred review)

During the period of the hollow peace [the post–Cold War era], the seasons will change.
—Prophecy of La Salette

"RECOMMENDED . . . [Jensen] turns her talents to storytelling on a grand scale, skillfully building suspense while exploring her protagonist's inner conflict of faith."
—*Library Journal*

The first angel went and poured out his bowl on the land, and ugly and painful sores broke out on the people.
—Revelations 16:2

"VIVID . . . Lovers of tales full of conspiracy theories, technology run amok, and ancient prophecies will relish Jensen's first novel."
—*Booklist*

The earth dries up and withers, the world languishes and withers, the exalted of the Earth languish.
—Isaiah 24:4

"AN EXCITING THRILLER . . . NONSTOP ACTION."
—BookBrowser

We have to expect a day when the balance of nature will be lost.
—Quetzalcoatl

That day has arrived . . .

Books published by The Ballantine Publishing Group
are available at quantity discounts on bulk purchases
for premium, educational, fund-raising, and special
sales use. For details, please call 1-800-733-3000.

JUDGMENT DAY

Previously titled *Millennium Rising*

Jane Jensen

THE BALLANTINE PUBLISHING GROUP • NEW YORK

A Del Rey Book
Published by The Ballantine Publishing Group
Copyright © 1999 by Jane Jensen

All rights reserved under International and Pan-American Copyright Conventions. Published in the United States by The Ballantine Publishing Group, a division of Random House, Inc., New York, and simultaneously in Canada by Random House of Canada Limited, Toronto.

Del Rey is a registered trademark and the Del Rey colophon is a trademark of Random House, Inc.

www.randomhouse.com/delrey/

Library of Congress Catalog Card Number: 00-107273

ISBN 0-345-43035-2

This book was previously published under the title *Millennium Rising*.

Manufactured in the United States of America

First Edition: October 1999

First Ballantine Mass Market Edition: October 2000

10 9 8 7 6 5 4 3 2 1

To Arjuna, a rogue scholar

ACKNOWLEDGMENTS

I have many to thank for their inspiration and help. My gratitude to John Hogue for his books *777: The Millennium Book of Prophecy*, *Nostradamus: The New Revelations*, and *The Last Pope*. John's work not only kindled my fascination for millennial prophecy, but he later became a good friend and offered advice, insight, and the use of many of his prophecy translations in this work. Thanks also for permission to use quotes from the Edgar Cayce Foundation (from the Edgar Cayce Readings, copyright 1971 and 1993), and the Osho International Foundation (from Osho's book *The Land of the Lotus Paradise*, copyright 1984), www.osho.org. I would also like to acknowledge Michael Talbot's marvelous book *The Holographic Universe* as the inspiration for some of the ideas in this novel.

Among the others who helped with research on this book are Gerry Jones, Beth Farley, Norman Dizon, and Melissa Sullivan from the Archdioses Library Media Center in Seattle; Janet W. Burns, Mark Geisel, and Bernard Nadeau, who each helped with translations; Ann Weissenburger of the Rockaway Township Free Public Library in New Jersey for location reconnaissance; Jon Michael Smith and Dr. John D. Rather of NASA for their technical expertise; and Marcos Silviano at ipanema.com for his help with Rio de Janeiro research.

On a personal note, I'd like to thank Lois and Jim Gholson, Adam Bormann, and Philip Cayting for slogging through early drafts, and my husband, Robert Holmes, for listening to endless hours of brainstorming (as always). Special thanks to my agent, Shawna McCarthy, for her diligent efforts in selling this manuscript, and my editor, Shelly Shapiro, along with her reader, Eric Miranda, for their invaluable help in shaping the work and their staunch belief in *Millennium Rising*.

ACKNOWLEDGMENTS

Before these events many rare birds will cry in the air. "Now!" "Now!" and sometime later will vanish.
—NOSTRADAMUS, EPISTLE TO HENRY II

Food and Agriculture Organization of the United Nations

F A O

FOOD OUTLOOK REPORT
No. 100 Rome, May/June 2005

SUMMARY
Widespread drought, now entering its third year, leaves the world food supply in critical condition.

CATASTROPHIC DECLINE IN RICE PRODUCTION
Worldwide production of rice (milled) has fallen from 557.3 million tons in the peak year 1996 to 420.9 million tons last year to an estimated 398 million tons this year. Asia, by far the largest producer of rice, continues to face severe drought conditions in prime paddy territory.

WHEAT AND COARSE GRAIN YIELDS IMPACTED
Wheat and coarse grain yields have also decreased steadily for the past two years. The world's largest producer of coarse grains, the United States, lost yields at a rate of 10 percent each of the past two years. This year they hold steady at 237.4 million tons. Asia and Europe have suffered losses of 20 percent and 30 percent, respectively, since the drought began.

Some relief has been provided by C.I.S. (Russian Independent States), South America, Canada, and Oceania, where intense rains have produced slight gains in wheat and coarse grain productions. Total coarse grain production this year is estimated at 742 million tons (down 16 percent from 1996). Wheat production is estimated at 514 million tons (down 10 percent from 1996).

WORLD TRADE RISES AGAIN THIS YEAR BY 19 PERCENT
To offset the decline in rice production, many Asian countries have sought increased imports of wheat and coarse grains. Last year's imports hit a record high of 332 million tons. The demand is expected to rise this year to 360 million tons.

The United States raised their export levels by only 5 percent during the past two years, pointing to their lowered yields. Had it not been for the recovery of the C.I.S. region from its all-time low production levels in the mid-1990s, the trade demand would not have been met last year. C.I.S. provided 35 percent of the 139-million-ton increase in trade. The rest was provided by South Africa, Oceania, and South America, where record prices encouraged dangerous overexporting.

WORLD FOOD SUMMIT IN AUGUST
Since 1988, when FAO produced their *Projections to 2010* report, it has been recognized that we were without surplus cereal reserves and were therefore unprepared for an emergency. The stated goal of building a surplus did not occur, but the emergency did. This August a World Food Summit will be held in Geneva to discuss and hopefully address the situation, both for the coming year and the coming decade. The key issues will be how to fulfill the 360 million tons of trade anticipated this year and a discussion of Food Aid Relief for those countries that cannot afford to purchase imports at current trading prices.

ACT 1: WHITE

The great famine which I sense approaching will often turn [up] in various areas then become worldwide. It will be so vast and long-lasting that they will grab roots from the trees and children from the breast.   —NOSTRADAMUS C1 Q67

During the period of the hollow peace [the Post–Cold War era], the seasons will change.
                    —PROPHECY OF LA SALETTE (1846)

We have to expect a day when the balance of nature will be lost.   —QUETZALCOATL (A.D. 947)

[At a time when there is a] great nation across the ocean that will be inhabited by peoples of different tribes and descent . . . many nations will be scourged by want and famine.
                    —ST. HILDEGARD (1141)

All public cult will be interrupted. A terrible and cruel famine will commence in the whole world and principally in the western regions, such as has never occurred since the world's beginning.—JOÃO DE VATIGUERRO (THIRTEENTH CENTURY)

These conditions have not changed. For the hardships for this country have not begun yet, so far as the supply and demand for foods are concerned.
                    —EDGAR CAYCE (1943), NO. 257–254

The earth dries up and withers, the world languishes and withers, the exalted of the Earth languish. The Earth is defiled by its people: they have disobeyed the laws, violated the statutes and broken the everlasting covenant. Therefore a curse

consumes the Earth: its people must bear their guilt. There-
fore Earth's inhabitants are burned up, and very few are left.
                                                    —ISAIAH 24:4,6

CHAPTER 1

The first thing Deauchez noticed when he woke up was how quiet it was. He arose from his makeshift bed on the couch and went to the window of Father Espanza's office, pulled back the heavy drapes, and blinked in the glare of the midday sun. The streets of Santa Pelagia were empty. Discarded blankets in dirty doorways, food wrappers, and other, more personal cast-offs, like the baby shoe perched on a nearby flowerpot, were the only evidence of the crowds that had so recently inundated the small village. Even the thick pall of fear was gone, leaving an aftertaste like that at the scene of a day-old car wreck.

Deauchez checked his watch. He'd been out for ten hours. He wished Martinez or Espanza had awakened him, but then they wouldn't unless he'd requested it, would they? And he hadn't said a word to them when he'd stumbled back through the dark last night; hadn't spoken, hadn't even checked the statue in the vestibule. To what end? It had bled, of course. Certainly the thing had bled—his own clothes had been covered with the stuff. He looked around now and noticed that the bloodied suit he'd left on the chair had been taken by someone; somewhere a middle-aged woman scrubbed his things, watching mesmerized as the water turned red, all the while muttering breathless, endless novenas.

A shrill bleeping sounded from his black leather bag. In a moment, Deauchez had the computer on the coffee table and opened it with a single smooth gesture. On-screen was the red-capped visage of Brian Cardinal Donnelley.

"Just getting up, Michele?"

"A moment ago, yes."

"How are you feeling?"

3

"I'm perfectly well."

Donnelley managed a distracted smile. He tapped a manila folder on his desk. "I read your report. Any further thoughts now that you've had some rest?"

"I have nothing to add, Your Eminence. Except that from what I can see of the town, most of the pilgrims have already left."

"Last night's was understood to be the final message, wasn't it?"

"Even so, the crowds must have been quite eager to get home. It's unfortunate. I was hoping to interview some of the witnesses."

Donnelley leaned forward and studied Deauchez keenly. "There was something I missed in your report. You didn't specify . . . that is, you didn't exactly come right out and say whether or not you *yourself* saw . . . Well, I don't want to put words in your mouth."

Deauchez had a brief flash of the old cypress in Sanchez's field: the leaf-laden, oddly twisted top branches shaking violently in a wind that made no sound. "Nothing," he answered sharply. "That is, as I wrote there, the, the, the . . . *mood* in the crowd was thick with an almost opaque fear. Until you have been in such surroundings you really cannot imagine how difficult it is to think clearly. It was a classic case of crowd hysteria."

Donnelley was looking at him with an odd expression. Deauchez found he didn't much care for it. He told himself it was only because the lighting in the room was difficult, with the bright sun hitting him from behind. The laptop's inboard camera was not the best.

"Be that as it may, it would be more thorough, I should think, to record *all* observations from the site."

"I beg your pardon, Your Eminence, but I saw nothing of relevance other than what I already mentioned in the report: that a few people in the crowd did appear to have the wounds of Christ spontaneously appear; and that the statuette I brought from the Vatican did bleed also, apparently independently, though there was blood on my own hands so I cannot absolutely confirm. It was very dark."

"Any traces of stigmata on you now?"

"None. If there had ever been wounds they were closed by the time I got back here last night. The blood on my clothes was real enough."

Donnelley was suddenly cool and remote, as if he'd given up on his questioning. "His Holiness wants to see you as soon as you return. He wants a firsthand summary. I think he's a bit concerned about Santa Pelagia."

"I don't blame him. The situation here was extremely fragile, though it seems to be over for the moment. But . . . does that mean you won't grant my request to continue?"

"No. As you say, Deauchez, Santa Pelagia is obviously significant . . ."

"The most significant case of mass hysteria this century, if not ever." Deauchez felt a renewed sense of scholarly excitement and dread at those words, a combination this place had engendered in him from the start.

"I would be careful before you lock yourself into that position, Deauchez. This thing is not going to be easily dismissed."

Deauchez was taken aback by Donnelley's icy tone. "That's . . . why it's imperative that we learn more."

"Agreed. You know His Holiness leaves for Israel on Monday. I think he would like to make some sort of statement about Santa Pelagia before his trip. Be back by Saturday, will you?"

There was no shower at the church. Father Espanza took Deauchez across the street to the single hotel, Las Rositas Blancas. It hadn't had so much as a broom closet available when Deauchez arrived the previous day, but the recent gold boom had crashed. The owner, a short, plump man with a slickness to his hair and a toughness to his skin that spoke of cigarettes and alcohol, was not mourning the loss of business. He had the look of a man wrestling with much larger questions. He sent searching glances at Deauchez throughout the ritual of signing in, as if he wanted to question him. *Father, what do you think about . . . Did you see . . . ?* Deauchez avoided his gaze.

He was troubled about the phone call. It gnawed at him as he soaked under the hot water in his room's cracked, mildewed stall. He had the distinct feeling he'd stumbled into one of those painfully political imbroglios where fates were altered and careers ruined by a single, ill-chosen word. He'd seen it happen to others at the Vatican, but he himself had always been spared.

Ten years ago Brian Cardinal Donnelley had been a bishop teaching at the Pontifical Gregorian University in Rome, and Deauchez had been one of his favorite pupils. When Donnelley was appointed to head up the Vatican's Congregation for the Causes of Saints he'd asked Deauchez to go with him.

Any spot in the Vatican was a choice career move, and Deauchez was immensely flattered. But he hadn't anticipated how much he'd love the work or how well suited for it he'd be. As it turned out, one of the bureau's jobs was investigating supposedly preternatural phenomena presented in support of a sainthood candidate; healings, mostly, but also such Catholic standards as bilocation, the aroma of sanctity, and visions. The Church required hard-core evidence of the divine to declare a saint, and these days they were not disposed to find it. Deauchez's undergraduate major in psychology, as well as his skeptical bent, caused him to excel in his new post.

And for all these years, Deauchez had assumed that Donnelley appreciated him for *precisely* what he was: a priest more apt to find psychosis than saints. Donnelley always praised Deauchez's logic and reasoning, the "unemotional clarity" in his reports.

Until now.

There was only one main drag in town, the paving so old it had nearly reverted to baked earth. Deauchez walked it slowly, taking a foray into an alley or two and finding precious little on the other side. Not only were these nominal causeways cleared of visitors, but the locals had also gone to ground: a white face glimpsed behind a tattered curtain, a dog that darted away anxiously, the sound of a baby's cry.

It wasn't until he returned to the hotel that he noticed the young Asian man seated on a bench outside the town's single restaurant. His bronze head was cleanly shaven, his legs were tucked up under him, and his cumin-colored sari covered everything except his bare right shoulder and arm.

"Hello. I'm glad to see someone's still here," Deauchez greeted the man in English.

The man's peaceful smile widened. "Hallo."

"Have you been in town long? " he asked, trying Spanish.

It was no use; the man only grinned at him blankly.

Admitting defeat, Deauchez went into the restaurant. A young waitress glanced up skittishly at the sound of the screen door. The place was otherwise empty except for a lone black man who occupied a table near the window.

"How ya doin', Father?" the man said. He looked anxious for

conversation. He looked as interested in sitting alone as Deauchez was.

"Mind if I join you?" the priest asked.

"Hey, yeah, no problem! Goddamn ghost town around here,
huh?—Oh, sorry."

Deauchez drew up a cane chair. "So it is—Coffee please, uh,
café con leche y dos huevos, favor," he told the waitress. He
turned to his companion. "Are you on a pilgrimage?"

"Me? No. Reporter. Simon Hill, *New York Times.*" The man
held out his hand and Deauchez shook it. Hill looked to be in his
early thirties, just a few years younger than Deauchez himself.
He was on the heavy side, with dark, babyish skin on his round
face, and wire glasses that badly needed cleaning.

"*New York Times.* That is a good post, Mr. Hill."

"Most of the time. Where ya from, Father?"

"France, originally," Deauchez evaded. "I came to see what
all the fuss was about. I assume for you it's the same?"

"So you weren't, like, brought here by a vision?"

Deauchez laughed. "No. And you?"

"Just doin' my job. My editor sent me down."

The girl brought Deauchez's coffee and refilled Hill's cup.

"Have you heard anything official from the Vatican yet, Father?"

"I'm afraid not."

Hill leaned forward intently. "So what're they gonna say?
Some of the people here weren't even Catholic. I mean, they
weren't even seeing the Virgin Mary, they were seeing Hindu
gods and stuff."

Deauchez looked up sharply from stirring his coffee. "Oh?
Who did you talk to?"

Hill shrugged. "Actually, most people I talked to didn't see
anything. I mean, they saw like a light or something, but not, you
know, Mary or anything. But I heard that some of the people
who *were* seeing visions, weren't seeing Mary. I heard one
woman talking about Isis or something."

"You did not speak with any of them personally?"

"Not exactly. I had a couple of them pointed out to me, but
usually there was a language problem or . . . well, the few that
did speak English were too freaked out to talk about it." Hill
looked disappointed. "I only got here two days ago and there
were so many damn people around. Most of them were locals,
anyway. Gawkers."

"I heard that the first ones to arrive were foreigners who claimed a vision led them here," Deauchez said casually, stirring his cup.

"That's what I heard."

"You didn't get any more details? How many there were? Where they were from?"

"Not . . . not really." The reporter's voice held a trace of hesitation.

He probably wasn't used to being on the receiving end of such questioning, Deauchez thought. He relented while his salsa-covered eggs were delivered and tasted, his French palate struggling with the unaccustomed spice.

Hill cleared his throat. "Don't mean to, like, ruin your eggs or anything, but what did you think of the miracles? Did you see 'em?"

"I thought I saw a few cases of stigmata in the field, yes," Deauchez answered neutrally. "Yourself ?"

Hill nodded. He continued to nod, his eyes staring out at the street. "Damn weird. We got some of it on tape. We filmed the statue in the church bleeding, too."

"Have you ever studied stigmatics, Mr. Hill?"

"No."

"The first one was St. Francis of Assisi. He displayed the signs of Christ's passion on his hands and feet. After he died others also exhibited the phenomenon, though it's quite rare."

"It's linked to hysteria, right?" The reporter looked at him slyly. "Or is that heresy?"

Deauchez smiled. "Not to me. Stigmatics are classic hysterics, which is to say that they have an enormous capacity for emotion and imagination. They are not just pious, they are fanatically devout, even to the point of flagellating themselves and others. Not something the church prints up brochures about, but I assure you it's true."

Hill perked up. "If stigmata's so rare, how come so many people got it here?"

" 'So many' is relative. I would say ten to twenty people showed signs of it last night, *oui*? Out of . . . shall we say two thousand? Given the mass fear and excitement of the crowd, it's not all that inexplicable."

"What about the statues?"

"Bleeding statues and paintings are actually *more* common than stigmata, though they are usually fraudulent."

Hill was frowning, perhaps at Deauchez's explanation or perhaps at his own thoughts. "Even assuming your mind could cause wounds to open in your own flesh, how could it produce blood on a statue across town?"

It was a question Deauchez himself was interested in. "Stigmata-hysteria linked with telekinesis? I honestly don't know. But a few classic stigmatics have not only caused statues to bleed, they went for years without food—a feat we call *inedia*. It, too, implies some kind of matter transference, although it's possible a few of those good saints were sneaking down to the kitchen."

Deauchez smiled, but the reporter apparently didn't get it.

"Huh. Do you think the original people that showed up—the foreigners—could all have been hysterics?"

"Unlikely. Not only is it rare, it's a phenomenon reserved for Catholics."

Deauchez began looking around for the waitress. The reporter had managed to turn the tide, and the priest was now on the losing end of this information exchange. It was probably ill-advised to be talking to the press in any case.

"Father, you answered the wrong question. I asked if the first ones could all have been hysterics, not stigmatics. The thing is, at least a couple of those people, the first ones, they were *famous*."

Deauchez's hand, which had been trying to get the girl's attention, dropped as Hill's words registered. "Famous? Are you referring to Maria Sanchez?"

"Not just her. I mean, she's not even really famous, is she? Or wasn't. Probably will be now. No, I mean, like major personalities. I saw a few faces in the crowd I'd seen before—on the news or magazines or whatever."

"Oh? Who? Who did you see?"

Hill's mouth opened to say something, but nothing came out. After a moment of studying Deauchez he shook his head. "Man, I'm sorry. Rules. Never tell anybody your stuff before it's in print. I know you're a priest and all, but . . . you know. Just read the *Times*, okay?"

Deauchez was annoyed, but he could see that the younger man was serious. "All right. Thank you for the company, Mr. Hill."

"Hey, yeah, Father—you, too. Take my card, why doncha? In case you hear any news."

Deauchez took the proffered bit of paper without much interest.

"You do have a name, right?" The reporter's eyes were sharp and inquisitive in that baby face.

"Deauchez. Father Michele Deauchez."

As Deauchez drove over to the field where the alleged visions had occurred, he was thinking about how quickly a name could change connotations. Maria Sanchez, for example. For almost a year, that name had been on one of the many case files on Deauchez's desk, and in such capacity it had provoked nothing more than mild curiosity and stress—one more thing that he had to find time to look into. Now Santa Pelagia had reached out and sucked Deauchez in as if impatient at his dawdling.

The Sanchez field bordered either side of a long dirt driveway. In the harsh, unimaginative light of day, it was nothing more nor less than six acres of parched grass. A few dozen stragglers were still camped out in the field. One family had confiscated a roomy canvas tent with COUGAR CAMP written in military-style lettering on the side. It was one of the few reminders that foreigners had swept through this field mere hours before.

The house itself was a white-walled stucco affair. According to Fathers Martinez and Espanza, Maria had married into the wealthiest family for miles around after being so instructed by the Virgin herself. She had also claimed divine direction when selecting this property, saying that the field would one day be needed for the Virgin's own plans. Her prophecy had been most propitiously vindicated of late.

Inside, the mood was that of a death vigil. Adults sat and wept or stared at nothing with swollen, blank faces. Children wailed intermittently and listlessly, not expecting a response.

Deauchez found his way down a hall lined with Catholic pictures in dusty frames. Sanchez's death would have been the crowning finale of this week's Passion play, and Deauchez's heart sank as he pushed open her bedroom door and saw a doctor leaning over the bed. But when the doctor turned, the middle-aged Sanchez was revealed to be wearing a petulant expression and a fleshy vitality that belied any such outcome.

"But I need to *see* her," Sanchez said, her whining tone evident even in Spanish.

"I understand, *Pequita*! But Dr. Janovich has patients in Washington, too. She said she hoped to be back in a few weeks' time."

Deauchez rapped lightly on the open door and they both saw him. Sanchez's face was overwhelmed with an angelic expression. "Father Deauchez, isn't it? Oh, Father, do please come in."

"*Gracias, Señora.* I hope this is not a bad time."

"Of course it is a bad time, Father. It cannot be helped. Please, pull the chair closer and sit with me."

Deauchez did as he was asked.

"I don't mean to be familiar, but we have so little time left to love one another." Sanchez reached out one hand with a grimace of pain. He took it gingerly and smiled at her.

The hand Deauchez held was wrapped in clean white gauze that precisely covered Maria's palm the way a boy might wrap tape on his hands to play football. As he looked, a bright red dot appeared in the center of the dressing as if responding to the mere weight of his gaze.

"Do you mind?" Deauchez asked, nodding at her hands.

"No, Father, of course you must. Doctor?" Sanchez held up her hands with a supplicating air.

The wounds were flowing copiously by the time the doctor finished unwrapping them. Deauchez turned one of her hands carefully, trying to see the wounds. They were on both sides of each palm, in the center, and were the size of a half-dollar. They appeared to be genuine. How deep the wounds went he could not tell without probing, and he did not need to put either one of them through that at the moment.

Looking at the bleeding palms, he had a flash of memory. *Last night.* He'd lifted his own hands in the midst of everything else in that field, and there it was, on his very own flesh—such an unaccountable, terrifying, joyous, *chosen* kind of wonder. He knew there were nuns who prayed for years for the stigmata—priests, too—yet never received it. They lacked some essential gift, some chromosome that enabled their desire to be made manifest in their flesh, that hysterical, unknown "Faculty X." And there Deauchez himself had stood, with the wounds *in his very own flesh.* But he knew better. It had been an illusion, and if it wasn't that, it was the hysteria of the crowd affecting his subconscious mind. He had not been chosen for anything.

"Thank you, *Señora.*" Deauchez nodded to the doctor and the hands were redressed. Maria bore the treatment with a pained, faraway look in her eyes.

"*Señora,* would it be possible for you to answer a few questions?"

"*Sí.*"

"Could you tell me about the stigmata?"

"It was not the first thing that happened to me. I don't know if Father Espanza told you or not."

"I would like to hear it in your own words."

"My father was killed before I was born. My mother told the Virgin that I was to belong to her because I would never have a father. The Virgin began appearing to me right away. I often saw a glowing woman standing next to my crib in the dark."

Deauchez nodded encouragingly.

"Then, when I was fifteen, I was praying every day and going to church every day, and I became very upset that other people in the village did not seem to care about God the way that I did. Some even made fun of me! Then I had the first sign, Father. On my arm, the word appeared: 'God.' "

"*Dios?* On your arm?"

"The skin raised in bumps and spelled it out: *'D-I-O-S.'* "

"And then what happened?"

"Well, I showed it to Father Espanza. I didn't know what to think! He gave me some books on saints, and I read about the stigmata. I realized the Virgin was trying to speak through me, too."

"I see."

"After a while, the name on my arm went away and I began instead to get red spots on my hands, like blood under the skin. Now they are like you see."

"Do they ever fully close?"

The doctor spoke up. "Yes. Monday through Thursday the wounds close completely."

"But today is Tuesday."

"Oh, but now they will never close again! Not ever!" Maria said tearfully.

"All right," Deauchez soothed. "Now tell me about what has happened here recently."

"The Virgin told me a few weeks ago that people would be coming. You can ask Dr. Carlos or Father Espanza, I told them!"

Dr. Carlos nodded gravely.

"I said to my husband: 'Go out and clean up the field, because soon there will be people sleeping out there and we must make it as comfortable as possible.' So he and the boys cleared away the sticks and stones."

"How did the Virgin tell you about the people coming?"

"In a dream," Sanchez said wistfully. "She said those that would be coming were the *final seeds*. The *witnesses*."

"Is that all?"

"Yes, Father."

"All right. Can you tell me what you saw in the field?"

Maria studied him. "Didn't you see her?"

Deauchez cleared his throat. "I want to hear . . . I want to hear what *you* saw."

"The Virgin appeared in the sky. She was dressed in a black robe and mantle as a token of her grief. She told me and everyone. *Revelation 16:2*."

A spike of pain passed behind Deauchez's eyes. He felt something whelming up inside him, some kind of irrational panic attack. He resisted it. "I'm sorry. Revelation . . . ?"

Maria was watching him with bright crow's eyes. "16:2."

"16:2. Yes." Deauchez cleared his throat again. "Was there anything else?"

"I am to stay here, that's all I know. Catholics of Mexico and the United States can come here to wait for the end. It is not promised that we will survive the ravages that are to come, but whether or not we are martyred, we shall soon be free."

"Ravages?"

Maria's face began to twitch with distress. "Father, do not ask me what will happen! I do not know, I'm only a poor mortal woman!" Tears streamed down her doughy cheeks. "Oh, I am so very afraid, Father! Mary, Mother of God, have mercy on those who love you!"

Maria's sobbing increased, her face reddening. Deauchez watched, at a loss for a response. He'd never been a parish priest, never learned the skills to handle situations like this, and they made him extremely uncomfortable. Watching Maria was like watching a storm build, as if an ocean of grief had found a crack in the dam and was slowly pulling down the walls. The doctor moved to Sanchez's side and mumbled calming words, pressing her face with tissues from a nearby dispenser and then, defeated, calling down the hall for a warm washcloth.

"Maria," Deauchez said with a gentleness that masked his growing unease. "I'll leave you with the doctor now. Thank you for seeing me."

Maria nodded her head but couldn't manage words. Deauchez ducked out of the room, a bit faster than was dignified, and moved toward the living room. He got a glimpse of Maria's emotional state passing like a brushfire to the others in the house. The sound of wailing swelled.

When he reached the car the sun was setting, turning the sky red. Deauchez leaned against the compact for a moment, taking deep breaths and trying to clear his head. *That fear.* It was only a small taste of what he'd felt in the field, that tingling panic that demanded to pull him along, like a river current sucking at his soul. That he'd felt it in Maria's room convinced him more than ever that she'd somehow triggered the event—triggered it, or was still manifesting something the event had planted inside her.

The first angel went and poured out his bowl on the land, and ugly and painful sores broke out on the people who had the mark of the beast and worshipped his image. Revelation 16:2. Deauchez stared at the screen of his laptop. It was perched unevenly on the hotel bed, a Bible CD-ROM spinning silently in the D drive. The pain struck him behind the eyes again. There was something about last night that made him feel ill, horribly ill. He kept seeing that damned tree, and he didn't want to think about it because it really *wasn't* a good idea. He had to stay rational, not let himself get hooked by the emotion of this thing.

He wiped his forehead and stared at the verse, trying to decipher where all this was heading. It described the pouring out of the first bowl. There were seven bowls in all; all of them plagues rained down on man during the course of the apocalypse. There were also seven trumpets, which sometimes matched up in content with the bowls and sometimes not—it was one of those inconsistencies of John's.

Deauchez was of the school that believed St. John of Patmos had experienced a classic "visionary dream," probably aided by hallucinogens. He'd risen from his sleep and written it down, trying to pull the pieces together into coherence but afraid to change much since it was, after all, God's message. The evidence was there for anyone to see. The dream imagery of Revelation was nonsensical at times—always drifting toward a pattern, then breaking down with the equivalent of a white rabbit hopping through the scene. The fact that the author had expected it to all come true in his own lifetime—sometime around A.D. 90—was yet another card against credibility.

For all of those and other reasons, the Catholic Church didn't harp on the end of the world these days. Even if the scholarly issues *weren't* so iffy, the Protestants and Pentecostals already did it better than anybody else. But officially, of course, Revelation was positioned as a quite literal description of inevitable events— there was just, as the pope himself might put it, no reason to *dwell* on it.

What else had Maria said? Something about final seeds? Witnesses? On a whim, Deauchez entered "seed/s" and "witness/es" into his Bible search routine. There were over a hundred of each individually, but only one verse contained both words. Isaiah 43:5–9. He pulled it up.

Fear not: for I am with thee: I will bring thy seed from the east, and gather thee from the west; I will say to the north, Give up; and to the south, Keep not back: bring my sons from far, and my daughters from the ends of the earth; Even every one that is called by my name: for I have created him for my glory, I have formed him; yea, I have made him. Bring forth the blind people that have eyes, and the deaf that have ears. Let all the nations be gathered together, and let the people be assembled: who among them can declare this, and shew us former things? let them bring forth their witnesses, that they may be justified: or let them hear, and say, It is the truth. Ye are my witnesses, saith the Lord, and my servant whom I have chosen.

The sound of motors interrupted his thoughts. Deauchez went to the window and looked out over the main street. Several vans had appeared, the dust from their arrival still clouding the air. A beautiful blonde was looking around the place with an expression of disappointment while her crew unloaded equipment. He recognized her first, then the van: WWN, World Wide News. Deauchez felt a flurry of irritation. He supposed it was inevitable. Simon Hill had gotten a head start on the others, but they *would* come. It was fortunate that the "visions" and the "miracles" had lasted only seven days and news of them had been slow to travel outside Mexico. Perhaps the fact that there was nothing to look at anymore would discourage the story from spreading very far.

He went back to his computer and booted up the Web. He brought up the *New York Times* page and there, close to the bottom of the list of stories, was the heading THOUSANDS GATHER FOR MIRACLES AT SANTA PELAGIA. But before he read the story, he was drawn to the headline WORLD FOOD SUMMIT BEGINS NEXT WEEK. He'd been following news of the summit carefully, and he double-clicked on the header to get the latest.

On Friday, world leaders and experts in agriculture and nutrition will convene in Geneva for the World Food Summit. President Fielding will attend, along with several of his key advisers. The White House press release states that Fielding fully supports the U.N.'s FAO, and that he's confident that the crisis can and will be dealt with. What the press release didn't say is that enormous pressure will likely be put on the U.S. at the summit, pressure to raise export levels this year in order to help those hardest hit by the drought. Last year the E.U. countries implemented modest rationing plans. Opinion polls in the U.S. are strongly against any sort of rationing, and Fielding has said that rationing in the United States is not necessary. Most world leaders will be attending, with the exception of Israel's and Jordan's heads of state, who have scheduled water talks with Pope Innocent XIV early next week.

Deauchez frowned. Why was Fielding being so stubborn about the rationing? Even the Vatican was serving more meat and less bread these days.

The Santa Pelagia story had Hill's byline.

Santa Pelagia, Mexico. One felt transported back in time to the sixteenth century witnessing the bizarre scene in this tiny Mexican village. Over two thousand people sat in a field and stared into the sky, supposedly hearing a message from God. Most in the gathering were native Mexicans, but a select group of early arrivals included Hindus, Muslims, Christians, and members of other faiths from around the world. Besides the message itself there were the "Santa Pelagia miracles" on display, including the seeping of red fluid from several religious statues and paintings in the town and the wounds of stigmata appearing on a number of those present. By late last night the crowds began to disperse, apparently satisfied that the message-giving

was at an end. Exactly what it was all about, we are sure to
soon learn. Though no one has made a public statement yet, the
presence of highly visible religious leaders such as the Reverend Raymond Stanton, a televangelist and founder of the Christ
Spirit Network, and Mohammed Khan Abeed, the controversial
African-American Muslim leader, assure that the message will
not be long withheld. Stanton's and Abeed's offices had no
comment.

Next to the body of the article was a video camera symbol.
Deauchez double-clicked on it and watched the numbers at the
bottom of his screen flip by as it downloaded. He really didn't
want to watch the thing, but he supposed he ought to know exactly what was reaching the public.

The cameraman was obviously overwhelmed himself. The
images cocked at times and wavered. The sky was nearly dark.
The lighting was bad. Still, the dim images of the crowd: people
swaying and crying out; close-ups of an old woman's face, blood
streaming down her forehead from wounds, hands clasped in
prayer and bleeding; an older man, blood dripping down his
arms; a young woman, her white dress stained red, eyes rolled
back in ecstasy . . . Yes, the video conveyed the terror all too
well. The camera swung to focus on the cypress tree, and
Deauchez abruptly terminated the playback. There was that
wave of sickness again. *Damn it.*

Catholics everywhere would be screaming for an answer. It
was up to Deauchez to make sure the pope had the right one.

Yet even as his logical mind was fuming at the press for
spreading this hysteria, he found that his emotional response
was not following the program—it was, in fact, feeling something else altogether.

It was on the tape. The stigmata. It really happened.

Yes. In some unmannered corner of his heart, he was simply
terrified.

CHAPTER 2

The Reverend Raymond Stanton threw down the *New York Times* in disgust and wrestled with one of his chief demons, that ol' entangler, Rage. Stanton knew the lineup of his own personal attacking team so well by now that he could have drawn you a picture and given you their jersey numbers. Rage, Lust, Greed, Conceit, Envy. Those were the stars, the ones who led the offensive push for Satan every time, in Stanton's own private Cotton Bowl of the soul.

Stanton was almost always trounced.

Outside the thick oak door of his office, he thought he heard the phones start ringing. It *might* have been his imagination, but there were a million or so good Christian folk out there who would soon be asking, if they weren't already, *What was a fine Southern Baptist minister like the Reverend Stanton doin' at one of them Catholic Mary sighting things?* He could almost hear the gleeful chortle of that faggot-phony O'Neal—wouldn't he get a snoutful out of this mess?—as he waved the *New York Times* around like a Christmas cracker, *Whoo-ee, that boy's goin' down!* O'Neal'd be preparing a sermon specifically to point out any possible angle on the affair, any remote drop of betrayal and pagan idolatry, that any one of Stanton's flock might be apt to miss on his or her own. Because, he would say, that was the kind of responsible guardianship that O'Neal himself practiced, but in reality it was because O'Neal couldn't keep awake a couple of thousand viewers with his show, while Stanton routinely spellbound several million a broadcast, if you didn't count football season.

Stanton's phone buzzed. The blinking light indicated the desk of his secretary, Sarah Smith. He pressed the intercom button.

"Sarah, yes, I was in Mexico. No, I *didn't* tell you. I was plannin' on it! Mohammed-on-a-motor-car, Sarah, if I could just get four or five hours to collect my thoughts, I could explain everything!"

"Mrs. Southerby just called threatening to stop payment on that check for ten grand! I'm not sure we *have* four or five hours, Reverend. If we were a bank, I'd say 'shut the doors.' "

Sarah was one of those modern young women who never missed a pitch. Stanton had learned that it was wiser to accept her suggestions than to ignore them out of what his mother called "sheer male stubborn-nation." It had not been an easy lesson.

"I need that time, Sarah. Can you help me out?"

"Just tell me this—did you see Mary?"

"No, not Mary," he snapped at her. He took a deep breath to quell his irritation. "I was plannin' to do a big sermon on the whole thing Saturday, if that idiot reporter hadn't opened his gosh-blame yap!"

"Why *were* you there?"

"It wasn't Mary, it was an angel of God. Look, I know it sounds like a load of horse manure, but this is *really* important. I need to be able to tell people my own way. You gotta buy us some time, sweetheart."

"An angel. Right. I think I can fend them off with that. Do you really think you'll have something ready for Saturday's broadcast?"

"I've *got* to."

"Right. Okay. I've got it covered." Sarah disconnected.

Stanton's finger dropped from the button dejectedly. An angel of God. Funny. He'd watched other ministers pull that trick, like Roberts with that "build-me-a-new-church-or-God's-gonna-kill-me" routine. He'd even used it himself, rather shamelessly, because—or so he'd thought at the time—if you get an idea about something, and it sticks with you, like, say, an idea about raising a couple of mil for a new satellite transmitter so that you can overpower the other guy's signal, well, who's to say God *hadn't* put it in your head? That the idea *wasn't* an angel? Up until a few weeks ago, that had been about as close to divine revelation as this good ol' boy got.

But, and here's where it got absolutely, foot-stompin' hilarious, he, Stanton, had really, *truly* had it happen this time. He'd lain in that field helpless as an infant, pants soaked in mud and, yes, even piss, tears streaming down his face, and he'd *seen the face of God.*

He began to shake, remembering it. His throat constricted and he was overcome. He went to his office door and locked it, not wanting to be seen this way. Then he crossed to those big windows of his that overlooked the park and unbuttoned his cuffs, took his shoes off carefully, and knelt down. He turned his face to the clear blue heavens and the tears began pouring down again, like a river flowin', the river of the blood of the Lamb.

HOSANNA, HOSANNA, BE YE WITHOUT FEAR, FOR GOD HAS SENT ME AND YE HAVE BEEN CHOSEN OF MEN.

He heard it still, and would hear it and *hear* it until he did his part. He'd been chosen to lead God's people, even though he didn't deserve it, and lead them he must. If everything else in his entire life had been one big bag of bull-patties, this thing shone clear: the Reverend Raymond Stanton had to lead God's children to the Rapture, and somewhere, somehow, he had to pull from inside himself the right words to make that happen, the message that would make the people believe. And as if that weren't enough, he had to figure out how to explain why it was that Catholics and Muslims and even honest-to-Jehosafat pagans had seen the angel, too.

God commit that reporter to hell for making it more difficult than it was already bound to be.

SANTA MONICA, CALIFORNIA

In the midst of the flurry that was Trish, Tyna, and Melanie, all of whom were packing boxes and issuing panicked calls to utilities and rental companies, or leaving urgent voice mails for L.C.N.'s nearest and dearest, Trent Andrews was attempting to still his mind and type up a cohesive, compelling, and urgent message to what he hoped would be the ears of the world.

It would, at least, be the ears of Internet surfers who frequented the Light Consciousness Network—one million hits and counting. It would also go out in the printed newsletter for those who wouldn't take the time to access the Web site, but might spend sixty seconds browsing a piece of L.C.N. mail at their kitchen counter—which included most of the Hollywood community.

The Light Consciousness Network boasted quite a few stars and film executives. You might even say the L.C.N. had become de rigueur in the past few years. "L.C.N." was one of the acronyms people threw around at their power lunches, and if you didn't know what it meant you were *way* out of the loop.

This sudden popularity was something Trent spent countless visualization hours trying to support while, on the other hand, using meditation to detach himself personally from it, knowing that at any moment de rigueur became passé and it did not happen quicker anywhere in the world than here, in L.A.

But that was an eventuality he would never have to face now.

"Trent?" said Tyna.

Andrews looked up and saw that a visitor had entered the room, and that the visitor was wearing a Roman collar. The priest was a youngish man, midthirties, with shortly trimmed hair and expressive eyes in the same chocolate brown, silky shade. He was of medium build and his gaze was intelligent, yet Trent sensed his aura was wounded somehow, wounded or perhaps just innocent—innocence being something Trent had little opportunity to observe in this town. Something about the priest looked European, but not Italian. Despite his many distractions, Trent realized he was waiting to hear an accent to complete the picture. He did. The priest was French.

". . . Father Deauchez," the man was saying. "I was hoping I might speak with you about Santa Pelagia."

"Sit down. Please."

The room was a mess and Melanie had to dig a chair out from under half-stuffed boxes.

"You are moving your office?" Deauchez asked.

"Yes. We're going to Sedona. It's in Arizona."

"Ah, yes. I have heard of it. They say it's beautiful."

"It's supposed to be *safe*. Did you get a message at Santa Pelagia, Father?" Trent watched the priest try to formulate an answer to this question through a haze of discomfort.

"I'm investigating the Santa Pelagia sighting for the Vatican, Mr. Andrews."

If Andrews had had the time or motivation, he'd have told Deauchez that his aura indicated he was hiding something. He had neither, and the priest hadn't come here for self-elucidation.

"So what can I do for you, Father? I'm afraid I'm really rushed trying to get this uploaded, so . . ."

"Something for your Web site?"

Trent was surprised. "Yes. Do you read our page?"

Deauchez smiled. "Only very recently, I confess. Someone in Santa Pelagia gave me a tip that a few of the early visitors might be ... well, public figures. I'm afraid I convinced the hotel owner to let me look at the register and I did some searches on the Web with the names. That is how I found *you*, Mr. Andrews."

"I'm impressed. It seems like a lot of effort, though, for what will soon be public knowledge. For the record, I'm writing the whole thing up for the Web site right now."

"Ah, but I would not have known about your Web site unless I had searched on your name, yes? One must start somewhere. There were so many people in Santa Pelagia. It was difficult to identify who might really have something to say."

"What makes you think *I* do?"

"You had a room at the hotel, so you must have arrived early. I, myself, had to sleep in the church."

Deauchez's smile and accent were charming. Andrews was struck by the man's innate sexual appeal and recognized that the collar only amplified it. Indeed, there were dozens of aging actresses who would follow just such a handsome young guru to hell and back, martyrdom and beyond, should he only beckon. Trent knew; he had built his entire organization on the phenomenon. Now for the first time he was seeing his own potency across the desk instead of in the mirror. And Trent responded, though he rarely swung that way. There was more than a little narcissism in it.

"I suppose I did arrive early," he said. He cleared his throat self-consciously. "There were only a handful of people around when I got there; a couple of Americans, a few Brits. A group from India showed up the next day. After that it gets hard to keep track."

"*Why* did you go to Santa Pelagia, if I might ask?"

Trish began taping a new box and the noise was grating. She shot Trent an apologetic look.

Trent sighed and hit CTRL-FI2 to save his file. "Look, I could use a quick breakfast. Do you mind if we hop out? There's a café downstairs."

Why he wanted to continue this discussion with the priest was a mystery. But then, Trent believed in mysteries, and in synchronicity, and in following his instincts, even when they were hormonally goaded.

Santa Monica Boulevard was as loud and colorful as ever, as if nothing ever changed.

"Has the drought been bad here?" Deauchez asked as they walked.

"Yeah. For four years now, really. We got hit a bit sooner than everyone else. Lots of neighborhoods in the hills have been lost to fire—over five thousand homes this summer alone. They've put heavy restrictions on water usage. That's why everything looks so dead. Those brown patches edging the sidewalk *used* to be grass."

Deauchez nodded sympathetically. "It's not much better in Rome."

"Is that where you live?"

"Yes."

"I wouldn't go back there, if I were you."

"I'm sorry?"

"Rome. I wouldn't go back there."

Deauchez squinted at him blankly, then a slight tilt appeared at the corner of his mouth that might have been a smile. "Oh. Yes, I see. Thanks for the warning."

The café was little more than a hole in the wall with baked goods, coffee, and a small sandwich selection. But the food was decent—lots of sprouts, veggies, and fat-free grains, and there were little metal tables and chairs outside that were made for soaking up the sun and people-watching. Andrews found it amusing that people kept staring at Deauchez. They probably thought he was dressed for a film and might be someone famous. De Niro, perhaps. Funny. People in L.A. could have green hair and no one would look twice, but an old-fashioned priest's collar was something to gawk at.

They made it through the line and carried their lattes and muffins over to a table. When they were settled Trent resumed their conversation.

"Okay. You asked me why I went to Santa Pelagia, right?"

"Yes, I did."

"You said you scanned our Web page?"

"Yes."

"So you know about L.C.N.'s philosophy about the aliens?"

Deauchez unfolded his napkin with great care. "I'm afraid it was a bit like picking up a book in the middle."

Trent began cutting up his muffin. He shrugged. "It's not that difficult, it's just cosmology. You have your saints and angels, right? So think about this. What if *you* were looking at those saints and angels, even God, from one perspective, and *I* was looking at the same beings from a totally different perspective? We'd have different descriptions of them. You see?"

"How so?"

"They're divine. Meaning they're entirely unfathomable to our minds in any case, so we just sort of pull brain patterns out of our memories somewhere and attach them to these . . . these *entities* that we are perceiving and yet don't really know how to perceive."

Deauchez thought about that one. "I think I understand."

"Well, they're really aliens."

Deauchez nodded slowly. "What makes you think so?"

"Look, people have been seeing fairies or demons or angels or Egyptian gods or whatever since the beginning of time. Chances are they're seeing *some*thing. Now all of these abductions that have been going on in the past twenty years? They're not myth, they're *real*. Some of us are just now figuring out that these beings—the ones that abduct—they're the same ones people have been seeing all along. They just called them by different names because of cultural expectations. Back then people couldn't even *imagine* space travel."

Deauchez took a bite of his muffin and pondered. "Why do *you* call them aliens, Mr. Andrews? Are they from another planet?"

"Most definitely. But they're so far beyond that, that's no longer what defines them. The point is that they're so advanced that they're like gods to us, the way that the Europeans were like gods to the primitives. And they've been around forever, I mean, at least as long as man."

Deauchez's openly accepting gaze was all the encouragement Trent needed to continue. "People don't believe, Father, because they think it's like science fiction, aliens suddenly arriving for the first time from some other planet in a spaceship. But it's *not* science fiction, it's *theology*. These are incredibly advanced beings who have been looking out for mankind, and who have literally been our 'gods,' the basis for all of our religion, since the dawn of our species!"

Deauchez wiped his mouth delicately with his napkin. "Are you an abductee, Mr. Andrews?"

"Yeah. I knew a long time ago that I'd been chosen for something. I thought it was L.C.N., but now I see that was only the beginning, only the *ladder*, if you know what I mean."

Deauchez shook his head. "The beginning of what?"

"Santa Pelagia. I was one of the seeds and L.C.N. is my sowing ground."

Deauchez glanced up sharply. For a moment only, he wore the most penetrating gaze, then he gently asked, "Could you try to think what made you use the word 'seed,' Mr. Andrews, just now?"

"I don't have to think about it. Imrlll used that word when she told me to go to Santa Pelagia. That's what I was, a seed. That's what we all were."

"Imrlll?"

"She's the head female alien presence."

The priest seemed to dismiss that tidbit of wisdom in favor of something more urgent. "Did you ever speak to Maria Sanchez?"

Trent was surprised by the question. "No. I knew it was her field, but I never got to meet her."

"Had you heard of Maria Sanchez before going to Santa Pelagia?"

"No."

"You had not read about her in the papers perhaps, or on the Web?"

"Never."

"Did you discuss this seed idea with others at Santa Pelagia?"

Trent hesitated, a bit put off by the energy of the priest's demands. "A few, yes. I mean, we talked about what was going on, didn't we? Wouldn't you? It was incredible."

Deauchez's eyes narrowed as he studied Trent. "And how did Imrlll tell you about Santa Pelagia?"

"During a visitation a few weeks ago."

"A visitation? Is that like an abduction?"

Trent sighed. "Yes. We don't like to call them abductions. I mean I do, like earlier, when I'm talking to the general public. The word 'abduction' is well known, but the connotation is negative. It implies kidnapping. We believe that aliens never take anyone against their *subconscious* desires."

The priest's expression remained neutral as he studied Andrews. "I see. Are you entirely conscious for a visitation?"

Trent shook his head. "They don't operate very well in our time-space dimension. That's why they have to take us in an unconscious state. We remember them as dreams, or they come out in therapy."

"Therapy? A therapist helped you remember this visitation?"

Trent shifted uncomfortably at the priest's tone. "Not this one, no. My therapist got me started recalling memories through hypnosis, but lately I've been able to remember visitations myself, as dreams."

"Like an ordinary dream?"

"Kind of. More vivid, though. Very real."

"And this Santa Pelagia one was like that?"

"Yes. I was taken onboard a craft and examined. Then, when I was in a very relaxed state, Imrlll came in and talked to me. She told me about Santa Pelagia and she said I was to be one of many seeds, many witnesses; that she'd be appearing to give the world a crucial message. She warned me that others would see her in different guises."

"She did?"

Andrews smiled at the priest's naiveté. "Yes. That's what the aliens *do*, they appear to people in whatever mental form of them is in that person's mind. The Virgin Mary, an angel, whatever."

"And what *was* the message of Santa Pelagia, Mr. Andrews?"

Trent looked off down the boulevard and smiled lazily. "Come on. Someone must have told you by now."

"I would like to hear it from you."

Trent waved a hand at the street. "All of these cars, all of these people running around? They think they're important, as if what they're doing today matters. It doesn't. In a very short time, all of this—Hollywood, L.A.—it'll all be gone, just like the Roman Forum, the Greek Parthenon, even Atlantis. They had their day, and now they're so much dust."

He leaned forward and locked the priest in his gaze. "This, too, shall pass away—and suddenly, and violently, and very soon."

Father Deauchez did not look surprised. "So therefore Sedona?"

Trent nodded. "I'm to get as many people to follow me there as I can, and believe me, I intend to."

Deauchez took a sip of coffee, his eyes never leaving Andrews. "So the whole planet will not be destroyed, then?"

Trent laughed bitterly. "No. This isn't *your* apocalypse, though Revelation saw part of the truth, the way you see part of God. Humankind isn't going to disappear, Deauchez, but it *will* be changed forever. The aliens have been working for years to make certain individuals ready for a shift in consciousness. Now it's time for the New Man to be born."

Deauchez put down his cup and pushed it away. His expression was inward and grim—whether with confusion or disapproval, Andrews couldn't quite tell. Trent let him stew while he finished his muffin.

"Tell me about these disasters," the priest prompted when Trent was done. His voice sounded calm, but his aura was hopping.

"*You* know the prophecies. What do you think this drought is, a coincidence? Famine will annihilate millions before we're through—maybe even billions. But hunger and thirst won't be the worst of it, not by a long shot."

"Is that all?" Deauchez was watching him keenly.

"What do you mean?"

"There is nothing more . . . *specific* in the disaster line?"

It took a moment for Trent to realize what the priest was fishing for. "Ah! You want me to tell you about the sores. Yes, it's true. It's not a *huge* disaster, but it *is* the sign."

"The sign?"

"The sign that the message of Santa Pelagia is true. I intend to publish it today in my article. Imrlll told me to get the prophecy out quickly, because it will be happening very soon, and I need to be on record when it happens. So people will believe."

"You intend to spread this message?"

Deauchez's brown eyes challenged him. Trent looked back unwaveringly. "With every breath I have."

The priest looked away, putting a hand to his head as if it pained him. He'd apparently gotten everything he wanted out of the interrogation. Trent felt oddly used.

When Deauchez spoke again it was in a weary tone of voice. "Mr. Andrews, do you realize how much damage you could do—you, and the others like you, by spreading this hysteria?"

Trent looked at Deauchez with disbelief. "*Father* Deauchez, do you realize how many millions of deaths you will *personally* be responsible for if you try to suppress this message?"

Deauchez flinched. Trent stood up and put his hands on his hips.

"In case you hadn't noticed, the ship is going down and it's time to hit the lifeboats. I suggest you lead, follow, or get out of the way. You guys try to block the doors, and you'll have a hell of a lot more to answer for than the Spanish Inquisition!"

Andrews strode away, feeling the exultation of a really *nailed* exit line. His triumph was short lived. Even as he realized that the priest was not going to stop him, was not calling out or following, he regretted the parting. There was something about the priest that wasn't easy to dismiss.

But it was too late, and too pointless, to turn around.

Deauchez was not having a good day. He sat at a bank of phones in the L.A. airport and ruminated, trying to figure out exactly where he was going next. Stanton's office had refused him a meeting. The young woman on the phone told him absolutely, positively, that the reverend was not seeing or speaking to anyone about Santa Pelagia, and that he could watch their broadcast Saturday for the official response. Abeed's office laughed him off the line. The woman there informed him that if he dared bring his "bone-white Catholic ass" into their part of town, he'd be lucky to make it to the church doors, and if he did make it inside, Abeed would probably shoot him for trespassing personally; he hated priests.

And Andrews—Andrews had called him on the Spanish Inquisition!

Deauchez had gotten a couple of other names by crosschecking the hotel registry with the Web's search routine. "Dr. T. Kratski, Moscow" was a popular book author from Russia. He'd been a physicist with the government, but had left a few years back and was now "free to openly promote" his theories. Those theories, as near as Deauchez could make out, had something to do with viewing the universe as a hologram. Deauchez fired off an order for Kratski's new book using the article's link to the publisher. Kratski might or might not turn out to be a player in this, but his ideas at least sounded interesting.

Then there was Sister Mary Magdalen Daunsey. Deauchez couldn't believe it when he saw her name on the registry. He'd questioned Martinez and Espanza and they vaguely remembered her—yes, she'd come into the church and introduced herself. They hadn't thought it important enough to mention. Obviously they had no idea who she was.

Daunsey was well enough known to Deauchez. She had either renovated or started a number of charities in Dublin: soup kitchens, ex-con reform, shelters for homeless and battered women, even job training. She was a Benedictine, and her order in Dublin had been shaken to the core by the young, fire-breathing sister in their midst. For years she rocked the convent until, finally, those who were too traditional to take her transferred and the ones who were left were practically disciples. Now she was busy rocking larger institutions.

Daunsey had charisma all right, and opinions—lots of them. The problem, as her superiors in the order soon learned, was that she uttered even her worst heresies with such youthful passion and compassion for others, and was so tirelessly driven, even obsessed, to serve the poor, that it was extremely difficult to censor her. In an ugly incident a few years back, Daunsey made a widely publicized, tearful appeal to the pope begging him for mercy on the birth-control issue. The press clip was taken outside the front door of a poverty-stricken family in which the mother had just died birthing her tenth child. Daunsey had assisted with the woman's labor for twenty exhausting hours and was covered with the woman's blood.

How did you fight someone like that? If it had been anyone else, they would have been out of the order. But for Daunsey, the best one could do was "no comment." And so she went on. He'd even heard recently that the police used her to negotiate with the IRA. Negotiate with the IRA! A Catholic nun! That was the kind of power Daunsey wielded in Ireland: even the terrorists respected her.

Deauchez knew all this in part because one of his friends at the Vatican worked in the Congregation for Institutes of Consecrated Life and for Societies of Apostolic Life—the office that monitored the Benedictines, among others—and in part because he'd found himself intrigued and always paid close attention whenever he saw or heard anything about Daunsey. In a way, he admired her, with her waiflike appearance and power-punch personality, but he thought she was foolishly idealistic. The Church was what the Church was—it was old, it was traditional. Those could be wonderful things and usually were. They could be frustrating things, too, but you couldn't change them without also ruining the things that were beautiful about the Church. It was like love, or so he imagined; you had to accept people the way they were because you were never going to change them.

But whatever Daunsey was, saint or misguided idealist, she had been at Santa Pelagia, and that scared Deauchez pretty much where he lived. He could only guess at the influence someone like Andrews wielded, but Daunsey? He knew. He also knew that if she got her jaws locking around this thing, if she *bought* it, she would shake that puppy until all of their necks were broken.

While he was thinking about it, Deauchez fired off an e-mail to Donnelley telling him he'd be dropping by Dublin on his way back to Rome and mentioning that Sister Daunsey had been in Santa Pelagia and that he hoped to interview her. He wished he could see Donnelley's face when he read it!

But Daunsey would only take a day, and Russia was too far away. That meant he still had a bit of extra time. There had to be something else he could do in the U.S. before he left.

A TV hung from the ceiling nearby. It was playing a familiar commercial that showed a man trudging through a sandy desert, dying of thirst. The man pulls out a Telegyn cellular phone and orders a pizza delivery with an extra-large Coke. Deauchez had seen the spot before and a similar one where a man on a desert island uses his laptop to catch up on some bills by connecting it to a Telegyn cellular. Telegyn had an effective slogan given the modern dependency on the Internet: "We Can Plug You in from Anywhere on Earth." Deauchez had even found himself wanting one of the blasted things.

The news returned and aired a statement by President Fielding. He said he was about to leave for the World Food Summit. He invited everyone's prayers for a productive and speedy session and made a warm appeal to Americans to "be sensitive about your use of grain products and eat a little less in the spirit of global concern."

Deauchez *hrmph*ed at this, finding it typically weaselly. Fielding's speech was obviously aimed more at the U.N.'s ears than at his actual constituents. Deauchez closed his eyes and tried to think. He could e-mail Simon Hill. Hill had implied that he knew more names, probably was working on verification before printing them . . .

But something else clicked in his brain. He opened the search menu and paused for a moment, trying to remember. He typed "Camp Cougar" but nothing was returned. "Cougar Camp" was next. He opened up the search to include all home pages, figuring it might be a small operation.

It took a while, but something did come back.

LARKSPUR LAKE, EASTERN WASHINGTON

Will Cougar felt the fire burning in his muscles—a gift from the Spirits, this adrenaline. The Spirits would give him the life force to do what needed to be done, channeling it into him so that he could, in return, channel it back out to the project at hand. He was grateful. It would be a long time before he saw much rest.

Tents were filling up in the east meadow and all along the lake's western shore. The east shore they didn't own, but Will Cougar knew that in time their tents would be lined up on that side, too. Private property, that invention of the white man, wouldn't mean anything in the days to come. Mr. Charles O. Wannemaker, the chief landowner on the other side and perpetual complainant about Cougar Camp, would have to live with that fact. Or, more likely, he wouldn't. Those who could not realign with the Sacred Path would die, if only from the inability of their minds to switch gears. Wannemaker, like so many of his race, would never be able to deal with a world that was not defined by *I* and *mine*.

"Will Cougar?"

Sacred Dance jogged up to him. He appreciated the beauty of her approach the way he might appreciate a landing bird, but with a bit more of his anatomy participating. She was dressed, as he was, in worn jeans and a Cougar Camp T-shirt. Like his, her long black hair was tied back in a ponytail. And Sacred Dance's skin tone and features reflected white blood not too far back in the family tree, as did his own. Some people commented that they looked like father and daughter. This was funny, because Sacred Dance shared his bed on occasion. Age was not something Will Cougar thought about, particularly when it came to the Spirits' greatest gift, the pairing of male and female.

"I spoke with Ben Mark in North Dakota," Sacred Dance said, just a little out of breath. "He said he appreciates the warning, and that they're ready for anything. We also notified the Sun Tribe in Alaska and Red Man's group in New Mexico."

"That is a good thing."

"And the mailing is ready to go. We're loading everything in the pickup. Brownie is going to run it out to the post office."

"Have him drive it to Spokane. It will get to the people faster if we send it from Spokane."

Sacred Dance's eyes went wide at this unexpected indication of how short the time really was. "All right."

"And send someone with Brownie. We should pick up the perishables in Spokane now. Take the list. It is in the files. Triple the quantities."

Sacred Dance nodded. Her lower lip trembled.

"You are very afraid," he observed.

"Yes. I'm sorry."

"Ask the Spirits to take your fear. Soon, you will be too busy to be afraid, and that is a good thing. You must always be too busy living to fear life, too busy dying to fear death."

"Yes, Will Cougar."

"Remember when the Spirits told us to come here? We left our home at the base of Little Sister and then Little Sister roared, just as the Spirits said."

Will Cougar's accurate prediction of Mount St. Helens's eruption had changed many things—not just their address. It had been the beginning of his acceptance as a legitimate shaman by those outside the tribe.

Sacred Dance nodded. "I remember."

"It is the same now. Keep your heart on the Sacred Path. As long as you are listening to the Spirits they will tell you what to do."

Sacred Dance smiled gratefully. "How long before they start arriving, do you think?"

"A few days. More will come in a week or so, after the sign."

"I hope we have enough room. There're only a few thousand tents and the mailing list has two hundred thousand names."

"Not all of them will come. Those who do not get tents will sleep on the ground. That is not important. What is important is that we are here together, and that we keep this area sacred through the coming storm. When it is over we can worry about building more shelters."

"Yes, Will Cougar."

Sacred Dance ran off toward the office. Will Cougar headed for the underground storage facility. He was in the cool, dim log building speaking with Jim Broken Claw about making room for the perishables when he heard someone enter.

He turned and saw a Catholic priest standing in the doorway.

"Can we help you?" Jim asked.

"Hello. The office said I might find Will Cougar here?"

"I am Will Cougar."

"My name is Father Deauchez. I was hoping to speak with you for a few moments about Santa Pelagia."

Will Cougar looked the man over and found that he didn't get any negative feelings from him, except that the man was very anxious; but then, most white men were. "I must work, but you can walk with me if you wish."

He gave Jim Broken Claw a few more words of instruction, then headed out of the building and toward the corral. The priest followed, struggling to keep up with Will Cougar's long gait.

"I read about you on the Web," the priest said.

"We don't use it."

"I'm aware of that. It was a survivalist home page. They had a review of one of your training camps."

The priest paused, but Will Cougar felt he had nothing to add so he didn't say anything.

"Are you a survivalist group?"

"We are Indians."

"Do you train a lot of survivalists here?"

"We help people remember how to live off the land; how to hunt, recognize food and medicines in the forest, build shelters. We do not turn away anyone who wants to learn."

Deauchez smiled disarmingly. "Because this home page was aggressively antigovernment. I was curious . . ."

"I have no politics, Deauchez, but if people want to learn how to live *without* the U.S. government, I think it is a very smart thing. Nothing lasts forever."

They arrived at the corral, and Will Cougar ducked through the split-rail fencing and went in among the stallions. He couldn't resist checking a few of the beautiful animals, feeling their throats and bellies for signs of swelling. They all looked healthy. Stone-Gazer came out.

"I want you to slow down the mating program," Will Cougar told him. "We may get sickness here and the newborns will have a hard time fighting it. Keep the birthrate low for the time being. Once we are certain things are over, we will be breeding all the time. And be on the lookout. If you see any signs of sickness anywhere, even in the birds or in the insects, if you smell anything unusual on the wind, move the animals inside and shut the flaps on the barn. The Spirits of the Air will be carrying bad things."

"Yes, Will Cougar."

Stone-Gazer looked nervous, as Sacred Dance had, but Will Cougar didn't have time to speak with him about it. Better he learn courage by example.

The priest was waiting outside the fence. "Will you tell me what led you to Santa Pelagia?" he asked, as soon as they began walking.

"The Spirits told me to go."

"The Spirits?"

"Yes."

"How do you talk to the Spirits?"

"How do you?" Will Cougar said with irony.

"I'm sorry. What I mean to ask is do you use any . . . substance?"

Will Cougar looked at the man sharply and didn't answer.

"It's not a question of legalities. I'm interested in the process."

Will Cougar shrugged as if to say there was nothing he could do about that.

The priest's expression belied his patient tone. "Did the Spirits tell you about Santa Pelagia in a dream or was this a waking vision or . . . ?"

"You do not understand spirit walking. Perhaps you should ask me something else."

"Very well. What did the Spirits say?"

"They said I should go there. There a message would be given. Do you not know this already?"

"What message was given to *you*?"

Cougar stopped walking and looked at the man. He was starting to feel annoyed, and that made him realize this called for more of his attention than he was giving.

"Since you ask, I will tell you. At Santa Pelagia the Spirits spoke to us, they spoke to the white man, they spoke to other red brothers from different parts of the world. It was Hopi prophecy that this would happen, that the spirits would tell the whole world, and the prophecy has come true. The Great Purification will begin very soon."

"The Great Purification?"

Will Cougar spoke with firm, clean gestures. "Hopi legend tells us that there have already been two purifications, long ago. This is the third. When people lose the Sacred Path and too many are harming the Earth, our Mother, then the Spirits must cleanse the world. It is beginning again. The Spirits will protect some humans, those who walk the Sacred Path, and we will be ready to start life over. But those who do not and cannot, they are going to die. This is not my will. I have nothing to say about it."

The priest's jaw tightened, sharpening the bones high on his cheeks. "You plan to tell people this? I noticed boxes of fliers back at the office."

"We have been preparing for this for a long time. The Spirits told us to come to Larkspur Lake. Now we have this place and we have everything we need to take care of ourselves. Those who come here may survive."

"How will people know it's true?"

Will Cougar grunted. "You know the answer. You have all of the knowledge that you need." He resumed walking.

"There is a sign, is that correct?"

Will Cougar didn't say anything.

"Is it named in the flier?" the priest persisted.

They'd arrived at a small cement bunker in the ground. Will Cougar opened the hatch, slipped down inside, and pulled it closed, leaving the dazzling, cloudless sky and the priest behind.

Deauchez found Sacred Dance back at the office. He couldn't help noticing that she was very attractive. Much of her beauty, he decided, came from a visible glow of general health and recent excitement.

He'd visited reservations in the U.S., but this place and its people felt entirely different. It was not marked government land on the map, for one thing. And they were strong here and fit and they looked extremely motivated. There was not the least scent of poverty or despair to the place. No doubt all of this had been achieved by Cougar. He was commanding in an aging Clint Eastwood kind of way. He obviously didn't give an inch to anyone.

Deauchez strolled over to a wall of the office where books were for sale—Cougar's *Walking the Sacred Path*, *A Shaman's Journey*, *The Coming Purification*.

Sacred Dance reentered the office with a flier. "I had to dig it out of the boxes. We haven't had time to print a batch for ourselves."

Deauchez skimmed through it. Yes. The sores were mentioned. Will Cougar was calling people to give up their jobs and come to the camp for good. "Where do you get the names for your mailing list?" he asked, hoping his voice didn't betray his anger.

"We have our own list, from the books and the camp. Plus, a few years ago Will Cougar bought lists from magazines—*The Modern Shaman*, *Esoterica*, magazines like that."

"And survivalist magazines, too, I suppose?" Deauchez smiled to take the edge off the query.

"A few. They like our living-off-the-land training camps, but most of our sessions draw the shaman crowd."

"I see."

"New Age people have been good to us. A lot of them come to take our spirit path training. We have a totem animal quest that's been popular, too."

"You do well, financially?"

Sacred Dance grinned. "We do *very* well. But much of it goes back into the camp and our publications. Will Cougar says it was Hopi prophecy that one day the white man would turn to the red man in order to find his soul. The white man knows technology, but the red man knows Spirit."

Deauchez watched her until she shifted uncomfortably. He realized he was staring—not really *at* her, beyond her. He was having a hard time keeping his mind focused lately.

"How does he talk to the Spirits? . . . May I ask that?"

Sacred Dance laughed. "It's no secret. A few weeks ago, Will Cougar went into the sacred hut and when he came out he told me about Santa Pelagia."

"What happens in the sacred hut?"

Sacred Dance smiled as if thinking of something pleasant. "It's dark in there, and warm and smoky. It's a good place to go and open your mind. We all use it when we want to try to listen to the Spirits' voices. Will Cougar is just better at it than anybody else."

"Smoky?"

Sacred Dance rolled her eyes and didn't say anything.

"Was there anything else about that day that you can remember? Was Will Cougar reading a magazine or newspaper, perhaps? Did he ever talk about a woman named Maria Sanchez? She has been in the press."

Sacred Dance frowned. "No. Will Cougar doesn't read newspapers much. Besides, we were busy that week—he wouldn't have had time."

"Busy in what way?"

"Some people came out and gave us shots. Hantavirus inoculations. They've had some outbreaks near Spokane."

There was nothing in any of this that Deauchez could hold on to—not a hole anywhere in the dike. He sighed. "Very well. Thanks for allowing me to speak with him."

He turned to go and felt a hand on his arm. He looked back.

"You're welcome to stay here, if you want," Sacred Dance said, her face troubled. "Maybe it would be a good thing."

He smiled sadly, touched by her concern. "I'm afraid I cannot do that right now. But I will keep it in mind."

She nodded, but her eyes said she knew better. Her eyes said she was looking at a dead man.

CHAPTER 3

"Father Deauchez!"

Simon Hill rose from his seat at the lounge table and waved Deauchez over. The priest caught sight of him and struggled through the crowd.

"Thanks for meeting me, Father. Any problems finding it?" Hill took Deauchez's overnight bag, placing it on the extra seat.

"No. It's a good thing you know the airport so well."

"What can I say—it's a second home. How long do you have?"

"An hour. My plane leaves at noon." Deauchez sat down and nodded at a second glass of red wine on the table. "Is that for me?"

"Yeah." Hill pushed it toward Deauchez. "I thought, you being French and all . . ."

Deauchez ignored the implications and took the glass gratefully. "Thanks." He took a sip. The stuff was horrid, but he needed it, nonetheless. "Your e-mail said you had new information?"

"Uh, yeah. Hey, you didn't tell me you were with the Vatican, Father."

Deauchez grimaced. "So *that* is why you wanted to meet. How did you find out?"

"I looked you up. Father Michele Deauchez. You're with the Vatican bureau that deals with saints, right? You're even said to be a favorite of the Man himself."

Deauchez laughed bitterly. "Your sources are prone to exaggeration."

"So set me straight."

"I cannot. My report is not final, and I could not discuss it with you if it were."

38

Hill's fist lightly pounded the table. "Come on! Do you have any idea how big this thing could be?"

Deauchez couldn't meet the reporter's eye. He looked at the wineglass instead. "I don't see why. The sighting is over."

"I've been checking it out! Abeed's called the press to a sermon he's giving at his Harlem church Saturday morning. He's not a nice man, Father. He's one scary person, believe me. He *sells* hate. Unless the message of Santa Pelagia has caused him to have a *big* change of heart, he could cause a lot of trouble."

Deauchez didn't say anything.

Hill went on. "And Stanton . . ."

"Is going public Saturday, too."

"Yeah. How'd you know?"

"I rang his office. Who else is there?"

"I have a few names."

"Will you tell me?"

"I'm still checking. It'll be in the paper as soon as I'm sure."

Two could play at that game. "Then I suppose I will read it then," Deauchez said dismissively.

Hill rolled his eyes. "Come on! Just tell me what you guys think. I mean, this is up your alley, right? Prophecy? Mary sightings?"

"I don't know *what* to think, Mr. Hill. And that is not an official remark, by the way."

Hill scratched his head. He had the bright eyes of a mouse searching for a crack in the footboard. "So *un*officially then, maybe as sort of an expert consultant. You know the Bible, right? Do you really think the apocalypse is coming? Will it interrupt cable service?"

Hill giggled nervously at his own remark. Deauchez did not. What he did was push his wineglass away.

"Mr. Hill, I cannot be your consultant. Do you know why? Because I don't want news stories on this event. I think it's dangerous. Do you understand? It's really *not* a good idea."

Deauchez realized that he sounded angry. *Was* angry.

Hill stared at him blankly, as if unable to comprehend such a sentiment. "Why not?"

"Do you remember what it felt like at Santa Pelagia? Are you blind? Deaf ? Did you not feel the fear there?"

Hill looked resistant, like he didn't want to think about it. "I *guess*."

"Do you know what that kind of fear can do to people? Maybe you have never seen people who are out of their minds. Panic kills. Do you want to spread it? Do you really? You can do it without me, Mr. Hill, but I do wish you would think twice."

Deauchez grabbed his bag and stood up. Even as he was letting his anger control him, he knew that it wasn't really Hill he was angry at. He was upset about what Cougar and Andrews were doing, what others like Stanton would probably do, too. Hill was only the channel—*they* were the voice.

"Hey, wait a minute." Hill smiled brightly, completely unscathed. "Just one more thing, okay? Come on, look at this."

Hill was fishing in his pockets for something. He found it just as Deauchez was about to walk away. "*Look.* Someone sent it to me anonymously. Over the Web."

Deauchez reluctantly took the piece of paper. On the e-mail header the recipient was Hill, but where the sender's name should be there was just a blank. He supposed Hill could have doctored it—after all, it was just a printout—but something told him the reporter had not.

The body of the e-mail was a quote.

Famine, plague, war; in the Twenty-Four;
Is seeded a warning for the whole world.
                    —Nostradamus

Seeded. A ribbon of ice snaked up Deauchez's back.

"Does it mean anything to you?" Hill asked. "Have you seen it before?"

Deauchez shook his head and handed the page back.

"Does it have any Scriptural relevance, maybe?"

Deauchez was walking away.

" 'Twenty-Four'—does *that* mean anything to you?" Hill called.

But Deauchez was already moving through the crowd. He did not turn around.

SOMEWHERE OVER THE NORTH ATLANTIC OCEAN

The flight to the European continent was going smoothly. The weather was clear, which is to say that they weren't flying through one of those intense, thunderous, drenching storms that seemed to be the only alternative to dry, baking heat these days.

Fielding, with his tan, lean-into-his-sixties, ex-Hamptonite body, was stretched out in a leather recliner, reading one of the endless flow of reports that trickled into and out of his briefcase like salmon heading upriver to spawn. Unlike other presidents, Fielding did not do trips like this in tennis shorts. Fielding never let down his guard like that; the most he ever did was loosen his tie. The jacket and shoes did *not* come off, not in the presidential plane, not anywhere.

The other men in the president's entourage found it prudent to follow Fielding's example. This was exceedingly to Anthony Cole's advantage. For while Ross and Macum, Connor, and even General Brant sat and sweated, visibly itching to at least roll up their cuffs in the swamplike temperatures that Fielding preferred, Cole was always as cool and powdery-dry, as impeccable as if he'd just stepped out of a *Vanity Fair* ad.

It was not the reason Cole was secretary of state, but it sure as hell didn't hurt.

The folding door between the presidential cabin and the section most of the staff were crammed into shook with a light tapping knock. Connor slid from his seat and went to the partition, opening it a pinch. He and a press undersecretary exchanged a few quiet words.

"Mr. President," Connor said, "I think we may want to turn on WWN."

Fielding glanced up without lowering the report in his hands and nodded toward the large screen on the cabin wall. It jumped to life.

"*. . . extraordinary reaction. In grocery stores across the country, people are lining up to buy as much food, particularly grain products, as they can get their hands on . . .*"

Cole felt a stab of adrenaline. His muscles tensed imperceptibly against the leather seat.

The images on the television screen showed grocery stores in the process of being gutted. Stores with eight, nine, ten checkout stands in full swing had carts backed up, clogging the aisles. The cameras caught families pushing into line with not one, not two, but three or four carts piled high with sacks of flour, cornmeal, loaves of bread, economy-size boxes of cereal, packages of meat, and everything else imaginable. Cameras panned aisles where the racks were emptying out. On the floor here and there were white piles of dust where a bag had not held up to the exuberance of the shoppers.

The report in Fielding's hand slipped unnoticed to the floor. "God*damn* it!" he said.

Cole glanced coolly at the others. Connor looked like he'd just swallowed a mouthful of shit pie, General Brant was turning purple, Ross, being Ross, looked mostly afraid that Fielding would spank him, and Macum, being Macum, just didn't get it.

"*. . . similar reports from Chicago, the Los Angeles area, the Bay Area, the Northwest, really all over the United States. Isn't that right, Marilyn?*"

"*Yes, John, that's what we're seeing, and news of the rush only seems to be making matters worse.*"

A woman in a Minnie Mouse sweatshirt blinked into the camera outside a grocery store. "*Yeah, well, I saw on the TV? That people were doing this? And I thought, 'I'm not gonna wait until there's nothin' left.' So I got in my car, you know? And came right down here? 'Cause I called my husband and he said, 'Go on and get everything you can,' that he'd pick up the kids, you know?*"

"I don't goddamn believe this!" Fielding exclaimed.

"We aired your request! I mean, it went out to *all* the major news affiliates!" Connor sputtered.

"Goddamn *civilians*! They're making China's point *for* them!" said Brant.

"Shut. Up," said Fielding.

"*. . . no word from the White House yet. President Fielding, as you may recall, is on his way to the World Food Summit.*"

"*Marilyn, any word on what started this panic?*"

"*John, from what we've been able to learn, people are very concerned about the news that broke earlier this morning: China, India, and many of the Middle East and North African countries have signed a proposal they plan to present to the U.N. at the summit. The proposal was leaked to the press. The first re-action was the commodities market dropping by fifteen percent by closing time, and now this.*"

"*For those of you listeners who haven't heard about the pro-posal, it calls for the U.N. to step in and mediate all grain distri-bution until the drought is over. The proposal suggests that all cereal crops from all countries be accounted for, and that the U.N. distribute that food between nations based on population, at a single, agreed-upon international rate.*"

"*So you don't think this rush is related to the president's ear-lier speech at all?*"

"Well, one would hope not, John. He can't be very pleased about this, having just asked Americans to exercise self-moderation. In fact, we asked some people about that specifically."

"I feel bad for the president and everything," a young yuppie-type male was saying into a microphone. *"It was a nice gesture and all, but, bottom line, the food is disappearing as we speak. I mean, I don't really think that China and Iran and those guys will get their way. Or that the drought's going to get worse. But . . . hey, I'm not taking any chances, either."*

"Turn it off," barked Fielding. The screen died.

"Mr. President," Brant said with earthshaking gravity, "I suggest that we *immediately* launch the level-one rationing program we discussed earlier."

"I don't think people would blame *you*, sir, not after this," Connor offered.

"Rationing will only promote the idea that there's not enough food in America, and that's absolutely not true!" Fielding snapped. Cole knew that what he really meant was, *Of course they'd blame me!*

The president turned to his secretary of state. "Cole? What impact is this going to have?"

The entire cabin was silent as Cole steepled his fingers thoughtfully and considered. "I don't need to mention the phrase 'bad timing.' It's a good thing you decided to make room for this summit, Mr. President. You'll have a lot more ruffled feathers to smooth now. A decisive move on your part against this . . . outburst . . . could pull us through politically."

"Do you have a *suggestion*, Cole?" Fielding asked icily.

"Yes, sir. I do." Cole's hazel eyes blinked lazily at the president's insulting tone, but his voice was calm. He told the others his suggestion, but it wasn't what he *wanted* to say at that moment. What he wanted to say was, *Yes, sir: I suggest you put your head between your legs, you son of a bitch, and kiss your ass good-bye.*

MARACAÑA STADIUM, RIO DE JANEIRO

There was a tentative knock on the dressing room door. Blade, who had his feet bent up and over in his scorpion handstand, ignored it for a moment, then slowly lowered his legs toward the floor, breathing out. The knock came again.

He finished the exhale in a burst and rolled lithely to the right and then to his feet. Fortunately for whoever was knocking, he'd been on the last posture of his preperformance routine.

"Yeah, it's open," he said. He did a few quick knee jogs in place, stretched down to his toes.

He could sense the door opening behind his bent head. Rather, he detected the increase in volume of the distant crowd and the wailing of the warm-up act. He straightened up, shaking out his muscles.

In the doorway was Nigel, his PR flunky, looking appropriately nervous about interrupting His Bladeness before it was time. Next to him was a good-looking blond bird Blade had seen around here before. She held a creature with an amazing white round face set in black fur. It was one of those Brazilian moon monkeys that had been in the press of late. The beast clung desperately around the blonde's neck.

"Absolutely fuckin' brilliant," Blade said, breaking into a grin.

Nigel flushed with pleasure and relaxed, like a dog realizing it's not about to be struck. "Thought you might like to meet our guest."

" 'Ello," Blade said to the monkey. He clucked his tongue and held a hand out. "Hey, little man."

The monkey shrank back for a moment with big, shy eyes, then made a leap of faith, grabbing Blade's finger and leveraging itself into his arms. Blade uttered a startled gasp and found himself staring into deep brown eyes six inches from his own. The monkey apparently liked what it saw, for it lay its cheek against his and put its frail arms around his neck.

Blade was charmed. "He's absolutely brilliant, isn't he?"

The blonde laughed. "It's a *she*, which probably explains why she's fallen in love with you."

"Hey, you remember Gillian? She's with Greenpeace," Nigel offered.

"Brilliant. That's absolutely fuckin' where you need to be, sweetheart."

"Yeah, well, she was thinking . . ." Nigel continued nervously, "you know, that you'd probably be sayin' somethin' to the crowd tonight, right? About the Heart of the Amazon bloody gang rape, that is."

"Absolutely, babe. You got it." Blade gave the blonde a manly, it's-under-control wink.

Nigel looked at Gillian with relief, but she wasn't having any of it. "That's great," she said. "I thought you might want to take the monkey onstage with you. The crowd would love it. And she's very photogenic."

Her eyes pinned him, level and steady. Most birds didn't get within a thousand yards of him without going all gaga, much less tell him what to do onstage. Must be a dyke with a cause, Blade decided.

"Could be fucking brilliant," he admitted warily. He studied the creature. She was very infantile, and infants were notoriously unreliable, weren't they? And there was some yellowish mucus around her small, flat nose. Getting sick? Naturally phlegmy? He didn't know, but it was too gooey for his tastes.

"You sure she won't shit, bite, run amok, anything like 'at?"

"She usually does her business right after meals," said the blonde, unfazed. "Certainly never when anyone's holding her. And she wouldn't bite or try to escape. With that crowd, you'll be lucky to get her off your neck at all."

"She *is* the affectionate one, isn't she?" Blade tickled the monkey's belly hesitantly. The monkey laid her head on his shoulder and sighed as though weary. Her bright eyes never left Blade's face. Adoration, of him in particular, always read well on camera.

He nodded. "I don't know how you got ahold of her, sweetheart, and I'd rather *not* know. I'll take her on. Nigel, have . . . uh . . ." Blade snapped his fingers.

"Gillian."

"Right! Gillian backstage. When it's time I'll come back and get the monkey. I'll take her on for a few, then bring her back and you'll get her off my neck. All right, luv?"

"Absolutely fuckin' brilliant," the blonde said.

GREENPEACE SHELTER, RIO DE JANEIRO
The television in the staff room went through its paces unobserved. The early evening news released its tidbits to no one. Next, the major Brazilian station, *Rede Globo,* covered—Live!— the preparations for the rock concert to be held this evening in Maracaña Stadium. A helicopter showed the crowds arriving for the spectacle: thousands of people, sixty thousand to be exact—a sold-out performance in Brazil's largest amphitheater. Coverage of the opening act was cut into frequently by a montage of Blade's early career. No one cared about the opening

act; it was a time to build anticipation, and the station played it well.

But this program, although earmarked for much staring this evening, had gathered no audience here. The twenty-seven-year-old staff manager, Jennifer Mallard, and the five other people in the Greenpeace shelter had forgotten all about it. They were too busy running around in a panic.

During the evening feeding it had been discovered that one of the extremely rare Brazilian moon monkeys had disappeared: Number Ten, a.k.a. Princess Di. The monkey had been so christened by an American staffer—not so much for the late British belle but for another Diana, the Greek goddess of the moon.

The truth was, if any of the other monkeys had gone missing, Jen would have simply called the police at once. But it wasn't another monkey, it was P. D., the sweetest of the lot, the girl who'd stolen their hearts. P. D. was particularly fond of the boys on the staff and of the ant-covered bananas they fed her after arguing over the privilege.

And since it *was* Princess Di, there was always the chance that someone had just . . . what? Taken her out for a stroll? Decided to smuggle her home for the evening to show the kiddies? Or something equally brain-dead?

Jen was both furious and worried. She was worried for P. D.— of whom she was particularly fond, despite her professional distance with the monkeys. And she was worried about getting in hot water with HQ. She'd worked hard to convince them she could shoulder the responsibilities of this job, despite her age and her petite size. If something happened to P. D., her superiors would assume she couldn't handle the position after all.

They'd searched every cabinet and cranny in the building ruthlessly; triple-checked the cages to make sure P. D. hadn't been put in the wrong place. Nothing. Jen gave up on finding her in the building and went to the office to start calling through the list of volunteers. She grilled them, as she had grilled everyone in the building, and with as little success. P. D. had disappeared sometime in the afternoon. No one admitted to having seen or heard anything.

Not halfway through the list, Jen observed Deirdre and Manny sneak guiltily into the staff room through the open doorway to the hall. There was nothing more they could do, of course, but they probably felt that entertainment was somehow inappropriate at a time like this. The familiar chords of one of Blade's hits echoed through the hall, a fact Jen's brain had not registered until now. So he was onstage then. Jen sighed. She had been so looking forward to the concert—if only as a breath of pop culture from home.

She picked up the phone and moved on.

She was still working through the list when a sharp scream erupted from the staff room. Jen tossed down the phone and raced, expecting the worst.

"Did you find her?" she demanded, as she and the other three staffers crammed into the doorway. Deirdre and Manny didn't answer. They were staring at the screen. Deirdre pointed a shaky finger.

There, in the arms of the mega–rock idol Blade, was Princess Di. She looked for all the world like a tiny lost soul.

"Bloody hell!" said Pritch, an Aussie.

"Oh, my God!" said Jen.

"This little baby," Blade was saying in his cockney drawl, *"is homeless now because of people's bloody greed!"*

The crowd roared.

"There's only twenty or so left of this species now, 'cepting those what fled from the bulldozers. And we don't know if any o' them will survive, what with their natural habitat being destroyed."

Princess Di, as if on cue, looked directly into the camera as it zeroed in on her. Her scared white face filled the monitor. Her eyes looked bright and feverish. She gave a heavy, heart-wrenching sigh.

"Oh, geez," Richard muttered, tears in his voice. "Give 'em hell, sweetheart."

Jen stared at him in disbelief. "Are you crazy? She's in quarantine! All of them are!"

"I know that, Jen, but . . . Christ! I hope those a-holes in the agricultural bureau are watching. I hope they get protesters up the ass tomorrow."

Jen started to retort, then closed her mouth. In truth, there was a small, irresponsible part of her that felt a similar satisfaction. But Maracaña Stadium of all places!

They fell silent and watched Blade do his save-the-Earth shtick. Princess Di looked like she was holding up all right. She just clung to the singer's neck and kept her eyes pretty much on his face. Sweet thing.

The cameras panned the enormous crowd. They were with the singer one hundred percent. They were mesmerized by Princess Di.

"*Look* at that! There're thousands of people there!" Jen wailed. "Do you know how many viruses there are in that audience, not to mention what Blade himself is carrying!"

"Dunno, Jen, I hear he's really into meditation and stuff," Manny said seriously.

Jennifer rolled her eyes. "Jesus, who's responsible for this?" She was looking at Richard.

"Don't look at me! Just because I think it's a damn fine idea!"

On the monitor, the camera was going in for another poignant close-up while Blade talked about the sacredness of trees. Princess Di sneezed.

"Uh-oh," Deirdre muttered.

"Gillian was around this afternoon," Manny said. "And I heard she had a friend on Blade's staff. She got a couple of people tickets to the show."

"Who told you that?" Jen asked.

"Um, um, um . . . Pete?"

"Rain, get on the phone and see if you can get ahold of Pete. I tried him a while back but—"

"Uh—Pete's at the concert," Manny interrupted. "I told you, Gillian got him tickets."

"Crap," Jen said. She wasn't thinking well. "Where's Gillian from anyway?"

"She's only been here, like, about a month," said Rain, a Californian. "She's from New York or something. She's *really* cool."

Princess Di was framed in the lower part of the monitor now, beneath the singer's rakishly handsome face. He was beginning a rendition of "We Are the World" when the monkey sneezed again. The singer glanced down and Princess Di met his eyes, licked some snot that had run down from her nose. Blade kept singing, but he glanced behind him, offstage.

"Jesus, you guys!" Deirdre interjected loudly. "Aren't you *watching* her?"

They looked. The cameras were panning the audience now. The crowd was on its feet, everyone singing at the top of their lungs with the rock star.

"We are the children . . ."

The camera switched back to Blade. Princess Di sneezed again.

Jen drew a sharp breath. "Oh, *Christ*! I'm going down there. Richard, call the police, tell them to meet me there. I don't know who's responsible for this, but whoever it is, their ass is going to be *deported*."

DAY 4
ROME, ITALY

Deauchez's flight into Rome touched down at 7:00 A.M. local time. The car that awaited him was not empty. Donnelley himself was in the backseat, and Deauchez knew things were going to be tense as soon as he saw him. That Donnelley, a cardinal who did not take his rank casually, would come out to the airport to meet Deauchez could mean only one thing: the pope wanted to see Deauchez as soon as he arrived at the Vatican, and this would be Donnelley's only chance to debrief Deauchez beforehand.

"Michele, it's good to have you home," Donnelley said. He embraced Deauchez a bit awkwardly from his seated position and pressed his rough cheek to Deauchez's in the adopted Italian style.

"I'm glad to be back, myself," Deauchez replied, and he was, despite his apprehension. He held his questions while the driver eased the car out of the airport loop. Donnelley would run the conversation. He always did.

"Did you get any sleep on the plane?"

"About four hours, yes."

"That's good. I'm sorry about Dublin."

"I understand that you needed me here, Your Eminence," Deauchez replied, smiling to show that he was sincere. "Has anyone heard what Sister Daunsey's story is yet?"

Donnelley looked out the window and cleared his throat. "She's here, Michele."

"She is *here*?"

"Yes. She'll be in our meeting with His Holiness. We've just been waiting for you."

Deauchez was so stunned that it took him a few moments even to form words. "I don't understand. Did she . . . *ask* to meet with him? Sister Daunsey is not an investigator!"

"No, but she was *there*. His Holiness is quite keen on hearing everything he can about Santa Pelagia, and I thought . . . Sister Daunsey *was* an eyewitness."

Deauchez stared at him. Had Donnelley himself invited Daunsey? He could scarcely believe it, nor fathom why.

Donnelley must have seen something on Deauchez's face, for he said, "Michele, this is not *your* situation to control—nor question!"

Donnelley's tone was not unremittingly angry, but it did hold a warning. Deauchez tried to collect himself. He knew he shouldn't be reacting this way, but the whole situation was so bizarre! That someone like Daunsey, a vocal, rebellious Benedictine nun, would suddenly be stealing Deauchez's own briefing with the pope! And on so critical and sensitive an issue!

"I . . . I have no idea what you want me to say."

"Just tell me what you plan to tell him, and allow me to advise you." Donnelley patted Deauchez's hand encouragingly.

". . . It is my opinion, after an admittedly cursory examination, that Maria Sanchez's stigmata are probably psychosomatic," Deauchez told the pope. The triple caveat made him sound like a complete idiot, but Donnelley had insisted that he qualify his "opinions."

Across the table, a sound escaped from Sister Daunsey. With horror, Deauchez realized it was a snort of derision. Pope Innocent XIV pretended not to have heard it. He nodded thoughtfully, one finger to his lips, as if considering Deauchez's words. "Go on, Father Deauchez."

"I'm still investigating what connection might be shared among the initial pilgrims to Santa Pelagia, the foreigners. The few I *have* met claim to have had visions or dreams telling them to go there. I thought perhaps they might have heard of Maria Sanchez through the press, and that this might have been at least subconscious inducement for their . . . visions. But I have not run across any proof that this was the case."

"And these people with the visions? What were they like?"

"The ones I know of so far include a Native American shaman, a Southern Baptist minister, a Black Muslim, and a . . . hmmm, I suppose you would say a New Age guru in Los Angeles who believes the aliens that allegedly abduct people are the same beings as our saints and angels. And then there is Sister Daunsey here, of course, although I have yet to hear her story."

"Unbelievable!" Sister Daunsey said, glaring at him with disgust. "You're makin' this up, aren't you?"

"Sister Daunsey?" the pope asked, confused.

"All of this nonsense about aliens; he's only tryin' to make these people sound ridiculous. He's tryin' to make a mockery of the whole thing!"

Deauchez felt himself flush, more at the impropriety of her response than at the insult. "I assure you, I'm being as accurate as possible."

"It's all right, Sister," Donnelley said calmly. "We already know there were people of many faiths there. The individual beliefs may seem odd, but that's not the point."

"Perhaps it is not *the* point, but it is certainly *a* point," Deauchez argued. "After all, if we are to consider the validity of God's message to Santa Pelagia, we must consider, as we do when considering sainthood, *whom* he said it *to*. Or, I should more precisely say, one must consider the reliability, the authority of the witnesses."

Sister Daunsey snorted again. "And *you* are qualified to judge that reliability, that authority? *You*, who couldn't see the Blessed Virgin when she was right in front of your blessed nose!"

Donnelley glanced sharply at Deauchez, perhaps in warning. He needn't have bothered. Deauchez could only stare at the nun in amazement. It wasn't, couldn't be, that Sister Daunsey was stupid. She wasn't even, he was certain, being *intentionally* sacrilegious. She simply had no respect for authority, nor any sense of decorum.

"Well, it doesn't sound particularly ridiculous to me, Sister Daunsey," the pope said in a cheerful voice. "I wouldn't let it upset you. Now would be an ideal time, I think, for you to tell us your story, since that is why you are here."

There was a slap on the wrist in that remark, Deauchez thought. The pope was telling Daunsey *why* she was here—to tell her story, *not*, therefore, to express her opinion. But Daunsey seemed oblivious.

"*Papa*, I saw the Virgin in a dream. I'm *not* hysterical, which I'm sure is the opinion of Father Deauchez. Psychologist priests think every female is an hysteric." She shot him a baleful glare.

Deauchez took a deep breath and said nothing. Someone, perhaps Donnelley, had obviously briefed her about him.

"She told me in the dream to go to Santa Pelagia and I did. I certainly had never heard of Maria Sanchez *or* Santa Pelagia. In Santa Pelagia I received the stigmata, as did others in the field. I witnessed so many miracles, *Papa,* so many *miracles*."

She wrapped her arms around herself and shivered. With her pale, pixie face and her large, dark eyes, this gesture was most effective.

"God was there. *She* was there—the Virgin. Oh, I wish you could have seen her! Anyone who has ever felt the Holy Spirit would have known they were in the presence of the divine!"

Deauchez moved to defend himself, but the pope put a warm hand on his arm to still him.

"What did the Virgin tell you?" the pope asked Daunsey gently.

Sister Daunsey faltered. She sighed heavily and looked around the room as if to avoid answering. Deauchez could see her defiance, her self-assurance, being overcome by a dark cloud, an element more akin to sadness than fear.

When she looked back at the pope it was with an expression of deep regret.

"*Tell* me, Daughter," Innocent XIV urged.

Daunsey pushed herself back in her chair and sighed. Her every fiber shouted how reluctant she was to speak.

"Is this necessary?" Deauchez blurted out in exasperation. "I'm sure His Holiness would get the full impact even *without* the histrionics."

As soon as he'd said it, Deauchez would have done anything to take it back. What on earth had possessed him? All three of the people around the table looked at him as if his behavior was entirely inappropriate. He, Deauchez! After all the things Daunsey had said! Deauchez cursed himself silently and looked down.

But his words seemed to give Daunsey strength, for she spoke up clearly. "*Papa,* the Virgin was dressed all in black and she told me that the end of the world has come. It's *here*. It's *now*. It's not soon, it's not a threat, there's no 'if.' It will begin at any moment, and there *is* no appeal. I'm to assemble the Catholics of Ireland and England together in London and wait."

Daunsey and Innocent XIV gazed at each other for a long moment; Daunsey, with earnest sadness, and the old man, searchingly, as though trying to judge her words through the light in her eyes.

After a moment, Innocent XIV held out his hands to her. "Kiss me now, and leave us for a bit. I wish to speak to Father Deauchez alone."

Sister Daunsey stood and bent to his upraised arms, kissing him on the cheeks instead of on the ring, a gesture Deauchez found entirely too familiar, though the pope himself had invited it. She and Donnelley headed for the door. Deauchez avoided looking at Donnelley as he passed, knowing that his superior would be rightfully furious. Daunsey's presence had pulled out of him the very things he'd been warned to suppress.

When they were gone, Innocent XIV leaned forward and gave Deauchez his full, gentle attention. "Sister Daunsey strikes me as being most sincere in her beliefs about this event."

"Yes, Holiness."

"Were the others you spoke to equally sincere?"

"They appeared to be. I have only interviewed three so far, including Sanchez."

"And there were miracles? Stigmata? Bleeding statues?"

"I—I saw some, yes. Some were even caught on film. But nothing was scientifically tested, Your Holiness. It would take years to verify even one of the miracles. In my opinion . . . Do you recall the *convulsionaries* of St. Médard?"

Deauchez had done his doctoral thesis on the subject. In the early eighteenth century, much to the Vatican's embarrassment, a fanatical group of Jansenists began displaying "miraculous" behavior as they gathered around the tomb of a newly deceased deacon at the St. Médard cemetery in Paris. They became known as *convulsionaries*, because members would enter violent trance states, often convulsing. In such states they were witnessed by hundreds to heal suppurating wounds, broken limbs, and other ailments. They were personally impervious to injury, whether by blade, fire, mace, or any other weapon. Several of them even delighted in being crucified. It was the Church's first pronouncement of hysterical causes for the kinds of behavior they would have normally accepted as divine. What else could they do? The pope had just issued a bull saying the Jansenists were heretics.

"I'm well aware of how cautious the Church is about miracles these days, Michele, as well as your own *psychological* focus. Even so, I hardly think Santa Pelagia need be compared to the *convulsionaries*." There was a hint of reproach in the pope's tone.

"Yes, Holiness. I'm only suggesting that similar crowd dynamics may have been a factor in producing the apparent miracles at Santa Pelagia."

Pope Innocent XIV sighed. "Yes, I saw your initial report, though Cardinal Donnelley was most reluctant to give it to me. He said it wasn't complete."

Deauchez said nothing, but found this an ill omen.

"You wrote that it was all mass hysteria."

"Yes, Holiness."

"Do you still think that?"

Deauchez hesitated. "My most honest response is that I no longer know what to think. There was mass hysteria at the site, without a doubt. Sufficient, in my opinion, to account for the so-called miracles. What interests me more are these dreams and visions."

"In other words, if *not* divine, how could so many unrelated people have had the same revelation to go to Santa Pelagia at the same time? Your crowd dynamics wouldn't have been a factor then. Yes, it is a critical point."

Hearing the pope so clearly nail the weak spot in his case gave Deauchez an immense sense of failure, and not a little desperation. "If I could only investigate further, I could make an educated assessment of 'the call to Santa Pelagia,' if we want to name it that. But Your Holiness, the message of Santa Pelagia itself speaks against the event. I find it ludicrous that we are to believe the *apocalypse* is at hand. People have claimed that since before Christ was born!"

Deauchez found he was breathing hard. His palms were hot and damp.

"Do you believe in Revelation, Deauchez?"

"No, Holiness. I don't."

The pope smiled sadly. "I've always liked you, Deauchez. A pope needs to surround himself with all kinds of people, like a microcosm of the world. Christ did with his Twelve. You . . . you are my doubting Thomas, did you know that?"

Deauchez was embarrassed. "No."

"And Daunsey . . . I suppose she really *is* our Mary Magdalen, as she herself must have known when she chose her name. More passion for God than any of us knows how to deal with propitiously."

"Yes, Your Holiness."

The pope hesitated thoughtfully. "We Catholics are not historically renowned for our tolerance of other faiths. And yet it occurs to me . . . If you were God, and you wanted to send this particular message to the world, would you not call the leaders of many different faiths together?"

"I don't know. I . . . I was not exactly impressed with his choices, if that is the case. Sanchez is nothing more than a spoiled manipulator. Andrews is licentious, egotistical . . ."

Innocent XIV took Deauchez's hand in his own, which was warm and soft. "And Sister Daunsey? Ah, but who of God's creatures would ever be pure enough, *worthy* enough, for you, Michele? Even you yourself, as sinless as you are, cannot fathom God inside you. So how could you accept that he might enter lesser vessels?"

Deauchez, deeply confused at this analysis, didn't know what to say.

The pope dropped his hand. "But thank you for your effort, my son. I know you have done your best."

GENEVA, SWITZERLAND

The back of Fielding's neck was beet red and corded with tension of the capital "T" variety, tension of the sort only a man like Fielding could birth, namely the outrage of a man who believed he was king of the world and that someone had just farted in his presence.

Cole, who was seated directly behind the president, knew exactly what Fielding was thinking—what he would be *saying* if they were in a room filled with *his* people instead of in a U.N. assembly hall that contained at least a few dozen people that weren't on Fielding's payroll and weren't prepared to nod and smile at anything he said.

He'd be saying, *I'm the goddamn president of the goddamn United States, I don't have to sit here and listen to this shit!*

But he *did* have to sit here and listen. At least, it would be extremely bad form to walk out in the middle of opening statements—hence the muscles in his neck. Whatever the muscles were doing, there was no doubt a slight, interested smile was pasted on the other side of Fielding's head. Half the leaders in the world were sneaking glances at Fielding, trying to gauge a reaction. They should, Cole thought, have had *his* seat.

". . . it's time for the West to take responsibility!" China's President Lee was saying. His adamant face at the podium was strangely detached from the voice coming through their translating headsets. "They have spread their materialism all over the world! In the past fifteen years, China and India and many of the other so-called third-world countries have had their farmers leaving the agricultural regions by the tens of thousands to move to the city. Why? In search of the *car*, the *television*, the *stereo*, the things they see promoted by the corporate pirates of the West. They push these things the way an opium dealer pushes opium! So that now, when we have a crisis like this drought, there are no reserves, no way to ride the difficulty and stay afloat! The United States has done this for their own financial gain. Yes, *they* are responsible for the condition of our agriculture! *They* have taken billions in business revenue from our countries and given us their toxic waste and global warming to swallow in return!"

A number of delegates—mostly those who had signed China's petition—pounded on the table with a light fist, their sign of approval and agreement. Cole had never seen things so cleanly divided down have and have-not lines. On the nonpounding side were the U.S., the E.U. countries, Canada, Australia, Japan, and Israel. And making up the pounders, almost everyone else—*including* the Russians. Cole was not surprised to see them siding with China: they were too close to the Asian giant, and too weak politically, to risk invasion if China decided it *had* to have grain.

"We cannot deny any longer the situation! We are right now facing very limited food resources to feed billions of people! Most countries are suffering and want to work together to do what is right, but not the United States, the largest exporter of grains! The United States wants to distribute their crops however they wish, but we know what this means. They will feed their own people at their usual gluttonous levels and push a few crumbs from the feasting table to the rest of us. President Fielding will not enforce any discipline of the American people out of fear of election year, and the American people will never discipline themselves. A few days ago they raided the stores at the least mention of self-control. Fielding responded with this so-called moratorium on grain warehouse shipments, but the moratorium is *only* for ten days. What happens when this summit is over, I ask you, and the crops are harvested in a month or so? There will be no moratorium then!"

Fielding leaned back and hissed over his shoulder. "You said that moratorium would make them feel warm and fuzzy about our intentions, Cole!"

"It was the best gesture we could make under the circumstances," Cole answered in a low, calm voice.

"Do you know who that guy is on the platform?"

Cole knew to whom Fielding referred. Seated directly behind and to the left of President Lee, in a seat of honor, was an unusual-looking political delegate: an old Chinese man with a long white beard and black robe. He faced the crowd stonily, and yet, without so much as a hint of a frown, he still managed to convey self-righteous wrath.

"Tsing Mao Wen. He's a Taoist monk. He and a few thousand of his followers were fugitives under the Red Guard. But Lee discovered him and brought him back into the limelight. I hear he's quite the political philosopher, and his ideas just happened to coincide with Lee's own."

"Is he a commie?"

"That would be putting it too simply, but . . . yes. I'll brief you later."

Lee was summing up. "This is the truth: there has been a glutton at the table for a long time; a glutton not only eating more than its fair share of food, but eating up too much oil and wood and other finite resources of this planet we all share! The question is, is the United Nations prepared to consider the well-being, the lives, of *all* the people of this Earth? Can they take decisive action? We have submitted a plan that we believe is a fair and unbiased distribution of food resources. We seek a confirmation on that proposal before we leave this summit. Thank you."

Lee stepped down to thunderous applause. Cole looked over to see Prime Minister Billingsworth staring in slack-jawed, glassy-eyed astonishment at the sheer number of delegates who were standing up in support of Lee. The British dignitary looked rather like a housewife who'd just caught her first glimpse of a porno flick.

And Fielding's neck, well, it just kept getting redder.

VATICAN CITY, ROME

Father Angelico Carnesca's office was tucked away off the Vatican library. Deauchez had always envied its cozy warmth, its proximity to the endless walls of books, and its window overlooking a cobblestoned and fountained inner courtyard.

Carnesca grinned when he saw Deauchez, his eyes sparkling with curiosity.

"*Buon giorno,* Michele! I heard you were back! I was going to come bother you myself after supper."

"So I have beaten you to the mark, for once?" Deauchez teased. "How does everything go?"

"The same: slow but steady. We're up to the thirteenth century on the data entry. There's been some interesting material found, but nothing to compare with *your* adventures."

Carnesca and Deauchez might have been brothers, for they were similar in height and build, and both had dark coloring. But Carnesca was Italian and could not be mistaken for anything else. His hair had that black sheen that Deauchez's French genes could never match, and he had unusual gray eyes, one of which had a tendency to wander, particularly when the scholar was worked up.

It was probably this slight defect that had driven Angelico to books as a child, and he loved them still. But the man had as voracious an appetite for modern intrigue as he did for medieval history. His nose for gossip made it difficult to keep anything to oneself. Conversing with him was rather like sharing a bed with a cover-stealer.

"What do you know about my adventures?" Deauchez asked, curious to hear the grapevine version.

"Santa Pelagia." Carnesca whistled. "Big deal, eh? The pope wants to know, the press wants to know, everybody wants to know what happened."

"*Oui.*"

"So? What happened?"

"You have studied prophecy, am I right?"

"Ah! That's why you came to see me. I should have known it wasn't a social call."

"Well . . . I do have a *few* questions."

Carnesca considered him critically, as though judging horseflesh. "All right. But first fill me in, yes?"

It was the price of admittance, so Deauchez did, briefly. Carnesca sat through the whole thing without saying a word.

"So everyone who was there agrees the message was apocalyptic?" he asked at last.

"I don't know about everyone. Four that I know of so far."

Carnesca tapped his chin. "Of course you realize that a lot of prophets—as in all of them—have predicted massive upheaval at the turn of the millennium."

"They said that last millennium," Deauchez said dryly.

"Some did, that is true. But the tricky part is that the best prophets usually don't pin precise dates on their work."

"How convenient."

"Not really. The thing about prophecy is that dates are not that relevant."

"What do you mean?"

"The best prophets have more of, well, a kind of *genius* at future-trend surfing. For example, say I ask you what would happen if you had a wild, flagrant love affair with a woman."

Deauchez raised an amused eyebrow. "What?"

"No, just pretend as if you did, what would happen?"

"I would lose my post, probably be defrocked if I persisted."

"All right. Then the possibility of you being kicked out of the priesthood is there. The question is, how likely are you to do something like that? What's the probability?"

Deauchez grunted. "Nonexistent."

Carnesca winked teasingly. "You never know—a pair of pretty eyes, perhaps . . . ? Let's say very low—five percent. On the other hand, what is the probability of you becoming pope?"

"Ha! Even less likely."

Carnesca made a *comme ci, comme ça* gesture. "Let us say the most probable future, then, is that you will be just an ordinary priest for another forty or so years and then die, eh?"

"You make it sound so appealing."

"We all have our crosses to bear. The point is, that's the way future-trending works, only on a much larger scale. You must take into account what all individuals, or at least all societies, will *probably* do, what the responses will be to *those* actions, what the responses will be to the responses, and so on."

"Like chess."

"*Sì*, exactly! But it gets worse!" Carnesca's lazy eye jittered. "Sometimes two or more actions are just as likely to occur. Will the king pardon the traitor or behead him? Maybe the decision hinges only on how accommodating his mistress was the night before. And so from that choice there begins what are essentially *two separate paths* into the future, one for each possible outcome, and each one is as complex as the one we were just discussing. Multiply that by the too-close-to-call choices made by the entire planet, and soon you have thousands if not millions of potential futures."

Deauchez nodded appreciatively. "You put it very well. But if there is no 'absolute fate,' as some would believe, but only these millions of possible paths, then prophecy is *not* possible."

"Not at all! A great prophet not only *can* envision most of these paths—intuitively, the way a great chess player can sense all possible moves on a board—but he can also spot similarities, things that develop on *almost all paths*. If you think about it, you might say it was inevitable that man developed the airplane, the car, the atomic bomb. And think of this: given that it was inevitable that man *developed* the atom bomb, and given man's history of warfare, how likely is it, do you think, on all future paths, that we will never use it for mass destruction?"

Deauchez decided he'd rather not think about it. He changed the subject. "If the great prophets *could* see all that, why not dates?"

"Well, say for example that Nostradamus foresaw the invention of the airplane. But exactly when, that would depend on many factors: when each of the components was invented, when the right kind of scientific mind would be born that would be obsessed with the problem, and so on. Perhaps you could pin it down within a few decades. One thing you *would* know, however, is that there would be other events that were highly probable that couldn't happen *until* the airplane was invented. So the *sequence* of events is much easier than dates."

"Did he? Predict airplanes?"

Carnesca grinned, the widening of his eyes highlighting their discord. "Nostradamus? *Sì, sì!* And submarines, nuclear weapons, Napoleon, Hitler, WW II . . ."

Deauchez huffed. "Come now! I admit, I'm no expert, but his wording is completely vague, is it not? Can't you read just about anything into it?"

"You tell me."

Carnesca went to one of his shelves and pulled a book on

Nostradamus. "Okay, airplanes. Remember, this man died in 1566 . . . 'Weapons will be heard fighting in the skies . . . People will travel softly through the sky over land and seas.' "

Deauchez frowned thoughtfully.

"Submarines, let's see . . . 'Through lightning in the box of the central life fire, gold and silver are melted. The two captives will devour each other . . . When the fleet travels under water.' "

"What was that first part, fire in the box?"

"Maybe a sixteenth-century attempt to describe nuclear-powered submarine engines?"

Deauchez looked doubtful. "And nuclear war?"

"I'm getting there. 'At sunrise one will see a great fire, noise and light extending toward the North. Within the earth death and cries are heard, Death awaiting them through weapons fire and famine.' And another: 'There will be let loose living fire and hidden death, Horror inside dreadful globes. By night the city will be reduced to dust by the fleet. The city on fire, helpful to the enemy.' "

"Which city?"

"Who knows? One large enough to be called *the* city. Paris? Rome? New York? Wait, here's another. 'The sky will burn at forty-five degrees latitude, Fire approaches the great new city. Immediately a huge, scattered flame leaps up.' That one must be New York. It's not only new, it's at that latitude."

Deauchez found it difficult to hide his annoyance—the subjectivity of these things always irked him, and he was rawer at the moment than usual. "How do these read 'nuclear weapons'? He talks about fire."

"Of that magnitude? In dreadful globes? Coming from the sky?"

"He could be talking about a comet or asteroid. Or making it up, for that matter."

Carnesca shrugged with a defensive stiltedness. "I find the predictions on Napoleon and Hitler fascinating, personally. They're described as the first two Antichrists. He names both of them."

"The first two?"

"There are three all told."

"What do you mean he *names* them?"

Carnesca turned back to the book. " 'Pau, Nay, Loron will be more of fire than of blood. To swim in praise, the great one to flee to the confluence. He will refuse entry to the Piuses. The depraved ones and the Durance'—France—'will keep them imprisoned.' Napoleon *was* more of fire—that is enthusiasm—than of blood; he wasn't a royal, he was a commoner. If you recall your history, he persecuted both Pope Pius VII and Pius VIII, imprisoned them both on 'the confluence' of Isere and Rhone in 1799. It's a remarkable prophecy."

"Pau, Nay, Loron?"

"Nostradamus was fond of anagrams. He was so disturbed by what he saw that he didn't want just anyone to be able to figure out his message—only those who took the time and were scholarly enough to decipher his words."

"It just, coincidentally, makes him invulnerable to being proven wrong since things can be read so many ways," Deauchez remarked dryly.

Carnesca made that *comme ci, comme ça* gesture again. "Pau, Nay, Loron becomes Nay Pau Loron or Napaulon Roy—Napoleon the King."

"Hmmm," Deauchez rumbled, but he was not unimpressed.

"Oh, Napoleon is absolutely not an issue. Nostradamus was very precise about his rise to power, his wives, his victories, Waterloo, Elba, the whole thing."

"I'll take your word for it. What about Hitler?"

"He calls him 'Hi*f*ter,' the second Antichrist. 'Great discord in the Adriatic, warfare will arise . . . unions will be split apart . . . including England and France in '45 and others in '41, '42, and '37 . . . In that time and in those countries an infernal power will rise against the Church of Jesus Christ, this shall be the second Antichrist.' *Dates*, Michele, and Hitler is named specifically in a number of quatrains, such as this one: 'The shocking and infamous armed one will fear the great furnace. First the chosen ones'—Jews—'the captives not returning: The world's lowest crime, the Angry Female Irale'—could be Israel—'not at ease. Barb, Hi*f*ter, Malta.' 'Barb' is short for Barbarossa, Hitler's disastrous Russian campaign. Malta was key to his defeat."

Deauchez leaned forward to look at the book. "If he predicted *three* Antichrists then he was not following Revelation, correct?"

"Nostradamus was a Christianized Jew. Some of his prophecies match up with Revelation, but not all. He's undeniably heretical. Even so, you can't say you know prophecy *at all* unless you've studied Nostradamus."

"What does he say about the third Antichrist?"

"He calls him 'Mabus,' and he's to come from Babylon, which, if you interpret it geographically, is now Baghdad, Iraq." Carnesca was flipping through the book again.

" 'The third Antichrist very soon annihilated, Seven and twenty years of blood will his war last: The heretics are dead, captives exiled, blood-soaked human bodies, water, and a reddened icy rain covering the entire earth.' "

Deauchez digested this thoughtfully. "Was there not a verse about 'Twenty-Four'?"

"Twenty-Four?"

"Yes. Check the index."

Carnesca did and found it. " 'Famine, plague, war, in the Twenty-Four, is seeded a warning for the whole world.' "

"Do you have any idea what that refers to?"

Carnesca shook his head.

"Is that the only verse that talks about Twenty-Four?"

"It's the only one in the index." Carnesca turned to his computer and booted up a Bible CD-ROM. Deauchez already knew what he would find there. He'd looked it up himself on the plane.

"Revelation 4:4," Carnesca read. " 'And round about the throne were four and twenty seats: and upon the seats I saw four and twenty elders sitting, clothed in white raiment; and they had on their heads crowns of gold.' "

Carnesca looked at Deauchez curiously. "It's the number of elders seated at the throne of God to witness the apocalypse."

Deauchez nodded.

"Is this relevant to Santa Pelagia somehow?" Carnesca's eyes were as bright as a ferret's.

"Probably not," Deauchez answered with a poker face.

Carnesca stared, waiting for a hint. He obviously smelled something not being said and he didn't care for it. "Let me tell you something, Michele. I know better than anyone that prophecy must be taken *cum grano salis*. But if there were ever going to be an apocalypse, it would be soon. Prophets from all over the world have predicted it, including many of our own saints. Did you know that according to St. Malachy, Innocent XIV is the second-to-the-last pope?"

"No."

"It's true. St. Malachy came to Rome on a pilgrimage in 1139. When he topped the hill and saw the city he fell to his knees and went into an ecstatic trance. He uttered 112 Latin phrases, one for each of the popes to come. We're on number 111 right now."

"What do you mean 'phrases'?"

"Descriptions of each pope. John Paul II, number 110, was referred to as *'De Labore Solis,'* 'labor of the sun.' That's a classical term for eclipse and Karol Wojtyla was born during one. He also labored tirelessly to bring the 'light' of democracy into the 'dark corners' of communism. Innocent XIV is called *'Gloria Olivae,'* or glory of the olives."

"Meaning?"

"I don't know. Olive branch? Peacemaker? He is a world-renowned mediator."

Deauchez grunted, dubious. "And the last pope?"

" 'Peter the Roman,' he's called. St. Malachy said, 'During the last persecution of the Holy Roman Church, there shall sit Peter of Rome, who shall feed the sheep amidst many great tribulations, and when these have passed, the City of the Seven Hills shall be utterly destroyed, and the awful Judge will judge the people.' "

"I take it you have studied Malachy."

"Of course. After all, I *live* in Rome, and so do you." Carnesca leaned back and studied him, a have-I-frightened-you smirk on his face.

"You realize, of course, Angelico," Deauchez pointed out, "that none of these predictions match each other?"

"Not always in the fine print, I'll admit. Still, what they all see is a whole lot of suffering, some cataclysmic rip in the fabric of life. The good news is that most prophesy a golden era beyond the devastation."

Deauchez rose. "I'm grateful for the lesson. It may prove useful. But I must tell you my honest opinion about all of this prophecy business."

"Please do."

"Est quaedam flere voluptas," Deauchez said. *There is a certain pleasure in weeping.*

Carnesca winced and laid a dramatic hand on his chest to show where the blow had fallen. "Ah, Michele! I hope you are right and the prophecies are nothing more than dark bonbons of titillation. But remember, they also say *mus non uni fidit antro,* eh? A wise man has a backup plan. I, myself, have a packed bag waiting in my closet—just in case things in Rome get sticky."

"Is that so?" Deauchez said with wide-eyed sincerity. "Given what you have dug up about Santa Pelagia, I'm surprised to find you still here."

He meant it facetiously and expected a laugh, but Carnesca didn't even smile. He just stared at Deauchez with sucked-in cheeks, his left eye jittering to the side and back again like a fish hooked on a line.

CHAPTER 4

DAY 5
ATLANTA, GEORGIA

If there was one thing that Reverend Raymond Stanton could *not* abide, it was a doubting Thomas. He sat in his dressing room chair putting on makeup and shooting disgusted glances at his wife, Mimi, who was doing her nervous flutter routine over in the corner.

"Ray? Hon? I'm sorry, sweetie. I . . . I *do* believe in your revelation, darlin', it's not that at *all*—"

"Mimi, for the love of Christmas, will you just shut up!"

Mimi's fuchsia lips closed into a chin-trembling, heartbreaking, martyred kind of pout. He'd seen it a million times. For that matter, so had everyone else in America. Her eyes glistened, but he knew she wouldn't cry. No, she'd just finished three hours of makeup and he'd seen her break an ankle and not shed a tear when her Revlon was fresh. Mimi had perfected the art of crying without real tears, and yes, now the handkerchief came up and dabbed at the inner duct of her eye to pick up that camera-ready glisten before it smudged her eyeliner.

He heard Jerry call out in the hallway. "Ten minutes!"

He was going to be ill.

"Mimi, would you please get on outta here and give me a minute to myself?"

"But, *hon*," Mimi protested in her most whining voice, "I think we should *resolve* this . . ."

"Mimi, listen carefully. There's not a single gosh-blame word you can say that's gonna change anythin'. I'm askin' you to leave and, darlin', I mean *now*!"

Mimi, who was wringing out her handkerchief like it was the

fabric of life itself and she was trying to squeeze out a few more drops, took her pout and left the room.

And then he *was* ill. He felt it coming and hurried over to the bathroom; lost it in the john.

He stumbled weakly from the bathroom, went back to his chair and tried, with hands barely able to function, to blot some more face powder over his newly perspiring skin.

He had the sermon, that was no problem. It was, in fact, a master play, assuming he could summon up the kind of presence necessary to pull it off. True, he'd been condemned from at least a dozen pulpits since the Santa Pelagia story broke, but he could handle that. Heck, it was almost a challenge, taking those other guys' holier-than-thou bull-crappie and making them look like on-the-bench wussies when he proved that it was he, Stanton, who was playing quarterback for God. Which is exactly what this sermon *would* do because it was ballsy, oh yes. Nothing *any* of those other guys could say would be as ballsy as this.

No. The Santa Pelagia story wasn't gonna finish the Reverend Raymond Stanton.

But if he gave this sermon and the apocalypse didn't *come, that* would.

He could see it in Mimi's eyes, the thought of standing on that mountaintop, praying *hallelujah* and waiting for God, while God takes a later train. Or even, heaven forbid, decides to go to the Bahamas, instead. Weren't those idiotic scientists always saying it took billions of years to create the world when Genesis called it six days? Not that he *believed* any of that evolution bull-pucks, but, still, what time zone was God in, anyway?

YOU MUST PUBLICLY GIVE THE MESSAGE OF SANTA PELAGIA AND THE PROPHECY OF THE SORES WITHIN THE NEXT FIVE DAYS.

That, at least, was clear enough. Stanton had to assume the angel *didn't* mean five billion years.

"Five minutes!"

Stanton's stomach clenched in terror.

It's not too late to back out.

No! I know what I saw!

Why did Mimi have to point out this morning that other preachers had given exact dates for the Rapture and had been wrong; had been left, in fact, standing there holding their Roto-rooters. But Mimi was bound to look at it that way. As exciting as the "new message" would be for a time—the angst, the drama, leading people up that hill—the bottom line was that either the message would turn out to be *true*, in which case their beautiful home, cars, clothes, trips, and Mimi's chance to get onstage three times a week, would be gone. Forever. Their life over. Or, the message would turn out to be *false*, in which case they'd look like morons and lose their ministry.

Yes, he could understand her reluctance. Anticipating God's glory was one thing, but they had it pretty darn sweet down here on Earth, too. Mimi didn't *want* to believe. Would his flock? Or would they, like Mimi, be prevented from believing simply because they wanted to live?

Then a voice spoke inside his head, clear as a bell. *If the sores come, they won't doubt anymore. Not them, not you, not Mimi. And the sores* will *come.*

Stanton stared at his reflection blankly for a moment, feeling a strange euphoria descend. The thought of it, of his giving this prophecy and then the sores appearing! For a moment, he caught a glimpse of what it would be like—he, Stanton, not just a preacher for show, not just some slick talker, but a true right-hand-of-God religious prophet, like John the Baptist maybe. A living vessel, emblazoned with God's spirit like some kind of—

There was a tap on his door. "It's time," came Jerry's muffled voice.

"I'm ready," Stanton whispered.

NEW YORK CITY

Simon Hill looked at the few familiar faces around the assembly hall and realized that none of his competing reporters had any idea what it was they were covering. They were there, and they looked interested, sure, because Abeed always said *something* controversial, was always good fodder for the public, whether people agreed with him—which most of the people living in Harlem did—or were outraged, a category which included virtually all whites and not a few of those Abeed called "whitey-fied blacks," referring, Hill supposed, to people like himself. Even had his fellow reporters known that this speech was regarding Santa Pelagia, they probably wouldn't know what that meant. But Hill knew, oh yes. His stomach was clenched so tight that it was causing the occasional jolt of nerve-pain. He knew indeed.

He heard the crowd hush, then burst into applause and trills and shouts of adoration. From a side door, a line of men emerged. They were dressed in black velvet robes with neon-colored satin banding. Six walked in and then Abeed himself entered, wearing a robe of solid gold satin.

Hill had covered Abeed before, and this frenzied worship of the man always terrified him, but today it made him positively ill. God only knew what they'd do when . . .

"Brothers and sisters," Abeed shouted as he reached the pulpit. He held out his arms to silence the crowd. It took a while, so intent were they on showing him their love, particularly in front of the press. They finally calmed.

"Brothers and sisters, this is a momentous day! A day unlike any you have ever seen, I will promise you that. And this day is only the beginning of many others unlike any you have ever seen!"

The crowd *amen*ed and stomped in approval.

"For I have somethin' *mighty* to tell you, something *profound*. And you may not thank me for telling it to you when I'm done! No, I say you may not be happy *at all*! You may be frightened! You may be aggrieved! You may wonder why! But look around you, my people, and you will *know* why!"

People hooted and stomped at the implication.

"But before I tell you what it is I must tell you, brothers and sisters, I first have to know! Do you believe in God?"

The crowd screamed. *Yes!*

"Do you believe in the truth of the everlasting *word* of God?"
Yes!

"Do you believe God punishes the wicked?"
Yes!

"Do you believe that the last shall be first and the first shall be last?"
Yes!

"Do you believe God led his people out of bondage in Egypt?"
Yes!

"Do you believe that *you're* in bondage now?"
Yes!

"Will God set you free?"
Yes!

"But when?" Abeed shouted in a trembling voice. " 'When!' cries the mother holding a baby racked with cocaine! 'When!'

cry the schoolchildren watching their friends dying in the streets! 'When!' cries the old man, homeless and sick and hungry! I'm here to tell you today that God has *given us an answer*! Listen carefully, my children, and I will tell you a story . . ."

ATLANTA, GEORGIA

". . . They *mocked* Abraham, they *mocked* Moses, they mocked *Christ himself*! A prophet is never acknowledged in his own land, my friends. Why? Because those whom God has not *chosen* cannot abide bein' left out! And so they mock!"

Stanton wiped his face with one of his embroidered handkerchiefs. The gosh-blame studio lights made it difficult for him to read the audience. He could make out faces only in the first few rows, but he sure *felt* resistance out there.

"And so they mock," he repeated in a soft, sorrowful voice.

He held the moment for a beat, then spoke up loud and clear. "You have heard other ministers speak out against me this week. They say I was down in Mexico for a Mary sightin'. Let me tell you two things right now. I *was* in Mexico is the first thing, and I praise God that I was chosen to be there! The second thing is that they have *no idea* what happened in that little village! None! I come before you today to give you the message from God that was given in Santa Pelagia, just as *he instructed* me to do!

"Be all the *world* against me, I will stand by God! I will do as *he* requires! Not what Ernest Marshall requires, not what Gentry O'Neal requires, but what *God* requires! When Jesus walked the Earth his disciples said, 'Lord, Lord, why do you sup with tax collectors? Why do you counsel harlots? Why do you bother preachin' to the gentile?' "

Stanton glared accusingly into the lights. "And the Lord replied, 'Doth not the shepherd leave the ninety-nine sheep in his flock to go find the one that *is* lost? I come not to save the saint but the sinner!' "

The audience was a bit restless. He heard some chairs groan as fleshy burdens shifted. Stanton wiped his face.

"I have a verse to read to you, my precious friends . . .

"Isaiah 43:5–9. 'Fear not: for I am with thee: I will bring thy seed from the east, and gather thee from the west; I will say to the north, Give up; and to the south, Keep not back: bring my sons from far, and my daughters from the ends of the earth; Even every one that is called by my name: for I have created him for my glory, I have formed him; yea, I have made him. Bring forth the *blind people that have eyes*, and the *deaf that have ears*. Let *all the nations* be gathered together, and let the people be assembled: who among them can declare this, and shew us former things? let them *bring forth their witnesses*, that they may be justified: or let them hear, and say, It is the truth. Ye are my witnesses, saith the Lord, and my servant whom I have chosen.' "

Stanton paused, moving his Bible around for a moment to make sure it sank in.

"I'm here to tell you that this verse was made flesh in Santa Pelagia, Mexico, my friends! From the time way back some five hundred years even before Christ was born, when Isaiah *wrote* this prophecy, it had lain unfulfilled, a bit of poetry, that some might not have thought would ever relate to an actual event. But like all God's prophecies it *came to pass* exactly as written in that little Mexican village just a few days ago. I know! I was there!"

Now there were some murmurs from the crowd.

"This is what the verse means, and this is exactly what happened: God had a message to give to the world! Not just any message, but a message of *ut*most importance, of *ut*most urgency, the most important message since the angels announced the birth of Jesus Christ over two thousand years ago! And this message isn't just for Christians, oh no. It is for *all nations*! It's for the unbelievers, too, which is what he means by 'the deaf who have ears' and 'the blind who have eyes'—those who have the *capacity* to understand and *accept* his message, even though they had never before known the light of Christ!"

His voice continued to swell in timbre. He had his rhythm now; it was like boxing; *jab, jab, jab*, the words like hammer blows: confident, hard to the mark, without thought.

"It was a *mir*acle that this prophecy came to pass in our own lifetimes! It was a *mir*acle of faith, a *mir*acle of God's final mercy and compassion toward this wayward planet. And I, your humble pastor, was chosen by God to receive this message for *you*, for *our* nation of Christian brothers. So when I tell you now that I have somethin' to give you today, somethin' precious, somethin' more important than anythin' you have ever received in your life, you will know that it *is* the truth. What I have for you is nothin' less than God's final message to mankind!"

He let that sink in; he could feel the tension mounting. The rustling had stopped and the audience was hushed expectantly. Yes, now there was nary the scrape of a heel.

"You may ask, 'Reverend Stanton, how were *you* chosen to receive this message?' I'll tell you. Many of you will remember that I was in the hospital a few weeks back for a minor procedure. I want to thank you for all your kind cards and letters, and especially for your prayers. It was while I was in the hospital that I had a vision . . ."

NEW YORK CITY

". . . And the angel said to me, Mohammed Khan Abeed, stand up and *raise* your head! Stand up and re*ceive* the power! Stand up and *face* the God who made you in his image, and prepare yourself to be *his* warrior!"

The crowd rumbled in ecstasy.

"Now when I say 'an angel appeared to me,' I'm not sayin' that I *wished* it had happened! I'm not talkin' 'bout somethin' I dreamed up from my own *head*! I'm *talking* about a blazing, enormous, beautiful angel as real as you are right now! And you want to know something? That angel was *black*!"

The crowd clapped and *amen*ed in glee.

"Now hold on, now, before you get too excited." Abeed's pale palms came up to still the crowd. " 'Cause this wasn't the *friendliest sort* of angel. This angel did not *come* to pass the time of day! *This* angel was an angel filled with the *wrath* of *God*! And, brothers and sisters, you know as well as *I* do what God has to be wrathful about!"

The crowd's feet shook the building for a good two minutes. Abeed had to shout "hold on" repeatedly to get them to quiet down.

"The angel told me 'Go down to Mexico, to a place called Santa Pelagia. You are a *wit*ness, a *seed*. In you will be planted a message from God for your people.' And what do you think I did?"

A few people in the crowd shouted, "You went!"

Abeed gazed around at his audience, a big grin on his face.

"You're darn *right* I went! Let me tell you something: when an angel of God appears to you and tells you to go somewhere, y'all gonna go on an' go! Y'all ain't gonna *ar*gue with no ten-foot-tall black angel! You say, 'yes, sir!' and you pack your bags that very hour! And that's exactly what I did!"

There were some laughs and amens from the crowd, but most of them were hushing their neighbors now, getting anxious to hear the next part of the story.

"And when I got there, brothers and sisters, there were people from all over the world. I say, from everywhere. Even from Africa, yes! And places like India and China, too! What message God told whitey there, I couldn't say—but there *were* a few white folk, and I wouldn't have wanted to be in *their* shoes 'cause I can tell y'all right now, they didn't get good news!"

The crowd laughed nervously.

"But what message he gave the people of color, I *do* know, because I asked them, and because I heard it myself. That same blazing, beautiful angel floated above a field, high in the trees, every night for seven nights. And what he told us was that it was *time for the end of life as we know it!* It was *time for the birth of a New World!*"

The crowd was speaking back to him now; things like "Whacha mean, Brother?" "What's it gonna be like in this New World?" He had their attention, all right. He had Hill's, too. Hill watched the crowd anxiously, but mostly he was just trying to hear over the pounding of blood in his ears.

ATLANTA, GEORGIA

"The apocalypse of Revelation is *beginnin'*! We've *known* about it, we've *talked* about it, we've been waitin' with fear and wonder. Well, the waitin's *over*. The seven plagues are about to begin, accompanied by famine, plague, and war, the Antichrist, the persecution, all of the events of the Great Tribulation. And when they're over, my friends, God will *return to rule the world!*"

From somewhere to Stanton's right, a woman burst into tears. Someone in the rear of the room groaned loud and long.

He could feel the flame in him now, all doubt gone, all nervousness gone, he was a flaming fire. And it was better than it had ever been before because he was aflame with the spirit of the angel of Santa Pelagia.

"The angel told me to lead all true Christians to Kittatinny Mountain in New Jersey. There, we'll await the Rapture. It's comin'! It's gonna happen! Nothin' on Earth or in the heavens can stop it! And those on that mountain will be showin' their absolute faith and love, and they *will be taken first*, God has promised me this!"

Someone in the crowd said, "Oh, my word."

"I know it's difficult to have faith! I know it's difficult to believe! My own beloved wife, Mimi, showed me this. She doesn't want to leave our life, our friends here, like you."

Mimi shot him a murderous glance, her face as pasty as cream cheese, even through several applications of "sunny glow." He ignored her.

"We *want* heaven, but we're afraid to let go of Earth. Well, I'm here to tell you, you *must* believe that what awaits us in heaven is so beautiful, so wonderful, it's beyond our powers to comprehend! *There'll* be no want. *There'll* be no aging! *There'll* be no sickness! *There'll* be no sin, no crime! We'll have all of our loved ones all of the time! That's what heaven is, my friends, it's a place where you want for nothin', can imagine nothin' better! So what is there to fear? I tell you right now, within the space of *a few months at the most*, everyone in this room will be in heaven—heaven . . ."

He paused dramatically. "Or hell."

Most members of the audience were crying now. He could hear their muffled sobs even if he couldn't see them. And he sensed something else . . . a touch of anger, perhaps, from the willful? One man in the front was fixed on him, his jaw set in a particularly stony way.

Stanton hoped he got the sores but *bad*.

NEW YORK CITY

". . . And when whitey is destroyed by his *own* sins, by his *own* technology, by his *own* neglect of the Earth and his *own* rape of his brothers, then it will be time for us to take over and build a New World! I tell you, the apocalypse that's coming will wipe out most of the First World that whitey lords over. He will be destroyed! And then the balance can be turned! He who was last shall be made first! He who was first shall be last!"

From under the pulpit, Abeed brought out a globe. He held it aloft, perched like an egg between his splayed fingers.

"This is gonna happen now! Within the next few weeks it will start! I'm charging you with this! Forget about your jobs! Forget about school! None of that matters now! There will be a new education! Your slavery jobs will be gone! Your landlords, dead!"

The crowds cheered and stood up with a roar. Abeed didn't bother to hush them, he shouted over them.

"The world will be turned *upside down*!"

In a fluid gesture, he flipped the globe one hundred and eighty degrees on its axis.

"We will gather right here, in Harlem, and prepare ourselves for the future! When whitey goes down—and I don't just mean *our* whitey, I mean the Establishment all over the *globe*—we will be ready to march in and take up the throne!"

ATLANTA, GEORGIA

"You may doubt! You may say, 'Reverend Stanton, how am I to quit my job and take m' kids out of school and follow you to some mountain? What if you're wrong?' I tell you, you must have faith! Christ said to Thomas, 'Blessed are those who believe and have *not* seen me.' But God is merciful! He knows you need more authority than one ol' Southern Baptist preacher's word. So he's sendin' a sign! A sign so that you will *know* it's time to get yourself right with God and be where he's *asked* you to be for the Rapture!"

NEW YORK CITY

"God will *smite* the land with sores!" Abeed spat, shaking now, possessed by the Holy Spirit. "Just as Revelation predicted as the first sign of the apocalypse! And then you will know that IT HAS BEGUN!"

VATICAN CITY, ROME

When Donnelley's secretary found Deauchez, he was in his room. He'd been glued to an Internet broadcast of Stanton's sermon for over an hour, and now he was going over it for the second time.

"Cardinal Donnelley would like to see you in his office," Father Addison said.

Deauchez nodded, distracted and disheartened by the broadcast. He shut his laptop's cover and headed out across the courtyard and lawn to the Apostolic Palace.

As he walked, his amorphous turmoil about Stanton was lost to a more specific apprehension of the next few minutes. Though he did not rank high enough to have living quarters in the Apostolic Palace, Deauchez had an office there, in the bureau's rooms, and he'd been avoiding it. More accurately, he'd been avoiding Donnelley. It wouldn't surprise him terribly to be transferred. He'd embarrassed them both in the pope's office, and he knew it.

But when Deauchez entered his superior's office, Donnelley was smiling. "I see Father Addison tracked you down. Fine, fine. Have a seat, Michele."

"Thank you, Your Eminence." Deauchez sat warily.

"The pope has reached a decision."

"He has?"

Donnelley was smiling affably, but Deauchez got the feeling he wasn't too pleased, nonetheless. "Yes. He's decided to release a statement saying that we are very aware of Santa Pelagia and that we're putting a great deal of effort and care into investigating the matter. At least, that's all he's planning to say before his trip."

Deauchez was relieved. "That seems wise."

"So it appears you've convinced him to caution."

Was that a compliment? Deauchez shifted uneasily in his seat.

"And His Holiness wishes to continue the investigation. He wants *you* to continue with it."

Deauchez felt a mix of elation and disbelief, as when you win something you did not expect to have a shot at winning. The thrill mixed with a fear that they'd made a mistake, perhaps, and would withdraw the offer, or that the "but" would show up sooner or later and be a real doozy.

"Thank you, Your Eminence."

"Thank His Holiness, Michele. He seems to feel that a cool head is what's needed on this side of the equation, and he believes you provide that."

"On *this* side of the equation . . . Your Eminence?"

Donnelley stared at him with a blank look, as if realizing he'd let something drop that perhaps he had not intended. He was frozen that way for a moment; then he pursed his lips and put on an avuncular air.

"I suppose I should tell you, Michele, since you'll no doubt hear news about it here and there." Donnelley rose and crossed to the window. The office had a coveted view overlooking the back of St. Peter's Square. "You weren't the only one who impressed His Holiness at the meeting. He's very fond of Sister Daunsey. He believes she is adamant about what she believes, and one of the things she believes is that she must lead the

Catholic people of Ireland and England to London in the immediate future to prepare for what's to come."

Deauchez felt dread slip through him like a gulp of hot milk.

"His Holiness isn't prepared to stand in her way. He gives God the benefit of the doubt, as he puts it. Sister Daunsey will lead her mission without any inference from the Vatican."

Please, no, Deauchez thought.

"On the other hand," Donnelley continued, as if discussing some minor theological point, "he's not committing the Vatican to her position, either, at least not yet. He wants *you* to continue to gather facts, if you can. When he returns from Israel, he'll look at the matter again."

"But . . . what is Sister Daunsey going to accomplish other than to terrify a few million Irish Catholics?" Deauchez tried to keep his voice reasonable, despite his wish to shout, throw something, and otherwise evince his disapproval.

Donnelley held up a single fleshy hand in warning. "Michele, that is His Holiness's decision. Do you feel capable of carrying out your part?"

"Yes, Your Eminence."

"Good," Donnelley said brightly. He sat back in his chair. "Try to keep the traveling expenses reasonable, as always. And send daily reports to me via e-mail, please. I have something that should make that easier."

Donnelley pulled open a drawer and brought out a compact black cellular phone. The word "Telegyn" was molded into the plastic down the side. "It was a present from my niece, but I'd feel better if you took it with you. After all, you'll be in more remote locales than I."

Donnelley smiled warmly and held out the phone, making Deauchez feel like the most ungrateful soul who ever lived.

"That is extremely generous, Your Eminence. I have been wanting to try one of these."

"Well, we clergy must keep up with the times. We'll assess where you are near the end of the week. Of course, I encourage you to stay for tomorrow's mass. His Holiness will be leading the morning services and Monday is soon enough for you to start."

Deauchez took a small table in the cafeteria and ordered a pot of tea and some baked goods. Sister Daunsey arrived, reluctance screaming from every step. Deauchez stood up politely at her approach. She paused at the table, her hands on the back of an empty chair.

"I very much appreciate your meeting with me, Sister Daunsey," Deauchez said in his most welcoming tone.

She studied him suspiciously for another beat, then sat down.

Once she had made the decision to join him, Daunsey's attitude—quite deliberately, Deauchez thought—moved from suspicion to indifference in the space of a heartbeat. It must be a tactic she'd grown as a defense mechanism, he thought, a shield for all those times she'd faced an authority figure who disagreed with her. She pushed her chair back and slouched down in it, facing to the side, away from him. Her body language was so rebellious he had to suppress a smile. One would expect such a posture from a sixteen-year-old boy, but hardly from a Benedictine nun.

"I did my best to simulate an Irish tea. I hope it will do."

Daunsey glanced at the table briefly, then returned her gaze to Anywhere Else. "Very thoughtful of you, I'm sure."

He poured some tea into her cup and sank back in his seat. "I'm not your enemy, you know."

She didn't respond verbally, but she scooted up a bit in her chair and turned her body toward him a few degrees. She busied herself with cream and sugar.

"You said it was important on the phone," she said in her lovely Irish lilt, "but I can't see what you and I have to chat about. You made your position clear in the meeting, as did I."

"I know. I wanted to apologize for any . . . emotionalism on my part."

She shot him another suspicious glance but didn't say anything.

"Do you know about the pope's decision?"

"Aye. He told me himself."

Deauchez blushed at that, but didn't rise to the bait. "What do you think of it?"

Daunsey was looking over the baked goods. She selected two muffins, a croissant, and a lemon tart and put them on her plate, using her fingers. She licked powdered sugar from her thumb.

"He should endorse the Santa Pelagia message. It would make a lot of difference to the older Catholics. But I've grown used to workin' around the Vatican. I can do so again." She took a large bite from the lemon tart.

"I was surprised, actually, that you had not yet left. I thought you would need to make a statement or . . . something."

"I already did," Daunsey replied, speaking around yellow custard.

"Really? I'm sorry I missed it."

Daunsey's look said she found that about as likely as his saying he was sorry he'd missed being castrated.

"Where . . . uh . . . where might I find a copy of that statement?"

"Father, if you want to know what disaster I've already wrought, why don't you just ask me?" Daunsey took several large gulps of tea and began ripping the croissant into pieces.

"Very well," he said levelly. "I would like to know what you have released to the public so far. Is that not a valid question?"

Daunsey shrugged as if to say she couldn't care less if he knew one way or the other. "I made a press statement just before my flight here, and I e-mailed an article for our newsletter back to the order. It's gone out, so they tell me. I also gave a phone interview to *Catholic Digest* this mornin'."

Deauchez very deliberately picked up his cup and sipped.

"That makes you angry, doesn't it? *Catholic Digest*."

"Not at all."

"You're a terrible liar."

Daunsey was chewing the croissant, curiosity and amusement on her face. It transformed her, somehow, and for the first time Deauchez realized what Sister Daunsey was: she was *simple*, not intellectually, but emotionally. She was like a bright, willful child, incapable of duplicity or of suppressing anything, just as passionate and compassionate and curious and wide-eyed. If you stepped on a bug in her presence, she would probably respond exactly like a five-year-old, with equal parts of biological curiosity and devastation at the cruelty of life. This childlike quality could be viewed, as no doubt the pope *did* view it, as a sign of God's favor. How particularly irritating.

"The *Catholic Digest* usually only prints stories approved by the Vatican."

"True enough."

"I thought the Vatican was staying neutral for the moment."

Daunsey shrugged. " 'One nun's experience at Santa Pelagia.' That's the title. The Vatican is neither confirming nor denying my experience."

Deauchez didn't say anything. He didn't trust himself to open his mouth. Neutral indeed! If it was in the *Catholic Digest*, millions of devout Catholic mothers and grandmothers would read it as God's own truth.

"Why are you so sure nothing happened at Santa Pelagia?" Daunsey asked him. Her tone was genuinely interested for once, instead of being challenging and derogatory. "Is it because you didn't see anything, and you feel that God should have—*would* have—spoken to *you*, if he'd really sent Our Lady there?"

Deauchez flushed, uncommonly upset by her remark. "You are so far from the truth, you have no idea."

"Meanin' what?"

"Listen to me," he said, leaning forward. "In my job I have investigated many cases, cases where everyone was sure either God or Satan himself was present. And in every single one of those cases, it was clear to anyone with an unbiased position and a . . . *rudimentary* understanding of psychology, that the people involved had simply worked themselves into a frenzy. They would seize any mundane occurrence as a sign: a raven lands in a tree outside and it's an omen of evil! There is blood in the yolk of an egg and it's a sign of Satan's presence in the village! And when people get panicked and afraid, it's very easy for them to believe they see things, or even act out in bizarre ways, which are, of course, interpreted as further proof of the presence. We can devolve in an instant from modern people living in the age of science to the superstitious peasants of the Middle Ages. It only requires the right trigger!"

"I cannot speak for your other cases, Deauchez, but that's *not* what happened to me. I was not hysterical or afraid or even thinking about anythin' other than work the day I had the dream. And I wasn't panicked in Santa Pelagia either. I knew what was happening. It was *the Virgin*. It didn't have anything to do with me, any more than you, sitting there, can appear or disappear simply by my wishin' it so."

Deauchez leaned back in his chair and sighed. They clearly weren't going to change each other's minds. "As you say. So what are your plans?"

"I fly back to Dublin tomorrow, after mass." She popped the entirety of one of the muffins into her mouth. Fortunately, it was a small muffin.

"And?"

She shrugged and shook her head, chewing busily. "Dumpno,"

she mumbled, swallowing. "I have a lot of details to work through."

"Can I ask you something?"

She rolled her eyes and nodded.

"I wondered about you, I mean before all this. Don't take this as criticism, but . . . If you have such deep disagreement with the Church on fundamental issues like birth control and the role of women, why do you stay?"

"I was *born* Catholic, Father. There are millions of Catholics in Ireland. I won't abandon those who believe they must still follow Rome, and I won't apologize for my faith. I decided to try to make the Church somethin' I could be proud of, to try to make it stand for what it *should* stand for, for myself, and for Ireland."

"Oh," Deauchez said lamely.

"Can I ask *you* somethin'?"

"Certainly."

"Why did *you* become a priest if you don't believe in God?"

Deauchez swallowed some saliva down the wrong pipe and convulsed with coughing. "I—*do* believe—" Cough. "—in God."

Daunsey looked irritatingly smug. "As you say."

She stood, grabbed the last muffin from her plate and another tart from the tray, and turned to go. "I'll be seein' you, Father."

"I would like to keep in touch."

"So you can spy on me?"

"I will anyway. Do you have an e-mail address?"

After a moment's hesitation, she gave it to him.

"But I'm going to be very busy, and I'm not sure where I'll be." And with that cautionary note, she walked away.

Yes, Deauchez thought sourly, *I'm sure you'll be* very *busy.*

NEW YORK CITY

Hill slipped from Abeed's meeting a minute or two before it broke, about the time his fellow reporters also began edging toward the door. If they hadn't smelled what they were covering before the meeting, their drawn faces told him they had, at least, caught a good strong whiff of it now. The *Times* van was circling, and he caught it a block or so from the church.

"Hey, man! Not a good idea to go wanderin' around here at night," Bucky, the driver, complained as Hill ducked inside. "I'd a been around in another minute. I saw you grabbin' for the door and I *about* had myself a heart attack!"

"I don't *have* a minute, Buck, old boy." Hill grabbed his laptop from behind the seat, booted up his word processor, and began typing furiously.

"Where to?"

"Circle out a little wider. I wanna see what the crowd's gonna do."

Bucky grunted as if to say Hill wasn't going to be seeing much of anything with his nose stuck in that computer screen, but he didn't interrupt again.

Ten minutes later, Hill had finished his first draft. It needed work, but it had a nice energy—energy, Hill supposed, that came from the adrenaline that was only now beginning to chill in his veins. He bumped the file off to his editor and looked up for the first time.

The van was crawling now, and the traffic was horrendous, mostly heading the same way they were.

"We goin' *toward* the church or *away* from it?" Hill asked.

"Toward it. Next street." Bucky sounded nervous. Hill realized why. Besides the cars, there were walkers and runners on the sidewalks, also heading toward the church. Some of them were young, and they carried baseball bats or broom handles. Some were older folks, tired-looking men, and women, too, their tight polyester shorts and tank tops spread over bulging bodies. The pedestrians didn't seem to be paying each other any mind, though the young ones were dodging through the old, provoking the occasional curse.

"You got the time to tell me what's goin' *on* now?" Bucky asked in his own lovable way.

Hill opened his mouth to speak but the shrill bleeping of a cellular cut him off. He patted down his jacket, found nothing; lifted his considerable bulk off the seat to get at the lost regions in the pockets of his jeans.

Meanwhile, Bucky plucked a cellular from his shirt and answered it. "Hullo?" He shot Hill a dirty look. "Oh, yeah. He's here." He passed the phone to the reporter.

"This is Hill."

"It's Jeanine. Why aren't you carrying your phone? I've been trying to reach you for the past half hour."

"Um . . . left it on my desk." Hill grinned apologetically at Bucky. The older man rolled his eyes.

"You still in Harlem?"

"Yup. Any news?"

"I'd say *so*." Jeanine sounded excited.

Hill's heart rate, which had just come down after he'd spewed out his guts on the electronic screen, kicked back up into high gear. He began feeling his pockets for a pen, then realized his laptop was still booted. He put his fingers on the keys. "Talk to me, baby."

"Pastor Fortune Simnali, Zaire. He's a faith healer and minister of a large Protestant church. Sagara Bata, Calcutta guru. He's got a big following in India and can supposedly levitate and produce things out of thin air. Father Polo Dimish, ex–Russian Orthodox monk and recent reviver of the Skoptsy traditions. Ever heard of Skoptsy?"

"Nope. But keep going."

"Dame Wendy Clark, London—astrologer and psychic to the royals. 'Sister Mercy' from Sidney, Australia. She looks like a born-again preacher type."

"Any more?"

"*Oh,* yeah. Yoshiko Tanomaru, Tokyo, cult guru. Sister Mary Magdalen Daunsey, Dublin, Benedictine. Jürgen Hefner, Germany, founder of some kind of magic cult based on Rosicrucian and Illuminati traditions."

"Really?" Hill wiped his hands on his shirt—they were perspiring like mad, getting slippery on the keys.

"Oh! You won't believe this one: Walter Matthews, Canada. He started this church called First Church of Jesus the Blessed Redeemer and is high up in the National Race Alliance. You know, the neo-Nazis."

"Christ!" Hill's stomach did a flip-flop like a trained seal jumping through a hoop.

"That's it."

"Wow! Major score. How many is that, J.?"

They reached a cross street, and down three blocks to their left, Hill saw the church. There were swarms of people outside. The crowd almost reached their intersection and looked even longer on the other side. And it was gaining momentum. Some people were screaming and crying and having religious fits, but most were busy smashing things, raising their arms in rebel yells.

"Uh . . . Look, man, I really don't think . . ." Bucky sounded scared.

Sirens sounded in the distance—a *lot* of sirens. A rock hit the side of their van. If either he or his driver had been white, Hill knew, they'd be even more fucked than they already were inside this marked news van.

"Back out to ten blocks at least," Hill suggested. Bucky looked relieved.

Hill turned back to the phone. "What?"

"I said that's *nine*," Jeanine shouted.

Hill squeezed his eyes shut and counted in his head. He'd already known about seven: Sanchez, Stanton, Andrews, Giri, Abeed, Kratski, and Levi. Now there were nine more. That made sixteen total.

"I think there's a few more, J., keep looking. And make sure you pull all the press clippings or footage on whatever you find. Leave 'em on my desk. I'll be back there tonight."

Hill's eyes were fixed on the people in the street. "Man, they are goin' *nuts* down here, J."

"Really? Be careful. Oh, I got a little more on Father Deauchez, too." Jeanine raised her voice to overcome the mounting cacophony.

"What is it?"

"I mean, it's probably not relevant, but . . ."

"*What*, Jeanine?"

"Just some stuff from when he was a kid. Press clippings. He was involved in a big custody battle between his father and grandmother. His father claimed mental abuse on the grandmother's part. He won and she killed herself."

It was a weird background for a favored Vatican priest. "Nasty," Hill said.

"I'll leave those clippings on your desk, too."

"Thanks. And do me a favor, would ya? Pop your head into Ralph's office and tell him I'll probably have a much better version of what I just sent him by press time."

"Will do."

Hill clicked the phone off just as another rock struck the back of the van. This time it cracked the glass.

"This is *not* my idea of a good time," Bucky growled. "Is your door locked over there?"

Hill pushed his lock down with an elbow. They were farther out now, but they were still crawling, mostly because of emergency vehicles. He had a feeling roadblocks would be going up any minute.

"Park it, and we'll wander on over there on foot," Hill said.

Bucky put on the brakes and gaped at him. "Man, are you plumb *crazy*?"

"Come on, you can look non-whitey-fied, can't you?"

"What?"

"Never mind. Bring the camera."

Bucky pulled to the curb, grumbling all the while. "You *know* we ain't s'posed to leave the van alone down here. We're gonna be lucky if there's a *motor* left by the time we get back. And there sure as hell ain't gonna be no *camera* left, neither. I'm gonna be carryin' it for about five seconds before some big mother grabs it."

But Hill was already reaching for his door handle, his news instinct erect and raring to go. "These are momentous times, my friend. Momentous times call for momentous actions."

Bucky did not look particularly inspired.

VATICAN CITY, ROME

There was something in the corner. In the dark. He huddled down in the bed, put his head beneath the covers.

But it didn't matter. In fact, it was worse, because now he couldn't see what the thing was doing; whether, perhaps, it was moving toward him. He was shaking with terror, that panic like an overfriendly second cousin that slept with him, curled around him, like two peas in a pod.

"Tell me what you see, Michy . . ." came the voice, the old, scratchy voice. He felt her weight beside him, smelled that peculiar mix of warm, funky, old-age smell and lavender. Under the covers he shook his head. No.

"Look! Look at him now! He's beckoning, beckoning! Michy, he wants to tell you something! Look!" The voice was cajoling, squealing with excitement, like it was a carousel he was being invited to see.

But the voice was a big fat liar. He dug deeper under the covers, desperate to get away. And then the hands came, pulling at the blanket, trying to unsheathe him, like a board being pried off a slug, and he struggled and struggled, knew he couldn't win.

"Michy! Uncover your head. Right now." Firm now, the voice. Annoyed.

And the hands, old but strong as iron, were pulling down the blanket and he was losing his grip.

"Now look, Michy!"

The blanket was no longer over his face. He couldn't help himself. He opened his eyes and looked in the corner. And there, in the dark, oh, in the dark dark dark . . .

He whimpered.

"Don't be a scaredy-cat! It's only a spirit."

The boy began to cry with terror, but he kept the noise of it to himself as best he could.

"It's a gift, Michy! You have to learn to speak with them. Listen and you'll hear what he's saying. Listen!"

And his mind obediently churned up whispering words; words from the comics owned by the boy down the street, words from the old tales his grandmother told, words from his nightmares. They were words, mostly, about the delicacy and juiciness of little boys.

"Grand-mère, please!"

Deauchez sat upright in bed like a shot. The room was dark, save the corridor light that made its way under the crack of his door. But he could see a little of that terrible place where forms mounded into shapes of black and gray and things had another character entirely from their innocuous ones of the waking day. He was staring into the corner beyond his bed. His eyes did not blink. He did not move. Slowly his heart rate slipped into second gear, his breathing eased from its rabbit pant.

"There's nothing there," he said out loud. The words sounded odd in the dead of night, alone.

He cleared his throat. "There's nothing there." He said it more loudly this time, and more firmly.

There was no response.

He reached over a shaking hand and turned on the bedside lamp. There was a moment, a fumbling moment, just before the bulb clicked to, when he thought for sure something was reaching up from under the bed. But the light came and it banished the dark, and all that came with it, in an instant of shining reason.

He studied the corner again, but there was only his desk and chair, a wastepaper basket. He got out of bed and went over to the small area that passed for a shrine in his room. There a picture of Christ—a smiling Christ, not a bleeding Christ—hung on

the wall. Below it was a small table with half a dozen candles
and a rug on the floor. Deauchez lit the candles and knelt. How
long since he'd done this? Two years? Three?

He folded his hands and looked at Christ.

"There's nothing there," he said.

Christ smiled, in seeming agreement.

And Deauchez began to chant the mantra for the first time in
what would doubtless be a very long night.

"Our Father, who art in heaven . . ."

CHAPTER 5

The mass was splendid. No matter how many times Deauchez saw it, he never grew jaded to the magnificence, the glory, the thrill of it. St. Peter's Basilica was so vast, with its marching marble walls and endless floors, its soaring vaults and even higher dome, with the colossal papal altar surrounded by the bronze enormity of Bernini's baldachino. It all but dwarfed the tide of humanity within, as if reflecting how God dwarfed man.

Oh, but the tide was splendid, too! The cardinals in their crimson ceremonial dress and white lace, the priests with their solemn black overlaid with snow-white vestments, the pope himself, in his shining cream and gold. The ceremony was weighted with a splendid ponderousness: the ritual, the vibration of all those voices pouring forth in response, the unearthly magic of the boys' choir.

When it was over, feeling very full and satisfied, as though he'd just eaten a tremendous meal, Deauchez could not resist the beckoning blue of the day. He left the Vatican to wander outside in the Sunday market.

The mass had enabled him to let go of all that was troubling him, nightmares both old and new, and he refused to pick that burden back up. Tomorrow would be soon enough.

A few blocks away the Sunday midday ritual was unfolding. Sunday market lasted only a few short hours instead of the day-long spree of the working week, and it had a lazy feel, a picnic feel—fresh bread and salami for lunch, perhaps, or a pig to take home for Sunday dinner; a newspaper full of fresh flowers, a bunch of asparagus tied with twine. Children played around the carts, mothers easing church finery from their darkly tanned limbs and pulling up cotton shorts in the gloom behind the carts. The little ones tugged and yearned, impatient to join the others.

The drought showed its gaunt face even here. The carts of apples, instead of being filled to overflowing, had room to spare. The apples themselves were not the plump, bursting specimens Deauchez recalled from his youth, but were instead tired-looking, as though complaining that it was just too damn hot.

And it *was* warm, even for August. The gentle touch of a light breeze gave little relief. He wished he'd taken the time to change before coming out. Perhaps he could have sneaked past his fellows in a pair of shorts and a T-shirt. How luxurious that would be! But the sun was on his face, at least, and despite its recent incessantness, he found himself drinking it in with the joy of a child.

He purchased some red grapes from an old man and a split roll smothered with Brie a few carts away. He found a stoop on which to sit, ate the bread and cheese, then munched some grapes pleasantly—they were only a tiny bit withered—and watched the people enjoying the day.

There was a pretty young girl selling flowers at a booth across from him, hair thick and black and glossy and pulled back in a casual ponytail to reveal a long, graceful neck. Her eyes were a bottomless black. The breeze ruffled the wisps of hair at her forehead and made the loose cotton bodice of her dress dance a bit, like a sail. She caught him looking at her, and smiled; it was a warm, shy blush of a smile. He felt his heart do a long-forgotten leap and he grinned back at her, before it even registered.

Embarrassed, he looked away. No use fueling some penchant for priests in the poor girl. Absently, he popped another grape into his mouth.

And spit it out. A horrid, rank, rotten taste bloomed like a noxious ink upon his tongue. Without the least thought of dignity, he raised a hand and spit into it repeatedly, searching for and expelling any remaining trace of that bitter fruit.

Having gotten rid of the worst of it, he examined the grapes in his hand and saw that several in the bunch had black, cancerous-looking spots. Rotten! He dropped the whole lot onto the street in disgust and wiped his hands on his pants.

He looked over toward the cart where he'd purchased the grapes, thinking he would take them back. Then he noticed that a cart much closer, a cart of apples, their faces upturned to the sky,

also had the black spots, and, as he looked at them with puzzlement, three or four more of the ugly spots suddenly appeared on
previously pristine apples *right before his very eyes*.

He looked around with growing alarm at the other carts in the
market and saw the spots starting, yes, on a bed of corn's green
jackets, on a barrel of strawberries whose keeper was peering at
the fruit nearsightedly, reaching out a hand to swat at a growing
spot on a strawberry basket as though it were a fly. His eyes returned to the booth with the pretty girl. She gave him a broad
smile again, looking up shyly from under her lashes in an unmistakable invitation. And as he watched, a black spot began to grow
on the caramel flesh of her neck, spreading out like a burn on a
piece of film. Something in his face must have registered, for her
look turned to one of puzzlement and unease, followed an instant later by pain as her hand rose to her throat.

But Deauchez was no longer watching. He had risen and was
now sprinting for the Vatican.

Behind him, he heard the first screams begin.

NEW YORK CITY

"Hill! . . . *Hill!*"

Somewhere on the fringes of his consciousness the name was
registering. Probably not the first time someone called, but by the
fourth or fifth it was distracting him and he was getting annoyed.
Couldn't they see he was busy? He was scanning the Internet
press, namely his competitors, reading all the Santa Pelagia–
related stories, and he was almost done. *Los Angeles Times* . . .
laughable.

None of the other newspapers or magazines were treating
Santa Pelagia very seriously yet, and although the name was tied
to several of the prophets individually—Abeed and Stanton,
namely, and Andrews in the *Los Angeles Times*—no one had put
them together or talked about the bigger international picture.
No one except Simon Hill.

He grinned. No, nowhere on Earth was there anything close to
the piece the *New York Times* had run this morning; not the front-
page headline, but a few paragraphs and a title on the front page,
with the rest, half a page's worth, on page four. He'd run sixteen
names with it, as well as summarizing each prophet's slant on
the whole thing. He'd been up all night, he and Jeanine, but he
was still jacked. Looking at it like that, all the Santa Pelagia

prophets together, even if he *was* probably still missing some, well, it made one pause.

And all over the country on this fine Sunday morning, *New York Times* subscribers would be doing just that. They would be standing up from their sofas or kitchen counters, putting down their coffee cups, and they would be wandering over to the TV or radio, newspapers in hand, to check out WWN and see what this thing meant. But WWN hadn't lined up their ducks yet, and they were getting phone calls telling them so. They were scrambling, and the name on that scramble was Simon—

"For Christ's sake, Hill, get your ass over here *now*!"

That voice belonged to Ralph Bowmont, managing editor, and he sounded upset. Hill looked up and realized that everyone who was in on this Sunday morning—which was about ten people—was lined up against the windows that faced West 43rd. Hill got up.

"Oh, my God!" Nancy said. He heard the distant sound of a car crash. He quickened his step.

Four stories down something was going on. It was early on a summer Sunday morning, and the traffic was at perky but hardly rush-hour levels. There were people on the sidewalks, mostly people out enjoying a Sunday-morning jog or walk, churchgoers on their way to services, and tourists in for the weekend and out to see the sights. Of course, the inevitable homeless were sprinkled liberally throughout.

Rather, that's the way it *should* have looked, but someone or something had cracked the otherwise normal picture. Cars were blaring their horns at drivers who had simply stopped for no apparent reason. Three or four vehicles were crawling onto the sidewalk in an effort to move around the blockages. Where these cars were going *to* wasn't clear, but they apparently did not at all like where they were at. Hill saw one driver abandon his Volkswagen Jetta entirely and take off running down the street, swatting at the air as if fanning himself while he ran.

And he wasn't the only one. Joggers were getting heavier use from their Reeboks today. Sweatsuited men and women were sprinting down the street, as were men and women in Sunday finery. Some were ducking inside any building they could, some were diving down subway steps, some were pushing into already-occupied taxis, and some were just running, going for broke. Across the street at ground level was a small bakery—Hill knew it intimately—and people were packing into the place. The owner was at the door, trying to lock it, but people were still pushing in. Every time the door opened, Hill could see the faces of the people inside stretch—they were screaming.

Behind him, the phones started ringing, all at once and unceasingly.

"What is it?" Hill asked no one in particular.

"Look at them!" Ralph exclaimed. There were dashes of excitement on his cheeks.

And then Hill saw one teenager, a punk with green hair. He was just standing in the middle of the sidewalk watching people run. He took off his leather jacket, revealing a T-shirt that matched his hair, and held his skinny bare arms up to the sky in a defiant gesture, fists clenched. Hill noticed that the boy's face had dark spots on it, and his pale arms, held out like that, began to blossom similar dark spots. Hill squinted.

"Christ, what *is* it?"

"You should know, Hill, if anybody does. Tim, call security. Tell them to lock the doors downstairs."

"Really?" Tim, who was barely twenty, was impressed.

"Do it! Move!"

Tim took one last look out the window and took off.

"No one's goin' out there to cover this. Not until we find out what these things are," Ralph said. Not a single reporter objected.

Susan came running over from her desk. "Just talked to Dr. Mackleby. They're on the West Side, too. He's examined a couple—said they're basically *rotting* the flesh. The ones he saw were quarter-size and didn't seem to be getting any bigger. He said they 'hurt like a son of a bitch.' "

"What's causin' it ?" Ralph asked.

"A chemical accident?" Nancy suggested.

"Mackleby said he doesn't know, but it must be airborne."

"Great. Get back on the phone," Ralph ordered. "Call Johns Hopkins or the university. Mackleby's a good writer, but I wouldn't bet my *cojones* on his medical expertise."

"Right." Susan took off.

"Everybody else—on the phones. If you were leaving, too bad. This has A-number-one priority. Mayor's office, Austin. White House, Frank. Police, Allison. The rest of you, start calling your regions. Anyone who's not in, call 'em at home and get them checking *their* regions. I want to know if this thing is anywhere other than the Big Apple, and what people are doin' about it."

"Why would it be anywhere else?" Nancy asked, confused.

Ralph didn't answer; he assigned her. "Go call the super and see if we have an air-recirculation feature. He'll know what I'm talkin' about."

Nancy seemed to know what Ralph was talking about, too, because her eyes widened and she hurried off as if her life depended on it.

"Frank, go tell Susan to ask her medical guys if it can get indoors, and see if she can get 'em to make up a list of emergency dos and don'ts."

Below, the streets were reaching an eerie sort of stabilization. Most of the pedestrians had found shelter; there were lots of faces peering out through windows at ground level. More drivers had abandoned their vehicles for buildings, while others had their windows rolled tight and were honking, trying frantically to drive on. At the bakery, the door was finally locked, but many inside were examining themselves and, apparently, were not happy with the results.

Hill started to return to his desk. He was itching to call Stanton or Abeed. He knew what Ralph was thinking. He was thinking it, too.

"Hill: in my office! Now!" Ralph snapped. Hill did a one-eighty and padded obediently behind his editor.

"Talk to me," Ralph said as soon as his office door was closed.

Hill was at a loss. "Wow."

"You're gonna have to do better than that, son."

"I can't believe this!" Although the thing happening in the streets scared him, Hill's state of shock was, at least for the moment, more akin to that of a man who's just been told he's this month's big jackpot winner and is having difficulty getting it to sink in.

"I know that you're probably up to your soft spot in self-kee-gratulations, Hill, but do you know what's gonna *happen* here, at this very building, when people begin to connect this with your article talkin' about the sores prophecy? They're going to be on us like flies on donkey doo-doo."

"Is that why you had them lock the doors?"

"Hell, yes! And they'll be callin' up here in a minute for a better explanation, so we don't have much time. Right now, Buckaroo, you may be the only man in this city who can answer these folks' questions, and those questions, this topic, is the only thing they're gonna care about for the next forty-eight hours or so, maybe a hell of a lot longer, if we can keep it juiced."

"I wouldn't say I'm *that* important," Hill said, but he couldn't suppress a smile.

"No, you're not. It's bullshit, and I know it, and you'd *better* know it. You probably don't know a damn sight more than you've already printed, but the public, they don't know that. And you'd better work your ass off getting new information so they don't find out."

"I'm all over it," Hill said ardently.

"You'd better be. Startin' about five minutes ago, you've got a couple a thousand reporters on your heels, includin' all the big boys at the networks, so if you want to keep your lead, you'd better start runnin'."

"Right." Hill got up.

"Not quite done," Ralph remarked. Hill sat.

Ralph was a shrewd native Texan of a size that proved that everything in Texas *was* just plain bigger. Hill knew Bowmont had gained his coveted post through his exemplary news wiles and not, as some of the whiners in the office liked to claim, because his family name had OIL written all over it in huge diamond letters. Hill had too much respect for Bowmont not to hear him out, even if he *was* feeling like the cat who ate the canary.

Ralph looked thoughtful. He hit his phone's speaker button and dialed out to the newsroom. Susan answered.

"What kind of coverage are we looking at?"

"It's all over the U.S.—at *all* the major affiliates I've talked to so far," she said breathlessly. "Hold on."

Susan hit her own speaker button, and Hill could hear the sounds of the newsroom outside.

"Ralph wants to know where it's at!"

"Munich and Berlin have been hit!"

"Middle East has it, according to Haifa!"

"Western Russia's affected—still checking."

And the voices chimed on. *London, Paris, Beijing, Calcutta, Tokyo, Johannesburg, Mexico City, Warsaw, Hong Kong, Jerusalem*, all affirmative.

When it was over, the newsroom outside was stunned to silence, as were Ralph Bowmont and Simon Hill.

"Good job, keep going," Ralph told them. He hit the speaker button to disconnect. "K-rist!" he breathed, a strange excitement in his eyes.

"I really didn't think . . ." Hill said guiltily. That glow of satisfaction over being, well, *right* about the potential of the Santa Pelagia story was fading fast in the realization of the enormity of it. In its place was emerging a horse of a much darker color. "Christ, what *is* it?"

"Don't go losin' your nerve on me, Hill. This may be pure co-inky-dence. It may have nothin' to do with your Santa Pelagia story—probably doesn't. But just in case, I'm puttin' your story on red alert. You have a team, Hill. You can take the second conference room for your command post, toss the travel budget out the window. Whatever you want, you've got, but I want the *Times* to stay number one on this thing. Are you ready to ride?"

"Yes, sir!"

"Good."

Hill was just getting up when the door opened, sans knock. Susan's face, drained to a pasty white-blue, peered in.

"What's up?" Ralph asked, alarmed.

"It affects animals, too, Ralph," she said, her lips drawn back cruelly from her teeth. "And . . . and plants."

They both just looked at her.

"It's getting the *food*, Ralph," she said. "It's getting the *food*."

GENEVA, SWITZERLAND

"It's *WHAT*?" Fielding roared, looking for all the world like he was about to execute General Brant for being such an inappropriate joker, such a bold-faced liar.

Brant looked loath to repeat himself, but he did. "It's rotting our crops, Mr. President, right in the fields."

"How the hell can it do that?"

What Fielding meant, thought Cole, was, *Who gave it permission to do that?*

Cole looked out the open window toward the streets of Geneva. He'd never seen a room empty as fast as the U.N. summit room had when the announcement came in about the sores. Every delegate had run for their country's private conference room, desperate to get on the phone and find out what was going on back home. Not that anyone regretted the abortion of Prime Minister Billingsworth's long, posturing ramble about Good Will and Trust and the Inadvisability of Sending the Entire Planet into a Police State.

"It's August," General Brant said.

"I know what goddamn month it is!"

"What I mean is that we're at the *height* of the fall harvest season. Corn, wheat, potatoes—all of it—it's in grave danger of being wiped out! That's eighty percent of our annual total."

Fielding's face turned various colors as he mentally went through the paces of this particular pony ride. He sank wordlessly into a chair. He looked the way Cole had always known he would look when the going got really tough—like a twelve-year-old bully who's finally been socked a good one.

"Who *did* this?" Fielding asked bitterly.

General Brant's chin tilted ever so slightly up as if defending his honor; he did this whenever he had to concede ignorance. "Mr. President, we just don't know. The scientists are saying it's some kind of spore-borne bacteria. They've never seen anything like it."

"Somebody *had* to do it! Was it that bastard Lee?"

"Unlikely. China's been affected, and the Middle East, the Russians . . . We haven't found anyone who hasn't been hit as hard as we have. And we don't even know yet if it *could* be man-made."

No one in the room said anything for a moment. They were still trying to absorb the enormity of the thing. But Cole had absorbed it. "Mr. President," he began, in a grim and concerned tone. "I know we're all devastated by this news. But I'd like to offer a suggestion."

"Yes, Cole?"

"The source of this toxin can be determined later. Right now it's critical that we focus on the crops."

"And what is it you suggest we *do*?" Brant said in a mocking tone.

"If these spores *are* airborne, they probably couldn't get through a filter—say, for example, sheets or canvas. We could construct quick shelters for the crops."

Brant stared at Cole as if he'd just suggested that they turn on the Bat signal.

"If you put ten- or twelve-foot poles around the edges of the fields," Cole explained patiently, "then hang sheets or blankets or military canvas between the poles, that would keep the wind from blowing through the crops. Some spores might still get in over the top, but there would be far less damage. Perhaps your military engineers could fine-tune the idea, General."

Brant shook his head, but Cole could tell he was warming to the idea. He would. It had military operation written all over it.

"There are millions of acres of crop fields," Brant said dubiously.

"Exactly. I suggest we issue an emergency press statement over all major U.S. affiliates instructing farmers and any civilians living near fields on how to build shelters using sheets and stakes. Meanwhile, we can mobilize the military, including the National Guard. They can go out and assist. They'll have better materials."

Brant sat there, thinking about it.

"It's unlikely we'll salvage everything, Mr. President," Cole pressed. "But time *is* of the essence if we're to do any good at all."

"Well, go on, Brant! Go! *Now!*" Fielding said. He looked like he'd just found his nerve lying on the floor like a pair of fallen trousers and had hitched it up.

The general rose and trotted from the room.

"Good suggestion, Cole," the president said, giving Cole a smile as if he were awarding him a congressional medal. Cole watched as the breeze from the window ruffled Fielding's silver mane. A tiny dark spot appeared just below Fielding's left eye.

Cole smiled back, watching it grow. "Mr. President, I only hope it helps."

SOMEWHERE OVER THE MIDDLE EAST

Sunday evening's flight from Rome to Delhi had numerous cancellations. Deauchez was able to get a seat without undue difficulty. Next to him, two Italian businessmen, both of whom had the painful, discolored spots, were—gingerly—discussing the theory that the sores were a biochemical accident and the apocalypse story just a government cover-up.

Nearby sat a Slavic grandmother who looked like she'd never been on a plane in her life. She was dressed in black and praying with a crucifix. She was going somewhere urgently, perhaps back to the homeland to live out the planet's few remaining days. Or maybe she was going to join one of the prophets. Nearly everyone on board looked a lot more nervous at the least bump of turbulence than was to be expected on an international flight.

Deauchez had no stomach for any of it. He pulled the Russian prophet Kratski's book from his briefcase and began to skim through it, as interested in avoiding conversation as in the research.

He was quickly drawn in. Kratski was explaining how certain properties of a hologram could explain age-old mysteries about our brains, our bodies, even physical reality itself. A hologram is constructed by using a split laser beam aimed at the object you wish to make a hologram of, such as an apple. The light from the laser and the light reflected back from the apple pass through an unexposed film, and a holographic plate is made of the *difference* between the two wave patterns. In other words, a laser hologram is a light *interference pattern*. The holographic plate looks like a bunch of squiggles or waves; not like an apple at all to the naked eye. Yet when another laser beam is directed at the plate, a three-dimensional apple is projected.

Kratski suggested that our brains work this way, too. Objects in everyday life, like tables and chairs, are constructed from billions of quantum particles of pure energy, but scientists have never understood how these particles are organized. Perhaps the energy frequencies are organized as interference patterns. It's our brain that automatically *interprets* the patterns, acting as a laser that allows us to "see" a table or chair. The fact that the other senses—hearing, taste, touch, and smell—have already been shown to operate as frequency analyzers supported the hypothesis.

Many unexplained properties of our brains fit the holographic model. When scientists tried to locate the place of memory in the brain, they found that memories are *nonlocal*. They don't reside in any particular cell but seem to be present everywhere in the brain. Similarly, if you break a holographic plate up into a hundred pieces, each piece will still project a full-size apple. *Each piece of a holographic interference pattern contains the information of the whole.* Just like our brains. Just like our very DNA—a fact which is the basis of cloning.

The theory also solves certain mysteries of quantum physics, such as why an electron changes its form from a wave or frequency, the building blocks of interference patterns, to a solid, which is what the brain interprets it as, based on *whether or not it's being looked at by a scientist.*

But Kratski went beyond a scientific analysis. He thought the holographic model explained the paranormal. If the world of matter consists of energy frequencies arranged as interference patterns, and if the subconscious mind is able to read them, might it not also be able to alter them? If so, it could account for cases of bodies being spontaneously healed by faith, people lifting heavy objects in times of crisis, telekinesis, stigmata, and many other physically impossible events.

And if all that was about to be proved, as Kratski believed, what might it open up in the intersection of the supernatural, the religious, and the scientific? Forget cloning! Perhaps future technology would permit humans to alter the fabric of reality itself by simply modifying the interference patterns of matter.

It gave Deauchez a chill, and a strange thought popped into his head. *If we're truly about to uncover the face of God, maybe he does not like it. Maybe we've eaten once too often from the Tree of Knowledge, and that is why . . .*

He pushed the thought away, slipping the book in the seat pocket as though he were shelving the entire subject. He felt a surge of anger. If God was doing this, then Deauchez would really be pissed off. But God *wasn't* doing this—and Deauchez made himself pack that thought up in a bundle and send it somewhere far away, somewhere excessively nonlocal.

It was the sores that had shaken him. He honestly had not expected it. Not even in the farthest reaches of his *what if*s. The occurrence of the sores had settled a weight on his chest with such force that it was difficult to know where to go for relief. It changed the urgency of everything, of the need to disprove and, paradoxically, the need to believe. So he was doing what Cardinal Donnelley had told him to do. He was going on with the pope's mission; had decided, in fact, to leave right away.

Deauchez sighed and took the printout of Hill's *New York Times* story from his pocket for the hundredth time. The story was available in many international papers now, Hill's byline still on it, but this was the original, downloaded from the Web.

Hill had found more of the Santa Pelagia prophets, as he called them, quite a few more, though he apparently didn't yet know about Will Cougar. Hill had rummaged through each prophet's press statements, summarizing how they were each defining the rules of the game. Kratski himself, for example, had the mission of gathering all of the intellectuals and artists of Russia and taking them to Siberia to wait out the coming apocalypse.

It was the same with each: some were staying put, some were going to remote regions, some to cities, but they were all calling people to them. It was likely that some number of people would go, especially now that the sores prophecy had—to all appearances—been fulfilled.

And then what? Deauchez didn't know. Perhaps he would find out in India. He'd chosen India because there were two of them there: Sagara Bata in Calcutta and Dishama Giri, a Hindu yogi, in Allahabad. And there was one more reason why he'd chosen India to start. It was an e-mail that had been forwarded to him from Donnelley. It was from a Father Hanley in Goa, India. The body of St. Francis Xavier, incorruptible for hundreds of years, was decaying.

CHAPTER 6

Old Goa was still the city it had been in the sixteenth century, when its populace outnumbered both London and Paris, and when its charms were so seductive, it was called the "Rome of the Orient." It was the world itself that had changed, making Goa appear to Deauchez's eye as a small and old-fashioned jewel, however dazzling it still might be.

In the midst of gilded palaces and baroque Indian temples lay *Sé Cathedral*. And within the cathedral complex was the Basilica of Bom Jesus, with its devoutly carved and slightly exotic wooden interior. It was here that the body of St. Francis Xavier was on display.

St. Francis Xavier had come to Goa in 1542 and was responsible for innumerable Catholic converts among the local population. He was one of those men who had dedicated his life and his fire to breaking the will of those with belief systems different from his own, to molding their minds in his own image, and he had been very successful at his mission. But, as the nearby Shri Mangesh Temple showed, his success had its limits.

Today there were very few people in the streets of Old Goa, and those who were out wrapped themselves tightly in veils and scurried from one place to another, as though the very air were poisonous. Deauchez saw a few dark eyes shooting glances at him from beneath thick dark cotton, and it struck him how fortunate he was to have escaped contracting the sores himself. Thank God he hadn't been outside that long in Rome and that the spores were mostly gone by now.

He arrived at the cathedral and found that the sanctuary was quite warm, for all the windows were closed. There were only a few older people in the pews, praying silently. He felt a surge of disappointment. Why had he come here? He'd expected . . . what, hysteria? Terror? Something about the body—yes, he'd expected something more.

He passed through the side door and crossed to the basilica. That smaller chapel, too, was hot and underpatronized.

The coffin of St. Francis Xavier was one of the old-fashioned kind that Deauchez found both fascinating and repellent. Its glass walls allowed easy viewing of the corpse, which was dressed in finery. A silver and bejeweled casket surrounded the glass walls, and an outer stone tomb enhanced the effect further still.

Slumped in a pew next to the glass coffin was an older priest. He was just sitting there, staring at the body. Deauchez approached the coffin and peered in through the glass walls at the object of the older man's attention. The saints' bodies he'd seen usually looked mummified, though some did look remarkably lifelike thanks, at least in part, to wax and makeup. This particular corpse was turning into dust. Next to the golden sleeves, where a hand had once been, there was a grayish pile, one long finger bone still sticking up. As Deauchez watched, the face, which was caving in, caved in further still. One of the eyeballs fell back into the head and disappeared.

Deauchez uttered an unconscious syllable of surprise and disgust.

The priest looked up. "Who are you?"

The man's face was covered with the black sores. He looked like he'd lost an altercation with Jack Frost.

"I'm Father Deauchez from the Vatican. Are you Father Hanley?"

"Yes. Didn't think they'd send you so soon for *this*. Surely there's more important things going on right now." The priest looked sadly at the corpse. "More important things than one crumbling old saint."

"You might say I was in the neighborhood."

"We've not opened the case since January," Hanley said, as if defending himself. "We open it once a year to clean. It's not been touched since then."

Deauchez sat down next to the man. "When did it start?"

"Saturday."

"Was there anything else going on then?"

Father Hanley nodded. "We were hearing rumors. About Santa Pelagia. About the prophets."

"What did you hear?"

"I think it was maybe Thursday. People came to the church, upset, wanting to know if the stories were true. I myself, and Father Pavar, had not heard anything from the Vatican, or anything about Santa Pelagia, and we said so. But they kept coming and asking. They were hearing stories from other people, and they were frightened.

"Up until yesterday, the church was full. All day, all night, people were praying and crying . . . It was a scene. I didn't know what to tell them! I was hoping the Vatican would say something, but the pope only said it was being investigated."

"Oui."

"Then the body began to fall apart, and everyone could see it. What was I to do, cover it up? That would only make it worse. And when the body started to go, it made the people even more upset. You know, it has been said for a long time that when the body of St. Francis Xavier begins to decay . . ."

"I know," Deauchez said. "It is the end of the world." Similar beliefs were held about a number of Catholic relics around the world. "When did someone first notice the change in the corpse?"

"As I said, it was Saturday night, during the midnight mass. There were maybe three hundred people packed in here. They'd been whispering all day, you see, 'Watch the body!' 'Watch the body!' They knew the prophecy, and they wanted to be in *this* chapel so they could watch for it. Lo on about midnight, it began to go."

"You hadn't had any of the sores here then?"

"No. They came on Sunday, toward evening."

"Where is everybody now?"

Father Hanley looked down, ashamed. "Where did they go? They went to their prophets: Sagara Bata or that yogi in Allahabad. Even the ones I thought were really . . ." He heaved the sigh of a man who had failed at his life's work. "They said God had sent two prophets for India, and neither one was Christian, so what were they to do? Most went to the yogi, I think. That Sagara Bata, some find him questionable with his magic. I told them *both* were of the devil, *pagans*. They wouldn't listen."

Deauchez stood up to go. "I appreciate your help."

"Are you *leaving*? But what am I to do? His Holiness hasn't said what we're *to do*."

The older man's face was lost, lost as only a man used to following orders can be when no orders appear. Guilt burrowed into Deauchez like a puppy seeking a teat. Hanley was right, the pope hadn't given his flock much instruction about Santa Pelagia; and who was responsible for that?

"Just pray, Father Hanley. Trust in God and pray."

KITTATINNY MOUNTAIN, NEW JERSEY

The picture was static for a moment, then slightly cockeyed, then it cleared. All over America, people sat and stared at the man with the bad two-hundred-dollar blue jeans, white shirt, checked casual vest, and incongruous dress shoes. His fleshy face looked overly white in the bad lighting. His stiff, blue-tinged silver hair was mobilized in flaps by a sturdy breeze. He stood, a little unevenly, with one foot propped against a boulder on which a 225-foot war memorial obelisk was mounted; it was the centerpiece of High Point Park, a 10,000-acre wilderness, and the center, too, of Stanton's Kittatinny wilderness encampment. He looked like some weird hybrid of Billy Graham, Charleton Heston as Moses, and John Travolta in *Urban Cowboy*. Beyond him, dressed as if for a country-and-western hoedown, was a woman with an enormous head of matching silver hair. She was dabbing the corners of her mascara-laden eyes with a wadded handkerchief.

And the American people—more of them, that is to say, than were currently watching an original episode of *The X-Files*—sat nursing their Cokes or putting microwave popcorn in their mouths or absently swabbing aching black spots on their flesh, and they stared.

Most of them were skeptics. Even so, the least interested among them were more curious, more glued to their sets than they'd been in a long, long time. And all of them were trying to judge what this man was made of.

Unfortunately for the Reverend Raymond Stanton, he was not having a good day. Trying to set up camp and get the broadcast equipment working in "a day or two" had been about as smart as a defensive tackle who'd seen one too many dog piles. And Mimi was not helping. She was not one for wilderness, wilderness being anyplace where actual soil came into the picture. Two hours ago he'd sent Sarah—whom he gosh-blame needed here—back down to Port Jervis to purchase one of those RVs. Mimi had always turned up her nose at them, said they were tacky. Her idea of traveling was a good, honest, four-star hotel. But after getting her first true whiff of tent life, Mimi had had a change of heart.

And the people! A few hundred drove up with them from Georgia, a long convoy that had been fun for the first hour. More were arriving every day. And to his astonishment, there were already nearly a thousand people just *sitting* here by the time they'd arrived, no doubt inspired by that wonderful, marvelous, sure-as-syphilis-can't-deny-it plague God had sent down just like he'd promised. Hallelujah!

As powerful as it all made Stanton feel, it made it damn near impossible to get anything done. There was always somebody at his elbow desperate to introduce themselves like they were putting their name on God's recruiting list or something, or wanting to have long, shuddering conversations about how terrified they were, and what did he think was going to happen to Miami or Phoenix or Timbuktu because they had relatives there and blah de blah de blah? Praise Jesus and his angels, the fulfillment of the sores had been a real blessing, not to mention an utter rush, but now everyone expected him to know *everything*. Who did they think he was, Christ on the cross?

And Mimi, too, was having a difficult time being "on" and keeping her hair and makeup and outfit just so, twenty-four hours a day. What she wanted to do, he could tell, was vent at him like a steam train, but there were a few thousand people here making it impossible for her to do anything but smile. And the final out of the inning: Mimi had gotten those sores herself. *Bad.* Not that most people hadn't, but she, for crying out loud, was *his* wife. She'd been pasting makeup over them—particularly over a nasty one on her jawbone—all day long.

"Friends," he said into the camera. "This is Reverend Raymond Stanton broadcastin' to you live from Kittatinny Mountain, where we have begun the Lord's work. We have begun the gatherin' together of God's people in prep'ration for the Rapture.

"I know many of you out there have been afflicted by these terrible sores which were prophesized by me the day before they appeared anywhere in the world. And I didn't get this information through some kind of magic or New Age divination, no! I was called to Santa Pelagia, Mexico, and there I was given the word by *an angel of God*. So won't you come join us? If you believe in Christ as the risen Savior, this is where Jesus wants you to be in the days ahead.

"Now, many have asked me, Reverend Stanton, how come the plagues of the apocalypse have begun and we haven't been Raptured? Many have been taught that God would take his people *before* the start of the Great Tribulation. Well, friends, I will tell you what I believe, after havin' seen the sores do their work. I believe that many of us *were just plain not right with God!*"

Behind him, the gathering crowd gasped in protest.

"The Bible says the sores will appear on those *with the mark of the beast and who worship his image.* What is 'the beast'? Normally, we think of the beast as the Antichrist, and perhaps he *is* already among us and *does* already have your loyalty, I don't know. But in this particular verse it *could* mean somethin' else. It could be *money*—do you worship money, friends? Is that what drives your life? Or it could mean the devil himself and any sin therefore counts as *worshipin' his image.* Sex, drugs, greed, ego? Friends, *look* into your hearts! That's why God's kept you here through this plague, so you can see written on your own flesh whether or not you're ready for the trumpet's blow! This is your opportunity to get right with God before the Rapture comes because, I'll tell you what, once it's come and gone and you're still here on Earth, there'll be no second half!"

Those on the mountain behind him began to cry and ask God for forgiveness out loud, obviously because they had the gosh-blame things.

The good reverend put down his microphone and rolled up his sleeves. He held his arms up to the camera and turned them back and forth, invited the camera in for a nice close-up of his unmarked face.

"I do this to show you that it *is possible* to be right with God! And I'm not braggin'! To be honest, before my trip to Santa Pelagia, I might have been afflicted myself! But the experience in Santa Pelagia burnt me clean, like a blade purified in fire, and I want that for you, too! You *must be purified* before his return!"

The crowd increased their volume at this remark, praying for forgiveness. Stanton began to sweat. He wasn't used to this level of responsive vocalization during his sermons. What did they think this was, a Promise Keepers rally?

"It's true! Even ministers like Reverend Gentry O'Neal have

been afflicted. I hear he's been so struck in the face, there's hardly any unmarked skin left a'tall! What secrets do *you* harbor, friends? Now we're going to pray in a minute; pray for poor Reverend O'Neal's soul, and for all of our brothers and sisters who have been shown that they have hidden sins to make right with God. We'll pray for you out there, too. But first, there's somethin' I need to read y'all."

Stanton opened his Bible to a marked page.

" 'And the second angel poured out his bowl upon the sea; and it became as the blood of a dead man: and every living soul died in the sea.'

"Friends, these sores, as terrible as they are, are not the *end* of God's plagues on man! They're the *very beginnin'*! If you don't want to be left here on earth to face the *Antichrist*, and *Armageddon*, and the *final persecution*, and all of the terrors of the end times, then you must do two things! You must pray *deeply* for God to forgive your sins and come into your hearts. And you *must* come here to Kittatinny Mountain! I don't know how we'll find room for y'all, but God's been known to be handy at logistics, friends, and I know a way will come! Bring any campin' gear you need and food supplies for a couple of weeks, please, more if you've got it to spare. Now let's pray together for the souls of those afflicted . . ."

And many viewers *did* pray that night. Many prayed for the first time in years, maybe in their whole lives. A few even prayed for forgiveness. But what most of them were praying for, those who watched the broadcast who would, in better days, have flipped by Stanton with a flick of the remote as sure and fast as the answer of a Jeopardy finalist, *they* were praying for something else altogether. They were praying *Don't let this wacko be right*.

JERUSALEM

Pope Innocent XIV was having a difficult time finding that place of peace and openness from which he could give full attention to the rambling speech being given by Benzo Zahid of Jordan and being duly translated by Zahid's slim aide. Full attention was deserved, he believed, for the least of his interactions with others, much less what was rightfully due these men, leaders of nations, who were concerned enough about these water disputes to bypass even the World Food Summit.

But the pope could not stop thinking about Sister Daunsey and about the sores and the news from America about the salvage effort for the grain and, most keenly, about the fact that he should be in Rome, leading his flock at a time like this.

As was to be expected, the initial suggestions the pope had made regarding the fair sharing of the dwindling water supply—which had seemed promising enough to create this meeting—were now being picked to shreds with such stubbornness and pettiness that it seemed at any moment someone would give up out of sheer frustration and walk away.

It was his job to prevent that. It was not going well. Perhaps, he thought, that was because these men also had larger questions weighing on their minds?

"What has this got to do with your forefathers? We agreed to discuss this from a twenty-first-century perspective, that is all!" Israel's Prime Minister Shimon interrupted Zahid.

Innocent XIV held up his arms in a calming gesture. His huge white sleeves did wonders for drawing attention at times like these.

"We will not dwell on ancestral rights," he said soothingly. "This is not the purpose of our meeting today, nor is it relative to what we are seeking, which is the optimal use of water for all peoples in this region."

It stopped the course of the argument. The two men leaned back in their chairs in postures of distrust, both breathing a bit harder than normal. The pope sighed. Israel and Jordan's portion of the talks had the simplest issues. He was not looking forward to his meetings with Ethiopia and Egypt over the Nile, nor Turkey and Syria over the Euphrates next month. Both Ethiopia and Turkey, desperate for water, were overtapping their respective rivers. The countries downstream, their topsoil baking rock hard in the sun, were thirsty, hungry, and ready to go to war about it.

"Gentlemen," said the pope, "we all know that there are many things in our respective domains which require our attention at the moment, yes? There are urgencies we all feel. Can we not find a way to put this to rest quickly so that we can each move on to other matters? Perhaps, Benzo, points three and four, which you have found questionable, you might concede in return for Avraham, my friend, your agreement to points twenty and thirty-three? It is my feeling that these would not be items which would lessen either of your countries' benefit from this agreement."

"The underground aquifers are on our land. I will never submit to more than a ten-percent siphon in return for the pumping equipment. It's *our* water. Ten percent is a fair price!" Zahid said.

"We'd be dead at ten percent, and you well know it!" Shimon's face was livid. "We've been using that water supply since Israel began! Just because we've allowed you to stay on the land, you have the impudence to suggest—"

"Please!" the pope interjected. "Benzo, ten percent is no solution for Israel."

"Then let them find their *own* water supply!" Benzo said angrily.

It was at this stellar moment that a rock crashed through the palace window and landed on the thick Persian rug. Tiny shards of glass made their way to the conference table. Everyone jumped.

"We will be heard!" a loud male voice cried up from the street.

The four Israeli soldiers who were Shimon's bodyguards went to the window. They peered out from the sides cautiously, drawing their guns.

"It's Levi," one of the guards said. There was a touch of awe in his voice.

Prime Minister Shimon squeezed his eyes shut for a moment as though the name caused him a headache.

"He's the one from Santa Pelagia?" the pope asked softly.

Shimon nodded.

"There are two hundred with him at least," another soldier reported.

"Ask them what they want," said Shimon.

Zahid and his men were getting nervous. The pope gave Zahid a reassuring wink, as if to say they were all world leaders, above being aggravated by a few rabble-rousers.

"He says he wants to speak to you about the water treaty. He seems rational."

"Rational! Of course he's rational! He's a rabbi, not a terrorist," Shimon said tiredly. He went to the window and looked out.

"Shimon!" a man's voice called out challengingly. "Why do you waste our government's precious time with such idle pursuits? We will never agree with the Arabs, and we certainly do not need advice from the Roman!"

"Rabbi Levi, *shalom* to you also! Where did you learn to throw such a stone?"

Some in the crowd laughed.

"Where did you learn to dodge one? I tell you, Israel needs *action* now, not talking! Give up this waste of time and meet with me. We have much to accomplish! Water is the least of our immediate concerns."

"I have heard your new philosophy, Rabbi, and I respect your right to believe it, but as for me, the living must go on as always! *Shalom*."

Shimon tried to leave the window on that note, but the crowd in the street roared. Then Levi's voice rang out clearly. "Shimon, one more thing!"

The prime minister turned reluctantly back to the window.

"If I were you, I'd get the Roman and the Jordanian goat out of here! This is not a good time for a crusade!"

Some in the crowd laughed. Innocent XIV felt a clammy sweat break out over his skin. He couldn't even see Levi, but *the voice* . . .

Shimon turned away from the window and motioned to his men. They began to pull the heavy drapes together. In the next room they could hear the tinkle of breaking glass and the thud of a rock.

Shimon gave quiet orders to his men and returned to his seat, his jaw set with anger—and fear.

"He has many followers, this Rabbi Levi?" the pope asked quietly.

"Before, a few. He was a radical with a good voice. Now?" Shimon shook his head. "Some even say he's the Messiah, of course. He doesn't deny it."

"Shall we continue? Perhaps another room is required?"

Zahid stood up and threw down his pen. "No! I, for one, will not continue with such threats being made by my host!"

"It's not I—" began Shimon.

"*Israel* is my host!" Zahid spat in Arabic. No translation was necessary.

Zahid was gone. His storming out had been somewhat moderated by the pope's pleading insistence that he take the proposal home and think about it, and Zahid's own reluctant agreement to do so.

Shimon led the pope out into the corridor, as well. As the two elderly leaders walked toward the central foyer, they could hear the crowd outside getting louder. There were troops out there now: the unmistakable sounds of jeeps screeching to a stop, the clatter of boots, and barked orders.

"We are grateful for your efforts. Perhaps things will calm down," Shimon suggested.

"We will pray it is so."

"I think . . ." Shimon said carefully. "I believe it would be wise if we found a nice ship for your journey home, yes? It's a pleasant voyage to Athens, and the airport . . . it can get so crowded this time of year."

Innocent XIV was shocked at the words. Was the situation really that precarious? "Whatever you think best."

"Yes. I think a ship. And from Athens it's only a short flight to Rome."

They'd reached the central foyer. One of Zahid's soldiers, a teenage boy, was crouched there tying his shoe. He stood up, smiled at them charmingly, and ran off to find his leader.

DAY 8
GREENPEACE SHELTER, RIO DE JANEIRO

Jennifer Mallard and Pritch Gainer sat in two of the visitor's chairs in the monkey observation lounge. They had pulled the chairs up to the large window and were drinking bitter Brazilian coffee while they kept bloodshot eyes on the animals and on the staffers beginning the morning feeding. It had been another grueling shift of all-night nursing. Even so, both found it difficult to let go, to go off to sleep and leave the monkeys to their fate, or, rather, to the hands of the morning crew.

"D'ya think we should call someone, ey?" Pritch asked in a hesitant voice. His Australian accent got thicker when he was tired.

"The vet's coming round at ten," Jen replied, yawning.

"Yeah, but . . . d'ya think maybe we should *call* someone?"

Jen's brain was too dulled with lack of sleep to get his point immediately. She was watching Allison trying to get Apollo to eat some of the hot gruel they'd made up this morning. Apollo, a.k.a. Number Seven, was pushing the spoon away and wrinkling up his face with disinterest. His nose was crusty with congestion. Across the room, Joanne was trying to rouse Hermes for breakfast, but he only pushed her away and rolled onto his side in his cage, wanting to go back to sleep.

"Call someone? Like who?"

"Maybe," Pritch said enigmatically.

Jen was not in the mood. "Make some sense, please!"

"WHO—World Health Organization."

She looked at him sharply. "What for? We have the best vets in the organization right here."

"Yeah, but . . . Din' you read about some of those new viruses? Ebola 'n that? Maybe we should have someone who really knows their shit come in 'n check this out. Make sure it's just, you know . . ."

"Pritch, these monkeys have colds! Princess Di caught something when she was out and she infected the rest of the monkeys. That's what the vets say."

"What do they know? We isolated P. D. the minute she got back, din' we?"

"Airborne viruses can travel through vents. This place isn't *that* secure."

Pritch shook his head. "I saw a few other runny noses that night we was searchin' for P. D. Whatever this is, I don't think they got it from her."

Jen shrugged. "So they all caught it from a staffer. What difference does it make?"

"Have the vets even considered that it might be somethin' else?"

"*Look* at them, Pritch. They have *colds*. Bad colds. It's pretty damn obvious." Jen was angry. Pritch sighed and looked down at his white tennis shoes.

Jen went on in a more rational tone. "They were perfectly fine in the rain forest. They were perfectly fine when we picked them up. Whatever they've caught, they've caught it from *us*. Dr. Jim says they'll be bouncing back soon, they just need time to build some antibodies."

"I'm not sayin' you're not right, Jen. You're probably right as rain. I'm just sayin' we oughtta be sure."

Jen looked at the monkeys. Number Three, Venus, had roused and was clamoring—somewhat less enthusiastically than normal—for attention, climbing the chain-link walls of her cage in a sure sign of wanting to be held. Joanne went over and took her from the cage.

"Look at that. Venus is doing better," Jen said, brightening.

"Seems like it, don't it?"

They sat there for a moment, both lost in thought.

Jen didn't respond well to unpleasant suggestions, she knew herself well enough to know that, but if she was given time to think about it, roll it around, she sometimes came over to the other person's point of view. She was rolling this one around big-time.

"Pritch . . . did you hear about that one case—those monkeys in Washington, D.C.? The ones they'd imported for medical research from Asia that started getting sick in the holding facility?"

"I read the book."

"You remember what they did to *those* monkeys when *they* got ill?"

"I remember," Pritch said, but his expression indicated that he'd *just* remembered it, and it wasn't a pretty picture.

"That's right, Pritch. The CDC or USAMRIID or whoever they were *slaughtered* those monkeys. *All* of them. Then they found out that the virus they carried wasn't communicable to humans after all."

Pritch bounced his leg nervously, face pinched. He was watching Venus tug on Joanne's hair between bites of gruel. "You're right, Jen. It's just a cold."

OUTSIDE CALCUTTA, INDIA

From Calcutta to the Tarakeshwar Temple was thirty-five miles west along a narrow road. The scenery was voluptuous with distant mountains and rolling mounds; the landscape was still green with trees, though the grasses and native flowers had withered and many of the fields they passed had been abandoned to their fate in the sun.

For the length of the hour-long drive it was rare not to have some group of foot-travelers in sight, many in families that included the very young and the very old. Some carried heavy earthen pots on their heads. Deauchez's driver explained that the pots contained water from the Ganges, being taken to the temple to pour on the *lingam* of Tarakeshwar Babu, an avatar of Shiva. Normally this was a pilgrimage taken during certain Hindu festivals, but this current batch of penitents was walking toward something not on the annual schedule of events.

Long before they saw the actual encampment, their roadside companions had thickened, both cars and pedestrians. When they drew closer, the congestion made it difficult to continue. Deauchez's driver, a middle-aged Hindu, pulled the car over and declined the invitation to walk to the encampment. He would wait, he said. He did not meet Deauchez's eyes.

Deauchez had dropped the collar for the day, but he could not so easily disguise his skin color. Still, no one on the road paid him the least attention. He slipped along with the procession, which moved quickly now, as if sensing their proximity to the goal.

He heard voices raised in a chanting response long before he saw anything. Then the crowd slowed, and looking up ahead, he saw that they were passing through some kind of inspection point. He hesitated, then moved around the queue, trying to reach the head. He was a visitor. He wasn't interested in being officially processed.

When he reached the pass-through, he found that a group of about thirty men and women, most wearing blue traditional saris or pants, were taking names, handing out tags, issuing brief instructions, and moving the arrivals forward to another line that entered a large white tent. Parked next to the tent were white vans with red caducei painted on their sides. Those emerging from the other side of the tent seemed to be free to disperse, for they hurried toward the dip whence the chanting voices came.

Deauchez endeavored to pull one of the processors, an older woman, aside, but she didn't speak English. After a frustrating ten minutes—they tried to convince him to get back in line, Deauchez tried to show them his Vatican card—he found himself speaking with a young woman they'd called from the tent. She was dressed in a doctor's white coat and her thick black hair was kept back in the traditional braid. She approached Deauchez, wiping her hands on a towel. She looked tired and overworked and was quite pretty.

"What is it you need?" she asked him, using her coat sleeve to push her hair off her damp forehead.

"I'm with the Vatican. My name is Father Michele Deauchez."

"You're not here to join us then?"

"I'm just observing, I'm afraid."

"Well, if you're not staying long you can bypass the check-in. Come on, I'll take you round the tent."

As they walked he said, "Can I ask what all this is for?"

"The government. It was one of their conditions for this gathering. They want everyone registered."

"And the tent?"

She smiled. "Yes. Many of these people have no access to health care, yet here we are doing preventatives. I suppose you might call it a miracle."

"You're doing medical exams?"

"No, inoculations. Typhoid, typhus, tuberculosis. With the unprocessed water being consumed these days, and a crowd this size in close proximity . . . Well, the offer was made and we're grateful."

"It sounds as though the government is going to great lengths to support Sagara Bata's movement." Deauchez found this both surprising and alarming.

"Not especially. They just want the names. It was an international health group that offered the inoculations. We will be fortunate if the government simply lets us be. Sagara Bata says they will."

They'd reached the rear of the medical tent. Someone stuck their head out and motioned to the woman anxiously.

"I really must . . ." she said.

"I understand. Thanks for your time."

"If you go to the far west side of the gathering, you'll find English translators." She was already backing away. Then she turned and was gone.

Deauchez topped the rise and found himself looking down over a natural basin. People were seated or squatting down the sides of the basin the entire way around the expanse. It was a huge natural amphitheater needing little or no help from man to complete the function. No wonder Sagara Bata had chosen it.

And the man himself, Deauchez supposed, was the figure seated on the stage below. The stage was a simple wooden platform, perfectly round. Sagara Bata sat, cross-legged, in a high-backed, oversize armchair that looked like a bad prop. He, the chair, and a microphone were the only things on the stage.

In the distance, the temple was visible, but this crowd had little interest in it. They were taking their water jugs to the stage. Long lines of new arrivals, like spokes, formed down every aisle. A group of men stood around the stage, accepting the jugs and taking them, one at a time, to Sagara Bata. Without disrupting his discourse, he would dip a hand into the jug and sprinkle a few drops of the water into the air. The jug would then be delivered back to its owner. Occasionally, a person was allowed onstage to receive a blessing personally, though Deauchez could see little of that process, his view being blocked by the person's back.

Now he could reconcile what he'd heard of the man's teachings with the choice of locations—if indeed Sagara Bata *had* chosen it, and it had not been ordained by the voice of the Universe, as he claimed. Sagara Bata was not strictly Hindu, but Tarakeshwar Temple was. Sagara Bata referenced the *Upanishads*, and many believed he was an avatar, a living god come to Earth—a Hindu concept. Yet most of Sagara Bata's teachings were Buddhist, and some, as it was vaguely put, were teachings "for this time alone," which meant they were modern, almost New Age. At the core of all of Sagara Bata's teachings, so Deauchez had been told, was love.

That it was an effective gospel was evident. Those who were gathered here knew all too well whom they were here to worship: Sagara Bata, *not* Tarakeshwar Babu.

On the western side Deauchez found the group the female doctor mentioned. They were not difficult to pick out, even if the drifting sounds of English hadn't audibly pointed the way. There were several hundred Westerners here, listening to blue-saried translators dotted among the crowd. Deauchez tried to slip innocuously down onto the dry grass in the rear, but one of the translators tugged at his sleeve and motioned to the long line in the closest aisle. Deauchez tried to say that he had no interest in approaching the stage, but the translator just kept repeating Sagara Bata's words in English and motioning relentlessly for Deauchez to go. It was like trying to have a conversation with someone who was talking to someone else. Deauchez went.

He had plenty of time, as the line plodded forward, to observe the meditative crowd and take in Sagara Bata's message.

". . . When you have accessed the *watcher*, the third eye of your consciousness, you will be able to not only view *yourself* remotely and unemotionally, you will be able to view the entire fabric of life this way. We have seen the ripples in the fabric for a long time. We have felt the approaching tremors in the pattern. Now we see that the labor has begun. Is it the labor of a birth or the labor of dying? Ask the watcher. He will tell you simply and without emotion that it is both. What dies that is not reborn? What can be born if it is already alive?

"Like love and hate, sickness and well-being, fear and security, birth and death are dualities that are relative only to the unenlightened mind. The *watcher* knows that they are the same thing—they are *one thing*. Dying and birth are part of a continuous flow, as when a stream passes over first one rock and then another. It is silly for the stream to fear either rock. You are part of the stream, and nothing can alter that, nothing can stop the flow that is the Universe, and each of you in it, from moving forward in the direction in which you are intended to go."

Deauchez caught something out of the corner of his eye and turned to see a white male taking his picture. The man was in his early forties, lean and tan. He wore khakis. Deauchez frowned at him, and the man turned and took more pictures of the gathering, of the stage and various angles of the crowd. Deauchez relaxed.

". . . So what we must do is think unselfishly. If you are attached to your own physical body, if you are attached to this duality-driven concept called 'life,' to the shell of personality that overlays the infinite *watcher* that is the true core of your being, then you are not focused on the stream. The stream is the Universe. The stream is God. The stream is the combined essence of all of our watchers. What we must try to do is reach our watchers and plug into the stream purely and with absolute love. We allow ourselves to be pulled along by it rather than trying to alter or direct its course. We do not say, 'I want to keep living in this body, so do not cause anything bad to happen here.' This foolish sentiment is constructed of dualities. You are not your body, you are the stream; identify with the flow, not the rocks. If the flow wishes to pull you from your body, go with it effortlessly. And likewise, there is no such thing as 'bad things happening.' When your body is sick, a fever comes. Is the fever a bad thing? This is the simple judgment of a child. A doctor knows that a fever is the body's way of killing the organisms that threaten it. The fabric of life must heal itself; the stream must heal itself. We must give in with utter love to the healing. If we fight the healing we are like children fighting the doctor who wishes to give them a shot. If the healing requires famine or sickness or earthquakes or floods, we will welcome the healing, for we identify ourselves with the stream, the pattern, and we must focus all our joint energies on encouraging the stream to heal itself, by whatever means it must."

Oddly enough, Deauchez could feel the energy of which Sagara Bata spoke. Not the energy of the stream or the Universe, whatever that might be—what he *could* feel was the *focus* of the people around him. Everywhere he looked sat those with their faces slack in that peculiar blank look that indicated inward reflection, unself-consciousness. Some had their heads tilted slightly back to face the sky; others were slumped like marionettes with unmanned strings. Some had subtly joyous expressions and others reflected nothing. And for the most part, they were not afraid. Oh, there were tremors of fear here and there in the crowd, like the twitching of a muscle that is overstrained, but this was not a reenactment of Santa Pelagia. This gathering was not consumed by massive, hysterical fear.

Looking at the blank faces, Deauchez could not find relief in this fact. In truth, this new reality, this *focus* on "encouraging the healing" was, in some unfathomable way, even worse.

". . . We are one with the stream. The stream needs your energy to heal. We lend the stream all of our energy to heal. We go with the course of the stream and encourage its swift running, wherever it leads."

He was nearing the stage. Another Caucasian, a young woman a few feet ahead of him, was lifted up to see the guru. She approached Sagara Bata and the man handed her something. Deauchez realized that he didn't have a jug of water and he was, like the woman, a relative oddity in this crowd. What if they sent him up, too?

He looked for a way to slip from the line, but even as he did so his reasoning was confirmed. His arms were grasped by two of the blue-saried disciples and he was led toward the stage.

"No, really, I . . ." Deauchez began, but he was already being lifted up.

Well, there was nothing to be done. He approached Bata, smiling politely, wanting to get it over with. At least he wasn't wearing his collar; that would make this twice as embarrassing—a priest going to a guru for a blessing.

Sagara Bata was a short, round man with long, wavy black hair that fell to his waist and angular, hawkish features that contrasted with the roundness of his fleshy chins. He smiled at Deauchez and motioned him closer. His voice never faltered in its steady discourse, and Deauchez could still make out the words of the English translators in the section to his left.

As Deauchez stepped to Sagara Bata's chair the man held up his two hands. The sleeves of his blue robe were wide and they fell back to his forearms as if to reveal that his arms were bare and his hands contained nothing.

"Fear is a closed door that lies between us and the truth," Sagara Bata was saying to the crowd. His eyes gazed limpidly into Deauchez's, noting him, dissecting him. "Fear is our mortal ego's immature struggle to retain its selfness, to fight the stream. The only cause of fear, the only *source* of fear, is *our struggles against the stream*. When we fight the current of life, we begin to drown, we cannot breathe, and we have great fear. When we realize, finally, that to breathe and be safe we only need to stop our struggling, then all fear vanishes. Once we stop struggling there is nothing but the flow, and the flow is always in the perfect eye of God."

Sagara Bata brought his empty palms together in a clap and rubbed them vigorously. Slowly, his palms expanded as though cupped around something. Then Sagara Bata opened his hands and held them out toward Deauchez. Lying in the center of his palms was a small statue of the Virgin Mary. It was a benign thing, the kind of little resin statue that one could find in a hundred icon shops, except for the fact that Mary's mantle was black, for the Virgin of Santa Pelagia, and except for the fact that lying in those large, brown, intensely lined palms it was one of the most frightening things Deauchez had ever seen in his life. It struck terror in him inexplicably; it could not have been more frightening had it been a serpent or a human heart.

Deauchez tore his eyes away and looked up at the guru's face. Sagara Bata smiled, lifting the item, urging him to take it. Then he saw the priest's expression and his smile faded. He gazed at Deauchez, brows puzzled, eyes searching. His face, so open, so blank, was like a mirror that promised doors sprung and curtains lifted on realms that Deauchez could not bear to see. He backed away and stumbled off the stage. It was all he could do not to run.

SEDONA, ARIZONA

Trent Andrews was staring at himself in the mirror. He was sitting cross-legged on the cabinet sink. He felt it creak under his weight, but he had to get close, had to get right up close to that mirror.

He was naked. His face showed the stubble growth of a week without razors, and he wanted it that way. He needed a beard, he felt. It seemed right. What else did he need for where he was going, what he was turning into?

And what is that, Trent?

Perhaps the mirror would tell him.

Outside, there were already six thousand people gathered. Some of them were kooks, he knew—crystal-rubbers who would go anywhere the spiritual breezes blew. And some didn't even believe. They were sitting out there right now in exactly the same spirit as they would stand in line to sign up for a life insurance plan—mindless robots with their primary function set to "safety."

But none of that changed the fact that there were six thousand out there, calling his name. Not out loud, at least not often, but calling it nonetheless, sucking at his vortex. *Andrews, Andrews, Andrews.*

I Want, Need, Help.

Even now they were gathered below, as he had instructed Tyna; they crowded in the streets of the tourist village that didn't know what had hit it, down there beneath his hotel window.

The radio was set to WWN in the other room and it was going on and on, as it always did. Trent *had* to hear the news. In that respect, he was not unlike most of his countrymen who kept one eye on any and all sources of news these days, as they had during the Gulf War, the O. J. thing, and the presidential sexcapades that so characterized the '90s. Trent had the *New York Times* delivered every morning. He'd heard on WWN yesterday that the circulation of the *Times* had tripled in the last three days. The newscaster had called it, with an audible smirk, "miraculous."

"The White House repeated again at the lunch-hour conference that they do not have official numbers for the crop damage caused by the toxic spores. Estimates from the National Farmer's Alliance have put losses as high as sixty percent of this year's fall harvest. But Press Secretary Marshall Connor, who flew back from Geneva on Sunday, denied that these numbers were accurate, saying that the salvage effort has been deemed 'a great success.' He would not answer questions about how the crop

damage might affect the food summit or this year's exports of grain."

There isn't going to be any grain, Trent thought calmly. People around the country were beginning to think about survivalists. They were starting to think about how they wished they'd *been* one and that, if it wasn't too late already, they'd better get on with that stockpiling agenda real quick. They were thinking that even *before* the spores, weren't they? With that grocery store crash a week or so back? And now they were thinking about it with a *lot* more intent.

But those people had to worry only about themselves, maybe a handful of loved ones. Trent, he had six thousand mouths to feed, and more were coming every day.

He put his hands up to the mirror and studied the lines of his palms. He knew the standard palmistry interpretations, but none of that seemed worth a damn now. His death line hadn't been cut in half overnight. Nothing had changed.

Those Rapturists, Stanton's group, they were expecting to be picked up any minute. What did they care about food? But Trent, he'd told these people they were going to survive, to start a new world, that they'd be safe here.

What was he supposed to do? Would Imrlll give him the power to turn rocks into bread?

He shut his eyes tightly. He needed his therapist! He needed to go into a hypnotic state and search for the answers. Had Imrlll told him something he had missed?

There was a hesitant knock on the bathroom door. Tyna, no doubt. The natives were getting restless.

Trent leaned forward and kissed his own reflection, met it forehead to forehead and tried to send himself images of peace.

It really felt as though he were kissing, touching, someone else. He didn't recognize himself anymore. He was amazed and afraid of what he was becoming. The Change—the New Man—was descending. It was thrilling. It was terrifying. What would He be like?

Trent unfurled his legs and swung down from the sink. He strode to the bathroom door, and on past Tyna, whose shocked look he ignored, then to the double doors that accessed the small balcony. He opened them and strode out onto the patio.

Below, the noises of the crowd stuttered then dropped off to utter silence as they stared up.

Trent pulled a metal chair over to the railing and stood on it so that the crowd could clearly see his legs. He raised his arms in a victory V and turned, slowly, so that they could see him in each and every part.

It took a long, embarrassing moment for them to get it. Then they did.

Below, the crowd burst out into applause and screams of adulation. For their prophet was perfect and without blemish. He had not been plagued with sores, and surely this was a sign of his—*their*—favor?

Trent felt the energy of it buoy him, nearly lift him off his feet. It felt like lightning entering his veins. His chrysalis cracked open a few inches more.

THE MEDITERRANEAN

By dark that evening the *Queen of the Sea*—so named in both Hebrew and English on her prow—was well under way off the coast of Israel. She was a huge, private yacht, a two-hundred-footer, all white and gleaming teak. Besides her rather ordinary-sounding name, she was unmarked.

The discreetly boarded passenger of this ship, Pope Innocent XIV, had retired shortly after launch. He was exhausted in a deep, consuming way that made him feel quite ancient, quite incompetent. He had wanted, needed to read his Bible, and he had done so as long as he could; the darkness in the images of Revelations competed with the darkness of sleep stealing over his mind. In this particular battle it was Somnus, not St. Michael, who won.

The sheets on the elaborate bed were fine, white, starched, not unlike his aged skin. The disquiet in his soul slipped into dreamland behind him like a shadow. There was something about an earthquake. He was watching the ceiling of the Sistine Chapel crack and fall in plastered gems while he stood beneath trying to catch them so they wouldn't smash to powder on the floor. They could be reassembled if whole, he thought, if he could only . . . He ran about, arms outstretched, sick at the destruction, not able to move remotely fast enough.

At one o'clock a persistent knocking woke him. He was used to having his sleep interrupted, and it took him a moment to realize, after calling out rather stupidly for his secretary to come in, that the knocking was not coming from the stateroom door. It was not being made by human hands at all. It was a light, thudding sound, and it came from the walls of the ship, intermittently, and accompanied by a mild stirring feeling. The ship was running into things.

He tried at first to go back to sleep, but the sound would not let him. It was subtle, muffled, yet bothersome. He could not imagine what it might be. Were they not well into the Mediterranean by now? It might have been driftwood or remnants of a downed ship, but it had gone on for so long—he looked at the clock—twenty minutes, at least.

Then it occurred to him: what if they weren't in the middle of the Mediterranean at all? What if the ship had been hijacked? Was even now working its way in an ominous detour up a debris-clogged rivermouth?

That got him up. His slippers were next to the bed; he slid his bare feet into them and they scuffled against the thick white carpet. On the far wall a round teak porthole shone with moonlight. He looked out.

The stateroom porthole was about ten feet above the water. For a long moment he could see nothing on the black, rippling surface of the sea. Then something appeared, a vague shape at first, growing distinct as they closed the distance to pass it. He knew first that it was a carcass—a dead, bloated shape bobbing passively on the waves. And as the object slipped slowly past his window he saw a long, gray nose, sharp white teeth, red lolling tongue, turned black by moonlight or death. It was a dolphin. He turned his head to follow its passage, and by the time he had lost it and turned back, several smaller fish were floating by, flanks to the sky, silver and flat-eyed. From the other side of the ship a soft thump declared its intersection with some larger mass.

He donned his shiny red robe, slipped a rosary into his pocket as unconsciously as a layman might slip in his keys, and hurried topside.

The dim glow of the control room above him outlined capped heads and braid-trimmed forms. Captain Janus, who had escorted him aboard, was no doubt up there. But the rear deck was clear, and the pope had no need for company. He had no need to question Janus on when this had started or where or what he had seen. For in his heart there was already too much knowing.

Instead he walked to the rail and looked out like Moses looking down from Sinai. The rosary was wrapped around his hand, though he could not have said when he put it there. It took a moment for his eyes to adjust to the view.

The moonlight off the water was bright, sparkling. He could see amazingly far, though not very clearly. Where the shining caps failed to glitter, there he knew dark shapes covered the water, absorbing rather than reflecting the light. There were many dark spots off toward the horizon. And close to the wake of the ship he saw the bodies themselves, floating like crackers on soup—rotten, flesh crackers on salty brine.

He had been reading the words before sleep, and he did not need his Bible to retrieve them now. He spoke them, whispering, out loud. " 'And the second angel sounded, and as it were a great mountain burning with fire was cast into the sea: and the third part of the sea became blood; And the third part of the creatures which were in the sea, and had life, died; and the third part of the ships were destroyed.'

"Mother of God, have mercy on us!" he cried piteously, and he sank to his knees as though the rail were his altar. The only reply was the splashing wake of the ship and the dull thud as another corpse was bumped aside.

CHAPTER 7

DAY 9
ALLAHABAD, INDIA

Allahabad is where the two most sacred rivers of India meet, the Ganga and the Yamuna. It was an unmatched pilgrimage destination for this reason, and the home of a particularly virulent society of ascetic yogis, called *sádhus*, or holy men of the Hindu faith.

The *sádhu* encampment was perched on what Deauchez could only assume had once been an isolated spot; the top of a barren hill just outside of town. Now lines of pilgrims moved up and down the hill, dragging bleating goats or sheep or carrying live fowl. They were silent or praying in muttering voices. They had swollen faces and blank eyes.

They were in the realm of Kali.

Deauchez had been warned not to go to the hilltop by his innkeeper. The innkeeper explained to the priest that they were at the end of a twenty-five-thousand-year cycle. They were in the *Kali Yuga*, the age of Kali, the goddess of time and thus of death and destruction. He pointed to a picture on the wall that showed a black female deity with an open, fang-laden mouth dripping with blood. Around her neck was a necklace of tiny human heads and in her four hands were a sword, a noose, a blood-filled skull, and a severed head.

Now the holy men were saying it was the end of the *Kali Yuga* and Kali was coming to reap a bloody harvest. So many would die that the cycle of reincarnation would be broken for thousands of years. Kali would simply eat most of the less-advanced souls, destroying them forever. The people on the hilltop were reverting back to Kali worship in hopes of appeasing her and thus avoiding this fate. Kali worship was no place for Westerners.

Of course, Deauchez had no choice but to ignore him.

There was something specific that he was searching for. When he retraced his encounters with all of the Santa Pelagia prophets he'd met so far, he could find nothing tangible to put his finger on, and yet . . . something kept nibbling at his mind, like a whispering voice that was still so low, he couldn't hear it, only sense its breath on his ear. The body of St. Francis Xavier, Sagara Bata's gathering . . . What was it he was *almost* seeing?

Next to him on the slow, crowded climb up the hill was Chitra, the teenage son of the innkeeper. He'd been sent along graciously as "guardian" and translator for the foolish white man who wouldn't listen to good advice. Chitra's English, as his father's heir in the tourist trade, was fairly good, and Deauchez appreciated his services. It was unlikely that the *sádhus* would speak a language Deauchez could understand.

As they topped the crest of the hill, Chitra stopped and gripped Deauchez's arm. What greeted them would make a seasoned warrior's blood run cold. The large, dusty plateau was crowded with people. Every ten feet or so was a fire where one or two or three of the *sádhus*—easily recognizable by virtue of their nakedness, their long matted hair and curling nails, their spectral white body paint, and their blood-spattered limbs— were busy sacrificing animals for waiting penitents. The plateau ran red with blood and viscera. The pilgrims were dipping the ends of their saris or scarves in the stuff. The *sádhus* seemed to go out of their way to let the blood spill over their bodies. And around these fires and often tumbling into them or the people around them were worshipers in ecstatic trances, most often not the *sádhus*, but men and women who, smeared with the blood of sacrifices, were communing with Kali directly. Some simply stood and shook violently, eyes rolled back in their heads, but others whirled about, irrespective of the fact that there was no place to do so. And those of the *sádhus* who were not sacrificing animals were committing acts of self-mortification that Deauchez found sickening. One was hanging from hooks buried in his back. Another was in a headstand position, his head buried in the choking dust. A third was passing a flaming torch over and over his skin. Yet another was piercing his cheeks and tongue with long iron skewers. It was a scene that might have been conceived by Hieronymus Bosch.

"I have never seen this," Chitra whispered in a shaky voice. "This is not like the worship of Vishnu."

No, Deauchez thought, *this is the worship of Santa Pelagia.*

"Do you know which one is Dishama Giri?" he asked.

"No, but . . ." The boy raised his arm and pointed.

In the center of the plateau, nearly hidden by a crowd of people, was a single bare tree. Deauchez didn't recognize the species. It was a smooth, barkless gray, and it had many winding branches that bore no leaves. It wasn't all that tall, perhaps twenty feet.

Sitting on the branches were three *sádhus*; two on upper branches and one on a lower branch. This third *sádhu* was nearly hidden by the line of people who were approaching him and kissing his feet, which hung down, dirty and swollen. Yes. Three *sádhus* had gone to Santa Pelagia: Dishama Giri and two others. It had to be these three. The men in the tree appeared to be entirely unconscious of what was going on around them. Only the whites of their eyes showed between thinly parted lids.

"I believe you are right. But he does not look very talkative, does he?"

"You want to talk?" The boy looked at him as if to say that only a fool would want to talk to such people or even imagine talking was possible in a place like this.

"I *must* ask some questions about Dishama Giri. What would you suggest?"

The boy searched the plateau for a moment, his hand shielding his eyes from the sun. Then he took off right into the center of the melee. Deauchez stood there for a moment, horrified, but he had little choice. He plunged into the tumult, following Chitra as best he could.

By the time they'd reached the other side of the hilltop, Deauchez was bruised from people falling into him, or stepping on his feet, or pushing him out of the way. Blood and excrement were splattered on his clothes, even on his face. He pulled out his handkerchief and tried to clean off the worst of it.

Then he saw where the boy had taken him. Cleared off to one side of the plateau were hovels made of sackcloth propped up with sticks. A few battered pots lay nearby, and tattered flag banners of orange were stuck in the ground. Three *sádhus* squatted there, naked and bloody and sweating, two smoking hand-rolled cigarettes and one a filthy pipe. From the smell in the air and the look of their eyes, the substance wasn't tobacco.

Chitra approached one of them, an older man with a fat, hanging belly. The man's genitals swung in the dust between his enormous purple feet. Chitra got on his hands and knees and crawled forward to kiss the man's filthy toenails. The *sádhu* grunted at the boy and glanced blearily at Deauchez.

The boy began speaking—pleading Deauchez's case to the *sádhu*, the priest assumed. The *sádhu* kept grunting and occasionally said something short and sharp. Finally the boy motioned Deauchez forward. Deauchez bowed his head briefly in greeting.

"What are the questions?" Chitra whispered.

"What made Dishama Giri go to Mexico?"

The man listened to Chitra repeat the question and answered shortly. "Kali appeared to him in a dream," Chitra said.

"How did he get the money to fly to Mexico?"

At this, the boy and the *sádhu* spoke for a while, the ascetic tiredly speaking in quick bursts, as though pausing for rest in between.

"He says when Dishama Giri told their guru about the dream the guru thought it was only a man-dream, not a god-dream. So he told Dishama Giri he must beg for the money to go, and he must also beg money to take two of his brothers because he could not travel alone. The guru thought this would not happen. But in three days, Dishama Giri came back with the money. Then the guru knew it was a god-dream and he let them go."

Deauchez felt his heart sink. Just like the others who had been "called" to Santa Pelagia. And what else was there? "Was Dishama Giri smoking like this before the dream?"

"*Chilam?*" the boy asked, pointing toward the pipe.

Deauchez nodded and the boy asked the question, but the *sádhu* only looked at him pityingly.

"Ask him if he remembers anything unusual that might have happened around the time of the dream."

The boy spoke for an even lengthier time to the man. He seemed to have trouble making the question understood. Deauchez wasn't at all sure the boy himself understood it.

"Nothing happened. It was just . . . like every day. They were at the festival in town, like everybody."

"What festival?"

"*Mela*. Holy men come from everywhere—and people, too. *Mela,* Hindu festival."

"Is that not unusual?"

"Not in Allahabad."

"Did anything happen to Dishama Giri at the festival?"

The boy looked doubtful, but he turned to the older man and asked the question. The older man clearly thought as much of the query as the boy had. He immediately began shaking his head and frowning. But one of his companions began rattling off a counterpoint.

The two argued for a moment, then the younger man appeared to trigger something in the older man's memory. He slapped the dirt with one bloody, pudgy hand as though in revelation. Smiling and nodding, he jabbered enthusiastically to Chitra.

The boy looked impressed. "He was hit by a truck."

"What?"

The older man was still going on.

"Dishama Giri and another *sádhu* were struck in the street by a truck which drove away. A . . . uh . . . medicine truck came and took them to hospital."

The younger *sádhu* spoke up.

"But he says they weren't hurt bad. They came out again in a few hours."

Something was slipping through Deauchez's mind like a shark getting ready to surface. He sat and thought for a moment, poised on the edge. "Find out which hospital, please."

The boy spoke again to the *sádhus*, who made some geographical-looking gestures.

"Yes, I know it," said Chitra. "St. Cajetan's."

NEW YORK CITY

Simon Hill was staring at the computer monitor, perplexed. He tapped his lower teeth with the erasing end of a No. 2.

"Something good?" Susan asked. She'd been strolling by his chair on her way to the conference room and was now sidling up to hover over him.

"Dunno."

The e-mail was from the priest, Father Deauchez, the one who had blown him off at the airport. Either he'd had a change of heart, or he was intentionally trying to send Hill on a snark hunt.

Would he, could he be that manipulative? It was certainly a possibility: the man was with the Vatican, after all, Hill thought wryly.

"Deauchez claims we've missed a prophet right here in River City. Will Cougar in Washington. The state, not the D. of C. Native American. Runs some kind of shaman-slash-survivalist place called 'Cougar Camp.' "

Susan looked doubtful. "How could we have missed that?"

"Maybe the guy isn't big on talking to reporters. Besides, we've mostly been looking overseas."

"Anything's possible. I'll call our Seattle correspondent after the meeting." She turned to go.

"No . . ." Hill said thoughtfully. "I mean, yeah, see if he can get a bead on this Cougar guy, but don't send anyone in. I might fly over there myself."

"Really?"

"Deauchez wants us to check out some hantavirus inoculations that were given at Cougar Camp a month or so ago. What organization gave them, where else they inoculated for hanta, stuff like that."

"What has *that* got to do with the price of tea in China?"

Hill chewed absently on the eraser. "Good question. I'll put you on the record-checking end of it, but I think . . . I dunno, I have a feeling there's something there. I wanna check this out myself."

And as much as he was unsure of the priest, the reporter in him *did* feel it: that strange, urgent sensation that was notable primarily because it defied logic, did not fit the known facts of the matter in its intensity, and therefore seemed to be coming from someplace else entirely—not from the mere black-and-white text of the e-mail, for example, but from some subconscious intuition; from his "gut," as Ralph might put it.

Susan, apparently, was not getting the same signals. "They're waiting."

"Right." Hill's large frame bounced up from the chair, casting a spin on the wheels and causing it to bang noisily against the desk. This maneuver was so inherent in every such rise Hill made that one could only assume the bang acted as some sort of psychological signal to the reporter that, yes, he really was on his way. Such tricks, as well as Hill's incongruent lightness on his feet, gave him the air of a pudgy, nerdy prepubescent.

But today, the action drew a wince of pain, and Hill abruptly slowed down and began to mince carefully toward the conference room. Perhaps it was too much to expect to remain sore-free, he thought bitterly to himself, but somewhere on the arms or legs would have been nice, or even his chest or back. Damned bathroom vent.

He glared at Susan, who was chewing back a smile.

They were waiting in the conference room—Hill's senior reporters: Kevin, Marta, Frank, Austin, and Susan made five; Jeanine, the team's research assistant; and Ralph. Hill's boss was leaning up against the wall near the door, as usual, as if to make it clear that he wasn't here to run things, only to observe and help out as necessary. Hill knew how lucky he was to have a boss like Ralph on this story. Most bosses he'd had in the past would have shoved him aside days ago to grab the glory for themselves.

"Let's run down the prophets," Hill said. He crossed to the whiteboard, where a numbered list of names appeared.

"Sanchez?"

"There're over five thousand in Santa Pelagia," said Marta. "Mexicans and some Americans, mostly Catholic. Felix says it's pretty quiet. There haven't been any more visions, but the mood is—quote—'very morbid.' "

Hill wrote "5000" and the date next to Sanchez's name. They proceeded on down the list. Stanton had drawn six thousand so far to Kittatinny Mountain, Andrews, about sixty-five hundred to Sedona.

"Any spaceships show up there yet?" someone joked.

"No," said Susan, "but supposedly Andrews is fond of parading naked. He doesn't have the sores."

"None of the prophets do so far, am I right?" Hill asked.

The reporters each nodded and looked at each other. You could feel the mood in the room turn solemn as the oddity of this sank in.

"Abeed's still giving the same speech every night," Hill contributed. "Harlem's under heavy police patrol, but nothing more's erupted. We're guessing about four thousand African-Americans have shown up from outside the city, and they're mostly camping out in the streets."

The other prophets were following similar patterns: three to six or even eight thousand followers had joined the prophets in their appointed places. Dame Wendy Clark was set up in Scotland; Jürgen Hefner in Regensberg; Walter Matthews was near the U.S. border at Montreal and drawing skinheads from both countries; Levi's followers were "practically running the streets" in Jerusalem, giving daily speeches at the Temple construction site; Dr. Kratski, who had the smallest group, was appealing to "intellectuals" to gather in Siberia; Father Dimish's gathering was outside Kiev.

He's getting Russian and Greek Orthodox from all over Eastern Europe," said Kevin. "And get this—he's advocating castration for men and cutting off one breast for women. It's a tradition from an old Russian sect called Skoptsy. He says it'll prove to God their readiness to leave life."

"Lovely!" Hill quipped. "Get someone in there. We need pics. For tonight, do a small feature on what Dimish is doing—our readers will love it." In the rear of the room, Ralph nodded approvingly at Hill.

The last three names on the list were recent finds. "Mohammed Rahman?"

Frank answered. "He's calling Muslims to a Sufi monastery on the coast near Beirut. He did publish the sores prophecy before they broke out—we just missed it."

"Dig up the original coverage if you can. Taruma Sakarro?"

"He claims he's the prophet for all of South Asia," said Austin. "Do you have any idea how many people that is? Indonesia alone has over one hundred fifty million."

"He's in Singapore, right?"

"Yup. At least twenty thousand have already gathered and there're more coming every day. They're religious people, and he's really nailed their fears. They believe the entire world is going to be broken up into tiny islands like Indonesia. Singapore is one of the few cities he claims will survive."

"And Philip Constant?"

"South African Mormon," said Frank. "Says he's there for the whites *and* the 'negroes' of Africa—as long as they'll agree to act like Mormons. He's also got his spiel going out to all the Mormons around the world. Utah's put out feelers and they're giving a tentative nod to the guy. He's telling Mormons either to go to Salt Lake City or to join him in Cape Town."

Hill nodded and looked at all the numbers he'd written down

next to the prophets' names. "Interesting. It's not a bust, but it's not exactly a cattle run either."

Marta spoke up. "Last night's phone poll showed that only ten percent of our readers say they believe in the message of Santa Pelagia, but another forty percent 'aren't sure.' "

Ralph whistled. "Perfecto. That means they'll keep buyin' newspapers until they make up their minds, right, kids?"

Everyone grinned. They were on the best ride this paper had had in decades, and they knew it.

"Okay," said Hill. "Write up your briefs and send 'em to Susan. I want new info for tonight's edition—stuff like the castration angle. I wanna know what these prophets are *doing*, and so do our readers."

They'd reached the bottom of the names on the list. At the end were five blank places numbered twenty through twenty-four. Hill chalked in a tentative "Will Cougar" and explained Deauchez's e-mail.

"We're checking Cougar, but we still have four prophets missing, guys. There's *gotta* be four more. Any luck in South America?"

Marta looked cross. "I've had three people scouring the press. The Brazilian papers have been looking for someone, too. There's *nothing*."

Hill turned to the global map on the wall. "We *have* to be missing one in South America. It's a huge area and none of the prophets are covering it. Ditto China. Austin?"

" 'Fraid not, Kemosabe. But the food summit has everyone distracted. Most of China's leadership is there, and that's all their papers are talking about. With over a billion stomachs to feed, they're pretty much focused on the food thing."

"All right. Stay tight. I *don't* want to hear about someone we've missed on the CBS evening news."

They'd been forced to take a risk Hill abhorred. By last night's edition they still hadn't located all of what Hill was sure were the "Twenty-Four." Ralph insisted they print the Nostradamus quote and the tentative suggestion that there were twenty-four such prophets. It had been a grand slam with the public—the phones had gone nuts—but now every other reporter on the planet knew there were prophets missing and was out searching for them.

Hill moved to the other side of the whiteboard, to a list entitled "Events."

"Okay. Sores. Susan?"

"Dr. Robert Tendir released a statement this morning from Telegyn labs. The spores are carrying a kind of superbacteria that affects both plants *and* humans—very rare. It produces enzymes that cause cell walls to decompose. It's a bit like soft rot in plants, but it affects humans more like streptococcus. And its affects are accelerated—occurring on contact, as some of us well know." She raised an eyebrow at Hill. "Tendir insists that the bacteria is a natural substance and, in his opinion, could not be lab-generated. Tendir's the Nobel prize winner who runs Telegyn's research facility."

"Sure, but what's Telegyn's angle on it?"

"Apparently they just decided to run the tests since they had the capability. It's the first real report I've seen. Also, the EPA says that ninety percent of the spores are gone, according to their air tests. There're still a few floating around, but there hasn't been a new flow."

"Good, but see if you can get someone official to say 'It could happen again at any moment.' Just to keep people's blood pressure up."

"Right." Susan made a note. "Also, there are *some* areas that haven't been hit at all—Greenland, Siberia, and certain parts of our own Rockies, too."

Hill tapped his tooth with a pencil. "Get me a list of areas that weren't hit at all, and I mean *at all*. I'd love to get a quote from someone like Stanton explaining that one. Frank, any update on the crop damage yet?"

"All of our sources say it's destroyed at least half of this year's crops, despite Washington's denials. Europe, the Russian federation, and most of Asia were hit *really* hard. They started building crop shelters about ten hours after we did. And from all accounts, it was a critical ten hours. Estimates are that there's been more like a sixty- to eighty-percent loss in most countries."

"Jesus! When is Washington s'posed to make an official announcement?"

"Tonight, in Geneva, right after the president addresses the summit."

"Hold a slot for it."

Everyone in the room looked a little green at the implications of what they'd just heard. Hill took a deep breath and tried not to think about food, it being a substance particularly near and dear to his heart. He went over to where "Red Tide?" had been written in on the event list.

"Kevin? Tell us about the red tide."

Kevin flipped to his notes, leaned forward in that macho, gap-kneed way of his. "Last night Stanton went on and on in his broadcast about how the red tide outbreak was the second sign."

Austin spoke up. "Yoshiko Tanomaru pointed it out as a sign just this morning."

"But the story about the tide itself just broke in the U.S. late yesterday," Kevin added with a smug arrogance, "*and* none of the press has connected it to Santa Pelagia."

"Not yet," Hill said intently. "We have to break this one tonight in a big way. We just got a bunch of new footage, didn't we?"

Ralph nodded.

"Great. Kevin and I will go over it right after the meeting. Anybody else have any input on it?"

No one spoke for a moment, then Austin said, "It's not going to make the food situation any better."

Hill nodded. The fishing issues had not been lost on him. "Thanks. Bust the phones to get some quotes for tonight's editions. For now let's break: we've got tons to do."

Marta raised a quick hand. "Simon? On the Web, Greenpeace posted their own 'seven signs of the apocalypse.' Number one is something that's recently happened in Brazil. Greenpeace designated a couple of hectares as the 'Heart of the Amazon.' They've been working for ten years to protect it. It was home to several rare species, including the Brazilian moon monkey."

"I remember." Hill nodded.

"Well, about six weeks ago the Brazilian government overturned the hold order and bulldozers went in. Greenpeace got a forty-eight-hour stay to remove whatever they could, including some of the monkeys, but that was it. Greenpeace is calling it 'the final violation.' "

"Wasn't there some brouhaha last week about Blade stealing one of those monkeys for a rock concert?" Frank said with a snicker.

"That's right. He claims he didn't *steal* it, though, and Greenpeace isn't pressing charges."

"What a press-hound!"

"Hey, don't dis my man!" Kevin said, slipping into his street voice. "Blade is righteous! He's playing the Palladium on Friday, and yours truly has backstage passes!"

"All right, all right!" Hill interrupted playfully. "I see their angle, Marta, but I'm not sure it fits in with Santa Pelagia. Kevin? Video room?"

"Just thought I'd throw it out there," Marta mumbled, with a tinge of disappointment, but Hill was already on his way out the door.

Good ol' Ralph. He'd shown his commitment to this story in numerous ways, and now here it was again. Not only did Hill and Kevin have the video room to themselves, but Ralph had called in an expert, an earthy-looking biologist from nearby Rutgers. Normally they'd have to do the research legwork on their own.

The biologist's name was Fendmann. His dark, ungroomed beard and glasses were right in keeping with his sockless loafers and his backpack. He looked silently over Kevin's list of the areas hit, but his head kept shaking back and forth as he turned pages. "This is unbelievable."

"Let's take a look," Hill said. "Whadda we got, Carl?"

Carl turned dials on his video console. "First one is from this morning, Sea of Japan. WWN footage."

It had been shot from a helicopter, high and moving over the sea. Carl turned down the volume on the sound of the blades. As the camera panned the water there was no mistaking the huge swatches of red.

"That's it, huh?" Hill asked.

Fendmann was peering raptly at the screen, Kevin's paperwork still clenched in his hand. "That's the algae, yes. It's very small—you're looking at billions of dinoflagellates."

"Have you seen this before?"

"Once. In the Gulf of Mexico. But it was nothing like this."

Fendmann gave them a rundown on the red tide, a lot of scientific jargon, more than they really needed. But even as he droned on, the video was moving, and Hill heard Kevin utter a stifled curse. He didn't need to look at the younger reporter to know there was a lump in his throat; Hill was fighting one the size of a baseball himself. It wasn't the wide swatches of red that got to him. He didn't have enough science to get emotional, as Fendmann apparently was, over a bunch of algae. It was the corpses that littered the ocean's surface like the scene of some astronomical plane crash that hit home.

The sea was dying.

They reviewed footage for an hour, all the while some part of Hill dying, too. Fendmann lectured, and Kevin was too numb to be much help. But perhaps his uncharacteristic emotionalism *was* a help, for Hill knew that when this footage aired on the news, people everywhere would be feeling what Kevin felt, what he himself felt. He dictated the beginning of his story into a mini–tape recorder as his coworkers listened. As usual, his writing voice sounded like he was channeling some far more educated, more sophisticated soul.

"There are no little white fishing boats on the Sea of Japan today. Even if they'd had the heart to try and the courage to risk food poisoning, their way would have been blocked by thousands of corpses. As the bubonic plague swept Europe in the fourteenth century, so have the living beings of the sea been harvested on this day. But it isn't a virus that has taken this dreadful toll, it's tiny dinoflagellates—a type of algae that produces nerve toxin. Like the *E. coli* bacteria in our bodies, these dinoflagellates are always present in the sea, but usually in such small doses that they don't cause a problem."

He glanced at Fendmann for confirmation. Fendmann nodded his approval.

"For some reason we do not understand, this kind of algae occasionally has an outbreak of population growth, forming such vast colonies that it becomes visible to the naked eye, turning red as the algae dies. In such states, it attracts the creatures that eat algae. The attraction is fatal."

He clicked the recorder off for a moment and watched again as the 'copter approached the beaches near Seoul. In the water, wading through the dead fish, were Buddhist monks and a host of the devout, making their way into the sea to offer libations. The video didn't get close enough for Hill to see their faces, but he could sympathize with their grief even if he could not fathom their actions: How could they fight the stench and horror as the dead fish butted against their thighs, their chests? Some carried incense, perhaps praying to the gods of the waters, and some waded straight out, arms up, symbolically offering themselves instead.

He had Carl pause the film on a frame, thinking about what he wanted to say. He took Kevin's hit list from Fendmann and held it open as he spoke.

"What makes this particular event such an enormous tragedy is its scope. In the depths of the vast Pacific and Atlantic Oceans, life goes on unchallenged. The Arctic Ocean and mid–Indian Ocean are still loving hosts to life. But hundreds of thousands of miles of coastline and inland seas have turned deadly. Overnight, the Sea of Japan, so warmly contained by islands, is completely contaminated. The Yellow Sea, East China Sea, and South China Sea have all been infected. Off Australia, the Coral Sea is littered with the dead, and stained with dying dinoflagellates. The Bay of Bengal off India, the Mozambique Channel off Africa, and the Mediterranean Sea—all are infested with an explosion of red tides. The Caribbean Sea, the Gulf of Mexico, the eastern seaboard of the United States, and the Gulf of Alaska take the tragedy to the continental U.S. Never in the history of mankind have red tides broken out so suddenly and so devastatingly in so many unrelated areas."

He turned the recorder off. Kevin looked fortified, as if given courage by the act of reporting on the tragedy. He signaled Hill for the recorder and turned to Fendmann.

"What exactly is *causing* it?" he asked.

Fendmann answered, and Kevin summarized his response into the machine.

"Some say red tide is caused by global warming; that the toxic algae explode in warm weather. Some say it's caused by human and livestock sewage, the high nitrogen content acting as a fertilizer. Some say it's toxic dumping, that the chemicals we spew into the oceans upset their natural balance."

Hill nodded at him approvingly. Fendmann looked pensive, stroking his beard and looking down blankly at his khaki-clad thighs. Kevin took a deep breath and plunged on.

"We dump our manufacturing chemicals into rivers. Our lawn fertilizers, pesticides, car fluids, all are known to leak chemicals deadly to sea life into our subsoils, sewers, and landfills, eventually making their way out to sea. We've tested nuclear weapons in the oceans as though they were some remote planet, not the foundation for life here on Earth."

On the screen, a close-up of a dead pilot whale, stomach white and bloated in the sun, cut abruptly to black. The end of the reel.

"So maybe the environmentalists are right," Kevin was saying. "Maybe red tides are the first sign that our seas are sick to the teeth from our toxic runoff. The truth is, we just don't know what causes red tides."

Kevin clicked off the recorder. Hill took it from him and spoke. "We only know that the monstrous death that has resulted on this day is a tragedy beyond our ability to comprehend or fully mourn."

He clicked it off and they sat in silence for a while.

"I've got two more reels," Carl offered. Hill shook his head. He'd seen enough.

He knew Ralph would scrap most of Kevin's contribution, the last few paragraphs anyway. Newspapers didn't print admonishments. It's not what people wanted to read. The environmentalists would print it, their own version of it, in small presses and on the Web.

But nobody listened to them anymore.

GENEVA, SWITZERLAND

President Fielding had been briefed on the new red tide situation only moments before his speech was to begin. He'd looked at Cole rather helplessly, as if to say, *What else could I possibly have to deal with?* and Cole had told him to go on with their prepared plan, to ignore the red tide issue. It wasn't all that relevant to the grain problem. It wasn't their concern at the moment.

Except, Cole suggested, it might be wise to strike the part in the speech about each country being responsible for harvesting *all* of their own available resources—particularly the line about fully utilizing the gifts of the life-sustaining and ever-bountiful sea.

As they entered the summit room, Cole noted that everyone else was already there, including President Lee and, next to him, the ever present, ever shadowy Tsing Mao Wen. And the press was there, a select few. There was a reporter and photographer from the *New York Times*, along with representatives from several television channels.

"Ladies and gentlemen of the U.N., my fellow dignitaries, members of the press," Fielding began briskly as soon as he reached the microphone. An attitude of haste and untouchable firmness was what was needed here, or so Press Secretary Connor had advised over the phone.

"We, the United States, have recognized the importance of this summit and the issues behind it. We have desired to do whatever we can to ensure that this year and for any year to follow those who are hungry will be fed. We have taken precious time from other vital national issues to attend and support this conference.

"But I'm sure I will be voicing the opinion of *many* of the leaders seated here when I say that the cost of this summit is beginning to exceed its value—at least for the present moment. Because of this most recent danger to the crops, my leadership is best utilized at home, working with the farmers and scientists of the United States to make sure that we both fully *comprehend* and fully *maximize* our food production this year. I'm sure all of you are in similar situations."

Fielding, the Man Who Did Not Sweat, wiped his brow—whether out of sheer nervous energy or genuine need Cole could not tell. He was standing behind the president, watching his neck go apoplectic. He could see Lee over Fielding's shoulder. The Chinese president's face was getting grimmer and grimmer.

"Many nations have lost crops to the toxic spores. We extend our mutual grief over this untimely event." Fielding took a deep breath. "Our best estimates of the loss of crops in the United States is . . . around forty percent of our fall harvest. This is *only* an estimate."

Cole heard some gasps from the audience. *Liar,* Cole thought calmly. It was fifty percent gone of an already low harvest year. The forty percent figure had been sweatingly debated. There was a painful dichotomy between convincing the foreign powers that the U.S. was in a bad way and could not export and causing another panic back home.

"On the other hand, we have a vast greenhouse system around the country that produces food year-round and some areas that were not hit at all. The truth is, we no longer have sufficient data to conduct these discussions. I plan to go back to the United States and work with a group of dedicated Americans to determine what yield we actually *will have* this year. I assure you that the United States will continue to coordinate with the FAO to determine the most appropriate plan of action. Under no circumstances will any U.S. grain be auctioned to the highest bidder. When we have determined what exports are available this year we will be taking prices similar to last year's closing prices from each recipient nation."

There was the bone. Commodities holders back home would be furious—the situation was a seller's wet dream. But the U.N.

was listening a bit too thoughtfully to China's proposal, and who knew how far the situation had further deteriorated because of the spores?

President Lee did not look mollified. He folded his arms tightly against his chest, his lips whitely pressed, his eyes dull with hate. Next to him, the monk was as inscrutable as ever.

THE MEDITERRANEAN

The *Queen of the Sea* was approaching Athens at long last. In his stateroom, Innocent XIV was putting the finishing touches on a speech he wanted to give tomorrow, after he'd talked to Father Deauchez once more. His pen trembled over the page as he read the draft, just as it had trembled as he'd written it, the words coming in fits and starts, his mind torn between religious instinct and political caution.

How the delay of this trip had confounded him! He was needed so desperately in Rome! The journey by sea was not fast in the best of times, and with the ship slowed down by the wrenching offal . . . But God had put him here for a reason, and he knew what that reason was. He was to be an eyewitness to this sign and witness he was; he was a veritable prisoner in the midst of it. His eyes were to see the scope and reality of it; his nose was to experience the smell, the smell of death and putrefaction that swept onboard with every waft of the breeze, even down here behind closed doors.

So he had witnessed. He understood it in his soul the way he could never have understood hearing it secondhand. Now it was time to return to his post. From Athens a quick plane ride to Rome. The private jet was ready, his secretary said, and several of his favorite cardinals were in Athens waiting to join him for an in-flight meeting, as he had requested.

He sighed and gave up on the speech; he was not being productive with it anymore. He rang for his secretary and gave him the draft to type up. The daylight and the blue of the sea beckoned from the window, but it was illusory. It was a graveyard out there and he had seen enough. He opened his Bible to Job.

He was still reading it when, twenty miles from their port, the physical world around him was torn asunder. First there was the sound, like a loud but somehow muffled cannon blast somewhere to the fore of the ship; the next instant there was fire.

He died quickly in the explosion, but not instantly. It took a number of seconds for the tremendous conflagration to take his life; long enough for him to recover from the brute shock and incomprehensibility of it; long enough to have the cohesive thought, *They've killed me.*

And then they had.

ACT 2: RED

In the meantime [there appears] so vast a plague that two-thirds of the world will fail and decay. So many [die] that no one will know the true owners of fields and houses, the weeds in the city streets will rise higher than the knees, and there shall be a total desolation of the Clergy.
—NOSTRADAMUS, EPISTLE TO HENRY I

Mankind will be decimated by epidemics, famine and poison. After the catastrophe they will emerge from their caves and assemble, and only few will have been left to build the new world. The future is approaching at a quick pace.
—SEERESS REGINA (PRIOR TO WW II)

And this shall be the plague wherewith the Lord will smite all the people that have fought against Jerusalem: Their flesh shall consume away while they stand upon their feet, and their eyes shall consume away in their holes, and their tongues shall consume away in their mouth.
—ZECHARIAH (160 B.C.) 14:12

A horrible war which is being prepared in the West, the following year the pestilence will come, so very horrible that young nor old, nor animal [may survive]. Blood, fire, Mercury, Mars, Jupiter in France.
—NOSTRADAMUS C9 Q55

The tropical forests support the sky. Cut down the trees and disaster will follow.
—SOUTH AMERICAN TRIBAL LEGEND

Without a doubt, diseases as yet unknown, but with the potential to be the AIDS of tomorrow, lurk in the shadows.
—THE UNITED NATIONS WORLD HEALTH ORGANIZATION REPORT, 1996

CHAPTER 8

Michael Smith groaned as the alarm clock blared for the fifth time that morning. He reached out and slapped the snooze button with deadly aim and then, after a moment of resistance, slid his lower body out from under the sheets, pointing it toward the floor. He landed, somewhat painfully, on his knees. That got his eyes open. He yawned, reached over, and turned the alarm clock all the way off, then stood, his joints creaking out their morning song. He stumbled blearily over the dirty clothes and magazines on the floor, heading toward the bathroom.

No one had ever mistaken the Ohio-born virologist for a morning person. It had driven his parents crazy when he was a teenager, it made him miss classes when he was in college, and it wasn't any better now, at the age of thirty-six. It was true that he worked twelve-hour days at PAHO's Disease Prevention and Control lab—the Pan American branch of the U.N. World Health Organization—but that wasn't what did him in. It was the four to five hours he couldn't resist in the late evening and wee morning hours *after* work, that precious self-time in which he pursued his twin passions of old movies and mystery novels, that made getting up so painful.

When he emerged from the bathroom fifteen minutes later, his thinning hair was newly washed and dryer-fluffed. He wore clean khakis and a madras shirt—both permanent press—and he was finishing off the knotting of a navy knit tie. He wandered out to the living room and headed for the front door, where his worn leather loafers had been left the night before. Callie, his Siamese cat, protested yowlingly at this maneuver, as she always did. Her sleeping habits were not unlike his own. She sat up, with a sharp-toothed yawn, from her favorite spot on the velveteen sofa.

"Callie, hon, I'm not leaving yet," Mike said with a hint of impatience, as he always did.

The cat jumped down and headed for her bowl in the kitchen.

Mike filled the bowl, gave the cat a few scratches down her back, and then headed for the door, this time in earnest. He had just opened it when the phone rang. He stared at it for a moment, then shut the door and headed for his car.

He arrived at the lab twenty minutes later. Josh Bergman jumped on him as soon as he walked in.

"Geez, where *were* you? We've been calling you for*ever*." The young Dr. Bergman, his Ph.D. so new it sparkled in his eyes when he heard his own name, looked like a white pencil with glasses and a reddish brown Afro stuck on top. He had the energy level of the very thin, and the combination of enthusiasm and naiveté that only the freshest interns had. He looked even more keyed up than usual this morning.

"I was on my way in, Einstein."

"Geez, lemme go tell Stanley you're here. Come to his office, like *now*, okay?"

Josh bounced off and Mike sighed. He stashed his briefcase in his office and grabbed a cup of coffee from the community pot in the hall. Something was up, that much was clear. Mike didn't know whether to be pleased or annoyed. It had been a while since he'd taken a field trip, and the prospect of a live case was always exciting. On the other hand, he was in the middle of tracing some viruses that he thought might be genetically linked to Ebola and might help explain the origins of the deadly disease. It was a bad time to leave the lab.

By the time he strolled into Stanley's office and saw the solemn, brightly intense look on both of his colleagues' faces, his curiosity had gotten the better of him. "So *tell* me."

Stanley motioned for him to close the door. Mike did, then took a seat.

"Mike, I need you and Josh to go to Rio. This morning."

"*Rio?* What's up in Rio?"

"We don't know yet. We got a call from Greenpeace this morning. They had twenty-five Brazilian moon monkeys in a shelter there."

The word "monkeys" immediately sent Mike's blood pressure up. "Uh-huh."

"They say they looked completely healthy when they picked them up six weeks ago, but they started getting sick. The vets said it was a cold virus. Yesterday they started dying. Ten have died in the past twenty-four hours. The final stages sound . . . well, it wasn't a cold."

"What *about* the final stages?" Mike was definitely wide-awake now, and he hadn't even touched his coffee.

"It's hard to tell. We have some information from one of their vets. He went on and on about *swelling* and *eruptions*."

"Eruptions? Like bleeding out?" It was a term imbedded in the myth and horror of Ebola. It described what happened in the last stage of the disease—the liquefaction of bodily organs and tissues and their subsequent expulsion from every orifice of the body.

"Don't know. But I'd like to treat this as a potential Level Four outbreak until we know better."

What Stanley wasn't saying, and didn't need to say, was that primates were known vectors for some of the most deadly viruses ever unearthed. Now they had an epidemiclike sickness in twenty-five monkeys of a breed never known to have had close contact with humans before.

"I agree," said Mike.

Josh nodded, as if he'd reached a similar conclusion but had been holding out on them.

"Good. Since it's in South America, PAHO has first crack. You'll be leading the investigation, Mike, and you'll have Josh. You'll also get some support from the local WHO office, PANAFTOSA. It's a hoof-and-mouth disease center, so don't expect too much. If it looks like real trouble we'll get you a team, probably from Geneva, maybe some CDC people."

Mike stood up. "I'm ready."

"Me, too," Josh said, bouncing up from his chair.

"Get to the airport then. Your flight leaves in ninety minutes."

"Feed my cat, will you?" Mike asked.

Stanley smiled gamely. "Have I ever let you down?"

THE WHITE HOUSE

In the Cabinet room at the White House, the secretaries of the treasury, state, defense, interior, commerce, labor, health and human services, housing and urban development, transportation, energy, education, and veterans affairs, as well as the attorney general, the vice president, and, of course, President Fielding himself, were all seated around the U.S. equivalent of the Round Table. They were silent, watching solemnly as the secretary of agriculture, Dr. Samuel Purvue of Atlanta, presented his emergency briefing.

A handsome young aide, a boy from Yale whom Anthony Cole had recommended personally, brought in a fresh pitcher of ice water with lemon. Cole smiled at the boy. The boy smiled back.

"Mr. President, I'm afraid there's no way around it," Dr. Purvue was saying with sonorous, earthshaking gravity. "Our utilization rate this year—*without* rationing—was forecast at 32 million tons of wheat, 197 million tons of coarse grains. That's 229 million tons total. We only have about 6 million tons in open stocks—we're just plain tapped out after the past two years. We've lost *half* of the fall harvest, meaning our total wheat and coarse grains production this year will be somewhere between 140 and 160 million tons, not the 303 we anticipated. Even at Grade Three rationing our utilization *domestically* would still be 190 million tons—more than we've got."

"Wh . . . wha . . . what about the greenhouses?" Fielding asked, with the enunciation of someone who has suffered a stroke.

"Mr. President, those greenhouses feed an elite specialty market; they supply dribbles of high-priced, out-of-season, organically grown produce. Pardon my French, but they don't add up to a piss in the Mississippi."

"Are you absolutely sure of your facts, sir?" General Brant asked.

"We have not yet heard from *every* farmer in America, General," Purvue said dryly, "but if this estimate isn't right to within a two-percent bandwidth, I'll be happy to resign."

"Can I resign, too?" the secretary of commerce, Mr. Arnold, muttered. There were a few nervous titters in response.

It was not the sort of flippancy one would display in front of President Fielding in ordinary times. The fact that it *was* said and, furthermore, did not even seem to register on Fielding, indicated how changed the times really were.

Cole spoke up. "In other words, we have no grain to ship overseas this year. *None.*"

"I'm afraid breaking that news is indeed our first challenge, Mr. Secretary. Our second will be to figure out what *Grade Four* rationing means." Dr. Purvue's voice was dark with irony.

"*Whatever* the rationing plan is, we have to implement it *now!*" insisted Liz Haron, the secretary of health and human services. "The half-shipment moratorium on grain warehouses is causing havoc. Stores are out of stock, people are scared to death about the entire situation, and the media is having a field day spreading nonsense about biblical prophecies!"

Wallace, secretary of the interior, leaned forward. "Some conspiracy theorists are spreading rumors that the spores actually got eighty percent or more of the crops; that we're *lying* to them. They say there *won't* be any end of the moratorium, *no* restocking. We have to do something to defuse the bomb before there's major trouble."

"Absolutely." Mr. Arnold nodded. "The business sector is calling for blood. If they can't ship, they can't make money. This is turning into an economic disaster."

"I think we're all in agreement that a formal rationing plan *must* be implemented in the next forty-eight hours," Dr. Purvue said loudly. "At this point, it will probably be comforting to our countrymen to see decisive action taken, even if it means they'll have to make sacrifices."

Everyone around the table concurred except Fielding. He looked like his mind was elsewhere.

"I *have* given this some thought," offered Purvue. "As you know, Grade Three categorized product types and allotted each citizen a certain amount per category per week. That amount was the *least* amount that would still cover the FDA's minimal nutritional guidelines. So it would seem we couldn't go any lower, and yet we must."

No one said anything. They looked too tired and shell-shocked to have any ideas at all.

"Now I'd like to make a suggestion," Purvue continued, "which I know Mr. Arnold isn't going to like one little bit. The truth is, many of the products on our lists provide little or no nutritional value. If we limit production to foods that are *optimally wholesome*, we could lower the amount of grain allotted to each citizen and *still* provide their minimum daily requirements. We could just eke through with 156 million tons."

"What are you saying, Mr. Secretary?" Mr. Arnold said in a tight voice.

"What I'm *saying* is that I'm not sure that in the current situation, when we're denying basic bread to starving nations, that we can really justify manufacturing products like Little Willie snack cakes!"

Mr. Arnold's jaw dropped and he sat there a moment, turning purple, as though he'd just swallowed an oyster shell. About the time that Brant, next to him, was about to administer the Heimlich maneuver, Arnold drew in a huge gasp of air and found words.

"Are you telling me we're gonna force a *multibillion-dollar* industry, with *thousands* of competing products and *millions* of American employees, to refurbish their factories and produce nothing but *nine-grain bread*?"

Dr. Purvue folded his arms across his chest. "Do you have a *better* idea, Mr. Secretary?"

"We're talking about *lives* here, Mr. Arnold," Liz Haron rejoined. "If Dr. Purvue has found a way for us to make it through this year without having our citizens dying in the streets then I, for one, think he's to be *commended*!"

"But . . . That's like telling our entire automotive industry that they all have to switch to manufacturing identical two-wheel bicycles! Forget how pissed off they'll be—particularly those who donated election funds for this presidency! Think about the country itself! We have no idea what a crash in that huge a business sector will do! It could cause our entire economic infrastructure to disintegrate!"

"I think that's a bit of an exaggeration, don't you?" General Brant said impatiently.

"*No*, General Brant, I *don't*!"

From out of nowhere a familiar voice roared with a rage and hubris that only that particular voice could muster: "Will the lot of you just SHUT the FUCK UP!"

Everyone turned to stare at the president.

"You! All of you! You're missing the GODDAMN POINT!" Fielding's face rumbled like a volcano about to blow. "Purvue says we can feed our citizens. FINE! I don't think the goddamn economic sector is our main problem right now, you FREAKING LAP BOY!"

This last was directed with force at Arnold. Spittle was flying from the president's mouth with every word he said. Arnold looked like he'd just swallowed a bug the size of Wall Street.

"Cole!" Fielding barked.

"Yes, Mr. President?"

Fielding just stared at him for a moment, composing himself. The room was so quiet, one could almost hear watches, pacemakers, and PalmPilots ticking.

"What do you think they'll do?"

"Are you speaking of China, Mr. President?"

"Hell yes, China! The goddamn Arabs! The freaking *U.K.* for God's sake. Any of them! All of them! *You're* secretary of state. What will they *do*?"

This was spoken with a quieter kind of venom than had been aimed at Arnold, and what passion there was, Cole knew, was not directed at him but at the world at large. Fielding was finally starting to respect him a little, perhaps even to need him. It was gratifying, though moot at this point. Fielding's opinions would not be relevant for long.

"Every country on this planet—with the exception, perhaps, of Canada, Australia, and South America—is worse off than we are, Mr. President," Cole explained. "*Much* worse off. China, the Middle East, India, Africa—none of them has enough food to keep a third of their population alive. Europe lost up to seventy percent of their fall crop to the spores, or so we've heard. And they were *already* on strict rationing. The Russians didn't fare much better. In my opinion, it's going to get very desperate this year. *Very.* Starving people don't have much choice. They'll do *anything* for food."

Fielding sat there for a moment, weighing these words. "*All* of them?"

"*Any* of them."

"Oh, my God," Fielding muttered.

"We *are* the number one military power in the world, Mr. President," General Brant said with great bravado.

"What about our allies?" Fielding asked Cole, ignoring Brant altogether.

Cole steepled his fingers and looked thoughtful. The room waited. "Mr. President, I have a suggestion."

Fielding didn't look surprised. "Go on."

"No matter what we do, we can't ship enough grain to make *everybody* happy."

"We can't ship any!" Dr. Purvue interjected.

"So we must choose carefully. We'll never provide China with enough grain under the current circumstances to prevent her from doing whatever it is she's going to do. Or any of Asia, for that matter, or even the Russians. They're too populous."

Dr. Purvue was shaking his head in a strong negative.

"But if we can reserve even *20 million tons total*—of wheat, corn, any grain really—it *might* be enough . . ."

"Enough for what?" Vice President Davies asked.

"It might be enough, if we're *very* diplomatic—to buy the continued loyalty of, say, the E.U.?"

"There *isn't* 20 million tons!" Dr. Purvue was shaking his head so hard that his long-as-a-liberal hair waved about, geek-like. "There's no possible way."

But Fielding was inspecting Cole with the every-fiber-tensed posture of a man lost in the ocean watching a dot on the horizon. *A boat? An island?* He sat up and sighed shakily. He took his water glass from the table and drained it.

"Let's discuss Grade Five rationing," Fielding said, wiping his mouth.

Dr. Purvue turned a delicate shade of chartreuse. "We can't."

"How are we with canned goods?" Cole offered by way of friendly suggestion.

"We can supplement with meat," Fielding said.

"Good idea, Mr. President! Particularly the first few months," Cole enthused.

Everyone looked at him.

"I know we've already thinned the beef herd because of their heavy grain intake, but I think it's time we slaughtered all remaining livestock—pork, too—except for a minimum reserve of dairy animals, of course, and perhaps poultry. Poultry can be fed the inedible remains of the butchering process."

"Good thinking, Cole," Fielding said appreciatively.

Mr. Arnold hid his face in his arms and began to cry.

ALLAHABAD, INDIA

Father Deauchez emerged from St. Cajetan's Hospital into the heat of the midday sun. He walked a few yards and felt his legs tremble beneath him. He tried to go on, for the inn was only about ten blocks away, but he could not. Dark things swam in his vision. His knees threatened to revolt.

Just down from the hospital, he spied a few rickety chairs and tables under a patched food-shop awning. He made it that far and sank onto one of the chairs, stuck his computer between his feet for security, and lowered his head into his hands, waiting for the dizziness to pass.

Some moments later, he became aware of the badgering voice of the waiter coming through what sounded like miles of cotton.

He managed to raise his head and order a *Nimbu*—a lime soda. The drink came and its sweet, citrus flavor, as well as the shade, restored some order to his senses. His head cleared.

Was it the heat that had swamped him so? Or the mixed astringent and putrid smells of the hospital? The sight of blood- and pus-stained bandages, perhaps? The limbless beggars who perched on the hospital's steps? Or the children who filled the hospital halls with their jutting ribs and their faces hollow from starvation? He'd never been able to stomach the sight of blood and suffering. An Indian hospital was no place for a weak-stomached Frenchman like himself. Yet he didn't think it was any of those things, nor last night's curry, either.

No. What was making him ill was what he'd learned inside that hospital. Although it was still all very vague, he had the distinct sensation that his fishing line *hadn't* come back empty this time; that he had, in fact, hooked the shark that had threatened to break the surface back there on that mountaintop.

God only knew if he'd be able to deal with the consequences.

When he had recovered himself enough to look around, Deauchez noticed an Anglo across the street, seated on a stoop. Deauchez smiled tentatively but the Anglo just looked away without response. Perhaps he was an atheist, if such a thing was possible in India. Deauchez pulled his briefcase onto the table, opened it, and booted up his laptop. He tried the Telegyn phone and got a link to the Internet without a glitch. Yes, he had three e-mails waiting. He opened his in-box anxiously.

One of the messages was from Simon Hill. Neither of the other two was from Sister Daunsey, as Deauchez had hoped. He'd written to her when he'd written to Simon, asking her one simple question. He was frustrated but not surprised at her lack of response. Of the two remaining e-mails, one was from Donnelley, and one was from the Vatican communications office—an official statement of some sort. They were both marked "urgent."

Deauchez felt a sense of dread about those two messages.

Some sort of official notice and Donnelley, no doubt, telling him about it. Had the pope announced something new, his full support of Santa Pelagia perhaps? Surely not; pray, pray not. He was so close to having something to barter with.

Deauchez opened Hill's missive first. It merely said:

I'm all over the Cougar Camp inocs. Will let you know. Hill.

Yes, it was foolish to have expected more. It would take time, wouldn't it?

With some trepidation, he opened Donnelley's e-mail.

My dear Michele:
   Terrible news. Pope Innocent XIV was killed when his ship exploded off the coast of Crete, 16:10 Crete time, 15:10 Rome time, yesterday. They say the explosion was so great that everyone aboard was killed instantly. We can thank God, at least, that he suffered no pain.
   Please return to the Vatican immediately. Your place is here in this time of trouble. All investigations are, as of this moment, suspended indefinitely. Come home, Michele.
   Your brother in sorrow—Brian Donnelley

It took some moments for the news to register. It sank in through a sea of resistance, like a lump of lead descending through thick goo. It was a sorrow broader and deeper than any he'd felt in a long, long time.

Tears didn't come, only the tremendous grief settling down on his chest for a nice long visit. Poor Antonio Girelli, a child, a young altar boy, who had risen so high in the world and had been stricken down for the audacity of it, for the blasphemy that a gentle soul could fly so unfettered in an ungentle world.

But even as Deauchez thought it, he knew he was romanticizing. Pope Innocent XIV *had* been gentle, and a good man, a *great* man. But he'd been a politician, too. He was a martyr, undeniably, but he was no saint.

Still. Yes, still . . . He'd been a friend to Deauchez, hadn't he? Even a father figure, perhaps. And he was the pope. Someone had murdered *the pope*. Who? And, for Christ's sake, why would they want to? And why *now*?

Inside his head, Deauchez had a message for the pope, a tiny spark that he needed to deliver, a consideration only, perhaps, or perhaps something more. Yes, he had dug this thing up; for the pope he had uncovered it. Who would take delivery now?

Deauchez pinched his shut eyes with his fingers, took a drink of soda. He stared at the monitor and sighed under the weight of that ponderous grief.

Come home, Michele.

He stared at it for a long, long time, the words from Donnelley blinking.

. . . suspended indefinitely . . .

Come home, Michele.

Before he could think too much about his decision, he maneuvered the mouse up to the menu bar and clicked DELETE. The e-mail disappeared. He deleted the PR office message, too, without looking at it. He knew what it would be: an official notice of the pope's death.

When both were gone his mouth was dry and his nerves jangled at the unaccustomed insurrection. As of this moment, he did not know the pope was dead. He had received nothing. Yet, it was time to leave India, Donnelley was right about that.

He began to make flight reservations on his laptop, but stopped. The travel service was the Vatican's, as was his credit card account. Was he being paranoid? Absolutely. But the pope *was* dead, and he *was* planning to disregard a direct order.

He hailed a taxi, feeling idiotically subversive, and directed the driver to a Swiss bank he'd seen in town. He would extract funds from his account in Rome and book a flight at the airport.

Of course, he had no intention of going home.

LARKSPUR LAKE, EASTERN WASHINGTON

Simon Hill hadn't expected Washington to be this dry and hot— wasn't it supposed to rain all the time? Or was that just Seattle? He had rented a car with no air-conditioning, and he was sweating by the time he found the office. It was one of many cabins at the far point of a circular dirt drive that ran through the camp. The door and windows were propped open to let in the breeze. Inside, it was empty except for a beautiful Native American girl who was seated at the desk, talking on the phone. It wasn't quite what he'd expected. He nodded at her with a hint of embarrassment. She smiled passively.

"No, it's fine. But we *do* have more coming every day. Monday will work . . . I think we're close to seven thousand."

Hill walked over to the bookshelves self-consciously and began scanning the titles. They were down to almost nothing; either they carried little stock or there'd been a recent buying frenzy. *A Shaman's Journey* was the only one of Cougar's volumes left, and it swam colorfully in a sea of blank space. Hill picked it up.

"Well, if we must," the beauty said into the receiver. "Will Cougar wanted me to make it clear that it's not a procedure we care to repeat every week. I can't imagine you would care to, either. All right. Thanks."

She hung up the phone with a grimace of annoyance and stood, stretching her back. "Can I help you?"

Hill turned a bit too fast and paid for it with a spike of pain that bolted up from his nether regions. He winced and walked to the desk in his new, bowlegged gait.

"Hi! Um, my name is Simon Hill. I'm with the *New York Times*." He switched the book to his left hand and stuck out his right.

"Ah!" Her face brightened as she shook his hand. "So you have finally found us, Mr. Hill?"

"You've been reading the *Times*?"

"Of course. You're the only newspaper who knows the first thing about what's going on."

Hill felt absurdly pleased. "Well, thanks. But . . . I think you have the advantage."

"I'm Sacred Dance."

She certainly was. "Really? That's pretty. Say—you guys should have called me."

"Will Cougar says we have done as the Spirits asked. There was no need to try to reach *everyone* in the world. That is not our mission."

Hill felt a rush of newsman greed. "What did he say about his mission? Does he think he's one of the Twenty-Four?"

"He knows the Spirits spoke to him. He knows they spoke to others. Beyond that, he would probably say he's not interested in your labels."

"Wow. That's almost a quote. Sounds like you know him pretty well."

"I know him."

"Hey, um, is he around, by any chance?" Hill shifted his weight from one leg to another. His eyes scanned the room, looking for a hint of an inner office door or maybe a pager or intercom. He saw nothing.

Sacred Dance got that dreaded regretful look. "Well, yes, but he's very busy. I don't believe he would see you. He gave me strict instructions about reporters. Anyone who shows up is to get a pamphlet. He says there's nothing else for him to talk about."

She took a mailer from the desk drawer and gave it to him. Hill looked it over. He wasn't impressed. "Wow. This is really, uh, thoughtful of you guys. Well done, that is, but um . . ."

"Yes, Mr. Hill?"

"Well, I flew in this morning from New York. I mean, I was really hoping to, you know, speak with Mr. Cougar. I'd be happy to publish an interview with him. In his own words, of course. People are *really* interested in what these prophets have to say, Miss . . . uh . . . Sacred Dance."

"It's just Sacred Dance, and you won't get anywhere calling him *Mr.* Cougar. 'Mr.' is a white man's title. His name is Will Cougar. Just Will Cougar."

"Sorry," Hill mumbled. *Let's all get P.C. down on the reservation.*

"It's not important. But I don't think Will Cougar would be interested in being interviewed for the *New York Times.*"

She smiled politely but crossed her arms and fell silent, a sure sign that she was waiting for him to leave. She obviously didn't know reporters very well.

"Okay. Look, could I just ask *you* a few questions, then? Just a *few*?" He smiled at her hopefully.

"I can't imagine what about."

"Well, let's see . . . Were you here when they did those hantavirus inoculations a month or so back?"

Her arms slowly descended in surprise. "Why would you ask me that?"

"*Why?* Well . . ."

"How did you know about the inoculations?" He could tell by her tone that she was not upset exactly, but she was tiptoeing around the borders of it, like a woman reluctant to get her feet dirty in a puddle.

"Um, Health Relief did them, right? It's a matter of record."

"I suppose. But why would you care?"

From the open doorway behind her a man entered. He was a startling apparition—dark, stern, and absolutely silent. His work gloves, boots, denim, and flannel did nothing to disarm the impression of a dangerous man. His black eyes were not those of a rancher but of a sorcerer, like something from a menacing dream.

The man paused at Sacred Dance's elbow, not making a sound, but she sensed him. Hill saw her back stiffen.

"Who is this?" the man asked, clearly addressing her and only her.

"Simon Hill. He's a reporter for the *New York Times*."

"Do you have something to tell us, Simon Hill?"

Will Cougar's voice was flat, neutral, but his eyes were not neutral at all. Hill had a desire to shrink back, but resisted it. He considered sticking out his hand and thought better of that, too. "Hi. You must be Will Cougar. I'm really glad to meet you, uh, sir."

"Do you have something to tell us about the hantavirus inoculations, Simon Hill?"

Hill thought about it. He scratched his chin. "No, sir. I don't believe I do."

Will Cougar grunted. He gave Hill an unreadable look and slipped from the room.

Hill sighed, glad to be free of the man's penetrating gaze, though a moment ago he'd have danced the Macarena to get to see Cougar, sores or no. He took his baseball cap off and wiped the sweat from his brow.

"I was going to close up the office, Mr. Hill."

Hill held up a dark finger in a pause. "One more thing. When I came in you were on the phone. That wouldn't by any chance have been about . . ."

Sacred Dance looked truly baffled by this line of questioning. "Since you browse records anyway, Mr. Hill, I guess I'll just tell you. The county is requiring us to inoculate our new arrivals. They say the drought is causing mouse populations to skyrocket. They won't let us have these crowds here without it."

"That's . . . uh . . . that's what I thought."

"Is there some problem?"

"Oh, hey, no. I mean, it's just a precaution, right? So, uh, nothing weird happened the first time? The last time, I mean?"

Sacred Dance studied him for a long moment. "Like what?"

"I dunno. Did the shots make anyone sick, maybe? Or . . ."

"Sick with . . . hanta?"

"Yeah. Hanta, or flu maybe? Anything? Any hospitalizations?"

She looked relieved. "No. Now I'm afraid I really *must* go. *Please,* Mr. Hill."

"Hey, sure. No problem."

He walked to the door, pulling out his wallet. He took a ten and a business card and gave them to her. "That's for the book, and the card is for you. You never know when a reporter might come in handy, right?"

He smiled. She took the offerings without smiling back and he felt a twinge of regret. It was a professional curse—pissing people off. It was particularly unfortunate when the pissee was a beautiful woman. He wandered back to his car, wondering what it was the pair of them weren't saying, and if there was any way he could dig it up. Somehow, he doubted it, but he reached for his cellular to call Jeanine anyway . . . and found he'd left it at the hotel.

On the shady side of the building, Will Cougar watched him go. Cougar was leaning up against the wall by an open window. He had been there, listening, since he left the office. He watched the reporter get into the car, watched him pull away, watched him disappear. Then the reporter was gone, but he was not gone completely. He had left something behind in Will Cougar.

And Will Cougar knew it.

CHAPTER 9

DAY 11
SOMEWHERE OVER THE MIDDLE EAST

When Deauchez awoke they were flying over dust-brown low hills and valleys that were randomly dotted with green irrigated fields. The green squares were dwarfed by the scale of the brown, including the brown of fields that had been abandoned to the dust. They were over the Middle East, Deauchez thought, probably Turkey.

He had at one point thought he might be going to the Middle East after India, not just passing over it. There was the prophet Levi in Jerusalem; he had longed to see Jerusalem again. He had even dared imagine that he might catch up with the pope there. Just he and the Holy Father, away from the Vatican, away from Donnelley's protective hovering, away from caveats ad nauseam.

Jerusalem was still there, Levi, too, for all Deauchez knew. The pope was not. After what had happened to Innocent XIV, Jerusalem did not beckon anymore. Not for the moment, anyway. Perhaps not for a long time.

Deauchez wondered, with a pang, who the pope's successor would be and how open he would be to what Deauchez had to say. *Peter of Rome* came into his head. He frowned, wondering where it had come from. Ah, yes. Father Carnesca. St. Malachy. Rubbish.

He stretched his back as best he could in the cramped tourist-class seat, wriggled his toes. Just across the narrow aisle, a Caucasian businessman was fast asleep, white shirtsleeves rolled up and tie loosened. There was a gauze bandage on his forearm—no doubt covering a sore—and a *Wall Street Journal* on his lap. He didn't look particularly troubled. His hand was loose in his lap inches from the newspaper, curled toward it the way a mother might unconsciously reach out to her child even in her sleep. No, this man's god was Mammon. His kind were the last who ever would be troubled about this prophet business. Thank the Lord there were so many of his kind!

As if purposely mocking Deauchez's unspoken thoughts, the man shifted in his sleep. A frown rippled across his face and his hand twitched in his lap. A slight, moaning sigh escaped his lips.

Annoyed at this betrayal, Deauchez glimpsed down at the newspaper to look for clues and saw that the headline was announcing the nosedive of the American commodities market. Deauchez slipped the newspaper carefully from the sleeping man's lap and scanned it. The American commodities market was recording record losses. All crop foods: grain, potatoes, corn, cotton; they were all diving through the floor. Fish commodities had turned worthless overnight. Even meat commodities—the infamous pork bellies for one—were plummeting. Kellogg, Post, Dolly Madison, Nabisco, Quaker, Keebler, Betty Crocker, Starkist, Bumblebee, and many other stocks were bottoming out. The U.S. had announced their new rationing plan; that was part of the reason why. And reports of the red tide damage—that was part of it, too.

Deauchez sighed and returned the newspaper to the sleeping man's lap. He'd first heard about the red tide outbreak at a newsstand in the Calcutta airport. It had hit him even harder than the sores. His first reaction had been a desire to get on his knees and repent. Terror, irrational terror. It was the second sign; there could be no doubt.

For a moment, in that airport, he'd seen the cypress tree in Sanchez's field, swaying in the wind. Panic had so seized him that he'd had to run to find the nearest men's room, where he'd discovered that the content of his bowels had liquefied. He'd sat there on the bowl while cramps racked him and dignity fled him, and he had stared up at the blaring light above and had muttered the mantra as fast as he could, over and over.

. . . thy kingdom come thy will be done . . .

It had been a bad attack, one of the worst ever. But it had passed, and in its wake was that defiance whose obdurate nature surprised even him.

Deauchez pulled his laptop up from its position under the seat in front of him. He pulled the Telegyn cellular out of his other bag and hooked it up to the modem outlet. After a moment of blinking PRIME ONE LINK, the phone's display cleared, and he found himself on the Internet. He went immediately into his e-mail.

Yes! There was something new from Hill. Eagerly, Deauchez double-clicked on the message header.

Father Deauchez:
    Hey, where are you? Tried to call you in Rome—spent, geez, twenty minutes or so getting the runaround and then they said you weren't there. I wanted to say I'm really sorry about the pope. You knew him personally, right? Well it just sucks. I thought for sure you'd be in Rome, what with the funeral and all.
    I went to Cougar Camp myself. Thanks for the tip about that. This is what I learned: They're scheduled for more of the inoculations this week to pick up the new people coming in. The county is requiring it (I checked). The group giving the shots is Health Relief. They do all kinds of work in disadvantaged areas, particularly on reservations in the Southwest. That's how they got into hanta, and why they're inoculating for it in new places like the Northwest where it's cropping up. Hantavirus is carried by field mice and people can get it if they stir up mouse droppings that are infected and then breathe in particles of the stuff. There have been a few cases of it in the Spokane area, which is why they've started the inoculations. The drought is causing a mouse population explosion all over.
    So . . . what? Nothing that interesting as far as I can tell. Still, it seemed like the woman I talked to at Cougar Camp was keeping something back, but I couldn't get it out of her because I didn't know what to ask. What are you looking for anyway? I can't do much more unless I know what it is you think is relevant about this stuff. So call me, okay? I'm back in New York.
    Simon Hill

Deauchez read the message over several times. There was both good news and bad in it. As usual, it couldn't break through the bonds of ambiguity that seemed to surround everything about this investigation. One glimmer of maybe something and lots of splashes of obviously nothings.

He pondered his response. Hill had gone to some trouble and he deserved an answer. And yet . . . Deauchez had this intuition that was driving him, this sense that he needed to talk to one of the so-called prophets, face-to-face, now that he knew what questions to ask. St. Cajetan's had left him with an idea of what might have happened in that hospital, but no proof. And Giri was too far gone to provide answers. Still, if he was right, any of the other prophets would do just as well. And if he was wrong . . . ?

But he didn't think he was. He had a feeling that if he could only ask the right person the right questions, he would learn everything. And there was no point discussing it with Hill until he did.

He clicked on the REPLY button and typed in a quick note.

> Mr. Hill: Thank you for your efforts—they are much appreciated. I am still investigating. I will let you know more as soon as I can. Deauchez

Nodding at the screen as if agreeing with his own approach, Deauchez rolled the mouse cursor over to the right to save the message until he was on the ground. Then he remembered the cellular. He clicked on SEND.

> Message sent.

NEW YORK CITY

Simon Hill cursed loudly enough to cause everyone in the newsroom to turn around and stare. Susan got up out of her seat and headed for him, an expression of curiosity on her face. But Ralph Bowmont had left his office, too, and he reached Hill first.

"What's up, cowboy?"

Hill pointed in exasperation at the monitor.

> Mr. Hill:
>   Sorry if I sent you on a wild-goose chase. I thought I had an idea, but it turned out to be nothing. Never mind.
>   Deauchez

Bowmont let out a long *tsk*ing breath. "Sorry, Hill. That's the way it goes sometimes. I thought this thing had a stink to it from the git-go."

"Man, it just *felt* like something."

"Anyone can get psyched out. Particularly on a story like this."

But Hill was still shaking his head as if rejecting what was now staring him in the face.

"Have you uncovered anythin' a'tall?" Bowmont probed.

"Okay," Hill said, leaning back. He enumerated his points on his fingers. "Stanton had chest pains and thought he was having a heart attack. He was in the hospital for two nights. They discharged him saying it was, like, a panic attack."

"Yeah?"

"Health Relief is funded by H.A.I.—Health Aid International. The county *did* require the shots, but only after Health Relief gave them a scare story. H.A.I. is paying for the shots; they're nonprofit."

"And highly respected, for what it's worth."

"But Health Relief *did* inoculate all over the county, and there *was* a fatality near Spokane from hanta this spring, so there's nothing that isn't kosher."

"Anythin' else?"

"Our contact in Moscow said he heard that Kratski and his group got booster shots before leaving for Siberia. Supposedly, though, that's not uncommon."

"And?"

Hill picked up a pencil, tapped it as if avoiding the question, then tossed it down again in disgust. "That's it. Most of our field agents haven't gotten that close to the prophets."

"Andrews?"

"Nothing we could find. Hasn't been to his G.P. in a year."

"Abeed?"

"Wouldn't talk to us."

Bowmont scratched his chin. "Looks to me, Hill, like that dog won't hunt."

Hill put his face in his hands and growled. *"Errrr!* I just . . . man, I thought it felt like something."

Bowmont looked sympathetic. "There's a whole lotta data to track on this thing. Everyone's workin' sixteen-hour shifts and still fallin' behind. The last two issues . . ."

"I know. We'll dump the medical checks," Hill said bitterly.

"Good call, son. What people wanna know is what the prophets are *sayin'*, what they're *doin'*, and who's fallin' for their act. And as much as we can find on the famine situation, of course, and the signs."

"I know."

Bowmont clapped Hill on the back in a Texan gesture of manly reassurance and wandered back to his office. Hill had to go tell his team not to waste any more of their time. But first, he looked at the e-mail again, shook his head in disgust, and deleted the damn thing.

RIO DE JANEIRO

The monkey's flesh was searingly hot. So hot, Dr. Michael Smith could feel it even through his thick protective gloves. The monkey wasn't putting up much of a fight under the virologist's hands. It lay on its back on the table, looking up at him with eyes that kept wanting to close—glazed, distant eyes. Mike wondered what the monkey was seeing when it looked up at him. Whatever it was, he was pretty sure Number Six was no longer aware of the gleaming chrome cages of the monkey room.

There were sixteen corpses in the next room, all of them stashed in the portable freezers the team had brought in. He would get to them soon, but the first thing he wanted to do was look at the disease while it was still doing its worst. He'd come straight from the plane, pausing only long enough to check the arrangements outside. It was clear that the local field office was taking this seriously, despite Stanley's misgivings. The building was cordoned off. A truck out front offered basic Level Four supplies, including suits, but he and Tony had brought their own.

The Level Four field dress was a wax-coated, long-sleeved white jumpsuit, several pairs of extra-thick rubber gloves, rubber boots, and a full-face respirator. Mike had a short conversation with Rodriquez, the man in charge from PANAFTOSA. He gave him brief instructions for setting up a lime box and the disinfectant "showers"—large buckets of bleach and warm water. Rodriquez was clearly worried about doing anything more visible on the street, but he agreed without question. Mike understood how he felt. It would be a shame to cause a local panic only to find the agent was innocuous, but they couldn't risk spreading a possible Level Four via the bottoms of their shoes either.

Inside, there were few people. The hoof-and-mouth folks clearly weren't comfortable getting close to something like this, and the shelter's staff had been taken to a local hospital. They learned from Rodriquez that half the shelter workers had serious cold symptoms and the rest were starting with sniffles. Mike had to get over there, too, and soon.

But first things first. If they knew what was killing the monkeys, they could test for it in the staff's blood. There was still a chance they would all be lucky.

The examination of Number Six was quickly dislodging that hope.

It didn't look like Ebola, that was the good news. Number Six was the sickest monkey of those that were left, that much was obvious just by looking at the creatures. In fact, Number Six was close to death, or so Mike thought. For the monkey's sake, he hoped very close.

Number Six had not vomited—neither blood, which was usual with Ebola, nor anything else during his entire illness; neither had the other monkeys. There was no bloody diarrhea, no diarrhea at all. Reportedly, the bowel movements had slowed down in regularity, then pretty much stopped. The monkeys weren't eating.

There was no blood in the mouth, an early telltale symptom of hemorrhagic fevers. There was no fluid sound coming from the lungs when Dr. Smith placed a stethoscope over the monkey's chest. Quite the contrary. Number Six looked like he couldn't produce a spare drop of fluid of any kind to save his life.

The primate's trunk was terribly swollen, his abdomen and genitals in particular, the former feeling taut and stretched, like a leather drumhead, when Mike probed the region. The creature's face and extremities were also swollen, but less severely. The flesh was hot and bone-dry; no sweat, no secretions. There were no visible rashes or wounds on the skin—Mike checked carefully, pushing aside the fur. The eyes were inflamed and irritated from a marked absence of normal fluid. There was nothing visible up his nostril passages except cracked, dry skin. The tongue was swollen from lack of saliva.

Mike shone a penlight into the monkey's eyes. The irises did not respond, nor would the monkey follow his moving fingers. He snapped his glove in the monkey's ear—nothing.

Mike backed away from Number Six and looked at the creature for a moment, the puzzlement on his face hidden behind the rubber mask.

"Is it Ebola?" Josh Bergman's muffled voice asked. Mike looked up. Bergman looked thinner than ever with his enormous Afro flattened under his surgical cap.

"Not unless it's mutated *a lot*," Mike answered. "There's none of the liquefaction of hemorrhagic fevers. In fact, he's completely dehydrated. Even the mucus from the cold is gone."

"What is it, then?"

Mike shook his head to indicate his befuddlement. "There's brain damage—it's probably swollen up like the rest of him. I wouldn't be surprised if that's what causes death."

"Encephalitis?" Josh gave the monkey a fascinated and horrified glance.

"Possibly, but the other organs are swollen, too, not just the brain. Look at how distended his stomach is. We'll know better when we open one of them up."

"Encephalitis is spread through an insect vector, isn't it? Mosquitoes, usually?" Josh looked around nervously as if expecting one to dive-bomb him as they spoke.

"The St. Louis encephalitis and California encephalitis outbreaks, yes, but swelling of the brain can also be postinfective—a complication of another virus. Measles, for instance. There's clearly more going on here than *just* encephalitis. I'd say it's more of a symptom than the cause."

"Then what's causing it? Heck, do you realize how infectious this thing is? Every single one of these monkeys caught it. And unless the twenty people who had contact with them turn out to have just *coincidentally* caught colds . . ."

Mike looked around. The last few living monkeys looked back. "Even if the staff did contract the primary infection, it might not progress as far in a human host. It might just peter out like a normal cold."

"It's possible," said Josh.

But he didn't sound convinced, and Mike realized that he himself didn't believe that either. Whatever the monkeys had, it was weird and it was lethal. Mike couldn't help remembering B virus—a herpes virus that infected rhesus monkeys. Between 1975 and 1989, twenty-eight animal handlers contracted B virus from monkeys and twenty-five of them developed encephalitis. Only five survived the disease. If the people who had handled these animals had indeed caught what the monkeys had, chances were high that it would play out just as it had in this room.

The only good news in any of this was that these monkeys were extremely rare and the number of staff here was under twenty. They had a chance of isolating this outbreak before it got much further—if they were very, very careful and very, very lucky.

LONDON

The wizened little nun was staring at him with the impersonal gaze of an entomologist. Deauchez shifted his bag to his other hand uncomfortably. The door to Daunsey's office was cracked open, and he could hear the conversation inside.

"I can't tell you how much we appreciate this," Sister Daunsey was saying. "It's an answer to prayer. We need housing *so* badly."

"The flats should be comfortable, as long as you don't mind the dust," a man with a British accent replied. "We weren't to open them for another month, you see. Things are still a trifle unfinished."

"I'm sure they'll be glorious. You're so very generous."

"Please, Sister. I have you to thank for convincing me that Santa Pelagia is the real thing. After your speech at the institute I began to think about what's really important. The end has a way of doing that to a fellow." The man laughed—it was an awful sound.

Deauchez cleared his throat, smiled nervously at the little nun. Her expression did not change.

"Don't think of it as the end, Mr. Friedalow. Think of it as gettin' a new prime minister . . . and he's *really* divine."

"Well, if he raises the rent, I'll want those flats back, Sister!" The man chuckled.

Oh, the delights of a little apocalyptic bantering, Deauchez thought sourly.

The door opened wide at last and a man in an old-fashioned bowler emerged. His alabaster face was shining and his eyes were damp; he was a man basking in the glow of a good deed.

Sister Daunsey had seen her donor to the door, and she caught sight of Deauchez waiting in the hall. First she gaped at him, then she slammed the door shut. Deauchez jumped and smiled sheepishly at the nun and the gentleman in the bowler as if to say, *She's just surprised to see me, that's all. I'm sure she's really thrilled.*

They both gave him a look as if he were a rare specimen of something particularly nasty. Then the man left and the nun tapped gently on the office door and let herself in. After a moment, the door opened and Sister Daunsey appeared. She had apparently recovered her wits.

"Father Deauchez. What a surprise." She made no effort to conceal her dislike, but she let him in.

"Sister Daunsey . . . I'm happy I caught you."

"You haven't caught me yet, Father."

Deauchez's smile wavered. "I mean . . . I'm so pleased I caught you in. Could you spare me a few moments?"

"I'm extremely busy, Father. I've had meetings and phone calls all mornin', and I must get out to make my rounds."

"*Please,* Sister. I flew all the way to London just to see you." Deauchez looked at her imploringly.

"All right, Father." She sighed. "I suppose I can manage ten minutes since you've traveled all the way here. Sister Rachel, it's all right."

The old nun was still in the doorway staring at Deauchez. She removed herself slowly, watching him until the very last second.

"What is it, Father? Why aren't you in Rome?"

Deauchez sought an explanation but found nothing except the truth, and that was not easily expressed. Before he could begin, Daunsey scowled. "What could be so important that you'd miss the funeral? You should be there for *Papa*'s sake if not for your own. Heaven knows, if I could be there . . ."

"Why aren't you?"

Daunsey smiled bitterly. "I'm just a radical nun. I'm not invited. Besides, I can't leave London right now. *Papa* would understand."

Deauchez walked over to her desk, looked at the laptop there. "I sent you e-mail."

"And I threw it away. I'm sorry, Father, but your theories don't interest me." Her words were courageous enough, but she looked a tad guilty. She smoothed the sides of her dress self-consciously.

"Did you?"

"Did I what?"

"Did you have any medical treatment within the month preceding your dream?"

"This is what you came all the way here to ask me?"

"*Oui.* Please answer."

Daunsey scowled. "The very idea! You should be ashamed! How can you continue chasin' phantoms when the evidence is so clear? What about the sores? What about the red tide? Don't you care about God? Don't you worry for your soul?"

Deauchez winced. The remark hurt, perhaps more than she'd even intended. He was indeed worried. "I would love to discuss all of those things with you, Sister, on my life I would. But you've given me ten minutes, and I must have an answer to my question."

"How can you expect me to take such foolishness seriously? I assume you mean anythin' from a dental appointment to a vaccination to visitin' the sick. I am a nun! I see all kinds of people every day. How can I answer when you behave as though the simplest, most ordinary occurrence would somehow belittle the most blessed act of my life!"

"I said nothing about belittlement."

"You don't need to. Every word from your mouth has screamed it since the day I met you."

She wouldn't meet his eyes. She meant to sound angry, but her tone was too dismissive, her words somehow evasive. *Methinks the lady doth protest too much.* "Did you have a vaccination, Sister?"

"No!"

There was something in her voice. He touched her arm. "You—you are trembling!"

She pulled away abruptly and walked around the desk, reached for her purse. He could see by the set of her face that she did not, *was* not, going to hear any more. What was she afraid of ?

"*Please,* listen! Only hear me out, then tell me if I'm being foolish."

She shook her head determinedly, hands still fumbling with her purse. He began talking anyway.

"Maria Sanchez had a personal physician with her when I saw her. Trent Andrews mentioned that he has had a therapist for years. Will Cougar had a hantavirus inoculation the week before his vision. Reverend Stanton was in the hospital when he received his dream. Dishama Giri, the Hindu yogi, was hit by a car days before his dream. He was taken to a hospital for treatment. And I went to visit Sagara Bata—they were giving inoculations right outside his encampment."

She put the purse down. She was gazing at him now, frowning. "I don't . . ."

"And while Giri was in the hospital in Allahabad, they were doing inoculations there as well. There was a holy festival going on in town, and the inoculations group told the hospital it would be a good day for vaccines because more people would be coming into the hospital than usual. Every patient that day got inoculated, which means Giri did, too."

"There's nothin' so peculiar about—"

"The group that did the inoculations in Allahabad was Health Aid International. They are the same ones—white vans with red caducei—that were doing the inoculations at Sagara Bata's encampment near Calcutta just a few days ago."

"Yes? And what does that mean? H.A.I. does work all over the world."

"But Allahabad and Sagara Bata's encampment are thousands of miles apart. Besides, in each case: why *then*, why *there*? Does it not seem a bit too coincidental?"

Sister Daunsey was shaking her head, two spots of color high on her cheeks. "I don't believe you. And even if it's true, it doesn't mean anythin'."

"How can it not *mean* anything? Don't you think it's all a bit too—"

"It doesn't *mean anythin'*!"

Her voice was raised; her words, her expression, suffused with anger. He stared at her, dumbfounded, like a child unexpectedly slapped. He did not know what he had expected, thinking that if he could only talk to her . . . He certainly hadn't expected this.

"Yes, you heard me correctly, Father Deauchez. *So what?*"

"I . . . I don't know. What if these dreams were brought on by drugs?"

"No! We all were told to go to Santa Pelagia! How do you explain *that*? Or what happened there? Your 'coincidences' are not very convincin', Father. Medicine is a part of our lives—you might as well say that everyone had *eaten* in the week before Santa Pelagia. You're clutchin' at straws!"

He searched for something, some rebuttal, some response, but he had no idea what to *feel*, much less what to say.

"It doesn't change Santa Pelagia," Daunsey continued. She was calming a bit now. "And it doesn't change what's happenin' right now. The *signs*, Father Deauchez. Have you forgotten the signs?"

Deauchez shook his head. He put a hand to his mouth, feeling as though he had to keep something in: words, perhaps, or maybe projectile vomiting.

Daunsey looked gratified. "Really, Father. You should pray to God to help you accept his will."

Deauchez swallowed and lowered his hand. "I'm sorry if I upset you. I don't know . . . No. I suppose you don't see it."

"Go home, Father. Go back to Rome and make your peace with God. Or stay here, if you like. You are *Catholic*."

"Catholic, yes, but not English, not Irish. What about the Catholics of Italy, Sister?" His voice sounded far away, like someone else's. "Or of France, Germany, Spain? Sanchez will draw the Catholics of Mexico and the U.S., but what about the rest?"

Daunsey faltered, as though the thought had occurred to her, too. "I—I'm sure God has his reasons, Father."

Deauchez could have pursued the theological argument, but he only nodded. He felt extraordinarily tired. "It's only—I don't want anything bad to happen here, Sister. To these people. To you."

Sister Daunsey made a *tsk*ing sound. "Father! *I'm* doin' what God has asked me to do. *I'm* not the one in danger."

He left her office, pausing to press her hand in his. But her eyes had already dismissed him—completely, irrevocably and, he thought, not without will, not without relief.

"Father Deauchez! *Tsss!*"

The words were hissed at him as he reached the front door of the brownstone. He turned and saw the wrinkled little nun who had spent so much quality time staring at him. Sister Rachel was peeking around the parlor archway. She looked around nervously, but there was no one else in sight. She motioned to him with an urgent gesture that was ludicrously conspiratorial.

He didn't want to speak with her. He was more exhausted, more disheartened than he could ever remember being in his life; sick to his stomach, sick at heart. Sister Daunsey was right. When spoken aloud, his "trail" sounded ridiculously meager. How had he gotten so lost? And could he ever find his way again?

He took two plodding steps toward the living room, and Sister Rachel clutched at him, pulled him along with an iron grasp. He found himself in the brownstone's parlor.

The nun pulled a sheet of paper from the side pocket of her habit and handed it to him. It was a letter addressed to Sister Daunsey's convent in Dublin. It was requesting an emergency blood drive because of "extremely low reserves" of blood. It suggested a tentative date, and that date was two weeks before Santa Pelagia began. The stationery named the organization: Health Aid International.

"I did see your e-mail, Father," Sister Rachel whispered. "I sort all her correspondence for her, ya know. 'N I tried to remind her of . . . what had happened. But she din' want to hear about it, Father! She wouldn't talk of it a'tall! Then you said that name in her office, Health Aid International!"

Clearly, the nun had been listening at Daunsey's door. Deauchez could have kissed her for it. "Did she . . ."

"Yes! She gave, she always does! But that's not the worst of it, is it? She passed out! 'N they took her back into a little area to recover. She never passed out before, did she?"

Deauchez had trouble getting his tongue to work. "H-how long was she gone?"

"Fifteen, twenty minutes, as I recall."

"Was there anyone back there with her?"

"None of *us*, Father, but a couple o' *them*. I was worried about her, wasn't I? 'N I stayed right outside there. But they said 'twasn't unusual, 'n she did come out of it after all. I thought she'd been overdoin' it, working day and night the way she does."

Deauchez's hands were shaking as he folded up the paper and stuck it in his pocket. "Thank you, Sister."

"Aye. But what is it, do you think, Father? Did they *hurt* her? Maybe they're tryin' to poison 'em off, the prophets! Maybe it's the followers of the beast!"

This statement made Deauchez feel better, somehow, as if by comparison his own theories sounded much less insane. "I don't know, Sister Rachel. But please, let me know right away if she seems at all . . . sick or . . . changed. Do you understand?"

Sister Rachel nodded, her chin thrust forward with determination. Yes, she would do anything to safeguard Sister Daunsey. Even so, her ingrained loyalty to the infallible collar had proven greater still. Deauchez gave her his card.

"Let her be for now, Sister. I will contact you as soon as I can. I'm lodging at Brown's Hotel if you need me."

"*Please* call me, Father. It's poison I'm afeared of !"

"I understand. Trust in God, Sister."

Deauchez slipped away from her and out of the brownstone. His nausea had miraculously disappeared.

RIO DE JANEIRO

It was quite late before Dr. Smith made it over to the quarantine ward at the hospital. At this stage of an epidemic, it always felt like he was playing beat-the-clock and everything was wildly out of control. He'd given cursory exams to the last two living monkeys. The least sick, the one still displaying cold symptoms, was just beginning to get feverish and wasn't swollen at all. The other had definite enlargement in the abdominal area.

He'd autopsied a few of the dead. When he cut open the monkeys' abdominal cavities, their organs spilled out onto the table. The stomachs looked like bulging purses, the livers were as big as a cow's, even the colons were puffed up like inflated inner tubes. When he dissected one of the livers it became clear that the organs were not enlarged because they were filled with fluid or gases—it was the tissue itself that had expanded, swelling up from some kind of poison or trauma, the way the tissue of a man's arm might swell to four or five times its size when bitten by a rattlesnake. The internal pressure of the swelling and the obvious soreness of the organs would have caused tremendous pain were it not ameliorated by the brain damage occurring at the other end of the body.

Immediately preceding death, the brain began literally streaming out of the skull like a PB&J sandwich overloaded with jam. The monkey he'd examined first, Number Six, hadn't yet reached that stage when he'd looked at him. His brain had no doubt swollen and was crammed against his cranial cavity in all directions, turning the creature into a mindless vegetable. But he hadn't yet done what they do at the end, these monkeys, the thing that had caused the vets reporting to WHO to mistakenly agree that, yes, the animals did "bleed out" when they died.

The brain, after having expanded in the skull far beyond the laws of displacement, eventually began squirting out of the ears and nose and mouth. The eyes bulged from their sockets. This was how he found every one of the monkey corpses, and this was what happened to Number Six, while Mike watched, two hours after his initial exam.

The virologist was thinking about this as he stood outside the quarantine ward at Hospital Municipal Souza Aguiar. Through the small glass window he could see the patients. Ten beds lined the walls on either side of the ward, and each bed was occupied. White linen drapes on ceiling runners—none of which were pulled—were the only remote claim to privacy these people had as they lay sick, most likely dying, amidst their coworkers. Maybe they'd been friends, maybe this one had had a crush on that one, maybe a few had hated each other, but whatever their feelings were, it was a cinch that none of them would have volunteered to play a round of pass-the-bedpan. They deserved better in these, what might well be their final days, but they wouldn't get it. Infectious disease left little dignity to the dying. Perhaps that was its most merciless face.

Welcome to Greenpeace Rio. For their trouble, these young people, these environmentalists, had been awarded a slumber party in jammies that had no backs—an office get-together with catheter bags and blood packs as the appetizers, hot stuffed sweetmeats as the main entrées, and fresh-squeezed brain for dessert. *Bring your own spoon!*

Boy. He was really getting tired.

Dr. Smith closed his eyes and forced the bad things from his mind. When he felt he'd succeeded as much as he was liable to, he pushed open the doors and entered the wing.

"Is this Jennifer?" He used the most upbeat voice he could muster through the respirator. He'd picked up the chart from the end of the bed, so he already knew that it was, indeed, Jennifer Mallard, manager at the late, great Rio Greenpeace shelter. But the young woman, a small, waiflike blonde, was turned on her side, staring at the wall, and he wanted to get her attention.

He succeeded. She rolled onto her back and scooted up in the bed, all the while taking him in with an intense, worried gaze. Her size was misleading. She was tough, her eyes told him that. "Who are you?"

"My name is Dr. Michael Smith, but you can call me Mike. I'm with the World Health Organization."

"Have you seen the monkeys yet?"

"Yes, Jennifer, I have."

"Are all of them . . ."

"Two are still alive."

"But not getting any better?"

"They seem to be progressing like the others, as far as we can tell," he replied neutrally. As a person he had a thing about telling the truth. As a doctor, sometimes that made things more difficult than they had to be.

Jen was watching him intently. "They said you were going to . . . *Is* it Ebola?"

Mike sat down carefully on the side of her bed. He could tell that a few of the other patients, those who weren't asleep, were listening to the conversation. "There's no trace in the monkeys' bloodstreams of Ebola. We're still testing, of course, but so far we've not identified what the disease is. We're not even sure if it's a virus or a bacteria."

"But whatever it is, we have it, right?"

"You have *something*. It's likely that it came from the monkeys, but even if it did, remember that we've never seen this disease in a human host. It may be benign."

He could hear nose blowing and belabored breathing from other quarters, but Jen herself didn't sound congested. He reached out a hand and felt her forehead. It was hot. He waved a nurse over and had her place a thermometer under Jen's tongue. He felt her neck and throat for swelling, looked at her arms. He nodded to the nurse and she pulled the white canvas drape around the bed. Mike pulled down the sheet that covered Jen's chest.

"I want to take a look at your tummy," he told her. Jen just stared at him from around the thermometer without blinking.

He pulled up her gown. She was no more than 105 pounds. Perhaps there was a trace of swelling in her small belly. It was difficult to say. He gently palpated the region with his gloved fingers.

"Umm!" Jen said, her back arching under his hands.

"That hurts?"

She nodded. The nurse took the thermometer from Jen's mouth and handed it to him: 101 degrees Fahrenheit.

He pulled Jen's gown back down. "Have you been having any abdominal pain before now—before I touched you?"

She nodded. "It was kinda sore this morning, when I got up to go to the bathroom. It's been worse tonight, like I ate something bad."

"What did you have for dinner?"

"Hideous noodle-something. I think it had chicken in it."

He checked her eyes with a flashlight. They looked normal. "Anything else unusual?"

"Something vaguely resembling peas."

He smiled. "No, I mean any other unusual symptoms?"

"Major headache." It was a simple thing to say, but her voice cracked as she said it, and he knew she'd seen at least one of those monkeys die.

He stopped his exam and took one of her hands. Damn the goggles and mask for making human contact so difficult! "Jennifer, I want you to remember that a monkey is a very different animal biologically from a human. Remember the swine flu? It killed lots of pigs, but very few humans died from it—they just got sick and then they got better. Those monkeys have very naive immune systems. As the world traveler that you are, you're super-resilient by comparison. Plus, you're young and healthy, and you have an entire hospital to care for you."

She looked down, frowning a bit as if to say that, be that as it may, she was in grave danger and she knew it. "Have you figured out what made the monkeys swell up like that?"

"No, but we will."

"Their brains swelled up, too, didn't they? Is that what killed them?"

He hesitated for a moment. "Yes."

She didn't say anything, just looked away, off into the white canvas of the curtain. "My cold is better," she said dully.

"Thanks to your antibodies. They're in there swinging away, so try to get lots of sleep and drink plenty of juice and water to help them flush out the poison, all right?"

For some reason, as lame as this was, it seemed to make her feel better. "I will."

He stood up and pulled the white canvas back around the bed.

Someone—a young man, from what he could tell through the suit—was waiting on the other side. "I'm Carlo with PANAFTOSA. I have the contact sheets for you."

"Did everyone fill one out?"

"*Sí,* Dr. Smith. One for each of the staff. Miss Mallard made out, too, a list of everyone who came to visit the clinic. And everyone we picked up from the contact sheets has also made out a sheet."

"Great." Mike took the pages and pen that were offered him and began leafing through the lists. If anything, they were sparser than one could possibly hope for. It seemed these kids did little except hang out at the shelter or with each other. It didn't look like any of them had family in Rio.

"What's gonna happen to the people on the contact sheets?" Jen asked.

"We bring them to the hospital as we find them," Carlo told her. "They stay down the hall."

"Can't they come in here? My friend, Lucretia—"

"No, miss. Not unless they get sick. I'm sorry."

Mike reached the bottom of the list.

"When . . . um . . . when exactly were the monkeys contagious, do you know?" Jen asked. Her voice sounded odd.

Mike shook his head. "Not yet. Just to be safe we'd like to contact everyone who's been exposed to them since they were brought out of the jungle."

"Oh."

"Why?" Mike glanced up. "Is there something you left off your form?"

Jen nodded. She looked scared. "I didn't know where to begin. I mean, I don't know who most of the people were. There were police and—God! I was going to tell you when you got here, Dr. Smith. They said you'd be coming right over."

Mike's pen was poised over the sheets as he stared at her, poised in digits that had turned into icicles. "Would you please tell me what you're talking about?"

Jen looked from Mike to Carlo and back again. "Well, uh, we *did* have the monkeys quarantined, but there was this girl on the staff . . . Gillian . . ."

CHAPTER 10

He hadn't meant to sleep through the night. He'd been so tired when he finally checked into the hotel after seeing Daunsey. A few hours, he'd thought, as he collapsed on the bed, and that's all, because there was so much to be done. He hadn't stirred again until morning.

He called down to room service and ordered a continental breakfast. He turned on the TV. When he emerged from the shower, his tray was waiting and the news was on. Prime Minister Billingsworth was saying that Britain supported the U.S.'s decision not to ship any exports this year. Their new rationing plan, he said, was more aggressive than any ever implemented in Europe, and they could not be expected to do more. Britain would immediately implement a rationing plan based on that of the U.S., and Billingsworth assured his countrymen that they would have enough food, despite their own crop damage, to weather the year on that plan.

An attractive female newscaster came on and said the Prime Minister's speech, and similar ones from the heads of Germany and France, were drawing clear lines in the sand. China had led many nations in a formal protest at the U.N. yesterday, with a repeat of their demand that all grain be pooled and divided based on population. A reply from the U.N. was still forthcoming.

Deauchez took a sip of coffee, his eyes glued to the screen.

War. There's going to be a war over this.

That's not your problem. Santa Pelagia is your problem.

Yes. He was hoping to learn something about Dame Wendy Clark today. The last *New York Times* he'd read said she was now in Scotland, but he ought to be able to learn something about her in London; then, whether or not to go to Scotland . . .

This train of thought was cut short by realization that the television screen itself was displaying the very name he sought. DAME WENDY CLARK: SANTA PELAGIA PROPHET. The words were underneath a video of an older woman with jet-black hair, ruby lips, and a gold-sequined black knit top.

"Yes, I *do* foresee war," she said in a stiff, nasally accent. "It wasn't outlined for me *directly*, mind you. Those sorts of details were not given to us, and for good reason! If we knew *everything* that was going to happen, I doubt that a single one of us could face up to it. Still, it was made *quite* clear that a series of devastations would rock the planet. Evidently, the famine is part of God's plan, and war—well! I, for one, hope Britain stays out of it, but that it *will* come, there's little doubt, really."

"But *will* Britain stay out of it?" The newscaster replaced Clark's image. "Certain parties are already criticizing Prime Minister Billingsworth for his speech. Clearly, the E.U. has made the decision to back the U.S. Why such a position was chosen so swiftly and so decisively is *not* clear, particularly when many are voicing their wish that Britain had simply . . . stayed out of it."

But Deauchez wasn't thinking about war anymore. He was thinking that he needn't worry about going to Scotland to talk to Clark, after all. He didn't need to ask her whether she'd had any medical treatment in the past few months. Dame Wendy Clark was in a wheelchair. She had multiple sclerosis, a condition that would ensure regular doctor visits.

Deauchez had gotten used to using the cellular. He took it now and strode over to the window, pushed back the heavy hotel drapes, and opened the sash. He dialed the number he found on Hill's card, the fresh air cooling his heated face and overheated nerves.

Down below, the day was still new. Only a few people were out this early. A taxi pulled up and let out a weary-looking traveler. Across the street a beige van was parked.

Deauchez frowned at the van as the ringing began in his ear. It was parked with its front facing him, but the glare of the sun prevented him from seeing if the van was occupied or not. Hadn't he seen one like it outside Daunsey's brownstone yesterday?

It's just a beige van, not the same *van. Don't be childish!*

He heard Hill's voice come on in what was clearly a recording, and he felt a surge of disappointment. Of course, it must still be the middle of the night in New York.

"Simon Hill, this is Father Michele Deauchez. I have that information on the medical angle for you now."

He quickly ran down what he'd told Daunsey: about Andrews, Cougar and Stanton, Sagara Bata's inoculations, and Giri's hit-and-run. He also told him about Daunsey's fainting at a blood drive days before her dream.

"I encourage you to print this information, Mr. Hill. It's about time we had some new theories in the papers. I'm still in London and I thought you might know the name of Dame Wendy Clark's physician. I could drop by his office, perhaps, see if he was contacted by anyone unusual who wanted to examine her or try some new drug. You can reach me at Brown's Hotel. *Au revoir.*"

SEDONA, ARIZONA

It was late August and it was hot, despite the whiff of fall in the air. In the streets of Sedona, temperatures were slated to reach one hundred four today, but it was a mere seventy now, at eight-thirty in the morning. In half an hour the grocery stores in town—two of them—would open their doors for the first time in several days.

Trent Andrews felt the warm morning breeze, felt it on his bare legs beneath his robe, felt it on his bare arms inside the loose sleeves. He'd had the garment made: calf-length white linen with a deep V-neck. It hung free; a thin, gauzy material through which the lines of his chest and legs were prominently outlined as he walked and a slightly darker mound was visible, when the breeze was right, at his groin. His blond hair was released from its ponytail these days, and it hung down past his shoulders in thick abundance. His face was tan and displayed an immature beard.

It was a look that felt right and had an appropriate impact on others. He was beautiful, and he was powerful, and right now he was a little bit scared.

The crowd that walked down the street with him contributed much to that feeling of power, and to the fear. There were a thousand or so pairs of feet with him on this walk, himself in the lead, and he'd not even asked them to come. They had followed him as he and his more personal entourage left the hotel, swarmed around him like moths batting at a lightbulb. And there were many more even than this crowd, parked around the edges of the town, setting up tents out on the fringes. They did not chant or sing as they walked; their creed had no anthem. There was only the vague, in-your-chest rumble of a thousand feet, walking quietly, and that felt a little bit frightening, too.

They passed the familiar restaurants on the main drag. Gibson's Grill was closed. A sign in the window said MAKING NEW MENU FOR RATIONING—OPEN??? Taco City was locked and closed and had the distinct air of desertion. The Desert Café was open. A sign in the window said COFFEE AND DRINKS ONLY. The owner, a hard-as-nails, fifty-something cowgirl, came to the open doorway and watched them with narrow eyes, cracking her gum in a tense rhythm.

"They're all closed! It's really happening!" a woman behind Trent called out in an awed, frightened voice.

Of course, you fool, was it not foretold to you?

These words were part of the larger Andrews, the one who was striding down the street in a robe of white. But farther back in his mind was another Andrews, one who still worried about things like logistics and responsibility, one who was still just a kid from Orange County who was as disturbed by the suddenly-here-and-now signs of famine as the woman who'd made the remark.

A few locals were already waiting out front of the largest of the grocery stores, a Maidway. They turned their heads as one and stared as the dull rumble of feet reached their ears. If they were intimidated by the crowd, they didn't show it. They clustered up close to the doors to mark their spots at the head of the queue and turned to Andrews with determined faces.

As Trent reached the store, two patrol cars pulled up in the small parking lot. The town sheriff and three uniformed officers got out. The sheriff was a thin, middle-aged man with desert-hardened skin and a beige Stetson. They took up a position in front of the store. Maintaining the peace, no doubt. First day of rationing and all.

They probably had not expected this large a turnout.

Trent stopped just short of the Maidway and held up his hand in a halting signal. Behind him, the sound of feet faded, like an echo dying away. Inside, his heart was pounding, but he showed no outward trace of it. He stepped onto the wooden platform and confronted the sheriff.

"I'm Trent Andrews."

"Yup."

"I wish to hear about the store's operation."

The sheriff scratched an ear and looked at Andrews with a level eye. "All right. When these here doors open, me and my men're gonna let people in. Seein' as how there's so many out here, I think we'll just let in a few dozen at a time. I'm sure Paul'd 'preciate that."

Trent tried to listen, but it was hard to concentrate through his nervousness, through the buzzing of thoughts in his head.

"You go on through the store like normal. Pick out what you want. Signs'll tell you what you can take outta the store with you. No point pickin' out more'n that. There'll be a table set up in front of the cashiers. They'll look at what you have, take down yer social security number, pull stuff from yer cart if it's too much, then you'll go on through ta pay. They'll be writin' down what you get, and you'll only get so much of some things a week."

"What if you don't have a social security number?"

"Gotta have a number. Gotta have a *card*. Them're the rules straight from the top."

The prophet's eyes had never left the sheriff, and now he stood mutely, trying to absorb it all. He made an effort to remain calm—calm and even, even and calm. He said, "I have people in my group who have flown from all over the world to be with me. They don't have social security numbers."

"That's gonna be a problem. Government says any foreign visitors should go on home. 'Course, they can go on down ta Tucson and apply for one of them exemptions. If they got a good reason ta be here, that is."

"*Tucson* is not the final authority on good reasons, Sheriff."

"I don't make the rules, son. This here rationing is for *real*. Lots of people ain't gonna be happy about it. But you can buy all the dairy you want, for now. Candy, too. Meat's still at pretty good portions."

Trent didn't glance back at his people, couldn't have faced them even if he wanted to, but he could sense their unease behind him like pressure building behind a valve. "So what's to stop me from buying my limit here, then hitting another store?"

"Yup, that's somethin' you all need to be aware of. Once you use yer social security number at a store today, it goes on a national registry. By tomorrow yer gonna be *stuck* usin' this store from now on, 'less you fill out an official change form to move it. Yer number's only good at one store, so they can keep track of what you buy. That might change, they say, once they have all the stores linked into a computer network, but for now, it'll take time. Which reminds me, Mr. Andrews: it might be a good idea if some of you sign up over ta Ray's. Maybe even send some folks down ta Phoenix once a week for theirs. How many you got now?"

Trent had been given a number this morning by Trish, and it fell off his tongue now. "Around twenty-five."

The sheriff raised a brow. For his stolid face it was evidence of surprise indeed. Surely he'd seen the tents and the cars, but he'd apparently been a little off in his own estimates. "*Thousand?* Oh, my, my. You see? Even gettin' that many in and out the store would be a trick. I don't think Paul could handle more'n maybe a thousand of you a day, leavin' room for the locals and all. That's, oh, six thousand a week since he's closed on Sundays? Another six over ta Ray's? Yup, I think yer gonna need to split up, Mr. Andrews, maybe send a good chunk down ta Phoenix once a week. I'm sure you all need other supplies down there anyway."

There were more of the locals now. A group of about thirty stood uneasily on the left end of the wooden platform, eyeing the man in the white robe and the crowd lined up down the street. Most of their faces were downright unfriendly. Trent tried to not see them, but it wasn't easy.

He was seeing those faces, and the sheriff's, set against him, and he was thinking about what he'd just heard. Sedona would feed only twelve thousand? *Twelve thousand?* That was less than half of what he had here now, and what the sheriff didn't seem to understand was that *this was just the start*. There would be more, many more.

"Didn't you all bring supplies up with you when you came?" the sheriff asked him in a low voice.

Trent wanted to strangle him. He whispered back, "Sheriff, I *cannot* send thirteen thousand people driving three hours to Phoenix every week!"

The sheriff nodded thoughtfully. He scratched his forehead. "Well, lemme see . . . Flagstaff has half a dozen stores. It's only a half hour north. Mormon Lake, Rimrock, Cornville, Cottonwood,

Clarkdale . . . They're small, but they're close, and they got at least one grocery store apiece."

It was not much, but it was a way out of this awful scene, a token face-saver so he could turn around again, at some point in the near future, and face that crowd. He nodded. "Twelve thousand a week in Sedona itself, then. I'll have my assistants take care of it."

"I 'preciate your cooperation, Mr. Andrews."

Trent turned to go. He felt his face burning and wished no one was there to see it. *What the hell am I going to do?* that logistical voice in his head was wondering, that little kid from Orange County.

But when he faced his followers they broke into broad grins and murmurs of encouragement and love, some holding out their arms to him. It was like a wave of pure energy, a spiritual transfusion. He drank it in, his eyes scanning the crowd from his raised position on the platform. He felt their desire, their confidence in him, saw the adoration in their eyes. His awkward shame melted away. What had he to fear? *What had he to fear?* Was he not chosen? It was Sedona that should be afraid.

He swung back around to face the sheriff, and this time, he did not speak softly. "You need to understand that what I'm doing here is of vital importance to the continuance of mankind. We *are* the future."

The sheriff didn't blink. "No one's tryin' ta stop you, son."

Andrews's eyes, his *being*, blazed at the sheriff. He could feel the power pouring through him like he'd just been plugged into Ma Bell. "I will do as you wish. For now. But more will be coming as the Earth changes intensify. If your arrangements cannot withstand the pressure they *will* collapse. We are loving people, but there are limits."

"I understand the situation quite well, Mr. Andrews." The sheriff spoke calmly and slowly, his eyes unwavering.

And that was all there was to say. Andrews nodded curtly and stepped off the platform. He held up his arms and walked into the crowd. His followers engulfed him, touching him as he passed.

LONDON

Someone was knocking on the door. Deauchez started, then remembered that he'd given the name of the hotel to Sister Rachel. Was it she, or even Daunsey herself with a change of heart?

He strode to the door and opened it, an eager greeting ready on his lips. But it was neither Sister Rachel nor Sister Daunsey, nor even a woman. Standing in the hall was a cardinal.

"Father Deauchez, peace be with you."

The tone of voice indicated anything but peace. The man pushed past him imperially. His long black vestment and his red cap made his office clear enough, and when the man turned and Deauchez got a second look at his face—a heavy, florid, middle-aged face—he recalled it vaguely, but could not find a name. He *would* not have found it, even had he not been temporarily stupefied.

"Your Eminence?"

"Cardinal McKlennan. I don't believe we've been formally introduced."

The cardinal held out his right hand in a clear request. Deauchez, embarrassed and awkward, bowed and kissed the bishop's ring. Such a practice was considered quaint by most bishops, and loathed by others. Cardinal McKlennan was obviously an exception. Either that or he was trying to make a point.

"It's an honor to meet you, Cardinal McKlennan," Deauchez said as he rose, "but I'm . . . deeply surprised to see you here."

It was an understatement. The name Deauchez knew, even if he hadn't placed it with the face. Cardinal McKlennan was the Archbishop of Armagh, a powerhouse, the most powerful cardinal in all of Ireland. And this powerhouse looked, at the moment, slightly cranky.

"Father Deauchez, let me get right to the point. Cardinal Donnelley contacted me early this morning. He's been unable to get in touch with you, and he's quite concerned. You were given orders to return to the Vatican two days ago, and not only did you not respond, you flew here instead."

"Well, I . . ." He was going to say he hadn't gotten the e-mail from Donnelley, but now, in the presence of the cardinal, lying about something like that seemed like a much more grievous sin than when he'd hatched the plan in the café in Allahabad.

"No excuses! I'm sure you have some misguided belief or other; they always do. I'm not here to take your confession, Deauchez, I'm here to pick you up. I'm flying to Rome in two hours, and I'm taking you with me."

The words were so unexpected that for a moment all Deauchez could do was gape at the cardinal.

"Well? Don't just stand there! Get your things packed. We'll miss the flight."

Deauchez stumbled for time. "How did Cardinal Donnelley know I was in London?"

"It's not important, Deauchez!" Cardinal McKlennan snapped. Then he sighed. "He mentioned something about the bureau's credit card. I assume that when you didn't show up, he was concerned and he called the credit card company to see if you'd scheduled your flight yet. Now come, get your things."

"But I didn't . . ."

"And you *always* stay at this hotel when you're in London, as do most of our officials."

"Oh. Yes, I see." But Deauchez didn't see. He hadn't used his credit card to buy the airline tickets; he'd paid cash. Why would McKlennan—or Donnelley—lie? And how *had* they known he was in London?

Then, of course, he knew. The knowledge was as obvious as finding one's glasses on one's head after searching for them fruitlessly. Daunsey. Had she *known* she was turning him in, or had she called Donnelley merely to complain about his badgering?

Deauchez walked numbly toward the bed and picked up his watch from the nightstand. "Why did Cardinal Donnelley not call me himself ? I'm embarrassed that you had to go out of your way, Your Eminence."

"You should be embarrassed. As for Donnelley, you'll have to iron that out with the man yourself. I really have no idea how angry he is." Cardinal McKlennan looked at his watch pointedly.

Deauchez was feeling more and more like a naughty little boy. He moved to his bag, began putting clothes and the cellular phone from the table inside it with unsteady hands.

"I'm surprised you are not already in Rome, Your Eminence."

"My goodness, but you do go on, Deauchez! Business detained me!"

Deauchez traveled light, and he soon found himself done in the main room. He moved toward the bathroom on leaden legs, trailing his bag along behind him. It was the oddest thing. Even as he went through these motions, a voice in his head was screaming that he did not want to go, was not *going* to go.

He was moving his few toiletries from the sink to the bag, ever so slowly, when it occurred to him to try another angle. "I know you probably think I'm simply being disobedient, Cardinal, but I do have vital information, information I was gathering for the pope himself."

"The Holy Father is gone, God preserve his soul." McKlennan genuflected. Deauchez followed his lead.

"Yes, it's a great tragedy. But I'm certain that whoever takes up the mantle next will be equally concerned about . . . about Santa Pelagia."

"No doubt." The cardinal's tone was icy.

"I found it difficult to talk to Cardinal Donnelley because he has been quite unusually inclined to view Santa Pelagia miraculously, but I *have* found some information that may prove supremely important to the Church in the days ahead. I felt it my highest duty to continue to follow my investigation."

McKlennan scowled. "Deauchez, I don't want to hear your little secrets. Whatever information you have, it's between you and your superior in the Curia. Is that clear?"

"I understand, Your Eminence."

"Are you done there?"

He *was* done, and he had no means to forestall what was coming. He took the step from the bathroom and set his travel bag down next to his laptop. He turned pleadingly to his superior.

"Your Eminence, are you not concerned about the Santa Pelagia message? Are you not alarmed that so many Irish Catholics are abandoning their homes and jobs and coming to London? Of what might occur when the apocalypse does *not* appear?"

"Father, you should be ashamed. You yourself were in Santa Pelagia and yet you deny!"

That pretty much shut Deauchez up.

"Let's go." McKlennan opened the door and held it ajar.

Deauchez swallowed hard. "I'm not going with you, Cardinal." The words sounded foreign to his ears, as though they weren't really his.

McKlennan stood there and stared at him, his face effusing with outrage. "The Holy Father is dead, Deauchez. You are needed in Rome. *That* is your duty. Do you refuse it?"

The words were uttered with the gravity and solemnity of the Supreme Judge himself. They were intimidating, incredibly so. Deauchez's stomach roiled with stress.

"*Please,* Cardinal, I only need one more day. I give you my word of honor that I will fly to Rome tomorrow, but I have one

more line of inquiry I can do here that may solidify my presentation to the new pope."

"Deauchez!" McKlennan sputtered, incensed. "Either you go
with me this very moment, or you'll face full repercussions for
disobeying *two* direct orders: Donnelley's *and* mine!"

Deauchez couldn't look him in the eye. He looked down at the
floor instead, jaw clenching stubbornly. "I will follow you to
Rome tomorrow, Your Eminence, and face whatever I need to
face there at that time."

Without another word, Cardinal McKlennan turned on his
heel into the hall, slamming the door shut as he did so.

Ten seconds ticked by in the silence following that thunderous
clap, ten seconds in which Deauchez's stomach continued to
churn until his entire body was trembling. For the first few of
those seconds his mind was utterly blank, then thoughts tumbled
in like clothes from an opened dryer.

You cannot do this! You will be excommunicated!

You are a priest! You took a vow to obey the Church!

*How much more will you get from the doctor? Nothing of im-
portance! You are afraid to present your case because you know it
might not be good enough, but there is nothing more you can do!*

His little room at the Vatican, the beautiful Vatican, beautiful
Rome. His friends there, the fellowship. How could he give that
up? It was the only life he knew. Would McKlennan seek the ul-
timate punishment? Would he lose even a modest position in
Rome? He had been so *very* angry.

"Wait!" Deauchez shouted. He grabbed his bag and his computer from the floor, opened the door, and raced out into the hall.
"Cardinal McKlennan?"

He turned into the main corridor, the one with the elevators.
There was no one at the elevators. Then he saw something move
at the end of the hall; it was a door opening. Behind it disappeared a figure in a long black garment. *The stairs,* Deauchez
thought. He ran for the door, bags bouncing against his leg.

The door did indeed lead to the stairs. By the time he'd
reached it and entered the stairwell, he could not see the man; he
could only hear soft leather-soled footsteps down below.

"Cardinal McKlennan?"

The thick stairwell dampened his voice, and the footsteps didn't
pause. Deauchez began running down the stairs as quickly as he
could manage with the bags.

He paused at the door to the third floor, but the footsteps continued below. He did the same at the door to the second floor and heard the footsteps. Naturally, Deauchez thought, the cardinal is heading for the lobby level.

At the first floor, Deauchez paused once more, and this time he heard a heavy door swing open and shut below him. He trotted down the last flight of stairs, moved his bags to one hand, and pulled open the ground-level door.

He stepped out into a short, red-carpeted hallway. It did not look at all familiar. He glanced around and saw no one, but down to the right was a set of swinging doors and they were slightly moving to and fro, as if they'd just been used.

Puzzled, he walked to the double doors and pushed them open.

He was looking into the hotel's kitchen. Preparations for lunch were under way; various young cooks were busy cleaning vegetables and pots. Immediately in front of the doors, two middle-aged men—obviously hotel managers of some sort—were having a conversation. They stopped speaking and looked at him questioningly. One of them was a dark-skinned man. He wore a long, black, wraparound apron.

"I'm sorry," Deauchez stumbled. "I . . . I got a bit turned around."

He backed out of the kitchen, cursing himself. He hadn't been following McKlennan at all! Now the cardinal was probably long gone, and Deauchez's career with him.

Deauchez looked desperately around the short hall. An EXIT sign shone clearly over a heavy, push-bar door. He ran for it. Perhaps, if God were with him, he could still catch McKlennan at the front of the hotel, waiting for a taxi.

The door let out into a brick-paved alley. Garbage cans and service trucks crowded his line of sight. He dodged around them, heading as quickly as he could for the hotel's front entrance.

When he reached the busy London street, he saw that he was half a block away from the hotel's front doors. He could see the smart green of the hotel awning down off to the left, the taxis waiting in line near the front door, the uniformed doorman, and *Cardinal McKlennan*.

He yelled the cardinal's name, but the words were lost in the street noise. Relieved, yet still anxious that he would be too late, he poised himself to run.

And all of this—the recognition, the shout, the tensing to

run—occurred in that first instant in which he recognized the cardinal's robe and hat, his heavyset frame. In the next instant, something else registered, and Deauchez froze.

Cardinal McKlennan was walking toward his car, a sleek, black car. He was passing the *beige van*, which had moved to this side of the street and was now parked a few feet from the hotel door. Men were getting out of the van, or, rather, the driver just had, and the man from the passenger side was walking around to join them. They watched McKlennan approach on his way to his car. As McKlennan moved past them he turned his head to the right to look at the two men, slowing down just a tad. He shook his head in a negative gesture, then made a slight motion with his hand, a thumb-leading gesture back toward the hotel.

The driver of the beige van nodded, neatened his coat, and put his hand in his pocket. The two men began walking quickly toward the hotel. McKlennan reached his car and got into the backseat. The car pulled away.

But Deauchez was no longer concerned about missing McKlennan. Instinctively, he ducked behind a signpost because the two men from the van were directly facing him as they walked toward the hotel. He peeked around the sign and got a good look at them: dark glasses, neat beards, elegantly casual dark suits and shoes. They could have been wealthy Italian businessmen in for a spot of international wheeling and dealing.

But they weren't. They were the men from the beige van. They ducked inside the hotel.

Truly confused now, and for some reason scared out of his wits, Deauchez edged toward the street. He managed to cross it, despite applying no more than subconscious attention to the business of car dodging. He reached the other side and backed up to get a good look at the face of the hotel.

Fourth floor. There was the window of his room, he was sure. It was right in the middle of the floor, as his door had been, and it was the only one with the window open. The white gauzy part of the curtain was fluttering a bit in the breeze. He'd left that way, hadn't even picked up his room key.

His mouth was dry.

He looked up at the window and then down at the hotel doors, not sure what it was he was expecting to see, and then he saw it. In his window something moved. The curtain was pushed back. A dark-suited man with a beard looked out, leaned forward to see if there was any balcony or ledge. There wasn't.

In the man's hand was something black. It glinted in the sunlight.

It was enough for Deauchez. He turned on his heel and ran.

MUNICH, GERMANY

Blade absolutely sounded like shit.

Georg, who was not a fan in the first place, stared down between his legs at the performer onstage and shook his head. The audience didn't seem to mind that the rocker obviously had a sinus cold from hell and was weak on his high notes, cracked on his sustains, and had the all-around tonal quality of wind passing over sandpaper. True, the guy wasn't Pavarotti at the best of times, but Georg could hear the sickness grating on his sensitive, operatic-trained ears like a scratchy recording.

You'd never find a *real* singer going onstage with a cold like that. These rockers—twenty cities in twenty days, and they'd never break a date even if they were dying because they got up to a half a mil a show. And here the fans were, desperate with adoration, paying full price for half of a performance.

Georg moved along the grid over to the yellow spotlights and tweaked their alignment. That was when he saw the man coming out of the ventilator room.

It wasn't one of the local crew. No one came up here except for him, not during a performance. It could be someone with Blade's band, but what would they want with the ventilator room?

The man was slim and dressed in black pants, a long-sleeved black T-shirt, and black gloves. On his head was a low-fitting black baseball cap, its bill shading his face. A hump on his back resolved itself, as he moved through a red light, into a backpack.

Georg felt alarmed and not a little protective of his turf on the high grid. He walked toward the man, moving quickly with long practice in stepping over lights and wires. The man saw him, froze, then gave him a jaunty little salute and began moving away, toward the rear ladder.

Practiced or not, he moved faster than Georg. But then, Georg knew a shortcut.

He was crossing the grid on a diagonal beam when the man in black—who was about thirty feet away—walked through the reflection off a white spotlight and his face was fully revealed.

What Georg saw was so strange and frightening that he stopped. The man-thing glanced at him from its grid beam, then turned and hurried to the ladder. Georg was suddenly pretty darn sure he didn't want to get any closer to whatever it was, so he just stood there and watched it get away.

Blade finished "Girl from Liverpool." Barely. Feeling like he was going to pass out, he weakly signaled to the band and they launched into an instrumental: guitar, drums, keyboard, and sax—some jazzy bit they'd worked up. Blade managed to get to the stage exit without falling over.

His manager, Jimmy, was waiting. "Blade! Sweetheart! How ya feelin'? Darlene, get a chair!"

"How'd I feel? Like a bleedin' dog turd. Christ, I'm sick."

Blade began sinking to the floor. Fortunately, Darlene was ready. He landed in a chair, flopped over at the waist, and put his head between his legs in an attempt to stop the spinning.

"I can't go back out there."

He couldn't remember ever feeling this sick in his entire life. His throat was on fire. His head was absolutely splitting. His body felt like it was made out of lead, and his gut was so sore he wanted to punch something.

Darlene felt his forehead. "Christ, Jimmy, he's burning up!"

Jimmy's hand came next. "Maybe a hundred. Not too bad really." He was trying to sound cheerful.

" 'S not a bloody hundred! More like a hundred and three. I got me some kids. I know a bad temp when I feel it!"

"Thank you so much for your opinion Darlene, now shut the fuck up."

"We'll cut out the last two songs and do one encore," Jimmy said to Blade in his best shot at a soothing tone. "We'll cancel the show tomorrow in Berlin if you want, but we *can't* just leave this one half-off, you know that. Here's your tea now."

Someone attempted to pull Blade into a sitting position. A hot mug was placed in his hands.

" 'M sorry, Jimmy. This came on from bloody nowhere. Two days ago it was just a fuckin' cold!"

"Yeah, yeah, I know. Save your throat." Jimmy—who was a bit congested himself—had gotten a cool rag from somewhere and was wiping at Blade's face.

"Swear to Christ, I don't think I can go back out there. I'm absolutely trashed."

He began to shake with the chills. Every muscle in his body ached and his stomach, his stomach was *killing* him.

"Yeah, sweetheart, I know." Jimmy's tone was full of that get-up-and-go spirit. "Three more songs and that'll have it, right? Then we'll get you tucked into bed straightaway. I'll call someone right now and have a doctor waiting when you come off, all righty?"

"Christ, Jimmy, look at him!" Darlene exclaimed.

Blade's eyes were closed. Somewhere in his right hand he still held the mug, but he couldn't feel it. He was so tired. He wanted to go to sleep—*please, God, let me sleep!*—but the pain in his stomach was so unbearable, he didn't think it would let him. He needed drugs. He needed a goddamn truckload of 'em.

"Come on, Blade! You're a pro—best there is. Three more songs while we're waiting for the doctor. You can do it in your sleep. Up we go now. Take a sip. Let's go."

The hand with the mug was moved toward his mouth. He wanted to finish the set, he really did. You didn't just walk off-stage in the middle of a show. He shook his head to rouse himself, took a sip from the mug Jimmy was holding up for him. His mouth was so hot the liquid felt cool on his tongue. God, he was thirsty! He slurped the near-boiling tea down like water.

"*That's* a lad. *That's* a good boy. *Three* more songs. *Nothin'* to it. Take a few secs."

"Jimmy?" a young, German-accented voice said.

"Fuck off !" Jimmy snapped.

"In the back there are men to . . . to speak with Blade."

"Not until the concert's over! Get the hell out of here."

"I know this is not a good time, but they are from . . . Well, I think you must see them now."

Blade opened his eyes and tried to focus on the speaker. It was a German kid, someone with the local crew. For some reason he looked scared. Blade tried to stand.

"*That's* it! All righty! *Here* we go!" Jimmy's arms were the only things holding Blade up. The rock star shook his head again to clear it. He locked his knees, steadied himself, signaled that he was okay.

"*That's* a lad! Instrumentals are gettin' old! *Here* we go! *Goin'* on!" Jimmy half-carried him a few steps toward the stage.

Then Jimmy let go and Blade took one step forward on his own. The world went spinning out from under him. He pitched to the left and Jimmy's speedy grab was the only thing that kept him from falling headfirst into an iron stage light.

" 'M sorry. Don't know what's wrong with m' fuckin' legs. Can't get m' balance."

"Give it *up*, Jimmy! Let him lie down, for God's sake! Do you want to kill 'im?"

"Shut the fuck up, Darlene."

"Jimmy Swan? I'm afraid we can't allow Blade to go back out onstage."

The voice was unfamiliar and the tone sounded very odd. For a moment, Blade thought his hearing was going, but then Jimmy turned and Blade, who was slumped against his chest, turned with him. Blade's eyes focused on what he thought was a hallucination. Ten men stood there, all of them decked out in goggles and white masks and rubber, looking like doctor dolls belonging to a child that liked to pile all the stuff in their bag-o'-tricks on at once. It was the mask that made the voice sound odd.

"Who the fuck are *you*?" Jimmy said.

"My name is Dr. Michael Smith. We're with the World Health Organization. We have a Level Four contagion on our hands, and we believe Blade has been exposed. We're going to have to take him into custody. In fact, we're going to have to quarantine the entire band and crew, anyone who's had exposure to him since the Rio concert nine days ago."

Darlene uttered a little scream. "Oh, bloody *hell*! What's he got?"

"Are you out of your friggin' mind?" Jimmy was belligerent. "Do you have the *slightest* idea who he is?"

"Mr. Swan, we know who all of you are. Have any of the other members of your party been displaying cold symptoms?"

"Colds? Christ, the whole bloody band's got it! And most of the crew!"

"Shut *up*, Darlene!"

The band out onstage, meanwhile, was getting very restless, as Blade could well hear. Their very notes were asking where the fuck he was.

"I have ta *go*," he muttered, pulling away from Jimmy.

One of the figures stepped forward. "Blade? I'm Dr. Smith. If you go back out on that stage you'll be endangering the lives of your fans. You have been exposed to a Level Four disease from the Brazilian moon monkey you held in Rio. If you have the disease, you're highly infectious."

"Oh, God!" Darlene screamed. She began backing away.

"That's it, I'm canceling the rest of the show," Jimmy said, trying hard to sound put out but actually sounding pretty damn terrified. Blade had never seen Jimmy terrified. "Fuck it. If this gets out and I didn't cancel, we'd have a goddamn slew of bloody lawsuits!"

"No!" Blade shouted. He moved toward the stage.

"Grab him," someone said.

He made a break for it, but his body betrayed him. He lost his balance again and crashed into the black curtains to the left of the stage entrance. Firm hands took hold of his arms, then his legs.

"I'm not sick!" he tried to scream. He found himself crying. He was carried away from the curtains by four of the men. The speaker, Dr. Smith, came over and looked at him. Blade stared up into the masked and goggled faces and felt real mortal terror. "I'm not dyin'!"

Dr. Smith felt his forehead, put two fingers against his throat to feel his pulse. "I promise we'll do everything we can to help you. The most important thing right now is that we get you to a hospital so we can get that fever down. The fever will kill you if we don't, do you understand?"

Blade shook his head, crying full force now. "I'm not dyin'!"

They brought a stretcher and put Blade on it. Darlene was staying far away, watching with huge eyes. Jimmy, too, the son of a bitch, was letting them just take him.

"Jimmy!" Blade pleaded.

"Got a bit of a cold meself," Darlene sniffled to no one in particular.

"We're putting him on a helicopter," Smith said. "The rest of you will go in vans; those with symptoms in one group, those without in another."

"No!" Blade cried out.

And then Smith was leaning over him and Blade was staring up at that terrifying face. He realized with horror who the man really was. "Dr. Smith!" A likely name! No, Blade knew him, even without the black hood and the scythe. This was the twenty-first century after all, and this rubberized, technological incarnation suited the times perfectly.

He was about to tell Death he wasn't fooled when someone else came into the picture. It was a young kid, one of the local crew. He tugged at Death's sleeve.

"Yes?" Death said.

"Eh . . . are you the one in command, Dr. Smith?"

"Yes."

Blade uttered a sharp, mocking *hah!*

"Good . . . eh . . . Did you have someone here before?" the kid asked nervously. "A man with black clothing? I saw something up by the ventilation room. I did not know . . . that is, now I think he maybe had some kind of . . . of mask on." The boy gestured with an open hand around his face.

"No, everyone on our team is dressed like this," Death replied with little patience. Blade could have told the kid that questioning Death was a bad idea.

"Oh. Okay." The kid drifted off uncertainly and Death turned back to him.

"Here we go, Blade," Death said.

CHAPTER 11

Stanton was awakened at 5:00 A.M. by someone knocking on the trailer door. He roused sullenly. Couldn't they even let him get forty winks in peace? It had better be, Stanton thought, Gabriel himself with his trumpet. He shut the door of the bedroom gently behind him—the last thing he needed was for Mimi to wake up and start her incessant whining—and padded in his slippers through what passed as the RV's fer-cripes-saken living room.

As it turned out, it wasn't Gabriel at the door, it was Clement Franklin, a slick young preacher who had begged the spot as Stanton's second, and who was as good at kissing you-know-what as anyone Stanton had ever seen. Despite his seemingly earnest—and justified—adoration, Stanton didn't trust Franklin as far as a Chinaman could throw a football. Clement Franklin, he of the oiled hair, scrubbed face, and oh-so-earnest suits, had a large white Bible permanently stapled to his right hand. It went *everywhere* with him, even to the john. It sat in his lap when he ate. He never put the gosh-blamed thing down. Stanton didn't believe any man could be that obsessed and not have an eye for the head quarterback slot himself. But Franklin was good at running interference, and these days, with the pressure on the mount—fifty thousand campers and counting—getting so thick you could serve it up on biscuits, Stanton could use all the help he could get.

"I'm sorry to wake you up, but you have to see this!" Franklin stepped up from the ground. The RV rocked for a moment with his added weight.

He had a videotape in his hand. Stanton huffed in begrudging acquiescence, but he found himself curious, sleepy or not.

"A good Christian friend of mine gave this to me. He's with WWN," Franklin explained as he loaded the tape in the VCR. It was the only introduction he gave.

The image that came up was harsh, bright video shot in a cheap TV studio. A flag, one Stanton didn't recognize, was on one dirty white wall. A cheap desk and chair were the only other props. An Arab man—young, maybe midthirties—was seated behind the desk. He was handsome, Stanton supposed, well aware of the value of looking good on camera. He was dressed in camouflage and had an orange beret on his head.

In the lower left-hand corner, words came up identifying the source of the video: Shebab Television, Baghdad. The speech, when it came, was dubbed over in a gruff, English-speaking voice that had clearly been added later.

"I am speaking to the followers of Islam everywhere. I am he who you have known as Mal Abbas. I have fought for the dignity and power of the Arab peoples all my life. I was part of the Muslim Brotherhood. I fought with the *Hamas*. With Izz al-Din al-Qassam, I let the world know that the Arab peoples would not relent under the powers of capitalism and the thievery of Israel. I waged many battles, made many strikes, some of which have made world head- lines, and some of which the United States, out of shame of their lack of control, did not allow to be made public!"

Franklin was looking from the tape to Stanton and back again with eager glee. Stanton had a feeling he already knew where this was going, why he'd been woken up in the middle of the night. Despite his immediate desire to doubt, he felt his pulse quicken.

"This assassination of the pope, leader of the barbaric Chris- tianity of the West, was only the first blow in the mightiest *jihad* the world has ever seen! I, Mal Abbas, come to you today on this, the thirteenth day since the Word of Allah was spoken at Santa Pelagia. I was instructed by Allah to reveal myself at this time. He said the thirteenth day would be the proper time, and look how true his words were, for has everything in the world not changed in these thirteen days?

"I am one of the twenty-four prophets, I, Mal Abbas! God has given me a mission unlike any other. I call for the unity of Mus- lims everywhere. Now is the time to forget our quarrels with each other. Now is the time to rise up in righteous wrath against the sinful dominance of the materialistic, corrupt West!

"To prove that I am what I say I am, I show you Mohammed Rahman, the Sufi master and the Santa Pelagia prophet from Iran."

The video changed to a handheld, amateurishly recorded segment showing that Sufi pagan bastard. Stanton recognized him, not only from the *New York Times*, which had repeatedly printed his picture along with all of the other Santa Pelagia prophets, but Stanton thought he might even recognize the man from Santa Pelagia itself. Rahman was putting his arm around Mal Abbas and kissing his cheeks. He took out a sealed envelope and passed it around to a group of waiting "witnesses." Mal Abbas's voice continued over the video.

"Rahman and I made ourselves known to each other in Mexico. I told him I must wait thirteen days to reveal myself, so he wrote a statement attesting to my presence with him at Santa Pelagia. This envelope is dated thirteen days ago, as these witnesses can confirm. In it are the words of Rahman stating that I am his brother-prophet of Islam, and my own statement prophesying the sores!"

The video went back to the sparse studio room.

"Rahman is Islam's prophet of the spirit, of the love of Allah. I, Mal Abbas, am the prophet of Allah's wrath! Forget your quarrels, my brothers! All those who worship the Koran and believe in Mohammed as Allah's greatest prophet are called to a Holy War! We already have many strong allies! Prepare yourselves! This is Mal Abbas, prophet of Allah."

The video ended abruptly. The silence in the trailer was profound.

High holy shit, Stanton thought, before he could adjust his language.

"So? What do you think?" Franklin was as proud as a kitten dragging a dead mouse to its mother.

"I think," Stanton said carefully, "I think we should study the Scriptures. We can't afford to throw the ball before our man's in place. It's too blessed important."

Stanton's warning brushed over Franklin's features like a momentary bad smell on the breeze. He quoted, " 'And I saw a woman sit upon a scarlet colored beast, full of names of blasphemy, having seven heads and ten horns.' "

Stanton clenched his teeth in irritation. The kid *would* want to start right finger-lickin' now! He began searching for his Bible.

" 'And the woman was arrayed in purple and scarlet color, and decked with gold and precious stones and pearls, having a golden cup in her hand full of abominations and filthiness of her fornications.' "

"Just hold on a gosh-blame second, Clement!" Where *was* his Bible? What had Mimi, in her infinite ineptitude or downright spitefulness, done with it? With a gleam of satisfaction in his eyes, Franklin held out his own white one. Reluctantly, Stanton took it. Franklin never missed a beat in his recital.

" 'And upon her forehead was a name written, MYSTERY, BABYLON THE GREAT, THE MOTHER OF HARLOTS AND ABOMINATIONS OF THE EARTH.' "

Stanton was flipping through pages hurriedly.

" 'And I saw the woman drunken with the blood of the saints, and with the blood of the martyrs of Jesus: and when I saw her, I wondered with great admiration.' "

Stanton found the page. Franklin was quoting from Revelation, chapter 17.

" 'And the angel said unto me, Wherefore didst thou marvel? I will tell thee the mystery of the woman, and of the beast that carrieth her, which hath the seven heads and ten horns.' "

"I see it," Stanton said impatiently.

Franklin ignored him: " 'The beast that thou sawest was, and is not: and shall ascend out of the bottomless pit, and go into perdition. And the ten horns which thou sawest are ten kings, which have received no kingdom as yet: but receive power as kings one hour with the beast.

" 'These have one mind, and shall give their power and strength unto the beast. These shall make war with the Lamb, and the Lamb shall overcome them: for he is Lord of lords, and King of kings: and they that are with him are called, and chosen, and faithful.' "

"Franklin, will you just stop for one for-pete's-sake minute?"

Franklin's mouth slowly closed. His eyes were deranged. Stanton read from the Scriptures, the Bible trembling in his hand.

" 'And he saith unto me, the waters which thou sawest, where the whore sitteth, are peoples, and multitudes, and nations, and tongues. And the ten horns which thou saw upon the beast, these shall hate the whore, and shall make her desolate and naked, and shall eat her flesh, and burn her with fire.

" 'For God hath put in their hearts to fulfill his will, and to agree, and give their kingdom unto the beast, until the words of God shall be fulfilled. And the woman which thou sawest is that great city, which reigneth over the kings of the earth.' "

The chapter ended there. Stanton sat for a moment, trying to think. Why did Franklin have to stare at him so?

"Babylon, that great whore, is now called Baghdad," Franklin said in an ominous tone.

"I know ancient Babylon is now Baghdad! But it says: 'the woman which thou sawest is that great city, which reigneth over the kings of the earth.' Baghdad doesn't reign over anythin'."

"Not now. But it *will*. Power will be given unto the beast and he will succeed, for a time, which means Baghdad *will* reign."

Stanton inwardly cursed and tried to focus on the Scripture. Wasn't it just like the weasel to have looked all this up before coming in, just to make Stanton look like an idiot!

But Franklin wasn't done yet. "The 'seven heads' are seven Arab countries 'where she sitteth,' and the 'ten horns' are ten leaders that will sign on with the beast. 'For God hath put in their hearts to fulfill his will, and to agree, and give their kingdom unto the beast, until the words of God shall be fulfilled.' "

How many Arab nations *were* there, Stanton wondered? Weren't there only three or four? But if he knew his own fist in the dark, he knew that wonderboy here would have researched it by now, if he hadn't already known it in the first place.

"But *if* the ten horns are ten Arab leaders, and *if* the whore is Baghdad," Stanton argued, "why does it say, 'the ten horns shall hate the whore, and shall make her desolate and naked, and shall eat her flesh, and burn her with fire'?"

Franklin nodded patronizingly, as if commending Stanton for having a single, cotton-pickin' thought in his head. "I wondered myself. Clearly, they're going to go against the beast in the end, but not until Mal Abbas has won many battles, otherwise why would 'the whore' be drunk with the blood of saints and martyrs? Either the 'ten leaders' will turn against Baghdad eventually, or they'll let Baghdad take the brunt of the counterattack. Maybe even a big old nuke."

Stanton considered it. It worked. More or less.

"Reverend Stanton, you know how much I admire you! You're God's prophet on Earth, I know that! But the people outside this trailer, they're *scared*, and they're wanting signs and miracles *every day* to keep them from being scared out of their wits!"

Stanton grunted noncommittally, but his heart rocked in his chest like a football in a bad spin. It was true! They wanted him to turn the very rocks into bread! They'd already directed hints at him in almost those very words!

"And they've been taught about the end times for years, Reverend. You *yourself* did most of that preaching, praise Jesus!"

That was also true. How could he have known he'd be sitting smack-dab at the head of it all and would have to live up to every single one of his own piss-fire pronouncements—most of which he'd uttered more for effect than because he actually *believed* them, at least back then. *Our sins do come home to roost.*

"They're looking for the other signs! They want to know: 'Who's the beast?' 'Who's the Antichrist?' They're scared that they've done something *unknowingly* to offend God! They want to hear that the Antichrist is not *our* president, and that casting a ballot for him two years ago didn't consign them to hell!"

Stanton shut his eyes. Why wouldn't this pup shut the frig up so he could ask the angel what to do?

"And here we are, moments from Judgment Day!" Franklin droned on. "You taught us that much, and I believe you with all my heart, Reverend. Armageddon is coming, and all we have to do is read the headlines to know who's gonna be on each side."

"Armageddon *is* comin'. *I* said that just tonight." Most of his "sermon from the mount" had been on that very topic.

"That's right, you did! Where do you think I learn—from *you*!"

What a toad.

"So think about that video you just saw. Isn't it clear? Mal Abbas has his headquarters in *Baghdad*—Babylon! He's gonna lead the Arab nations to war, probably in league with China and those Indians and Africans. Mal Abbas *is* the beast!"

Stanton found himself being swayed. He ran a hand through his hair, encountered dried hairspray, and tugged it out again. "But he says he got his message at Santa Pelagia," he said worriedly.

"Well . . . that's . . . that's something else."

Stanton glanced at the young man, surprised that, for once, he didn't have an answer. Franklin was actually staring at the bad gold carpet. It hit Stanton like a three-hundred-pound defensive tackle what the boy was thinking. He was thinking, *At Santa Pelagia, just like you; you in league with the Antichrist.*

"You're wrong about *that*," Stanton snapped.

"What?" Franklin replied, all innocent-like.

"Him bein' at Santa Pelagia is *not* a problem. Lucifer was one of God's angels before the fall, wasn't he? We know God controls everythin'. Of *course* he's engineerin' the apocalypse, right down to giving permission to the Antichrist to do his work. The Bible says that nothin' can be done but through his permission."

Franklin was shaking his head doubtfully. "We're treading on shaky ground here, Reverend. There's a difference between God *permitting* evil, and God giving it its *marching orders*."

Stanton was about to retort when inspiration struck. "Wait a minute—Judas was one of the Twelve, wasn't he? So why wouldn't the Antichrist be one of the *Twenty-Four*?"

"Hmmm."

"After all, Christ didn't *tell* Judas to betray him, he gave him the same message he gave *all* his disciples, it was the mind of Judas himself that warped it into some political message. But God *knew* he would, you see? It was part of the plan."

Franklin was nodding. "I like it."

Stanton felt a rush of triumph so strong, it was like the time the Falcons made the play-offs. Then something else occurred to him. He paged back through the Bible.

"But what about the whole other chapter, the chapter about the beast, the one where it says he has the 'feet of the bear' and all that?"

"You mean . . . *chapter 13*?" Franklin said knowingly.

Stanton had reached the page. It *was* chapter 13. His heart did another little lurch. "Praise *Je*sus!"

"Amen. I think all those events in chapter 13 are still to come. He'll wound his head and all that stuff as his power rises. You'll see."

"What about the number of the beast: 666?"

A frown creased Franklin's well-scrubbed face. "I haven't found it yet. He was the *twenty-second* prophet announced, and he announced himself on the *thirteenth* day, but any way you add it up, it doesn't make 666. Our friend who gave us the tape looked up their file on the guy. His real name is Rafael Abbas. He's a fanatic. Been associated with terrorist groups since he was a kid. The 666 is probably related to his birth date or his name in Hebrew or even a birthmark or something. Don't worry, we'll find it."

Stanton was drumming his fingers on Franklin's Bible. "We

should have *that* at least. That's the first thing people are gonna ask."

"I'll get it, but I don't think we should wait. This video hasn't hit the U.S. news yet. If we break the story first thing this morning, not only will you have found the beast before any of the English-speaking world has even *heard* of him, but . . ."

"I'll have found one of the Twenty-Four!" Stanton broke into a broad grin. The kid was right. Not only would he, Stanton, be the first God-fearing Christian to point out the long-awaited, infamous, Christian-heart-knockin' Antichrist, but he'd also steal the ball from that gosh-forsaken reporter, Simon Hill!

God *bless* Clement Franklin!

MUNICH, GERMANY

Dr. Smith had not slept since he'd landed in Munich the previous day. He sank into a chair in the doctor's lounge, his body shaking with fatigue and stress. Blade's temperature was 105 and his condition was advanced. His abdomen was distended and there were unmistakable signs of brain swelling. With the fever and the pain, his conscious moments were intolerable. He was delirious and the pain enraged him. They had to keep him pretty much knocked out with codeine. Mercifully, his pain would probably stop soon, once the brain damage advanced a bit further.

Mike had no doubt that it *would* advance. He thought Blade would live another twelve to twenty-four hours, max. Nothing they'd done had brought the fever down, or stopped the swelling. The other members of his band were, Mike calculated, about a day or two behind Blade. The traveling crew members, two to four days behind them. Not a one had been spared.

The doctors in Munich had followed the WHO team's instructions with little hint of ego—this thing had struck them too quickly and too heavily for ego. And as these doctors watched Blade and his quarantine-ward companions, Mike had seen them become more and more afraid. Mike, who knew more about it, was absolutely terrified.

Dr. Regar, the head of staff here, entered the lounge along with three of WHO's top people. Sam Richards was an American who worked full-time at the WHO headquarters in Geneva. Hilder and Fenson were from the EURO Copenhagen office.

"*Jesus*, Mike!" Richards commented. He poured himself some coffee and sat down at the table. He looked gaunt and unnerved.

"Obviously, containment is still the number one issue," Mike began as the others sat down.

"What about the concert last night? You picked up the stage crew, but the audience was sent home," Dr. Regar said worriedly.

"We *could* not detain the audience," said Fenson, a Swede. "A crowd of twenty thousand—you do not tell them they have been exposed to a plague worse than the bubonic! They would have made a stampede."

"But now those twenty thousand may be spreading it all over Germany!"

Mike shook his head. "I'm more concerned with people who had direct physical contact with the band: the airline crews, hotel staff, local concert crews, groupies, contest winners—people like that. The audience just doesn't get close enough to be in danger."

"But if it's airborne . . ." Regar insisted.

"Yes, well. Patently, it's a heck of a lot easier to catch than having sex or sharing needles. I'm only saying, I think the chances are quite low that audience members would become infected. The volume of air in even a closed concert hall is much greater than, say, an airplane. And the first row is forty to fifty feet from the band? We'd better hope that's the case, in any event. My God, including Rio, he's done ten concerts in ten days in ten cities! And most of them, so his manager says, were attended by ten thousand to sixty thousand people."

They all considered this uneasily.

"We should *warn* them at least," Hilder said.

"We will," Mike agreed. "We'll issue a press statement. By the way, we're bringing in the CDC and USAMRIID. They'll be particularly interested, since four of Blade's recent concerts were held on U.S. soil."

"A press statement isn't enough," Dr. Regar quibbled. "It leaves it up to the individual to respond if he or she gets sick. Who attends concerts? Teenagers. I have one at home. Responsibility is not exactly well developed at that age."

"But their *parents* will see the announcement. And, again, I think the odds of the audience being contaminated are low. I don't know what else to do. We've been taking names from Jimmy Swan all night. We'll try to pick up everyone he *knows* they've had contact with and that alone will be a nightmare.

There's simply no record of the actual concertgoers. We'll have to broadcast the announcement as aggressively as we can."

Regar didn't have any response to that one.

"We'll need a list of instructions for the hospitals, too," Sam Richards said. "Most of them aren't used to Level Four procedures. If these people walk into the hospital hacking away, they could infect everyone in the place."

"Yes. Absolutely," Fenson said.

"I agree," said Mike. "We'll issue a WHO procedural for the medical community. What we *really* need, though, is a blood signature. I haven't had that much time to look at the blood myself, but we've had our Washington offices working on it, and we've passed samples off to the CDC already."

"Nothing's been identified?"

"No. All we've done so far is confirm what it *isn't*. And until we have a blood test for it, I'm afraid there's going to be a lot of panicked people who end up having a normal cold."

"Better safe than sorry," Regar said grimly.

What wasn't being said, but what they all understood, was that until there was a blood test anyone on the contact lists would most likely end up in quarantine *together*—Level Four facilities being difficult to implement and space being limited. This meant that the chances were high of someone on the list who *didn't* have the disease contracting it in quarantine. Mass quarantine without a blood test, in effect, was something like a death sentence. That no one even brought it up for consideration spoke volumes about how terrified they were of this disease already. *Better them than me,* or, to be more altruistic about it, *Better them than the rest of us.*

"Mike, what *about* this contagion level?" Richards asked in an agitated voice. "The entire band and crew . . . I've never seen anything like it."

Before Mike could answer, the loudspeaker came on. A voice told Dr. Michael Smith to pick up line one. Regar pointed to a phone on the wall. Mike sighed tiredly, then went over and pushed the line one button.

"Dr. Smith here."

"Mike? This is Josh."

Mike felt a rush of relief. "It's about time you guys got up today! What the heck is going on?"

"Mike, I . . . I think you need to come back here. Right away."

Josh's voice was choked with tears. He sounded like he was on the verge of breakdown. He sounded incredibly young.

"What is it? What's happened?"

"Jennifer Mallard died this morning, Mike."

"I'm sorry." Mike shut his eyes. He'd wanted to be with her, with all of the Greenpeace staff. They'd been so frightened. But he wasn't exactly surprised at the news.

"And most of the other staffers are *really* bad."

"When she died, did it look like the monkeys?"

"I dunno. I mean, yeah. But worse. She was *human*, Mike, and she was only twenty-six."

"I know."

"At the end, her brain was *everywhere*."

Mike sank back against the counter, feeling sick. "I'm sorry, Josh. But we've got sixty people quarantined here—half of them already have symptoms. And we're not even *close* to containment."

"Mike, I'm not saying you need to come back here because of Jen, or even the rest of the Greenpeace staff." Josh's voice shook with emotion. "There's something going on here, Mike. God, I'm so scared."

"What is it?" Now Mike *was* getting alarmed.

On the other end of the phone line, Josh took in a deep breath. "People have been coming in to the hospital, Mike. A *lot* of people. The place is jam-packed downstairs. And we're getting calls from hospitals all over Brazil. I mean, *all over*."

"What are you saying?"

"I'm saying that these people seem to be *in the secondary stages* of whatever the hell this is. Their families say they've had a cold all week, now they've brought them in because they've got raging fevers and are in incredible pain. Some of them are already swelling. Mike, I swear to God, I think it's the same thing. It's gotten out. Somehow, it's gotten out, Mike. Jesus, my God, it's *everywhere* down here."

For a moment, Mike just stood there with the phone in his hand.

"Mike?"

"I'm on my way."

NEW YORK CITY

Simon Hill sat at his desk reviewing his team's proposed articles for tonight's edition. He yawned and took another drink of coffee. He was disappointed. Most of it was a rehashing with minor

updates of old material. There was a new piece about Dame
Wendy Clark's physician in London, a Dr. Frederick, having
been killed in a fire that burned down his office last night, but
that was pretty far afield. Dame Clark wasn't even in London
anymore. They had the "seven signs" list repeat, as usual, ripped
off straight out of Revelation.

Their readers couldn't get enough of what-might-happen-
nexts like the seven signs list. Still, the third sign, the rivers turning to blood, didn't show any promise of appearing. Red tide was
claimed by the prophets to have fulfilled sign number two—the
oceans turning to blood—and red tide did not infect fresh water.
No sign of prophets twenty-one through twenty-four either, except the rumor they'd gotten out of their China contact who said
that Tsing Mao Wen, President Lee's sidekick, was one of the
prophets. Apparently, the rumor was popular in China, but there
was no confirmation yet—not from Tsing Mao Wen, not from
anyone.

Hill had the sinking feeling they were losing momentum.
Bowmont didn't seem concerned, and why should he? They
were selling five times the number of newspapers they had been
a month ago. People were absolutely insatiable. They not only
bought the *New York Times*, they bought anything that promised
news about Santa Pelagia—most of which simply rearranged
New York Times information. Their opinion poll was frightening.
Twenty-five percent of the respondents now believed literally in
the Santa Pelagia message. Another forty percent were "not
sure." Surprisingly, the thirty-five percent that were sure Santa
Pelagia meant nothing were the worst. They called incessantly,
enraged that "the scientists" hadn't explained the sores yet or the
red tide. Where were the cold, hard facts? they demanded. What
they wanted, Hill knew, was a nice little box to put this whole
thing into. So far, they'd been disappointed and it maddened
them beyond belief.

Hill sighed and pulled a Kleenex from a box on his desk, blew
his nose into it. He cleared his throat and unwrapped another
Halls cough drop. Goddamn cold.

He shifted uncomfortably in his seat. Goddamn sores.

He got up with a sigh, too uncomfortable to settle down anywhere for long. A slight tug in his kidneys gave him someplace
to go. He headed for the john.

* * *

Hill was standing at a urinal, lingering a bit over his business because just having his pants down was a relief. The door behind him swung open and a man entered. Hill glanced at him in the mirror, then looked away. He didn't know him. The man looked like a tourist—baggy tan shorts, a Hawaiian shirt, sunglasses, tan sailor's hat.

This made Hill nervous, for although they had security down in the lobby that supposedly looked for anyone suspicious, the *New York Times* offices were open for business as usual, and they'd had more than a few kooks find a way up and try to cause trouble. So far, it had been with their mouths, not guns. Hill knew that could change at any time.

He finished up and zipped, turned around.

The man in the Hawaiian shirt was standing directly behind him. Close enough, in fact, for Hill to smell his breath; it smelled vaguely of anise. Hill gasped, more startled than afraid at first, and the man put a finger to Hill's lips at once. Something about the intimacy of this gesture made Hill suddenly quite afraid—like being known without knowing—but he was too taken aback to shout. The man pointed to the stalls, where Hill could see one pair of feet, as if to explain the need for silence.

Hill looked at the feet then back at the man slowly. The man reached up and pulled off his hat, removed his glasses.

It still took Hill a moment to put what he was seeing together because of the sheer improbability of it, and then he did. The man in the Hawaiian shirt was Father Michele Deauchez.

An hour later, Simon Hill was walking through the halls of the New York Public Library. He went to the far end and turned, going down the stone stairwell that led to the archive basement. It had been years since he'd been here. As a young reporter he'd haunted the stacks, a habit carried over from college. But between the *Times*'s own archives and the Internet's research capabilities, it never seemed quite worth the effort these days. The stairwell gave him a strange déjà vu sensation. He could almost feel the weight of his old green bookbag slung over one shoulder.

He went past the downstairs reading lounge and the research librarian. He slipped into the newspaper and document archive room. There, at a table among the stacks, he found Deauchez.

"All right, what gives, Father?" Hill asked, sitting down. "What's with all this cloak-and-dagger stuff?"

"You did not tell anyone you saw me?" Deauchez asked worriedly.

"No."

"Or that you were coming here?"

"No! Geez, I told you I wouldn't. What's all this about?"

"Someone . . . someone is trying to abduct me, I think." Deauchez's voice was low, frightened.

Hill raised a skeptical eyebrow. "Really? Who?"

"I have no idea."

Deauchez went into a long explanation about some cardinal's visit to his hotel room in London, a beige van, and two men with guns. He'd taken a cab to the train station in London and from there a train to the Liverpool airport. He hadn't dared Heathrow, he said nervously. He sounded paranoid as hell, but he didn't sound like a liar.

"The two guys must have been with the Vatican," Hill suggested. "McKlennan asked you to go nicely, but was prepared to take you by force if necessary. It's pretty rude, sure, but—"

"No, Simon. The Vatican would never use professional thugs."

"*Really?* Isn't the Vatican supposed to, like, have Mafia connections?"

Deauchez made a face. "I sincerely doubt it. And even if they did, why would they send such thugs after *me*? I have done nothing except try to research this event. Did you get my voice message?"

Hill frowned, remembering Deauchez's last message and his annoyance at it. "The last thing I got from you was an e-mail saying the medical angle was nothing."

"I said I was still *working* on it. You did not get the voice message I left on your phone?"

"I didn't get any voice mail, Father."

Deauchez looked freshly disturbed. "Could someone here be tampering with your voice mail, do you think?"

"Of course not! Are you sure you left it at the right number?"

"I heard your *voice*, Simon, on the message."

Deauchez looked so genuinely upset that Hill felt a twinge of suspicion himself. He'd never lost voice mail before that he knew of. But what could Deauchez be suggesting? That someone in the *Times* office was linked to those alleged thugs in London? That was absurd.

"I'll look into it," he offered. "Meanwhile, why don't you just tell me what the voice mail said."

Deauchez did. By the time he was through Hill had gotten a lot more interested in the priest and his story. He sat straight up in his seat, his fingertips tapping the table as if he were already writing.

"Jesus. I *knew* there was something to this medical stuff! H.A.I.—they're connected to Health Relief, the group that did the hanta inocs at Cougar Camp."

Now it was Deauchez's turn to be excited. "Are you sure? Because when I got your e-mail about Health Relief, I wondered . . ."

"I'm sure. Health Aid International is, like, a parent organization for Health Relief. I looked 'em up."

Deauchez was watching Hill, his brown eyes shining. "You *have* to print this, Simon. You must print this."

"Well . . . yeah. But what does it *mean*?"

Deauchez bit his lip nervously. "H.A.I. influenced the prophets somehow—*before* they went to Santa Pelagia. That was the part I could never decipher—how so many unconnected people were all suddenly drawn to Santa Pelagia."

"But *how* did they influence them? And why? And what about everything that's happened since—the signs and all that? And what about the shots they're giving at Sagara Bata's encampment? Or Cougar Camp for that matter? If the shots were just a cover-up to get to the prophets, why do 'em now?"

Deauchez shook his head, frowning. "I have no idea. But someone can maybe find the answers—*if* they look for them. Simon, I'm just a priest. I was hoping you and your newspaper . . ."

"All right. All right." Hill's thoughts were rife with budding possibilities. "I started this medical research stuff once before, but we didn't get very far. This definitely gives us more to work with. Heck, for that matter, there's no time like the present."

He got up and left Deauchez sitting at the table. He found what he was looking for and returned. "I checked out H.A.I. on the Web a while back, but there wasn't much there, just their logo and a brief summary of their mission. This should tell us a little more."

He plunked down a thick binder.

"What is it?"

"Charters for international groups. They're required by law to have everything spelled out." Hill began flipping through the volume. "Health Aid International. It was established twenty years ago. They have a board of directors that includes scientists and doctors from at least five of their host countries. They have a chairman. Their headquarters are in Washington, D.C. They operate, um, under the U.N. guidelines for international health groups. Their primary money source is private donations."

"May I see, please?" Deauchez pulled the volume from Hill and began paging through it urgently. Hill watched him with a hint of amusement. He could hear Bowmont now. He'd take one look at Deauchez and say, "There's one hound that's caught a scent." Hill was catching it himself.

"Every country that has a prophet is on their list," said Deauchez.

"Yeah? Doesn't mean much. H.A.I. works *everywhere*."

Deauchez kept turning pages. He stopped at something and studied it, his face tense.

"Father? What is it?"

Deauchez turned the binder around so Hill could see. It was an organizational chart with the names of the board members and lead doctors on staff. Deauchez pointed his finger at the name at the top, the chairman.

"So?" Hill commented. "Dr. Louise Janovich. Never heard of her."

"I have. The day I met you I went to visit Maria Sanchez. I heard her asking her own doctor when Dr. Janovich would be back."

Hill stared at the priest, eyes narrowed. Deauchez looked sincere, and Janovich was hardly a common name . . . Hill said nothing, just got up and headed once more for the stacks. When he got back, Deauchez was still absorbed in the binder, his hands shaking subtly.

"Dr. Janovich," Hill said, sitting back down with a large red book. It was a medical Who's Who. He opened it to a page he'd been holding with his finger and read.

"Dr. Louise Janovich, biochemist, psychiatrist. Graduated Harvard Medical School 1978. Chairman of H.A.I. for the past two years. Before that she worked in industry for eight years. Before *that* she taught psychiatry and did research at Harvard. Her specialties are, um, brain function, schizophrenia, pharmaceuticals."

"So why is she running H.A.I.?"

"Uh . . . I would guess the pharmaceuticals part?"

"I believe I'm more interested in the psychiatry part," Deauchez said fretfully.

"Here. It says, 'Dr. Janovich caught the attention of her peers with her controversial work on paranoid schizophrenia at Harvard in the mid to late '80s. Her presentation at the World Psychiatric Conference in Geneva in 1990 was the inspiration for much subsequent research.' " Hill snorted. "Guess I missed that particular party event."

"And I have not kept up with the psychiatric journals as I should," Deauchez said with regret. He shook his head. "No. It does not sound familiar to me. But I think we should see that presentation."

"Excuse me?"

"A conference like that would publish minutes, no?"

Hill was doubtful. "Do you really think that particular speech is relevant?"

"Oh, yes," Deauchez said. His eyes were determined. His certainty was catching.

"Yeah, okay, just a minute," Hill said, sighing for effect. He got up for the third time. He went to the research desk—a wasted trip, as it turned out. They didn't have it. He said as much as he slipped back into his chair.

"They did not make one?" Deauchez asked, disappointed.

"No, they *made* one. The reference desk has copies of the conference minutes going back to 1980, plus video of the presentations. But not for that year, not for 1990."

"Why not?"

Hill shrugged. "The librarian went to look for it, and it was, like, MIA. Checked out a month ago. Never checked back in. You know, like a roach motel, only vice versa."

Deauchez looked blank. "Pardon?"

"Never mind."

"But who checked it out, Simon?"

"There was no name in the log, she said. Didn't sound like standard procedure to me."

Deauchez began to wring his hands, his eyes staring off into space. "Someone took it, Simon. It must be incriminating. They knew that."

"*They?* They who?"

"I don't know. Janovich? I don't know."

The distinct feeling that he was caught up with a paranoid

nutball resurfaced. But the truth was, Hill wasn't absolutely sure. And he'd followed worse leads. "Look, I have to call in anyway. I can have someone in research look for a copy of Janovich's presentation."

"No!" Deauchez protested, as if Hill had just suggested burning a few babies.

"Whaddya mean 'no'?" Hill frowned.

"Check in if you must, but don't say you have seen me, don't say *anything* that would indicate this line of inquiry. Asking for the conference minutes would give us away in a heartbeat."

"Give us away to whom? Geez! With all due respect, Father, these are the people I *work* with. They're not gonna—"

Deauchez leaned over the table and put a warm hand on Hill's own. "My friend, I beg you to trust my instincts. I have been seeing men on my travels. In India one took a picture of me. When I landed in London to talk to Sister Daunsey there were two men at the airport that I now believe were following me. And the beige van I told you about was also in front of Daunsey's house. It did not quite penetrate until I saw those two men go into my room. I thought about this a great deal on my flight here. If someone *is* responsible for this, for God knows what reason, they are not—how do you say it—'small-time'? And they *certainly* do not intend to be found out."

Hill huffed. "Look, I can't just drop out! I'm, like, in charge of the whole Santa Pelagia story!"

"So tell them you are researching something else—ancient prophecy, perhaps. *Please*, Simon. We will find another way to get that video."

Hill heaved a martyred sigh. "Man! Fine, I'm not gonna argue with you. I'm too stuffed up and my throat hurts. Lemme just go phone in, see what's up, then we'll hunt down that video." He began rummaging for his cellular. By the time he reached his jeans pockets, he knew the cause was hopeless. Not even a wallet would fit between him and his Calvins. "Damn it! Left it at the office."

"Use mine," Deauchez offered. He pulled a cellular from his bag and handed it over. Hill dialed Susan's number and she picked up. She did indeed have news. Hill listened to her, getting that familiar rush. "Great! Hold on a sec."

He covered the phone's mouthpiece and passed the information on to Deauchez. "We've confirmed two more prophets!

Stanton announced the Antichrist on his broadcast today, now WWN's runnin' tapes of the guy. He's an Iraqi terrorist—calls himself Mal Abbas. Ever heard of him?"

Deauchez grimaced. "Not . . . not *exactly*."

"Supposedly he was at Santa Pelagia, but he says he wasn't s'posed to announce himself until day thirteen."

"And who is the other?"

"Tsing Mao Wen, the Taoist monk who's, like, the butt boy of China's President Lee? We'd heard rumors before, but he gave a speech to a group of Chinese military last night. He definitely announced himself as China's Santa Pelagia prophet. Said *he* was s'posed to wait until day thirteen, too."

Deauchez looked worried.

"Unfortunately, Stanton and WWN got the scoop on Mal Abbas. Damn that sleazebag! I wonder how he did it?"

But Deauchez was distracted. "Do Taoist monks wear orange saris?"

"Beats the heck outta me. Tsing Mao Wen wasn't wearing one—at the food summit, that is. I saw the newsreel. Why?"

Deauchez shook his head absently.

Typical, Hill thought. He went back to the phone and promised Susan he'd be back later that evening. As he returned the phone to Deauchez he said, "So there's only two prophets still missing. You sure you don't know anything about that?"

"No."

"What about that orange sari comment? Where'd that come from?"

But something else was clearly bothering the priest. He picked up the phone and tucked it into his bag, frowning uneasily. "Can we . . . do you mind if we get out of here, Simon?"

"Well . . . I guess not. Why?"

Deauchez tried to smile. "I don't know, but I'm suddenly quite famished, *mon ami*. And clearly we will not find the video here."

" 'Kay. Let's hit it." Hill was not exactly letting the priest off the hook, but he was always up for eating, cold or no cold. With the restaurants closed, they'd have to go back to his place. He'd picked up several T-bones last week, and he still had a bottle of wine from the last Fourth of July . . .

He realized Deauchez was already moving. In fact, he'd already disappeared among the books. "Geez, guess you *are* hungry," Hill muttered. "Wait up, hey, Father? Wait up!"

CHAPTER 12

RIO DE JANEIRO

Dr. Michael Smith was already wearing his Level Four suit when his taxi approached the hospital. He'd changed on the way from the airport, ignoring the puzzled glances in the rearview mirror. From what Josh had said on the phone, he wasn't sure he felt safe leaving it even that long.

Could the virus really have gotten out? Might it be, even now, floating like dust motes on the humid air of South America's largest city? Surely such a thing wasn't possible.

The driver pulled into the hospital drive in that hurried, wheel-rocking way the locals had. And as Mike reached up to steady himself, hand pressed hard against the passenger door, the signal his eyes were sending his brain finally registered.

They had put a sterilization zone up just *outside* the hospital doors. Suited personnel, plastic showers, lime pits—it all greeted his vision as though they were in some small village in the middle of nowhere and not in a parking lot in the middle of downtown Rio. It could mean only one thing: that the entire hospital was now considered contaminated.

The hairs on the back of Mike's neck rose like obedient cobras at a snake charmer's tune. He'd had his money out and ready before he'd put on his gloves, but his hands shook enough to make handing it over problematic. Then the taxi was gone and he stopped only long enough to identify himself to the WHO personnel manning the zone. Whatever was going on inside, he had to see it for himself. He went through the showers like a man late for an appointment and pushed aside the heavy plastic sheets that provided an extra barrier in front of the doors.

And confronted the main lobby. The lobby—and all he could see of the first floor—was a living sea of patients. Bodies were

217

packed in chairs, on tabletops, and over every square inch of
linoleum both in the front room and down every corridor in
sight. Through these bodies, wading like bathers through surf,
were staff personnel, identifiable by their masks, goggles, and
gloves. The few relatives that remained upright were hovering,
in grief and shock, at the sides of their loved ones. None of them
wore protective gear, though those with eyes to see and intelligence still undimmed by fear and grief held handkerchiefs to
their mouths. It was an ironically pathetic gesture, given that
most of the handkerchief holders were coughing into said same,
no doubt coating them with the virus that they already had in
any case.

The last remaining tendril of hope that Josh had been mistaken disappeared the moment Mike took in the scene. But he
ignored what his eyes told him. He began checking patients immediately, starting right inside the door. It was the only way he
could refrain from turning right around and walking out.

The patients were poor, ragged, and smelled of death. Their
fever warmed his fingertips even through his rubber gloves. A
man with red skin and a bowl-shaped haircut had an abdomen
and genitals swollen twice their size. A child of two or three
struggled to breathe through dry airways, legs and arms plumped
up like cooked sausages. A few already showed signs of brain
damage—pupils that didn't dilate, drooling mouths. Those who
were more coherent were in severe pain.

The truth was undeniable. The entire hospital was crawling
with whatever had been in the monkey room at the Greenpeace
shelter.

Inside his suit, Mike's skin was slick with sweat. He felt light-
headed, nauseous. He rose, slowly, from his inspection of a
young pregnant woman. He rose because if he did not, he would
fall over among these people, fall over and soil his suit both inside and out. He ignored the pleas and the hands and made his
way to the corridor, fighting for foot space the entire way. His
eyes scanned the suited personnel around him. He did not find
what he was looking for.

He made his way up to the second floor, where the original
quarantine room had been turned into a death room for those in
the final stages, those about to donate to the "squeeze-a-brain"
foundation. Blood and brains were splattered on the walls in a

few places that hadn't yet been cleaned. Mike recognized one or
two of the Greenpeace staffers in the beds, now busily dying—
the shock of seeing them, of realizing just how little time had actually passed, was considerable. But most of the beds were
occupied by people he'd never seen before.

Josh was standing at the end of the room. There was no mistaking him, despite the fact that his back was turned. He looked
like a coatrack on which someone had mockingly wrapped surgical garb. He looked as though he'd lost ten pounds since Washington. Ten pounds of *what*, Mike couldn't imagine. The boy was
too inexperienced to be thrown into something like this. Mike
felt a twinge of remorse as he walked up and tapped the young
doctor on the shoulder.

"Mike! Thank God you're here!" Josh clutched at him awkwardly through the gear. It was not the sort of thing one was supposed to do while suited. Mike pushed him gently away. "I didn't
expect you for another five hours at least!"

"I can't waste all my time flying! Stanley pulled some strings
and got me on a military plane. Nonstop."

"I'm sorry I had to call you back, Mike."

Mike shook his head in dismissal of this, pushing down his
own frustration. "I guess I never should have left. Can we talk?"

"Yeah, but not in here. The entire hospital's hot. It's in the air
system. We have a van downstairs."

"Let's go."

They passed through the tableau of death that lay between the
quarantine room and the front doors without stopping, without
saying a word. They stepped into the gray zone outside, and Mike
welcomed the dousing of the disinfectant hungrily and lengthily,
smell or no. They tossed the suits into a bleach pit, and their
hands and shoes were sprayed again with the caustic, stinging
spray. They took clean towels and fresh hospital greens with them
into the van.

The quarters were cramped but enormously comforting
somehow, perhaps because of at least the illusion of germ-free
safety. Velour-covered benches along each wall provided col-
lapsing points. Large sheets of paper lined the walls above the
benches. A whiteboard was propped up against the front seats
with a map of South America taped to it.

For a while, Josh and Mike simply looked at each other. Their

exhausted eyes said many things, and what it all boiled down to
was that this was some major funky shit. Mike could feel his
heart pounding as though he'd run a mile, his armpits already
dampening his fresh clothes.

"Those people in there," he began, "they can't all be connected to the Blade concert. Most of them look like farmers or
peasants."

"Most are coming in from poor villages outside of Rio, even
forest towns. We asked some of them about the Blade concert,
particularly at first. But it's pretty obvious they weren't at the
concert, Mike, and don't know anyone who was."

"Have you found *any* common denominators?"

Josh shook his head wearily. "We've mostly just been trying
to handle the flow. Christ, Mike, this is so unbelievable. It's not
just here, you know. We've been getting calls from hospitals all
over—São Paulo, Pôrto Alegre, Salvador, even Asunción,
Paraguay. Just a bit ago, Rosario, Argentina, called in."

"Argentina! God! Where's it *coming* from?"

"I don't know, Mike. But it's definitely not just from the moon
monkeys. It can't be. There aren't that many of 'em. Even if they
ran out of their natural habitat and scattered all over, even if there
were a lot more of the monkeys than we thought, we still wouldn't
be seeing contagion like this—not so quickly!"

Josh was right. Something was very unkosher.

"If the moon monkeys aren't the vector, maybe they caught
the disease from the same source as these new arrivals," Mike
suggested.

Josh nodded. "It seems that way, timingwise. These people
are in the final stages. But what could the source be? Why would
something so deadly show up so suddenly? We've never seen
this disease at all; now it's *everywhere*."

"Not everywhere, Josh. It's in quite a few places in *South
America*," Mike countered. It felt good. He felt his reason returning a bit. He got up, ducking his head, and went over to the
map. He searched for the names Josh had mentioned. São Paulo
and Pôrto Alegre were south of Rio, both on the coastline. Salvador was north on the coastline. Asunción, Paraguay, was at
least five hundred miles inland and southwest of Rio. Rosario,
Argentina, was four hundred miles or so southwest of Asunción.
There was no pattern. Or was there?

"Every name you mentioned is a big city."

"That's where the better hospitals are."

"But are the patients from the cities themselves, or are they coming in from smaller towns?"

"Smaller towns, mostly. We've been taking names and hometowns of everyone who's come in here. And I think I saw a fax with patient data on it from the hospital in Salvador. We've sent some personnel up there, so they're trying to get it organized."

"Good. Let's plot them."

Josh stepped outside and sent a message to the hospital. Five minutes later, they had a sanitized version of their own admissions file and the fax from Salvador. Josh began reading off names.

"Okay. These are the hometowns of the patients who have checked into the hospitals in Salvador: Juàzeiro, Curaçá, França, Remanso, São João do Piauí, Oeiras, Picos, Floriano, Paulistana, Bom Jesus da Lapa. Geez! Could these be *any* more difficult to pronounce?"

"They could be written in Russian," Mike said distractedly as he scanned the map. He found all the towns on the map and marked each with an X.

"Ready?" Josh asked.

"Go on."

"These are the hometowns of *our* patients: Pirapora, Bocaiúva, São Francisco, Carlos Chagas, Paranã, Nova Ponte, Centralina, Itumbiara, Tanabi—"

"Hold on." Mike was marking Xs furiously. He stopped and looked at the map.

"Want me to go on?"

Mike shook his head. Placing a finger on the map, he traced lines between the town names, first the Salvador names, then the names from the patients here. Except he didn't *have* to trace lines. Lines were already on the map: thin, blue lines that went directly past those towns.

"Josh?" Mike said in a choked voice.

"Yeah, Mike?"

"Do you have any idea where that area was—the one the moon monkeys lived in?"

"It was close to a town called Santarém. Geez, Mike, it was on fliers all over the Greenpeace shelter, don't you remember? It made me think of 'Santa Claus,' which is, you know, kinda ironic."

Mike wasn't listening; he was looking furiously at the map, searching for the name.

"It's not really the 'heart of the rain forest,' like they said," Josh continued, "just a dense, virgin area. It's actually quite a bit north, not central."

But Mike had found it. He found it by continuing up those branching lines on the map, the lines that connected the towns where the sickness had reared its head. He put a finger on Santarém.

"It's at the *head* of the Amazon," Mike whispered.

"Is it?"

"Jesus Christ!" It was almost a sob.

"Mike?"

Mike examined the map of South America, really looked at it for the first time. The entire map was covered with tributary lines, like a very old woman with broken veins under her parchment skin. The Amazon river bled into *everything* sooner or later. It bled into the São Francisco River, and the Paraná, and the Madeira, and all the other rivers and streams with which the continent was rife. He followed the thin blue lines with his eyes, across the breadth of the landmass and down, all the way to its tip. From there, the continental waters bled into the sea.

"God! It wasn't in the *monkeys*, it was in the *forest*."

"What?" Josh said, but his face blushed pink with a burgeoning comprehension.

"Now they've cut down the trees and let it wash out. Jesus, my God, Josh, it's *in the rivers*."

OUTSIDE NEW YORK CITY

The house was over in Port Chester; an upscale area, though the property itself was a few blocks and a few thousand square feet shy of the beachfront extravagances that they drove by on the way in. It was a quiet-looking brick Tudor with the air of a family home that had lost the bulk of its inhabitants to attrition. Now it gave the impression that a lonely widow lived inside. Perhaps it was the way most of the upstairs blinds were drawn with a dusty finality. But it wasn't the residence of a lonely widow; it was the home of a widower psychiatrist, Dr. Ernkin.

They parked in the driveway at 6:00 P.M. Hill wanted to check his messages with Deauchez's cellular before they went in, and Deauchez gave in to this American obsession with impatience. There was nothing earth-shattering in Hill's mailbox, and they were knocking on the door by 6:05.

Dr. Ernkin was in his seventies, a thin man dressed in the kind of sweater that men wore in the fifties, the kind that made Deauchez picture old men sitting in Paris cafés.

"Hello!" Dr. Ernkin said warmly. "One of you must be the gentleman I spoke to on the phone."

"That's me, Dr. Ernkin." Hill held out his hand. "I'm Simon Hill, and this is my associate, Mr. Deauchez. We really appreciate this."

"Not at all! I can't wait to see the final article."

Hill had told Dr. Ernkin a bit of a lark—a bogus feature article on influential psychiatrists—but it had gotten them in to see the video. Dr. Ernkin had been the thirtieth psychiatrist from the phone book they'd called. Deauchez was just grateful the man hadn't been named Zemeski.

"Isn't it funny how time flies?" Dr. Ernkin commented as he led them back into a family room. "1990! Seems like I was just there!"

"I know what ya mean," Hill agreed. Deauchez smiled politely. His mind was already on the video they were about to see. Ernkin and Hill continued the pleasantries as Ernkin loaded the tape, turned on the TV.

"Good conference, 1990. 'Course, I used to go every year. Haven't been for . . . oh, three, four years now."

"That's too bad."

"Geneva! What a beautiful city. It was Louise Janovich you wanted, right? She was brilliant, if I recall. 'Course you know that already or you wouldn't be writing about her."

Ernkin started the tape. Hill shot Deauchez a look as preliminary static filled the screen. He looked pleased with himself, that they'd found the thing. But Deauchez wasn't feeling pleased. He was feeling extremely anxious, even scared, and he didn't know exactly why except that he had a gut instinct about this tape: that it would be the nasty load of excrement he'd been opening lids hoping to find; that it would hold, perhaps, some surprises that he didn't want to see as well. His left hand worked the fingers of his right with apprehension.

White lettering on black appeared:

Paranoid Schizophrenics, dopamine, and
the biochemical world of fantasies
Lecture by: Dr. Louise Janovich, Harvard University

The video itself was amateurish; too dark because the room was lit for slides. Janovich wore a conservative beige blouse—the sort that had a big, bouffy scarf tie attached—and a calf-length skirt. She was full-figured, midthirties, brown hair, large glasses. She didn't look like the wicked witch Deauchez had expected without even realizing he'd expected it.

"The states we call 'mental illness' often include elaborate fantasies," she began. *"When a patient hears voices, insists upon some ludicrous global conspiracy, or conducts dialogues with people from Venus, they're diagnosed as paranoid schizophrenics. Yet so-called normal people have fantasies. At what point does the schizophrenic cross the line?"*

She described a questionnaire she'd developed for college students. She found that she could classify supposedly normal people as "fantasy deficient," "fantasy moderate," or "fantasy hyperactive." These classifications had no correlation to race or gender, but did predict occupation. Novelists, artists, and church ministers tended to test as "fantasy hyperactive," while engineers and ecologists were "fantasy moderate," and accountants and actuaries "fantasy deficient." She further found that the fantasy capacity seemed to coincide with at least one parent's test results. In other words—to be partially, if not wholly, genetic. Could schizophrenia be the result of this genetic trait run amok?

To test this theory, Janovich had looked at both antipsychotic drugs and psychedelics. She studied the effects of both on the brain's chemistry using BEAM scans. As her jargon got technical, Hill lost his focus and glanced at Deauchez, but Deauchez ignored him. *He* was following it well enough. He was leaning forward, still wringing his hands.

The research all boiled down to a neurotransmitter called dopamine in the brain's limbic region. Antipsychotic drugs *lowered* the level of dopamine, which was abnormally high in schizophrenics. Psychedelics raised it.

"Gentlemen," Janovich said, *"neurotransmitters act as activators or inhibitors. Chemically, our bodies are a series of*

checks and balances. When our biochemistry produces too much of a good thing, the inhibitor kicks in. When the inhibitor has lowered the levels past what is safe, the activator kicks in. This system can fail.

"Dopamine is an inhibitor. Could certain regions of the limbic system—specifically the nucleus accumbens—*act as a reality filter for the signals coming in from our senses, our emotional centers, and our memory? And could dopamine be the natural inhibitor for this process and thus, in the schizophrenic state, cause the 'reality filter' to be overinhibited? This might explain why the schizophrenic has difficulty separating reality and fantasy. His brain may literally be 'misfiling' events."*

A spattering of murmurs erupted on the tape. Dr. Janovich smiled and held up a hand for quiet.

"One way to try to prove this theory was to pose another question. If a paranoid schizophrenic's fantasies could be brought under control through antipsychotic drugs, could a normal person be made schizophrenic? Traditional psychedelics and hallucinogens cause overstimulation of the brain as a whole, with modest dopamine increase being but a side effect. What was wanted was a drug that targeted dopamine only, and that stimulated its production to much higher levels than a psychedelic could achieve."

Deauchez was unable to contain himself. He reached over and squeezed Simon's hand nervously, then withdrew it again and continued to wrench his own hands.

Janovich described her development of the drug, FI1 for "fantasy induction drug 1," and her initial testing on rats. The tests showed no long-term side effects, and she won approval to conduct her tests on human beings at Harvard.

A video began to roll behind Janovich. In the video, a young female, presumably a college student, was lying on a bed while Janovich gave her an injection.

"Meet Sandra, Harvard art student," the Janovich in Geneva said. *"She tested as a mild 'fantasy hyperactive' on our tests. I found it important to begin with someone who had less far to go to reach the level I desired."*

The video cut to a later time. Sandra was now out of her bed, or, to be more accurate, she was standing up on it while the video Janovich hovered nearby.

"I can't go with you now. Yes, I understand. Yes, thank you."

Sandra was speaking to someone, but clearly not Janovich, for her gaze was fixed near the ceiling. Her voice was choked with emotion, tears, reverence.

"All right. Yes. I promise. What do you want . . . Oh."

"Sandra? This is Dr. Janovich. Can you tell me who you're talking to?"

"My guardian angel," said Sandra. *"Shhhh!"*

The video moved forward in an awkward jump. Sandra was now seated on the bed, drinking water. *"This is after the drug has worn off,"* said the Janovich in Geneva.

"Sandra, can you tell me what just happened to you?"

"I saw my guardian angel. He told me a lot of things about my parents and about school and my boyfriend." Sandra looked dazed but elated.

"What did he look like?"

Sandra went into a long and coherent description of the classical angel. She was completely enamored.

"Do you see him now?"

Sandra shook her head dejectedly.

"You don't think you dreamed it, perhaps? Or imagined it?" Janovich prompted kindly.

"No! He was right here. I wasn't dreaming!" Sandra was upset at the mere suggestion.

The Geneva Janovich paused the video. *"Sandra, to this day, will tell you she really met her guardian angel. Our other subjects had similar experiences. Interestingly enough, what each one 'saw' changed. One boy had a terrifying episode in which he was taken into hell.Others spoke with dead relatives.*

"The impact of these experiences was resilient even to our explanations of what the drug did. The subjects simply refused to believe that what they 'saw' was not real. One young man even told me that the drug 'opened the veil' between worlds. Their capacity for self-delusion was really quite amazing. One can see where a constant dopamine surplus—in a patient whose brain is naturally producing it—would almost have to lead to mental breakdown."

Dr. Janovich paused thoughtfully. *"I don't need to point out what this research convinced me about so-called life-after-death experiences. I would guess that the level of dopamine skyrockets during the trauma of death, though I have not tested the theory."*

Hill glanced at Deauchez with a question in his eyes. Deauchez nodded, once, in reply.

"There is one further unexpected result that I would like to share with you."

The video behind Janovich began again. This time the subject was male. He was already in the throes of the drug.

"The suggestibility of the human mind is well documented in tests involving hypnosis. However, I found that FI1 caused suggestibility to be virtually limitless. If I gave the suggestion, for example, that a dragon had just entered the room, a dragon would immediately become part of the subject's fantasy. Again, we're seeing that the brain's filtering process that would normally categorize the idea as a verbal suggestion rather than sensory input is simply not functioning.

"Even more incredible, however, was the potential of the patients to induce physical manifestations of their fantasies."

The volume on the video went up. Janovich was talking to the boy.

"Mark? I'm going to try an experiment, okay? I'm going to rub some ice on your arm. It will be a little bit cold, but it won't hurt." From a tin nearby, Janovich used long tweezers to pick up a live coal and place it on his bare forearm.

"Ooh, cold!" the boy said, wriggling a bit, but clearly not in distress.

The camera went in for a close-up. The hot coal was pressed directly up against the flesh. After ten heartbreaking seconds Janovich removed it. The boy's hand came up and rubbed at the skin as though it tickled. Janovich held his arm straight for a long zoom in. The skin was perhaps slightly pinker but was otherwise unblemished.

"Now I'm going to try a hot stone. I'll just hold it there for a second, okay? I want to see how much the ice protects you, that's the experiment."

Janovich took a large piece of ice from a bowl. Now Mark looked nervous. His face screwed up in an expression of dismay, but he tentatively held out his arm.

Janovich moved the ice in with a swift gesture. It made contact with the boy's forearm, which the camera dove in to try to catch, but Mark immediately yelped and jerked his arm away.

"Okay. Thank you, Mark. Can I see?"

"Ow!" Mark held out his arm, his chin trembling. On the skin was a deep-red burn. In Geneva, Janovich turned to her audience.

"To conclude, I believe these experiments raise some very interesting questions. The obvious practical application is in the treatment and diagnosis of schizophrenia. As for other applications—I leave that, gentlemen, to your imaginations."

The video audience was on its feet with applause. Dr. Ernkin stopped the tape. "My goodness! I'd forgotten how good she was. That lecture was the talk of the conference, if I recall. Excited me quite a bit. It's too bad really."

"What's too bad, Dr. Ernkin?" Hill nudged Deauchez, but the priest was only half-hearing this. His mouth had gone dry; he felt sick to his stomach, sick to his soul. He needed some air.

"Well, goodness, I don't think she ever continued with any of it! Went off to work for a drug company or some such thing, but I never heard of a darn thing coming out of it—any drugs for schizophrenics, that is. Have you?"

"No," Hill replied.

"What has she been doing in the past ten years, anyway? Brilliant woman, really."

"She's chairman of Health Aid International now."

"*Is* she? My, my. Well, that's *something*, I suppose. But . . . well, they're more of a charity group, aren't they? Can't see as I get the connection. To Janovich's work, I mean."

"I have a feeling Dr. Janovich has made more of a contribution than you imagine, Dr. Ernkin," Deauchez said. He hadn't intended to say it. His tone was bitter. Hill nudged him worriedly.

"Huh? Oh, perhaps. Still, can't blame her. Would have taken a lot of fortitude, yes?"

"*What* would have taken a lot of fortitude?" Hill asked.

"Hmmm? Oh, as I said, that lecture was controversial, and that's like diagnosing a eunuch as having a 'slight hormone problem.' Some doctors didn't care for Janovich's methods *or* her conclusions. Thought she should be reprimanded for those tests on human subjects, even though she'd gotten all the necessary paperwork. Said it was a question of ethics. I tell you what the *real* problem was—it was a group of psychiatrists who fancied themselves religious men!"

Ernkin shook his finger. "I know what you're thinking, but they *do* exist, men who don't have any problem believing in science *and* God. They didn't like what Janovich's research implied—that all religious visions, that 'near-death experience' nonsense, and even religious practice were simply products of overactive dopamine production—no different than any other fantasy, and second cousin to mental illness. They didn't like it, no sirree, and they got their churches up in arms about it, too! Harvard was bombarded with outrage—from the Catholics, from the born-agains, you name it! And Janovich was the bull's-eye on the target. Can't blame her for taking the easy way out and simply quitting."

Hill nudged Deauchez again. The priest had shut his eyes, still feeling ill.

"Um—do you know where she went when she left Harvard?" Hill asked Ernkin.

"Some company. Did genetics research, as I recall."

"Genzyme?" Hill suggested. "Genentech?"

"No. Oh! I remember it had something to do with Dr. Robert Tendir—you know him?"

"Sure. He won a Nobel prize for his DNA research."

"Right. He was at the conference in '90. Can't think why, really. He's not a psychiatrist. Anyway, I remember because when I heard that Janovich was leaving Harvard, I thought he must have heard her at the conference and been impressed. She went to work for him is what happened. At that company. Um . . ."

"Telegyn?" Hill suggested. Deauchez opened his eyes at this. The name was familiar. His head was starting to clear. Water, he needed some water.

"Right! Telegyn. Don't know how long she was there, though. Don't know much about it, really, except that she was to work with Tendir. It seemed rather promising at the time—Janovich and Tendir, that is. Hell of a team, yes? But, as I said, I never heard of anything productive coming out of it."

Ernkin looked stubbornly at Deauchez as if bracing for another plea for Janovich's altruism. But Deauchez only cleared his dry throat. "Might I have some water, please, Dr. Ernkin?"

"Of course! Why don't I make us some tea? Should have thought of it a long time ago. Sorry about that. My wife died a few years back. I'm not the couple I used to be."

Hill glanced at his watch. "Um, I don't think . . ."

Deauchez shot him a look. "Tea would be wonderful, thank you, Doctor."

Ernkin went off into the house, presumably to the kitchen.

"Man oh man!" Hill whispered. "This is *way* the hell out there! I need a copy of that tape."

"You will print it, won't you?" Deauchez gripped Hill's arm.

"Father! Why *wouldn't* I? We're talking Pulitzer here! But if Janovich influenced the prophets, I need to know *why.*"

Deauchez was feeling better, and now the questions started flooding in for him, too. He got up, needing to move around. "I knew it! Somehow they . . . *implanted* those dreams. You heard what she said about susceptibility. Who could be more susceptible to dreams and visions than people like Sister Daunsey or Andrews or Stanton? You heard her say that!"

"Uh . . . Yeah. I heard. Religious people. Fantasy hyperactive. I see your point." Hill glanced at his watch again. "I'd like to get you on tape about all this, Father, soon as we get outta here. Why don't you just, like, hold it for a minute?"

But Deauchez was not capable of holding anything. "But the visions in Santa Pelagia . . . They must have . . . how could they make them *there*? I did not see any medical personnel in town, did you?"

"Nope."

"Well . . . I'm sure mass hysteria was part of it. It simply fed itself."

"Anything's possible," Hill said doubtfully. "But remember, that tape was made fifteen years ago—before Janovich even went to work for Telegyn. She's had plenty of time to finesse her drug since then. Maybe she used some time-release mechanism to, like, keep it in their bloodstreams or something. Still, the signs are a problem. Visions are one thing, but the sores . . ."

"It's not just Janovich, Simon! It has to be larger than that. She would never have the resources. Why, just the fact that she was appointed to head H.A.I.—the *exact* spot from which to reach the prophets—that alone shows that much greater forces are at play. Those two men at my hotel in London, for example. I can't imagine Janovich arranging that."

"So who else is involved?"

Deauchez pondered the question. "Do you know anything about Telegyn? Something like this, it must be planned for a long time, longer than two years. Janovich would have been at Telegyn then, correct?"

"Maybe. Telegyn's into telecommunications and genetics research. It's still privately held. Supposedly, they've got all kinds of millionaire silent investors. They're supposed to, like, *own* telecommunications in the next century because of their Earth-web stuff. Anthony Cole himself, the guy who started it, is stinking rich. Charismatic as hell, too. He's kinda regarded as a 'cyber guru' by Internet geeks 'cause Telegyn supposedly represents the fusing of satellite and biotechnology. But that's just hype. As far as I know, they don't actually do much cross-pollinating; it's just two separate divisions with Tendir at the helm of the genetics part. Anyway, he's our secretary of state now."

Deauchez stopped pacing, stunned. "You mean the founder of Telegyn is *that* Cole? The U.S. secretary of state?"

Hill frowned uneasily. "Well ... yeah. When Fielding was elected two years ago, he gave Cole the job. Used Cole as paragon of this whole election shtick he had: 'Don't use politicians, find the brightest people in the nation and put them in charge.' Cole's actually been pretty popular. People think he's really good. Speaks a *bunch* of languages."

"God in heaven. Secretary of state!"

Hill looked extremely uncomfortable at Deauchez's reaction. "So what about those two men in London? You think they're with Telegyn? You think Telegyn's behind this? Why would they be?"

"I cannot imagine."

"Look, lemme call the office and ask Susan to get some stuff together on Telegyn. We can swing by there and pick it up when we get to the city."

Deauchez nodded distractedly. For the third time that day, he handed his cellular to the reporter. Hill dialed his office.

"But don't mention me or any of *this*," Deauchez whispered.

Simon waved away the words impatiently. "Susan? Hi, this is Simon. I know, I know. Sorry. I'm really in the middle of something."

Susan apparently gave him an earful.

"What? What kind of virus?" Hill covered the phone. "There's been an outbreak of a new virus down in South America. Supposedly, the singer Blade's got it, and they're broadcasting warnings about his concerts. Good thing I didn't go."

Deauchez frowned. *Now* what was going on?

Hill went back to the phone. "Huh? Yeah. Leave space for it in the morning edition. Uh ... can you stop talking for just one sec? Sorry, but I need you to do some research on Telegyn: the company, current projects, staff, anything, everything. Yeah."

Deauchez was watching Hill and suddenly the phone in the reporter's hand registered. He stared at it with dawning horror. Hill must have read it on his face, for he tugged on Deauchez's arm to get his attention and mouthed *"What?"* Deauchez didn't answer. He grabbed the phone from Hill's grasp and hit the off button. He nearly threw it across the room, but he restrained himself, holding it instead in two fingers as though it were a snake.

"Hey!" Hill complained.

Without saying a word, Deauchez turned the phone around and pointed out the name on the side of the case: *Telegyn*.

Hill's eyes widened, but when he looked up his expression was skeptical. "Okay. But . . . you don't *really* think . . ."

Deauchez held up a hand in a "time-out" gesture, and tried to order his thoughts, which were threatening to run away with him. "Simon, I have been using this phone since I left Rome. Donnelley gave it to me."

"Who's Donnelley?"

"A cardinal. My superior."

"So? What, he's in on it now, too?"

"Please! I'm trying to think. You said you did not get my voice mail?"

"Sure didn't."

"And you say no one in your office would tamper with your messages?"

"No way."

"I left you a message asking for the name of Clark's doctor in London. That may have—"

But Hill's skeptical look had changed into alarm. "When did you leave that message, Father?"

"Uh . . . *merde*, yesterday morning around noon London time. It seems longer ago with the time change."

Hill's mouth dropped open. "Deauchez, Clark's doctor was *killed yesterday evening*. His entire clinic was blown up. They thought it was a terrorist bomb."

Now it was Deauchez's turn to gape. "That . . . that . . ."

"What about the e-mail you sent me? We talked about it this morning, 'member? I wrote to you about the medical stuff and I got back an e-mail that said 'It was nothing. Never mind.' You said you didn't—"

"Simon, *no*. I thought you were paraphrasing. My message said that I was still working on it and would get back to you."

"No *way*! How could they mess with e-mail? Jesus!" Hill began biting his nails worriedly.

Deauchez put a hand on the reporter's arm. "Simon, I think we should leave here. *Now*."

"Whaddya mean?" Hill glanced at the phone. Now he, too, seemed to regard it as a viper that might strike. "It wouldn't be able to trace us, would it? I didn't tell Susan where we were."

"It uses satellite transmission, correct? Would the satellite not be able to pinpoint the coordinates of a signal?"

Hill seemed to find this reasonable logic. "Right. We're outta here."

"Bon."

"What about Ernkin?"

"He should be fine if we leave."

Hill paused long enough to collect the videotape from the machine, then they both hurried toward the front door. Hill called out as they went. "Dr. Ernkin? We have to go, okay? I'll return the tape as soon as I've made a copy! Thanks so much!"

A voice saying "Wha . . . ?" and the tinkle of teacups came drifting to them from somewhere in the house, but they were already slipping into the night.

Hill's car was three blocks away when they felt it—an enormous explosion back in the direction of Ernkin's house. Hill faltered and the car rolled to a stop in the middle of the street. He had his hands up off the wheel as though he were being arrested. Deauchez turned to look out the rear window. A shout had left his mouth without his even being aware of it.

"Holy God! They bombed Dr. Ernkin's house! Christ forgive me, we should have taken him with us!" Deauchez sounded hysterical, *felt* hysterical. And something else—he felt a mortal fear so hot and sudden it felt like a bolt of lightning had fried through his body, turning his muscles to hot glue.

"It's not your fault, Father. You couldn't have known!" But Hill's face was frightened, too, and a bit uncomprehending.

And then Hill just sat there, dumbly. Deauchez stumbled in his haste to get the words out of his mouth. "G-go, Simon. *Go!*"

The reporter forced his shaking hands back on the wheel and

his foot from the brake. The car began moving again, and before long, he was driving as fast as the terrain would allow.

"I *told* you." Deauchez's voice trembled with emotion. He turned to look out the rear of the car again. He saw no headlights behind them. *He should be fine if we leave.* Idiot! "I told you they were there, that they were watching. I *told* you."

Deauchez knew he sounded demented and maybe he was.

Hill didn't answer. He didn't say anything at all, all the way back to Manhattan.

CHAPTER 13

WWN's breaking telecast on the new South American virus was aired in the early morning hours, East Coast time, of day fourteen. Their ratings were low at this time of day, consisting of early risers dressing for work or mothers feeding hungry babies with the TV on. The rest of the United States would hear the news throughout the day, many of them logging onto WWN's Web page after a nudge in that direction from coworkers. But those who were up and watching for the initial broadcast saw the pretty, off-hours newscaster read this:

"The World Health Organization has released an international press statement today. A new virus dubbed Santarém has been discovered in South America. The continent has been . . . apparently the continent of South America has been quarantined by a vote of the U.N. No flights except approved military and humanitarian flights will be permitted in and out of the country.

"Symptoms appear within five days of exposure. During stage one, the symptoms mimic those of a bad head cold. By stage two, eight or nine days after exposure, extremely high fevers ensue and steadily rise. D-death occurs by day ten to twelve, from encephalitis. No treatment is currently available.

"Santarém has already been exposed outside of South America. The rock performer Blade died late September 2nd of the disease. He was on a world tour when he contracted the virus from a Brazilian moon monkey in Rio. After his infection he gave concerts at the following cities: Los Angeles, Seattle, New York, Atlanta, Madrid, London, Stockholm, Paris, and Munich. All of these cities may have been exposed to the virus. At this

time, it is unknown if or how many concertgoers might have been contaminated."

The announcer stopped reading for a moment, her pink tongue licking her lip thoughtfully. She adjusted her scarf, as if unaware of the time clicking by. After long seconds of silence, through inner or outer prompting, she picked up the report and went on.

"Anyone who attended these concerts should report to their local hospital immediately. Hospitals have been issued procedures for handling this kind of Level Four contagion. Containment is now the top priority of the World Health Organization and the United States government. Full cooperation of the public is vital." She put down the report slowly, arranged it neatly on the desk. She put her hand to her ear and nodded. *"More on that story when we have it,"* she said to the camera. Then she picked up the next story and went on.

LARKSPUR LAKE, EASTERN WASHINGTON

Sacred Dance brought the last group of new arrivals into the mess hall and shut the double doors. Will Cougar watched the campers move into the inoculation lines from where he sat, unmoving, in the shadows. He liked the darkness at the far end of the hall. He felt anonymous there. Of course, they knew he was watching them. He had no illusions about that. He feigned laziness; his legs stretched out in front him, back leaning against the table. Sacred Dance came toward him. He both saw her and did not see her. He was watching the doctors.

There were four lines and each line led to a table where a nurse took information down on her pad. Then the person was told to go behind a rolling curtain. The curtain was there so that the others in line did not have to see the shots. But Will Cougar could see them. That was the reason he had chosen this spot to sit.

As Sacred Dance got close, he saw her draw back a little in surprise. She could probably see now that he was not relaxed at all, that he was watching.

"Stop, woman," he said, when she was ten feet away.

"Will Cougar . . ." Sacred Dance began. She sighed. She was worried. She had asked him what was bothering him before, and he had not answered her. She had good instincts, though. She had brought up the idea of calling that reporter, Simon Hill. That had made Will Cougar angry. He had gone to her desk, taken out the man's card, and ripped it up.

Sacred Dance slipped into a chair beside him. She gave him a needful look, a woman's look. She wanted to reach out to him, to comfort his soul. But his soul did not need a woman, any more than it needed to get drunk. What he needed was to make that bad feeling inside himself go away.

The four Health Relief doctors were all white men. They were the same ones who had been there before: polite, fake eyes. When the nurse was done taking information, the doctors took the forms and looked them over. Then they looked at the camper, up and down. Sometimes they asked questions. They took a syringe from a tray on the top shelf of an open silver cabinet. They put some alcohol on the arm and gave the shot.

"I called Spokane this morning," Sacred Dance said. "They said this will be the last time—unless we get more than five thousand new residents."

Will Cougar did not respond.

"Do you think we will? Get over five thousand more?"

"Yes."

"You do?" Sacred Dance did not sound happy about it. "How many more do you think the camp can handle?"

Will Cougar did not answer. He wished she would leave him alone. He had picked up something, something about one of the lines. It was that group of survivalists who had come in from Montana the previous day. They had come with their gear, driving around in loud trucks like they owned the place. With them they brought guns. Will Cougar had not made a point of taking weapons from the other campers. There was no excuse to take them now. He had not had any reason to *want* to until now. But on these men guns were a very bad idea. They were the kind of white men who thought a good time was going out to shoot wildlife and leaving the creatures alive to suffer. Their ancestors had done the same, shooting buffalo from trains until there were no buffalo left. Will Cougar could not understand the purpose of the Great Spirit in putting such men on Earth, but they *were* on Earth, and on it in great number. Perhaps that was why things had to end.

The survivalists were over there in line, making jokes and acting tough. They wanted to show they were not afraid of a shot, that they were not afraid of anything. The nurse frowned when they reached the head of the line. Frowned, maybe, at their camouflage and deer knives. The first of the group answered her questions in a mocking voice. Will Cougar sat up slowly, watching.

The man went around the curtain. He had heavy boots and a stride that made him look like he had full pants. He stuck out an arm and pushed up his sleeve. He gave the doctor a dull, gum-chewing stare. Will Cougar could see the death's-head tattoo on his arm.

The doctor took a syringe from the cabinet. Only it was not from the top shelf this time. It was from a box in the bottom of the cabinet. The doctor gave the shot to the man.

Will Cougar was out of his chair and walking toward the doctor, silently and quickly. As he got close, the next survivalist came around the curtain. Will Cougar pushed him back. The man glared hate at him, but he went.

"Why did you take the last shot from the box?" Will Cougar's words were low. The doctor was no more than thirty. He was startled, nervous.

"I'm sorry?"

"You were taking syringes from the tray. This time you took one from the box." Will Cougar pointed to the box.

Sacred Dance walked up. "What is it, Will Cougar?"

Will Cougar motioned her to be quiet.

"Ah, yes! I see what you mean." The man put on one of those fake smiles. "There's a higher dose in those. You see?"

He took a syringe from the box and one from the tray. He held them up. It was true, the one from the box had more liquid. It looked the same otherwise, except that the box-syringe had a red band around the top and the tray-syringe did not. One of the liquids looked a little bit pinker, too. Will Cougar studied them, saying nothing.

"The last patient was a large man. We want to make sure it's a good enough dose to do the trick," the doctor said, still smiling.

The man's friends burst into laughter on the other side of the curtain. *"He's a big man!"* one mocked. *"A biggy-wiggy, bad ole man!"* *"Oh, I want the* big *syringe! Please, doctor-woctor?"*

Sacred Dance flushed, but Will Cougar did not acknowledge the ridicule. He was still looking at the syringes. He was trying very hard to see them. But he saw nothing. He nodded once and turned away. He strode to the doors and left the building.

* * *

He was outside on the porch when Sacred Dance came out.

"He gave all of them shots from the box," she said quietly. "I don't understand, Will Cougar. What are you thinking? What's *wrong* with the shots?"

"It is not for you to worry about, woman."

"*Will . . .*" she said in a begging voice. She put a hand on his arm. He looked at her and saw hurt on her face. He would have to be blind not to see it.

He touched her shoulder and tried to smile. "I do not trust the government and do not like medicine, you know this. But this group is the last of it. Let us think about other things. Supper tonight is a good place to start. I am hungry and we must put the tables back in order. Sam can help you."

He saw that she did not know whether to believe in his change of heart or not. But she nodded and went off to find Sam.

After she left, Will Cougar stopped smiling. Watching the doctors had not made him feel better, as he had hoped. It had not stopped the thing that was eating him up inside. If anything, that thing was stronger than before.

But he still did not know what was wrong.

NEW YORK CITY

Hill awoke to find the hotel room empty. The priest's bed was turned out, but its occupant was not there. He was not in the bathroom, either, a fact apparent even from Hill's bed. The reporter sat up, heaving a snot-laden sigh. Just his luck. He'd lain awake most of the night dying to talk, but the priest's resonant snoring had put him off. Now the priest was awake and Hill had missed him.

He ran his hand over his close-cropped hair and got up to use the john. He stared sightlessly down at the bowl as his bladder went slack, the conversations he'd had in his mind during the night starting up again. Hill had plenty to say in these silent sessions; he'd assessed their situation, and not favorably. He saw two unarmed men: one, an overweight African-American reporter and the other a French priest. Their physical resources were few. Deauchez had a spot of luggage, most of which comprised two priest's suits, which he couldn't wear. Hill had nothing but the clothes on his back, already past gaminess. They had Deauchez's laptop and a phone they couldn't use. Hill had his car, but if it wasn't already too hot to keep driving, it soon would be. Deauchez had some cash, he'd said, but Hill himself had only twenty-one bucks.

Then there was the other side of the equation. The priest was being stalked by someone unknown. Now that someone was probably stalking Hill, as well. Ergo, Hill couldn't go back to his apartment or to the office.

Yeah, overall, it was a pretty sorry-looking situation.

And yet . . .

Hill tucked himself inside his shorts and turned on the taps to wash his hands, his dark, faraway eyes trained on his own reflection.

And yet, this man, this reporter right there, Simon Hill by name, might just be on the trail of the biggest you'll-fuck-all-know-it-when-you-read-it story the world had ever seen. If he could just fill in the blanks, form a solid theory . . .

If he lived that long.

The door opened and the priest came in, carrying two Styrofoam cups and a small brown bag. The smell of coffee invaded Hill's senses, even through his congestion. His stomach clamored loudly for its morning infusion of sugar.

"I didn't see anyone suspicious," Deauchez said, as if the true value of his trip out had been surveillance.

Hill grinned, thinking that the European, in that ridiculously American tourist shirt, was about as suspicious as they came. "Good. Good." He wiped his face with a towel to hide the smile, walked out of the bathroom, and took one of the coffees.

"Man, I hope that's edible," he said, looking at the bag.

"Unfortunately, no. It's cold medicine. The grocery was not interested in our misfortunes."

Hill groaned with disappointment. "Shit. I keep forgetting. I guess I'll have to grab us something later."

But could he? Wouldn't his assigned grocery store be one of the first places "they" would hang out? And he'd already ruled out his apartment. His stomach grumbled again in a kind of digestive panic attack at this train of thought.

"Have you had any thoughts about last night?" Deauchez ventured.

Hill rubbed his stomach protectively and sighed. "Lots, as a matter of fact. We should get a paper. Make sure it was Ernkin's house."

Deauchez produced a paper from the bag and tossed it to Hill.

It was the *Times*. The main story was the Santarém virus announcement. Hill forgot about his stomach as he skimmed the first paragraph. The prophets would claim it as the third sign, no doubt about that. Hill hoped to God someone got the damned thing under control.

Way in the back, on page ten, Hill found a blurb about the explosion. It had been Ernkin's house all right. He put down the paper reluctantly. "*Man*, I should be at work."

"Is there some way you could send in a story without going yourself?" Deauchez had obviously been chewing on a few ideas himself.

"Probably, but I'm not sure I *have* a story yet, not a complete one. I still don't have jack-all for a motive, or even much of a culprit."

"What about Dr. Janovich?"

"The video's great, but even combined with proof of contact with a few of the prophets, it's not enough for the *Times* to go on record accusing the chairman of H.A.I. of . . . of . . ." What, exactly, were they accusing her of?

"Of manufacturing the visions of Santa Pelagia," Deauchez said firmly.

"Right."

"Of trying to spread apocalyptic panic."

"Uh . . . I guess."

"Of causing thousands of people to leave their jobs to follow some religious fanatic. Of killing millions of sea creatures and wiping out over half of the planet's crops in a time of severe drought and famine."

Hill grimaced with doubt and disgust. "Jesus, Father. Why would *anyone* . . ."

"I don't know! I have been trying to understand for the past two days." The priest rubbed his temple, his mood dark with frustration.

"Look. We agree that Janovich could have induced the prophets' visions, right? Let's leave it at that and talk about the signs for a minute."

Deauchez nodded. They both thought for a while. Hill went into the bathroom and pulled some t.p. off the roll for his nose. He came out bleary-eyed, brain cranking.

"If anyone *could* do such a thing," Deauchez said, "it would have to be someone with biochemical facilities. Someone like the U.S. military or—"

"The military? Hmmm. I think Telegyn's the more obvious choice, though I don't know much about their research. 'Course, if they were engineering chemical weapons I'm sure *no one* would know about it. Here's one thing, though: Tendir was one of the first scientists to announce that the sores couldn't be man-made."

This was news to the priest. "Of course! With their authority, they are in a perfect position to cover up their own handiwork." He began pacing the room with new energy. "And if Cole is involved, then perhaps it's the government who—"

"Why would the U.S. government do it?" Hill whined, getting annoyed at Deauchez's second attempt to pin it on Uncle Sam. "Geez, the spores alone completely fucked up our food situation. The stock market is goin' nuts. Our foreign situation couldn't be worse. It's not exactly a *good* thing!"

Deauchez reluctantly agreed. "Some kind of subversive group within the government, then?"

"God, I dunno. Look, let's talk about *why* and *how* for a minute; maybe that will help pin down a who."

Deauchez nodded. "Very well. I cannot say 'why' as in why anyone would do this. But I have been thinking about the rationale behind the signs. First the sores: they fulfilled the first sign in Revelation, *oui*? But they also verified the story told by Santa Pelagia prophets."

Hill nodded.

"So that is two things the sores accomplished. And there is a third: the spores *also* destroyed a lot of the food supply."

Hill looked doubtful. "That might have been a side effect."

"If someone like Tendir invented the toxin, he would know *exactly* what it would do."

Hill had to admit that made sense. "But why would anyone wanna wipe out our food supply?" Hill, who would kill right now for a double cheeseburger and fries, could not comprehend anyone wanting to destroy something as benevolent and splendiferous as wheat and corn.

"Famine," said Deauchez.

It was more of a mutter, and when Hill glanced at him, the priest's face was lined with concentration, as if he were trying to put together a jigsaw puzzle in his head.

"Sorry?"

"Famine. It's one of the four horsemen of the apocalypse."
Deauchez set up his laptop and opened up a Bible CD-ROM program. "In the newspapers, you have only been listing the pouring out of the seven bowls from Revelation chapter 15. But there are also the horsemen."

"Yeah? So how do the horsemen relate?"

The priest was still working it out himself as he scanned the scriptures. "In many esoteric writings, the same thing is repeated, usually three times. It's supposed to give magical power to the message. Revelations is like this. The same series of events is repeated three times as the seven bowls, the seven trumpets, and the four horsemen. The four horsemen are really symbols of the entire course of the apocalypse, broad categories of the signs themselves."

Hill rubbed his eyes. The argument was hurting his brain. "Okay. And the first horseman is famine?"

"*Mais oui*. We were already bound to have famine in certain parts of the world because of the drought. Now it's destined to be a very *great* famine because the sores destroyed the crops. And the red tide fulfilled the second sign of the ocean turning to blood, but it *also* increased the famine by making fishing impossible."

"Hey, you're right!" Hill felt a rush of excitement.

The priest looked pleased with himself.

"Wait a mo. The environmentalists are saying that the red tide was caused by chemical dumping and sewage runoff. Which means it *might* have been manufactured."

"Exactly! They invented a fertilizer or a growth hormone for that particular type of algae."

"Man! This is actually making sense, Father."

"But what about *delivery*?" Deauchez looked troubled again. "The sores and the red tide appeared all over the world. How could they get such things into the air or water without being seen? And over such a wide area?"

Hill, admitting defeat, flopped back on the bed with his arms open. The priest paced.

The pause was a long one, but Hill finally had an idea. He sat straight up. "Lemme get on your computer."

He moved the laptop over to the cracked Formica table, took the modem line, and began looking for a jack.

"What are you doing?" Deauchez asked nervously.

"Surf's up."

"Do you think that's wise?"

Hill found the phone jack and plugged in his line. "Father, I don't think they can trace us unless we use your cellular, 'kay?"

Deauchez still looked apprehensive, but he stopped arguing. It took a few minutes for Hill to find what he was looking for—the Telegyn web site. Deauchez leaned over Hill's shoulder.

There it was—Telegyn—in all its corporate glory. Despite Hill's growing trepidation at the mere name, it didn't feel anything at all like looking the Gorgon in the face. It was, after all, just a Web site. Nice logo, professional layout.

"What are you looking for?" Deauchez asked.

"Stuff on the Earthweb."

It didn't take long to locate. In a position of corporate pride, the bottom of the main page, an icon for Earthweb appeared: a stylized symbol of a satellite and a little dome. Hill clicked on it and the laptop gurgled like a coffeemaker. The Earthweb page came up.

"Is that their cellular phone network?"

"Uh-huh."

Hill found a large diagram of a domed structure, looking like nothing more than a high-tech toolshed. It was called an "Earthweb hut."

"When Telegyn started the Earthweb, people said they were nuts, right? That it was way too expensive to shoot for full coverage of the planet, and too impractical. How many people wanna make a phone call from the Arabian desert? But Telegyn just kept their mouths shut and kept goin'. Now it's considered brilliant strategy. It's like when that phone company installed all the fiber optics lines? Obscenely expensive, but it sewed up their future as the number one provider. Until things went cellular. The Earthweb system is s'posed to do the same thing for Telegyn."

"How do you know all this?" Deauchez asked, his curious brown eyes inches from Hill's own.

"I have a little money with an investment broker. He's always whining about how he'd put my money in Telegyn—*if* they had stock. Telegyn is why he recommended that I *not* put any money in any other phone company. And Rembrandt, the PC clone manufacturer? They just made a deal to package Telegyn cellulars in their PCs. My broker had me buy some of *their* stock pronto. I'm telling you, brokers go gaga over anything linked with Telegyn."

They studied the diagram. Each hut was seven feet tall and six feet in diameter. It was encased in hard plastic, apparently to protect against vandalism. The satellite receiver equipment was housed inside. There was a small receiver dish at the top.

"So they have a number of satellites in orbit, *oui*?" Deauchez said. "And these Earthweb huts link to them from the ground?"

"Looks like it. According to this, there has to be an Earthweb hut within 100 miles of the caller; closer, if the land's not flat."

"And these huts are already installed everywhere?"

Hill squinted at the screen, scrolled down. "Um . . . It says their Earthweb is ninety-five percent com—" He stopped, a connection, a spark, knocking him flat. "Oh, shit!"

"What?"

Hill didn't answer. He hyperlinked to the "Earthweb Installation Map" and selected the United States, then Colorado. As the detail map began painting itself, Hill pointed to the legend with a shaky finger: yellow dots indicated huts that were active and green were for future installations.

"Yes, but I don't . . ."

Hill held up a "wait" finger, scanning the map intently. "Oh, man, *yeah*! Look at this! Up near Vail and Aspen, we have yellow dots, and down near Denver, and all the major cities, right?"

Deauchez nodded, looking confused.

"But near a few of these smaller mountain towns—Burns, for example—they're still green! They're part of that incomplete five percent."

"So? It makes sense from a business point of view, *non*? How many people visit Burns, Colorado?"

"I know! But Father, those are the exact areas that were not hit with sores!"

"What?"

"Yeah! We'd been getting in reports of areas that weren't hit. I had one of my reporters check it out. We were looking for some kind of explanation for a story—like, were the people there really holy or what? I mean, I know that the people who got sores were random—not everyone got 'em. But in some areas, *no one got 'em at all*."

Deauchez looked back at the map, his face tensed, his irises darkened to two black coals. "What other areas weren't affected?"

Hill could recall several others. Parts of Greenland, upper Alaska. They checked. Green dots.

"Ohmigod." Hill let go of the mouse and wiped sweaty hands on his pants.

"Excellent! This is proof, is it not?"

"Very circumstantial but . . . yeah. Hold your horses though. I wanna check out the red tide."

Hill backed up to the main Earthweb page. There it was, right below the hut info: "Earthweb buoys and ships."

The buoys were thick, plastic containers housing the receiver equipment. They were anchored to the ocean floor and, according to the information, covered only coastlines. The deep-sea capacity would be carried by the oceangoing vessels—or intercontinental airplanes—themselves.

"*That's* why the red tide only showed up on coastlines and inland seas," Hill said. "They don't *have* deep-sea buoys."

Deauchez nodded. "Very smart. With the huts and buoys it would be possible to release a toxin without many workers knowing about it. It could be built in at the factory, black boxes designed to be set off by remote signal or . . ."

He paused, staring at the screen as though he'd just noticed something. "Simon," he said uneasily, "can a Web site know who is logged on to it?" He pointed to his log-on on the screen: *deauchez@vatican.org*. Nothing subtle about that.

"Yeah, but I don't think it's a problem. The webmaster's probably some geek in the basement."

"Log off," Deauchez said.

"Father . . ."

"Please!"

Hill reached behind the machine and unplugged the modem. "There. Okay? We're off." He tried to sound patronizing, but *damn* if the man's paranoia wasn't catching. He shivered as an icy finger went up his spine.

"Time to check out, I think," Deauchez suggested.

"Right behind ya."

Hill was, in fact, ahead of him. As he waited at the door for Deauchez to collect his things, Hill said, "So the first two signs relate to the first horsemen, right? Famine? What's the second horseman?"

Deauchez scooped up the newspaper from the table and held it aloft, the WHO press release screaming through the headline. *"Plague."*

KITTATINNY MOUNTAIN, NEW JERSEY

It was no longer awkward to face the camera in the wilderness, away from the studio's protective support. In fact, Stanton found it difficult to tear himself away from that glassy eye, particularly if he had something new to say, and tonight, Praise Jesus, another touchdown was his to score.

"Children of God!" Stanton began with grim exuberance.

The crowd behind him moaned as one. It was a powerful rumble, an overwhelming force, the *thrum* of a hundred thousand.

"This day brings us the fulfillment of the third sign of the apocalypse!"

There were shouts of surprise and fear and, yes, even joy, from the audience behind him. He had to suppress a smile. Franklin was right. Wait to capture it live, on camera.

"Revelation 16:4 through 6. 'And the third angel poured out his bowl upon the rivers and fountains of waters; and they became *blood*. And I heard the angel of the waters say, Thou are righteous, O Lord, which art, and wast, and shall be, because thou has judged thus. For they have shed the blood of saints and prophets, and thou hast given them blood to drink; for they are worthy'."

Stanton tilted his head up as though addressing the heavens. "Thou hast given them *blood to drink*!"

The crowd moaned and screamed behind him. He paused, riding it. He held up a copy of today's *Times*. "Let me read somethin' to you from the *New York Times*."

He read the quotes in a booming, querulous voice, grinding the words like salt into a wound. " 'The *Santarém virus* is waterborne throughout the river system in South America.' " He paused dramatically, glaring into the camera to allow that to sink in. " 'Death ensues by day ten to twelve from encephalitis.' Do you know what encephalitis *is*, children? That means your brain literally *bursts* in your skull!" Another meaningful glare into the camera before going back to the page. " 'No treatment is currently available.' "

Stanton tossed down the newspaper with palpable disdain. "I know those of you who are sittin' in your comfortable homes want to ignore somethin' like that. Maybe you read your newspaper today and fear gripped your heart. But in the end, what did you do? You put down the newspaper and you said, 'It's happenin' far away. It won't happen here. It won't happen to me.'

"Well, pick it back up right this minute and read it *again*! That virus has *already* been slipped into this country like so much illegal cocaine! This is *God's* plague, and his will is far greater than we can comprehend! He chose as his carrier a rock and roll singer! His blade will fall first on those who commit the sin of licentiousness, of writhin' and dancin' and druggin' out to *rock and roll*!"

That "blade" part was quite a good, meaningful pun. He hoped at least a few of the pea-brains out there would get it.

"Sin and ye shall be judged! Perhaps you went to one of those concerts, or perhaps you, through the sin of permissiveness, will contract it through a son or daughter you allowed to go and be a part of such filth! Or perhaps a neighbor's sin will be visited on *your* house merely by a friendly conversation over the fence. You who live *among* sin shall also be judged!"

Stanton paused. He didn't have much choice. Behind him the crowd was raising its tongues in communal shouts of ecstasy. *Jesus have mercy on us! Lord God, please take us* now, *take us soon! I'm ready, I'm ready, sweet Jesus, come now! Destroy the wicked, wipe the Earth clean, Jesus I pray thy will be done! We joyously greet thy kingdom! Thy will be done, thy will be done, thy will be done.*

Thy will be done. It was coming to his ears more and more of late. He'd said it some days ago, in a sermon, when he'd painted a picture of the reign of the Antichrist and Amen. He'd accented his points of horror with *thy will be done*, and it had been an unqualified 7-pointer carry-and-kick kind of a sermon. Now his people on the mount—as he thought of them—had picked the phrase up like some kind of fight song. Destroy the wicked and *thy will be done*; torment eternally all those who won't accept your Son and *thy will be done*; consign to eternal flames the abortion doctors and homosexuals and *thy will be done*.

As for us, God, we on this mountain are doing exactly what you asked, so don't hurt us or let us suffer. Rapture us soon and thy will be done.

"And now that it's *in* the United States of America, that land that *used* to belong to God but now has fallen as Sodom and Gomorrah fell, now that it's *in* the bodies of her citizens, how long do you think it will be before it's in *our* river systems? The Mississippi, perhaps? Or the Colorado? The Ohio River? The Columbia? Or perhaps it'll be coughed up by some teenage rock 'n' roller and spit out into your local water supply. Does chlorine kill it? I ask you this, ye sons and daughters of the Most High, *can chlorine kill the wrath of God?*"

Thy will be done, thy will be done!

"But I want to rename this virus, this *plague* tonight. It's not *Santarém*, it has another name, one chosen by God, and by its fruits shall ye know it! It's described in Revelation 8, verses 10 through 11.

" 'And the third angel sounded, and there fell a great star from heaven, burning as it were a lamp, and it fell upon the third part of the rivers, and upon the fountains of water; And the name of the star is called *Wormwood*: and the third part of the waters became *Wormwood*; and many men died of the waters, because they were made bitter.'

"Oh, ye prodigal sons and daughters! That virus didn't simply appear from the rain forest! *God* cast it into the Amazon, at the head of that great river! And the name of that virus is *Wormwood*! And the waters it infests are *bitter indeed*!"

Thy will be done!

"I prophesize before you here and now that *millions* will die of this plague. God has told you where to be in these, the last days. If you refuse, if you insist on ignorin' his signs, you will surely perish! Your immortal soul will burn in hell forever!"

He had to shout over the audience now, which was rumbling en masse over and over, *will . . . thy . . . done,* like some horrible train a-comin' down the track.

"The Rapture is approachin'! You may or may not have time to reach us before it comes, but if you don't leave your homes, *leave now,* you will surely crawl up this mountain one day soon, crawl up on your diseased hands and knees, beggin' God not to be too late, and you'll *find us already gone!*"

He looked at the camera for a good sixty seconds while his people rumbled like a moving mountain behind him. His eyes were filled with the fire of the Holy Spirit. He sent that fire out onto the airwaves, sent it out with all the force of his mind. Then he slammed his Bible shut.

"Thy will be done."

CHAPTER 14

As it turned out, Reverend Raymond Stanton was wrong. The virus did not have the potential to kill millions of people. He was, in fact, off by a good decimal point, perhaps even two, perhaps even three.

Dr. Michael Smith, who had heard about Stanton's riveting performance on the U.S. airwaves the previous evening, was thinking about this. He was thinking that he could have told Stanton a thing or two about decimal points. He sat staring at the map in their new double-wide trailer cum control room; staring and thinking, wondering what it felt like to be a doctor in London when the Black Death swept through in 1349. How many had been killed then? A *third* of the population? *Half*?

However bad it might have been, he didn't believe it was as bad as this. There had *never* been anything as bad as this.

Mike had given up going into the hospital, even though it was not twenty feet from the trailer door. What was the point? It was the same story, played out again and again. Death, and it was always the same, no reassigning of cast members for the afternoon matinee. Plus the CDC was here now, and USAMRIID, and he'd let those doctors have their fun, coming in full of enthusiasm to "get things under control." He'd let them wallow in the blood and brains in there until they finally realized that control would never be theirs, until they crashed as he'd crashed into complete and utter hopelessness.

No, Dr. Michael A. Smith had seen enough of the inside of that hospital. And so he sat in the command post like some frozen vegetable, watching those around him fielding calls and taking notes and speaking in urgent voices and going over to a huge map on the wall and putting up or swapping out little pins with flags on them.

It was a global map. Green flags marked towns with one to twenty cases reported, yellow for twenty to one hundred cases, blue for one hundred to one thousand cases, and red for over one thousand. In addition to these familiar hues, a brand-spanking-new color had been commandeered yesterday in honor of their new friend the Santarém virus. It was pink—cheery pink flags marked those towns and cities with over ten thousand cases reported.

Mike gazed at the map with a face so stark it might have been smoothed by God's own finger. His uncomprehending eyes were fixed on the familiar outlines of the United States.

L.A. was pink. Concertgoers in stage two of the disease had begun showing up there as many as three days earlier, followed swiftly by their immediate families. Most of this first wave was already dead. Around L.A., like the rings of a bomb blast, clustered red flags, then blue, and farther out in places like Bakersfield and San Diego, yellow and green were littered like so much falling detritus.

Seattle and New York were pink, New York having joined the Big Boys about an hour ago. Portland, Boston, Philadelphia, and Atlanta were red. Blue stood at attention over Hartford, Albany, Concord, Vancouver, Spokane, Birmingham, and Charlotte. Green and yellow dotted areas as far away as upstate Vermont, Pittsburgh, and Washington, D.C., in the north; Florida, Tennessee, and North Carolina in the south; Idaho and southern Oregon in the northwest.

Did you hear about the Blade concert, man? He's only gonna be in New York. Let's drive out there and par-tee, you cool?

And in both apple-pie and mill-closed-desperate small towns, family doctors were dialing the CDC helpline number and saying, in shaky voices, *Uh, I believe I might have a case here? That is, this young man says he was at the Blade concert and, well, he's had this cold and his fever is 102 and he's hurtin' awful bad, and I, uh, was wondering . . .*

Mike could hear them now. *He's awfully scared and his folks're awfully scared and I'm awfully scared and my nurse just took off and what exactly am I supposed to do? Is a surgical mask and rubber gloves enough, 'cause that's all I have. Should I shut down my office? Should I fumigate? Should I take some vitamins? Give myself an injection of quinine? Make up my will? The hospital in town says they don't have Level Four facilities and they won't take him and what do I do now?*

Mike had been wrong about the contagion level at the concerts. Dead wrong. Far more than Stanton, he had underestimated the wrath of God. Several airplane crews and hotel staffs were in quarantine, pilots and stewardesses who had transported Blade and his band, maids who had stripped their sheets. Most were sick and, yes, he'd expected that. They'd hunted them down like rabies-infested dogs and they'd found them, were now in the process of finding those they'd touched. But the concertgoers were ringing in by the hundreds, by the thousands, by the tens of thousands, and he'd been so very, very wrong about that.

My God, he thought, *what is this thing that it can pass from a band onstage to thousands in a stadium in a couple of hours?*

And that was, as much as anything, the reason why he sat now and stared at the map like a frozen ear of corn. Because the virus was not contained, and, though most of his fellow virologists hadn't admitted it yet, it was highly unlikely that they *could* contain it. The hospitals and doctors were ill-equipped and fumbling. And with the concert infection rate so high, what did that bode for all of the people the concertgoers had been in contact with since? L.A. had it—*my God*, that concert was only one day after Blade had been exposed to the monkey. *One day!* Which meant that all the people at the concerts—those represented by the pink flags and the red—were *also* contagious on day one, and they'd gone back home and into their first week of school or back to their college dorms or their high-rise offices or family reunion end-of-summer picnics and then . . .

God. Mike was thinking about a simulator USAMRIID had developed called L5VS: Level Five Virus Simulator. It was created as a scare tactic to get funding for antibiological warfare research. But WHO had let their trainees play with it, perhaps to light a fire under *their* tails as well. L5VS was a hack job and had a simplistic kind of logic. A Level Five was a hypothetical agent that was one-hundred-percent lethal, airborne, highly communicable, and had a broad initial dissemination, most likely via bombs or other terrorist tactics. A contaminated patient passed on a Level Five agent to four new people a day. Like any exponential curve, the numbers of infected quickly escalated until all life on the planet expired. If one checked the little boxes in

L5VS to assume frequent air travel and a late effort at quarantine, the simulator had spread the disease to every man, woman, and child on Earth within twenty days.

But L5VS was only a simple C program and was, for any number of reasons—regional boundaries and other geographic barriers not the least of them—highly unrealistic. Or so Mike had always assumed.

"Mike?"

It was a tentative greeting. Mike turned stiffly, still doing his frigid organic matter imitation, to see Josh standing behind him. Josh's hands and pencil-thin forearms were bright red from a recent bleach scrubbing; he had clipped his Afro down to a patchy stubble in some fit of hysteria after trying one too many times to comb out the disinfectant. He looked like a concentration camp victim. Mike might have felt sorry for him, but at the moment he was too full up with feeling sorry for himself.

"We got word from Stanley. They're pulling command out of South America. They're moving it to D.C. and us with it, if we want. I already told Stanley I'd go. Said you probably would, too."

"Yes," said Mike. Going home sounded like a very good idea.

"They're putting together a really big joint task force on containment, probably at the CDC headquarters. We can be on it, of course."

"Of course."

"And they're gonna leave some teams here, you know. To try to get it under control."

"They won't."

The words were made more lethally blunt by the emotionally bankrupt tone in which they had been uttered. Josh just looked at Mike and then looked away, with eyes that were more than a little . . . *loose*, like a sheet flapping in the breeze.

"We can still stop it in America, though." There was a hint of defiance in Josh's voice.

Mike didn't bother to educate him. "When do we leave?"

"Four o'clock. Military transport straight to D.C."

And then Josh must have noticed something, for he walked toward the map in a tired but measured step. For some reason it reminded Mike of those documentaries where they always reenacted some near-death patient walking toward the light. But Josh wasn't walking toward the light, he was walking toward death, or

the flags that represented it, anyway. It had been several hours
since Josh had been in the command post and the map had
changed considerably. Mike heard Josh ask somebody what the
pink flags meant. The somebody told him.

Josh stood and looked at the map for a long moment. While he
stood there, people brushed past him, crossing from the phones
to the map and back again. Three yellows went blue. Green hit
Denver and Tulsa. Vacationers? Two yellows went up in Ohio.
San Diego went red.

When Josh came back, his eyes had *loosened* a little more. He
leaned down close to Mike and whispered in his ear. *"Jesus,
God, Mike: I'm so scared."*

Mike said nothing. What was there to say?

"You said . . . I thought the concert audience wouldn't . . ."

"They shouldn't have. None of it makes any sense." Mike
didn't want to talk about it.

"But a lot of them got it, right? In the audience? A *lot*? Even in
L.A.?"

"Yes, Josh. A lot of them got it. Even in L.A."

Josh sank down into a chair. He kept leaning toward Mike like
the freaking Tower of Pisa; his head was intruding in Mike's
space. Mike wished the cue ball would just *go away*.

"But *how*? I mean, even if he was coughing and hacking—
which he wouldn't have been in L.A. and Seattle for sure—how
could the virus have gotten to so many who were seated so far
away? And without coughing . . . I mean, *how*?"

"Josh, I have no fucking *idea* how!"

Josh blinked. His old pal Mikey had used the f-word. He
licked his nonexistent lips nervously and stared at Mike in mute
disappointment as if to say, *I once idolized you, now you're sitting there being pissy.*

And it was then, hearing it from Josh and seeing the look on
his face, that something sparked again inside Michael Smith. He
felt his original certainty stick its head back up like something
rising from the grave. *He's right.* I *was right. It's* not *possible.*

Mike stared at the map with eyes cleared of self-pity. What
they were seeing was the barest tip of the iceberg, but even so,
the numbers were huge. The L.A. concert had been eleven days
ago; Seattle, ten days; New York, nine days; Atlanta, eight days
ago. So all those flags had to represent concertgoers and their
immediate family and friends.

Which meant that the infection rate at the concerts was *astronomical*—at least a quarter of the average forty-thousand-member audience. But in halls that large even if the band's every breath were red hot, it still couldn't possibly spread out in that kind of volume . . . It was . . . it was almost as if . . .

The idea came from nowhere and with it a memory that had been buried under a stinking heap of despair. Mike stood up with a jerk. The chair he'd been sitting in crashed to the floor behind.

"Mike? What is it?"

"I have to get back to Munich. I have to get there *now*."

NEW YORK CITY

to: ralph.bowmont@nytimes.com
from: guest01@cyberjava.nyu.net
Ralph: Hi, it's me, Simon. I've stumbled onto a really huge angle on the Santa Pelagia story. It looks like the whole thing is a setup. I've got videotape of a woman named Dr. Janovich (CEO of H.A.I.) at a conference in 1990. She gave a lecture there about, like, inducing fantasies? It even demonstrates exactly how the Twenty-Four could have been implanted with dreams and visions. We also have evidence that many of the prophets had contact with H.A.I. before they dreamed of S.P.

There's more. Janovich worked for Telegyn for years before H.A.I. Telegyn has the biochemical know-how (Tendir) and the facilities (all the Earthweb huts and buoys—check out their Web page) to have both made and spread the toxic spores and the red tide. Ask Susan about the areas that didn't get the sores at all—they correspond with where the Earthweb network huts aren't working yet (again, see Web).

Also, Father Deauchez was being hunted in London by two guys with guns. The doc's house where we got the video last night was blown up as soon as we left—it was that Ernkin story. We think it's 'cause I used Deauchez's TELEGYN cellular from there to call in.

Anyway, I'm going on with this thing, right? As you would say: Yee-Haw. If anyone asks, say I've been missing since last night. A dead man tells no secrets, know what I mean? Also, the Father thinks we should make sure the FBI is on this, so will you get in touch with your contact there and pass on this info? I know it sounds strange, but the links are there. Obviously,

you can't get in touch with me, but as soon as I have a bit more evidence, I'll send in the first story. Hold the spotlight for me.
　　—Hill

Bowmont picked up the phone and dialed a direct line to a man named Ted Peterson. It was a number not many people had. It did not go through the FBI switchboard. Peterson answered the phone and Bowmont made himself known.

"What's up, Ralph? I see your team's been doing some A-number-one reporting lately. Been reading you myself every day."

"Thanks, Ted. Say, have your boys been pokin' around the Santa Pelagia story a'tall?"

There was a pause.

"Well, we've been keeping an eye on it. The way I see it, our biggest concern is the four prophets we've got right here in the U.S. of A. The others are out of our jurisdiction."

"I can see that."

"We've been watching them, making sure they stay nice and peaceful. No problems so far."

"What about the toxic spores? Have y'all popped the lid off that kettle?"

Another pause.

"Why, not really, Ralph. It seemed to be pretty much a global occurrence, and the State Department ruled out any possibility that it was some kind of bioweapon from overseas. Truth is, the scientists say it's entirely natural."

"Yup, that's what we reported."

"Is there something you want to tell me, Ralph?"

"I think there is, Ted." Ralph hesitated, but only for a moment. "I have a reporter named Simon Hill who believes he's onto some sort of conspiracy thing. He disappeared two nights ago, but I just got an e-mail from him on the subject. Seems he's gone to ground. He's got a damn fine nose, Ted. If he's caught a whiff a somethin', you can bet he'll dig it up."

Pause.

"Does anyone else know about this?"

"Not that I know of. I think this here e-mail should come to you straightaway."

"Forward it on right now, if you will."

"Sure thing."

"And if you hear any more from Mr. Hill . . ."

"You'll be the first to know. I'm a bit worried about him, Ted, to be perfectly frank. He was lookin' poorly last time I saw him."

There was another pause.

"Well, we'll keep our eyes out for him. Unfortunately, I don't have a lot of men to spare. We've had a rash of absentees ourselves just lately."

Ralph grunted. "We all do what we can and what we must, as my father used to say. I wish ya luck, Ted."

"You, too, Ralph. You, too."

WASHINGTON, D.C.

The blue hatchback was parked hard up against the curb, sandwiched between a red plumbing truck and a motorcycle. The man inside it was trying to look innocuous. He was not doing a bang-up job of it, between his anxious straining to watch the building across the street and his nervous flinching at every passerby.

The building across the street was H.A.I. headquarters and Simon Hill was inside. They'd borrowed a car—among other things—from a friend of Hill's and had decided H.A.I. was the next step. They'd had three choices really: H.A.I. and Janovich, Telegyn headquarters in Baltimore, or Cole at the State Department. Janovich, perhaps chauvinistically so, had been the least intimidating.

And the easier the better, because time was running out. As they were driving through New Jersey this morning they heard a radio story about the sequestering of the papal conclave. The entire car had suddenly disappeared from around Deauchez, leaving him floating in some state of intense introspection and conflict. What was he doing here in America? Why was he not in Rome? He should be speaking to the College. What if they chose the wrong pope, assuming that Santa Pelagia was divine when it was not? And if that happened, what would that new pope do? Send all the Catholics to London?

And then he'd had something like an embolism strike him, only it wasn't of blood, it was of words. *No, that's not what he'll tell them. Not London, that's not what he'll tell them!*

"No!" He'd spoken it out loud as if in protest against his very thoughts.

"What?" Hill, who was driving at the time, turned, fear on his

face. He looked around as though he expected to see the third
horseman itself clopping along behind the car.

But there was nothing, only the priest.

The driver's side door rattled and Deauchez jumped. It was Hill,
climbing back into the car.

"Did you find her office? Was she there?" the priest asked.

"Yeah. I saw her for a moment when her secretary opened the
door. She was on the phone." Hill sounded as skittish as Deauchez felt.

"She didn't see you?"

"Nope. But here's the bad news. There's not a chance in hell
we're gonna be able to break in after dark. Not without expertise
and equipment we don't have."

"Security men?"

"No doubt, but I'm more worried about the locks. There's a
lock on the elevators and stairwell doors. You probably need a
key to use 'em after hours. And up on the tenth, there's only one
entrance into H.A.I. It's got a major lock, and the individual offices have locks. I might be able to fumble my way into a house,
but not this, man, no way. We'd need TNT or something."

Deauchez squeezed his eyes shut. He prayed. *Please, God,
help us figure something out.*

In the pre–Santa Pelagia days, Deauchez hadn't been the sort
to pray for help. His view of God wasn't one where God was inside every mind, intimately manipulative in every life. Deauchez
believed in patterns. He believed in a universe that had rules and
laws—rules and laws as in, if you stand in front of a truck you'll
get run over. If there *were* miracles, they came from some subconscious part of ourselves, parts the Creator had given us just
as he'd given us the intelligence to invent trucks, and the kind of
bodies that could be smashed by them. Despite all that, Deauchez had found it a relief to ask for guidance just lately. Perhaps
it was because for the first time he felt truly small and powerless.

"And, to add one final twist of the ol' knife," Hill was muttering, "there are cameras all over the damn place."

"That's very disappointing," Deauchez said. If they couldn't
break into H.A.I., they couldn't get the data they'd hoped to find
in the H.A.I. files: something, anything more concrete than the
green-hut link and Janovich's fifteen-year-old lecture. Simon
needed it to soothe the *Times* lawyers. Deauchez needed it for

the Cardinal College. If he didn't have his ducks irrefutably in a row, Donnelley would have him locked up in a sanitarium.

"So—what might plan B consist of ?" Deauchez asked.

"Father, I have no frigging clue."

Even so, Deauchez sensed that the reporter *did* have an idea, and that he wasn't going to care for it one little bit.

THE WHITE HOUSE

The men and women seated around the table at the cabinet meeting looked like a very different group from those who had battled out the rationing plan nearly one week ago. *That* group had been worried and frantic and tight-lipped with grim concern, but their professional buff had been in place, from their lacquered hair and starched white collars to their see-your-face-in-'em polished shoes. *This* group was, well, beat to shit.

Most of them, Cole noted, had the blotched red noses, swollen, bleary eyes, and Elmer Fudd voices that indicated head colds which had, by their own accounts, "just come up out of nowhere." They were, more important, in the process of losing their D.C. polish to a darker, more pervasive sheen—that of desperation.

Secretary of Health and Human Services Liz Haron, for example, was apparently finding it difficult just lately to think of a good reason to put on makeup in the mornings. Her face had a surprised, eyebrowless look without her pencil liner. And Secretary of Commerce Arnold had found it not worth the effort to get his tie properly tied this morning, nor to fix himself the high-energy muesli that he'd recommended so highly to Cole in better days. From the look of his lapel, he had instead consumed a bowl of his son's Choc-o-Bit cereal and, further, had not considered it worth more than a halfhearted swipe when he'd dribbled some of it onto his jacket—and certainly not worth the effort of actually going upstairs and putting on a different suit.

The rest of the ensemble around the table had also taken hesitant steps down that spiral staircase, particularly Fielding, who was halfway to the bottom and had been for some days now. All of them, that was, save Anthony Cole. He looked impeccable, of course, like he'd just walked off a men's fashion shoot. But when he'd looked in the mirror this morning he had seen *something*, a hint of darkness under his eyes, the kind of dusky smudge a woman's eyeliner left behind.

Yes, even Anthony Cole had his demons.

"I think this Santarém virus is our biggest concern at the moment," someone was saying.

". . . rioting in L.A. and El Paso. Illegal immigrants are banding together in guerilla groups and raiding stores for food. We *have* to send out the National Guard, Mr. President. We can't afford to lose even a single loaf of bread to noncitizens. Isn't that right, Dr. Purvue?"

". . . stock market is going to hell. The crash of the food sector and all this end-of-the-world bullshit in the news has affected investor confidence about everything. There *is* no investor confidence. People are pulling their money out left and right. I'm afraid we're looking at another 1929."

"Do you think . . . perhaps we have the responsibility to at least *consider* . . . Polls show that a not-insubstantial number of our constituency is convinced that the Santa Pelagia message is *true*. Mr. President, if you don't respond to this . . ."

"India's government announced their support of Santa Pelagia today."

". . . new Cardinal College is sequestered and I hear that Santa Pelagia and how to handle it is their primary consideration in their choice of a new . . ."

"Our sources say that Palestine and Lebanon have already sworn allegiance to that Mal Abbas asshole."

The swelter of business continued to spew forth in chaotic non sequiturs. Everyone seemed to be having their own conversation with no one, although occasionally someone would say something angering enough to get a verbal slap back, something on the order of, *Screw you, Tom*. Oddly enough, no one seemed to realize this was not the normal mode of business, nor seemed inclined at all to stop.

Fielding, like Cole, sat and watched the rest of them as though he were sitting at a bench in the zoo. He was nursing a cup of hot tea with lemon, and he had a box of Kleenex with the presidential seal on it perched inches from his hand.

"Hold on a minute," he said at last. His voice, castrated by the cold, barely croaked out. It was ignored. He picked up a large binder that was on the table and slammed it down again, creating a loud *boom*.

"Shut up!" he croaked, as all heads turned to look at him. "Can we have some fucking order here, or is that too much to ask?" It was odd, but with his voice gone, he was like a lion without teeth or claws. It really was painfully tempting to ignore him.

Through supreme effort of will, no one did.

"You number types figure out what to do about the economy," he rasped to Mr. Arnold. "Lower the interest rate, print more money, whatever the hell you want. Just give me a report, and if it's not complete lunacy I'll sign it."

Arnold looked resentful, like a man left alone to save a sinking ship, but he gave a sharp nod.

"As for the riots, General Brant, send in the goddamn National Guard if you want, but only to those areas *having* riots. We can't afford to use them as fucking prophylactics. We may need them elsewhere.

"And I don't care what India or any other government is doing. Hell, I don't care if Prime Minister Billingsworth starts to levitate on the BBC; this government is not announcing any goddamn support of any goddamn inanity like this apocalypse nonsense."

"But the *signs* . . ." interrupted Mr. Grover. The secretary of transportation was from Alabama, and he was a religious man.

"Goddamn coincidence! I'm worried about two things, and two things only: this blasted virus outbreak and what China and this Mal Abbas joker are up to. Liz, I want WHO and CDC and US-AMRIID and anybody else who thinks they can get a handle on this thing to get whatever they need, do you hear? If they need more manpower, we'll consider using the National Guard for that. Round up people, quarantine, whatever. Let's be brutal. If we have to cordon off whole cities to get this thing under wraps then goddamn it, let's do it. We can't be weak now."

"Yes, Mr. President." Liz Haron turned pale, but she didn't argue.

"Now what's the situation overseas? Cole?"

Cole's slight, I-know-this-is-serious-but-it-doesn't-hurt-to-be-pleasant smile was bestowed upon each person in turn as he looked around the table. "Mr. President, China is on the move. Our satellites have been picking up convoys leaving Beijing and Shanghai for days. And they've implemented a very effective recruiting campaign. Any able-bodied citizen who enlists will get one food coupon, which they can pass on to parents, wives, or children. Anyone who's not enlisted, and doesn't have a coupon, will not be able to buy food in China."

There was a general intake of breath in the room.

"Early indications are that the Chinese people are accepting these conditions. The recruiting stations have been swamped, and there have been a rash of suicides among the elderly who either don't have a child, or who have a young grandchild who needs the coupon to eat. Of course, the limits on offspring of the past few decades have made this even more of a crisis for most families."

"Savages!" Liz Haron muttered.

Cole looked at her balefully. "That is how the food situation is in China, Ms. Haron. I know we've all seen the numbers. This isn't really that surprising."

"So how will they feed the troops?" General Brant asked.

"Yeah," croaked Fielding, his face hopeful. "How *can* they feed the troops?"

Cole gave Fielding a knowing look. "They can't and won't—not for long. Which is why I don't think they'll spend much time in training. They've got to get those troops off Chinese soil."

"On Chinese soil or not, they'll still have to *feed* them," Brant insisted, as if Cole were being stupid.

Cole raised one eyebrow at him. *Do they?* the look said. *Now who's being stupid?* "Tsing Mao Wen gave a speech to the troops in Beijing a few days ago. He told them they're embarking on a holy war and that their best ticket to the 'glorious new balance of the Universe' is to commit themselves to the fight. I think we can anticipate a kamikaze mentality from the government. They won't begrudge casualties."

Fielding's eyes were frightened behind their watery puffiness. "Who's with them?"

"India appears to be undecided. Mal Abbas has had several phone conversations with Tsing Mao Wen. We don't know what they said to one another, but it's pretty clear they're joining forces. So far we have solid confirmation that Pakistan, Afghanistan, Iran, and Saudi Arabia are going to sign on with Abbas, if they haven't already."

"What about Africa?"

"Like China, their people will have the choice to stay and starve, or fight for food. But the main problem there will be getting any of their men off the continent. Most of the African countries are pitifully stocked when it comes to naval or air transport.

Honestly, I don't think Africa adds much to the threat to us. They might make trouble for Europe."

"The Russians?"

Cole steepled his fingers. "President Yekov has spoken with Lee several times in the past few days. My guess is, they'll try to stay on China's good side without actually joining ranks."

Fielding paused to consider this a moment, then he gave a weird grin. "Say! Maybe we should send China and the Arabs some of our Santarém patients! *Heh, heh.* Say a prostitute or two? With a bit of luck, they won't have a food problem anymore. *Heh, heh.*"

Fielding looked around to see if anyone else was laughing. Ms. Haron's uncarmined lips tightened with distaste. General Brant grunted halfheartedly. Arnold was busy flicking dried milk off his lapel. Dr. Purvue and the V.P. just looked back at Fielding blankly.

Cole leaned forward. "Mr. President, I know you didn't mean that, but I think we should take a few moments to consider the facts. South America is completely infested. The virus is here, in the U.S., and it's been leaked to Europe, our allies. We would be wise to consider the unfortunate possibility that this virus may do a great deal of damage. Isn't that right, Ms. Secretary?"

"*Absolutely,* Mr. Secretary," Liz Haron said.

"Now if we and our allies are forced to commit resources to fighting this virus, containing it, it will at least cost us the National Guard. And if it's already infected our servicemen, it will impact the strength of our main fighting force. So if *we and our allies* are compromised in our ability to wage war, it might be wise to make sure that *our enemies* are compromised, also."

Every face around the table stared at Cole with sheer incredulity. *You cold, cold son of a bitch,* Liz Haron's expression in particular seemed to be saying. But she didn't say it. No one, not even Fielding, uttered one single, solitary word of protest.

EDGEWATER, MARYLAND

They drove through a seaside housing development, the kind of development that featured modern American monstrosities for the nouveau riche. The house they were looking for was designed like a Georgian in front, but the rear was all modern glass to take in the sea. It wore its exorbitant size as ungracefully as a large woman in a miniskirt, looking both extravagant and tawdry at the same time.

The woman who answered the door suited the house, as some owners suit their dogs. She was plump and middle-aged in her ribbed cotton sweats. She stared blankly at the two men on her porch, then glanced up, face puzzled, at the nonfunctional porch light. But realization had set in, even before the glance up. Her eyes hardly registered the broken bulb above, and by the time she looked back down her face was afraid—afraid and astonished, bushwhacked by the unlikely, like meeting one's maiden aunt from Toledo at a Hollywood coke party. She apparently knew very well who they were.

"Dr. Janovich, I presume," said Simon Hill. He aimed a gun at her chest, and she backed inside, not even trying to shut the door. Hill stepped in time with her as evenly as a dance partner. The priest followed and shut the door.

Inside, Hill checked the blinds; they were already closed. Janovich sat on the couch with Deauchez. When Hill joined them, they were studying each other like long-lost cousins or something, but ones with a grudge. Their faces held a kind of mutual fascination and loathing.

"What do you want?" Janovich asked Deauchez.

"To hear what you did to the Santa Pelagia prophets."

"I don't know what you mean."

"You visited Maria Sanchez before the visions began. I heard her speak your name."

"You're mistaken. I never met her."

"Are you telling me there's another Dr. Janovich?"

"I have no idea."

Janovich turned to stare blandly ahead, as if she'd gotten bored with the whole thing. But she was tense, hands stiff in her lap. Deauchez was getting flushed. Hill could see that her denials were angering him.

"Father," Hill said, pointing to a large stack of national and international newspapers on the table, all current editions. "Quite the newshound, aren't ya, Louise?"

Janovich pursed her lips contemptuously. Hill thought she looked much older in person than she had on the video, older than could be accounted for by the passage of time. She looked fifty at least, and the doughy shape under the loose sweats wasn't exactly threatening. Still, the priest seemed to think she was some kind of monster—maybe he was right. The guy had instincts like a dog had fleas, as Bowmont used to say.

"Come on, Louise," Hill said, "we *know* who you are."

"And I know who *you* are, Simon Hill." She turned to spear him with her eyes. "Does the *New York Times* approve of your tactics? Forced entry? Threatening with a deadly weapon? Is that how you get all your stories? If I'd known, I never would have read you."

"A fan! Wow, I'm flattered! Do you know all the reporters so well?"

Janovich looked annoyed and turned her eyes back to the wall. She crossed her arms defiantly.

"We should keep to the plan, Simon." Deauchez sounded nervous, like a twelve-year-old boy at his first graffiti vandalism. "We saw a video of your lecture in Geneva in 1990, Dr. Janovich. We know about the drug you invented and we know that H.A.I. had contact with the prophets before their visions. You implanted the Santa Pelagia visions. We want to know why."

"I had nothing to do with Santa Pelagia." Her eyes belied the control of her words. They darted around the room as though searching for a panic button. They rested lightly on the phone.

"Who asked you to do it? And why?"

Janovich's face was a blank mask.

Deauchez grew more flushed. His voice was getting louder, forced. "Did you know what they were planning? The damage to the food supply? The red tide? What reason did they give to you for so many deaths?"

Janovich turned on him savagely. "What is the *matter* with you! You're a priest! Don't you believe in your own faith? What's wrong with your mind?"

Deauchez drew back on the sofa as though he'd been slapped.

Hill coughed nervously. This was going nowhere, he thought, and if it wasn't going nowhere it was going someplace really funky.

"We should check the house," he said to Deauchez. "Maybe she has a home office, files, something."

Janovich looked straight ahead again, but her jaw clenched and Hill saw it.

"Yeah, come on," he urged. "There's gotta be something

around here. You wanna go look, or you wanna stay here with the gun?"

"I'll go." Deauchez got up quickly, as if afraid Hill might force the gun on him after all. He looked at Janovich again with a puzzled expression, then took off down the hall.

Janovich continued to stare at the wall, lips pursed tightly. It was A-OK with Hill if she didn't want to talk. Now that the first rush of the armed entry was over, Hill was starting to remember how crappy he felt. He moved his gun to his left hand so he could fish a Kleenex from a pocket. He wiped his nose.

"How long have you had that cold, Mr. Hill?" There was a sadistic lilt in Janovich's voice.

Now it was Hill's turn to flush. "Um . . . Deauchez?" he called out in a quavering voice. "See anything?"

"*Oui.* There's an office downstairs."

Hill motioned the gun at Janovich. "Okay, Doc. Let's go."

Hill led Janovich down the hall, the nozzle of the gun against the folds of skin at her back. There was something on her face, something calculated and quietly seething, that he didn't like at all.

The office downstairs was a large room with a cherry desk and bookcases lining the wall. There was even a fireplace, with tools and logs sitting next to it like props—it looked to Hill as though it had never been used. The house was on a grade and the room, though on the lower floor, opened onto the back lawn. French doors overlooked the sea. Hill could hear its rhythm, even though he couldn't see it in the dark.

And there was a computer and filing cabinets. Deauchez was already going through the filing cabinets when Hill and Janovich reached the bottom of the stairs.

"Only personal documents so far," he reported. "Taxes, receipts, copies of articles she published."

"Have you looked around for any wall safes? Stuff like that?"

"No."

Deauchez left the filing cabinet and checked the bookshelves, walls, closet. "I don't see anything, Simon."

But Hill knew there was something here. He could tell by the set of Janovich's jaw upstairs, the way she'd flinched when Deauchez had called out about the office. He glared at the frumpy psychiatrist and pointed the gun more meaningfully at her face.

"There's nothing here," she said. But her mouth was twitching in a nasal arc, like an Elvis impersonator. Her eyes were refusing to look at something.

"Deauchez, turn on the computer," Hill said.

Deauchez turned it on.

"There's nothing on the computer but personal data. I don't bring anything from H.A.I. home with me." Janovich's tone was an attempt at weary impatience. She would never win an Oscar.

Deauchez was poking around program groups and document directories with nervous speed, but he didn't appear to be finding anything.

"Have you been following your own paper, Mr. Hill?"

"What about it, Louise?"

"Read about the virus, have you?" Her voice was grating, low, hideous.

Hill was starting to sweat. He wiped at his brow quickly with his gun hand.

"Simon?" Deauchez sounded excited.

Hill looked over at the computer. On the screen was a white box that said "CONNECTING TO UPLINK." A wait cursor blinked green below it.

"What's that, a Web browser?"

"I don't think so. I clicked on an icon that looked like a red knife. It was under a program group called 'Personal.' "

"I don't hear dialing. Check for a phone line." Hill bent down himself to take a quick look under the desk.

It was a bad mistake. The pudgy placidity of the woman beside him came to a violent and sudden end. Janovich struck Hill hard on the back of his neck with two laced hands.

"Aahh!" His warning to Deauchez came out as an expelled breath. He went down on one knee. The gun wobbled in his hand. Janovich could have grabbed it then, but she ignored it, launching herself forward instead, literally flying past him.

Hill stumbled to his feet and saw that she had launched herself past Deauchez, too, or rather on top of him. The priest recoiled, startled at the flesh torpedo, then grabbed lamely at her thick hips. But Janovich wasn't trying to *go* anywhere, unless it was into the plate-glass window beyond. She was just lying across the desk. Before either of the men could react further, there was a *click* and a muffled *pop*. The smell of smoke, acrid and wiry, filled the air.

Hill reached for Janovich with one mightily pissed-off hand. The smell . . . Had she grabbed a gun? Had it gone off mistakenly? Deauchez must have had a similar idea, for he sprang up, his face ashen. But Janovich got off the desk willingly enough, if awkwardly. She had nothing in her hands. She didn't try to run or do anything at all for that matter. She had a secret, triumphant smile on her face.

Hill and Deauchez looked at the desk. There was smoke coming from the phone.

"What the . . ." Hill shoved the gun at Deauchez and sat down at the desk.

"What is it?" Deauchez asked.

"Ouch!" Hill jerked his hand back. "She blew up her freaking phone! It's, like, totally melted!"

"How is that . . ."

"Christ, Deauchez, it's a Telegyn cellular! It's got this base recharger thing, and there's a red button on the side, under a plastic shield. I think that's what did it. It blew the phone right the hell up." Hill was impressed; it was like something from an old Dick Tracy episode.

"That must have been the link," Deauchez said.

Hill glanced at the screen. Sure enough, the compliant message and the wait sign had disappeared. A new message replaced it: "UNABLE TO MAKE CONNECTION. NO UPLINK." Son of a bitch.

Hill stood up and took the gun. He waved it in Janovich's face and screamed, *"What did you just do?"*

Janovich's face warped under a wave of rage. She spat in Hill's face. "You're dead. You just don't know it yet."

Hill couldn't help himself. Sometime in the past twenty minutes he'd come to hate Janovich, hate her like the devil. He brought back his arm and struck her full force. The blow, mostly the side of the gun but also part of the hand that held it, landed against her right cheek. There was a horrible *crack* when they made contact. Janovich's head jerked back and it just kept going. She crumpled to the floor, unconscious.

Deauchez was afraid that the destruction of the cellular would have alerted the . . . well, those Bad Guys, the ones who had blown Ernkin's house to kingdom come. He wanted to leave—immediately. Hill utterly refused.

There's something on that computer. If there wasn't, she wouldn't have torched the damn phone.

They tied up Janovich, using extension cords they found in a Barnes & Noble shopping bag in the closet. They put her on the floor of the office where they could keep an eye on her should she regain consciousness. She never batted an eye.

The right half of her face was swelling up like a deep purple bubble blown from the side of her mouth. Deauchez wondered if she would die, if he was to be a cold-blooded murderer now in addition to being a manslaughterer—of Ernkin—an armed housebreaker, and AWOL from the Catholic priesthood.

Hill checked the back of the computer. He reported that the Telegyn recharger base was plugged into the modem B port. The Telegyn phone itself, being satellite linked, needed no wall connection. In the modem A port was another phone line, this one plugged into the jack in the wall.

They booted the Web. It worked successfully, letting them know, as it dialed, that it was accessing modem A. Hill checked the hotlists, saw nothing unusual. No inside link, for example, to the H.A.I. network. They logged off the Web.

"Well, the regular phone line's okay," Hill said. "Let's try plugging it into modem B and see if it'll work for that program you found."

He crawled behind the computer and swapped the phone cords. Deauchez brought up the Personal group window and double-clicked on the red knife. The hourglass appeared. Then: "UNABLE TO MAKE CONNECTION. INVALID COMLINK."

"It does not like the regular phone line."

"Crap!" Hill crawled out from under the desk.

Deauchez looked at the melted Telegyn phone. The thing had cooled a bit now. He took it out of the base, which looked relatively undamaged. The phone itself, though, was fried to a crisp. He hit the ON button, reluctantly, and got absolutely no response. He put it down.

"Damn it!" Hill sank down onto his haunches. He winced in pain, sighed the sigh of a martyr, and resettled his weight.

They both stared at the screen for a moment, at that irritating little icon.

"It has to mean *something*," Hill insisted. "She was practically hopping when you were poking around. What would a red knife mean? Something to do with surgery? Maybe it's the uplink to the H.A.I. network."

"It would probably be a caduceus, if it were H.A.I."

The red caduceus, like the one Deauchez had seen on the truck at Sagara Bata's encampment; the snake twining about the medical wand, symbol of medicine, symbol of Hermes . . . The red knife on the screen . . . Only it wasn't a knife exactly, not like a kitchen knife. This was more like a . . .

Deauchez leaned forward, squinted his eyes. "It's a red wand, not a red knife."

"Doesn't help me."

"Well . . . it *could* be H.A.I."

"Father, I have an idea."

Deauchez shut his eyes, aware of what was coming. Indeed, he'd been aware since the moment he'd picked up that fried cellular. "Simon, *please*."

"Father, we *have* to. Where is it?"

Deauchez turned angrily on the reporter. "Are you suicidal, Mr. Hill? Have you been watching too many Hollywood movies?"

But Hill was eager now. He had that hungry gleam in his eyes. "Look, we're not gonna get a damn thing more unless we can get an uplink to wherever that wand-thing goes. Am I right? Wasted mission, Houston, and all that?"

Deauchez waved a hand in concession. He felt the need to uncover something, anything, just as desperately as the reporter did.

"Right! So we'll just have to, like, time ourselves," Hill said. "We'll get on-line, poke around a bit, then take off. This isn't New York, it's Maryland. It took us an hour and a half to get here from D.C., Father. And I doubt they're any closer than that."

"And what if it does not work? What if it's on the wrong frequency or we need a code, or . . . ?"

"That's the easy part. If we don't get a link, we're out of here immediately. *Zoom*." Hill made a flying gesture with his hand and grinned. Deauchez was not amused.

He had never been so afraid in his entire life. He'd been *spooked* afraid, yes, more than anyone should ever have to be. But *this* kind of afraid, this sweating palms, wide-awake, light-of-day, afraid for your very physical life kind of afraid, never. What he wanted to say was, *You are right, Simon, it should be done, but* you *do it. I'll just wait down the street in some nice dark shadow. If you make it out alive pick me up on your way out of town.*

But he didn't have the guts to be that much of a coward. What he said instead was, "I'll go get the phone."

ACT 3: BLACK

A great change will come to pass, such as no mortal man will have expected. Heaven and Hell will confront each other in this struggle. Old states will perish and light and darkness will be pitted against each other with swords, but it will be swords of a different fashion. With these swords it will be possible to cut up the skies and to split the Earth. A great lament will come over all mankind and only a small batch will survive the tempest, the pestilence and the horror.
—PASTOR BARTHOLOMAEUS (1642)

The twentieth century will bring death and destruction, apostasy from the Church, discord in families, cities and governments; it will be the century of three great wars with intervals of a few decades. They will become ever more devastating and bloody and will lay in ruins not only Germany, but finally all countries of East and West.
—PROPHECY OF MARIA LAACH MONASTERY (SIXTEENTH CENTURY)

While in theory there is nothing which is absolutely inevitable, in actuality there are things which are almost inevitable. People believe that wars happen in the future, whereas in reality they happen in the past; the fighting is only a consequence of many events which have already occurred. Viewed from this perspective, all the causes of the Third World War have already happened. There is therefore only a very remote possibility that the conflict itself will not take place.   —OSHO (1982)

And after the second great struggle between the nations will come a third universal conflagration, which will determine everything. There will be entirely new weapons. In one day more men will die than in all previous wars combined. Battles will be fought with artificial guns. Gigantic catastrophes will occur. With open eyes will the nations of the Earth enter into these catastrophes. They shall not be aware of what is happening, and those who will know and tell, will be silenced. Everything will become different than before, and in many places the Earth will be a great cemetery. The third great war will be the end of many nations.

—*STORMBERGER (EIGHTEENTH CENTURY)*

The white men will battle against other peoples in other lands—with those who possessed the first light of wisdom. Terrible will be the result.

—*WHITE FEATHER OF THE HOPI BEAR CLAN, RECORDED BY REV. DAVID YOUNG (1958)*

Mabus will soon die, and then will come a horrible destruction of people and animals. —*NOSTRADAMUS C2 Q62*

CHAPTER 15

They settled Deauchez's cellular phone into the recharger base as though it were Cinderella's glass slipper. They looked at each other. Deauchez hit the ON button, then double-clicked on the red wand icon.

A box appeared: "CONNECTING TO UPLINK." The box told them to wait. They complied.

The screen went black. Then, a message appeared in a large red font.

PRIME ONE CHANNEL ESTABLISHED

Pause.

WELCOME, CARDINAL DONNELLEY

Deauchez, whose nerves were already on hyperalert, stared at the words with his heart suddenly in his throat and terror rich and steaming in his veins. For a moment there was the irrational fear that, somehow, he'd been pinpointed, found out, reported, trapped.

Then he realized—the computer wasn't *notifying* Donnelley. It was *addressing* him.

"What the heck is that?" Hill sounded disappointed.

"The network has identified us from the phone. They think I'm Cardinal Donnelley. The phone must be registered or tagged in some way."

"Registered? You don't have to register when you buy a phone. How do they know this one's Donnelley's?"

"Good question."

Good enough to make Deauchez feel very uneasy indeed. If the host system came up and it was the Vatican, then he would have to reconsider Hill's theory about the two thugs in London, have to consider the possibility that entire escapade *was* connected to the Church of Rome in some unfathomable . . .

But the words were disappearing now. They were replaced by a full-monitor image of an elaborate crest. The crest featured a king in old-fashioned knightly armor, seated on a throne. In one hand was a glowing red scepter. Deauchez realized now that the "red wand" icon had not been a wand at all, but a scepter. The king's feet rested upon a stone. Around the throne were various symbols: a skull and crossbones, blindfolded Justice, a globe with a kind of halo around it, a curtain or veil, a glinting sword. A Latin phrase was written across the top of the shield-shaped crest.

"What's it say?" Hill asked, pointing to the motto.

" *'Utrum deus sit necne, Sceptrum Rubrum.'* Whether or not God, the Red Scepter."

"Whether or not God, the red scepter *what*?"

"I think it's meant as a proper noun—the 'Red Scepter.' Whether or not God, the Red Scepter . . . *exists*, acts, reigns, governs, believes. The verb is implied."

"So it's some kinda group name?"

"Perhaps. I have never heard of it. Have you?"

"No."

They looked at each other then. It wasn't Telegyn. It wasn't H.A.I. It wasn't the Vatican. So what was it? Deauchez clicked the mouse button. The emblem screen dissolved and was replaced with an options menu.

THE RED SCEPTER
Utrum deus sit necne, Sceptrum Rubrum

CHARTER	WORLDWIDE COUNCIL
MEMBERSHIP ROSTER	ANNUAL SCHEDULE
ARCHIVES	CURRENT PROJECTS

"Man oh man," said Hill, no longer the least bit disappointed. "What *is* this, some kinda club? Secret society? Check out the charter."

But Deauchez hesitated. He could feel the time pressing on them, could feel its heft and its darkness, as though he were feeling the lid descend on his own coffin. "We don't have much time."

He had his own ideas about what was important, and he was the one wielding the mouse. He clicked on CURRENT PROJECTS.

"Okay," Hill agreed belatedly.

The Projects screen came up. And there, right at the top of the list, were two simple words:

PROJECT APOCALYPSE

"Holy shit!" Hill commented, chewing on his nails.

Deauchez took a calming breath and clicked on the title. The Project Apocalypse menu arose like a ghostly thing.

PROJECT APOCALYPSE
Those who make peaceful revolution impossible will
make violent revolution inevitable.
—John F. Kennedy

ANTHONY COLE'S PREAMBLE TO THE RATIFYING BODY
THE PROJECT GOALS
THE PROJECT CHARTER:
        PHASE ONE   PHASE TWO
        PHASE THREE   PHASE FOUR
THE NEW MILLENNIUM
CURRENT STATUS

They both sat transfixed. Hill's jaw was open, supported on his chest by his fleshy chins, and it was only partially because he couldn't breathe through his nose anymore.

"Jesus H. Christ, Father! Who the hell *are* these people?"

"I don't know," Deauchez answered grimly. He was ready to move on to try to answer that question, but Hill began looking around the desk frantically. He found a printer and powered it up while Deauchez impatiently hovered the mouse arrow over PROJECT GOALS.

"Just hold on a sec, okay? Let's see if we can find a way to print this screen first. I need something in writing. Man! No one's gonna *believe* this."

Deauchez didn't want to hold on a sec. He could feel sweat

sting the back of his neck. His scrotum lay tight and hard against his body the way a terrified kitten might push itself into a corner, trying to get as small as possible. He could almost feel the *whoosh* of the explosion starting at any moment, at his next heartbeat, and what would it be like? Would everything simply go black, or would he live long enough to experience the minutiae of roasting alive?

He moved the mouse to the top of the screen, searching for a pull-down menu. There was nothing. "I don't see a print," he said impatiently. "I don't think they would allow you to simply . . ."

"Okay! Just hit Print Screen then!"

Deauchez found the PRINT SCREEN button on the keyboard and pressed it.

A text box appeared on the screen: "PRINT SCREEN DISABLED."

"Shit!" Hill cursed. "Maybe Louise has got a camera around here someplace."

But Deauchez had had enough of that sort of thing. He moved back to PROJECT GOALS.

"What about Phase One?" Hill asked, as he tried to look around the room and keep an eye on the screen at the same time. "Wouldn't that be about the prophets? I'd like to see how—"

"Simon, please! We already *know* about the prophets! What we *don't* know is *why*."

Hill ran his hands over his skull and expelled a shaky breath. "I'm getting the idea that you wanna be out of here in about five minutes."

"Two."

"So run with it. You find out as much as you can, okay? I'm gonna go upstairs and grab us some food. I'll try to find a camera while I'm up there. I have to get at least one screen shot for the paper. Then we'll split."

"You want to look for *food*? *Now*?"

"Man, I'm *starving*! My stomach is killing me! And if we're not going back to New York where I can buy food, neither one of us will eat."

Hill was right. They hadn't eaten that day and wouldn't tomorrow if they didn't get food here.

"Very well. Go. But in two minutes we leave."

Hill was up the steps in a flash. The priest turned back to the computer, clicked the button, and began to read. Ten seconds later, he'd forgotten all about food, all about Simon Hill, even about the certainty that Death was riding toward him through the East Coast night.

It didn't take Hill long to find the kitchen. It was a warm, softly glowing area with a huge restaurant-style stove and copper pots hanging from the ceiling. The back door's window had a toile fringe that matched the tablecloth on the early-American dining set. It was straight out of *Architectural-freaking-Digest*. Hill's mouth watered at the visions of creaking sideboards it inspired.

On the counter was a large framed photograph that he glanced at, then returned to, picking it up. It was a wedding picture—Janovich's, and she hadn't been young at the time. Hill's eyes narrowed as he studied it. There was something familiar about . . . He sought and found some mail on the counter: Dr. Robert Tendir. She'd *married* Tendir! Which meant that Tendir lived here, too, and Deauchez and Hill had walked into the house not even knowing it. Their incompetence was frightening. Hill hurried to his task, feeling more anxious to leave than ever.

The pantry, when he found it, had a large door of solid steel. The interior was large, professionally equipped, and packed with food. There were rows of canned vegetables and soups, clear canisters of dry goods, and on one wall was a vacuum-tight crisper. Inside the glass, Hill could see boxes of crackers and cookies and loaves of bread. There was a freezer that held meat and more bread, frozen. No doubt about it: Janovich and Tendir were prepared. He was looking at the famine's equivalent of insider trading.

For a moment, Hill was so suffused with hunger and greed that he didn't know where to begin. He opened a box of doughnuts from the freezer and began stuffing them in his mouth, cold and icy. He stared at the rest as he chewed, unable to take it all in. After wasting precious seconds in mastication and mental disarray, he spotted a box of trash bags on the shelf and began to stuff them, too.

Tears were streaming down Deauchez's cheeks by the time he finished reading the project goals. It wasn't a lot of text; the difficulty was in getting what was there to push past the barricades that reason kept putting in the way of comprehension. The tears were an indication that it had finally sunk in. He backed up to the first Red Scepter options screen, his fingers so numb he could barely operate the mouse. He clicked on the MEMBERSHIP ROSTER button. What came up was not a complete list, but a simple box asking for a name. Deauchez cursed colorfully in French, words he hadn't used since grade school and words he didn't hear or recognize even now. He'd wanted to scan the entire list of members, but that apparently wasn't an option. He could learn what he most needed to know, though. He typed in "DONNELLEY" and hit ENTER. A second later, an entry appeared.

CARDINAL BRIAN DONNELLEY, VATICAN CITY
HEAD OF THE VATICAN'S CONGREGATION FOR THE CAUSES
OF SAINTS
TRAINING: MA PHILOSOPHY/THEOLOGY (OXFORD, '67),
          PONTIFICAL N. AMERICAN COLLEGE, ROME
            Ph.D. DIVINITY ('72),
          SECURITY TRAINING, R.S. HISTORY LEV 3,
          POLITICS LEV 4
BIRTHPLACE: DROGHEDA, IRELAND
PRIME ONE CHANNEL NUMBER: 10731, 12301
MEMBERSHIP: INDUCTED IN 1968, RED SASH
RELIGION COUNCIL MEMBER, UPPER BODY MEMBER
NOTES: USE 12301 NUMBER ONLY TO CONTACT
          DONNELLEY

Deauchez clicked CANCEL. He felt a black rage. The Red Scepter options screen appeared and he clicked MEMBERSHIP ROSTER again, angrily. He hacked in the next name with bitter thrusts: "MCKLENNAN."

CARDINAL JOHN MCKLENNAN, ARCHDIOSES, DUBLIN,
IRELAND
ARCHBISHOP OVER DIOCESE OF IRELAND
TRAINING: MA PHILOSOPHY/THEOLOGY (OXFORD, '66),
          ALL HALLOWS SEMINARY, IRELAND Ph.D.
           DIVINITY ('71),
          SECURITY TRAINING, R.S. HISTORY LEV 3,
          POLITICS LEV 4, ESPIONAGE LEV 2
BIRTHPLACE: BRAY, IRELAND
PRIME ONE CHANNEL NUMBER: 9381

MEMBERSHIP: INDUCTED IN 1967, GOLD SASH
CHAIRMAN OF RELIGION COUNCIL, UPPER COUNCIL MEMBER

"You bastards," Deauchez said with repugnance. Donnelley seemed so Romanized in the Curia that Deauchez had forgotten that he, too, was Irish. And he'd graduated from Oxford a year after McKlennan. McKlennan had probably recruited him into this thing. They'd each chosen a top Catholic seminary after that and had risen meteorically in the Church.

Why had they chosen the seminary? To infiltrate the Church, or because the Vatican was tied to the Red Scepter? Who else in Rome was in this thing?

But time, oh blessed time, he didn't have. No time to enter name after name into little white boxes as he thought them up. But he had to be sure of at least one.

He brought up the Membership Roster box again. Entered "CARNESCA."

MEMBER NOT FOUND

He closed his eyes gratefully. *Thank God. Thank God.* At least he had one contact he could trust. He clicked back, brought up the Project Apocalypse menu screen again. There was one last thing he had to know, though he'd give anything to pass this particular cup untouched. He prayed for strength, but it was a hollow, empty prayer, because the Project Goals screen was still lying too heavily on his heart for him to believe in any kind of a God at all.

He selected PHASE ONE. He'd lied to Hill about their not needing to know. There was something *he* needed to know, oh yes.

Hill had two garbage bags loaded with the choicest of the goodies and was opening a third when he thought he heard something over the rustle of the plastic. He froze.

Yes, there it was, ever so deliberately soft, ever so deliberately slow. It was the sound of the lock in the back door turning.

There was an instant of mortal terror so primitive that his bladder released a momentary warm jet and the bag slipped from his hands to the floor. Shaking from head to foot, Hill stepped over the bags and swung the pantry door closed, being careful not to latch it. He wasn't even sure he could get out again if he latched it. Then he picked up his gun from where he'd laid it on a shelf. He held it up next to his ear where one nail rattled lightly against it, like a distress signal in Morse code.

He heard the almost indiscernible creak of the back door, then there was a sound like a tiptoed footfall from inside the kitchen. Whoever it was, they knew full well that there were intruders in the house. No chance that it was a neighbor, or even Tendir coming home unaware. There would probably be more of them out front.

Hill squeezed his eyes shut against a wave of panic. He wanted to escape, to hide in the pantry or, better yet, try to make the back door after the footsteps passed. He wanted it more than anything in the world, so much that he was even willing to walk away from the bags at his feet, Pepperidge Farm and all, which was saying a hell of a lot.

But he *couldn't* sneak out the back door, even if he might get away with it. Because the priest was downstairs in the office, which was the first place the Bad Guys would head, and *he*, Hill, had the gun.

Damn Deauchez for insisting that they leave the bullets in the car!

Deauchez was gazing at the list of twenty-four names on the screen with rapt horror and dread. He'd been that way for perhaps sixty seconds. Time, for him, had become something liquid. His mind was far away, racing through events and conversations and meanings, and returning, always, to that field, that horrible field, returning to that damned, sickening cypress tree. It was one of those moments of epiphany where they say one's life passes before one's eyes, all of it, in a moment's flash.

Most scientists doubt such a phenomenon is possible, having no explanation for it. But perhaps, if Kratski's holographic model had any validity, one might hypothesize that the access mechanism that retrieves stored interference patterns in the brain has the capacity to simply . . . *shine* on all memory patterns at once, bringing them all into focus—not linearly, the way the conscious mind nearly always works, but like a sky full of fireworks, all memories bursting in one brilliant flash.

After that first shock-induced surge, Deauchez's mind might have slipped into that dark, fearful place that had been waiting to suck him in since he'd arrived at Santa Pelagia; that place from which there might be no return. But the demons were forestalled by something that broke Deauchez's concentration as sharply as a dart popping a balloon.

He turned his head abruptly to look at the stairs. From the upstairs hall came soft thumping, grunting sounds, like the scuffling of a dog that wanted to be let in. His self-preservation awoke with a vengeance, and Deauchez recalled where he was and what terrible danger they were in. He grabbed the phone from its cradle and stood up, looking around helplessly. The thought of them . . . of them simply opening the door and seeing him down here, alone and vulnerable, bathed in the harsh electric glow . . .

He grabbed the closest thing to a weapon he could see, slunk to the foot of the stairs, and turned off the lights.

Hill was struggling with a man. His considerable stomach was pushed up against the man's back and his arms were wrapped around him in a move that Hill hadn't attempted since high school wrestling. He'd peeked out into the hall and had seen a dark form move toward the office door, had seen the feet cross the threshold, blocking out the light that was shining from the crack. Then Hill had jumped him, the act coming not because he was brave, but because he was scared to death that if he didn't catch the bastard unaware, he'd sneeze or step on a loose board or do something else to flag his presence and would be summarily shot.

The man beneath the reporter's locked arms was of medium height and build, but he took his assailant's weight well. He fought wildly and furiously. He stepped back, slamming Hill's spine into the wall—staggered forward and then back; slammed him again.

Hill gasped for breath but held on, knowing that to let go meant death. His gun was in his right hand, but it might as well not have been there at all. He had no bullets, and its scare value against such an opponent and in the dark was questionable at best. Hill wrapped his left leg around the man's left leg and pulled back. The man staggered to keep his balance, but either he was strong or Hill's thighs were weak. He didn't go down. He was trying to get his right arm up and Hill partly sensed, partly assumed that it held a gun. Hill moved his right arm down so it pinned the man's right arm at the elbow. Hill's left arm moved up and around the man's neck, getting him in a headlock. That left the man's left arm free and he immediately began trying to punch Hill's left side with it, but it was a bad angle and his blows didn't hurt.

Hill forced his left leg back farther still and leaned his weight into the guy's left side, trying to get him to go down. He tightened his squeeze against the man's neck for good measure. He kept expecting at any moment for the guy's backup to come flying at him, but none came.

The man, like a tree that at first resists acknowledging that it has been severed from its roots, inevitably began to pitch forward. All the determination in the world couldn't hold up Hill's weight, not with the man's left leg being taken off balance. Hill had a moment of triumph, then the man stopped trying to strike out with his left arm and it occurred to the reporter, with the clarity of hindsight, that he'd overlooked one possible and extremely fatal move. The man had only to reach over and take the gun from his right hand with his left, and there was nothing Hill could do to stop him.

The hall light came on, bright, unexpected. The two struggling men were bent over and interlocked like mating bugs under a pried-up rock. They blinked in the glare, their faces red with strain, but neither dared to pause in the struggle. Neither acknowledged that they saw the priest.

Deauchez stood in the open office doorway, his hand still on the light switch, taking in the situation, nostrils flaring in alarm, prepared to flick the light off at any second.

There was a loud *bang*. The noise jolted the priest into action. He raised the poker from the office fireplace and brought it down in a mighty arc. The liquid *thunk* of it as it crushed into the assailant's skull answered the gunshot like an echo.

The man slipped from Hill's grasp and crumpled to the floor. Hill straightened up, trembling.

"Are you shot?" Deauchez asked.

Hill didn't have an answer. He examined himself, tested his legs. "No. Don't think he'd gotten it pointed at me yet, but he would have, in another minute."

Deauchez looked down at the poker in his hand. The skin of his arms was utterly white and flecked with blood and tissue. He was sickened by what he had done. The poker slipped from his grasp. "We have to get out of here, Simon. If there are not more now, there soon will be."

"I think he's dead," Hill responded, nudging the man on the floor. He rolled him over, gasped. "Christ! It *is* Tendir."

"Tendir? Are you certain?"

"He's her husband. There's a photo in the other room. He must have been on his way home when we logged on. I bet they called him on his cellular and told him we were here. The backup's probably right behind him."

Deauchez stared at the corpse. He had never seen Tendir before, but the man's bespectacled face was that of a scientist, not a hit man. For a moment, his revulsion at what he'd just done was replaced by something glad, yes, even proud. After what he'd read downstairs, he was very glad indeed. He supposed that was a terrible sin.

"Let's *go*, Simon."

And they did, but only after Hill went back to the pantry for the food.

CHAPTER 16

OUTSIDE BAGHDAD, IRAQ

His name had been Rafael Abbas. The angel gave him a new name at the time of his vision: Mal Abbas. It was a new life, a re-birth, and the name made this clear. The name was the least of what Allah had given him.

When he had been a young boy, Rafael wanted only to be a man. Not just any man, but a man like his older brother, who fought with the forces of the Hamas. For Iraq, his brother used to say, for the Koran. He said all the Arab peoples, all Islam, were being crushed by the Jews and their allies, the West. Rafael had listened to everything his brother said with unquestioning faith. And when his brother died in a bombing attempt, Rafael left home, said he was eighteen when he was three years younger, and joined the force. He had moved from one group to another since then. He could not find a people that matched his fervor, his drive to *do*.

Now he knew why. Allah had set him apart. He had chosen Rafael to lead his people from bondage. Like Moses. That was what the angel had said: "Like Moses." And before him, Allah would part the seas.

He was parting them even now. The people had accepted him as a prophet with hysterical gratitude. They had been awaiting Allah's justice for a long time, and they slipped as easily into the promise of Abbas as a Westerner slipped into a pair of jeans. Three days ago he had announced himself. Today he was here, in a concrete bunker, with the leaders of the Arab world, and on the conference phone was President Lee and Tsing Mao Wen of China. In three days, he had become the most powerful man in all of Islam. It was true, the prophet Rahman had followers, but they were a peaceful, elite gathering, and they were far away, in

Beirut. Peace was not what the Arab peoples needed right now and they knew it. They needed Abbas.

"Are you committed?" came President Lee's summons.

Mal Abbas rose from his seat. "Iraq is with you!"

Amin Hadar, Iraq's president, nodded brusquely in his chair, his cheeks hollowed by self-restraint. He was a revolutionary who had led the overthrow of Hussein. The West applauded him at the time, relieved to be rid of that old jackal. But those who felt relieved had never looked into Hadar's cold, gray eyes.

The others around the table leaned toward the phone, bobbing their heads in assent.

"Iran is committed."

"Lebanon is committed."

"Jordan is committed."

Saudi Arabia, Afghanistan, Pakistan, and Turkey spoke, as did several of their North African neighbors. They had all committed themselves before being invited to the bunker, but today it still had an air of momentousness, of an oath.

"We welcome you all!" Lee said. "I understand that Mal Abbas is to be your General Chief and China's main contact. Is that agreed among you?"

Abbas held his breath as he took his seat. Next to him, Hadar's cheeks sucked in further, as though the merest exhale might carry a protest. The others were more subtle but not necessarily less dangerous. Would they challenge Allah's prophet? No one did.

"Good!" Lee said. "I regret to say that India is hesitating. Their religion has strangled their courage. They listen more to their prophets than their bellies." There was a pause as he realized the insult. "Er . . . and *their* prophets are not moved to war."

"If Allah has not moved them to war, then we will not need them," Abbas said bluntly.

"It is true—our numbers are sufficient without them. Yet our task is not without challenge. We seek an open channel to discuss strategy with you and the others, General Abbas."

Abbas leaned forward anxiously. Strategy. Yes, he had something to say about that. "Please, speak, President Lee. Who do you list among our enemies?"

"The United States, naturally. And their allies in Europe have been bribed to stand by the Western whore. We must neutralize Britain and France. Germany still has American troops. We should attack them also."

Mal Abbas nodded vigorously, though Lee could not see him. "I very much agree. What about Eastern Europe?"

"Every indication is that they will remain neutral," Tsing Mao Wen's voice related.

"*No one* else will have the desire or resources to stand with the U.S.," Lee sneered. "With her stock market failing, even her blackmail will be curtailed. Our one question is Israel. We have been unable to gain intelligence as to their intentions."

"Your confusion is understandable, President Lee," Lebanon's ruler spoke up. "Israel has just had a change of power. Their prophet, Rabbi Levi, has overthrown their prime minister."

"So we have heard. Will they fight for the U.S.?"

"Levi has said that they will not go to war until their beloved temple is complete. That will take several more months at the very least." The Lebanese leader wore a look that said it could take much longer, if he had anything to say about it.

"That will be helpful if true," Lee mused.

"It *is* true," Abbas said. "Now let us talk about division of labor. We are close to Europe. We should infiltrate it. That is what I was told by Allah. And you—you will take on the United States."

There was a pause, a silent balking on Lee's part, perhaps, at Abbas's authoritative tone. But when Lee answered, he said, "As it happens, General Abbas, we were thinking along similar lines."

Abbas smiled, relieved. Then he noticed that around the table there were a few leaders, like the Libyan and, of course, Hadar, who were looking at him in angry disapproval. Their heated glances said that *they* wanted to tackle the Great Whore. Fools! They were brave enough sitting in this bunker, but they'd each had their tail between their legs before where the U.S. was concerned. Yet the majority of the leaders nodded approvingly. Let China wrestle the bloated demon that lived across the wide world. With the U.S. occupied, the riches of Europe would be theirs for the plucking.

Mal Abbas turned back to the phone. "Perhaps we can discuss your efforts, President Lee. I assume you will invade the U.S.?"

"We are still working on strategy, General Abbas, but it is time the Americans faced a war on their own soil. I think they do not have the heart for it—they are too spoiled and comfortable. And we *are* prepared for heavy losses. Still, America's border defenses are a problem . . ."

Abbas could barely contain his excitement. "That is what I wanted to discuss. Allah has given me a message for you, a prophecy."

"Is that so?" Lee said warily. "I have already discussed this with Tsing Mao Wen. He, too, had some interesting . . . ideas at Santa Pelagia."

"Yet," Wen interjected politely, "I also had the idea that our Western brothers would be most useful to us. Perhaps we should listen to General Abbas express his thoughts."

"Very well. I am willing to listen," Lee said, in a tone that was less than gracious.

The men in the bunker watched Abbas with suspicion. Prophecy? Like Lee, these men believed only so far.

"Thank you, President Lee. I have for you a day and an hour for your attack, and a promise of success. Allah has given his word that he will be with us, that he will shield your forces with his own wings if you prepare as he has instructed."

Lee said, coolly, "What is this day and hour? What are the instructions?"

"I will tell you the word that was given me in Santa Pelagia. But before I begin, I have a question. I was given *two* prophecies by Allah. The first regards your invasion. As for the second . . . might you not be able to obtain some weapons from your neighbors, the Russians? They must be eager to retain your friendship."

"Hmmm. It might be possible." From the tone of Lee's voice, Abbas knew that it was more than possible, that Russia had already offered it.

"Let's say we *could* get weapons," added Tsing Mao Wen in a deferential tone. "What would you have us use them for? The Russians have little technology that we ourselves do not possess, except for their advanced long-range nuclear capabilities. But any country that would use nuclear devices against America would be committing suicide."

Abbas felt a surge of joy, of glee, like a child about to reveal a wonderful secret. It was he, Abbas, who held the prophecies. He alone knew Allah's will. There was absolute power in the moment—with China waiting patiently for his instructions, and the leaders of Islam seated at his feet. "I am not suggesting that *you* deploy them . . ." he said carefully, unable to suppress a crazy smile at this tease.

There was a pause as Lee and Wen talked quietly together in

Chinese. Behind him, Hadar muttered low and furious, "We must discuss strategy *before* you make promises to the Chinese, General Abbas!"

Abbas turned to face Hadar; the revolutionary was on his feet, scowling in his characteristic and greatly feared rage. Abbas was taken aback at this rebuttal, at this interruption of his thought. It was a like a dash of cold water. Startled, he looked around the table. Yes, every face was with Hadar; they were angry about what he might say. Abbas suddenly realized how the prophecy would sound to them. Would his countrymen and neighbors be ready to accept the will of Allah? Would they have faith enough?

"What is it that you have in mind, General Abbas?" Lee said.

Abbas hesitated, confused. "I . . . eh . . . I must pray over the details, and . . . discuss the matter with my fellow leaders here. But I'm glad to hear you have access to such things."

Hadar hissed at him with a warning expression, exactly like a riled snake.

". . . eh . . . Yes. We can all discuss it later. For now, perhaps we can get back to your initial attack on the U.S.?"

Abbas cringed inside. He could hear himself yielding under the will of Hadar. Then a thought flooded on him like a beam of light. Had the angel not *warned* him to be discreet?

Yes, he remembered now, he had been warned about including the Arab leaders in his plans for the second prophecy. He was supposed to speak to China *alone*. Idiot! He had forgotten! He had been carried away by the power of the moment.

The panic of his disobedience, of his error, was overwhelming. He tried to convince himself he had not just ruined everything. *Like Moses. Like Moses.*

But Lee sounded willing to accept his postponement. "Very well," he said. "We shall keep that for another day. Let us hear your suggestions for the invasion then, General Abbas."

The moment of terror, the brink of disaster, passed. Abbas returned to his seat and began to tell them about the first prophecy.

INTERSTATE 40 WEST

It was noon before Hill stirred. He'd crashed before they'd reached D.C., staying awake only long enough to stuff himself with several peanut-butter sandwiches and a Danish.

Deauchez had had little appetite then, but he'd eaten a few pieces of bread around eight o'clock, more to keep himself awake than anything else. Once in a while, he checked the temperature of the man beside him with a worried hand.

Simon Hill was burning up.

When the reporter moved at last, it was one of these forehead-checking rounds. He pulled himself up groggily and moaned. He sat for a moment in the passenger seat, blinking, his eyes inward, lost in thought. He felt his own forehead with the back of a hand. "Fever," he said. "Headache, too . . . *Shit*." There was a flat sullenness to his voice and an odd look on his face, a stony, dull look that nevertheless managed to be bitter.

Deauchez felt an ache of hurt that was part sympathy, part regret, even grief. "Yes, I'm sorry. Do you want to stop to get some aspirin?"

"Got some in m' bag." Hill reached behind the seat and pulled out his black bookbag, the only thing from home he'd had with him the day Deauchez showed up. He took out a bottle.

He got lost somewhere in the middle of the aspirin-taking process. The two pills lay in his hand, the open bottle precariously tilted in his lap, little white tablets insignificant in the large dark weight of his hand. He stared out the windshield with that blank face of his.

"Maybe you should take three," Deauchez suggested gently.

Hill did not reply. He popped the pills in his mouth, shook another from the bottle, and added it to his gullet. He washed it all down with what was left in an old bottle of Coke.

They passed a large green freeway sign just as Hill was looking up. He turned his head to stare at it. "Excuse me, Father; did that sign just say *Memphis* eighty miles?"

"I believe it did."

"As in *Tennessee*?"

"Is there another in this part of the country?" Deauchez asked sincerely.

Hill glared at him. "Father, pardon my French, but what the fuck are we doing near *Memphis*? Cole and Telegyn are both in D.C., not to mention the FBI and anyone else we might care to talk to. And after that I'd *like* to get back to New York!"

This last was both complaining and adamant. Deauchez clenched his jaw stubbornly.

"Father Deauchez?"

"I thought we should drive to Sedona."

"Sedona? Are you nuts?"

"I thought we should investigate the inoculations that are still going on."

Hill looked confused. "You mean, like the hantavirus shots at Cougar Camp?"

"Those, yes, and the ones at Sagara Bata's gathering in India. I'm fairly certain they are taking place in Sedona, too, and Sedona is closer than Cougar Camp."

This didn't seem to elucidate the situation for Hill. He held his hand to his temple, wincing in pain. "What about Abeed or Stanton, they're a hell of a lot closer than—"

"They will not inoculate Abeed's group, or Stanton's. In this country it will be Cougar and Andrews, and Cougar and Andrews only. I . . . I think." Deauchez frowned worriedly. He was trying to sound more confident than he felt.

"All right. You read something on that network, I take it. But I gotta tell ya, whatever this lead is, I don't . . ." Hill paused. He turned to stare out the side window. "I mean, maybe you should follow up on it yourself, you know? Personally, I wanna get home. I mean—" He stopped again. "I'm not doin' too well, Father."

His voice was more than Deauchez could bear. He reached out and touched Hill's shoulder. "I know, Simon. That's *why* we must go to Sedona."

Hill turned, hurt darkening in his eyes. "I think you'd better tell me what you mean."

"Yes, of course. This is all speculation, I'm afraid. But it may be . . . well, perhaps I should just tell you."

"Go on."

Deauchez took a deep breath. "You see, the prophets had biographies on that system we broke into. And something else. I'm not sure what it means exactly, but each prophet had a designation after their name, in parentheses. It said either 'friendly' or 'nonfriendly.' "

"Friendly or nonfriendly?"

"Yes."

"Friendly or nonfriendly," Hill intoned, as if it were a foreign language.

"That's right, Simon."

"What the hell does that *mean*?"

Deauchez hoped to God he knew. "Well, as I said, I'm only guessing, but listen to who was designated as *friendly*: Cougar, Andrews, Sagara Bata, Kratski, Clark, Rahman, Hefner, and . . ."

"Yes?"

"I saw one more. His name was Lamba Rinpoche and he's a Tibetan Buddhist. According to the data on-line, he currently resides in Sierra Blanca, Texas, which is another reason why I thought it might be valuable to head this direction. Perhaps after Sedona . . ."

Hill pushed himself up in his seat, face eager now despite his own troubles. "Lamba Rinpoche? He's one of the Twenty-Four? How come he hasn't come forward?"

"I would like to know myself. It might be important."

"Okay, but what about the last one?"

A flush went through Deauchez. He could feel it burn his skin. "I'm sorry?"

"The *last* one. There were *two* prophets still missing." Hill wiped at his nose, though it was no longer running but red and dry. His eyes were relentless.

"I . . . did not have much time." Deauchez turned his head to check the driver's-side mirror, unable to meet the reporter's eyes.

Hill struck his door. "Damn it!"

"In any case, only those eight prophets were listed as 'friendly.' The rest were 'nonfriendly.' "

Hill sighed away his disappointment and turned in his seat. He rubbed at his nose again and looked out over the road as though he was trying to focus on the question at hand. After a moment, he shook his head. "Nope. I don't get it."

"I'm not certain I do either, but there *is* something those eight have in common."

"What?"

"They all have a metaphysical bent. Andrews and Cougar could be called New Age, Hefner is into Rosicrucian and other occult systems. Rahman is Sufi—a mystical branch of Islam and relatively liberal. Clark is a psychic and astrologer, and I saw Sagara Bata speak myself. He's a New Age Hindu who toys with Buddhist philosophy. And this new one, this Lamba Rinpoche, is a Tibetan Buddhist. Tibetans are very esoteric. They are pacifists, as well."

"I get it. All of them are, like, on the other side of the spectrum from Abeed."

"Exactly! Or Stanton, for that matter. Think about it. On the *nonfriendly* side we have Abeed and Matthews, both racists."

"Amen." Hill began wrestling with his bag to extract a notepad.

"We have a Mormon, a Baptist, and two Catholics in Daunsey and Sanchez. Tsing Mao Wen is atypical of his faith. Taoists tend toward the esoteric, but he's an anarchist."

"Absolutely." The reporter was scribbling furiously. "He's pushing China into war."

"There is also a Hindu, a Protestant in Africa, and a born-again Christian in Australia. Dimish is Russian Orthodox. Levi is an Orthodox Jew . . . Are you seeing the pattern?"

Hill drummed the top of his pen against his teeth. "Sure. But what's all this got to do with the inoculations?"

Deauchez was worked up now, intense, and it was an effort to speak slowly, to keep his eyes on the road. "Well, we know Cougar and Sagara Bata's groups are getting them—*post* Santa Pelagia."

"And you think *all* the friendly groups are getting them?"

"It's a theory."

"Why? What's in them?"

"This is only a *guess*, Simon, but . . . I have been thinking for the past few hours while you slept. I think the Santarém virus may get worse than anyone suspects. If that is true, then our finding out about those inoculations is crucial."

Especially for you, Deauchez finished the thought in his head.

Hill stared at him for a long time. When he spoke, his voice was firmly controlled. "Are you telling me . . . You think those inoculations might be a . . . a Santarém vaccine or a . . . an antidote or something?"

Deauchez nodded. He glanced at the reporter as much as he could while watching the road, wearing what he hoped was an optimistic and supportive expression.

But Hill's eyes were far away. "Still . . ." he said slowly, "they might *not* be."

"That's right, Simon. They might *not* be. But think: if it were the other way around, if it were the nonfriendly group getting the shots instead of the friendlies, I would suggest they contained just the opposite—the virus itself. Do you see?"

Hill's expression moved from self-absorption to dread as the words registered. "Oh, Jesus, yeah. Yeah, I *do* see."

"After all, this business with the prophets . . . Yes, they have spread the apocalypse story—quite effectively, too. But what is the purpose of this 'gathering together of believers' nonsense? Sister Daunsey, in London, bringing all the Catholics over from Ireland, and Stanton at Kittatinny Mountain, Andrews in Sedona. It must serve some plan of the Red Scepters, must it not? And what could that be but to assemble those who are of friendly or nonfriendly persuasion, getting them all together in convenient, isolated camps for . . . for . . ."

It was a thought he couldn't, daren't finish. Hill was fading. He lay back in the seat, notepad forgotten. But his eyes were still bright with that reporter's gleam of his. Even now, he was probably thinking of the story, of that idol of the printed page.

"If you're right . . ." Hill said slowly, thinking it through. "If they're doing Santarém vaccines at the friendlies, then that implies . . . Did you read about the virus on that network? Is it really s'posed to get that bad?"

Deauchez shook his head in frustration. "No. There was no time to look at the later phases. There was so little time."

"But you saw *some*thing."

Deauchez nodded reluctantly. He glanced over at Hill with an urgent fearfulness. "I will tell you, Simon, but you must write this up *today*. Send it to your editor. Can you manage that, do you think?"

"Of course! Just *tell* me."

"All right. On the network . . ." Deauchez took a deep breath. "I looked at the project goals. The number one objective of Project Apocalypse is to . . . to lower the global population."

Simon's eyes grew large. "No shit?"

"The population of the Earth is over six billion now, *oui*? Almost seven billion? Look at what they have done so far. You asked before, why would anyone want to destroy the food supply? At the time I thought they were just trying to fulfill the prophecies, but more important, the famine will kill, yes? Maybe hundreds of thousands."

"*Millions,* Father."

"Millions. Yes. Then there is the virus and, perhaps, war."

Hill watched him for a moment with those intense, boring eyes of his that Deauchez recalled from their first meeting, ages ago it seemed, in Santa Pelagia. "Okay. So did it say how many are s'posed to die?"

The priest looked at the road.

"Father? Did it say how many?"

"The goal I read, Simon, was . . . two billion."

As he said it, Deauchez felt a stab in his chest as deep and sharp and cold as the piercing of an arrow through snow. It was the first time he'd allowed himself to think about it since he saw it on the screen the previous night. Through the long night and morning of driving, he had blanked his mind with little conscious effort, and then there had been Simon to worry about, and he'd had the idea about Sedona. It had seemed a fine idea, because Sedona was far away, and there was even a very good, very noble reason to pursue it, so he didn't have to acknowledge the fact that he was simply fleeing.

"Christ!" Hill reached out a hand and gripped at Deauchez's sleeve. "Christ! Two billion dead, Father?"

But Deauchez's throat was constricted and the words would not come. The reporter shook him.

"Two billion dead?"

"No, Simon," the priest choked out. "Two billion *survivors*."

MUNICH, GERMANY

It was only four days ago that Mike had been in Munich; four days since they'd picked up Blade and shut down the local concert hall. But it felt like another lifetime, like memories from a past life, perhaps—a life that had been lived in an alternate universe where things actually made sense.

The München Universität Krankenhaus still held a few dozen technicians, caterers, promoters, and groupies, all quarantined in the wing where Blade had died. Outside, the hospital lawn was strewn with flowers and wreaths, farewells to the singer from grief-stricken fans. It was as close as the mourners were allowed to get. In truth, it was as close as they wanted to get. Inside, the last ten surviving members of Blade's traveling crew were busy dying.

The Germans were on top of this, Mike was told. It was clear that they were making a blitzkrieg of an effort. Sam Richards was still technically running the show for WHO, but the government had stepped in with heavy boots. They had over five thousand quarantined around the city—most against their will—and they hadn't tracked down a quarter of the original audience yet. The news from America about the horrific contagion rate wasn't making the rest of their quarry any easier to find.

The only real piece of luck, said Richards, was that the media and the general populace were supporting the manhunt enthusiastically, neighbors reporting neighbors whom they suspected of being, or having had contact with, concertgoers. This was not a uniquely German proclivity—it was happening in other cities around the world. Besides, the Germans could see what was happening in L.A. and Seattle, Atlanta and New York. Munich could hardly be blamed for taking no chances.

And thus, still twenty-four hours from the earliest possible sign of symptoms in those who had been in the concert hall that night, all of Germany held its breath to see if the Grim Reaper had gotten a bloody foothold among them or not.

Mike had no doubt that it had.

He found the young man—Georg was his name—smoking a cigarette in the day lounge. He looked haunted, sunken. It was the face of one awaiting death.

Munich was issuing white Racal biohazard suits to the staff—built-in air supply, pressurized closure, the BMW of disease control and a significant indication of their level of seriousness. Mike wasn't sure if he found it confidence-inspiring or frightening as hell, but he was fairly certain how those in quarantine would find it. So Mike did what was not easy to do in a Racal; he sat. He perched gingerly on the edge of a chair next to Georg and waited to be noticed. The boy's curiosity surfaced and he glanced over with red-rimmed eyes.

"Georg? Hi. My name's Dr. Michael Smith. I don't know if you remember me, but I led the team that picked you up four days ago."

Georg took a long drag on his cigarette and did not respond.

"There's something I want to ask you, and it's very important."

Georg rolled the lighted end of his cigarette in the ashtray. "I already said this a hundred times: I went to the hall just before the concert, so I could not have made contact with anyone, could I?"

"It's not that. You spoke to me that night. You asked if one of our crew had been near the ventilator room; something about a man with a mask. Do you remember?"

The boy's head shot up, his face oddly twisted. "It's about fucking time," he said.

* * *

An hour later, Mike and Sam Richards showed their IDs at the cordon in front of the concert hall. A man in a Racal came out and led them inside.

Suited and sprayed, they made their way into the guts of the auditorium and stared with amazement at the spectacle. The place was enormous, with seats for twenty thousand, and every one of those seats was either gone or currently being dismantled from the floor and bagged. The carpeting was being ripped up. Even the light fixtures were coming down.

"Jesus, Sam. Are they doing this in the States?"

"They are now," Sam said sourly. "USAMRIID's sent in decon teams. That's what I heard."

Now. Now that the numbers were going through the roof. It made Mike wonder what events had happened in those arenas between the Blade concerts and the time they were shut down. Home shows, perhaps, antique car shows, baby goods shows, ball games, crusades? It had not even occurred to him before. Mike shuddered.

"We'd like to see the ventilator room," Richards explained to their escort.

"Up on the grid?"

"Yes."

They were led to a ladder backstage and left to their own devices. Mike looked up at the narrow metal rungs and felt his heart sink.

"I hope this isn't a complete waste of time," Sam grumbled.

Mike gritted his teeth and started climbing.

They had little trouble finding the ventilation room; it was the only fully enclosed structure on the grid. They had a slightly harder time getting to it. When Mike looked down all he could see was the bottom of his plastic face shield. He had to feel his way along the steel beams with his feet, like an inexperienced balance beam walker. Behind him, Sam cursed loudly.

The door to the ventilator room stood open. It didn't lock, and there was no evidence of tampering. The room itself was about ten feet by ten feet, most of it taken up by a large air-processing machine.

"Now what?" said Sam, placing gloved hands on shielded hips. In the puffy white suit, the gesture read "Pillsbury Dough Boy" rather than "annoyance." If he'd still remembered how, Mike would have laughed.

"Let's just look around."

It was easier said than done. There were too many sharp edges in the room, too many chances of a rip or a puncture. Mike examined the fan system, trying to be careful. It was a large box, taller than he was and half again as wide. Two wide rubber vents were attached to the rear of the machine, each leading up and out through the ceiling. He lay on the floor to get a look at the bottom of the machine. A large fan under the unit sucked old air in from the auditorium below. Three pipes emerged from the body of the machine and headed off in various directions through the walls of the room, no doubt ending in output nozzles around the stadium where the "fresh" air was released.

"I don't see anything unusual, Mike."

Mike stood up. "Neither do I, except that this fan system obviously feeds the entire building. If it were tampered with . . ."

"It doesn't have to be tampered with. All the air recirculates up here. That explains how Blade's virus was spread among the audience."

"No, it *doesn't* explain it. Even if he'd been coughing like crazy and the virus got sucked up here, *some* of it would have been vented outdoors through one of those vents. And what did cross over inside the machine couldn't account for the sheer volume of cases. Thousands of people were infected at the U.S. concerts."

Sam didn't have a rebuttal. He put his hands on his hips again and stood as if waiting to leave. But Mike refused to be rushed. He ran gloved hands down the sides of the box. He didn't see anything unusual.

"Give me a hand, will you?" He pointed up at the rubber vents.

"Mike!"

"Come on. Just hold your hands out. I'll be very careful."

With a great show of reluctance, Sam locked his fingers and bent forward. Mike placed his booted foot gingerly on Sam's gloves and boosted himself up. He looked at the vents.

"What's *ausgang* mean?"

"Output, exhaust."

"And *eingang*?"

"Input."

Mike followed the input vent with his eyes down from the ceiling into the machine. About a foot above his own head he saw it. The vent had a piece of black electrician's tape on it. With

Sam squirming below, Mike tugged at the tape with his clumsy, gloved fingers, trying to get an end to come up so he could pull the thing off.

"Mike, I can't hold you!"

"Just a minute."

He caught an edge and tugged. Underneath the tape was a neat little hole, about an inch in diameter. It had to have been cut in the thick beige rubber with a knife or a razor. The inside of the duct was clean and new—unlike the duller, dusty surface of the vent's exterior. Mike lowered himself slowly, using Sam's shoulders for guidance.

"Can we please go now?" Sam whined.

Mike held up the tape with one finger and pointed upward.

Sam dubiously accepted the offer of a boost. He came sinking back down moments later. "It could be old," he said, but his face behind the shield looked shaken.

"It's *not* old."

"Mike . . . Have you been watching the news lately? All this business about Santa Pelagia and the prophets predicting the apocalypse?"

"Yeah. In fact, I just read the latest *New York Times* recap on my flight over here."

"They say Santarém is the second horseman—plague. A few of the doctors at the hospital . . . well, they're pretty scared, Mike. They say the reason it's gotten so out of control so quickly is because *God* planted it."

Mike held the tape up and smiled sardonically. "Looks like we have us another theory." But the bravado was a lie.

"Mike, I can't believe . . . The boy's story, it doesn't make any sense unless . . ."

"Unless what?"

Sam looked embarrassed. "They say sometimes angels take the shape of men."

Mike was filled with an annoyance so rabid he had a hard time not smacking Sam upside his Racal. "Sam! If God wanted to give everyone in this arena the Santarém virus, do you really think he'd have to resort to sending an angel in a mask down to dump a vial of the stuff into the air supply?"

Sam couldn't meet his eyes. "I—I guess not. But we don't know what the boy saw; it could have been anyone. Maintenance, maybe. As for the hole . . ."

"Maintenance! In a black outfit and a face mask?"

"Maybe it gets dusty around these vents."

Mike glared.

"For Christ's sake, Mike, think about it! Who would do such a thing? And even assuming they *wanted* to, who could have gotten ahold of it? We only just discovered the virus ourselves!"

At this, something seemed to drop on Mike from out of nowhere, knowledge as heavy and solid as only a newly born truth can be. He stared at Sam with the kind of surprise that precedes outrage like a handmaiden.

"*Did* we just discover it, Sam? Did we really?"

CHAPTER 17

INTERSTATE 40 WEST

The story—or, rather, The Story—was written on mass quantities of aspirin and sugar and carbonated caffeine. And despite these, Simon sat there in the passenger seat, laptop propped against the dash, and he sweat. It was a desperate stench that poured out of him in time with the letters that tripped off his dancing fingers and, after a while, the little grunting noises that also emerged, unbidden, as if Simon were climbing a mountain of stone instead of a pile of words. The smell filled the car and settled in as a funk that could almost be tasted; they could not crack the windows because Simon began to shake uncontrollably with the chills whenever they tried that.

And Deauchez was helpless to do anything but drive and try, with no success, to read the flat LED of the laptop from the side. That and fight to stay awake.

Sedona was still almost twenty-four hours away.

RUSSELLVILLE, ARKANSAS
5:00 P.M.

Deauchez filled the tank while Simon went inside to show the station manager his press ID and ask if he could pay to use one of the business lines. Such a simple thing, but the discussion about it in the car had been acrimonious and petty. Most public phone booths didn't provide modem access, and the cellular, that scrap of technology like a plastic tumor planted in their midst, was forcibly rejected by Deauchez, who refused to see the irony inherent in its use. Hill was right, they were certainly moving, but if Telegyn got a whiff of where they were headed, they might find someone waiting when they got there.

So the reporter, who seemed to have gotten fatalistic now that the story was birthed, held on with barely checked impatience until they reached a gas station.

The Story was a winged thing, and it seemed to be clawing at him to be sent on its way.

As for Deauchez: he, too, had a story to tell.

VATICAN CITY, ROME

The papal conclave had dragged on until nearly midnight. Father Angelico Carnesca had been waiting in his office for the news that they were retiring for the night. He was completely exhausted by the research they'd demanded of him. And when he'd finally been released, he'd walked straight to his room and removed his clothes, letting them lie where they dropped.

He was in his own room, for he was not part of the conclave. He had been called to speak to the assembly, and had been escorted in through the locked door by the Swiss Guards in order to do so, as he was escorted out again when it was done. He had seen many pained faces in that room, in that sea of cardinals, particularly after he had begun to speak. He could see them still when he closed his eyes. Despite his exhaustion, it was hard courting sleep.

The phone call came in shortly after 1:00 A.M., breaking through his first uneasy slumber. Semiconscious and weepy with frustration, he grabbed the receiver, wishing for once that he had no special privilege of a line in his room, the kind of privilege that came from being the chief library contact for clergy all over the globe.

"Carnesca," he managed.

"It's Deauchez," the voice on the other end began, and it continued ruthlessly. By the time two sentences had been spoken, Carnesca was wide-awake. By the time the regurgitation of information ended ten minutes later, he was sitting straight up in bed, tense as a rod. In the dark his weak eye jittered and jerked.

He put down the phone and tried to think what must be done. If Deauchez was not mad, this was vital information that the conclave, and the next pope, must have. He did not sound mad— at least no more mad than one would expect if all he said were true. And it was not Carnesca's duty to judge his news anyway, but the cardinals'.

Oh, God, could it really be? Could it be true?

Some part of him wanted to feel elated at the thought; he

could or should be greatly relieved if Deauchez were right. And yet, he did not quite believe it yet, did not understand the implications fully. For if it were *not* God, but the works of man, what then? Yes, what then?

And Cardinals McKlennan and Donnelley! It was too much!

He tried to calm himself, to pull himself out of the details and focus on the communication of the story. After much thought he put together a plan of action. He would gather a small group of trusted cardinals and discuss it all with them right now, tonight. He'd heard Deauchez's warnings of spies and interlopers, but he knew a few men he could trust. He had to speak with someone—had to have advice on this, and backing! When he faced the conclave in the morning, he must not face it alone.

Carnesca rose and dressed quietly. His exhaustion was still there, but overlying it was a nauseating anxiety that made his hands tremble. How could he get inside the conclave without being summoned? The conclave's sequestering was inviolable. But he, Carnesca, was not unknown in the Vatican. He would speak to Mystanza, Chief of the Vatican police, the *Vigilanza*. He knew Mystanza fairly well, and Mystanza had let him in before, when he was summoned. He would tell Mystanza that he had urgent news relevant to the conclave for one of the cardinals—Cardinal Talbot, perhaps. Would Mystanza admit him? Carnesca thought he would, if he looked desperate enough, and that would not be a problem. Mystanza would probably think it was news of some new disaster and, in a way, it was.

Carnesca bent his knees beside the bed in a prayer for guidance, for strength, for wisdom. Then he left the room.

NEW YORK CITY

When the call came in, Ralph Bowmont was sitting at his desk.

"Ralph? It's me, Simon."

"Well, goddamn it, son!" Bowmont stood up and went over to his office window to look over the newsroom. Most of the desks were abandoned. "Where the hell are you?"

" 'S not important. Look, I'm gonna e-mail you a story. I just wanted you to know it's on its way."

"What's all this about? You disappear on me, and your last e-mail—whoa, boy, I gotta be honest with ya—it came from outta nowhere."

"Did you check it out at least? Not that it matters—I've got the story right here. It's totally on the level. I've seen the evidence with my own eyes. You *gotta* print this. *Tomorrow.* Front page."

"Hell, I'll print it. Just get it in here."

"I will."

"Screw the piece, anyway, what about you? Where *are* you?" There was a pause. "I'm pretty sick."

"Yeah?" Bowmont said softly. "Well, that sucks bullets, but I'm not all that surprised."

"Are the others . . ."

"The whole dang office has it. It was Kevin. He went to the New York concert."

"I know."

"He passed on last night, Simon."

"Jesus."

"Most of the others are in the hospital."

"Shit." Hill's voice broke. Ralph could hear him clear his throat repeatedly on the other end of the line. "How come . . . how come they didn't quarantine you, Ralph?"

"They . . . uh . . . they've got their hands so goddamn full in this city—they've got a lot more to worry about than one screwy ol' news editor."

"So you're okay?" Hill sounded hopeful.

"I'm functional."

"You *sound* good."

"I'm all right," Bowmont said roughly. "Listen, son, why don't you tell me where you are? I'll send someone to help ya out."

"I *got* someone. Did you call the FBI, Ralph? I know this whole thing sounds nuts, but you have no idea what's going on. It's a major conspiracy—the whole thing. Well, you'll read my story anyway, but did you? Call them?"

"Yeah, I called 'em. I told 'em just what you told me."

"Great! Will you send 'em my new story as soon as you get it?"

"I'll take care of it, don't you worry."

"Thanks." Hill sounded greatly relieved.

There was a moment of awkward silence.

"That someone . . . are you still with the priest?"

"Yeah. Look, I'd better go."

"Hey, Simon? You know the rules, right? Make sure this doesn't

get leaked to anyone else. And make sure the priest doesn't tell
anyone, either. We don't wanna get scooped."

"Yeah, okay. But this is *really* important. A lot more important than getting scooped, right? So you've got to *promise* me it
will get printed in the morning. Front page."

Hill's words sounded suspiciously like a last request.

"Ralph?"

"Yeah, Hill. I promise."

"Thanks. I'll . . . um . . . I'll see ya."

"Take care of yourself, Hill." The words were sincerely tender
as Hill rang off. For a while, Bowmont sat at his desk, his face
blank. Then he picked up the phone and called Ted Peterson at
the FBI.

Hill pinched back his tears and hooked up Deauchez's computer.
He watched the story download and decided, almost as a treat, to
check his in-box on the New York host when it finished. There
might be something in there from one of his coworkers, maybe
even something e-mailed from the hospital. He thought about
the meetings he'd chaired just days ago—all those familiar faces
around the table, all of them on a grand ride and him at the
wheel. He thought of his desk, every stain and scratch known; of
the buzz in the newsroom when things were at full stride, like a
current that charged him, made him want to jump up and get out
there and sniff out, uncover, retrieve, and display proudly before
the rest of the pack. And his name rising from the classifieds,
marching up page after page over the years until that first time it
appeared on page one: it was a juice that addicted and filled and
satiated so that it became his life and there was nothing else
needed or desired. Nothing else, hardly, in his life at all for the
past twelve years. No wife, no child, not even more than a half
dozen conversations that didn't revolve around work.

It was easier, perhaps, to get that lost in it when you desired to
forget entirely where you'd come *from*, what you'd *been*. He did,
and he pretty much had.

By following the priest he'd unwittingly left behind everything and everyone that had sustained him since college. His
newsroom world had vanished forever even as he'd walked away.
Even if he could go back, it was no longer there. And he never
would go back, because he was vanishing, too. *Three* lives he
had lived: that first endless fat-black-and-nerdy childhood in

Mississippi; that blossoming, becoming time in college that his grandmother had paid so dearly to buy him, where he'd found his gifts and his voice; and his life in New York, where he'd been somebody. These lives seemed not really connected at all to him, but like biographies he'd read of other people, as if he were a cat going through incarnations instead of a human being growing old. And now he was in his fourth and apparently last life—this one brief desperate intermission before he winked out entirely.

He glanced out the window and saw the priest just emerging from the phone booth. There was still the gas tank to fill, so he had some time yet. He clicked on his in-box icon, needing to hear a word from any of his friends at the *Times*. Any one of them at all.

They reconvened outside the gutted, foodless minimart doors. Hill read Deauchez the e-mail he'd received from a WHO official named Dr. Michael Smith. It was a hysterical-sounding missive about standard airborne contagion rates and a man in black in a ventilator room in Munich. That is, it *would* have sounded hysterical if they didn't know better.

"Should we reply? What should we tell him?" Deauchez asked, excited.

"I already did. I told him to meet us in Albuquerque."

Deauchez gawked at Simon as if the fever were affecting his brain. *"What?"*

"He's a doctor. A virologist. If there's anything to your theory about the shots, he'll be able to tell, right? Besides, if those shots *are* a vaccine or antidote or whatever, someone like Smith will know what to do with it. If we get a sample, maybe he can take it back to WHO."

"I did not think of that," Deauchez admitted. He suppressed an enormous yawn. "I suppose we must take the risk. I only hope I'm not mistaken about the inoculations."

"So do I," Hill said softly, staring off toward the car.

"I did not ... I'm sorry, Simon. I think there is a good chance." Deauchez couldn't control another huge yawn, despite its ill timing.

"Let's get goin'," Hill said brusquely. "I'll drive."

"No, Simon. I know how bad you feel."

"Father." Hill faced the priest with a piercing scowl. "We've got more than another thousand miles to go. If you don't let me drive *now*, I might not be capable later, and we can't afford to lose road time sleeping. I hate to tell you this, but you're probably infected yourself—from me. You need those shots as bad as I do. And we *both* need to get to Sedona in one piece."

A guilty flush stole over Deauchez's cheek. "Very well," he said. They began walking toward the car.

THE FAR EAST

The first true act of World War III, though it would never make the history books, was not an attack on the U.S. by China, nor any official aggression from Mal Abbas and his contingent. It was committed by a handful of CIA agents and paid internal informants operating under direct U.S. presidential orders.

The timing had been Cole's idea. If they were going to act at all they must do so immediately. Wait even one more day, and chances were good that they would miss the military entirely, said military being sequestered somewhere unreachable or even, perhaps, enclosed in ships and planes headed toward their destiny. Not to mention how increasingly difficult it was getting to move in and out of some of these countries.

Ergo, there was no time for official haggling. While General Brant had a few of his boys work out the logistics, the speaker of the house was pulled into a private meeting with the president, Cole, and the V.P. He agreed to their plan with a kind of mute shock. He allowed that Congress should *not* be informed. He said he was glad to spare his fellow representatives such a terrible burden of complicity. He looked like he would never sleep again.

Twelve devices were smuggled through the usual channels to twelve agents. The devices were smooth steel cylinders, six inches in diameter and twelve inches tall. They'd been developed by a certain branch of the military that tinkered with biochemical warfare. When activated, the top of the cylinder rose and holes appeared around the circumference. A mist was propelled from these holes, atomizing finely to insure good air carriage. Each cylinder held one hundred cc's of, in this case, yellow blood serum obtained from Santarém patients.

Of the twelve devices, the following occurred:

Four were detonated in crowded streets near the capitol buildings of Iran, Iraq, Libya, and Jordan.

Three were detonated in street markets in Cairo, Algiers, and Calcutta.

Two were detonated in the largest airports in Shanghai and Canton.

Two were detonated at "strategic military locations" in China—a bar frequented by enlisted men just off the Nanjing base, and a small take-out restaurant that serviced half the soldiers in Changsha.

And one was dumped into the Grand Canal in Beijing.

These silent attacks would turn out to be a thousand times more lethal than those leveled at Hiroshima and Nagasaki. Yet, other than those who knew of the plan in advance, no one would even be certain that they took place at all.

DAY 17
VATICAN CITY, ROME
6:00 A.M.

Most of the sequestered delegates of the papal conclave were administering to their daily ablutions when the bells began to ring. Not only were the bells early, but their ringing was insistent and endless. Brian Cardinal Donnelley was waiting for those bells, dressed and seated on his bed in the room he temporarily occupied off the Sistine Chapel. At their first cry he started, splashed some water on his face as though he'd been washing, then exited his room. Down the hall, others were poking their heads out.

Cardinal Capras from Barcelona approached him. "What is it, Cardinal Donnelley?" His lumpy face was half shaven.

"I have no idea," Donnelley said with a mannered shrug. He grabbed a scurrying aide by the arm. "You there: What's happening?"

The aide bobbed from the waist in hasty deference. "Your Eminence. There's been a . . . uh . . ."

"Speak up!"

"I don't exactly *know*, Your Eminence. Several men have been discovered in their chambers dead this morning. We've been asked to check all the rooms."

"Dead!" Capras repeated, crossing himself. Donnelley crossed himself, too, and began walking down the hall. They seemed overly bright, these halls, and they swayed, like those in a fun house. The night had been one of horror—unrelenting horror—and he was exhausted. Cardinals, some he knew well and others he knew only from his private list of names and affiliations, were milling everywhere. He heard the word "plague" being whispered. Several asked questions of him as he passed. He repeated his denial again and again, like Peter, as he moved forward. Capras trailed behind him like an altar boy trying to carry his gown.

He turned the corner and saw men gathered around the closed door of a room. There were cardinals, of course, their red hats over faces middle-aged or better, plump, thin, scholarly, worried. A few secretaries mingled, too, probably sent by their superiors to gather information. Next to the door itself stood an officer of the *Vigilanza*.

"Is Cardinal Intiglietta inside?" Donnelley asked him.

The officer nodded respectfully. *"Sì."*

Intiglietta was the *camerlengo*, the chief of administration during the papal seat's vacancy, and head of the conclave. In another five or six years, Donnelley himself might have held the title, but there had not been another five or six years. So Donnelley had courted Intiglietta's friendship as a fellow member of the Curia. Intiglietta had been most cooperative. Not one of *them*, no, but not unmalleable.

"Then I will see him," Donnelley said, and he opened the door. The officer looked uncertain, but he did not stop Donnelley. The *Vigilanza* were not accustomed to disobeying members of the Curia. Donnelley shut the door on Capras's worried face.

Inside were five other men who looked as though they, too, had just arrived. And by Donnelley's calculations they would have. If he was correct, the first body had been discovered almost exactly seven minutes before. Dr. Barciento, one of the Vatican's most respected physicians, was examining the still figure on the bed. Also in the room were Captain Mystanza, chief of the *Vigilanza*, two of his officers, and Cardinal Intiglietta. Intiglietta was a slight, silver-haired Italian. He held a handkerchief over his nose and nodded, not ungratefully, to Donnelley as he entered. The corpse was that of Francesco Cardinal Marconi, his eyes staring up at the ceiling, his mouth a vibrant blue.

Mystanza bowed to him smartly and gave him a regretful smile. "Your Eminence, I'm afraid we have sealed the room for the investigation."

"I wanted to offer my services to Cardinal Intiglietta."

"Yes, it's all right," Intiglietta said.

"It's not Santarém," Dr. Barciento said, straightening from the corpse. "It looks like poison."

"Poison!" Donnelley said with convincing surprise. His heart was pounding loudly and his skin was clammy with fear, all of which added to his performance.

"I believe so, but it is difficult to tell without a postmortem. And that will have to be performed by the Roman authorities."

Donnelley wondered where McKlennan was. He had better arrive soon. "There are others dead? So I hear . . . ?" He addressed Intiglietta. The man nodded, still in shock.

"Yes, Your Eminence," Mystanza said. "We've found four this morning. We're still checking rooms. And the Secret Service and the Guard are combing the area."

"Who else has died then?"

Mystanza pulled out a notepad to check, but Intiglietta had the names ready on his tongue. "Cardinal Gazin from Portugal, Cardinal Simpson from America, and . . . Cardinal Talbot and Father Carnesca from the Vatican." His voiced was pained.

Before Donnelley could comment, the door opened and McKlennan entered. "Peace, Brothers," he said. His greeting was solemn and weighty. He gave a slight bow of deference to Intiglietta, ignored the others, and made his way to the bed.

Mystanza glanced at Intiglietta, mouth open to protest, but Intiglietta made a restraining gesture with one hand. Even Intiglietta respected McKlennan. The man was an Irish lion, a warhorse, and he had been vocal and strong during the recent proceedings.

McKlennan seemed to take control of the room. He leaned over the corpse and closed Marconi's eyes. He pulled the sheet up over the man's face, while Barciento watched, his face clouded with annoyance.

"Please touch nothing!" Mystanza pleaded, unsure of his authority.

McKlennan ignored him. "We must discuss this," he said, looking into Intiglietta's eyes.

"What do you mean?" Mystanza asked.

"This." McKlennan waved a hand at the body. "Were there any sightings of intruders last night, Captain?"

"No. We saw nothing, nor did the Guard, nor the Secret Service. We also saw no unusual activity outside the walls."

"Dr. Barciento was just mentioning the need for an autopsy," Donnelley interjected carefully. "He suspects poisoning."

"It seems so impossible!" Intiglietta said.

McKlennan nodded, his face ponderous and thoughtful. "Cardinal Intiglietta, may I respectfully suggest that Captain Mystanza carry out the investigation, and that no one outside of the Vatican City be informed?"

It was a bald assertion and everyone looked surprised by it. Barciento spoke first. "But Your Eminences, with all due respect, we are not equipped to conduct a proper forensic autopsy! Nor," he added, with an apologetic glance at Mystanza, "a thorough investigation. Four clergymen have been murdered in their beds!"

Mystanza grunted a reluctant assent. "*Sì*. It would be preferable to work with the Roman police. No one inside has much experience with homicide."

He was correct. Indeed, McKlennan had pointed out that fact to Donnelley earlier. The Vatican City was its own, independent state. It contained three distinct security forces: the Swiss Guard, the Secret Service, and the *Vigilanza*. The Swiss Guard was the remnants of the papal army. In jewel-colored costumes, armor, and plumes, they served the pomp and circumstance. Like the English Beefeaters, their function was the general protection of the Vatican grounds and of the pope against attack, but they mostly gave directions to tourists and posed for photographs. The *Vigilanza* was the standard police force for the city-state, small in number, accustomed to issuing traffic tickets and watching out for thieves and pickpockets. The Secret Service protected the pope. None of these three groups could conduct a proper investigation, though nominally the *Vigilanza* was in charge.

Intiglietta was nodding in agreement with Mystanza, but he asked McKlennan, "What is your reasoning, Cardinal?"

"If we notify the outside authorities they will descend upon us in droves, breaking our seclusion, and making demands that would severely delay the conclave. And we can in no way afford to lose the time. The conclave must reach a majority vote in the next few days. You know this is true. We *cannot* be interrupted."

"It is true, we are in a most critical phase," Intiglietta said slowly. "But it appears to me that we have had that decision removed from our hands."

"The deaths are tragic and much grieved, but they needn't impact the conclave if they are handled with care."

"But there *must* be a qualified investigation," Barciento insisted.

"And the police *will* investigate," soothed McKlennan. "I am merely suggesting that it be *our* police. Perhaps when you hear all the facts, you will agree that we can handle this case within our own society. By doing so, we can avoid impacting the conclave, and we can keep the news out of the press. Need I say that at a time like this, when millions of souls are in desperate need of their faith, that a scandal from the Vatican would be absolutely devastating!"

Donnelley nodded solemnly at this, as though he were hearing it, being convinced by it, for the first time. His heart was in his throat.

"You have information to impart to us, Cardinal McKlennan?" Intiglietta asked solicitously.

McKlennan heaved a pained sigh. "I'm afraid so. I believe our poor brothers have committed suicide, God have mercy on their souls."

"Suicide?" Intiglietta was appalled. "Why would men such as this commit a mortal sin—particularly *now*?"

"But the apocalypse is precisely *why* they were driven to it! Because the recent signs are proof of our Lord's imminent return, proof of the Apocalypse of St. John, and therefore proof of the inviolability of *every* word in the Holy Scripture, including those that describe what awaits the damned!"

Intiglietta considered this, a frown on his brow. Mystanza crossed himself, his face paling. He was a good Catholic, and he was apparently not unaware of what was going on in the wide world.

"Please continue, Cardinal McKlennan," Donnelley said.

McKlennan's face was the picture of sorrow. "I'm afraid Father Carnesca approached me yesterday and engaged me in the strangest conversation. He asked me what sins were unpardonable. Could God forgive something that was part of one's very nature? Even if you repented, he said to me, wasn't a sin like that still with you, inside you, the very moment after you'd made contrition?"

"Do you know what he might have been talking about?" Intiglietta asked.

"No. But he seemed quite agitated. I wish I had taken him

more seriously. I assumed he was asking rhetorically, but now it is clear he was talking about his *own* sin, about his *own* nature. His suicide is something that I shall have to live with for the rest of my life."

"Are you implying that Carnesca was a . . . a homosexual?" Intiglietta asked in a hushed voice. "I cannot believe it."

Donnelley spoke up. "To tell you the truth, I *have* heard rumors to that effect, though of course I dismissed them. But is it not too late to concern ourselves with Father Carnesca's sins? God knows what they were, even if we never will. I *do* know that Carnesca was convinced that the apocalypse was at hand, and he had a full knowledge of the horrors to come. Now that I think about it, he had appeared to be quite troubled lately. I, too, did not take the time to inquire into it, in all the madness we've been through."

Dr. Barciento was shaking his head worriedly. "What about the other three?"

McKlennan nodded. "They, too, must have had their reasons for fleeing the Judgment Day. As if they could!"

"But I knew Cardinal Gazin well! He was a pleasant, sincere man!" Intiglietta protested.

McKlennan nailed him with a baleful eye. "Your Eminence, you and I are both old enough to realize that you can know a man for years and never guess what lurks in his heart."

Intiglietta twisted his great ring, his eyes distant. Perhaps he was remembering Gazin, Marconi, and Carnesca dining together, as they often did. "Yes," he admitted slowly. "That is true enough."

"*If* it was a suicide pact, an investigation will find it out," offered Mystanza.

"Yes, but *whose* investigation?" McKlennan walked up to Intiglietta and placed a hand on his shoulder. This paternal gesture toward a man as scholarly and high-ranking as the *camerlengo* would have been absurd coming from anyone but McKlennan. "Do you think we could justify an internal inquiry? At the very least, Captain Mystanza might gather the evidence and prepare a preliminary report. Then, in a few weeks, if we are granted another few weeks, and if Mystanza's investigation finds it necessary, we can consider taking further steps."

"What about an autopsy?" Barciento asked, but his tone was already admitting defeat.

McKlennan turned to him. "You said you believed it was poison?"

"Yes, but . . ."

"And no poison was found?"

Mystanza's eyes lit up. "*Si!* We found, in the room of Father Carnesca, a bottle of Cognac, four glasses, and an empty bottle of strychnine."

"Ah!" McKlennan said, as if that solved everything.

Barciento reddened. "It *might* have been put there deliberately!"

"By whom?" McKlennan's tone was chiding, disdainful. "The conclave is sealed. Only the College itself and a number of secretaries and staff are inside. And the captain here has verified that there are no signs that the sequestering was violated. You can't seriously believe that one of our own would . . ." He did not finish. It was too preposterous.

Donnelley had listened to all this with nerves stretched taut and his own face feeling like a mask of calm concern that had been stapled to his head. McKlennan had operated so well, he hardly needed Donnelley's support. But now he added his weight to the shifting tide.

"I agree with Cardinal McKlennan. The conclave must not be interrupted, and this news must be kept from the public at all costs. It is vital that the people's faith not be shaken now by scandal or that—God forbid!—we encourage suicide among the flock by way of example. In fact, I think we should make it clear that no one is to speak of it outside these walls." He turned to Mystanza. "For the sake of the Holy See, can you trust your men's silence?"

Mystanza put his hand to his breast. "On my honor."

Intiglietta sighed and drew himself taller. "Yes. I see that we must not allow that to happen. The deaths are inconceivably tragic, but they have occurred and now we must prevent more tragedy. Let us put these poor souls to rest in the crypt and continue with our work. Captain Mystanza and Dr. Barciento, you will work together, quietly, to put together a report?"

Barciento bowed stiffly. Mystanza looked as though he were already writing it.

A half hour later, McKlennan and Donnelley were alone in Donnelley's room, picking at the breakfast they'd been served. For once even McKlennan looked depleted and old. Donnelley was thinking numbly that he had to change clothes before the conclave resumed. His frock was stained with sweat. Even his cap was damp.

"We were saved by the thinnest of circumstances," McKlennan fulminated, breaking the silence.

"I know." Donnelley stared down at his hands on the table.

"If not for Cardinal Evans . . ."

"Cardinal Evans befriended Carnesca because I told him to. I knew Carnesca was close to Deauchez."

"Yes, but it was sheer luck that Carnesca cooperated. Had he not awoken Evans last night . . ."

"But he did."

"He did not awaken him first!" McKlennan's hushed voice was furious. "Four murders, and inside the Vatican! It was a miracle that we managed it. It will be a miracle if we are not caught."

Donnelley studied his hands. They lay on either side of his eggs, and he could almost see the blood running off of his fingers onto the glistening skin of the cooked whites. That such a crisis had come at such a time—it was horrible. The conclave was sequestered. He and McKlennan and Evans had had to carry out the neutralizing themselves. *Themselves.*

How much had happened since the sun last set! He'd been fast asleep when Evans tapped on his door, his face bloodless. Evans had been called into a secret meeting with four other cardinals. *They knew. Carnesca* knew. Evans had excused himself to use the bathroom and come straight to Donnelley. Together they went to McKlennan.

Donnelley had proposed that Evans return with a laced bottle of wine, but McKlennan had opposed the idea. The men would not all drink at once, and when the poison began to work there would be cries, an alarm would be raised. No. They had to go in, the three of them, with guns, and guarantee silence. So they had. They had gagged the outraged, fearful churchmen. They had injected them with nitroglycerin and watched them die. The strychnine-laced wine had been poured down their throats later, when they were dead. The strychnine was to imply suicide. An autopsy would reveal the nitroglycerin, too, but only if done quickly. Of course, there would probably never be an autopsy now.

Donnelley had been trained to do it, yes. But he never thought he would have to. It had been vile, monstrous! Their eyes as they thrashed, trying to retch, mouths gagged . . .

"If Deauchez hears about these deaths, he'll do something even *more* extreme," McKlennan was saying. "God knows who he'll call next, or what evidence he managed to obtain at Tendir's house."

"The deaths won't get reported in the papers, " Donnelley said with a thick tongue. "He won't find out." But in his head he was repeating, over and over, *vile, monstrous, oh vile! vile! monstrous!*

McKlennan *humph*ed. "I cannot fathom why they haven't caught him. He's a time bomb, that priest. Moreover, he's *your* time bomb. He was your suggestion."

Donnelley just sat there, looking at his eggs.

LAS CRUCES, NEW MEXICO

Deauchez pulled into a gas station at dawn. He started the pump, then went into the minimart to buy a newspaper. He picked up the *New York Times*—it was today's edition.

The headline said:

WORMWOOD PLAGUE: DEATH TOLL SKYROCKETING

He started ripping through it right at the stand. Hill's story was not on page one, it was not on page two, it was not anywhere. Behind the counter, a teenage girl watched him with dull eyes, eyes that weren't surprised by anything anymore, and particularly not by some maniac ripping the newspaper apart at the newsstand.

Deauchez paid for the paper and gas and for three long extension cords picked up from the hardware section. He returned to the car, tossing the newspaper into the backseat in disgust. He was incensed, furious. He was sick and afraid and horribly disappointed. But he couldn't talk about it with anyone. The man in the passenger seat was asleep, and when he wasn't asleep he was delirious. Deauchez took a deep breath to calm down and began the work of tying the black man to the hatchback's seat with the extension cords, making it nice and tight so that he could not flail about.

As Deauchez pulled away, he saw that the girl was pressed against the minimart window, watching him. Or maybe she wasn't.

Her palms and forehead were against the glass; her face was as white and her eyes as blank as a corpse's.

That image, and the *Times* headline, would haunt him for miles.

ALBUQUERQUE, NEW MEXICO

The Albuquerque airport was small and the opportunities for confusion were few. Dr. Michael Smith wandered down to baggage claim. He looked around at the ten or so people who were in the large room, but none of them matched Hill's byline picture. Mike poked his head outside and looked at the cars waiting along the curb. He didn't see a pudgy, preppy-looking black man out there, either.

He caught himself on the lookout for colds. He wondered, for the thousandth time, what he was doing here—here, maskless, where the virus was loose.

It's not in New Mexico yet, at least it wasn't when I left Munich.

But *something* was here, or Mike wouldn't have been asked to come.

If there was anything that had made Mike feel safe from the virus on the journey itself, it was the sparseness of the travelers. For the first time in years, his commercial flights had been half empty. There were the businessmen, still in their suits, still flying about as though the world were not going to hell in a handbasket. But they had dark circles under their eyes, and their glances darted here and there, like trapped things.

At first Mike had a vague terror that the empty airports were a result of the virus, that there simply *weren't* more people out there. Then he realized that it was the food rationing. He himself had raided the WHO staff supplies and had a week's worth of stuff in his suitcase. Others wouldn't be so lucky. That was a good thing; if fewer people were airborne, fewer virus particles would be, too.

But that was little comfort compared to what he saw when he finally stuck his head up out of the sand. He'd been so lost in the virus, he'd not realized that it was only one problem of many. The world was on the brink of war. The papers announced the return of the U.S. draft. Rumors about China's intentions were prolific. Everyone he saw out here, including the airline employees, looked like zombies. He'd seen the look plenty in the past week, but

where he'd been, that look had been about the virus. He hadn't expected it to be out here, too.

When, exactly, had the world turned upside down?

But he knew when; it had something to do with that Santa
Pelagia story. That's why he'd written Simon Hill at the *Times*,
and why he, dumbfounded at the response he'd gotten, had
nonetheless arranged immediate flights. He took out the hard
copy of the e-mail. He'd read it many times, and now he studied it
again, trying to read between the lines.

*Am already working on something like this. Need your testi-
mony and help. Am on my way to Arizona to check into some suspicious circumstances involving the virus. Would love to have
someone like you along. We'll be arriving in Albuquerque, New
Mexico, sometime between 7 a.m. and 9 a.m. on Wednesday.
We'll drive by the airport baggage claim. We'll wait fifteen minutes. I think it'd be well worth your time if you can make it. Simon Hill.*

What did the message mean? *What* suspicious circumstances?
It couldn't be men-seen-near-ventilator-rooms, because there
hadn't been a concert in Arizona. And what an offer—to ask
someone to find their way across the globe in fifteen hours with
almost no explanation, and tell them you'll only wait fifteen
minutes for them to show up! He'd never have swung it if the
flights weren't so empty. There'd been no time to call in to HQ,
and no plausible explanation to give if he did call. So he'd decided to wait until he'd heard Hill's story before calling Stanley.

Mike saw his bag from across the room. He picked it up and
went outside to wait in the thin light of dawn.

Deauchez had been terrified ever since they'd approached the
Albuquerque city limits. He had a man in the passenger seat who
was tied up, for heaven's sake. If anyone reported them, he'd
soon have a police escort to quarantine.

And besides the fear was the guilt. *You're probably infected,
too.* If Hill only knew. The reporter lay literally cooking in the
next seat, moaning in pain. Deauchez had to keep the windows
up and the radio at full blast so Hill's cries would not be heard on
the slow city streets. The heat already building inside the cheap,
air-conditioning-devoid car was not making Hill's raging fever
any better.

By the time Deauchez pulled into the airport he was exhausted, sweating, and hopeless. The only person outside baggage claim was a thirtyish balding man with a naive, tired face. He carried only a large duffel bag and cloth briefcase. He stood as the hatchback approached.

Deauchez left it parked back a few meters and got out. The man was trying to peer through the front window of the car as Deauchez walked over to him.

"Dr. Michael Smith?"

"Yes! Are you with Mr. Hill? Is that him?"

"It's him and I am."

Dr. Smith smiled with relief and held out his hand. Deauchez gave a shake of his head. Dr. Smith withdrew his hand, a look of confusion crossing his brow.

"What's going on?" Smith looked less relieved now. He took a few steps toward the car, trying again to look in the window.

"I would not go any closer if I were you."

Smith stopped. He looked at Deauchez, then at the car. "Oh, my God."

"I'm afraid Mr. Hill has the virus."

"Oh, God!" Smith began fumbling in his pockets. He pulled out a paper mask and plastered it over his nose and mouth.

"Dr. Smith, please. There really *is* something going on. I think he was right to ask you here."

But Smith had backed up several paces from him, too, and was looking at both Deauchez and the auto with wide eyes.

"You, the car, him, you're all hot as hell."

"I know that. That is why it would be best if you rented your own vehicle and followed us."

"Follow you? To *where*?"

"Simon said you had suspicions that Santarém was planted."

Dr. Smith stopped moving backward. He blinked.

"Well, we have evidence that it *was* planted."

"In South America?" Smith sounded muffled behind the mask.

"Not just there."

The virologist's eyes widened. "Why?"

"We can discuss that later. We don't have much time now. *He* does not have time." Deauchez motioned his head toward the car.

"I'm sorry. There's nothing I can do for him."

"Yes," Deauchez said firmly, "there *is*."

CHAPTER 18

SEDONA, ARIZONA

It was midafternoon and the road south from Flagstaff, Interstate 17, was slowed by a steady stream of cars. Deauchez had seen so little traffic in his cross-continental trek, he'd reached the erroneous conclusion that this was the way traffic was in this part of the world—sparse and nonaggressive. He glanced at the map beside him, wondering if people were headed to Phoenix or even farther south to Mexico.

They were not.

This became clear when the exit for Sedona appeared, an hour into what should have been a twenty-minute drive. An off-ramp led down to a two-lane road that ran perpendicular to I-17. According to a gas station billboard, Sedona was five miles down that road. Cars began backing up long before the exit, and Deauchez assumed there must be an accident. He stole long, worried glances at Hill, who'd lapsed into a deathlike sleep. But when the hatchback finally rolled forward enough to see the road below, Deauchez realized that there wasn't an accident, only miles of cars: cars clogging the exit and swallowing that two-lane road below all the way into the desert horizon. And I-17 coming north was backed up waiting for the exit, too, as far as the eyes could see.

All the cars on I-17 were heading to Sedona.

Deauchez felt a chill of horror. *They're winning, the bastards.* He had plenty of time to brood about it. It took another hour to get within two miles of Sedona, and here people began abandoning their cars—BMWs and VW buses alike—in the desert sand, preferring to take the remaining distance on foot than to wait in the queue a moment longer. The desert looked like a huge car lot.

Deauchez glanced at Hill and stayed on the road, his car creeping forward. Another hour went by.

The town slowly became visible, rough shapes of man-made structures rising from the sand. The landscape had turned red—red rocks looming above, fine-grained red dust and sand like pulverized gemstones along each side of the road and running off into the desert. If it had been any other time, Deauchez would have stopped to appreciate the amazing scenery. As it was, he had plenty of time to take it in. He was still a half mile from the town when he got out of the car on one of the long pauses and tried to see what was going on up ahead.

It was a roadblock. A group of men were going through the cars. Whatever they were searching for—guns, food, Baptists—Deauchez was certain they would *not* like what they saw in his passenger seat. He looked around desperately. People walking by looked back. Fortunately, he'd propped a towel up on the window side of Hill's head. Hill could pass for an ordinary sleeper from the driver's side—if you didn't get too close.

Behind him, Smith got out of his car and stood there, watching him. His face said he had a thousand questions, but fear kept him from getting any closer.

"I have to get off this road," Deauchez called to him.

Smith nodded in agreement and pointed. Off to the right up ahead was a dirt lane. It ran north then swung back west around the town. Deauchez signaled affirmative and got into his car. He had to wait until the line edged forward a bit. When he was close to the lane he glanced at the checkpoint and saw a large, fluorescent ex-schoolbus pull up. The men who were manning the roadblock all climbed into it.

Deauchez didn't think twice; he turned the wheel hard and bounced over open desert. Behind him, Smith's rental followed.

They drove until the road swung west, kicking up dust in their wake. On their right were huge looming red rocks. In the glow of the dying sun the monoliths were bloodstained.

Two cars on a lonely road would be visible from town, particularly parked. Deauchez kept driving, looking for some kind of cover. He found it—a rock with a prominent overhang, its shadow darkening a good fifteen feet below it. Deauchez slowed and pulled over, flattening a few brambles, and slipped the car into the shade. The coolness of the desert shadows sank into the car immediately, relieving the dry heat of the day. Smith pulled in behind him.

The town was like a mirage across the red landscape. It would be a two-mile walk, at least. Smith hovered behind his own car, like a virgin at a dance, as Deauchez alighted. Inwardly, the priest sighed.

"I hope he will be all right here," Deauchez said. It was more invitation than statement.

"Is he conscious?"

"No."

"When did his fever start?"

"Early yesterday morning. Before that he had a cold." Deauchez studied the doctor for clues, but Smith absorbed this information with no change of expression.

"He wouldn't be any better off in a hospital, you know. There's not much they can do for them, except knock them out to avoid the pain."

Deauchez nodded in thanks, grateful for that minor attempt to release him from responsibility. He wanted to say, *Would you just* look *at him, please? See if there is brain damage yet or . . . something, anything?*

But he didn't. It wouldn't be fair. It might be *right*, but it wouldn't be fair. "Just a minute," he said thickly instead.

He opened the car and pulled a blanket from the rear, tucked it around Hill. He unwrapped the cord from the reporter's arms and moved one dark hand down to rest near an extra-large lemonade he'd picked up some miles back.

"Simon," he said. There was no response. He said it again: *"Simon!"* He dreaded the thought that Hill would have a sane, waking moment, perhaps even a last dying moment, and find himself left alone without explanation. But the reporter didn't stir. Deauchez glanced out the back and could see Smith standing awkwardly some twenty feet away, watching them.

Deauchez rolled up the driver's window, leaving it cracked just a hair. It was still warm in the car, but they were in the desert now. It would get awfully cold when the sun went down. Then he went to the trunk and pulled out a flashlight. He and Smith began to walk.

They went down an embankment of red dust and began their trek to town. Smith kept his distance. He had that damned paper mask tied around his head. Neither of those precautions kept him from talking.

"There're so many things I've been dying to ask you, back there in my car."

"Now would be a good time," Deauchez said with irony.

Sedona's borders were patrolled. The guards looked too unprofessional to be the military or the police, but they had guns, a hodgepodge mix of them from the looks of it. Deauchez and Smith followed the contours, staying out a ways, hiding where they could behind rocks or brush.

They could have entered the town at any one of several points, for the border patrol was spaced too far apart and the men were often distracted—talking or smoking with their buddies. It was less a true barricade than a performance, Deauchez thought, and he couldn't imagine why they bothered, unless they were expecting pissed-off government agents or the Chinese.

Or unless they want to make certain that everyone who comes in passes through that roadblock.

Deauchez didn't want to enter the town yet. He was looking for something, and as they edged back toward the blockade, he saw it. A large parking lot had been commandeered and was milling with people. They were being verbally escorted into queues by supervisors with bullhorns. At the head of each queue was a table and . . . yes! . . . people in medical dress. Then Deauchez spotted them, behind a strip-mall type building that edged the parking lot: three H.A.I. vans parked next to a large white truck.

He closed his eyes, overcome with relief. *Thank you, Lord, thank you! At least they're here.*

He'd drawn his assumptions about the inoculations of the "friendlies" with what seemed like reasonable logic at the time. But the logic, however reasonable it had appeared after looking at something as bizarre as the Project Apocalypse network, would never make it past Spinoza, or Sherlock Holmes, for that matter.

"Maybe we should just go back through the main entrance," Smith suggested. "They won't have any reason to stop us without Mr. Hill."

"They would send us right into those lines." Deauchez pointed to the parking lot.

"Isn't that what we want?"

"I want to get a sample of what they are giving out, but not intravenously. Besides, we need a syringe to take back to Simon."

"Yeah," Smith said uncertainly. He had an ill-at-ease expression. "Look, I didn't want to say anything before, but . . . a vaccine, even if this *is* a vaccine, it isn't the same thing as an antidote. To cure someone you need—"

"Shut up," Deauchez interrupted. His breath was coming hard. Smith stared at him, eyes wide.

"If they *created* the virus," Deauchez said in a self-addressing murmur, "they could certainly make one shot that would do both—some engineered time bomb of a weapon against the virus. They could not have infected people showing up at the camp and falling dead days later. It would ruin the illusion, cause a panic. People would leave. They would not want that."

"I guess it's possible. But usually . . ." Perhaps Smith thought better of pressing the point, for he shut up.

"And we need some syringes for you to get back to the lab," Deauchez said, as if the latter conversation had not occurred. "If we go through those queues I don't think they will give us extras, even if we ask nicely."

"No. I guess not."

"Besides, Simon is one thing—he has nothing to lose. But if I were *you*, I would not let them inject me with anything until we know for *certain* what it is."

They watched the distant scene for some minutes. There were several border patrolmen within sight of the vans—two down an alley on the other side of the strip-mall building, and another farther west toward town—but none of these looked especially keen-eyed or vigilant.

After a while a man in a white coat left the inoculation area, walked back behind the building, and went directly to the rear of the white truck. He took out some keys and opened the door. A few minutes later he emerged with a cardboard box—white with a red cross. The door banged shut and locked behind him, the solid thud of it very audible in the desert night. He carried the box around the corner of the building, back to the tables.

"The syringes are in the truck!" Smith whispered.

"I see that."

As if to mock their discovery of a target, a man with a gun appeared from the front of the truck. He looked like a much more serious animal than the border patrol. He walked to the rear doors and stood there looking around for a bit, looking right out into the desert, gun in arms, then he disappeared around the other side.

"And they're *guarding* the truck," Smith said, disappointed.

"But there is only one guard."

"You have an idea?"

Deauchez answered indirectly. "We will wait here until it's dark."

WASHINGTON, D.C.

Press Secretary Ross waited anxiously outside the door to the president's bedroom. He had a very bad feeling that he knew what he was about to hear, but he'd avoided facing it. Time was running out on that little trick.

Elissa Fielding was present, and he would be sucking up to her if it weren't for the fact that she had a cold. The first lady was a tiny woman—emaciated bordering on skeletal. Her blond hair was lacquered into a *That Girl* style, its youthful perkiness clashing with the stretched, preserved-hide age of her face. Her nose was red and a navy silk handkerchief was clutched in one manicured hand.

There were assorted underlings in the hall, too, but they were low enough in rank that Ross didn't bother remembering their names. There were no big brass present. Ross chose not to contemplate why that was. That the president himself had escaped this examination for so long was testament to his sheer South Hampton will—and cowardice.

The doctor emerged and Elissa Fielding hovered around him. "W-what is it?"

Dr. Kent looked grave. "We won't know for certain until we've done some blood work but . . . I'm sorry. It does look like Santarém."

Mrs. Fielding uttered a sharp cry and sank to the floor. She sat there, face slack, her stockinged legs poking out to one side like a doll's. Neither Ross nor anyone else in her entourage moved to help her up. Indeed, they all took a step or two back.

"I didn't think there was a blood test available yet," Ross said nervously. He found that he had backed himself into the wall at some point in the last thirty seconds. His buttocks were pressed up against it so hard it felt kinky. He did not even contemplate moving.

"There's no lab-response test, that's true, but if we send a vial to the CDC they can look for the virus manually. It's the *president*, for God's sake. We should have a car take it over right away."

"Oh. All right," said Ross, but he didn't step away from the wall.

Kent's dull glare motivated Ross to turn his head and order one of the underlings to have a car waiting and to phone the CDC to let them know they were on the way. The underling left the hallway gratefully. It was everything Ross could do not to run after him.

"We'll have to seal the blood in a couple of plastic bags or they won't take it," Kent instructed. "And the president should be moved to quarantine. George Washington's Level Four wing will do."

"No!" Ross cried out. For some reason he had not expected this suggestion. "If we move him to the hospital the media will find out!"

"And how long do you think you can keep this news quiet?"

"At least until we have a positive on the blood test. China's *invading*, for Christ's sake! I mean *for Christ's sake*!" He was shaking. The flesh of his butt cheeks danced against the wallpaper as though they'd been stuffed with Mexican jumping beans. "He should be in the war room right now! I've got everyone from the military to the British Empire screaming for him. This is a *very delicate situation*!"

Ross stared at the doctor, panting. Kent let out a long, impatient sigh. He opened his bag and took out a fresh pair of gloves and a mask. "All right, Mr. Ross. It's not as though . . ." He paused, looking at the first lady. "That is—the hospital won't be any more comfortable for the president.

"We'll tell the CDC we need an answer within the next hour. I'll go get the blood. I'll need two basins with rubbing alcohol or peroxide in them, fresh towels, and a box of large plastic sandwich bags. Pronto."

Another young man went scurrying off for these items. Kent took a syringe and two empty vials from his bag. "And the instant he's moved, you'll need to fumigate, then shut off his private apartment. The CDC can fax you guidelines. That probably goes for his office, conference rooms, anywhere he's spent time lately."

Ross nodded dumbly. On the floor, Mrs. Fielding heaved a great sob; thinking, perhaps, about certain places the president had spent time lately. "Do I . . . do I . . . do I . . . ?" she managed.

"There's no point worrying until we have the blood test back," Kent said gently. He glanced at Ross.

"It's . . . the *entire cabinet*," Ross whispered. The gesture was admittedly silly, since he wasn't willing to step closer and therefore had to raise the volume so that everyone in the hall heard him anyway.

"I know. I've been getting phone calls for days." Kent stepped toward Ross, looked around, and spoke low. "Mr. Ross, I recommend that you start making a list of the highest-ranking members of this government. We'll do blood work on them one by one right down the line until we find someone who's clean. Then we should goddamn well make sure they're put somewhere that's been purified and air-locked."

Ross stared at Kent blankly. Why was the doctor telling *him* this? He wasn't the one in charge. It wasn't *their* place to . . . Surely this was someone else's . . . There had to be *somebody* left who . . .

"Just a suggestion, Mr. Ross. I'm only a physician, after all."

"Uh . . . yeah. Thanks."

The doctor stepped over to Mrs. Fielding and offered her a gloved hand. She took it and stood, her eyes dead. Then Kent went back into the president's bedroom.

Ross, his buttocks still married to the wall, held his breath when the door opened, let it out in a sigh when it shut. Then for some reason he got the giggles. He laughed and laughed, accompanied by the sound of Elissa Fielding's dry retching.

SEDONA, ARIZONA

Deauchez gave Smith two choices: *a,* get inside the garbage bin or, *b,* wield the rock.

Smith didn't argue with Deauchez's plan, but the doctor in him clearly preferred crawling in garbage to causing someone bodily harm. A few days ago, Deauchez would have felt the same way. He would have experienced both terrible guilt at the prospect of violence and an abhorrent insecurity about his ability to commit it.

But any guilt had been quelled by what he'd learned on that computer; any doubt about his aptitude for violence had died with Tendir. It wasn't courage, he was just royally pissed off at their presumptuousness, their murderousness, their manipulation. It was, in fact, the latter that pissed him off the most, though he didn't acknowledge it. He couldn't stand theological manipulation when the Jerry Falwells of this world did it. These Red Scepter guys were *really* over the line.

They wandered to the right, until their angle of approach was hidden from the parking lot by the building itself. When they were sure none of the guards in the vicinity were watching, they made a dash for it.

And reached the Dumpster. It stood a few feet from the brick back of the strip-mall building, and it was a large affair, one of those that the truck itself picked up, slipping steel arms into the bin's metal sleeves. The Dumpster could have held half a dozen men, had it been empty. Unfortunately, this was far from the case. Deauchez helped Smith lift the heavy metal lid and gave him a boost inside. The smell was bad, and Smith accepted Deauchez's hand with an expression of revulsion on his face, no longer concerned about his proximity to the priest in the face of more immediate and overwhelming tactile input.

"Ugggh!" Smith exclaimed, trying to worm his feet down among the garbage bags.

"Shhh!"

There was the clinking of glass and the rustle of paper. It sounded incredibly loud to Deauchez's ears. *"Shhh!"*

Smith muttered something indiscernible, then settled down.

"Okay, I'm letting down the lid," Deauchez whispered.

Smith gave him an unhappy glare as the lid went down, his nostrils flaring in alarm.

Deauchez squeezed back between the bin and the building. He'd picked up a flat-sided, baseball-size rock out on the desert floor. It was one of the red rocks, and he had no idea what type of stone it was, but it felt solid, not powdery like pumice, not something that might fall apart when making contact with, say, a skull.

He heard footsteps approach. He peeked out.

A man went by, a man in a white coat. It looked like the same man they'd seen approach the truck before; and as before, he was alone. Deauchez moved around the bin so he could watch the man unlock the door, go inside . . . He held his breath.

The guard who was moving around the truck was at the back now. He glanced at the door, then stood looking out into the night. He seemed efficient, military, now that Deauchez could see his face: a hard man. He moved around to the truck's far side.

Hurry up now, Deauchez thought, *hurry!*

The man in the white coat emerged from the truck. The door banged shut, *thwunk!*

Hurry up! Hurry!

The man was carrying two cartons this time, both white with red crosses. He walked toward the Dumpster. Deauchez took one last look at the truck. He couldn't see the guard's feet—the tires were too massive—but he didn't think it had been that long since he'd gone around the far side. Out in the desert they'd counted sixty seconds for him to make one circuit around the truck—a long time, it seemed.

But that had been out there, in the dark.

Deauchez slipped along the back of the bin. He gave the bin a light rap as he did so, then he crouched down, holding the rock tightly in his right hand.

He heard the footsteps approach. They were light; the man's shoes were white with rubber soles and the parking lot was smooth. Deauchez hoped to God that Smith could hear them from inside the bin. He was about to rap again, for the man was near, when he heard it.

"Mew?" The voice was soft in volume, high and wavery, like the voice of a child or a very odd cat.

Deauchez's heart skipped a beat.

"Mew?" It came again, a sound so soft that the guard near the truck would never hear it.

The feet stopped. From his place in the shadows, Deauchez could see the white pant legs, the shoes. He held his breath.

"Mew?" This time it finished it off with a light scratching on the inside of the lid.

Two arms came into view, setting the cartons carefully on the ground. The arms disappeared. A heartbeat later, Deauchez heard the creak of the lid opening.

There was no time to go to the other side and look for the truck guard now. He had to take it on faith. Deauchez scooted around the side of the bin and stood. The man in white was still raising the lid, the heavy lid, trying to get a look into the dimness of the interior. He saw Deauchez around his raised left arm a split second before the strike. His surprised eyes met Deauchez's own, but the heavy lid filled both hands. For a moment, he was too startled to either drop the lid or cry for help. It was only a moment, but it was enough. Deauchez brought the rock crashing down on the man's head, striking him on the left temple.

The man did not go down.

"Ah!" he said. It was intended for a shout, but it came out at about the volume of a normal "hello."

"Ah!" he managed again. It was louder this time, just a little.

Horrified now at the entire scene, Deauchez brought his arm up again and struck the man in the same spot. Still the man stared. And again Deauchez struck. Revulsion washed over him.

I'm beating a man to death.

And then mercifully, on the fourth blow, the man went down, his eyes rolling up in his head like window shades flipped by an insolent teenager.

Deauchez glanced up and saw the feet of the guard emerging from the front of the truck. He grabbed the medic's arms and yanked him backward, into the bin's shadows. Smith lowered the lid. It made a small bang.

Deauchez crouched, panting like a dog, waiting for a shout or at least the approach of investigatory footsteps. None came. The body of the medic lay across him like an enormous bag of flour. The head was bleeding profusely—it looked mashed there, above his left eye. Deauchez felt sick.

Look at the work of thy hands.

He was Cain hiding with his brother's corpse. Then he looked up and saw that the two cartons were sitting there, out in the light, out in plain view. He pushed past the body, crawled *over* it, to peek around the front of the bin. The guard was standing near the rear of the truck, looking out into the desert. His gun was slung casually over his shoulder, a cigarette in one hand. He wasn't looking at the Dumpster at all. After a pause, he disappeared back around the side of the truck.

Deauchez tapped the side of the bin. "We must *go!*"

The lid began to rise. Deauchez helped Smith with it, pulled him out. There was no question of skin contact now. Smith landed on the parking lot surface, stomped his feet to dislodge a used coffee filter.

"Come!" Deauchez urged. He picked up one of the cartons and motioned to Smith to take the other. Smith gazed down with a curled lip at the man on the ground. Deauchez gave him a shove.

They couldn't see the other guards from the Dumpster, but there was nothing to be done for it. They sprinted out of the parking lot and ran like rats back out into the desert night.

The hatchback's flashlight was waiting for them back at the rock where they'd laid their plans. They crouched down and Smith pulled out a pocketknife. He slit open the thick tape seal.

He glanced up warily at Deauchez as he leaned in to look into the carton. Smith had gone back to maintaining a distance. That was just fine with Deauchez, given how the doctor smelled.

Inside were four clear plastic bags, each containing about twenty capped syringes.

"Jackpot!" whispered Smith. He picked up one of the bags, handling it carefully. "There's a code at the top in red: DS100."

"Does that mean anything to you?"

"No."

The serum itself was clear. Around the top of each syringe, near the plunger, was a thin red band.

Smith picked up the unopened carton and looked it over. There was no printing on the box, just the white of the carton and the red cross and something else. "There's a green circle on every side," Smith said. He looked back at the opened box. "Wait a minute, *that* box has red squares."

He cut open the second carton. The different markings seemed to make him nervous again, for he paused long enough to reach into his pocket and tie on that ridiculous paper mask. Inside the second box was another plastic bag of syringes, but this time there was only one bag and it filled the entire box. It looked like it held as many syringes as the four bags in the other box held altogether.

Smith lifted the bag up as though it were a snake. "WV103. Stamped in green."

Deauchez wished to God he'd had more time on that computer. He might have found out exactly what "DS100" and "WV103" meant. Somewhere under Phase Two and Phase Three there would have been a nice little bullet item about the virus, and maybe about the inoculations, too.

"Deauchez?" Smith prompted.

"*Oui?* I'm sorry."

"There are two serums here. This second one, the WV103, is tinged pink, and there's about half a cc less of it per syringe. Also, the first group of syringes has a red band at the top. These don't."

Deauchez retrained his flashlight beam on the larger plastic bag. "Does that tell you anything about them?"

"None of this is exactly standard. I can't tell squat without a microscope."

"Then you must take *both* back to your lab," Deauchez hoped he didn't sound as confused as he felt.

"Right. But what about Mr. Hill?"

It struck Deauchez hard. Yes. They couldn't very well give Simon one of each, could they?

"I—I don't know."

"Can you think of any reason they would have two different serums?"

What he's saying is, doesn't the fact that there're two serums blow your little hypothesis right out of the blessed water? If they were giving Santarém inoculations, there wouldn't be two serums, would there?

"No," Deauchez answered dismally. "No, I'm sorry."

"Well, then. Maybe we should take a closer look."

They slipped into town over a closed restaurant's pueblo balcony. Once on the street no one gave them a second glance, for the place was packed. Tourist shops selling Indian art and glass sculptures, closed Mexican restaurants, and Southwestern rug dealers lined either side of the long, curving main drag. Cars had been forbidden here—there was no room for them.

"They've come for one of those prophets, right? From the *Times*?" Smith whispered.

"Yes. Trent Andrews. He believes in aliens."

"Ah, yes," Smith said, licking his lips nervously. "Creepy, isn't it? I mean, this is like Jonestown meets Woodstock."

Deauchez couldn't help a smile at Smith's accuracy, though it really wasn't amusing. Most of the people were poster children for the West Coast New Age movement; some of them were dressed and groomed as though they'd never made it out of the sixties:

gauze skirts, Birkenstocks, long, unstyled hair, no makeup. Others clearly had money, but they had that glittery, flittery look all the same, with big jewelry that had every appearance of attempting universal energy accumulation—things out of an Atlantis crystal catalog.

There were "love circles" up and down the street: people holding hands in a circle, praying or chanting. Others sat alone, in meditative postures, or chatted with each other in hand-clenched earnestness. A few watched the skies with blissful expressions. Yes, as a whole, he thought, this was a group of people who had had their most extreme fantasies realized. The sky really *had* been falling, and they were gleaming-eyed with satisfaction at their proven intuitiveness, not to mention their *chosenness*.

But a few of them looked as if they wished they'd been wrong about the sky thing after all.

"This way," Smith hissed.

They passed a contingency of guards outside the nicest-looking hotel—where Andrews was staying, Deauchez guessed—crossed the street, and approached the parking lot.

The area was closed off with a portable plastic fence made from orange mesh. The main entrance to the lot was farther down, near the roadblock. Here there was only an opening to allow the inoculated to pass out into the promised land. A guard stood at that opening. He looked curiously at Deauchez and Smith.

"Hey," Smith said in a friendly voice. "We're waiting on a friend of ours. Mind if we look for her?"

"Sure, but stay on this side of the fence." The guard smiled before looking away.

From here they were only thirty feet from the closest inoculation table. The queue stretched back to the entrance, and the people in it looked alternately tired and excited. After giving information to a nurse, the man at the head of the queue stepped behind a portable white curtain.

Smith began walking back the way they'd come along the fence, trying to get a look behind the curtain. At the very edge of the building he could see behind it ever so slightly. The guard frowned at them. Deauchez noticed and tried to look nonchalant, but Smith was straining to see.

"I need binoculars," Smith muttered.

"You will have to get by without them," Deauchez said from the corner of his mouth.

Smith stood down from his tiptoes. He rubbed his face tiredly. "My eyes are all fuzzy. They do that when I'm beat."

"Allow me."

Deauchez changed places with Smith and squinted his eyes to focus on the doctor behind the curtain. Three people passed through the curtained area—a woman in her thirties and her two children, both preteens.

"Can you see anything?" Smith asked when the third came out.

"He takes the syringes from a tray on a cart. I can't tell which kind they are. Not from here."

Then luck befell them. A young medic in a white coat came over to the doctor with one of the cartons. He put it down and took the plastic bag out, opened it, and carefully placed syringes on the upper tray. The doctor didn't pay him the least bit of attention, but he took advantage of the pause. He stretched his arms. He looked like he'd been there all day.

"One of the medics is loading the tray from a box—it's definitely the green circle box; there is only one large bag inside it."

"Good! Because this guard over here is getting pretty irritated with us."

Smith smiled and waved at the guard.

The doctor walked around the curtain to take the next form from the nurse. He glanced up at the person waiting. It was a man, late forties. He was frail and wore a heavy brown turtleneck sweater. He followed the doctor behind the curtain as the doctor looked at his chart. When they were away from the eyes in the queue, the doctor asked the man a question. They chatted for a few minutes. The man pushed up his sleeve and the doctor reached down and . . .

Pulled a syringe from a box in the bottom of the cart.

"Mon dieu," Deauchez said in a hesitant voice.

"What?"

"This time he took a syringe from a box down below, below the tray." The man was looking away warily as the doctor injected the hypodermic. "It's one of the cartons, but the flaps are folded down. I can't see if it's a green circle or a red square carton."

"Damn!"

The man in the brown sweater approached the exit.

"Talk to that man, Dr. Smith. See if you can find any reason for the change."

"Right." Smith wandered away. Deauchez kept watching.

Teenager, teenager, tray syringe, tray syringe. Young women, one, two, three together, tray syringes all. Deauchez glanced behind him, his hopes sinking. He saw Smith talking with the man in the brown sweater.

The guard shot him a glance while Deauchez's head was up. He frowned and wagged a finger at him. *Why are you peeking around that curtain? Are you a pervert, into pain or . . .*

Deauchez squirmed, embarrassed. He pretended he hadn't seen the guard. He looked back at the doctor. Time was running out.

And then it happened again. Deauchez sensed it as soon as he looked back. At the table was an older woman, chunky, in her late forties, and she had with her a young man in a rugby shirt. She was talking to the nurse, a hand around the boy's shoulders, and something about the set of the boy's body, the protectiveness on the woman's face, and, yes, when he turned, the boy was a Down's syndrome child, maybe early twenties. The woman took his arm and walked him toward the curtain and the doctor took the chart from the nurse and glanced at the boy, no more than a glance, but suddenly Deauchez knew.

The doctor said something with a smile, something like *How are you* or *Aren't you a big fella* or *How was your trip, big guy,* and the woman smiled at the doctor gratefully and the back of the boy's head nodded, and the doctor reached down and took a syringe *from the box at the bottom of the cart.*

Smith stepped over to the fence. Deauchez could sense him, even though tears filled his eyes.

"That man's from Encino. He has prostate cancer."

"Oui," said Deauchez. He took a step backward. "What a godforsaken pack of Nazis!"

His voice was not particularly soft. His chest was heaving with choked tears. He looked like he wanted to start shouting.

"What?" Smith looked around uneasily. "Look, maybe we should take a walk."

"Yes, we are *leaving*!" Deauchez spat, louder still.

The guard who'd been watching them turned and began walking toward them at last, his face dark with annoyance.

Smith took Deauchez's arm—hot with plague or no—and steered the priest away.

* * *

Smith tried to stop once they were a safe distance from the parking lot, but Deauchez told him he was done here; that he wanted to leave. He didn't wait for an answer, merely headed back to the restaurant where they'd crossed into town. Smith followed.

Ten minutes later, they were back at the rock. The cartons had not been disturbed.

"Take one of the syringes from the green box and go inject Simon," Deauchez said, still breathing hard with anger.

"What is it? What did you see?" Smith's eyes darted over the two boxes.

"The syringes in the green boxes are the vaccines. Don't you see? They are choosing their survivors. Even in a crowd of 'friendlies' there are bound to be *some* that are undesirable."

Smith stared at him with a trapped look that said he knew damn well what Deauchez was talking about, but he didn't want to believe it, thank you very much. "Not . . . not really."

"Yes! 'Really!' It makes complete sense, if you can think vilely enough."

Smith looked off into the desert, scraping his lower lip with his teeth. "So what's in the red syringe?"

"I don't know. Placebo at best. Something fatal at worst— maybe even the virus itself."

Smith glanced at the red-marked box. "God."

"It's all right. You have the vaccine right here. A whole box of it."

"We're not sure of that."

"Sure enough to give a shot to Simon."

"Yes," Smith nodded. *After all, it couldn't hurt.* Deauchez could see the words on his face.

"Except *you* must do it, Dr. Smith. You must give Simon the shot. I have to go back to town."

Such a small thing shouldn't have surprised the doctor after everything else he'd heard today, but it did surprise him. "Oh, no! No, I can't . . ."

Deauchez grabbed Smith's arm, fed up. "God in heaven, will you stop thinking about yourself ! I *have* to go back there and try to make Andrews understand—try to *stop* this. And *someone* has to take care of Simon. He deserves it!"

Smith was shaking his head rapidly, his face stricken. "You

haven't seen what this disease can do! I don't have the proper gear, not anything!"

"If this is the antidote, or even just a vaccine, you will not have to worry about being contaminated. And if it's not, then *we are all lost anyway*. Don't you understand that?"

Deauchez realized he was gripping Smith painfully. He released his fingers. Smith looked down at Deauchez's withdrawing hands blankly. "Yeah. I guess I do."

"So please, I'm begging you—go give Simon one of the shots from the green box. Make sure he's as comfortable as possible. Then leave—drive back down to Phoenix with the rest of the syringes. Take them to your WHO or whatever you think is best. But be *very careful* who you trust. Don't take chances with them."

Smith looked exhausted and defeated. "All right."

Deauchez felt his anger drain away. He rubbed his eyes. If only he weren't so damned tired. "Perhaps you should leave a few syringes under the seat of our car, just in case. He's very bad."

"And you'll need one," Smith said. Deauchez didn't bother to answer.

Smith picked up the cartons, obviously not happy about touching the red-marked box. Deauchez helped him, placed the lit flashlight in one shaking hand.

"Thanks," Smith said. Deauchez couldn't tell if he meant it or not.

"Thank *you*, Dr. Smith. I'm very sorry to ask this of you. God be with you."

Then Smith was gone with the boxes, heading off toward the car. Deauchez made the sign of the cross and said a brief prayer for Simon as he watched him go.

CHAPTER 19

SEDONA, ARIZONA

Deauchez moved quickly through the streets to the hotel he'd noted earlier, gave the most reasonable-looking guard his name, and asked to see Andrews. He gave his full name, Father Michele Deauchez, fearing that Andrews would not recognize him otherwise. It made him feel paranoid—as though the Hawaiian shirt were a disguise and saying his title, "Father," stripped it off. But he saw no one who didn't look like an Andrews groupie—no one paid any attention to him at all.

He didn't know what to expect, even if Andrews recognized the name. They hadn't parted on the best of terms, and any hint that there might be more to discuss about Santa Pelagia, that *terra divinum*, would probably not be welcome.

The guard returned with a soft-eyed, bearded man whom he introduced simply as "Scott." Scott reminded Deauchez of what Americans had called "Jesus freaks" in the sixties—like he ought to be sitting on the grass, strumming a guitar, encouraging others to give peace a chance. He listened as Deauchez repeated his request and said he would "ask Trent." A few minutes later he returned, smiling warmly, and led Deauchez inside.

The interior of the building was stifling after the nip of the evening air. In the lobby, someone was stoking the blaze in a pueblo fireplace. People were lounging serenely about, mostly beautiful women, Deauchez noted, and beautiful young men. In the corridors of the hotel, he passed more of these passive, luminescent creatures. They looked either mad or stoned. He didn't see anyone who looked like hotel personnel. He wondered briefly what had happened to the people whose town Andrews had taken over.

"You're a priest?" Scott asked, as they mounted a flight of stairs.

"Yes."

Scott smiled. "Well, go for it. That's what Santa Pelagia is all about, isn't it? God loving all faiths?"

Deauchez was almost offended at the implication. Santa Pelagia? About *love*? But he stretched a smile in reply. He didn't trust himself to speak.

They entered a clay-tiled corridor on the second floor. The door in front of them, a once-ordinary oak hotel room door, had had its number removed, and someone—someone quite good—had painted a picture of an angel on it. There was nothing cherubic about this entity. The angel filled the door from the top, which the crown of the angel's head just brushed, to the bottom, where the first tentative touch of toe to earth took place. The angel's hands were held palms open and out, in a gesture typically associated with Jesus. Its masculine chest was exposed and magnificent. Its lower body was covered with flowing drapery. Its golden-maned head was tilted chin down, and its eyes stared up at the viewer. There was a triumphant, transcendent, yet somehow sexual expression on that face. It was the face, Deauchez realized, of Trent Andrews himself.

"Here we are," Scott said, in the voice of a born courtier.

In a moment of clarity Deauchez realized that he never should have come. But it was too late. He was ushered into the room and left there, alone.

By the time Mike reached the cars, his arms were shaking with fatigue from carrying the two cartons while trying to manage the flashlight. The awkwardness of it had at least kept him from thinking about much else. He lowered the cases on the top of his car and stretched his arms, wincing at the pain and quaking with relief. If he'd dropped the serum out there!

What was the matter with the priest, anyway—if he really *was* a priest? What was so urgent that he couldn't help Mike get the cartons back to the car and take care of Hill? To Mike, the town and everyone in it was completely gone, mad as hatters, around the bend and then out in left field about a mile. If Deauchez thought he was going to talk some sense into them, then he was mad, too.

But Mike was here now, and he hadn't dropped the syringes.

His irritation evaporated along with his sweat in the cool desert night. He picked up the flashlight from the car hood where he'd dropped it and swung it toward the other car, that horrid blue hatchback.

Not horrid: hot, *breathtakingly hot.*

The rear windows were thick with red dust from the road, but Mike could make out the dark head of Hill in the passenger seat. It didn't look as though he'd stirred.

How long had Deauchez said Hill had been in the fever stage? Twenty-four hours? It was possible no brain damage had occurred yet. Barely. Mike took a nervous breath and headed for his car door.

He pulled out his bag and began ripping through it. He donned a thick denim shirt, buttoning it to his throat. He put on an extra pair of khaki pants over his jeans. He placed a pair of underwear—unfortunately dirty; everything in his bag was dirty—over his head and tucked in his hair. He put his paper mask back on, took three syringes from the green box and placed them carefully to one side on the hood, then took thick white socks from his bag and placed them on his hands.

He walked toward the car, holding the syringes as lightly as he could without dropping them. He just hoped Hill didn't wake up and get a look at him during all of this, or they'd probably *both* die of fright.

The room was a sitting room, part of a small suite. Off to the left, an open archway led to the bedroom. The original Southwest touches—the aqua and coral stripes near the ceiling, the cream textured walls, and the aqua wall-to-wall carpet—were still evident. But the less permanent trappings had been replaced by items closer to Andrews's tastes: gold satin sheets, celestial paintings, and amorphous leather furniture.

At first, Deauchez couldn't see Andrews. The only light in the room came from one soft orb of a lamp near the door. Then his eyes adjusted, and he saw the prophet lying on a couch near the wall. He was wearing only a diaphanous white garment wrapped around his hips; his chest and legs were bare. He was stretched out on his back, his arms over his head, feet projecting off the other end. He looked like a cat lying in self-exposed luxury.

His eyes were open, but he didn't turn his head. "Father Michele Deauchez," he said, softly and without emotion.

"Mr. Andrews, thank you for seeing me." Deauchez was extremely uncomfortable. The change in Andrews was fascinating in a horrible way, but not conducive to the discussion he'd had in mind.

Andrews sat up slowly, swinging his legs down. He gazed at Deauchez from under half-closed lids. "Trent, please. You may give me your lecture now, if you must. Or have you come to your senses at last?" His felinity was so great, Deauchez thought that he might start licking his paws.

"I *have* learned a great deal since we last met, yes."

"*I* have learned things, as well."

Andrews stood, with measured lethargy, and walked to the bar. "How about a drink? You do drink wine, don't you, Michele?"

The intimate name seemed calculated to Deauchez. He cleared his throat. "Not at the moment, thank you. I'm rather tired, and it would put me to sleep."

Andrews poured two glasses anyway. "That's an excuse for little American farm girls, not Frenchmen. But you do look tired, Michele." Andrews walked over and handed him the glass. He didn't move away again, but stood studying Deauchez's face. "Yes. You look very tired and very old."

Deauchez fought the urge to step away from Andrews's too-near and too-bare presence. He changed the subject. "On my way here, the road was full of cars."

"Yes. They come. From everywhere they come." To Deauchez's relief, Andrews went to the window and looked out. "With each sign fulfilled the ignorance of the cattle loosens a little more. We shall have to close the border eventually. I warned them *days* ago to come. If they aren't here by now, they aren't truly ready for the Change." Andrews looked at Deauchez as if for validation. "I can't save *everyone*."

Deauchez refused to rise to the bait. "There is a group outside giving inoculations."

"Yes," Andrews said with little interest.

"Do you know what the shots are for?"

Andrews waved a dismissive hand. "Tuberculosis . . . something."

"Did the county require it?"

"Michele! I'm beyond caring about the pitiful laws of this country. The United States is already history to me! I do nothing that I don't want to do."

"Then who convinced you to allow the inoculations?"

"Why waste my time talking about the shots?" Andrews was growing annoyed. "They're for the body, and the body is at best a temporary vessel. You wanted to see me. I assume it's about something more important than that."

Deauchez walked over to the bar and put his wineglass down. "Of course. I apologize. I *will* tell you what I came here to say. I ask only that you listen with an open mind."

Andrews leaned back against the window ledge, a slight breeze ruffling his hair. He tilted his head in assent, his eyes full of mocking curiosity. Deauchez tried to ignore the implications of the look, and began.

Mike opened the car door slowly and stared at what was left of Simon Hill. The reporter's chubby, chocolate-colored face had deteriorated into a yellow puffiness that was putrefaction's foreplay. His lips were enlarged and pulled back from his teeth by the tautness of the skin stretched over his cheeks and skull.

Mike put the syringes on the floor under the passenger seat, then he pulled the blanket down gently. Hill's torso looked bitingly constricted by his clothes and the electrical cording. He moaned.

Trying to keep his face back as far as possible, Mike worked at the electrical cords with his sock-encased fingers, going over to the driver's side to complete the task. He understood why it had been necessary while Deauchez was driving, but the cords left deep, angry welts in Hill's swelling chest and abdomen. Mike loosened the reporter's jeans, as well. They really needed to be removed, but the best he could do was to open the waistline. Trying to shift Hill's bulk on his own would be lethal.

Hill's stomach was hot and hard, even through the makeshift gloves. It expanded out of the opened pants like the top on a baking muffin.

Mike pushed up the sleeve on Hill's right arm and picked up one of the syringes from under the seat. He uncapped it. Despite his resolve, he couldn't stop his hand from shaking. This serum could be pure Santarém for all he knew, whatever the priest thought.

But it was Hill's only chance. Mike jabbed the needle into Hill's arm and depressed the plunger. Hill's eyes opened as the needle went in, and when Mike glanced up he saw glazed, yellow orbs. He stepped back impulsively, banging his head on the roof of the car.

"Am I dead?" Hill croaked, his voice raw and dry.

"No. And I just gave you a shot that may make you feel better."

"Water?"

Mike looked around and saw a takeout cup. He put the empty syringe under the seat and picked up the drink. He held the straw to Hill's lips, trying not to get saliva on the sock. It wasn't a huge problem; Hill's mouth was as dry as an old woman's hands.

"*The* shot?" Hill asked feverishly after a few weak sips. "Was it *the* shot? Deauchez . . . ?"

"Deauchez will be back soon. He went to talk to Trent Andrews. But yes, it was *the* shot. Now *shhhh*—rest."

"*The* shot?" Hill muttered painfully, then he fell back asleep—abruptly—as though the short conversation had exhausted him.

"*The* shot," Mike said again, though he knew Hill couldn't hear him.

He tucked the blanket up around the reporter. It was the worst thing to do for a fever, but there'd be no one to cover him if he awoke with one of Santarém's bone-racking chills. He shut the door, walked back to the desert's edge, and shone the flashlight out into the night. There was no sign of Deauchez, nothing at all.

He took one last, guilty look at the hatchback, then stripped: everything he'd just put on and the clothes underneath them, too. Naked, he looked around helplessly, then rubbed the sand and dirt from the desert against his skin, rubbing it until his flesh screamed and his nose and mouth were choked with the stuff. He went back to his car and put on one of his last sets of dirty clothes, leaving the hot ones on the desert floor.

He put the cartons in his car and turned the vehicle around; began heading back toward the main road, where the lights of arriving cars were still coming on in an endless flow.

Deauchez talked without interruption. About the time he was describing the Janovich video, Andrews lost that absent studying of Deauchez's face, that amused quirk at the corner of his mouth. When Deauchez described the Red Scepter host, Andrews stood up straighter and his eyes took on a new look that was unreadable—except that it was not in the least bit mocking anymore.

When he'd finished, Deauchez leaned back against the bar and sipped the wine in his glass. He waited, watching Andrews for some clue.

For a moment, Deauchez felt a wave of empowerment. He and Hill *would* succeed in spreading the word. The Vatican would have a stronghold by now that believed his story, thanks to Carnesca, and perhaps Hill's boss had held the story to check a few facts—perhaps it would run tomorrow. Smith would take the vaccine to WHO and reproduce it. Hill would live to write and write about the conspiracy, and Deauchez would continue the fight—he'd talk to Daunsey next. He'd convince all the prophets one by one to release their people and they would, when the newspapers started admitting it was all a lie.

Andrews refilled his glass and topped off Deauchez's while he was at it. "I think you're right about the prophets receiving inoculations *before* Santa Pelagia—against the sores and Santarém. They could have done it when they gave us the message, as you say. But they didn't inoculate me in my therapist's office—you're wrong there. They did it in the mother ship."

Deauchez's budding smile faded out like a too-brief flower. "I . . . I suppose it's possible."

"I want you to give me the names of all the humans you mentioned, the ones you know are involved." Andrews went to a table and picked up paper and pencil.

Deauchez repeated the names uneasily: Janovich, Tendir, Donnelley, McKlennan, Cole, probably others at Telegyn. Andrews dutifully wrote them down.

"Great! Now what about the phone?"

"The phone?"

"The one that links directly into the Red Scepter host."

Andrews had definitely been listening.

"Er . . . I don't have it with me."

"It's in your car, perhaps?"

Deauchez hesitated. "I don't understand your interest in the phone."

Andrews tossed down the pad and moved closer. To Deauchez's astonishment, his face was grasped on both sides. Andrews had a bizarre, ate-the-canary grin, and an even more bewildering hint of pity behind it.

"You're so limited. You see everything and understand nothing!"

Deauchez squirmed.

"Your eyes gaze at truth and you deny it."

"But . . ."

"Shhhhh!" Andrews's face was inches from Deauchez's own. His eyes were carnivorous.

"I don't understand," Deauchez said piteously. He didn't like being held, not by such as Andrews, not with that look on Andrews's face. His heart slammed in his chest and struggled to get free as if *it* were being grasped.

"Our government has been in contact with the aliens since 1952 at least. Of course they would have some part in this procedure! It never occurred to me before, but it makes perfect sense."

"I don't think it is . . ."

"We *knew* a contingent in the government had knowledge of the aliens. *They've* held the true power. *They've* kept the truth out of even the highest office. Presidents are far too political to be trusted. So you've found out what this group is called—the Red Scepter. Good for you. UFO investigators have been looking for proof of them for decades."

Deauchez tried to shake his head, but it was trapped. "No, the Red Scepter is much older than the fifties, because their crest—"

"Shhhhh!" Andrews's eyes were wild, daydreamy. "So some humans have knowledge of this project—this Project Apocalypse. Telegyn is no doubt in with the aliens. Maybe even an alien company. Cole could be one of *them*, you know. There always was something superhumanly perfect about him. I wish I'd paid more attention."

The man was completely delusional, Deauchez realized. He tried to salvage what he could. "Very well. So a small group of humans is in on this . . . this alien conspiracy. But all of these signs have still been intentionally *set up*. They plan to kill off more than two-thirds of the population. You don't . . . don't *agree* with that . . . do you?"

Andrews looked at Deauchez ruefully. "Let me ask *you* something. What would you say if it were God doing it? Wouldn't you assume that God knew what he was doing?"

"No! No, I would not."

Andrews *tsk-tsk*ed. "You have such limited vision, Michele. Look at how shitty this planet has become. Don't you want to *evolve*? Don't you want to become like me? *Look at me!*"

He released Deauchez and stepped back. He lifted his arms

and turned, slowly, his skin glistening in the dim glow of the room. "Don't you see how I've been altered?"

"You look like an ordinary man to me," Deauchez said softly. He knew it was probably the worst thing he could say, but he couldn't help himself. He was tired of these fantasies.

Andrews looked down and shook his head in a bemused negative gesture, like a parent responding to a child's misperception. "No. You're not in tune enough to see. I'm *becoming*. Soon even ignorance such as yours won't be able to mask my glory. I'll be a being of pure light, capable of assuming any physical shape I wish, whenever I wish."

"What about the billions who will die? Does that not mean anything to you?"

Andrews smiled. "You've resolved my only source of doubt, do you know that, Michele? I couldn't figure out why the aliens would select people like Stanton. Now I know. Only a few enlightened ones have been selected—the 'friendlies,' as you call us. *We* will be the true fathers of the new millennium. The rest . . . gathered together so . . . *whoosh!*" He raised his arm as though wielding an angelic sword and brought it down in an unmistakable gesture.

"I can't believe you want that," Deauchez said, squeezing his eyes shut, but he didn't say it with much confidence. He took a step back.

"Our protectors know best. We *must evolve*; it's time! Those who are capable have been selected, and the number is *two billion*. That's more than I expected, frankly. They gave us thousands of years of reincarnation to be ready—those who are not have only themselves to blame. They've weighed down the human race long enough."

"I . . . I should leave." Deauchez felt bile rise in his throat. He backed toward the door.

But Andrews moved toward him. "Perhaps you can survive, if you stay here. I'm not sure if you're capable, but perhaps if you stay close to me, if you *try*." Andrews held out his arms, advancing. "Stay with me; let love and light fill your body and you may yet be saved."

Deauchez gasped with sudden comprehension. He took another step back and found himself up against the door. He felt around for the knob, but before he could turn it, Andrews was on him. He grasped the priest's face in both hands, as he had before, and this time he pressed his lips to Deauchez's. His body, oiled and hard, pushed against him. Deauchez was locked: his muscles, his lips, locked. With a cry of revulsion he thrust Andrews away. He wiped his mouth with the back of his hand, breathing hard. "Please!"

Andrews's face contorted with an ugly rage. He called out, "Scott!" The blond man opened the door.

"Put this 'visitor' in the jail!" Andrews took a deep breath and expelled it, as if to cleanse himself of the entire scene. He turned away.

"What are you doing?" Deauchez protested.

"Put him in isolation, please. I don't want him talking to anyone."

"Yes, Trent." Scott took Deauchez's arm. Deauchez looked at him imploringly, but the young man's face was set in a neutral silence. He would not meet Deauchez's eyes.

"But why do you do this? What right—"

"Since you are so unenlightened, I'm concerned that you might tempt others to negative thoughts. Things are very delicate right now. *Very* delicate."

"I will leave at once, I swear! I won't talk to anyone."

"I'm afraid that's just not good enough." Andrews's voice was so cold it had already dismissed, buried, and forgotten him.

As he was walked through the building and out into the street, Deauchez offered up a prayer he knew would not be heard. He'd walked into this mess out of blind desire to prove to Andrews that he was wrong, to hear him *admit* that he was wrong, to hear him tell all those people out there that he was wrong.

It was pride, stupid intellectual pride, and now he would pay. Who knew how many others would now be condemned to death, as well—all for the sin of his pride?

The cartons were in the backseat, covered with Mike's coat. He'd thought about putting them in the trunk, but he'd wanted to keep an eye on them—the backseat felt safer somehow. The rental car jostled on the dirt road, and now and then Mike imagined he heard a light *clink* from the boxes. That was silly, of course; the hypos were plastic and snug inside the cartons' lining.

Get on the main road, he told himself, *and you'll be home free.* There was little traffic headed back the way he was going, so he could be back at I-17 in half an hour. And from there to the airport in Phoenix . . . why, he could be in Washington by dawn.

The entrance to the main road was within the beam of his headlights now, and he saw that there were five men standing there, at the edge of the asphalt, waiting and watching his approaching lights.

Mike took his foot off the gas and touched the brake, slowing the car to a crawl. What were they doing? They hadn't been guarding the dirt road when he and Deauchez drove on to it. Had they seen his headlights?

Mike began to sweat. He wished he'd put the syringes in the trunk after all, but he couldn't very well do it now. Or could he? He stopped the car and pulled up the emergency brake. He took the keys from the ignition and, after a moment's hesitation, left the lights on.

Hurrying now, fear priming him, he got out of the car, ran back, and opened the trunk. It took four tries to get the right key in the slot, seconds ticking away. He ran back and grabbed the boxes from the backseat, taking them to the trunk as hastily as he dared.

He thought he heard shouting.

He arranged his coat over the white cardboard, slammed the lid shut, and dodged back to the driver's seat. He got in, turned the ignition.

Yes, the men were running toward him. Now they were halfway between him and the main road, and still they came, not pausing when his car rolled forward. He thought about turning off into the desert, but that terrain—its vastness and unevenness—made the choice intimidating. Besides, there was no time to think it through. They intersected twenty seconds later.

Several of the men held up their hands, indicating that he should stop. Heart pounding, he did. A man opened his door.

"Step out of the car, please!"

"I'm sorry? I was just heading out to the freeway, and I realized I didn't have my map out—"

"Step out of the car! Now!"

Mike's legs were like water. He stumbled getting out. A flashlight shone in his eyes.

"What are you doing out here?" The man with the flashlight had thick white hair and a youngish face. His tone wasn't angry, but it was determined. Two of the others began searching the interior of the car.

"I'm local," Mike lied. "I was just trying to make my way down to Phoenix. The roads are so packed."

White Hair's face was barely visible over the glare of the flashlight. It was stony, blank. "Can I see your driver's license, sir?"

"Sure." Mike dug out his wallet. "You know I, um, I'm still registered in D.C. for tax purposes. Sedona's more of a vacation home, but I pretty much live out here. *Heh, heh.* You know how that goes."

The man looked at Mike's ID, then at Mike. He handed it back. "What kind of physician are you, Dr. Smith?"

"G.P."

"We need the keys for the trunk, Hart," said one of the men who'd been searching the car.

Mike glanced toward the speaker, letting a panicky expression slip through. White Hair—a.k.a. Hart, apparently—took the keys from Mike's hand and tossed them.

"Where are you coming from? There're no houses back on this road. There's nothing. I've driven it myself. It just skirts town and ends up on the other side."

"Yeah, well I was *on* the other side of town. I was just trying to avoid traffic."

The popping of the trunk echoed in the darkness. Mike looked toward the noise, his face set in a pleasant smile.

"Dr. Smith, can you explain why you've been rolling around in dirt?" Hart's voice tightened perceptibly.

Mike grinned; he couldn't help it—it was nerves. He wiped at his face. "It was my dog. She . . ."

"Shit!" said one of the other men. "Hart, get back here!"

Mike's knees buckled and he leaned back against the car door. Hart grabbed his arm and pulled him to the trunk.

"It's just some medical supplies," Mike said.

No one spoke as Hart surveyed the boxes. Mike heard someone's feet shuffling restlessly in the dirt. It triggered an odd memory of being backstage at a recital of his sister's; hearing her step with her ballet shoes in the sandbox, assuming a professional air, the way young girls do.

Hart shone the light in his eyes.

"We should tell Scott," said one of the men.

"Those cartons are from our inoculations." Hart's voice had a new edge that Mike could only identify as *bad*.

"No. They're some supplies I had at the cabin, and I thought—"

Hart struck him, a blow across the face. It made a loud, cracking sound in the night. Mike raised a hand to his stinging cheek, eyes wide.

"How did you get them?"

Someone whispered. "Geez, we should go get Scott."

"We're not getting anyone!" Hart ordered, his eyes never leaving Mike's face. "Now *tell me*."

"Yes. We took them."

"Why? Because you thought they might be good drugs? Want a little fix, did you? Want to sell the stuff ?"

"No! I'm a doctor! I wanted to . . ."

"Yes? "

"To take them to some friends who didn't want to come to the camp," Mike finished awkwardly.

"Bull. Shit," one of the men muttered.

"He's just tryin' to make a buck stealing supplies," someone said. "Let's take him to the jail."

"Yes," Hart agreed. He stepped back and looked at the others. "I'll walk him over there. You guys finish searching the car—rip out the seats, everything. And get those boxes back to the H.A.I. people. Be *careful* with them. Have one of the medics make sure there're no syringes missing. If there are, I want to know how many."

"I'll go with you," a small, wiry man said.

"No, thanks. I can handle him. Why don't you go find Scott? I think I saw him by the main gate a few minutes ago."

"Are you sure you don't need me?"

"I have a gun, don't I?"

Hart took Mike's arm and tugged. He led him, not back along the dirt road, but across the desert directly toward town.

They said nothing as they walked. Hart's left hand guided Mike, and his right held the gun. Mike was lost in thinking that he'd possibly just lost the Santarém vaccine for the human race, or at least for that portion the Red Scepter let die before they released it themselves.

It was true: Mike had never completely bought into Deauchez's story. It was like watching a really convincing UFO documentary. While you watched it you had that creepy feeling that it just might be true. The next day, it seemed much less plausible. Two days later, you'd forgotten it completely.

But Mike had still been in the middle of this particular UFO story, and even while his rational mind sent up warning flags, he'd believed in it enough to risk his life getting that serum, to be desperate to get it to the lab. It wouldn't be a hard test to run—simply put some Santarém virus in a sterilized petri dish and squirt in a few drops from the syringe. If it killed the virus, he would have just paid for his existence on this planet a thousand times over.

And then he'd inject himself with the very first dose, because God knows he'd been exposed. In fact, he *should* have gone ahead and injected himself back at the car. Even if he wasn't sure it was the vaccine, the chance was better than certain death. And there couldn't have been anything too bad in it, according to Deauchez—not the syringes in the green-circle cartons, not the stuff being given to the fine and strapping young friendlies.

They were well away from the dirt road when Hart stopped. Mike glanced back and saw his rental car being driven away. There was nothing else out here in the dark but him and his escort. He wondered why Hart had paused, but he wasn't afraid. In his mind, he was already in that jail cell, sans vaccine, and that was enough of a disaster to contemplate.

Hart apparently didn't think so. He brought the gun up in front of Mike's eye and removed the safety very deliberately; pointed it at his forehead.

"I want you to tell me the real reason you took those syringes." Hart's face was utterly calm; his voice held not a trace of emotion.

Mike's heart began to pound; the fear he'd experienced at the car whelmed back up in a reprise. "What do you mean?"

"You didn't go to the trouble of stealing those syringes because they contained a tuberculosis vaccine. So why did you take them?"

Mike tried to read the man's face and could not. He had no reason to trust Hart, it was true. Yet what was in the end more compelling was Mike's history of always being able to convince others of his point of view. Basic moral rectitude—he had faith in it the way others had faith in God. And this man, surely this man couldn't know what was *really* going on, could he?

"All right. The syringes might contain a vaccine for the Santarém virus. We have proof that there's a human conspiracy behind these apocalypse signs. The virus is certainly man-made. Have you been reading the papers? This thing could kill every man, woman, and child on Earth. I know it sounds unlikely, but I can explain *exactly* what's going on. I can explain it to you, to Trent Andrews, to whomever you'd like."

"Who's 'we'?" Hart asked calmly. "Who helped you steal those syringes? Who told you all this?"

"I . . ." Mike hesitated, sensing that things were not going well. "Well, a couple of guys I met. They've already left the area."

Hart stared.

"Look, you can take me back to town if you want, let me go over all this with Andrews or whoever. But if you *really* want to save people, just give me a couple of syringes. I actually work for the World Health Organization—I can get them tested. Every hour I lose might cost millions of lives. You can say I ran away."

Hart gave an almost imperceptible nod. "Yes. You *did* try to run away."

"Huh?"

The man's grip on Mike's arm relaxed and fell away. The gun straightened and firmed ever so slightly, the muzzle like a black tunnel in front of Mike's eyes.

"Run," Hart said.

Mike realized what was coming. Without a thought, his only impetus sheer terror, he did as he was told. He spun around and began churning through the dirt as fast as his feet would carry him. A brief cry of fear erupted from somewhere in his belly.

One, two, three, four steps.

Mike heard the report, like a slamming door, even as he realized his feet were no longer on the ground, that he was flying through the air. It was the last sound he ever heard. Not even the falling of his own body registered on those deaf ears.

CHAPTER 20

DAY 18
WASHINGTON, D.C.

They came for Anthony Cole at his home in Georgetown at 3 A.M. The team was suited, efficient, respectful. A doctor examined Cole in his bedroom. A young woman, her body hidden in the papery folds of her white suit, drew his blood, thick latex gloves slapping cool rubber against the inside of his arm. He could tell, by subtleties in their demeanor and by their in-and-out productivity, that he was only one of many officials roused this morning—not *the* official, not yet. Afterward he was asked to put on a suit similar to theirs. The new Racals were slim and flexible, but still a nuisance. He did not tell them that he had no need for one.

He was driven in a chauffeured car to an emergency session at the House. The committee consisted of senators and congressmen. Several who were present were in the first stages of Santarém and knew it. The sickness in their midst, behind the face shields, only made the committee's task that much more urgent. Their aim: to get some vestiges of a noninfected government in place before the leadership of the free world disappeared entirely.

The president and vice president were busy dying. The Speaker of the House and the president pro tempore of the Senate were also riding the Santarém express. This much was outlined in the first half hour. In the second, they debated whether or not the normal rule of succession applied in a crisis like this. They decided that it did apply, at least until it was clear that all reasonable candidates on the list of succession were infected. Cole, next in line, was visibly clean, though his blood test would have the final say on that score.

No one indicated, or even seemed to feel, that Cole would not be at least a *reasonable* president. He had been a visible and popular secretary of state. Certainly, none of these men would doubt his ambition. And, of course, he had his supporters in the group, those who shared his vision—and his loyalties.

At this juncture Cole was dismissed from the proceedings so that the committee might retain impartiality. More important, his duties called him elsewhere. The members all rose as he exited, deferential in their silence, resembling a delegation of astronauts. Cole was driven to the Pentagon, where other emergency sessions were afoot.

By 5:15 A.M. what was left of the National Security Council was gathered in the war room. That meant Anthony Cole and Norman King. King was not only an old friend of Cole's, he was the director of the CIA, a far from coincidental conjunction that had proved invaluable in the past few months. The general who was temporarily replacing Brant was named Myers. He was the highest-ranking general in the United States Army, and he was not an old friend of Cole's. Whether he'd been infected before he donned his suit was anybody's guess.

"They're coming in from both directions," Myers said, pointing out the images on the electronic map display. "The east wing of their attack will be approaching over the North Atlantic; the west, from the Pacific. Both wings are about two hours away, and they're already starting to fan out. My guess is it'll be a scattershot formation. They might even position some units to cross the border over Mexico and Canada."

Myers looked calm, confident, deeply in his element. Not since Pearl Harbor had America faced an invasion, but Myers didn't appear to be particularly worried about it. "We'll launch an immediate counterattack from some of our deep-sea carriers, knock out at least a few of 'em before they get close. But most of our force will be positioned at the twenty to thirty miles offshore range. Everything we've got is headed that way right now."

"How do we stack up against their hardware, General?" Cole asked, although he knew quite well.

"The SU-27 is the best they've got, and that's about half their fighter division. The rest are a mix of older models. They're bogged down, though, by large carrier planes—the kind that hold four to five hundred men apiece. The fighters are in front of the carriers and sticking close, a kind of protective vanguard.

Based on this configuration, I'd say China will be less interested in engaging in air battles than it will be in getting those carriers over land. They've got a lot of men in the air, and they can't do a whole lot of fighting strapped in."

"Is that likely, General? That they'll get those carriers over-land?" King asked.

"About as likely as tits on a choir boy. We've got radar up and down the coastlines. We can spot a *pigeon* in the air, and our fighters are twenty years ahead of their best. No, they don't have a chance of comin' in, but it'll be bloody. There's gonna be a lot of well-fed sharks today."

Cole tented his fingers—white glove tips to white glove tips. "I'm glad to hear that. We await your lead, General, of course."

"Of course," Norman King echoed, with a smile.

6:45 A.M. EST, 2:45 P.M. IRAQ
UNITED ARAB FORCES COMMAND CENTER, OUTSIDE BAGHDAD

The display was crude by American standards—a row of seventeen-inch CRTs with yellow blips and chunky lettering. But they served their purpose. Mal Abbas could see China's strike force as it approached U.S. airspace.

He was sweating inside his green and gold uniform, his nerves strung as tightly as Gabriel's lyre. He did not doubt the prophecy's veracity exactly. Had he, Abbas, not been at Santa Pelagia? And had Allah not given other prophecies there that had already been fulfilled? What he did doubt was his own worth as Allah's mouthpiece. He worried that he had done something wrong again, something that would cause Allah to abandon him. And he worried that he had somehow misunderstood the angel's instructions.

He voiced none of these fears, to China or anyone else. China had agreed to his request—to the appointed day, the appointed hour. Abbas eyed the clock on the wall nervously even now, to confirm this for the hundredth time. Yes, yes. The hour was approaching and the planes were in the air. But Abbas knew Lee assented to the timing because it suited him, not out of any real respect for Allah. Would Allah offer his protection to a man like that?

Abbas looked at the clock again and expelled a held breath. It came out as a moan. He clamped his teeth shut over it. *Soon,*

soon. Allah, I have followed your will. Make good your oath. For my people. For the Koran.

He asked the radar operator, "Any sign of unusual activity?"

"Like what, sir?"

Abbas shook his head sharply in a *never mind*. Why had he even asked? It was not yet time.

In the next room, Iraq's titular leader, Hadar, was coordinating the United Arab Forces' attack on Europe—within certain parameters, of course. Abbas had insisted that the prophet centers remain unscathed for the time being and China had agreed. Still, Abbas ought to be in there; Hadar would gain too much control. But Abbas could not get himself to leave these displays, the live blips that represented China's advance. The Arab attack was only human warfare. With China flew the Heavenly Host.

A private cleared his throat behind him. "President Lee is on the phone, General."

Abbas picked up the handset, his palm slick against the cool plastic. "This is Abbas."

"General Abbas!" Lee sounded like he was trying very hard not to scream. "We are getting close to the American border."

"Yes. I'm watching it from here."

"So where is this miracle you promised us?"

Abbas bit back a remark about Lee's godlessness not being worthy of a miracle. He looked, instead, at the clock. One moment the black second hand was crawling and the next it lunged forward, his heart lunging with it. "It will be soon, President Lee."

Abbas felt a presence at his elbow. It was Hadar. The revolutionary looked at him with cold eyes, then at the clock, then at the monitors. He said nothing, but there was a smug tilt at the corner of his lips. If Abbas's prediction failed, Hadar would make sure every man, woman, and child in Iraq knew it. More important, there would be no chance of getting cooperation for the second prophecy—not from Hadar, from whom he did not expect it, but not even from China.

"General Lee, I must go . . ." Abbas began, feeling ill.

"You will stay on this phone until this is over!" Lee said. Then he added in a more moderate tone, ". . . If you would."

"Certainly." Abbas licked the sweat from his lips.

They stood in silent apprehension. Abbas's eyes went from

the CRT display to the clock and back again, as alert as a cat watching a fly bat around the room. At 3:00 P.M. the second hand fell into place with the finality of an axman's blade. Abbas could barely hold the receiver in his hand, thought he'd surely pass out if he didn't put it down, if he didn't *sit* down. His eyes went to the display with a dry rasping shift.

Nothing had changed. On the CRTs the blips were nearly on top of one another now.

"Abbas . . ." Lee began, on the edge of panic. Beside him, Hadar grinned spitefully.

Then the display went blank.

THE PENTAGON

Anthony Cole was watching with the others when the radar went out. One moment the Chinese blips were present and were approaching the blips that represented the American defenses, and the next, every indicator on the map was gone. General Myers communicated pungently with the computer operators, but they could not get the signals back.

What followed for the next ten minutes was eminently professional chaos. Cole offered little input, waiting for Myers to figure it out. One of the Air Force's chief radar experts was finally patched into the room's speaker line.

"Captain Wilson, what the *hell* is going on?" Myers screamed at him, as though Wilson had not only fucked up personally, but was responsible for debilitating the entire U.S. military.

Wilson's disembodied voice was high and tight. "The Chinese fleet has just passed our line, General. But ten minutes ago all of our U.S.-based radar systems went down. They just—just went down. Our satellites' infrared and optical capacities are still operational, but they're not gonna be a whole lot of help. We're blind, sir."

As panicked as Wilson sounded about this, he'd at least had time to assimilate it. Myers, on the other hand, grabbed his stomach and gasped as though he'd just been kicked in certain tender regions. "Holy Christ! Are we under nuclear attack?"

"Unlikely, sir. The BMEWS station in Greenland is still operational. There are no ICBMs in the air. I repeat: no ICBMs in the air. However, the radar problem *will* interfere with our ability to detect hostile subs. There's also the problem of what China's birds might be carrying. But as of this moment, we're facing a conventional force."

Myers looked over at Cole. "Jesus," he said, but he sounded relieved. "The Chinese wouldn't have a snowball's chance in hell of knocking out our nukes using subs and planes. So I doubt they'll start any of that shit."

Cole exchanged a look with Mr. King. "That's good to hear, General," he said.

Myers nodded repeatedly; too repeatedly.

"Did any of our boys get in the air, General?" Cole prompted.

"Right. Wilson? What's going on at the line?"

"There was a . . . um . . . lot of confusion. An awful lot of our birds were already up. Radios went out—we couldn't communicate with them. Most of them tried to come in. We . . . we lost a couple dozen due to malfunction or . . . uh . . . collision. We do have fighters up now, General. But without radar they've only got their eyes. On some of the new bombers the visibility from the cockpit is not . . ."

Myers's scowl had been deepening with every word. "Bottom line, Captain!"

"Yes, sir. Bottom line—they're getting through. I'd say we have about a third of our capacity in the air, and their effectiveness is severely compromised. Some of our weapons systems— the Stealth missiles, for example—use radar for targeting. We've had to fall back to the manual guns, which require a much closer range and—again—visibility."

"I can see that, Captain."

"The West Coast is even more of a problem. It's still dark over there, and there's supposed to be a heavy fog this morning along . . . um . . . the California and Oregon coast. That'll make visibility a real—"

"We get the point!" Myers barked.

Since no one else was saying it, and Myers looked too stupefied to think it up on his own, Cole had to make the suggestion himself, "Excuse me, General. Could this be HAARP technology?"

Myers's face flooded with understanding. He headed for the idea like a bull charging a matador, spinning on one of his own men. "That's it, Lieutenant—Chinese HAARP! Why the *hell* didn't we see it coming?"

The young man shook his head, once, sharply. "Negative, sir.

China's HAARP program is rudimentary. *We* couldn't pull this off."

"It *has* to be HAARP, Lieutenant! That's what HAARP *does*—heat the ionosphere, scramble radar waves. Right? Our intelligence missed it. They must have."

"General, *we've* only got a few ground-based HAARP stations. China doesn't have even that much on-line. To cause this wide an effect you'd need a satellite program at least."

Norman King shot a glance at Cole, but Cole didn't return it—he was busy examining his manicured nails. He was thinking that the lieutenant was right: the U.S. HAARP program *was* rudimentary. It wasn't that the military strategists didn't understand the potential: all wave signals bounced off the Earth's ionosphere. By aiming unusually high amplitudes of power at it, the ionosphere could be heated, affecting the signals that used it as a transmission medium. But HAARP was a legacy of Reagan's Star Wars, and Star Wars had never gotten off the ground politically—it was too expensive. The solo HAARP efforts that sprang up later were hampered by protest from environmentalists—greenies who worried about such things as fucking with the ionosphere. That was how democracy worked, Cole thought. Telegyn, on the other hand, was nothing like a democracy.

Captain Wilson's voice came from the speakerline. "General Myers, sir, there *are* some similarities to HAARP, but I guess you haven't heard yet . . . This phenomenon appears to be occurring in all daylight areas, not just the U.S. Our German bases have reported similar difficulties. Televisions and radio are out, civilian air traffic control is down . . . And we're getting reports of . . . um . . . well, some kind of . . . of sun activity causing burn damage in the cities. If the sun *is* undergoing an intensification or . . . uh . . . flare activity, it might heat the ionosphere coincidentally and have the same effect as HAARP."

Myers looked at Cole, a bewildered expression on his face. "Burn damage?"

And then those words rang a bell in the general's mind. Cole could see it in his eyes—as he'd already heard it in Wilson's voice. Like everyone else on the planet, they would have read plenty about the prophecies by now. He could see a connection being made and the hurt and denial that connection evoked.

"We need details on this sun activity," Cole said, addressing one of the secretaries. "See what you can find out."

The woman started to reply, then lost the words in the intensity of Cole's gaze. She did a rough, curtsylike nod and went out.

"As for the invasion . . ." Cole turned to Myers, taking control with an air of crisp efficiency. "It looks like we have to be prepared to fight inland. Do we know where the Chinese force is heading?"

"Not yet," answered Wilson. "We can't see them on—"

"Yes, we know!" Myers snapped.

"Yes, sir. I was going to say that we *do* have ground reports that they're moving well inland."

"Find them," Cole ordered. "Send out patrols from our bases. Whatever it takes."

"Of course," Myers said with frustrated determination. "We'll make 'em sorry they ever touched U.S. soil." He issued orders to his lieutenant, who picked up the phone and passed on the command.

Cole nodded approvingly and gave Myers a reassuring, "we're-in-this-together" smile. But Cole knew that it would take days to locate all the Chinese, because they would be scattered in places unanticipated.

It was a strange sensation, and he was perhaps the first leader in history to ever experience it. He was standing behind the lines of one army, having designed the strategy of another, and playing, meanwhile, for stakes neither one of them could even fathom. He knew China's plans, had helped construct the details.

At the heart of the Chinese invading force were numerous independent teams the Chinese called the *Pa woo* or "Creeping foxes." By nightfall, somewhere between two hundred and six hundred teams would have taken over American farming towns throughout the bread belt, according to project estimates. The *Pa woo* would take hostages, commandeer the local groceries, and become as entrenched as the Nebraskan Freemen. And all the while the American military would be flocked along the coast like seagulls or hunting for the enemy near strategic targets. The U.S. command was not expecting trouble in the middle of nowhere, in places with no military significance, where grain silos instead of missile silos rose to the sky.

If General Myers and his advisers had really thought about the Chinese, thought about their psychology, their motives, they might have anticipated something of the kind. That was why the strategy implanted in Tsing Mao Wen and Mal Abbas was so brilliant. The Chinese were not really interested in *mano a mano* combat with the Americans, not essentially. They were interested in the grain belt, in getting their hands on the production of *food*.

In the spring, the *Pa woo* would supervise the farming activity, collecting and stockpiling the harvest for whatever distribution their superiors devised. That was the dream that had been lodged in the Chinese mind, anyway. That was the promise. There were, of course, strategies the Americans could use to dislodge the *Pa woo* in time; even China understood this. But what China did not understand was that there was a third player in the game, Santarém, and it was even hungrier than the *Pa woo*.

The secretary Cole had dispatched returned. She had a videotape in her hand. "All the TV stations are down, but WWN sent us this footage by courier. It's going on outside, you know. The sun. It's going on *right outside*."

She stood motionless after this revelation, her lip pursed as if very put out. It took Myers some effort to pry the tape from her hand. "Will someone put this on?" he ordered. A young corporal took it from him and put it on playback. All eyes in the room turned to watch.

Footage from the street outside the Capitol. There were twenty or so people moving up and down the wide marble steps. A dozen more stood talking. Who knew why WWN had been there? To the casual eye, it almost looked like a normal scene—with the sun shining down so benevolently. Or it would have, if it were not for the paper surgical masks and white rubber gloves worn with the tailored suits; if not for the policemen standing on the sidewalk, on the lookout for anyone with a cold; if not for the coffee vendor selling lattes made with goat milk for $20.00 and some forgotten stash of plastic-wrapped biscotti for $50.00 apiece. Perhaps that's what WWN had been there to capture, for the camera zoomed in on the vendor and the long waiting line. Cole could almost hear the banal commentary that would air with such footage.

Very quickly, the scene changed. The camera wavered, and over the live feed came the cameraman's voice: "Ouch. What the fuck?"

Cries rose up around him. The cameraman turned in time to

capture the people on the steps screaming and running for the doors. A balding man raced by with his leather folder raised to protect his pate. The people in the latte line scattered. Then the cameraman himself was running. He said, "Oh, my God! It's *burning like hell* out here!" There were several minutes of jarring footage, insensible video of people fleeing. Then the cameraman stopped. He steadied the instrument on his shoulder and panned the scene.

The area in front of the Capitol had been deserted except for a homeless man who'd been asleep or drunk on a bench. When the camera found him, he was smoking. Then he burst into flames. He stumbled off the bench with agonizing cries.

"Something's going on," the cameraman panted. "I can't feel it here, but over by the steps it's burning hot. It might be sarin gas or some kind of . . . I don't know."

But it wasn't sarin gas. Cole felt an enthralled satisfaction watching the video. It had been the greatest challenge, no question.

The camera left the stumbling, burning pyre that was the drunk and scanned the sidelines. The people who had fled the scene now lay on the ground, their faces and hands covered with second- and third-degree burns. On some of them, the hair on their heads had been singed down to brutal nubs. Some of the police were injured, too. One was trying to use his radio and appeared to be having little success.

The injuries, to a trained doctor's eye, might have been identified as laser burns, had that doctor seen diffused laser burns. But Cole knew most doctors who had used lasers at all had used them in a single, focused beam—a beam that sliced flesh open with its power. A diffused beam didn't slice, it scalded. The more diffused the beam, the more subtle the damage. There had never been much medical use for a beam like that.

Into the melee on the video walked a neighborhood doomsayer. Perhaps he'd been drawn by the scent of roasting meat. Cole could hear his litany before the camera found him, and when it did it showed a wild-looking man with a placard that read THE END IS HERE. He stood on the sidelines where the injured and the bystanders alike gathered and watched the drunk blacken like a hot dog on a grill.

"Repent! Repent! Before it's too late!"

Paramedics shoved him aside. A young hotshot in white held

his hand out, then stepped slowly into the burn zone. He took another step, and another. "There's nothing. It's gone," he called out, waving his men forward. They went to put out the drunk.

"Stay back!" shouted a policeman, but the paramedic was right. The burning on the courthouse steps *had* stopped, even as screams of agony rose, distantly, from a nearby street.

"And the fourth angel poured out his vial upon the sun," said the doomsayer, *"and power was given unto him to scorch men with fire. And men were scorched with great heat, and blasphemed the name of God, which hath power over these plagues: and they repented not to give him glory."*

"It . . . it's true," one woman said to the strangers around her. Her lips were pulled back tight over her teeth in a hot pink outline as if a child had ringed it with a crayon. "I read it in the *Times* this morning! The sun! It *is* the fourth sign!"

In the war room, Anthony Cole allowed himself a deep, heartfelt sigh.

The rest of the morning and early afternoon Cole fielded the twin crises of the invasion and the burning sun with great aplomb. By late afternoon, he had gone a long way toward claiming the position in spirit that would soon be his in fact.

It was after 5:00 P.M. before he had a moment alone. They gave him rooms in the Pentagon, but Cole did not sleep. His mind was too active, and he had gotten the code number on his pager.

He did not believe that the suite, or the phone, would be bugged, but he used his Telegyn cellular anyway. They would not be able to pick up the voice on the other end that way, and he could be discreet about what he said out loud. Anthony Cole believed in taking risks, just not stupid ones.

He called the Baltimore headquarters of Telegyn, his brother Peter's personal line.

Peter Cole had been with Telegyn since he graduated from Yale, and he'd been promoted to CEO when Anthony left for a political career. At thirty-three, he was three years younger than Anthony, and his only living relative. Their father had been a banker and a member of the Red Scepter's Upper Body. He'd died of prostate cancer, never seeing his sons' work come to fruition. Their mother had died young.

Although Anthony remembered little about his mother, he imagined that Peter was like her. Peter was emotional—loyal to a fault, certainly, and deeply committed to their plans, but still emotional. Anthony, on the other hand, was his father's son: brilliant, methodical, even dedicated to the cause of the human race as a whole; but on a personal level, he was cold.

There'd been a time in Cole's life when he'd regretted this lack of feeling, considered it an impairment. But later, when he became involved with the harsh necessity that was Project Apocalypse, he realized that only a man like him *could* do it; that his lack of emotion was exactly what was needed for what had to be done.

Once on the line, Peter conferenced in their head of security, a man named Ted Rodgers, and Tendir's replacement, Dr. Morton. Peter explained the reason he'd sent the code. That reason was Dr. Michael Smith.

"The source of the leak has been confirmed as Deauchez and Hill," Peter said. "Dr. Smith flew into Albuquerque. They must have either met or phoned him there and passed on what they knew. What we don't know is if they went to Sedona with him or not."

"That's most unfortunate," Cole commented in a neutral voice. But despite what would have been a grueling day for any leader, this was the first time during its long hours that he was touched by real threat, real dismay. He could not comprehend why the priest and reporter had not been eliminated long ago. Telegyn had been prepared to act swiftly at the least sign of leaks, yet Deauchez and Hill had outwitted or outlucked them for days. Cole felt a sour frustration suffuse him. It was not directed at the two men, any more than he would have gotten angry at rats for trying to escape their cage. The bitterness he felt was at his own team's incompetence.

"But the good news is, there have been no other leaks," Rodgers was saying.

"That you've identified," Cole corrected him.

"There's no reason to think that there might be additional leaks," Peter said. "Smith talked to a stagehand who saw our man at the concert in Munich—that explains the e-mail he sent to Hill. Hill's reply asked him to fly to Albuquerque. We also have the Russellville stop to confirm that Hill and Deauchez were headed that way."

"What *about* that stop you mentioned?"

"The filling station in Russellville has been cleaned," Rodgers said. "Even though they seemed totally uncontaminated, except by the virus that Hill was carrying."

"Good. There must have been other stops, no?"

"We haven't confirmed any yet. We know about Russellville because Hill called the *Times* office from there. That's also where Hill got the e-mail from Smith and where Deauchez called Father Carnesca."

"That e-mail was a mistake." Cole's voice was slow and matter-of-fact, but he heard the flinch in Rodgers's reply.

"He wasn't using our phone, so it takes time for his mail to register on our system and for us to delete it."

"As I said, a mistake."

"May I suggest . . ." Dr. Morton said conciliatorily, ". . . Deauchez and Hill unlikely to have made it to Sedona due to Hill's illness. Perhaps a hospital? They may have used false names."

"We're already checking that," Rodgers said.

"And we can assume the reporter is no longer a threat. He's either dead or close to it."

Cole gave his voice a deliberately thoughtful twist. "I think not. This person who was encountered last night had something in his possession, you said?"

"Yes," Rodgers answered. "Two boxes of syringes: one WV103 and one DS100. There were three syringes of WV103 missing."

"Then I suggest that we not count *anyone* out just yet. Those missing items *will* be found, won't they?"

"You have my word."

"How many men do we have in Sedona?" Morton asked.

"Three," said Rodgers, "but they're top-notch, especially Hart. If Hill and Deauchez are anywhere near the place, alive or dead, he *will* find them."

Cole was getting impatient, a fact he hoped he relayed in the clearing of his throat. This was urgent, and dangerous, and if he could have handled it himself he would have. But he could not; his part was to be played out elsewhere now. "Gentlemen, I don't think I need to indicate the thoroughness which is expected of you. Not by me; it's *demanded* by the very importance of what we're about."

"Of course, Anthony," said Peter. That reverential note of his was in his voice.

"Yes, sir," Rodgers said.

"Now I have to go. I wish you luck."

"And you . . . Mr. President," Morton answered. Immediately, the words broke from the others: *Mr. President, Mr. President.*

They were a bit premature, it was true. But it was the first time Cole had been addressed in this manner, and it pleased him. He might even have smiled had it not been for those two names, lingering like shards of glass in his mind: Deauchez and Hill.

SEDONA, ARIZONA

Deauchez had slept through most of the day. When he awoke it was late afternoon, and the light coming in through the single tiny window was the heavy, golden light of a waning sun. For a while he lay on his cot, studying the walls around him. Last night, a door had opened in the darkness and Deauchez had been thrown into a room, alone. Now he could see that the only furnishing was a cot mattress on the floor. The floor was cement; the door, solid wood. There was a bare toilet against the wall, its pipes rusty, and outlets for what might once have been a washer and dryer. From the view he saw through the window—passing feet—it would seem he was in a converted basement, probably an old utility room.

With nothing else for him to look at, his mind began to wander. He began to think about Sister Daunsey. He recalled, with preternatural detail, each encounter he'd had with her, the things she'd said. He remembered her face, so unadorned and energetic, and her childlike mannerisms.

The memories hurt deeply. He knew all the reasons why the thought of Daunsey should be painful: her being so completely fooled, so heartlessly wrong, responsible for misleading so many. But there seemed to be something more personal in it than that. Perhaps, in her failure, he saw his own.

What was sadder than a man or a woman dedicating their entire lives to a God that didn't care, maybe didn't even exist? Pushing their lifestyle, goals, personal choices, even their thoughts, their very *perceptions* about the world, through a filter that was completely fallacious?

Nothing was sadder than that. What might Sister Daunsey's energies have done had they been directed toward medicine or social reform outside the confines of religion? Because for all the good she'd done, long ago in that soup kitchen, her foundation had been shifting sand. Her mercy had been built on the concept of God, and because that concept was illusory, unknowable, it could be warped and twisted, as it had been, as so many of those who wreaked havoc in the name of God throughout the centuries had been.

Better to harbor no illusions at all.

No illusions. He'd been thinking a lot about himself in the past few days, about why he had become a priest, about his own filters. How ironic that some of the conclusions he'd reached had come to him so late. Too late.

Deauchez found himself crying. He pressed his arm against his mouth to muffle the sound, refusing to give anyone the satisfaction of hearing him, if, perchance, there was anyone out there to hear. It wasn't the threat of his own personal danger that broke him. It was the *finality* of it, of his situation; how literally he'd been silenced. No one knew he was here. No one cared. No one would let him out, certainly not Andrews. And God? Did *he* care at all about what was going on down here on Earth? Apparently not. He was not going to help Deauchez get out of this. No, Deauchez and his investigation were stopped dead, no way around it.

He supposed that meant he had lost. And poor Simon—poor, poor Simon, out there all alone. He had lost, too.

Simon Hill was dreaming about a town, some strange, European gingerbread town, but menacing, like something out of *Fantasia*. Somewhere in the maze of streets was a *Times* correspondent office, and he had to get there because he had to send in his story, this amazing and horrible story—he had to tell the world what was going on. But he couldn't find his way and someone was after him, devious little hooves clicking behind him on the cobbled streets. He ran and ran and . . .

It was the cold that finally got to him. It kept plucking at him with frozen fingers, and he eventually realized that giving in to it meant *the surface*, waking, and he went with it gladly—anything to get out of that endless maze.

He opened his eyes and stared straight out the front windshield of the Honda. In the distance, off a bit toward town, the sun was well over the eastern horizon. Its golden glow lit the desert rock and made it gleam in a soft, warm, pinkish hue. But the glow did not extend to the Honda, which was deep in the shadow of the rock wall just outside his passenger door. He couldn't stop shivering. His teeth rattled.

He was dying of thirst.

He fished around weakly and found the lemonade, managed to raise it. He parted cracked, dry lips for the straw and sucked at it greedily. He finished the drink, the air rasping loudly in the straw, but it had been enough for now. He tried to sit up but his head hurt. Was it possible that it hurt *less*? Yes, he thought. He remembered feeling like his head was in a meat grinder at some point; now it was a dull, thudding ache, a *sore* ache, like his entire brain was one big bruise. Bruised was decidedly better than ground meat.

He had to pee.

He found electrical cord loose around him. He pushed it away. He opened the car door and managed to get one leg out—a quaking lump was all it was—then the other. He struggled to his feet, using the door for leverage. The hatchback canted to the right.

The rock wall outside his door went straight up, swinging out over the car far above him. It was a huge rock, almost a mountain really. He staggered—one step, two—on those kitten-weak stumps. His stomach spasmed, his intestines racking up in a cramp that felt as though he had Montezuma himself in his bowels. He gave a gasp of pain and tried to move faster. He reached the side of the rock and went around it, out of sight of the car.

He struggled with his pants. They were extraordinarily tight, though at some point his fly had been opened. He felt like the Incredible Hulk, like he'd gained twenty pounds while wearing the same clothes. He got the material down finally and sank, quivering, to the desert floor.

And voided. It was the biggest, most painful goddamn mess he'd ever made in his entire life. His stomach rippled with dagger-like shock waves and rumbled loudly as the mostly liquid stuff gushed. The stench reached him on the morning breeze and it made his gorge rise. He clamped a hand to his nostrils and kept riding this particular tiger. It wasn't as if he had a choice.

Many minutes later he'd recovered enough to stand, on visibly quaking limbs now—like a ninety-year-old with severe palsy—and step away from the stuff. He tugged his pants up weakly. They stuck somewhere around the bottom of his suddenly enormous ass and he gave up. He managed to get back to the car by leaning against the rock. He sank down through the open passenger door, wondering where Deauchez was and why he'd been left alone to be so very sick.

He had some vague notion that he'd been given the shot, and that Deauchez had been wearing underwear on his head at the time, but surely that was pure hallucination. He wondered how long he had to live, and if he would die here in this stinking, cheesy economy car, alone. These things flashed through his mind quickly and with surprisingly little emotion; then he was once again asleep.

WWN BROADCAST

The plague of the sun lasted exactly twelve hours. It was twelve hours without television or radio, and most of the people in the United States had no idea what was going on. They kept checking their sets like anxious hostesses checking pot roasts, staring at the static uncomprehendingly. They'd heard that the war was coming, and with the news blackout, many feared a nuclear exchange. Movies of the week had made them aware of EMP, and it was the best excuse they could think of for the lost reception. Those who had shelters and basements used them, but they kept checking the tube.

At the end of the twelve hours, WWN was broadcasting for anyone who tuned in. Millions did. The news channel appeared to be having difficulty choosing a lead story. There were downed civilian planes, the war's first rapacious thrust, and nature's sunny disposition turned murderous. But there was also the continuing Santarém saga. Santarém was not a new story, but it still won the day's highest honors. The latest statistics on the dead and infected were staggering, brutal. The pretty newscaster stumbled over them, darting her eyes off camera, as if suspecting her coworkers of handing her the wrong paper.

Twelve million dead in the U.S. alone, an estimated forty million in stage two, and an estimated one hundred million contaminated. The admonitions from WHO had changed: the newscaster did not say one should turn oneself in to authorities at the first sign of a cold; she said one should quarantine oneself in one's own home, hanging a white rag or sheet or towel from a window on each side of the house to let potential visitors know. The newscaster didn't say it, but the alert viewer understood that the change in public procedures meant one of two things: either there were no more authorities to hand oneself over to, or said authorities had their goddamn hands full.

The American television audience listened to these figures with bewilderment. They had tuned in to hear about the war. The Santarém numbers were a surprise bonus—a scorpion in a Cracker Jack box. Many in rural areas knew nothing about the sun plague. They watched the details of the day's events with a sense of unreality, as if they were watching an elaborate fiction—an Orson Welles hoax with Spielberg production values.

The burning sun had struck only large cities. Sydney, Tokyo, and Hong Kong had suffered the least because they'd been on the dark side of the planet for most of it. The U.S. East Coast, on the other hand, had taken the full twelve hours right up the backside. The burning did not occur everywhere at once in the cities; it fell in blots and bursts, always in areas of about a hundred square feet, and the locations on which it fell changed randomly and without warning.

In Paris, a metropolitan railcar had lost power on a high span that fell into the path of the searing rays. Everyone in the aluminum tube had been roasted alive. In Madrid, a fifty-by-fifty-seat section of an open-air amphitheater had been hit; six hundred died in the stampede that followed. In Atlanta a gas plant exploded from the heat. In L.A., the fires began at dawn, spreading from strips of landscaping where sprinkler use had been abandoned, leaving tinder standing where green things had once thrived. Worldwide, four large commercial flights were lost due to the failure of air-traffic control.

But the civilian casualties were minor compared to the implications for the military. The Chinese had had the luck of the devil in their timing. Hundreds of Chinese planes had been shot down, but an unknown number *had* penetrated the border, the anchorwoman said, particularly on the West Coast. Initial reports indicated that the Chinese targets were farming communities.

The cumulative effect of these stories sank in slowly. Many viewers sat through five or six renditions before they had any thoughts at all. But the impact, when it came, was hard. The fourth sign had been confirmed in a spectacularly undeniable way. The rationalists who'd managed to label the sores, the red tide, and the virus as coincidence had no place to put this one.

And then many did get up off their couches and move. Twenty million Americans packed a few things in their cars or on their bicycles or on their backs and left home in search of their own personal front-running candidate of the Twenty-Four. Agnostics were converted. Atheists were tormented. And ten thousand people, some with sniffles that might or might not be anything, and some who were just plain terrified, took their own lives.

The world was beginning to believe.

CHAPTER 21

KITTATINNY MOUNTAIN, NEW JERSEY

Stanton was half asleep, and in his mind's eye he saw the crowds. He'd been on the air nonstop for almost two full days, and even in an exhausted doze his mind could not stop thinking about the massive audience just outside his door and just beyond the camera lens. He could not stop calculating his own worth, ticking off the points of his fame the way a miser will count his coins. He had watched football games on TV since before he could talk, and now his brain produced *auto replay* and *slow mo* of its own accord.

He was thinking that he was the Number One prophet of the Twenty-Four. After all, wasn't he in the most important country in the world, the U.S. of A.? Wasn't he the only U.S. prophet with his face on the TV every night? And wasn't he pulling the kind of ratings that would make a network executive cry like a baby? The news hardly ever covered that Abeed weirdo in New York—*his* followers had a mind to take over something, and the newspeople seemed to think that maybe if they didn't mention 'em they'd go away. The media didn't seem to know much of anything at all about that pagan, Cougar, except for flashing his picture around. As for Andrews, that New Age, half-baked freak, well, the press had to know *he* was off in outer space. They covered his gathering occasionally, but they hardly ever gave him airtime to speak.

No, it was he, Stanton, who'd won the play-off. He could see now that God had foreseen it all along. All those years ago when Stanton was struggling with his ministry and getting that television show started, why, it had been God's hand urging him onto the field. God had given him that television career in preparation for this day, so that he would be Number One. God had spoken to non-Christian faiths down there in Mexico, sure, but it was clear that he had his real money on the Baptists.

When the knock came, he was more put out to be separated from his visions of glory than from sleep. He answered the door with a growl. "What the blazin' angels is it *now*?"

"TV," Franklin said, and pushed his way inside.

They'd had a big-screen brought up for the double-wide, though it hogged most of the living space. It sprang to life with the image of a huge, black plain. Black smoke roiled upward in great, gusting billows.

"Jiminy Christmas," Stanton said.

"Yup." Franklin looked like he'd just awarded himself the grand prize for cleverness.

They didn't have to say what it was they thought they were looking at. Two days ago the fourth sign had occurred, and Stanton had been preaching on the fifth ever since. *"And the fifth angel sounded, and I saw a star fall from heaven unto the earth: and to him was given the key of the bottomless pit. And he opened the bottomless pit; and there arose a smoke out of the pit, as the smoke of a great furnace; and the sun and the air were darkened by reason of the smoke of the pit. And there came out of the smoke locusts upon the earth: and unto them was given power, as the scorpions of the earth have power."*

"Where is it?" Stanton asked.

"Paks, Hungary. A nuclear power plant blew up a little while ago. I think it's—"

"Shhhh!" Stanton waved an impatient hand. The newscaster was speaking.

". . . reports of a grave emergency started coming in from the plant half an hour before the explosion. They reported that their spent fuel pool was overheating. Apparently, it had been overheating all morning, but the temperature gauge continued to register normal. By the time they noticed the steam rising off the surface of the pool, it was too late. The main reactor was shut down, but the temperature was already exceeding . . ."

"Locust . . . rads . . . get it?" Chortling over a disaster was a bit too much, even for Franklin, but he came close. "Radiation— *rads*—that's the stinging locust that Revelations is—"

Stanton stopped him with a look that said, *You get ahead of me on this one, you son-of-a-bee, and I'll kill you.* Franklin's glow faded like a TV going bad.

"Neither sabotage nor negligence has been ruled out. There have been no official estimates on damage or loss of life yet, but the blast area alone encompasses most of the city of Paks. This level of nuclear disaster could release as much as three hundred million curies of radionuclides into the air. That's just over three times the radiation released during the Chernobyl disaster, and that plant was located in a remote area. There does appear to be a modest wind blowing at the site, from the look of the smoke on the video. We have reached the president of the Nuclear Regulatory Commission, and we do expect him to be on the air with us in a few . . ."

Stanton lowered the sound with the remote and settled back on the leather sofa, frowning.

"Reverend, if we record tonight's broadcast a little *early*, I can get the footage over to New York. Heck, we can probably get a slot on WWN this afternoon if you're up for being interviewed. Do you think we should wait, and hit it hard with tonight's broadcast instead of . . . no. If we go on WWN that'll only get more people tuning in tonight to get the full . . ."

"No," Stanton said.

"Huh?"

"I said no."

Franklin stared at him with a bewildered expression as if to say, *I hear you talking, but there must be something wrong with my ears, because what you're saying makes no sense.*

"Cheese-whiz, Franklin, will you just let me *think* for a minute? Is that too much to ask? Just *time out* and lemme *think.*"

Franklin pressed his lips together. He turned his eyes to the TV and watched the footage. Stanton watched it, too.

Hmmm. Yes, it looked nasty all right. It was a *big* area. Blasted black, smoke billowing out like the skirts of Dallas Cowboy cheerleaders. No, those were white. What team wore gray? He was shocked that it wasn't on the tip of his tongue, then thought to himself . . . ah, fudge it. He concentrated on the screen. A nuclear reactor. That was bad, no doubt about it. A nuclear plant exploding—that was a bad thing. Still . . . it wasn't exactly a *pit*, was it?

"I don't know," he said out loud.

"The Scripture says, 'And he opened the bottomless pit; and there arose a smoke out of the pit . . .' "

"I *know* the Scripture, Franklin."

"Then what's wrong with it?"

Stanton tried to formulate words. "It . . . it doesn't seem big enough."

"Not *big* enough?" Franklin looked in confusion at the monitor. "Reverend, I really don't think we can afford to miss a chance to . . ."

"Was it *you* at Santa Pelagia or was it *me*?"

"Reverend Stanton, it was you, of course."

"Then can we trust my instincts for a minute here? Just for one cotton-pickin' *minute*?"

"Yes, sir."

Franklin shut up. Stanton looked thoughtfully at the tube. "I was thinkin' *bigger*. The sores, the red tide, that virus—holy crowly, that virus! Then that sun thing helpin' the invasion. Now those were *big*."

Franklin agreed that they had indeed been big.

"I'd thought it'd be somethin' more like . . ."

"You've been predicting volcanoes," Franklin prompted. "Or maybe a big ol' earthquake that would open up a pit. Or a comet."

"That's right. I thought it would be somethin' more like that." Stanton crossed his legs, shifted his weight on the cushy velour. He had a niggling suspicion that he was being childish. God could do a gosh-darn nuclear disaster if he wanted to. Yet, something didn't feel right.

Stanton turned up the volume. They both watched the broadcast for a while.

"You know . . . it's pretty big," Franklin said.

Stanton didn't answer.

Two hours later, he was in the pissant-size bathroom dressing for his nightly broadcast and worrying about what he was going to say. Nuclear disaster or no nuclear disaster? Or should he hedge his bets and weasel around it with a couple of veiled references? Despite his firm line with Franklin, he *wasn't* sure. It would look pretty bad if he said it was the fifth sign, then a comet hit. Then again, it would look like he'd dropped the ball if he didn't name it and, lo and behold, that was what it was.

He was snapping the rhinestone fasteners on his red shirt when the word "volcano" floated over from the living room and grabbed him by the short hairs. He wandered over and stared at the screen. The first pictures he saw were of a huge, smoking, lava-streaming fissure in the top of an enormous mountain. The words below the pictures said "Mount Semeru, Java." The voice-over said the massive volcano had gone off without warning. The blast was so great it was heard twenty-five hundred miles away. All six hundred thousand residents of the nearby city Malang were dead. They were probably poisoned by gas, the experts said, well before the lava reached the town.

Semeru's explosion appeared to have had its roots deep in the Pacific plate, for almost simultaneously two other volcanoes had erupted: Mount Talakmau, in Sumatra, which was in an uninhabited area of peaks, and the Philippine volcano, Mount Pulog. Pulog's eruption was minor compared to the force of Semeru's, but it was the end of the world for the few thousand people in the nearby villages of San Fernando and Bauang. The announcer used those words—"end of the world"—and the pictures of the smoking, spewing craters fit the bill. WWN was calling it the "Ring of Fire triple-play."

For a long time Stanton stared at the footage. Then, slowly, a grin spread across his face. He'd been right. *He'd been right!* Bless God, Hallelujah, and a thumb o' the nose to that fancy-pants little cake-boy.

"You see that, Franklin?" Stanton said triumphantly to the empty room. "You see that? Now *that* is *big*."

WASHINGTON D.C.

The swearing in occurred in the Oval Office. Cole hardly recognized it, for in the past few days it had been completely stripped, sterilized, and refurbished. It was an unusual ceremony, with everyone in their white suits and with so few people present—only members of the committee, a few judges, and his brother Peter by his side in lieu of the spouse he did not have. But it was being filmed for later broadcast and, Cole liked to think, for posterity.

Years from now, when people watched the film they would talk about how close to complete breakdown the world had been—the white suits alone would remind them of that. They would talk about how fortunate it was that Anthony Cole had been spared; that he'd been there to take the reins; that he'd been just what they needed. They would muse at seeing him so young, so new to his power, like watching a legendary star's first film. That would be later, when he was no longer just the American president but chairman of the Worldwide Council.

At least, that was the future Cole was imagining as he repeated his oath of office. He had not anticipated being much moved by this ceremony. When you work for something long and hard enough, its fulfillment can be anticlimactic. After all, his mind was already past this day, already chewing on events far down the line. Yet he did feel something. He was, after all, being placed in the highest office in the land. When he turned to Peter for his congratulations, and saw his brother's shining face behind the clear plate, Cole actually felt something like joy, something like love.

Afterward, he was allowed to take off the suit in a sterilized room for his televised speech to the American public. He had written the speech himself, and its platitudes were not uninspired. After the speech, there was a brief reception. Brief, because it was impossible to eat in the suits. Brief, because everyone had been up for days.

It was odd, but within two hours of becoming president, Anthony Cole was alone with his brother in his temporary quarters in the White House. They weren't supposed to remove the suits—not until they were safely installed in the presidential bunker. But Cole took off the helmet anyway, unable to stand it. Peter mimicked him, as Peter always did. They turned to WWN to watch the coverage of Anthony Cole's ascension. But WWN had not yet learned of the swearing in, had not yet gotten the footage—they were not as efficient as they used to be. They were covering volcanic eruptions out in the Pacific.

Cole frowned and flipped the channel. Stanton's broadcast had just started, and he was proclaiming the volcanoes as the fifth sign. Cole was not pleased. He looked at his brother.

Peter shrugged. He knew enough of Anthony's cautionary ways not to speak loosely, but his "who knows?" expression conveyed more than words. Out loud he said, "Did you hear there was a nuclear plant explosion this morning in Paks, Hungary?"

"Is that so?" Cole flipped back to WWN, where the volcanoes were still on.

"WWN was covering it earlier, but then these volcanoes went

off—three of them at once. One took out a good-size city. Ironic, isn't it?"

Cole watched the screen, his cheeks hollowing as they did whenever things were not quite going as planned. "Hmmm."

"It's quite a coincidence, but—" Peter stopped short, unable to piece together what he wanted to say without actually saying it.

But not a big deal, Cole finished the thought. Their fifth sign had been upstaged, but what did it really matter? The fifth sign had not been one of the most difficult or impressive, and there had been *a* fifth sign, after all.

But it *did* matter. At first Cole attributed his sense of discomfort to his perfectionist vanity. When he made a plan he expected things to happen as laid out, right down the line. But as he watched the volcano coverage he began to realize that there was more to it—that the events really were *too* ironic. The glow on the day—*his* day—began to fade.

WWN finally got a clue. The volcano coverage was cast aside in favor of the hopeful report that America had a new president. But somehow it didn't seem that important anymore. Cole flipped the channel back to the Reverend Raymond Stanton.

"Hey!" Peter complained.

"Shhhh," Cole said.

KITTATINNY MOUNTAIN, NEW JERSEY

"Dear *penitents*! I want to give you the revelation that has come to me, that has made itself *clear* to me as I watched the unfoldin' of this latest sign . . ."

The live audience was hushed. Thanks to generous grants from his followers and free satellite time from Telegyn, huge screens dotted the rocky landscape, giving his words to the millions on the mount as well as the viewers at home.

"*Satan is rulin' the world right now!* Yes, I know it is a dire situation to be on this planet while it is Satan, not God, who's callin' the plays! But it was prophesized, dear ones, and do not think for a moment that ol' Lucifer will have the advantage for long!"

The crowd called out their praises and amens.

"We have watched the signs bein' fulfilled. The fourth plague: the plague of sun. The fifth plague: these volcanoes. People ask me about the sixth plague, and I'm prepared to speak on that tonight. I believe the sixth sign has to do with this war, folks.

Revelation says, 'And the sixth angel sounded, and I heard a voice from the golden altar saying, Loose the four angels which are bound in the great river Euphrates. And the four angels were loosed, which were prepared for an hour, and a day, and a month, and a year, for to slay the third part of men.' "

"Now, there's some important words here. First he's 'loosin' angels that have been bound.' What angels have been bound, friends? You know it: Lucifer and his rebellious angel army. The other word to remember is *Euphrates*. That river runs right through Iraq, right near Baghdad, also called Babylon. I think the sixth sign is talkin' about the war of the Antichrist; the war we're in right now. God's gonna loose the powers of Satan, and they will rise from the Middle East and have victory for a time."

"The Bible says that Satan is to have his *winnin' streak* before he is defeated for all of eternity. Now let me tell you somethin' about the Chinese: they will *not* be our primary opponent! The Chinese will have died in the millions just to weaken our strength, because *Satan* is a coward. When both China and America are exhausted, *Mal Abbas* will come in and rout 'em both!"

The crowd roared in despair.

"America will be conquered by the demon forces of the Antichrist, and God will allow it to happen. Look at how the fourth sign abetted the Chinese invasion! And why? Because it's time America ate some humble pie! We have strayed a mighty long way from God since our ancestors came to this country to worship his name!"

"Praise Jesus! Amen! Thy will be done!"

Stanton paused, sweating. He knew his face was beet red on camera. It "didn't read optimally," that weasel Franklin had suggested. As if the prophet of God should have to worry about reading optimally! No doubt Ezekiel got a bit red in the face, too, seein' that wheel. But Stanton's red face and tendency to spit when overwrought were minor compared to Mimi. Franklin had started putting her as far into the shadows as he could, but he hadn't dared take her off the broadcast entirely. So back there Mimi stood, her face plastered on badly, her mouth clamped shut. Mimi's eyes—if you got close, which the camera never did—were so off-track they practically pointed in opposite directions. She was takin' more and more of those nerve pills of hers, which, as it turned out, was a blessing.

"Now many of you have been askin' about the Rapture—when's it gonna be? You know as well as I do that no man is privileged to know the mind of God completely. But this is what I see dimly, dear ones . . . and I pray to God for guidance as I give this prophecy to you . . ."

The crowd was listening with all their hearts, and they were trying to be quiet as Franklin instructed, but on many faces tears streamed and sobs broke out as irrepressibly as hiccups.

"This is what is to come, and I believe it'll play out fast. These signs have not been slow in comin', and maybe that's God's mercy. I already mentioned that the sixth sign has to do with the war—the victory—of the Antichrist. But as I read over my Scripture tonight, friends, I was inspired to see beyond that, into the seventh sign. Listen to me read now. 'And the seventh angel poured out his bowl into the air, and there came a great voice out of the temple of heaven, from the throne, saying; It is done. And there were voices, and thunders, and lightnings; and there was a great earthquake such as was not since men were upon the earth, so mighty an earthquake and so great. Every island fled away, and the mountains were not found.'

"Now this is *catastrophic*, friends. This will make every sign we've had so far seem like Little League! I see massive earthquakes and violent upheavel up ahead—and I know why! The very Earth itself will *rebel* against Satan's victory, because she is God's creation, friends. When the Pharisees asked Jesus to stop up his followers' adulation he said that if they didn't call out his praises, the very rocks and stones would do it! This is what I'm talkin' about. The very *fundaments* of the Earth will rise up and protest the Antichrist's reign!"

The crowd was listening, mesmerized.

"We will live through the takin' over of America by Mal Abbas, because I believe he'll leave this mountain be. We already see how he doesn't *dare* attack London or Rome. *That's* why you were called here—to be placed under God's protection!"

"Praise Jesus! Thank you, God! Thy will be done!"

"We'll live through the sixth sign, and we'll start to see tremors and quakes appearin' around the world. And they will increase. Then, as the battle of the Antichrist peaks, the faithful will be Raptured up to spiritual bodies in the blink of an eye, because what will follow next, no Earthly flesh could survive! *The world will shake itself apart!*"

The crowd groaned as one.

"Revelation says the entire face of the Earth will change, it will be the *power of creation come again*! God will reshape the Earth, cleansing it of all evil and sin and pollution! Every livin' creature will die, as they did in the great flood, including every minion of the Antichrist! After all, do you really think Christ would come back to be king of a dirty planet?—no, it must be *wiped clean*!"

The crowd was with him now. He knew they were hungry and cold and tired of camping out, but his words had the power to make all of that disappear.

"We will be Raptured up just as Noah was placed in the ark. The world will be *destroyed*, shaken to its foundation, and *recreated*! Then we will return, along with all of God's faithful through the ages, to live in the new paradise!"

"Praise Jesus, come and cleanse the Earth!"

"Make a new paradise!"

"Thy will be done!"

"The world as we know it will be destroyed!"

"Thy will be done!"

"By earthquake!"

"Thy will be done!"

"By fiery volcano!"

"Thy will be done!"

"By the ocean obeyin' no shore! New York, Los Angeles, San Francisco, Seattle—all will be buried under the waves of the seas!"

"Thy will be done!"

"The continents will split asunder!"

"Thy will be done!"

"Molten rock from the Earth's core will wipe the slate clean with the fire of righteousness, and all sin and sinners will sink into the fiery depths!"

"Thy will be done!"

Behind him, from the shadows, came a strange shrilling scream, like that of a rabbit when the trap springs shut. He couldn't resist. He turned to look. It was Mimi, her carmine lips spread apart, her inch-long fingernails tearing at her own face.

Then the ground underneath his feet moved in a gentle ripple.

LARKSPUR LAKE, EASTERN WASHINGTON

Inside the sacred hut, Will Cougar was sitting with folded legs and bent head, utterly oblivious to the waking world around him.

He was on the third day of a spirit walk and he was deep within what some might call the subconscious mind, and which Will Cougar knew as the Spirit World. He had imbibed nothing since he began, his bodily functions being slowed to a crawl by his alpha waves. He had, in fact, not moved.

It had taken him a while to find the path this time because his head was clogged with worry about the camp, with Sacred Dance's need for him to take control and her frustration at his increasing withdrawal. He was weighted to the Earth by thoughts of things to do and far deeper, self-doubting blockages. But he had at last found a way down late yesterday. Now he sought the truth.

He'd been following a woman for hours—a beautiful Spirit woman, daughter of the wolves and of the wind. She was dressed in gray, mistlike robes. It was she who had told him about Santa Pelagia and she who had spoken to him once he was there. He was determined to catch her, to put an end to the disruptive, worrying doubt for better or worse.

He followed her into terrain he'd never seen before: frightening, crawling terrain. He'd come someplace *bad*, and he wanted to leave more than anything. But he wouldn't give up his pursuit. He chased her on and on.

She ran and he followed, over barren landscape, blackened by fire, stubs of trees like charred bones sticking up from the ground and threatening to pierce him through. There were bodies, human bodies, animal bodies, stuck on the swordlike trees and littering the ground. Under his bare feet he felt the crunching of bones. This world was one vast, stinking abattoir.

They passed a river of blood. In the heavens the stars screamed and wailed and shook, as though being pried from their orbit.

Still she ran.

This place was Death, he knew. Not death, but Death. The *world's* Death. Why did she lead him here? What did she want him to see? Why did she want him to see it?

And then the ground was cracking open as he ran, beneath his feet, dirt and bones and bodies tumbled into the chasms as he leaped over them. She was up ahead, maybe two hundred feet, when a mountain emerged from the ground in front of her, ripping, rending the earth like a thrusting phallus. It rose and rose, booming, expanding. Black rock, rising, towering. The rumble of it vibrated his very soul.

The mountain blocked her path, *ate* her path. She stumbled backward, away from the growing summit. It was his chance. He ran on as the world beneath his feet bounced. It was like running on a trampoline. He grabbed for her and caught hold of one cold, slender arm.

He spun her around and stared at her face, her sweet face. But he was so close to her now, he could see that it wasn't a face at all, but a painted mask.

He reached forward and pulled it from her face and stared . . . at his own visage.

He screamed, its echo loud even through the roaring of the hell she'd brought him to.

Will Cougar emerged from the hut into the cool night air. It was September and the nights in eastern Washington were crisp. The breeze dried the drops of sweat on his skin.

In front of the hut, Sacred Dance was asleep in a camp chair. A sad smile crossed Will Cougar's lips. He squatted down in front of her and gently shook her arm. Her eyes opened.

"Will Cougar?"

"It is I."

She sat up, rubbed her dark-lashed eyes. "Have you finished your spirit walk?"

"Yes."

"Did you find what you were looking for?"

He nodded solemnly. "Yes. I want you to tell people that they do not have to stay here anymore. They can stay if they wish; we have food. But they are free to go."

Sacred Dance's eyes clouded with hurt and panic. He felt sorry to see it, sorry to have put it there—not by the words he just spoke, but by everything he had done wrong from the start.

"What do you mean?"

"I myself must leave. Tonight."

"But the people are all here—for *you*!"

"The message of Santa Pelagia was a lie." Will Cougar said it flatly, although he felt a surge of anger when he spoke these words aloud.

"Oh, no," Sacred Dance said despairingly. "Oh, Will Cougar, no!"

"Larkspur Lake is not safe."

"No!"

"No place is safe."

She began to cry.

"The Earth is sick. She is very, very sick."

"*Why,* Will Cougar?" Sacred Dance sobbed.

"I do not know. That is why I must leave. I must go on a death walk. Perhaps if the Spirits will forgive me, they will tell me what to do."

"Will Cougar," Sacred Dance pleaded. "*Please,* don't leave. What if you don't survive? A death walk is . . ."

"Then nothing will be lost," he said simply. "Help me now. I will need warm clothes and some water."

He turned toward camp, his eyes already journeying.

ACT 4: PALE

Then shall the elements of all the world be desolate; air, earth, sea, flaming fire, and the sky and night, all days merge into one fire, and to one barren, shapeless mass to come.
—THE SIBYLLINE ORACLES (SECOND CENTURY B.C.)

. . . and when the seas rise . . . every soul will know what it hath made ready [for the Judgment Day].
—MOHAMMED (A.D. 620–30) QUR LXXXI, 12, 14

The balance of nature will be lost when the ocean tides shall obey no shore. *—QUETZALCOATL (A.D. 947)*

Now, at the appointed time, the Midgard serpent [who encircles the Earth and seas in Norse lore] is shaken with tremendous rage. It trembles and quakes on the Ocean's slimy floor, so violently that its motions cause waves to sweep across the . . . Earth, as high as the mountains . . . At the same time, the world's mountains shake and the rocks tremble . . . Mortal men . . . are killed in great numbers, and their shades crowd the path to Hel [the Viking underworld]. The sky begins to stretch, and finally breaks in half.
—FROM THE RAGNAROK: ANCIENT NORSE PROPHECY

The earth shall reel to and fro like a drunkard, it shall sway like a hut in the wind; so heavily upon it will lie the guilt of its rebellion that it shall fall, never to rise again. *—ISAIAH 24:20*

South becomes North and the Earth turns Over.
—FROM AN EGYPTIAN PAPYRUS (B.C.)

And every island fled away, and the mountains were not found.
—REVELATION 16:20

CHAPTER 22

DAY 23
SEDONA, ARIZONA

The man stumbling toward town through the desert had a posture and gait not unlike Charles Laughton's in *The Hunchback of Notre Dame*. He favored his left leg heavily and swung his upper body with each step as though the extra propulsion was integral to his progress. His pants were a few sizes too large and were held up by electrical cord. His face had a gauntness and a grayness of pigment that reminded one of graveyard ash.

He smelled horrible.

He had an idea of *where* he was—the red rock landscape alone told him that—but he was still shocked and amazed at what greeted his eyes. He hadn't seen the town up close before—not in the days before it had become a sanctuary for UFO aficionados and New Agers, and not some number of days ago, when he'd arrived. Even without the comparison, the sight was astonishing.

He was not the only one heading toward town on foot, though he was probably the sorriest looking. *Hundreds* of people were walking toward town, from every direction conceivable. The town itself was a tumult of people, even from this distance. Beyond the confines of the permanent structures a vast new outer city had sprung up: a circle of tents and trailers, RVs and automobiles. And trailing from this tent-city layer, like the tail on a sperm, was a line of parked cars that stretched back, back, along the main road, cars driven into the desert and left there. As far as the eyes could see—which was quite far in this flat-horizoned land—the glint of metal went on forever.

He guessed there was something like a couple million people here. He never had been good at the gumball-in-a-jar thing.

He desperately wanted a newspaper.

He was close to the outer tent circle now, and he was among people again. The people, walkers-in like him, mostly got one whiff and shied away. He was getting the vague idea that he really needed a shower, though his nose was not functioning at all.

Apparently, neither was the proboscis of a fine older gent in a tweed jacket and trench overcoat. He and the man intersected just inside the tent encampment, and the man did not shy away.

"Excuse me," said Simon Hill, "can you tell me what the date is?"

The man gave him a long, appraising glance, though not unfriendly for all that. "You look like someone's stolen your soul, lad."

"I've been sick."

The man raised a quizzical brow. "I wouldn't say that too loud, if I were you. Not that you'll fool anyone, looking like *that*." The man studied him. "You don't *sound* as if you've got a cold."

"I don't have a cold."

"Fever?"

"I don't think so."

The man reached out a hand and touched paper-light fingers to Hill's neck.

"No. No fever. It's probably not Wormwood then, but you might want to clean up a bit. Where I've come from—*out there*—they'd burn you in the street for looking like that. Just as well I left then, you might say, and you're absolutely right."

Simon was struggling to keep up, though the man had slowed his pace. He was getting enormously tired, and he wondered if he could make it after all. He'd been practicing around the car for two days. That is, he thought it was two days ago when he'd had a good period of clear thought, and he'd been working on getting some strength back ever since, eyeing the distance from the car to the town warily, as Evil Knievel might have viewed the Grand Canyon.

"Where *do* you come from?" Hill asked.

"Oakland. I taught there. The entire city's hysterical, absolutely hysterical."

"They're . . . they're not really burning people in the streets, though, are they?"

"If they look like they might carry the virus, they are!" The man glanced at Hill with a bemused expression. "They shoot them first, of course. Say, where have you been? It's happening all over the country, according to the news."

"Geez. So . . . um . . . what day is it again?"

"Oh. Right. Forgive me. I'm an old man with the memory of a monoped. September twelfth."

"Oh." Hill's face fell. He had a terrible feeling. Everything had gotten worse since he'd been out of it, and he'd been out of it for quite a while. Why had everything gotten *worse*? His story should have broken. The entire conspiracy should be over by now, or at least severely damaged.

"What date did you *think* it was?"

"Um, dunno really. Guess I've been out of touch."

"Why am I not surprised?"

"So you came to follow Andrews, right?" Hill asked, thinking of another way into the real questions he had dangling.

"My dear friend, I expected to get the faith test eventually, but not from such a one nor in such a place."

"Sorry."

"Yes, it's true. I came to follow Andrews. And I will pledge allegiance or whatever else they require."

"Do you believe it, though? *Him?* You don't look like the type to buy into aliens."

"Never thought I'd *be* the type, if you must know. But people are dying out there, particularly in California . . . like they weren't human beings at all, but blades of grass under a lawn mower. My God, it's . . ." The old man controlled his contorting features with effort. "My dear boy! I'm a stubborn old goat, but I know when to get on my knees and start begging as well as the next man."

"The plague is that bad?"

The man in the trench coat shot him another disbelieving look. "You *have* been out of touch, haven't you? Son, there are *bodies lying in the gutters*. Do you know how strange that looks in the twenty-first century? In a city like Oakland? And not just the homeless either—people are being thrown out by their own families."

"Jesus Christ," Hill muttered.

"Apparently," the man said, with considerable bitterness. "Some say the plague will take everyone who's not intended to stay for the new millennium. Which, if we're judged by our merits, is very few of us indeed."

"But . . . there's a *cure*, an antidote. Haven't you seen anything about that?"

The old man stopped walking abruptly and turned to stare at Hill. "What do you mean?" There was no trace of amusement in the man's face now.

"They . . . they haven't found a vaccine?" Hill asked cautiously.

"No!" the man snapped. "President Cole says they're putting everything they have on it, but there hasn't been any progress. Why should there be? It's not like it's a *normal* disease, this Wormwood! It's the wrath of God!"

"President *Cole*?" Hill asked, horrified.

"Get with the program!" the man screamed furiously. He turned and ran away from Hill as though he might be carrying something even worse than Santarém.

Hill walked on through the canvas-and-aluminum suburbs. He was still thinking about that newspaper, and he noticed a number of mini–satellite dishes on top of RVs and pickup trucks. Groups were gathered around portable television sets. More people were listening to boom box radios. He wanted to listen himself, but people grew squeamish when he drew near. He finally spotted an RV where a paunchy, middle-aged man was asleep in a lawn chair, head thrown back, snoring lightly. A heavyset woman was cooking hamburgers over propane and watching a TV that was perched on a plastic picnic table. No one else was around. He moved in behind the woman, downwind. She was watching the BBC.

". . . war-torn landscape of England, Scotland, Ireland, and Wales. The United Arab Forces unmercifully hammered Glasgow, Dublin, and Liverpool today. At least a hundred people were killed and three hundred injured. The downtown area of Liverpool is close to ruin, priceless cathedrals, art museums, and historical architecture have been destroyed by six intense days of air strikes. The best efforts of the RAF have not kept the bombers out of English airspace. One can hardly blame the battered survivors for turning resentful eyes to their larger sister to the south, London, where not a single shot has been fired nor a single bomb dropped."

The TV image moved from bomb rubble to aerial shots over the Vatican. The streets teemed with people.

"The other European city to have escaped the wrath of Mal Abbas is Rome, where millions of Catholics have gathered as

they have here, in London. Could it be that the 'madman of Baghdad' has respect for his fellow zealots? Or is it truly divine protection?

"The new British prime minister, barely two days in office, had no comment about London's apparent immunity, but he left early this morning for Scotland, saying that he had to go where he was needed most.

"Whatever the politicians think, the people's *thoughts on the matter are crystal clear. They continue to flock to London, despite the danger of Santarém from the Blade concert there weeks ago. The bombs have done what faith alone could not: made them believers in 'Saint Mary of Dublin,' London's patron saint of Santa Pelagia."*

The monitor showed a film clip of a wiry, brunette nun amidst a sea of followers. She had an otherworldly expression about the eyes.

"Sister Mary Magdalen Daunsey is a Dublin nun and former soup-kitchen founder turned prophet. Her followers claim she has the gift of stigmata, a gift she 'shared' during her recent prayer service on the BBC."

Daunsey praying. Her chin was tilted back. Her eyelids were mostly closed, but a band of pure white showed between her dark lashes. She mumbled incoherently. Her palms, which were pressed together on the desk in front of her, began to leak blood onto the polished oak surface.

"This display has a few skeptics crying 'fraudulence' and flimflammery but it seems to have earned the nun more converts than critics. The real controversy came when Daunsey publicly contradicted British health officials, who are advising all travelers to steer clear of London as one of the potential Santarém outbreak points. But with the rest of the world seemingly engulfed in chaos and terror, comfort and hope is worth more than gold. Apparently, more than life itself. The people do *come—they come on Saint Mary's instructions, and they'll die happily in the streets, if need be, just to be close to their prophet."*

The monitor showed video taken in the hallways of a brand-new apartment complex in London. People lay on blankets in the hallways, dying. The camera panned one of the apartments—it was packed with the sick and the dead. "Irish Catholics," said the words at the bottom.

"Apparently, Saint Mary cannot guarantee her followers any-thing but hope. Although the number of cases in London has not followed the pattern so horrifically exhibited in other concert cities, there has been sickness here. About the outbreak of the so-called Wormwood plague among her own immigrants, Saint Mary would only say that God did not guarantee anyone immu-nity from the signs of the end times. But it would seem her fol-lowers are offered, at least, an immunity from war . . . for the moment."

The footage changed to show an encampment from the air, a sprawling mass of humankind. Dotted throughout the landscape were strange shapes made of flesh and wood.

"The loyalty to Saint Mary might be considered tame compared to the obsession of some. In Kiev, followers of Father Dimish have turned to crucifixion as a means to declare their faith, no longer satisfied with castration and the excising of breasts. They are said to have little food."

The monitor changed to a night scene; a vast shantytown was on fire.

"In Africa, the followers of Pastor Simnali have rioted, choos-ing to mutilate others rather than themselves in their hunger. No one can say whether Simnali himself escaped alive.

"In India, where a series of small quakes have rocked the land, Allahabad has been taken over by the Kali-worshiping supporters of Dishama Giri, Hindu prophet. Near Calcutta the group of Sagara Bata is now in the tens of millions, but still rela-tively peaceful, despite a lack of food.

"And in the United States, President Cole has alleviated the food woes of the prophets by sending in the National Guard. He's guaranteed that anyone going to one of the U.S. prophets shall have their food rations transferred immediately."

The film showed thousands of people in line. Behind long tables were Guardsmen, giving out boxes of rations and check-ing off lists. Words came up beneath the image—"Salt Lake City, Utah."

"It is not, says the new American president, that he neces-sarily endorses the message of the prophets. But in this time of global crisis, respecting the beliefs and desires of his people is the least he can do."

"Bull*shit!*" Hill muttered.

The woman at the grill turned and saw him. She backed away, shooing at him, grease flying from her spatula.

He moved on. Now his physical weakness was compounded by turmoil. What in God's name had happened to his story? And where was Deauchez?

He pushed his way into the streets of Sedona at last. In the distance, he could hear bullhorns. *"If you have not yet registered, make your way to the Maidway parking lot, where your name and social security number can be listed for food. Rations are immediately available for new registrants. Inoculations are required."*

Inoculations. He was panting now. The shot had saved him, *must* have. But if Deauchez had given him the shot, where was he now? With a start he remembered the doctor, Smith. They were supposed to meet him. But Hill had no memory of anything after he'd sent that story. *His story.*

The crowd was dense and people shouted angrily at him to take a bath. He pushed on, growing more and more upset and more and more tired. He spotted a bookstore and elbowed his way inside.

Although the shop was small, and there were a half dozen customers crowding the aisles, it still felt like a peaceful haven after the streets. They were woefully low on stock, and there were no newspapers at all. He walked up to the counter and the man behind it—a fifty-something white man with skin spotted from too much sun—tried to hide the wrinkling of his nose.

"Do you carry the *New York Times*?" Hill asked, his words blurring in his haste: *Newktimes.*

"What?"

"New. York. Times."

"Buddy, there's a line outside that door about three blocks long ever' mornin'. Ever' copy of ever' newspaper I get is sold out before the sun comes up."

"Oh," Hill said. He felt tears of frustration threaten. He couldn't go on, couldn't keep searching.

"Don't worry. You didn't miss much this mornin'. 'Specially in the *Times*."

"Yeah? What'd it say?"

"Mostly goin' on about how great President Cole is and them other new leaders overseas? They convinced me the first time. I wish they'd start sayin' what he's gonna *do*."

"He can't . . . can't have been president for long," Hill said tentatively, half expecting another outburst.

The man only looked at him funny. "Noooo . . . But time ain't what it used to be."

"That's true enough."

"The *Times*'s lost its edge, if you ask me. Don't even talk about them earthquakes much. Now the *San Francisco Chronicle*? It was quotin' Reverend Stanton, sayin' that we're seein' the first rumblin's of the seventh sign. 'Course, them folks in San Francisco are right on top of the fryin' pan, ain't they?"

"There hasn't been anything in the *Times* about . . . about some kind of conspiracy?" Hill asked, already knowing the answer.

Now the shopkeeper did look at him queerly. "Guess you *do* need a paper. Not to mention a bath, beggin' my pardon."

Perhaps it had been the grail of the newspaper that had kept him on his feet. But Hill's legs, which had been shaking since he'd hit tent-city, gave up the ghost. He felt it coming and backed up against a nearby wall, slid to the floor.

The shopkeeper came around the counter and looked down at him. "What is it, food?" he asked, almost whispering. He glanced uneasily at the other customers, but they just gazed at Hill dully and looked away.

"No. I've just . . ." He recalled the warning from the man in the tweed jacket. "I think I've got a touch of food poisoning. A guy gave me some meat last night. I think it was bad."

The shopkeeper remained wary.

"It's not Santarém, really. I don't have a cold." Hill demonstrated by breathing loudly through his nose. Dry as a bone. "Or a fever either—go ahead and check."

The man, looking a bit embarrassed about it, checked Hill's forehead. He grunted. "Follow me."

The shopkeeper led Hill past a storage room and up a flight of wooden stairs. Upstairs was a small apartment, obviously the man's own. He looked nervous.

"Look, I hope you won't be takin' advantage of this. You can't tell anyone I let you. I don't wanna crowd of people up here . . . No offense."

Hill felt obscenely grateful. "I won't tell anyone. It's very kind of you."

"Well . . . it just looks like you could really use a shower 'n a decent rest. I'm no saint now, God knows, but in times like these, when ideas about doin' somethin' nice come into your head, you think twice about ignorin' 'em."

The words touched Hill. He was overwhelmed by a feeling of sorrow at the state they were all in, as if this small kindness had tipped the scale. Or perhaps it had just been so long since he'd had a break from anyone.

"So . . . the shower's in through there, 'n you can rest on the couch. Please don't touch the food, though. I only have my own rations for this week. You can get somethin' out in town when you're ready. Have to stand in line, though."

"I had food in my car, actually. That's the least of my problems."

"And . . . uh . . . well, you seem like an educated man. I've been keepin' my own copies of some of the papers? They're under the bed. Please keep 'em neat and don't take nothin'."

The man looked at Hill with a nervous vulnerability. It was the look of someone who was hoping not to have his newfound humanitarianism prove foolish, as he'd always suspected in the first place.

"I will, I promise."

He showered first. The water was hot, and it felt better than just about anything he could ever remember—even chocolate. He examined his wet body under the stream, sliding his hands across his hips, his sides, over his stomach. Beneath his fingers, his skin was loose and his own shape was unfamiliar. His stomach no longer hung over his pubic hair—the crease where it had folded was still there, but above it was only a slight bulge, not several inches of protruding flesh. He lathered and rinsed, feeling as though the filth of the tomb was pouring off him and down the drain.

When he was done, he would have given anything for fresh clothes, but he had none. He put his old ones back on and sat down on the bed with a stack of the *Times*.

He went back to the last issue he could remember and read on from there. There was nothing but continuing support, even mawkish coverage—he could see that now—of the Santa Pelagia story, of the prophets, of the signs. Every front page was blitzed by it, the entire first section held little else. Had he started this? Had he been that bad, that gloatingly irresponsible, when he'd been on the story? Yes, he had.

Nowhere was there any mention of the conspiracy—not even

the slightest "it's been rumored" hint. There was a new pope, he noted, Pope John Peter I, and he had declared Santa Pelagia divine. He was calling all Catholics to London, Santa Pelagia, or Rome. So Deauchez's phone call had come to naught, as well. He cursed vehemently under his breath. Had Bowmont thought him mad, or had *they* gotten to him? A story he found in a five-day-old issue made the latter seem likely.

It was about the murder of several WHO doctors. In Munich, virologist Sam Richards and two of his closest colleagues had been gunned down in a hospital parking lot. In Washington, a Josh Bergman and Stanley Hughes had been assassinated in an apparently unrelated event. Another WHO doctor, one Michael Smith, was missing. According to the *Times*, resentment and rage against the impotent medical profession was thought to be the motivation for these attacks.

Hill let the paper slide down with a stifled sob. They had gotten Smith. And they'd managed to get to his story, too. No one knew. *Still, no one knew!* No one but himself and Deauchez.

Hill had never felt more miserable in his life. He sincerely wished that he had not returned from the dead, that he had been spared this resurrection. He collapsed on the bed, chest heaving, but found that he felt too wretched to cry. Maybe that was why he leaked at the little things; the real sorrows were too big for tears. He wanted to talk to Deauchez. He wanted the priest. Where was the priest?

A glimmer of memory came to him. Maybe he'd been dreaming, or maybe it had really happened, but . . . hadn't someone told him that Deauchez went to see Andrews? But that made no sense. Why would Deauchez do that? And what if Andrews, or someone close to him, was one of *them*?

Hill had the thought that he must get up, must go look for the priest, that Deauchez might need him. But even as he thought it, he was falling asleep.

SPRINGFIELD, IDAHO

Inland. He'd traveled south, but inland. He was heading south very deliberately, though he did not yet understand where he would end up. He *did* know why his route was inland. The coast was dangerous. The coast was a very bad place to be.

Will Cougar was tired. He had walked for three days without food. Once upon a time, a man on the road could have gotten a ride in this land. Once upon a time, people might have given him a bite to eat. It was no longer that way. There were few cars on the roads here, in Idaho. And he didn't care to travel the main roads anyhow. When he did see a car the driver sped up as soon as they caught sight of a stranger. He knew why: they thought maybe he was sick, maybe he was carrying that virus with him like an invisible companion, or maybe he was some crazy person. He had seen more than a few crazy people on the road himself.

Springfield was just a small farming town, but as he neared it he knew that something was wrong there. He had planned to walk another hour or two before finding a place to sleep, even though it was dusk. Usually, he curled up in the woods, scavenging branches and leaves to make a bed. They were warm and they kept you hidden, too.

But Springfield would not be easily passed. Trucks with canvas tops and camouflage paint rolled past him. When he got to a place where he could see the town, he saw many such vehicles. The streets were crowded with machines, lights, soldiers. He did not know why.

He decided he would not go on tonight after all. He found a deserted farm down a dirt lane, still in view of the town. The house was dark, and a broken array of laundry lines in the yard added to the air of abandonment. The screen door on the front of the house was hanging from its hinges. Will Cougar did not enter the house; he went to the tall, red barn.

He must have been tired, for he had made a mistake about the farm. He was still looking over the inside of the barn when he heard a footfall, soft, behind him, and a flat sound that was the drawing back of a gun's hammer. Will Cougar turned to see a desperate-looking young man in overalls aiming a shotgun in his direction.

The man looked him over in the dim light, his bloodshot eyes wide and staring, as though trying to figure him out. He maybe decided Will Cougar was a vagrant, for he raised the gun. "Get out," he said, in a low, urgent whisper. "You can't stay here!"

"I only want a place to sleep."

"I said *get*. This ain't no hotel."

He must want people to think no one lives here, Will Cougar thought. *A visitor is the last thing you want when you are hiding.* He lowered his hands. "I will go."

He was walking past the man when he heard a sharp intake of breath. "You . . . you . . ."

Will Cougar waited. He saw the man's gaunt face struggle for words. None came, and Will Cougar turned once more to go. A hand grasped weakly at his arm.

"Wait! You—you're that prophet. That Indian. A-aren't you?"

The man looked as afraid that Will Cougar might say yes as that he might say no. Will Cougar nodded once, sharply.

He was surprised at the reaction. The man dropped his gun and raised his hands as though to ward off something. He backed away, then slammed to his knees as though someone strong had pushed him down. "Oh, my God," the man blubbered. "Oh, sweet Jesus!"

Will Cougar frowned and left the barn, but the man followed him into the yard, shuffling, grasping at him. "No. I—I'm sorry. Please! Don't be mad. You can stay. I—I got some food hid, if you're hungry. Please! You can stay if you want."

Will Cougar stopped moving. He did not like this man's face, so afraid of him. It worried Will Cougar. It bothered him very much. But it had been a long time since he had eaten.

He took the man's hand from his arm and nodded. "Yes. Thank you. I would like some food."

"Okay." The man's face brightened as though he had been granted a pardon, as though maybe having Will Cougar mad at him was a pretty terrible thing. "Y-you can make up a bed in the barn. I got blankets. I'll go make the food. I-I'll just go make it."

In the barn, Will Cougar watched the town from the high window. The man brought him blankets and food. The food was good. He ate, then watched the town some more, but he could not tell what was going on. He had not wanted the man to stay, so he had not asked him about it, and anyhow the man looked anxious to get away.

With his stomach full, and nothing happening in the streets beyond, Will Cougar's mind wandered. On his long walk he had put one foot in front of the other. One foot in front of the other pressing, solid, into the earth. On a death walk, you took nothing with you except some matches and a knife, maybe some water. On a death walk, you made your mind smooth, like a piece of paper, and as you planted your foot you reached down deep into Mother Earth, *felt* her. You watched yourself walking on the face of her like a teardrop rolling down a woman's cheek. And if your mind was quiet and your feet were seductive, she would speak to you.

Within her voice, Will Cougar climbed as well as walked; he walked with his feet and climbed with his mind, hand over hand, down the rope of the past few months to find the point where things stopped being right. It was like searching for the exact moment when an itch began. But he found that moment and at that moment was a face—a dark face, the face of that reporter who had come to ask about . . . yes, about the shots.

When the reporter had asked that, Will Cougar remembered what had happened that day he was given *his* shot. He had forgotten about it, and at the time it had happened, he had not felt anything about it at all. But when the reporter asked those questions, it was as though Will Cougar were a third person, watching himself getting that shot and passing out all over again. He knew then that something was wrong, that something had been done to him . . . *maybe* something that had to do with Santa Pelagia. But he did not know what it was, and he did not know how to doubt what he had so fully believed in the breath that came before that reporter's words. It took him a while to learn how to shed that skin.

When he found the face, he knew that he must see that man again. He had stopped yesterday at a small market and called the *New York Times*. He was passed on to a man, a Bow-mount he'd called himself, who had told him that Hill was dead. Will Cougar asked Bow-mount to repeat it. Bow-mount said again that Hill was dead. He was lying. Bow-mount then wanted to ask Will Cougar questions, but Will Cougar hung up. He checked the *New York Times* at the store and did not see the name of the reporter—Hill—anywhere on it. So the man in New York could be telling the truth. But Will Cougar knew that he was not. He also knew that Bow-mount would not tell him where Hill was, even if he asked.

But Will Cougar's feet were being pulled south. He was a fish on a line being drawn through the water, and whenever he thought about Hill, that pull grew stronger, as though the line had grown taut. Another thing happened when he thought about Hill. He saw another face, the face of that priest who had come asking questions at the beginning. That priest had not started anything bad in Will Cougar the way that Hill had. Will Cougar had been too full of the visions back then. But now, now that he thought about it, that priest had been the only other person who acted like maybe something was wrong with Santa Pelagia. But Will Cougar did not know where the priest was, either, did not even remember his name. So he moved south.

Out in the night, a voice crackled large, mechanical. It was a bullhorn. At first Will Cougar thought he was hearing funny, then he realized that he was listening to Chinese. He knew then what was going on in Springfield, Idaho, and why the farmer who owned this house hid like a rat inside. He watched through the window as the searchlights danced across the face of a big white building in town, a church. The voice of the American translator went on and on, but there was no response.

Will Cougar rolled onto his back with a knowing grunt. So this was the white and the yellow men's war. It was a curious strategy on the yellow men's part, but not very wise. His own people had tales of similar barricades in their long history. The stories never ended well. The men inside the church would wait and the men outside the church would wait: wait until the spring, or until that virus came, or until the world ended. Or maybe they would wait until someone got tired of waiting and started to shoot.

They would not wait long, probably not even long enough to grow tired. For the world *was* ending, and it would happen very soon. That was another secret the Earth beneath his feet had told him.

CHAPTER 23

Anthony Cole was not the kind of man who ignored bumps in the smooth surface of his world. He was the kind who sought them out and worked at them with heavy fingers until they disappeared. Still, he was president now, and there had been a great deal of urgent business.

The war was the least of it. The Chinese had not sent any more troops, and there was little for the military to do except sit on the *Pa woo*. But there were appointments to make, a cabinet to fill, and every day Santarém grew, on and on and on, requiring strategy, maneuvering, crisis control. Entire platoons were consigned to bury the dead and patrol the cities against the sick and the looters. The sight of their new, military camo spacesuits probably did little to instill a sense of security in the citizens, but it couldn't be helped.

So Cole had not had a spare moment to follow up on this particular bump, this strange thread. He was not entirely oblivious to it, but he *had* filed it in the "maybe it will go away" box in his mind. It was a form of indulgence he rarely allowed himself.

On day twenty-four the issue emerged, ripe and stinking, and demanded his attention.

When the news came in, Cole was in the middle of a working luncheon with his new cabinet. His personal aide, a Mr. Ashe, read the report. Mr. Ashe was the bright young Yale grad who had paid his political dues as waterboy at another cabinet meeting two weeks ago. He read the details to the silent room, forks hanging in the air like conductor's batons.

403

The nine-point-three L.A. quake had started with a whip-lashing jolt, and it grew into a screaming roar. Freeways groaned and collapsed like exhausted dogs. Buildings fell in upon their center soufflélike, and entire blocks disappeared into fissures that erupted in the middle of boulevards, buildings, and school-yards. The coast had not split off from the mainland at the San Andreas, as some predicted would happen with a quake this size, but cliffs and beaches had slipped away, multimillion-dollar real estate consigned to the sea.

L.A.'s population was, mercifully, greatly reduced at the time of the quake. Gone from their numbers were those who had left to join the prophets, those who had fled Santarém, and those who had succumbed to it. Other cities in California were less de-serted. San Diego and Fresno faced seven- and six-point quakes minutes after L.A. The seismic distress rippled outward and up-ward, the Pacific and the North American plates straining against one another like bedmates having bad dreams. San Francisco, for the second time in a hundred years, was rocked by an eight-point-plus shaker. Rows of brightly painted houses splintered like colored matchsticks. Along the wharf, entire streets, includ-ing the touristy Pier 39, slithered into the bay. Lower floors pan-caked into subgarages. And, in another repeat of history, fires had followed the quake like night follows day.

After Mr. Ashe had read the report he stood quietly, waiting for Cole's instructions. Cole did not speak at once. He showed no outward reaction at all. Even internally, he held his reaction in check like some wild thing locked in a barn. He looked around the room to gauge the others' responses.

His cabinet had been selected with infinite care, the names laid out years ago. Every one of them was loyal to him, and every one of them had excellent credentials. Yet despite their high intelligence, despite their understanding of the events now shaping their world, not one face in the room showed real dis-tress. He saw confused bemusement mostly, a kind of "*Well, how about* that?" and here and there a shadow of regret. All of them had secured family and possessions far from the fray months ago. All of them were steeled to expect tragedy. No, none of them looked particularly perturbed.

But this was different; this wasn't about tragedy. Cole could see that none of them got that.

"We should send in a relief force," said the new secretary of human services.

"It'll be hell to dig one up," said the secretary of defense. "The virus is starting to have a real impact on our National Guard, and those who are still standing are needed where they are."

"It's going to be a problem getting food to the survivors, too," the secretary of agriculture said. "There's nothing left in emergency relief, so what we really need are troops to get the grocery stores back on-line and the normal rationing chain flowing again."

They looked at Cole, expecting some input on these tactical issues, but he did not offer any. Instead, he turned to Mr. Ashe. "I want a report on every volcanic eruption and earthquake—large and small—that's occurred in the past two weeks. Worldwide. Get it in here as soon as you can."

Mr. Ashe vanished.

"There . . . *have* been a number of quakes recently . . . haven't there?" the new attorney general said with a frown. It wasn't a very deep frown.

"There was that Kobe-size quake in Japan, and several near Allahabad in India, I think," the secretary of agriculture recalled.

There was a bit of discussion about this, aimless, before they settled and waited for Cole to say something. But he had nothing to say. He would not even let himself *feel*. He was not going to open those barn doors until he had a damn good idea what was behind them.

Mr. Ashe returned. He handed a single page to Cole, then went to the computer, where he called up the file for projection.

Cole looked at the page in his hand and sucked in his breath. "Get my brother and Dr. Morton on the phone please, Mr. Ashe," he said in a still voice.

When he glanced up, he saw that something in his tone had laid a cold finger of dread, at long last, on the faces of the men and women around the table.

SEDONA, ARIZONA

Hill was afraid. Deauchez had disappeared, had abandoned him out at that car, and the only plausible explanation was that the priest had been picked up—picked up by *them*. Now Hill was following in his footsteps, just like Janet Leigh retracing her sister's road trip in *Psycho*, and everyone knew what a great idea *that* had turned out to be. But what choice did he have? Only one: he could leave town without Deauchez, give him up for dead.

Not an option.

At Andrews's hotel, he was eventually passed off to a young guy named Scott. Scott was the first one he'd talked to who didn't look stoned, and when he repeated the priest's name, Scott's bearded face lit up with comprehension. "Right! And I bet you're Hill, huh?"

Hill blinked at him. "Uh . . . yeah. Simon Hill. Have you seen Father Deauchez?"

"*Simon* Hill—the reporter?"

Hill nodded.

"Ah!" Scott exclaimed again, apparently further enlightened. "You know, a guy named Hart was looking for you two. Wanted to know if you'd come by here. 'Deauchez and Hill,' he said, said you were traveling together. I was kinda wondering if you'd show up looking for Father . . ."

Hill did not know who Scott was talking about, but he had a pretty good idea who it *might* be. His skin broke out in goose bumps, a feeling his grandmother used to describe as someone walking on your grave. "When was this?" he interrupted.

Scott took a deep, contemplative breath and let it out slowly. "Um . . . let's see. Almost a week now? Something like that. I'm pretty sure that was the day after the priest showed up, if that means anything."

Blackness threatened to swamp Hill. He grabbed at the air for something, any kind of support. Scott met his hand in midair and steadied him with a strong arm. "Whoa! Don't freak out, man. It's cool."

"Where's Deauchez?" Hill managed.

"He's over in the jail. Trent had him locked up." Scott rolled his eyes. "Don't even ask."

"But you said—you said someone came looking for us."

"Yeah, and by your reaction I guess you didn't wanna be found. Don't worry. I told him I hadn't seen either one of ya."

Hill stared at Scott's pleasant, innocuous face, unable to grasp what he was being told. "Why? Why would you do that?"

Scott's smile faded. Resentment flickered in his eyes. "That Hart—he's a real psycho. He shot someone for stealing vaccines about . . . well, yeah, I guess it was the night the priest showed up.

Trent didn't wanna do much about it. The guy who got shot *was* stealing, I guess. But it sure pissed me off. I wouldn't turn a *dog* over to that asshole after something like that. Not that I ever liked him much in the first place. Too slick—reminds me of an agent I had once. He's still around here somewhere, unfortunately—Hart, I mean." Scott ended this amazing diatribe with a sad shake of his head. "Seriously bad Karma, man."

Scott looked so guileless, so completely incognizant of what it was he was saying, that Hill didn't know whether to laugh or scream or cry. He decided the best plan was just to get the fuck out.

"I have to see Deauchez," he said.

He'd regained his equilibrium, and Scott let him go with the care of someone putting down a glass figurine. "Well . . . sure." He shrugged. "Tell ya what. Why don't I go ask Trent? That poor guy's been locked up for a week, and Trent hasn't mentioned him. He . . . um . . . tends to forget things sometimes. He's under a lot of pressure, ya know. Maybe . . . Look, I'll just go ask him."

He did, as promised, go ask. When he returned, jogging lightly up to Hill, his face was hopeful. "Hey, you wouldn't happen to have Deauchez's Telegyn cellular, would ya?"

Hill was not surprised by anything anymore. He reached for his black bag, opened it carefully to make sure Scott didn't see the gun that was in there, and held the phone up as if offering it at auction. "Deauchez?"

Scott smiled. "Deal! But you guys have to leave town—*immediately,* Trent said."

Hill wanted nothing better.

As Scott led him through town, Hill was thinking, hoping, that he was about to see Deauchez. He had no idea why Andrews had locked him up, though the priest was certainly more than capable of making himself a nuisance. But unless Scott was really out of the loop, Deauchez was alive at least, and that was the main thing.

He was impatient with the crowd, impatient with Scott's popularity. Every few feet someone stopped them, and Scott always maintained his ebullient generosity, never brushing them off. Hill was about to interrupt one such conversation when it was interrupted for him. At first he thought he was having another wave of fatigue, then he realized that the ground was literally moving beneath his feet. It was an earthquake.

Within seconds it was clear that it was a very big earthquake. The crowd reacted with screams, people shying away from buildings, from each other. Scott grabbed his hand and shouted, "This way!"

They pushed through the panicking crowd. It was like trying to walk in a washing machine. The ground's back-and-forth jarring threatened Hill's balance, and several times he felt the sickening resilience of flesh beneath his feet. He didn't look down. The crowds swept him away so fast, he *couldn't* look down. It was all he could do to keep hold of Scott's hand.

Street signs, business signs toppled. The light, Southwestern-style buildings did not hold up well. Chunks of textured plaster came raining off of them like scabs peeling away. There was a swamping terror in the crowd—much worse even than at Santa Pelagia, because it was more immediate. God's wrath was not *coming*, it was already here, already shaking them silly like an enraged parent, and it might never stop.

But it did stop. By the time Hill and Scott had half pushed their way, half been carried into a side street, the quake was over. The panic was abating, too, fading into a kind of traumatic aftershock. People were no longer running and screaming. The cries that came now were muffled, purposeful—they were coming from under the rubble.

The dust of broken plaster danced in the air, floated like a halo around Scott's head. He looked around, dazed by the destruction. "It's here," he panted. "Ohmygod. I—I have to go. Best of luck, man."

He started to leave but Hill grabbed his arm. "Wait! *Where* is it? I don't see . . ."

Scott pointed to a heap of broken wall immediately in front of them. "He *was* in there. In the basement. I'm sorry. I really have to go."

"Christ!" Hill ran to the building, stumbling over debris. He screamed Deauchez's name over and over, not even pausing for an answer.

He finally recognized the front door, but there was nothing around it but air. He kept calling for the priest as he searched for some clue as to the building's design, some more profitable entrance or egress. As he moved around what he thought was the side of the building he found a section of wall with a window, low and barred. The window's frame and bars were intact, but next to it was a gaping hole where the plaster had imploded. Hill knelt down to look through it, still calling out. It took a while before he could see inside, dust frustrating his efforts. Then he saw that he was looking into a small cell with a dust-covered cot on the floor, a toilet, a door . . .

The cell was empty.

The tents and RVs had fared better than the buildings in town. Charcoal broilers lying on their sides and clothes dumped from makeshift lines were the worst casualties. Deauchez wandered through the campground, avoiding the clusters of fearful neighbors. He could scarcely believe how much the place had grown since he'd arrived. It was beyond comprehension. He wondered if it were the same for the other prophets, for Daunsey. He wondered if Hill was dead.

In his haste he began to trot, legs weak from his confinement, from the terror of the quake and of his escape. One moment he had been lying on the cot, his heart full of black, rotting despair. The next, the world had shuddered and a hole had opened up in the wall, debris raining down on his head. He had not paused to contemplate the situation; he had hoisted himself up and run.

It seemed to take forever, but he finally hit the open desert and spotted the place where he knew the car was parked. He ran faster, the rock looming tall in front of him. He squinted, trying to see, desperate to see, but the shadow was falling in such a way as to completely hide the vehicle. He was beginning to doubt that it was there at all.

Then his eyes picked out its shape in the darkness and he sprinted as fast as he could. He was only a few yards away when he saw that there was a figure in the passenger seat, a figure under a blanket.

"Simon!" he shouted, his heart sinking. Surely the reporter would not be here after all this time—and be alive.

Of course he's dead. He got the vaccine so late! Even if it could have worked, it probably would not have worked so late.

He reached the car and dashed around it, pulled open the passenger door.

"Simon . . ." he repeated softly. He didn't smell anything horribly foul. He uttered a silent prayer despite his newfound fatalism and tugged anxiously at the blanket's edge.

A hand grabbed his wrist—grabbed it with a cruel power. It

was a white hand. Something was terribly wrong. Then the blanket was pushed aside and there was a gun, its black barrel staring straight at him. Holding the gun was a brutal-eyed man with white hair.

"You even *think* about moving and you're dead." The man's features were tensed in hard, furious lines. A grimace of a smile twisted his mouth.

The world swayed beneath Deauchez as though the earthquake had returned, but it was only his knees giving out. He leaned, panting in sudden terror, in that awkward position of reaching into the car. "Who—who are you?"

"Vengeance."

"You're one of *them*, aren't you? The Red Scepter?"

"Shut up." The man swung his feet out of the car and, as he stood, he pushed Deauchez backward until the priest's head struck the sheer rock walls of the monolith. Then he stepped forward again into Deauchez's face. "You know I just found your car this morning. A jogger mentioned it to a friend of mine. I looked at this road a hundred times from town, never saw it. Pretty neat trick."

"Was it?" Deauchez hadn't thought it all that clever at the time.

"Yes," White Hair said, his smile fading. "You've been fucking lucky, Father. But all luck runs out. I knew you'd come back here—soon as that earthquake hit. You or *him*. Now I'm going to kill you."

Deauchez felt rage burn through him at the futility of it all. And he'd thought he'd been *lucky* to have escaped—that his prayers had been answered! He'd only been coaxed to his death by that open wall, a lamb to the slaughter.

"Then do it," he said, and he realized that he meant it. In his fury at God, at the whole wacky, wonderful way of things, he had found bravado.

"Do you know I killed that friend of yours, Dr. Michael Smith?"

A moan escaped Deauchez.

"He was trying to leave town at the time. He was carrying syringes—*stolen* property, I might add. We knew immediately who had been chatting with him, but we couldn't find you. Where have you been, Father Deauchez?"

"Why don't you get this over with?"

"Where is Simon Hill?"

"I don't know!" Deauchez suppressed an angry sob.

The man's face was reddening with . . . irritation? anger? The gun jammed into the priest's ribs. "I don't want to hold you up from those pearly gates. I can see how anxious you are. But I do have one more thing. I got a phone call a few days ago from a lady—a very great lady. Perhaps you remember her. You beat her up and killed her husband."

"Janovich," Deauchez said tiredly.

"*Dr.* Janovich. She wanted to know *why you didn't believe?*" Despite his phony smile, hatred glittered in White Hair's eyes like some sharp implement, even here, even in the shadows.

Deauchez didn't answer. The man struck him across the face. The blow was unexpected and heavy with rage.

"Why didn't you believe?"

Deauchez turned his head and spat out a tooth. His cheek shrieked with pain. Blood dribbled down his chin. He felt his chin tremble and stopped it with an effort of will.

"Go to hell," he said. He voiced it deliberately and blankly to make it clear that the conversation was over. Then he turned his head and looked away. He looked off to the left, out where the desert was still untouched by Andrews's sorry carnival. He fixed his eyes on the stark beauty of the landscape and prepared to die.

There was a gunshot and Deauchez crumpled to the desert floor.

"What did he mean?"

Someone was shaking him. When Deauchez opened his eyes, it took him a moment to realize that Simon Hill was crouching beside him and that he was neither spirit nor hallucination. Next to them was a dark form.

White Hair's corpse. Deauchez looked up at Hill in shock. "Simon!"

"Yeah, I *know* that," Hill said, breathing hard. His face was drawn and scared. In fact, the reporter still had his gun clutched in his right hand; it dug painfully into Deauchez's shoulder where Hill was trying to grip him. Deauchez pushed Hill away.

"Let me stand."

He got to his feet carefully, using the rock behind him for guidance. He could see that Hill, too, was trembling. Alive, but not necessarily well. Deauchez reached out a hand to help him.

The white-haired man, on the other hand, would never rise

again. There was a small amount of blood on the back of his head. Deauchez stuck his foot against White Hair's side and began to turn him, then saw that his face was mostly gone. He grimaced in disgust and let the corpse fall back on its front.

"Good shot," he said in disbelief.

"Don't ask me how I did it, because I have no friggin' clue."

They stared at each other, wide-eyed. Deauchez was numb— he had gotten a little too used to the idea of being dead. Still, he knew intellectually how thrilled he was to see Simon Hill, even if his emotions were temporarily moribund. He stepped forward and hugged his friend.

"You have lost a lot of weight. Are you all right?"

Hill, still oblivious to the live gun in his hand, patted the priest's back awkwardly. "Yeah, well, I wouldn't recommend it, but it sure cleaned me out. I think I'm okay."

"I'm so glad, Simon. Really—so happy."

But Hill didn't seem to be sharing the moment. There was something more than wary in his eyes. He was looking at Deauchez as though he wasn't sure who he was.

"Father, I want to know what that man was talking about. Why did he ask you why you didn't believe? Why would Janovich be asking you that?"

"Simon . . ." Deauchez began. He stopped with a sigh.

"If you don't tell me, I'll—"

"Wait! Don't say something we will both regret. I will tell you, I promise. But we must get on the road first, yes? There will be more where he came from, and I don't think I can work up enough anger to die twice in one day."

Hill glanced at the dead man as if he had forgotten he was there. His gun hand was shaking uncontrollably as it hung at his side. Deauchez reached over gently to take the weapon. At first Hill resisted, and it made Deauchez's heart grieve to see the suspicion on his face. But at last Hill did release the gun. He turned as if to get into the hatchback.

"We should take another car," Deauchez suggested. "They know about this one now." He looked across the desert at the trail of automobiles. "Surely we can find one with keys in all of that mélange."

Hill opened the door anyway. He pulled out the garbage bags of food from Janovich's house, now visibly lighter, and then he groped around on the passenger's-side floor.

"There were some syringes under here. I found 'em when I was looking for aspirin. Damn! They're gone." Hill stood, upset.

"That is unfortunate. We could have sent them to a lab." But the loss of evidence really didn't surprise Deauchez anymore. It was like a cruel joke in its improbable consistency.

Hill closed the door. "I was thinking *you* might need one. Did you get a shot at the camp?"

"No," Deauchez said wearily. "Come *on*, Simon. I don't need an inoculation. I think you know that. We must *go* now. We can talk about it later."

Hill just stood there, his face a mask of hurt and distrust.

"Please," Deauchez begged. "There may be more of *them* arriving any moment."

The reporter rolled his eyes. "Glad to see you're still as paranoid as ever," he grumbled, and the two of them began to walk across the desert.

CHAPTER 24

INTERSTATE 17 SOUTH, ARIZONA

Hill chose an ice-blue Lexus with blue leather interior and the keys dangling in the ignition. Deauchez drove and he headed south, toward Phoenix. He said nothing, and Hill didn't feel like talking either until they were free of Sedona. He didn't feel safe until then.

Their leaving was faster than their coming had been. Northbound, the traffic was backed up for miles and miles, but there were few cars southbound, on their side of the road. Most of the cars pouring into Sedona had California plates. Hill watched the traffic gravely, wondering how the hell Andrews and his pals were going to deal with all of them, glad he didn't have to stick around and watch them try.

As the last trace of Sedona faded from their rearview mirror the sun was going down.

"Where're we heading?" Hill asked.

"El Paso."

Hill gazed out at the color lapping the horizon. It was a beautiful sunset, and he was grateful to be alive, but that couldn't assuage his anger. "What's the point? Someone at the *Times* snuffed my story."

"I guessed as much. But you still have it, do you not? The story?"

"On your computer."

"Then we could go to a smaller paper. Phoenix, perhaps." The very tilt of the priest's head was hopeful.

Hill scowled. "No. We can't."

"Why not?"

"They'd never print it. And even if they did, no one would believe it. Not now."

The priest said nothing.

"The volcanoes and earthquakes, Father," Hill said bitterly. "That one back there was just a ripple, you know. L.A. had a nine-point-three this morning. They're happening all over."

"I did . . . hear some things. People talking in the street." Deauchez sounded reluctant to admit it.

"Well, I don't understand how the Red Scepter could be producing earthquakes like that. Do you?"

"No. But they *must* be." The priest looked at him, imploring.

Hill shrugged coldly. "Maybe, maybe not. But until we can explain it, no one will believe the rest of our story. It has to *all* make sense, or *none* of it will. You do see that, doncha?"

Deauchez did not answer, but his hands on the wheel were white-knuckled in their grip. The woundedness of the priest begged Hill's sympathy; not intentionally, not manipulatively, but it begged it nonetheless. Hill refused to feel sympathy. Instead he said, "And I don't see how this Rinpoche guy is going to explain it to us. Besides, why bother with him? He's not the *only* missing prophet—*is* he, Father?" His voice was spiteful.

The priest's jaw clenched. "No, Simon."

" 'No, Simon,' " Hill mocked. "So *spill* it."

The priest sighed. He gave Hill a regretful smile. "I'm truly sorry. I only found out myself at Janovich's house and . . . you were sick. There were more important things for us to talk about."

"Just *say* it."

Deauchez nodded. "Yes. I'm one of the Twenty-Four."

Hill struck the dash with his fist. "Damn it! God *damn* it!"

Deauchez flinched. "I'm sorry. I swear I did not know before I looked at that computer."

"Jesus Christ, Deauchez!"

"I know."

"I mean, Jesus Christ!"

Hill stewed for a bit. Although he'd had his suspicions since that encounter with Hart, the confirmation stung—stung his sense of pride as a reporter, that this thing had been right under his nose and he'd been off in frigging wonderland or something. But it also hurt because he'd thought he knew this man. Now he understood nothing about Deauchez at all. "I don't get it. The whole thing. It doesn't make sense!"

Deauchez smiled sourly. "Unfortunately, it does. I had a lot of time to think about it, locked away in Andrews's jail."

"And?"

"Cardinal Donnelley told me about Santa Pelagia right after the first sighting. Normally it takes months, if not years, before the Vatican works up enough interest to send an investigator. But Donnelley wanted me to leave at once. And I would have, if not for the pope. He was blessing a group of Franciscan initiates, and he asked me to be there. I don't even know why, except that it was to be a special service and he, too, did not see the hurry. If he had not insisted that I stay, if I had arrived in time to witness *several* nights of visitations, I might not have been able to . . . I don't know what would have happened."

"Geez. So do you have any idea how they, you know, implanted it?"

"I *think* so. I had dinner with Donnelley about a week before Santa Pelagia. We had wine, and I remember feeling very tired. I went back to my room and fell asleep without even removing my clothes. The wine must have been drugged. I think they came that night and . . . did their work." Deauchez shuddered.

"You remember nothing?"

"Nothing."

"What about a dream? Didn't you dream about Santa Pelagia?"

"They did not have to implant a dream telling me to go there. I was to be sent as an official investigator. They only had to program the visions I was to have at Santa Pelagia itself. And they probably gave me the Santarém and sores inoculation then, too, as they did to all their prophets. It would ruin their plans to have us discredited or dying early on. You see?"

Hill thought about it, his fingers tapping on his leg. "What about the Santa Pelagia visions, then? What did you see when you were there?"

Deauchez shifted awkwardly in the driver's seat. "I—I have not allowed myself to think about it, to tell you the truth. It makes me feel . . . sick."

Hill was in no mood for excuses. "Uh . . . it's pretty important."

The priest nodded. "All right, Simon. For you I will try."

He appeared to be steeling himself. His back straightened, hands gripping the wheel at ten and two. The daylight outside had been dimming steadily, and Hill could make out little of Deauchez's face, but his voice grew remote, daydreamy. "I went to the field that last night. I knew there would be much hysteria at the event—I could feel it the moment I arrived. So I tried to prepare myself. I anticipated . . . I don't know what I anticipated. Some kind of melodramatics, I guess. I thought Sanchez was at the heart of it."

"Yeah, I was there that night. I remember."

"But when I got to the field she was not . . . I did not see Sanchez, at least, I was not aware . . . The *people*. There were so many of them—crying, begging. And there was something . . . was there not? I think there was something about the trees."

Deauchez's voice sounded ever more eerily displaced in the confines of the car, as though it weren't originating from him at all, but from a turned-down radio or from somewhere outside. They went by a lighted billboard and for a moment the interior of the car was bathed in flat gray illumination. Hill, who had been watching Deauchez peevishly, suddenly froze.

The priest was staring blankly out the windshield and on his forehead droplets were forming, like water appearing at the lip of a leaky faucet. The globules, though large, might have been sweat, but they were not—they were crimson. Hill watched as one bead grew fat and overflowed, running down into the Frenchman's dark brow in a long streak of gore. The priest's eyes were set in a glazed look.

Hill sat up abruptly. "Oh, shit! Father? *Father?*"

Deauchez turned his head slowly to look at Hill. His eyes were unfocused.

"Pull over and lemme drive, okay?"

"I'm fine," Deauchez replied. But he wasn't bothering to look back at the road.

"Pull *over*!" Hill reached for the wheel.

With some mutual fumbling and panic, not unlike that involved in the rescue of a drowning dog, Hill managed to get the car onto the shoulder. When the vehicle was well and truly stopped, he turned to scavenge in the backseat for a towel. Deauchez sat there, looking faintly troubled.

"What is it?" he asked, as terry cloth was thrust at him.

Hill didn't answer, just turned the rearview mirror to the driver's seat. Deauchez's eyes grew huge when he saw his reflection. He brought the towel up to wipe at the stains and turned his face away as though ashamed.

"I think maybe we . . . uh . . . we shouldn't talk about that night," Hill said. He didn't feel betrayed anymore. He fought against a sense of frightened revulsion, as though he'd just learned that the person sitting next to him had strange and fearsome powers.

As, indeed, he had.

On the road again, it was Hill who resumed the discussion, unable to hold back a flood of questions. "I still don't understand why they picked *you*, Father. The first day I met you, you were talking about how stigmata aren't divine. You don't fit Janovich's profile."

"They risked a great deal choosing me, I'm certain," Deauchez answered in a dull voice. He wouldn't look at Hill. "I made up many conversations in my head while I was in that cell—discussions between Janovich, Donnelley, McKlennan . . . All complete nonsense, no doubt, but . . . It's true, I *was* close to the pope and I was a known skeptic. If I had gone to him and confirmed Daunsey's story then he would have been convinced. Yes, I think he *would* have been.

"But . . . there may be more to it than that. I think I took their fantasy potential test—a number of us did, under Donnelley's prompting. He called it 'a little personality quiz.' I took many such tests in my psychology courses, so it was nothing new to me. Perhaps I scored high, and that convinced them I would be receptive to their implant, despite my rational facade."

Hill was confused. "But they killed Innocent XIV. Why bother to make him believe?"

"*Because,* Simon. Have you not noticed how intricate their plan is? Everything is calculated down to the very *hour*. If Innocent XIV had fully endorsed Santa Pelagia, back then on day three or four, why then millions *more* Catholics would be in London or Rome right now. As it is, this 'official blessing' did not occur until days ago, so their desired number of Catholics will probably not be reached."

"Rome?"

"That was to be *my* gathering place," Deauchez said, with pain in his voice. "I saw it on the Red Scepter host. I must have been positioned to cover most of Europe. Daunsey was intended for Ireland, Scotland, and England."

"And Santa Pelagia was for Catholics in the U.S. and Central America?"

"*Oui.* I had a great number of them to . . . to 'hook,' and I refused to play. They are *now* going to Rome, though. I heard two guards joking one day about the new pope's blessing. 'Too little, too late,' they said. But it will matter profoundly to the Catholics."

"I know. I read about it." Now Hill did feel sympathy, spurred by not a little guilt at his own behavior. He hadn't thought about what being chosen for Santa Pelagia had put Deauchez himself through. "I'm . . . sorry you didn't get your message across to the Vatican, Father. I know how much it meant to you."

"At least I cost them some time," Deauchez said with contempt.

They were both silent for a bit, lost in thoughts of futile exertions, shipwrecks on the shore of obligation.

"So why *didn't* you buy it?" Hill asked. "You obviously saw *something* that night. You told that guy back in Sedona that you didn't know."

"I told him to go to hell. I meant it quite literally."

"But . . . *why?* If that's not going to trigger—"

Deauchez got a pained expression and held up a hand to stop the warning. "It's a long story, Simon."

Hill glanced over at the priest, but now his features really were lost in darkness. He hesitated, then asked, "Does it have to do with your grandmother?"

Deauchez turned, startled. "How did you know about that?"

"I dug up some press clippings on you after we met. Um . . . sorry."

But Deauchez neither absolved nor blamed. He turned back to the window. "Being a skeptic doesn't mean you have no imagination, Simon. Sometimes it can mean that you have had to fight a very big imagination indeed."

His voice broke a little, and Hill didn't push. He waited, and after a bit the priest began to speak.

"It was my father who was French. My mother was Hungarian. She died when I was very young. My father was so devastated he let my grandmother take custody.

"She was from the old country, my *grand-mère.* Her family had made a living for generations as mediums and fortune-tellers. She believed we had a natural talent for communicating with the dead—a talent that was inherited, like brown eyes or long noses. She thought it was her duty to teach me how to use the talent so that I could earn a living."

"Weird," Hill murmured. Deauchez cocked his head as if to say that wasn't the half of it.

"My earliest memories are of my *grand-mère* trying to convince me to speak to the spirits. Usually at night, in bed. I slept in her bed. She kept the room very dark."

Hill bit a fingernail. He was suddenly not at all sure he wanted to hear this story.

"I was terrified." Deauchez's voice was even, but there was emotion poised behind it like water behind a dam. "My father found out when I was seven. I was visiting him, and when it was time to go I broke down, pleaded with him to save me. My *grand-mère* resisted. It turned into quite a famous legal battle, for its time. I suppose now such things are commonplace, but not where I came from, not in Épinal, France."

The words were simply put, but not simply felt. Hill waited while Deauchez studied the evening landscape and composed himself.

"My father won the case and she died. Hung herself."

"That must have been awful."

"I had a very bad time then, yes. I thought she would come back and haunt me. Maybe even kill me. I was only seven. I had to . . . to testify on the stand that I did not want to live with her, to tell about the things she did that scared me. 'Blood secrets,' she called them. She was sitting right there in the courtroom, staring at me like I was . . . urinating on the family tree."

The priest turned to look at Hill, his eyes big black pools of shadow. "I did love her, Simon, even if she terrified me."

"I'm sure you did."

"And when she died, I knew I had killed her." He stopped.

"That *sucks*," Hill said with great feeling. It was so idiotically American that Deauchez laughed. The tension cleared a little.

"After that my father had to sleep with me for a year—a fact his new wife did not appreciate, I can tell you. Still, I awoke a dozen times a night, screaming. I think . . . yes, I think my stepmother had almost convinced him to lock me away."

"But that didn't happen, right? You got over it?"

Deauchez's dark head bobbed in acknowledgment. "When I was eight I found the Church. An aunt took me. How to describe it? It seemed like magic to me then, *good* magic. I had long talks with the priest. He told me I could banish evil spirits with the light of God. He taught me to pray."

Hill heard tears in the priest's voice at the memory. "I would lie in the dark and pray over and over and over. If I filled my brain with prayer, the spirits could not get into my thoughts. I really felt like I was creating . . . I don't know, maybe a kind of 'magic bubble' around me. I know it sounds ridiculous."

"Not to me," Hill said. He'd had magic bubbles of his own as a kid.

"As I grew up, I knew this was just a mental image, not any *real* magic, but it was effective. You know, when you are very scared any relief will do."

"I get it. Religion protected you, so you became a priest. So how'd you, like, end up such a *skeptic*, if you don't mind my asking?"

Deauchez didn't answer for a moment. He reached out and put a hand on Hill's arm, as if for strength, or perhaps just a bit of human warmth. "It was not just my *grand-mère* telling me there were things there, in the dark . . ." His voice was heavy with some undefinable emotion.

"Yeah?"

"Simon, I *saw* them."

"Saw what?"

Deauchez made a plaintive gesture. "Spirits, demons, monsters? Whatever they were, the prayers worked like a magic talisman to keep them away. But as I got older—around eleven or twelve—I began to think about it. At that age, you form your views of the world, *oui*? You begin to separate fantasy from reality."

Hill nodded.

"Until then, I believed the spirits *were* there, that I was protecting myself from them with the prayers. But my best friend laughed at me. 'There are no such things as ghosts,' he said. Yes, and others confirmed this. I asked my father, my teacher. 'There are no such things,' they said.

"And being a curious boy, a boy concerned with being normal, I began to examine my own beliefs. You see, I had memories, *clear* memories . . . But by then I had been fighting *not* to see them for a few years, and I could no longer be certain that I ever had. I did not want to . . . to *try* to see them again. I was afraid that I *would*."

Hill watched the road, lips pursed thoughtfully.

"It became an obsession for me. Were there such things or not? I began to read everything I could find on the occult, ghost stories, and so on. Then in college, I discovered psychology. Here was a new kind of talisman! The books told me that I had not seen *real* things; it was my subconscious mind projecting Jungian archetypes, it was my Oedipus complex trying to appease my *grand-mère*, it was hypnotic suggestion, mass hallucination. Psychology, too, became my shield."

"But didn't psychology, like, *clash* with your whole religious viewpoint?"

Deauchez sighed. "Ah, Simon. Our motivations are never so simple. I have thought about little else these past few days. I would like to tell you that I became a priest because I believed in faith, believed that man needs God in order to be moral, to be kind, to be good—even if it's only an illusion. The example of Christ's life, what genuine love and pacifism it teaches! I could tell you that I believed in faith intellectually, as long as it did not get hysterical, did not dip into the dark side. But I also loved the Church. I felt safe there—safe with the rituals and the candles and the choir. Perhaps the greater truth is, my shield of psychiatry had cracks, and underneath it still lived the little boy who needed magic to keep out the dark."

At this, Deauchez trailed off. Hill adjusted the mirror and played with some dials to give him privacy.

"I think . . ." the priest said when his voice steadied, "I can now see that all my schooling and all the work I did at the Vatican, it was all about the same thing: investigating the supernatural so that I could prove to myself over and over that it did not exist, that I did not have to be afraid."

The priest heaved a huge sigh, but there was something cleansing about it, as if the festering was at last expressed, and the places where it had lain could now heal.

Hill reached over and patted Deauchez's leg. "I appreciate your honesty and all, Father, but . . . I gotta tell ya, that's the most fucked-up story I've ever heard."

Deauchez chuckled. "You should read Freud's journals. His patients were *really* 'fucked up.' They make me look most unfucked by comparison."

They rounded a bend in the road, and the lights of Phoenix appeared below them like a valley of glittering stars.

"And you didn't even have to pay for twenty years of therapy," Hill pointed out.

"True," Deauchez said. He placed his outstretched hand on the glass as if to touch the lights below. "But I have the feeling, Simon, that the bill for this one is still in the post."

THE IRAQI COUNTRYSIDE

Since the success of his first prophecy, the prophecy of Allah's shield, Mal Abbas had been a great hero among his people. The news of his success got around quickly—Hadar was not the only one who knew how to play the game. Now the people vied in the streets for scraps that clever vendors claimed were his clothes. Hadar was all but forgotten. Abbas almost felt sorry for him.

But not quite. Abbas would remember that moment for the rest of his life: the moment when the radar went out, when his fear turned to triumph, when Hadar's face lost its mocking look and flickered with real fear. He, Abbas, had put his neck on the block for Allah, and Allah had not let him down.

Now there was the matter of the second prophecy.

Abbas had come to recognize the angel's wisdom: his fellow Islamic leaders would never accept the proposition. Not even after the display of Allah's favor during the Chinese invasion; not though Mohammed himself came back and ordered it. They were not strong like he was—not willing to put their necks on the block. Their faith was not the people's faith. The people would follow him anywhere—Abbas believed that. So Abbas had simply not told Hadar and the others.

China, of course, was quite willing. The risk to be taken was not theirs, after all, and they saw that something had to be done. Europe was pushing back the UAF. China's invasion had succeeded, but their war was at a stalemate. Now the plague of Allah—*Wormwood*—had appeared in China and the Middle East. Something drastic was required to finish the West, and Allah had given Mal Abbas the key.

He was driving out now to inspect their progress. Three days ago, a discreet convoy had picked up a shipment from a Chinese plane at an abandoned airfield. Hadar had been in the war room at the time. Abbas had given him rope there, allowing him to manage their troops, feeding his need for control. Hadar believed he was holding on to power, but in reality Abbas was only keeping him occupied. Abbas cared little about the war against the Europeans. The power lay in the prophecies and the prophecies alone.

When he reached the site, Abbas was pleased with its appearance. The launcher was settled into a wooded area, and it was almost impossible to see until you were right on top of it. At the site were *his* men, compatriots from years in the trenches. Radicals, warriors for Allah, like him. They were willing to put their necks on the block, too.

"We have run through all the tests," Kamar told him. Kamar's passion was explosives, and he was jubilant at having such a specimen. "Every test passed. The system survived the relocation beautifully."

"Good. And the others?"

"The same. We will not need to use either of the two spares."

Abbas nodded, pleased. But up close, the size and cold power of the thing frightened him a little. "What about targeting?"

Kamar showed him the portable computer that had come with the shipment. "This targeting system has a CEP of one mile," he boasted. "That means we can select any square foot within its range and it will hit—worst case, that is if *everything* goes wrong—within one mile of that exact spot."

"Amazing! And all our targets are within its range?"

"Oh, yes! She can fly nine thousand miles."

As the maps came up, Abbas sighed with anticipation. There they were, the names of cities that he'd heard so often: San Francisco, Chicago, Liverpool, Paris. He could destroy any of them if he wished. But Allah's plan was even better.

"We hook the bombs up to the interface and then download the instructions," Kamar said. "It's only a push of a button. Are you sure about the targets?"

Abbas covered his mouth, his hands trembling, and nodded. Sure? Oh, yes. He was sure. He had lied to China, of course; agreed to the targets they'd set in exchange for the bombs. When it was done they would see how much more perfect Allah's vision was than their own.

"And—Allah has promised. There will be no retaliation?" Kamar was watching his face intently. The question might have been a challenge if not for the look in Kamar's eyes. He was not questioning the prophecy. He only wanted to hear it spoken again, the way a woman craved being reminded of love.

"There will be . . . no retaliation," Abbas said with slow, deliberate enunciation. He, too, thrilled at the sound of it. "Now. Shall we set the targets?"

PRESIDENTIAL BUNKER, FAIRFAX, VIRGINIA

When Peter arrived that evening, Cole had cleared his schedule. In truth, he was interested in little else. Mr. Ashe escorted Peter into the office and shut the door. Immediately, Peter removed his Racal helmet and tossed it onto a leather chair. He was one of the few allowed to enter and exit the bunker at will, but the price was the suit—at least as long as anyone was watching.

"Everything's set to go," Peter reported. "The sixth sign numbers have been exceeded at every site—except for Rome and El Paso, of course. But Rome's made a strong recovery."

He poured himself a glass of water from the pitcher on the credenza, then came over and sat down.

Cole remained impassive at his desk, fingers steepled together. "Exceeded by how much?"

"A hundred percent in some cases! We projected three to four million for Sedona, for example. It's almost twice that and still growing. Stanton's site is even higher."

Peter went on quoting numbers, but Cole knew the figures already. He'd spent the last few hours poring over the data at the Red Scepter host. He held up a hand to stop the flow.

"You seem quite pleased about it, Peter. I don't think you understand. Those projections were rock solid."

"Of course they were!" Peter said placatingly, as though Cole's ego were the issue. "Things have gone better than we ever anticipated, that's all. But it's not a problem. The inoculations stopped at their target numbers. All the H.A.I. groups have either pulled out or are giving placebos. As for the overflow at sites like Stanton's—it will simply mean we'll reach our target quicker. We ran some rough calculations a few hours ago. Based on the latest site numbers and the deaths in the recent quakes, we might reach our target *within three weeks*."

Peter said this enthusiastically, as though this were a great thing. Cole couldn't believe his own brother could be so dim. There was no point in even trying to make him understand. Cole rubbed his eyes tiredly. "Never mind that for now. I want to hear about the Scientific Council conference call. Did you reach everyone this morning, as I asked?"

"Yes. Dr. Morton chaired the call. Everyone except for Gounot was present."

"And?"

Peter looked less certain of this news. "The consensus is that it must be a . . . a fluke. We could have had a rash of seismic activity at any time. It just happened to be now."

"They're *certain* it has nothing to do with Paks?"

"Paks couldn't have caused anything like this. It couldn't have been caused by *anything* we've done."

Peter looked adamantly, ignorantly confident. Cole suppressed a desire to shake him.

"I don't believe that," Cole said, reigning his words in tightly. "In fact—do you know what I think?"

"What?"

"I think the great scientific minds of the R.S. *want* the problem to go away, that's what I think. They haven't the first clue, so they'll pretend it doesn't exist."

Peter shook his head. "But—every model has shown that, on purely physical grounds, the nuclear explosion in Hungary couldn't have caused the eruptions in the Pacific. Not to mention the quakes we've seen today on the West Coast!"

"Yet it *is* happening."

Peter shook his head stubbornly, not debating the fact but Cole's insistence upon it.

Cole sucked breath in through his teeth. "So what else? What else is going wrong?"

Peter flushed and looked down at his hands. He always did that when he had something to tell his older brother, something he didn't want to admit. "Well . . . it's Deauchez and Hill. Hart and his men found their car yesterday. The syringes were recovered. One was empty—probably used on Hill."

Cole waited.

"So, uh, Hart and his men went back into town to look for them. There was a quake there today—in Sedona. Hart must have gone back to the car . . ."

"Go on."

"They found him a few hours ago. He'd been shot."

For a moment, Cole did not trust himself to speak. Then he said, with utmost calm, "Deauchez and Hill have been in Sedona for a week and we just found them? And now they've gotten away *again*?"

Peter glanced up from under his lashes, hurt. "Anthony, I just told you how many *millions* of people are in Sedona! And we had no idea if they were even there or not until yesterday."

"Where are they now?"

"We don't know."

"Peter, you've failed me. The entire team has failed me."

"No! Don't worry about Deauchez and Hill. No one will believe them. And most of the papers and TV stations aren't even on-line anymore because of the loss of personnel. We *will* get them, but they're harmless—believe me!"

Cole did not respond to this pointless excuse-making. He was so terribly angry. Yet he knew that Peter was only a fool, not the real problem. Somehow he himself had missed something, was missing it even now.

"We're almost finished, Anthony," Peter insisted. "I told you, the goal will be reached in another few weeks! Then we can disseminate the antidote and begin to build the New World. Anthony, you should be *proud*."

Cole laughed, incredulous. "Proud?"

"There's nothing wrong! Really!"

Cole didn't bother to correct his brother. It would take a lifetime. When he left, Cole called in Mr. Ashe.

"I want you to find the names of the top seismic scientists in the U.S. The very best. Bring them in, Mr. Ashe. And be quick about it."

"Yes, Mr. President?" Mr. Ashe looked confused.

Cole heard the question mark and realized that he was not at all being clear. "The best—Mr. Ashe—who are *not* R.S."

"Yes, Mr. President. Right away."

VATICAN CITY, ROME

McKlennan opened the door to Cardinal Donnelley's office. His ruddy complexion was blotchy with stress. "By God, Brian, I'll grow mold waiting for you! Whatever is taking so long?"

Donnelley, looking uncharacteristically unkempt, was stuffing papers into a briefcase. "Forgive me. I know I should have gotten ready days ago, but there simply wasn't time. Just another moment."

"Brian Donnelley, we must leave *now*!"

Donnelley blinked at his visitor distractedly. "All right. Yes.

Just let me . . ." He opened one last drawer and peered into it, but his blank face did not seem to register the contents.

"We should have left last night!" McKlennan berated.

"But there was so much to be done and we couldn't get a car to come, isn't that what you said? Is it all arranged now?"

"Yes, damn it! I had to offer a king's ransom because of the crowds. They're meeting us outside the entrance to the museums."

Donnelley looked alarmed. "So close! Will the driver be able to get through?"

"He *must*! I've offered him a fortune. But he'll not stay a wee moment if we're late. *Come!*"

Hands shaking, Donnelley closed his briefcase. McKlennan grabbed impatiently at his sleeve and pulled him from the room.

They strode down the corridors of the Borgia Apartments and out across the gardens toward the Pinacoteca. As they walked, Donnelley's gait was stumbling and uncoordinated, and McKlennan had to grip his elbow to keep his old friend on his feet. Priests, a monsignor, a nun who served dinner, all greeted Donnelley by name. He appeared not to notice them. They walked by the Pontifical Academy of Sciences. In the distance they saw buildings that housed some of the greatest art treasures on Earth.

With every step, Donnelley grew frailer.

"Have strength," McKlennan whispered. He shot a worried glance at his friend, really *seeing* him finally—seeing that Donnelley's slowness this morning was about something far deeper than procrastination and muddleheadedness. *"Have strength!"*

They reached the Pinacoteca and skirted the building. Beyond lay a courtyard and on the other side of that, the Egyptian and Etruscan museums exit. But Donnelley's faltering walk had slowed terribly and now ground to a halt, his will expended and extinguished like the mechanical springs of a windup toy.

He stood panting, refusing to be pulled forward, then sought refuge on a nearby stone bench. "I can't," he gasped. "I simply can't."

McKlennan's eyes darted around nervously. There was no one close by, no one staring at them—yet. Impatience and a desire to pacify—if only for expediency's sake—warred on his face. He sat down.

"Listen to me," he hissed. "It's only a little farther. Soon we'll be in the car, then out of Rome. You'll feel better when we're away from here."

Donnelley shook his head, his face looking very old. He looked nothing at all like the vigorous young man McKlennan had befriended years ago. "No, John. It's over for me. I've nothing left. The cause has taken it all. I have no heartlessness left—no will, no desire. *Oh, God!*"

To McKlennan's horror, Donnelley began to sob. Although his tears were soundless, his face was twisted in pure anguish, and there was nothing subtle about that.

"That's not true!" McKlennan urged quietly. "Look inside yourself! Surely you can find the strength to reach the car. You don't even have to do it—simply put one foot in front of the other and lean on me. I'll get you there."

"You don't understand," Donnelley managed, his breath hitching softly. "I'd rather stay."

"You don't mean that!"

Donnelley's eyes raised to McKlennan's in a gaze of sheer misery. "Look around you, John! These people . . . the priceless works of art and history! If this is truly the price, then at least my staying says that I fully understand the loss. Yes, *I understand it*!"

"You're a fool! You knew the cost—as did we all! And you know, too, that it was the only way!"

"But my stomach for it is gone. All gone. Whatever atrocities I have committed, I have done my last."

"Don't be such a martyr!" McKlennan glanced at his watch. He was very, very angry now—angry at Donnelley's weakness, yes, but also because he could feel the man's spinelessness sucking at him, at his own will and conviction, trying to drag him down a path to hell.

"Brian, I'm going to the car now. If you don't come with me this instant, I *will* leave you here."

Donnelley's face was contorted with indecisive agony, but he said, "Go on then, John! Go. *Go!*"

McKlennan went. He left Donnelley crying on the stone bench and hurried on past the museums and through the gate. When he emerged from the other side, outside the Vatican's walls, he saw nothing but people, throngs of people on every side. There were no cars—taxis or otherwise. He looked at his watch again. He was five minutes late, but he didn't think the car had been here or was coming. No, the press of the crowds was thick—too thick, even here, on the opposite side of the walls from St. Peter's square.

He'd underestimated the logistics, and he'd allowed Donnelley to delay him; he should have left yesterday or even two days ago, with the other cardinals. His skin was slick with the sweat of terror, with a sure and certain knowledge that things had gotten out of his control. He began to push his way furiously through the crowd.

OUTSIDE THOMPSON, UTAH

Will Cougar had jumped a train that took him south, past Salt Lake City. On foot or even by car, he would not have gotten far. Interstate 15 was overflowing. It looked the same every time the train got within sight of it—the road filled with cars that were moving slow as snails. Highway 70 was no better. In many places, drivers had parked off the road, giving up. In some of these cars the people were dead, the glass stained with the blood and brain splatter of Santarém.

He thought it was fitting that those cars proved so worthless, that they could not help people run away. People had gotten so used to running away. But he experienced little satisfaction about it.

The train turned east and he got out, walked some more. Now he waited at the place where east/west 70 met southbound 191. In his hands was a sign he had made. It said NEW MEXICO.

There were many cars going by on 70, but no one turned south.

Across from Will Cougar, in the dry landscape out in the middle of nowhere, was a mass burial. A digging machine was parked off to one side near a big pile of dirt. It had made a wide trench. Inside the trench were bodies. Men in too many clothes shoveled lime into the pit. Around the edges, back away from the smell or maybe from the virus, were the families. Everyone's face was hidden behind paper masks. Even the children wore them.

Several of the gravediggers kept looking at Will Cougar. They were suspicious, maybe, because he did not wear a mask. But no one came near him.

A red VW Rabbit with California plates made the turn south and glided to a stop beside him. The dust from the tires made it difficult to see, and when it cleared a young Hispanic boy, no more than nineteen, was standing at the open driver's door.

"Get in," he said. Will Cougar did.

At first the boy said nothing as he drove, and Will Cougar said nothing. Then the boy asked, "What's your name?"

"John," Will Cougar lied.

The boy glanced at him with liquid brown eyes. "*Verdad?* You kinda look like that Indian prophet. The one from the papers."

"People have said that before."

"Where are you going?"

"South."

"New Mexico, the sign said."

Will Cougar nodded.

"I have friends near Las Cruces. You going that far?" the boy asked.

"Las Cruces. Yes."

"They have a ranch."

"That is good. A ranch is good."

The boy's tongue was loosened, and he began to talk, talk without thinking, the way foolish people do. "I left L.A. a couple of days ago. There're too many sick there. I can't believe it. Have you heard about the quake? I was listening to the radio. I'm glad I left, man."

Will Cougar grunted.

"*Mi madre* took my little brothers and sisters away a few weeks ago. They went down to Santa Pelagia. Me, I didn't wanna go. Then some *amigos* of mine got it—the virus. I was going to go down and try to find my family, but the border's closed now. Did you know the border was closed?"

Will Cougar grunted.

"I thought I should get out of there. Maybe stay for a while with these friends, you know, in Las Cruces. Then go down to Texas. There ought to be a way to get over the border in Texas. I heard you can sneak over there. What do you think?"

Will Cougar thought about it. "I think if you want to see your family again, you should go down to Mexico right away. As soon as you can."

The boy stopped talking. Will Cougar did not look at him, but he could sense that the words had drawn blood. Truth was like that sometimes.

"Mind if I listen to the radio?" the boy asked.

"You should listen if you want to," Will Cougar replied, although he did mind.

The boy turned it on. There was nothing there but awful noise.

The boy turned and turned the dial to find something. Turned and turned. Finally he got a Salt Lake City station—some white man praying.

Will Cougar leaned back against the seat and closed his eyes. He knew the boy had stopped to pick him up because he was lonely. He had stopped because he needed someone to talk to. But Will Cougar could not help that—he had more important things to do than talk. He was not in the sacred hut, and his feet were not even planted on the earth. But things were moving very fast now. He could not afford to be picky.

The urgency of it helped him. Sometimes he felt that he never completely left the spirit world at all anymore. He went down and soon he forgot about the praying on the radio, and about the boy and the car. He went down, seeking out the image that he kept seeing. Yesterday he had seen it, arcing over the mountains, fuzzy and shimmering. When he rubbed his eyes, it had disappeared. And this morning he saw it again from the train, hanging over the cars on the freeway in the clear morning sky. It was not real, it was a vision, and he had to find out what it meant.

So he went down again, seeking the rainbows.

CHAPTER 25

DAY 25
SIERRA BLANCA, TEXAS
4:30 A.M. LOCAL TIME, 11:30 A.M. GREENWICH

The early morning was dark, clear, and bitingly cold. Tall halogen lights illuminated the parking lot of a huge brick building that might once have been a school. Half a dozen vehicles were strewn about in a lot meant for a hundred. The Lexus slid smoothly into a slot near the door. A man rose from the front porch and came down the steps to greet them. He was a small, brown man, completely bald, and dressed in a cumin-colored sari. One shoulder was bare.

Deauchez was overwhelmed with a sense of curiosity and dread. He had his door open and was striding toward the man before Hill had turned off the engine. He could hear his own shoes on the pavement, as though from some great distance, and the colors of the man's robe were overly bright with meaning. It seemed to the priest that he'd been waiting a very long time for this moment. Unnameable hopes surfaced so unexpectedly and so pungently that he was afraid for his own sanity. For all he knew, this man was a time bomb, the final waiting "prophet of doom." And yet, somehow, Deauchez knew that he was not.

Under one of the lampposts they met. The man was much shorter than Deauchez. His brown palms pressed together in a bow. On his aged face—which was as open as a babe's—was a gap-toothed smile.

"Howdy!" he said, with a mild Asian accent. "So nice to see you!" He clasped Deauchez's right hand in both of his own and shook it. His flesh was hot and soft.

"We are looking for Lamba Rinpoche."

"Well, thank goodness, because that's who I am!" The man

433

giggled. He greeted Simon Hill with the same cheerful warmth. "Come in! Come in! I'll take you to the kitchen and make everyone some tea, okay? We'll just tiptoe through the hallway because everyone else is still sleeping, all right?"

"Um . . . sorry we're so early," Hill said, giving a puzzled glance to Deauchez as they climbed the steps. "We're lucky you were up."

"Oh, I knew you were coming! I've been waiting for you for some time, and now you are here. Thank goodness!"

PRESIDENTIAL BUNKER, FAIRFAX, VIRGINIA
7:00 A.M. LOCAL TIME, 12:00 P.M. GREENWICH

He'd had a fitful night, managing to sleep for an hour of the four he'd allotted himself. And then he'd been called early, as he'd requested. Now he was finishing his second cup of coffee and trying to prepare himself. The day would be grueling. The day would be dangerous—the most dangerous part of the whole plan. Would Abbas come through? Already, Janovich had failed completely with two of the prophets. Then there were the unknowns: China's reaction, for example. Reactions could be unpredictable in a situation like this. They had laid out all the variables with care, but there was still a degree of risk.

The knock came a few minutes early. The cup rattled in the saucer as he put it down. "Come in!"

Mr. Ashe entered and told him that he had found three of the best seismic scientists as requested—he raised his eyebrows as if to indicate the further caveat on that request. The scientists had arrived and were quite anxious to speak with him. Cole blinked at Mr. Ashe. This was not what he'd been expecting. He glanced at his watch.

"Not just now," Cole said. "Perhaps later today."

Mr. Ashe looked puzzled. Cole read the look: there was nothing on this morning's agenda, and he had been so adamant about the visit. But Mr. Ashe said nothing. Mr. Ashe would never think of correcting Cole on anything, hence his appointment to this post.

Mr. Ashe was not gone five minutes when a second knock came. This time it was what Cole had expected—three men in military dress, followed by a white-faced Mr. Ashe. In charge was General Starkey, a four-star ex–Naval Intelligence man, Cole's official replacement for General Brant. With him were two of his lieutenants.

"Mr. President," Starkey said in a bleak, Boston-edged voice, "we need you in the war room right away."

Cole stood up with a sense of déjà vu. Had he played this out before? In his imagination, certainly, and no doubt in his dreams. He followed the general from the room. They passed the president's waiting room, where three suited men sat with briefcases and charts. One of them tried to get Cole's attention and was hushed by Mr. Ashe.

Although he didn't respond, Cole was keenly aware of the men, and knew them for the scientists Mr. Ashe had so recently announced. Cole had a bizarre image of the three witches from Macbeth huddled around their stinking pot and calling out to the future king. He had a mesmeric desire to look into their black kettle, to taste their strange brew, but it would have to wait.

In the war room, Starkey pointed the way to the main con. "Mr. President, if you please."

The command post lay front and center before a huge curved screen. About thirty men were already in the room—staff, military, and cabinet members. Most of them, too, had just been summoned from their quarters in the bunker, and they stood in a line behind a curved mahogany rail, facing the display like business-suited Greeks facing the Trojan ranks.

On the screen was the global map. To the left lay the United States. To the right, across the broad expanse of the North Atlantic, were Europe, the top of Africa, and the Middle East. Cole's eyes found the four red blips over the aqua blue of the Black Sea. His pulse skipped erratically.

"Mr. President," said Starkey, "about ninety seconds ago, our BMEWS stations in Greenland, England, and Alaska detected the launch of four ballistic missiles. They're live and flying, sir. I suggest we go to DEFCON 1."

Starkey's eyes were full of tense resolution. Like Cole, he understood more about these events than anyone would ever guess. But he and Cole would play it out as written—for the sake of those in the room who did not know; for the sake of the historical moment. Cole took a step toward the display and placed a white hand on the mahogany railing to steady himself. He felt a sense of timeless calm, as when a worried-over event finally arrives and any opportunity for alteration is past.

"So be it," he said.

The room was bathed in red light. The words "DEFCON 1" came up at the top of the screen. A siren cried out and died away.

"Who launched them, General?"

"They were fired from remote locations—probably using mobile rocket launchers. One came from Turkey, one from Syria, and two from Iraq. All four launch points are along the Euphrates River. They're in the upper atmosphere, Mr. President, which means they're long-range—ICBMs. In other words . . ."

"They could be headed our way."

"I'm afraid so. The Arabs don't have intercontinentals of their own, so they're store bought. Over the polar cap we're in range—and that's exactly where they're headed. Show the trajectory, Lieutenant."

The map changed from a lateral view of the world to a polar view. And, yes, the line from Iraq to the East Coast of the United States that was now being illustrated went right over the Black Sea and Russia. It would skim Sweden and Denmark, touch the tip of Greenland. A bit of Canada, too, was in its path, before it ran smack into the heart of New England.

Lieutenant Harker spoke up excitedly from his console, "General, sir, one of the birds is losing altitude."

Starkey swiveled to the board, his jaw clenched. "I was going to say they could also easily veer off to Europe. That now appears likely."

Mr. Ashe spoke up. "British Prime Minister Allen is on line two as soon as you're ready, Mr. President."

"In a minute. Can we shoot them down, General?"

"Unlikely. Our PAC-3 and HAWK programs are designed for short-range missiles like SCUDs. ICBMs are too high and too fast. And they may have avoidance technology. The truth is, we're still not sure what the Russian birds were capable of. Hell, we don't even know what the *payload* is, Mr. President. Worst case—they could have up to ten MIRVs per missile, with a payload of 25 megatons or more each."

"Shit," one of the staff members muttered aloud.

"Do we know *where* in Europe, General?"

Harker answered. "The bird that's falling is starting to swing to the south, Mr. President. So far, it could be anywhere on the continent."

"We'll know more soon," Starkey said. There was an ominous irony in the statement.

"Less than ten minutes to impact if they're aimed at Europe," Harker confirmed. "Twenty for the U.S."

"I'll take that call now, Mr. Ashe."

Ashe punched open a speaker line to the main con. "Go ahead, Mr. President."

"Prime Minister Allen?"

"Yes, Mr. President. I'm here." Allen sounded anxious but, like his American counterpart, prepared to deal with the situation.

"I'm in the war room. Our hearts are with you."

"Thank you, President Cole. We're prepared for extensive retaliation and so is France. We won't wait to see where or *if* the bombs fall."

"Of course."

"Will you retaliate immediately?"

Cole looked at Starkey. The general's mouth was downturned in a grim line. He nodded firmly as did most of the heads around the room.

"Yes," Cole said. "We should coordinate our efforts, Prime Minister. We don't want to knock out half the globe with radiation."

"Agreed."

Cole looked at the map. His calm was slipping away now. Things appeared to be going well, but the event itself was so close. His fingers were tingling and he rubbed them; they were cold. "Close in on the Middle East, please."

The screen zoomed in to show the Middle East in great detail. The origin points of the four missiles were designated by bright indigo dots along the Euphrates.

"There's no point in being half-assed," Starkey said. "They've launched one nuclear attack. We want to make sure they don't get a chance at another."

"Mr. President, we mustn't harm Israel," Secretary of State Johnson spoke up gently.

Cole pressed a finger to his lips and bowed his head, as if considering deeply. But his answer came at once. "We should strike all primary and secondary military targets. We could give you Syria and Turkey, Prime Minister. We can take Iran and Iraq."

"No missiles came from Iran, sir," Lieutenant Harker pointed out.

"No one said they did, *Lieutenant*," Starkey growled. Harker shut up.

"Jordan and Lebanon will be spared," Cole continued. "They're too close to Israel. Indeed, Prime Minister, you might stay to the northwest when striking Syria."

"Agreed, Mr. President."

"What about the rest of the alliance?" Starkey asked. "Egypt, Libya, the Saudis? China?"

Cole studied the map. "There's not much in Saudi Arabia worth damaging except oil, and we should keep the radiation localized. As for China . . . she didn't launch the bombs herself. But if we attack her directly she'll launch whatever she has. No, I think not. But put intelligence on hyperalert, General. We'll want to gauge Lee's reaction *carefully*."

"Yes, Mr. President."

"What say you, Prime Minister?"

"I concur. We'll cover Turkey and Syria. We shall not be gentle. I—I must go now."

The blips were visibly separating now, two continuing on the U.S. trajectory and two moving south, one sharply and one more moderately so. Cole's eyes were glued to them, heart pounding.

"Good luck, Prime Minister."

"Goddamn Arabs," Harker muttered bitterly as England rang off. There was a note of hysterical rage in his voice.

For some reason, that voice sank into Cole like blood into cotton. Although he thought he'd been prepared, that he understood what was happening even as recently as a moment ago, the truth of it suddenly became much clearer, like binoculars focusing. He saw the blips through Harker's eyes, and felt, in a low, hideous thrill, the absolute violence, the rending, that was about to occur.

He turned and looked at the men around the room and saw the same stark abhorrence in their eyes, even in those who'd been primed for this day, as he had. Their faces were so pale they were like impressionistic dashes of white paint decorating the theater.

"Mr. President, the authorization code," Starkey urged.

Cole turned and took the keys that were offered him.

BALTIMORE, MARYLAND
12:00 NOON GREENWICH

While Anthony Cole watched the fireworkslike parade of ICBMs cross the map between east and west, Peter Cole was at Telegyn headquarters overseeing other scheduled flights. He could not track them on the map, of course, for his targets were small planes, often rented from local crop dusters for large sums of money, and they flew low and within country borders. It was, in fact, a most desirable thing that the planes not show up on any radar at all.

So Peter could only watch the time tick by anxiously, perhaps as anxiously as his elder brother, even though he had a much less public role to play. He didn't have to wait long. A few minutes after the twelve-o'clock hour the pilots began calling in their reports.

Outside Kiev one of their pilots had made several passes over a ragged encampment, the plane spraying its liquid from nozzles spread out across its wings. The plane flew high for a crop duster, and by the time the clear liquid reached the earth it was hard to detect. The encampment was a zoo anyway, the pilot noted, they wouldn't have noticed if the stuff had doused them like inmates being hosed. Most of the people on the ground hadn't bothered to look up at all. The few that did disregarded the plane almost as soon as they'd seen it.

The followers of Canada's Walter Matthews had paid more attention to the plane, being military types, but had not done anything but stare at it. Its lack of government or Air Force markings must have been reassuring. Perhaps they thought it was a routine fire hazard check, or possibly a disinfectant due to the crowds. The pilot who'd flown over Pastor Simnali's group in Zaire said the area was already in smoking chaos, but he'd sprayed it anyway. The fliers who'd been assigned Sydney, Jerusalem, Iwamizawa, Singapore, and Cape Town reported no problems. The crop duster in Allahabad had completed three passes and one to spare.

Over Santa Pelagia, the millions gathered in and around the Sanchez field had been bored, perhaps. They had looked up and squinted into the afternoon sun and, when the dumping was observed, they had applauded it cheerfully and waved. Perhaps, Peter thought, someone below had suggested that it was holy water.

Apparently, no one had suggested that it might be Santarém.

SIERRA BLANCA, TEXAS

They were sitting in the kitchen. It was a large room, and in the center was a table and a group of backless stools. On these stools sat Deauchez and Hill. Lamba Rinpoche brought them each a mug of sweet, milky tea, smiling and bowing as he handed them their cups. Then he sliced a fresh loaf of bread on a cutting board and put it on the table.

"This is to keep you until our cook wakes up, all right?" Rinpoche said, as if afraid they might waste away before his eyes. Hill stared at the bread with a kind of disbelieving greed. His hand darted out of its own accord and snatched a piece.

But Deauchez was interested only in the monk. At last Rinpoche sat, impervious to any need for haste.

"You were at Santa Pelagia, Mexico," Deauchez began.

"Oh my, yes. Yes, indeed!"

"Did a dream or a vision tell you to go there?"

"It was a dream," Rinpoche said, raising a finger heavenward.

"And did you get a message in Santa Pelagia?"

Rinpoche looked at both of them with a head-tilted, birdlike interest, as though considering how to answer. "Yes. I think I will tell you. I was informed that it was the end of the world, okay? You understand?" The monk looked from one to the other of them expectantly.

Deauchez nodded. "Was there anything more?"

"Were you, like, s'posed to ask people to go somewhere?" Hill suggested.

Rinpoche's face brightened. "Yes! I was to tell them to come here."

"Here?" Deauchez looked stunned.

"Were you s'posed to wait before telling them?" Hill prodded.

"Hmmm . . . I believe I was to tell the reporters within four days. Yes, that was it."

"But you didn't."

"I did not. You are correct." Rinpoche raised both hands in a gesture of supplication. "It didn't seem like a good idea at the time."

He was still smiling. He looked at Deauchez with kind eyes, as if it all should make perfect sense. Deauchez, on the other hand, was beginning to think the monk was a few spins short on his prayer wheel.

"I don't understand."

"Well . . ." Rinpoche tried to remember. "Ah . . . yes. It would have upset people, okay? Don't you agree?"

"Yes, it *would.*"

"Yes, it would be upsetting! People do not like to think about dying, for the most part. Am I right? And also, why should they come here? It's a long way for some of them, and I'm sure they have other things to do. You understand? You know where I'm coming from?"

Deauchez felt an odd smile spreading across his lips.

"But . . . didn't you understand the message to be, like, a *command*? From *God*?" Hill asked, a piece of bread flopping in his hand.

Rinpoche made a dismissive *pshah* gesture. "Oh, my, Mr. Hill. God does not speak in such a way." He giggled. "Goodness, no! God is a quiet voice in here—" The Tibetan tapped his chest. "Not some big thing that hits you over the head like a hammer, okay?"

Rinpoche demonstrated with an invisible blow directed at an invisible tiny human on the table. He repeated this gesture several times, making his face look angry and wrathful, then he laughed and laughed as if this were the funniest thing.

Deauchez and Hill stared at each other incredulously.

"But . . . what did you think it *was*, if not God?" Deauchez asked.

"What was it?" Rinpoche repeated, wiping his eyes. His smile faded. "What was it . . ." He thought seriously about it, then his forehead cleared and the smile returned. "Illusion. Yes, my friend. But you see, to a Tibetan, *all* is illusion, *maya*. Therefore, I recognized it right away!"

"Ah," Deauchez said blankly.

"Is that all you came to ask me?"

"No. Well, yes, but . . . What is it you plan to do?"

"Do?"

"If you know the message of Santa Pelagia was just an . . . an illusion, don't you feel a responsibility to tell people that the apocalypse is *not* coming?"

Rinpoche's face clouded. "It *isn't*?"

"You just said the message wasn't true!" Hill said.

"No," Rinpoche said patiently, "I said it wasn't *God*."

VATICAN CITY, ROME
12:11 P.M. GREENWICH

In an annex of the Sistine Chapel, Cardinal Donnelley was lying facedown in front of a giant crucifix. He was literally throwing himself at God's feet; he, who had dedicated his life to atheism; he, who had vocalized a thousand unfelt prayers in order to fool his fellow clergy. They say there are no atheists in emergency rooms. They say Voltaire begged God for forgiveness on his deathbed. Voltaire was not such a very great Rationalist that he could not change his mind, when the chips were down, and neither was Brian Donnelley. He was calling on the Lord Jesus Christ, whom he had always believed to be a radical messianic screwball not unlike a dozen others of his age. He was calling on Mary, that bewilderingly illogical mother-goddess, on the saints and martyrs, on anybody else who might do him some good.

He'd once believed that he was privileged to dedicate his life to a good cause, to a noble and necessary cause. He'd never believed in a power higher than man, and he'd bought into the subterfuge of their work, and ultimately into the sacrifice that Project Apocalypse had demanded—for man's sake. But he no longer knew what that meant. He could not see past the faces of the men he held down, struggling, while McKlennan injected poison into their veins. *Villain. Monster.* He had learned, too late, that he did not have the strength of will of a true Machiavellian.

Now he was begging that his self-sacrifice be enough; that his own blood be enough to wash away his sins. But, like Voltaire, he was mad with the thought that it was not enough, could never be enough; that the deepest reaches of hell were even now being prepared for him. He sobbed and moaned and pleaded for mercy from beings he'd claimed did not exist, and he found that their faces were turned from him.

When Gabriel descended, Donnelley was surprised by an intense, blinding light that exceeded all expectation or experience. So bright was that light that Donnelley could not even see his own hands, which were on the floor just below his eyes. And following the light, as night follows day, was utter darkness.

John McKlennan was twenty miles from Vatican City when Gabriel fell. He, too, saw the light, through the windows and even the walls of the stone house where he had taken refuge. But for him it was a light that would not fade, for it was burned onto his retinas. He would survive for days in a shelter where there were many just like him. He would lie on a concrete floor, a thin blanket sticking to his melted flesh, unable to move, unable to see, unable, even, to say his own name. *McKlennan.*

He was a warhorse of a man, was John McKlennan, and it would take him a long time to die.

LONDON
12:13 P.M. GREENWICH

Sister Mary Magdalen Daunsey was in the kitchen of the London brownstone trying to fend off yet another food crisis when the word came in. She was playing that old trick, performed so well by J.C., of making food for ten feed a multitude. Daunsey herself took less and less. She was flying high most of the time anyway, on the pure energy of mystical union. Stigmatics had been known to not eat, reputedly for years. Daunsey could bear it also. Under her heavy black robe, her ribs and hipbones vied for prominence.

It was Sister Marguerite who burst into the kitchen, prattling incoherently about something she'd just seen on the telly. Through stammers and wails and run-on words they deciphered the fact that there was a nuclear bomb headed for the British Isles. No one knew just where it would land. Everyone was to take shelter, particularly those who lived in London or other prominent targets. Then they heard the air raid sirens go off in the streets, the sound building, slowly, spreading out through the neighborhoods beyond like a chorus of banshees.

"Now just calm down," Daunsey told the panicking sisters. "The good Lord has spared us thus far, has he not?"

And she did believe that. She had no fear. Her presence in London had held back the enemy's hand until now; she had no reason to think that God's immunity would stop here.

So they did not go down to the basement of the brownstone. They did not seek out the nearest bomb shelter, the names and locations of which were being flashed across the telly's screen in long white lists. Instead they went to the church a few doors away, Sister Daunsey leading her clan down the sidewalk. She had reverted to her black nun's habit full-time now. She thought it gave her followers confidence in her, and it comforted her as well; its cotton sheathing had become a symbol—to be visibly clad as the bride of Christ. She'd once heard a fellow sister call her own habit "good theater" and had admonished her harshly. But in truth, it was.

Out in the street, the locals were emerging from their flats and burrows, dazed with fear and urgency, crying out to each other, offering news and instructions. Most were planning to head for shelters as they'd been instructed. Cars clogged the narrow, one-way street. But some of their neighbors, seeing Daunsey, abandoned their course and fell into line with her. When she pulled open the old wooden doors of the church, there were nearly a hundred on her tail.

The church interior was quiet and dim. It filled up quickly. Daunsey herself wanted to go to the head of the church, to the foot of Our Lady, and pray alone. But she could not, because the others in the church needed her. Father Hardy was there; he and Daunsey had formed an uneasy truce some weeks earlier. After a moment's consultation, he began preparing mass while she, standing at the head of the congregation, took up her rosary and led the congregation. Those in the church who knew the words joined her. Those who did not got to their knees, bowed their heads, and logged silent entreaties for their own survival to whatever God they knew. The terror in the room was palpable, but Daunsey's words—passionate, loud, steadfast—held it at bay like a lion tamer's whip.

Perhaps it was that emotional tide in the room that pushed her over, but by the time she'd gotten through three Hail Marys, Daunsey felt herself being drawn into a trance. She felt the familiar and much anticipated itching in the palms of her hands, on her brow. Her face was uplifted, transfixed, but in some still-conscious part of her brain she detected the slippery feeling of the blood as it began to stain her moving fingers, heard the *ping* as the red drops that hung from her beads like newborn pearls dripped slowly to the floor.

Her lips continued to move, but the volume of her words died away. Sister Francis came to stand beside her. She took up the prayer as one taking a handoff of the torch, and Daunsey could let herself completely go.

Come my beloved, come! she prayed. She was seeing again the beautiful woman of Santa Pelagia. And she begged to be granted a vision of Christ himself. He came to her, so radiant and beautiful that she trembled and wept, crushed in the throes of an unbearable passion. *Let me be with you. Grant me a place in your shadow in Heaven, I pray!*

Her request was answered by Raphael. When he fell he brought the light, the light that Daunsey, in her ecstasy, took for *His* radiance. And after the light came shattering oblivion whose depths she had never imagined fully, despite her meditating upon it almost every day.

PRESIDENTIAL BUNKER, FAIRFAX, VIRGINIA
12:25 P.M. GREENWICH

Cole watched the map, jaw clenched, as surface-to-air missiles were launched in defense from the Hughes Air Force base in Virginia. Standard procedure demanded them, and their targets were the two remaining ICBMs. The one at fifty thousand feet was approaching the U.S. over the middle of Canada, and the other one was already at twenty thousand feet over Goose Bay and dropping rapidly.

The surface-to-air missiles, to Cole's relief, appeared half-hearted in their efforts. As Starkey had pointed out, they were ruthless against aircraft, against even cruise missiles, but at fifteen thousand miles per hour, the ballistics were simply out of their league. Most of the STAs, losing a sense of their target, fell harmlessly into the Atlantic. The rest crashed, with bright little blips, in rural parts of Canada. The Russian ICBMs didn't even get singed, by the look of it. They continued on their paths faster than the Concorde, faster than the fastest jet plane the United States Air Force owned.

The bomb that was already falling fell a little bit more. It crossed the border to upstate New York.

WWN BROADCAST
12:26 P.M. GREENWICH

WWN was broadcasting, live, from New York City. It was pure pandemonium. The streets were filled with people screaming and running, violent and frenzied in their desperate need to get out. All bridges and tunnels were jammed with cars. Perhaps it would have been better if the TV had given them no warning at all, for there could be no escape. In New York there were few exits and still plenty of people—the entire escalating contingent from Harlem, as well as those who had either elected or been forced to remain close to the commercial, financial, and publishing hub that was the city. Those who could get out had been gone for weeks. Those who could not had long abandoned any pretense of civility. Motorists were pulled from their cars and thrown into the streets so that others might take the wheel and drive, smashing into everything, up sidewalks, over people, whatever it took.

And across America, people were watching. Waiting. Breath, thought, suspended.

The fires of hell were on their way.

KITTATINNY MOUNTAIN, NEW JERSEY
12:28 P.M. GREENWICH

Franklin had told Stanton about the TV announcement more than
ten minutes ago. Stanton was now standing in front of his people,
live and on the air from Kittatinny Mountain. He planned to be on
the air when the bombs struck their targets. Outside, he was the
Wrath of God. Inside, he was gleeful. He knew the bombs were
the sixth sign—there was not a shred of doubt. Either New York
or Washington would be hit by the first bomb, he thought. And
the other one would get L.A., probably, that morass of celluloid
sin; or maybe San Francisco, that modern-day Sodom.

It didn't really matter to Stanton where the bombs hit, except
that if he'd had his druthers he'd like the first to strike Washington. New York City was close; they might have to deal with radiation. Besides, Washington *really* deserved it.

But the Reverend Raymond Stanton was gracious enough
to allow God to pick New York if he really wanted to. After all,
the signs were nearly over now. Mal Abbas would finish off Europe and cow the West with his bombs. The battle of Armageddon in Israel would begin any day, maybe even today. And
Stanton himself had drawn more people than he'd ever thought
possible, more than he'd ever even wanted. Most of them had
come since that sun thing, camping out not only here but all
along the mountain road and down in Rockaway and Montville,
too. No, this thing was getting down to the wire, even God could
see that. Maybe the Rapture would come even as the bombs
struck, and he'd have been *on the air*! What a great testimony!
Not even those ignorant scientific Ape-y-ists could argue with
their own eyes.

He was standing on his now-familiar rock and preaching to
the crowd, praying, chanting, and the crowd was swaying, too.
He was preaching Antichrist. He was preaching the takeover of
America. He was preaching the Rapture. But mostly he was
preaching about the fate that awaited those who did not accept
Jesus Christ into their hearts as their personal savior. Hell, that
everlasting torment, was like a nuclear bomb, Stanton said—he
never had been one to pass up a timely allegory. Hell was a rending fire, only it lacked the bomb's mercy, for its torments went on
and on and on, just like the Energizer bunny.

Thy will be done!

Stanton had just seriously warmed up, the spittle beginning to fly, when their equipment stopped functioning. One moment he was on the air and the next, the friendly red light was gone. He screamed for Franklin. They *must* be on the air now! It was *the* big game and Franklin had dropped the ball!

He was still screaming for a go at 12:29 P.M. Greenwich, when the first of the two remaining ICBMs—Uriel—struck the United States. Its epicenter was not Washington or New York City but fifty-three miles to the northwest.

High Point Park, Stanton, and his born-again Christians all disintegrated in a fire hotter than Dante foresaw. Their very molecules burst apart as though matter itself had forgotten what glue bound it together, each particle striking out to do its own thing. Atoms of soil, rock, tree, grass, and human blood and bone had an ecumenical reunion in the mushroom cloud that billowed up where the summit once had stood.

And, as Stanton himself had promised, every single one of them was taken up.

PRESIDENTIAL BUNKER, FAIRFAX, VIRGINIA
12:35 P.M. GREENWICH

Cole watched as the final bomb, the one dubbed "Metatron," moved over the continental U.S. It looked as though it could be heading straight for L.A. But the bomb wouldn't reach Los Angeles, or even California. Its height readings were too low for that. It had begun dropping over Montana. Now it descended even lower, crossing into Idaho as it fell, fell, still hurtling south. It was like a game of pass-the-hot-potato, or would have been, if those below could have tracked the bomb's flight. By the time it passed over Logan, Utah, it was low enough that those in the streets could have looked up and seen its white plume.

Salt Lake City was not on the list of areas being evacuated. There were over nine million pilgrims gathered there, and even if they'd been told to evacuate they wouldn't have gotten far in the crush. Nine million! Only about five million American Mormons even existed, according to Cole's data, so the rest had to be West Coast and Southwestern hangers-on. He watched, his hands gripping the railing at the con, the room utterly still, as the blip's height readout plummeted, and then came the illuminated glow, right on target.

Cole sighed and closed his eyes. All targets hit. He had anticipated this moment for a long time, with a sense of duty and even dread. But he did not feel dread now. The loss of life was terrible, of course. But at the moment, he felt only an incredible sense of power, of triumph at having pulled it off. It was no minor feat.

And of no minor consequence. He knew exactly what the bombs would do. He even knew the model numbers. One of their own had participated in the Russian sale, of course. They could not afford Abbas being handed duds—not with plans so finely honed.

Each of the four angels was a twenty-five-megaton blast. In Salt Lake, the crowds had probably been on their knees when the scythe of Metatron fell upon them. Of that nine million, only the farthest fringes would suffer at all. Salt Lake City had simply disappeared. Where it had stood, there was a conflagration so intense that already nothing remained but cinders. Within a twenty-mile radius, the wind and heat of the blast were whipping in a furious firestorm. At forty miles out, windows were shattering and combustibles were bursting into flame. And at sixty miles, up in Logan, the residents were right now turning their heads in the direction of a tremendous sound, a sound so deep that it rattled their teeth. Those who were outside would feel a hot breath that stirred the hair and brushed the cheek with a poisonous, caressing finger.

And on the wings of that breath would come the birth of the new millennium.

UNITED ARAB FORCES COMMAND CENTER, OUTSIDE BAGHDAD
12:45 P.M. GREENWICH

Mal Abbas had chosen to be in the UAF Command Center when Allah's four angels were loosed. There was nothing Hadar or anyone else could do about it once they were gone, and he had wanted to watch it all on the map display. He'd wanted to be there, too, when the second prophecy came true, when Allah gave him the victory—in front of Hadar, in front of all of them.

Shortly after the angels were fired, one of the radar operators noticed them. He called them to Abbas's attention, frantic, but Abbas only smiled. His ears were buzzing and nothing in the room seemed quite real. *He had loosed the angels.*

Things grew more frantic. Someone figured out that four ballistics had just been fired from Arab territory, two from within their own borders. Abbas watched the screens, a skull's-head

smile on his face, and told them it was Allah's will. Allah was going to smite down the infidels.

They fetched Hadar. He ran to the consoles and screamed at
Abbas, red jowls shaking. *What have you done?* But he did not
seem real either. Nothing Hadar could do mattered now. He might
have been a buzzing fly. Abbas kept grinning. Abbas told him it
was Allah's will. Allah was going to smite down the infidels.

Naturally, Hadar began screaming about retaliation. Coward,
fool! Allah would shield them, as he had shielded the Chinese
invasion. They were Allah's *chosen*. He told Hadar this, but
Hadar only looked at him as though he were mad. And when the
host of blips appeared bright on the screen—first from England,
then France, then the United States, dozens, *dozens* of them,
Hadar cursed and ranted and screamed bloody hell. The things
he said! To Allah's prophet!

But somehow, none of that was real either. The blips were real.
Abbas could not stop smiling. He told Hadar, told all of them:
*Watch! Allah will stop the bombs. He will erase them in flight, as
easily as a child erases a drawing.* They all looked at the console, but the blips kept coming.

For a moment, he thought Hadar would shoot him. The maniac
withdrew his revolver, pushed it in his face. But even *that* was
happening to someone else. And at Abbas's laugh Hadar did look
afraid. He backed away and holstered the gun, muttered a curse
or a prayer. Then Hadar ran. They all ran. Abbas was left alone in
the control room. Still grinning. Still watching those blips.

Waiting for them to disappear.

SIERRA BLANCA, TEXAS

"What do you mean?" Deauchez asked, incredulous. "The
prophecies are being *faked*! It's *not* the apocalypse!"

Lamba Rinpoche tried to smile, but his face had been growing
increasingly pale for the past few minutes. "My dear ones," he
answered quietly. "Many signs and portents have been fulfilled
in the past few weeks, have they not?"

"But . . . the Red Scepter is *mimicking* them!" Deauchez was
frowning intently in his effort to get his point across. "They want
to make people *believe* . . ."

Rinpoche raised a finger to his lips. "I have a riddle for you.
Okay? Ready? Which came first, the chicken? Or the egg?"

The monk looked at Hill knowingly, and the reporter felt a

sense of confusion. It wasn't that he couldn't get what the monk was saying; he wasn't sure he *wanted* to. Even Deauchez's tongue was silenced.

Rinpoche rose, slowly, as though his entire body were made of glass. "Excuse me, please. I must go outside for a moment. There has been—" He took a deep breath. "Oh, my goodness. Many souls have just been liberated."

Deauchez and Hill exchanged apprehensive looks.

"Lamba Rinpoche?" Hill queried.

But the monk was already heading for the back door. He looked about a hundred years old. "The television is in the next room, friends." He opened the door and went out.

Deauchez and Hill jumped up as one and headed for the TV. Dawn was about to arrive outside, and as they settled around the static-laced set, two monks came downstairs. They pointed to the strangers and conferred about them in Tibetan. Hill paid them no heed, trying to find a signal on a sea of static. More monks entered.

Soon the monks, too, were caught by what was coming in intermittently on the flickering screen. They all gathered around and knelt on the floor to watch as though it were some sort of international pajama party.

"Oh, my God," Hill said when the picture cleared. He could not accept what he was seeing.

"S'il vous plaît, s'il vous plaît non," Deauchez whispered.

Although they had no pictures yet, a disheveled, red-eyed WWN announcer said that Rome, London, Kittatinny Mountain, and—they were still unsure of this one—possibly Salt Lake City had all been destroyed in a nuclear strike. The Middle East was being laid waste in an all-out holocaust of retaliation.

The monks began to chant a death vigil. Deauchez began to scream. He didn't stop. He wouldn't stop. Hill grasped him first by the arm, then was forced to take the priest entirely in his arms to prevent Deauchez from tearing into his own face with his nails, from ripping out his own hair. He got the priest in a bear hug on the floor, a wrapping move not unlike the one he'd used on Tendir. Deauchez's back was pressed against him and his arms were pinned down as he screamed and screamed and screamed. Hill was crying, tears slick on his face, wet on Deauchez's neck. He kept saying in his ear, *it's all right, it's all right, it's all right.*

But, of course, it wasn't.

CHAPTER 26

PRESIDENTIAL BUNKER, FAIRFAX, VIRGINIA

Cole had not been to bed since before the nuclear strike began. The war room commanded his attention for hours, all of them waiting and watching to see if more missiles would come, bright blips from the Middle East or China. After his initial pleasure at seeing their four targets hit, Cole had been gripped tight with—if not fear, exactly, then something like an expectant father's trepidation.

But no more missiles came. Lee, through the instructions planted in Tsing Mao Wen, or through his own instinct for self-preservation, did not join the conflagration. And no more missiles were launched from the Middle East, not even the two extras that Abbas had been given as backups. Then there came a point where there could be no more missiles, no more planes, no more anything from the Middle East at all. Not ever.

There were the reports of damage to hear and frantic calls from world leaders to field, including Israel's messiah, Levi. It had been midafternoon before Cole had been able to do what he felt he must—what he *insisted* he do—which was to take the presidential plane up north to look at the damage.

As he approached the place where Kittatinny Mountain once stood, what he saw was a melted black wasteland. Cole looked over the devastation with a deep and honest regret. It was not regret as in wishing one hadn't done it; it was a regret that it had been necessary, the way a stern parent might feel after imposing a warranted but harsh discipline. The park and its surrounds were a great, poisonous wound. Miles from the epicenter bald trees lay side by side and atop their neighbors, like stalks of flattened wheat in a crop circle. And beyond that they still stood erect, black and splintered, jagged teeth in an immolated skeleton's mouth. Cole did not have much empathy for Stanton's followers, and as for the theologically innocent who'd been caught in the region—they were the unfortunate but inevitable casualties of war. No, his heart did not bleed for the people who had died here, but he did lament the trees.

In the WWN presidential broadcast, Cole spoke to the American people from the plane. He appeared to be intensely moved. He assured his fellow countrymen that the war would soon end. The Middle East had paid dearly for their violence, and they would surely surrender. In fact, Benzo Zahid, whose small country of Jordan was, like Israel, dangerously close to the reeking, leaking hell zones of Iraq, had already called to offer unconditional surrender.

Then live footage aired, footage taken by American military planes flying over the Middle East. It showed the damage caused by the American, British, and French counterattack: very little appeared to be moving.

President Cole himself had given WWN the go-ahead to air the film. He thought it would allow Americans to salve their grief with revenge. He thought it would show them that he, Cole, was in control, that they were winning the war; that they had all but won it.

But the American television audience who was watching WWN did not receive the footage in quite that way. By now there was such a growing sense of universal peril that the wreckage playing across their screens only made those who'd paid for the bombs with their tax money feel worse. It was true that many Americans did not understand the old-world ways of the Muslim countries. It was true that they'd been attacked first. But these days God was watching. These days the planet Earth was a very small place. These days any and all bad news tipped the scale of reason a little bit more toward the Looney Tunes side, and what they were seeing was very bad news indeed. What the footage showed them was that they had just fought a nuclear war, might still be in the middle of it. What the footage showed them was that millions of human beings had just died, and that it was their president who held the smoking gun.

SIERRA BLANCA, TEXAS

Hill had a folding chair next to Deauchez's bed. It was a seat of vigilance, a "next of kin" kind of a place, and he'd held on to it determinedly through the night. He hadn't realized how much he'd come to depend on Deauchez—on his direction and his dogged persistence.

But he had. Deauchez had saved his life, not once, but possibly three or four times. Now Hill was helpless to close the maw of despair that had opened under the priest. He could not imagine what comfort he could offer, except for his presence. Every word of hope that came into his head rang false. There were neither words of hope nor hope itself. And so he sat.

Just after dawn, Lamba Rinpoche came into the room, holding a tray with a bowl of soup. He greeted Hill with a bow of his head and went to Deauchez's side. Something about the way he settled on the edge of the bed begged privacy, though he didn't ask for it. Hill slipped into the hall, leaving the door ajar.

It had been Rinpoche who'd settled Deauchez yesterday. He'd returned from outside at some point, looking calm once more. By then Deauchez had stopped struggling, but Hill had not dared let him go, for the priest's face was set in a wretched grimace, a shriek that had gone silent, and each time Hill loosened his grip, the priest began to scream again, in a voice that was ragged and raw.

Rinpoche had sat next to them on the floor. He'd leaned over and touched Deauchez's face with the tips of his fingers, tracing lines while talking in a quiet, musical voice. What he'd said—or sung—Hill hadn't a clue, but after a while Deauchez's face had relaxed. He'd shut his eyes and gone to sleep. He'd been asleep ever since—perhaps, Hill hoped, that sleep was giving his brain time to build neurological bridges over the fissures that gaped in his reason.

Hill sat down on the floor outside Deauchez's room so he could listen. He rested his head back against the wall and closed his eyes.

Lamba Rinpoche held the spoon up to the priest's lips. Deauchez's eyes stared back at him from within bruised, hellish circles. Rinpoche waited with infinite patience, the spoon like a car at a stoplight. After a moment, breeding won out. Deauchez's mouth opened. Rinpoche began humming a low, singsongy tune.

"I can feed myself," Deauchez said, his voice as lifeless as a shark's eyes.

"I'm so glad," said Rinpoche, handing over the spoon.

He took back up his singing. Deauchez's hand, moving like an automaton, managed one spoonful. "What is that song?"

"This? Oh, hmmm. Let's see. 'You are here. All is well. All is good. God is here.' Yes, it goes on and on, something like that." Rinpoche giggled. "Tibetans are not . . . how do you say . . . not really the very best lyricists."

Deauchez did not smile. He let the spoon clatter onto the tray. "I'm not hungry."

"Oh. Maybe you could try again in a little bit, okay? I made it for you especially." Rinpoche moved the tray onto the nightstand.

Deauchez lay back, those devilish eyes fixing on the monk in a disquieting stare.

"You are here. God is here. You are safe. All is well."

For a while those eyes remained on the monk, but they lost their focus as the priest's mind wandered to blacker shores. Rinpoche's voice went on and on, and gradually it pulled the eyes back into the here and now.

"How can you go on?" Deauchez asked bitterly.

Rinpoche paused his singing. "How can one not?"

"I cannot. I will not."

"Why not?"

"Because I failed."

The monk tilted his head. "Really?"

Deauchez squeezed his eyes shut. "I should have convinced the pope that it was not true! If he had told Catholics that, none of them would have been in London or Rome, and they would not have been slaughtered."

"I see. And what *did* you tell the pope?"

"I told him it was not true, but I had no proof and he did not believe me!"

Rinpoche held up his palms. "Dearest one, what proof could you have had besides your own convictions?"

Deauchez covered his eyes with his forearm. Despair floated on and around him like a heavy scent. "I was one of them, too— one of the Twenty-Four. Like you, I should have known it was some kind of trick."

Rinpoche put a warm hand on Deauchez's chest and patted. "Oh, I was not as clever as all that. But tell me what happened to *you*."

Deauchez revealed the details, as he had to Hill in the car.

"The truth is, the only reason I didn't believe in Santa Pelagia was because I'm incapable of faith! Even now, I *hate* God when I think he exists at all. My entire life has been hypocrisy, and *that* is why I failed. The others blindly accepted it because they believe in anything! I blindly rejected it because I believe in nothing! And because I believe in nothing, it was inevitable that the pope would dismiss my opinion. My entire life, my entire *being*, has led to this terrible place. I killed those people as surely as if I were one of *them*."

Rage and self-pity whelmed up like a cancerous pool. For a time, Rinpoche let Deauchez cry. When it subsided he spoke lovingly. "You are trapped in your own pain, and that narrows your understanding of events. Try for a moment to look at the entire whole, okay?"

Deauchez's sniffing quieted.

"You and I were two of those destined to receive this message. Do you not think you were chosen for a reason? Do you not think you were chosen for exactly *who* and *what* you are?"

"Chosen by whom? The Red Scepter?"

"No. That is *not* what I mean," Rinpoche said with a hint of firmness. "If another priest had gone, it is likely that he would have behaved as the other receivers behaved, you see? We cannot know for certain, but I find it unlikely that anyone would have accomplished the task you set for yourself: to see through it all and perceive all that was behind it at that very moment. Dearest one, do not put me in a position of enlightenment in this regard. You know far more about it than I do. That is why you came here, I think. You understand?"

Deauchez uncovered his face. His eyes, perhaps a little more human now, glared into the monk's own. "But what about God! How could he let this happen? How could he let the Red Scepter kill all those people whose only crime was to believe in him!"

Rinpoche nodded sagely. "Ah, this is another kettle of fish entirely! Are you really angry at yourself for *not* believing? I think, maybe, you are angry at God for not being *worthy* of your belief!

"Let me tell you something, okay? You asked me, when you came here, why I had not acted. I didn't understand you. Sometimes your Western ideas are very confusing, you know?" Rinpoche smiled. "You see, it is not in the Tibetan mind to think of such kind of 'acting' any more than it is in our minds to think that we should go move a mountain because we want to put a road there! You Westerners think this way, yes, I have seen it! Big blasted tunnels right through the mountain. Tibetans? We go around!"

Unwillingly, the corner of the priest's mouth turned up.

"You have been trying to make everyone believe you when you say the apocalypse is not here, my friend. You are frustrated because they have not heard you. The problem is, of course, that it *is* here. You see? You know what I'm saying? You said it was not God who spoke at Santa Pelagia and perhaps that is true. Nevertheless, he *has* spoken."

"What do you mean?"

"It *is* happening. Therefore, God *has* spoken."

A look of pain washed over Deauchez's face. "But that . . . that is so unjust!"

"Many have suffered, yes, and I'm afraid it is far from over. But we Tibetans believe that evil does not just appear any more than good does. You dig a hole, you plant a seed. The Universe— God, if you prefer—grants us the natural process of germination and growth, but the Almighty does not reach down his finger to make an avocado tree grow from an apricot seed! Do you know what I mean? *This* tree does have bitter fruit, oh, my, yes. But we *did* plant the seed ourselves, Michele. We *must* have. You understand?"

Deauchez nodded, his mouth twisting with emotion. "I think so."

"I'm glad." Rinpoche took Deauchez's hand in his own and squeezed it. "These are things we could debate for decades, you and I. For now, you might be better served to think on this—"

Deauchez nodded in anticipation.

"All of us alive on Earth right now are part of this pattern. There are those who have created their part *deliberately* and *ruthlessly*, and there are those who have contributed without even being aware. I am part of this pattern, too, and so are you, Michele. You believe your childhood scars—these things you call your 'character flaws'—you believe they prevented you from believing. Very well. But *perhaps they were supposed to do just that.* You understand? Sometimes our deepest flaws are our only salvation."

Deauchez's eyes were large and clear and filled with a kind of puzzled sorrow. Rinpoche leaned forward and kissed him on the forehead.

"Now take a shower, dear Michele, and come downstairs. All right? Okay? We have much to discuss, and I believe a visitor is on the way."

PRESIDENTIAL BUNKER, FAIRFAX, VIRGINIA

When the news came in about Mount Rainier, Cole had just settled down to his first real meal in days. He took the communiqué in the manner of one who has just been smashed in the face after the referee stopped the fight. He carefully put down his fork and napkin and forced the potato in his mouth down a newly constricted throat.

The colossal 14,410-foot peak, which had been visible on clear days from just about anywhere in Washington State's Puget Sound, had been split apart by massive internal pressure. While ash and detritus skyrocketed upward, lava flows descended. And although the towns closest to Rainier had evacuation programs, the day's events had proven inarguably that they were not fast enough. A relatively minor five-point quake had jolted out from the mountain as ash commingled with the ever-present Seattle rain. But the disturbance in the plate would not seem minor to Japan. It had started a tsunami in the Pacific, scientists predicted, that would make life interesting in Hokkaido in about ten hours' time.

Cole listened carefully to all the details. Then he asked Mr. Ashe to bring in the three scientists whose presence he had nearly forgotten.

Mr. Ashe introduced Drs. Childs, Mang, and Prescott. Childs and Mang, behind their face shields, looked young and nerdy—looked like they belonged at Berkeley, which, indeed, was precisely where they were from. Prescott was an older, more tightly strung fellow. He was an oceanographer from Scripps Institute.

"I'm Anthony Cole," the president said. He got up and shook their hands through their rubber gloves. "I'm sorry you've been kept waiting. And I do apologize for the discomfort of those suits."

His voice sounded banal, in control. It was the performance of a lifetime.

"No sweat, Mr. President," said Mang.

Dr. Childs was already withdrawing a paper from his briefcase. "My colleagues faxed this to me here this morning."

He handed it to Cole. The fax was of a telegram.

To: all oceanographic and seismology labs
From: N.O.A.A. research vessel *Malcolm Baldrige* R 103
Indian Ocean oceanic rift expanding at abnormal speeds off the
horn of Africa. Stop. Four inches recorded since yesterday,
3:00 GMT. Stop. Recommend emergency testing commence
along all rift and fault lines. Stop. We have also recommended
to South African government evacuation of high population areas on coast of horn. Stop.

"That came in about five hours ago," said Childs. "Since then
we've taken calls from the French and the Japanese. And it's
happening at the rift off Baja, too. Our station there started picking up minor changes in measurements several days ago."

Cole leaned back against his desk for support. In his hands the
paper ruffled, lightly, as if there were the merest breath of a
breeze. "What does this mean? I'm not sure I understand."

"Dr. Prescott can probably explain the basics to you better
than I can," Childs said.

Prescott unfolded a large tectonic map, fumbling in his nervousness. Cole motioned to the conference table and they all
helped to arrange it there and gathered around it.

"I'll try to make things clear, Mr. President," Prescott said.
"The Earth's crust is separated into what we call plates. These
plates sit on top of the liquid magma of the Earth's core. Where
two separate plates meet can be either a point of subduction or
induction. Most of the induction occurs under the ocean at the
oceanic rifts."

Prescott pointed out the large blue rift marked in the middle of
the Atlantic and another cutting in a rough diagonal through the
Pacific.

"*Induction* means that the plates are moving *apart*. As this
happens, new molten rock boils up, cools, and hardens, becoming new ocean floor. Essentially the Earth is expanding at the
rift."

"I understand."

"*Subduction* is where two plates meet and one slides *under*
the other. When that happens, the portion of the Earth's crust
that's being subducted gets sucked down into the core and liquefied. Depending on the thickness of the crust, this might actually

be *more* material than the Earth can handle and some 'new magma' will erupt back out at weak points—volcanoes. That's why volcanoes are usually found at subduction areas. The Pacific Ring of Fire is an example."

"What about the faults—like the San Andreas?"

"Fault lines are like stress cracks running out from induction and subduction sites," Mang said. "Most of the faults in California run off the Pacific rift. The rift runs right up into the American continent at Baja."

"I'm with you so far. So what does this telegram mean, gentlemen?"

The three scientists exchanged glances.

"The problem, Mr. President," said Childs, "is that this entire process is normally incredibly slow. Normally, we get a couple of *inches* of new ocean floor a *year*."

"Which means a couple of inches of crust are *subducted* a year," added Prescott.

"But a few days ago, the spread at the oceanic rifts began speeding up. By yesterday, its speed had increased dramatically."

Cole licked his lips. "How much?"

"Depends," Mang said. "Sometimes it's slower, sometimes it's faster, but right now it's averaging about an inch an hour."

"And Mr. President, all the induction in the world can't make the Earth *bigger*," Prescott said in a meaningful tone.

Cole frowned. His fingers picked unconsciously at the edges of the map.

"What Mr. Prescott is trying to say," Childs explained, "is that the Earth is still the same *mass* it's always been. When new ocean floor is created that means material must be *subducted* to balance it out."

Cole put a finger along the chief lines of subduction. "Hence the volcanic eruptions?"

"Yes, sir," said Childs. "And the quakes. It's like time-lapse photography. Every movement the Earth's crust was going to make over the next few hundred years is suddenly happening *now*, all at once."

"The stress it will cause on *all* existing faults will be unprecedented," Prescott said.

"It'll probably create *new* stress fractures," added Mang.

"And we're likely to see even midplate quakes with stress like this, like the Oklahoma quake of '63."

Cole was quiet for a moment. He straightened up, not meeting their eyes, put his hands in the pockets of his suit pants, walked around to the far side of his desk. He turned away from them, as though thinking. But he wasn't thinking. He just stood there, trying to stop his insides from shaking. His abdomen, which was hard and ribbed from his morning calisthenics, was quivering as though a current were running through it. He tried to stop it, tried to get it under control. He was cold, terribly cold. Even his brain was cold, and it was thinking sluggishly.

The scientists waited silently behind him. When the president turned at last he had his arms crossed in front of himself, hands gripping his elbows tightly. "Thank you for the explanation, gentlemen. Do you have any idea what's causing this acceleration?"

"Mr. President," Childs said carefully, "I'm afraid we don't know. But we *can* tell you what will happen if it doesn't stop."

Cole stood at his chair feeling strangely exposed. He felt like a prisoner in the sentencing box. "Go on, Dr. Childs."

SIERRA BLANCA, TEXAS

"There now. Isn't this nice?" Lamba Rinpoche said with a sigh.

Hill glanced at him, surprised. It was a hell of a thing to say while settling down to discuss the end of the world. Still, the monk had a point. The day outside was a light, listless gray—a result, according to the TV, of ash from the recent volcanic activity. By contrast, the community room was quite cozy with its roaring fire, colorful blankets, and tea service. Then there was the company: Rinpoche, several of Rinpoche's smiling monks, and, of course, Deauchez. The priest's presence cheered Hill considerably. Though pale and quieter than usual, he appeared to be otherwise recovered. And if Deauchez could recover from his shock, thought Hill, might not the human race?

Hill cleared his throat and looked around the group. "So what does everyone think?"

Rinpoche held up a finger. "There's an old saying: If a man is not careful, he will end up where he is going. The trick is to know where that is. Perhaps it is true that very few of us knew where we were heading before this began, and that is why it has happened. After all, events can only be results, so the cause must exist. The question is—where are we heading *now*? What is the result of *this* cause?"

Hill scratched his head. "Well . . . we *thought* we were trying to expose the conspiracy. I s'pose we hoped that if people knew the truth, things would go back to normal."

Deauchez spoke quietly. "It's rather late for that now."

"To 'go back to normal,' yes," agreed Rinpoche. "But perhaps not too late to go back to living, eh? You see what I mean? When *I* think about where we are *going*, I think . . . yes! I think of a *snowball.*" The monk stopped and looked at them in a satisfied way, as if this was supposed to make perfect sense.

"A snowball?" Hill repeated.

"Why does it remind you of a snowball?" Deauchez asked.

"I was hoping *you* could tell *me!* You see, when I was in Santa Pelagia I kept thinking about a snowball. Yes, and when I watched the news over these weeks—*snowball.* Can you think why?"

The monk looked sincere enough, but Hill sat back, his brow cocked with irritation. It sounded screwy to him.

Deauchez appeared to be taking the question seriously. "What is the snowball doing?"

"It is rolling, this snowball."

"Downhill?"

"Yes! Exactly!"

"Ah, geez," Hill muttered.

Deauchez stared at Rinpoche, a curious confusion on his brow. "You are talking about the phenomena."

"I don't know." Rinpoche shrugged. "What are *you* talking about?"

Deauchez began wringing his hands. "The *fear* that was at Santa Pelagia . . . Did you feel it, Lamba?"

"Certainly. Very much so."

"I remember it truly scared me. Remember, Simon? I told you that day in the airport that you shouldn't write about it."

"I remember."

"It felt . . . *wrong* somehow, terribly frightening, almost like . . . a living thing." Deauchez looked fretfully at Rinpoche. "Is that what you mean?"

The monk had his head cocked to one side. Despite the smile on his face, his eyes were far away. "Please continue."

"The statues."

"The statues! Very good point!"

"What about the statues?" asked Hill.

"A few of the statues bled. Did they not, Simon? Did you see them?"

Hill remembered it clearly, though he didn't see the connection at the moment. He shrugged. "Sure. We got the big one at the church on tape. It *looked* like it was bleeding, but we didn't have time to, like, pick it up or anything. It could have been rigged."

"By whom?" Deauchez shook his head. "By the Red Scepter? Why risk something that could be so easily discovered? If the statues had been proven fakes the entire event would have looked bad, and they did not *need* the statues. The stigmata they programmed into some of the prophets would have been enough!"

"But some of the people who had stigmata weren't members of the Twenty-Four," Hill pointed out.

"Oui!" Deauchez said. "Exactly!"

Hill frowned at him. "But what does it *mean*, Father?"

"A wise man never picks up a sword," quoted Rinpoche, *"until he's counted all of the enemy."*

"Jesus and Mary," Deauchez said. He put a hand to his temple. "Santa Pelagia got out of hand. They planned it, but it got bigger. *It got bigger!"*

"How?" Hill's palms were sweating. There seemed to be something in the air, some kind of communication that was deeper than words humming in the circle. Neither of the prophets responded.

"How did it get bigger, Deauchez?"

Deauchez shook his head, his eyes squeezed shut. "I don't know. Something to do with the crowd, with the hysteria. I tried to tell the pope it was dangerous—and you!"

"Oh," said Rinpoche. He straightened up, his eyes clear. "Of course. You are quite correct. Thank you."

PRESIDENTIAL BUNKER, FAIRFAX, VIRGINIA

"Mr. President," Childs said, "there's still disagreement among our colleagues. Some are insisting this is a rare but natural occurrence, and that the whole thing will eventually settle down."

"You don't agree?"

"It goes against everything I've ever learned about tectonic plates," Prescott said with some disdain. "There *is* no historical record of abrupt growth in a short period of time. It's just not there."

"Mr. President," said Childs, "if it doesn't stop, the induction will cause major quakes over much of the Earth. But the *really* bad news is—that's not the worst problem."

"It's the volcanoes," piped Mang. "With all that subduction going on, there's gonna be *lots* of partially melted crust that's forced upward."

"I don't know if you're aware of it, Mr. President," Childs said, "but new volcanoes can sprout up almost anywhere. They erupt where the crust is weak, like leaks in an overfilled balloon. There was one that erupted in the middle of a field in Mexico in '46. Within a week there was a brand-new mountain standing there."

"And with volcanoes, it's the ash that's the real killer," said Mang. "We already have tons of it in the air, even from the volcanoes that have gone off in the past few weeks, right? And the more explosively they pop, the higher the ash goes. So if we have enough of these big blasts, we're going to have a volcanic winter, man."

"The ash and debris from a volcanic eruption can travel all the way up into the stratosphere," Prescott explained, "particularly if the explosions are violent, which these will be. Once it gets up there, it doesn't come down. It'll block out the sunlight."

"And block out the *heat*, as well—for years," put in Childs. He sighed, tried to wipe his brow and found plastic in the way. "If enough volcanoes go off, our biggest problem won't be people dying from quakes and tsunamis. Those who survive the surface activity will starve and freeze to death. There'll be another ice age, and it will happen *quickly*."

The three men fell silent. Cole clenched his jaw, which seemed determined to either quiver or grin in nervous agitation. "Well. I see."

The scientists glanced at each other. "I'm afraid our only suggestion, Mr. President," Childs said apologetically, "is to evacuate anyone within a hundred miles of any existing fault or volcano. Prepare food rations, shelters . . ."

"Yeah," Mang said earnestly, "and if you have any, like, supersecret contingency plans for an ice age—like sending a bunch of people to Mars or something—now would be an excellent time to go for it."

Cole looked at Dr. Mang in disbelief. Something between a

sob and a laugh broke from him. He put his hand to his mouth, only just refraining from biting it.

After a moment he was able to thank the men politely for their advice, as befitted even a doomed commander in chief.

CHAPTER 27

SIERRA BLANCA, TEXAS

"You first," Deauchez said.

"Okay, then," Rinpoche said pleasantly. "Dear ones, when I think about what you've told me of the Red Scepter's plan, I think three things. First, I think it is very, very daring. Second, it took great resources and great *strength of will*. Do you know what I'm saying? Therefore, we must assume that their purpose is one of great importance, at least as they perceive it."

"Sure," Hill commented dryly. "They, like, wanna rule the world."

"Ah! But what a very great deal of fuss just to rule the world. You smile, Mr. Hill, but if you think about it you will see it is true. Let us agree, at least, that the reason was very important to very many people. All right? The third thing is that their game is a dangerous one. Oh, yes, I'm afraid *very* dangerous."

"You mean, besides the obvious?"

"I do not refer to the loss of life, Mr. Hill. I say it is dangerous because it has never been played before—not ever! They say there is nothing new under the sun, and generally they are right! But not in this case. The Red Scepter is playing with nothing less than global consciousness. And because it is such a *new* game, I cannot help wondering if even they know the rules!"

Hill bit a nail worriedly. He looked at Deauchez, who was nodding with a kind of hurt understanding.

"They have been following Revelation," the priest said. "But many of the other religions' prophecies echo Revelation. They only had to pull off a small number of phenomena to convince nearly every culture on Earth that the end had come." He counted them off on one hand. "The sores, the red tide, the virus, the burning sun, the Paks nuclear disaster, and the four ICBMs."

465

"What about the earthquakes and volcanoes?" Hill asked. "Aren't they the seventh sign?"

Deauchez and Rinpoche looked at each other. The monk smiled encouragingly.

"Remember, Simon, we could not understand how the Red Scepter was causing the earthquakes and volcanoes?" Deauchez said. "Well . . . I don't believe they are."

Rinpoche nodded in agreement.

Hill was getting irritated at being the only one lost. "Could you *elucidate* that point, Father? Uh . . . *anyone*?"

"They probably planned to stop at the sixth sign," Deauchez said thoughtfully. "After all, how could they produce the seventh sign, and why would they want to? They already destroyed four of the prophet centers with the bombs, so it's no use trying to get more people to believe now. Nor do they need to reduce population. Wormwood alone will suffice."

"I see your point." Hill pinched his lips with his fingers as he considered it. "But if they're not causing the quakes—what *is*?"

Deauchez poured himself some more tea. He picked up the porcelain cup and warmed his hands. "The same thing that made those statues bleed in Santa Pelagia."

"Yes," Rinpoche agreed with a tranquil smile.

"What? *God*?" Hill asked dubiously.

Deauchez frowned at Hill's comment, his eyes reflecting pain. The monk leaned forward gently and patted Deauchez's hand. "Come, now! You know what it is. *Tell* him."

"No . . . not God, Simon. Not the way *you* mean. It's hysteria, global hysteria."

Rinpoche put a finger to his lips. "I think a better name for this particular snowball would be *Karmic suicide*."

"Karmic suicide?" Hill huffed. "What's that supposed to mean? We're, like, killing ourselves?"

"If a man has faith like a grain of mustard seed, he can move mountains," Rinpoche quoted. "Smartest thing the Nazarene ever said!"

Deauchez flushed with excitement. "*Oui!* When people have gone to Lourdes and they come away with their bones mended or their lungs cleared of tuberculosis—it's *faith*, Simon! And I don't mean some kind of mental idea, I mean a *physical force*. It happens so infrequently because people don't really believe. They may pray a thousand rosaries; they can say over and over 'I believe, I have faith'; but in some inner part of them that truth never descends. In their truest heart, they *don't* believe."

"Faith is the most difficult thing," Rinpoche agreed, nodding. "The conscious and the subconscious minds are like two separate continents. Between them lies a gap. We call this gap *bardo*."

"And it's the *subconscious* mind that is linked to the fabric of the universe, the holographic pattern. The subconscious mind *can* change physical reality. *That* is Faculty X!" Deauchez exclaimed.

This seemed to be something of an enlightenment for the priest, but this time, Hill wasn't the only one who was lost.

"Faculty what?" Rinpoche asked blankly.

"Excuse me," said Hill, "so you're saying the Red Scepter made people really *believe* that the world is ending, so now it just . . . just *is*?"

Deauchez's excitement faded at the thought. "Heaven help us, I think so."

"But that's not possible!"

"Let us try an experiment, okay?" Rinpoche asked Hill. "Ready? One, two, three, four, five, six . . ."

The pause was as heavy as a grand piano.

"Seven," said Hill. His eyes widened as he finally got it. "Oh, shit. People have been reading about the seventh sign since the beginning—since our first lists in the *Times*."

"Just as the people in Goa expected St. Francis's body to decay, and so it did," Deauchez muttered to himself. He looked up, eyes bright. "Or the way a voodoo practitioner might die when he knows some powerful priest has cursed him. *Faith!* It's not just an illusion of the mind—I was wrong about that. It can be very real."

"But . . ." Hill scratched his head. "Even if people are *expecting* the seventh sign, how can they affect the Earth? How can they actually *cause* earthquakes?"

"The subconscious mind *can* affect matter," said Deauchez. "As it does in faith healings—or as it did with those statues. It never has on this scale, true, but then millions—or even billions—of people have never before agreed on what was going to happen."

"The saddest thing, Mr. Hill," Rinpoche said gently, "is that if the Red Scepter had told everyone 'It's the apocalypse! End of the world! So sorry!' and everyone had a clear conscience, they would say 'You're crazy, man!' "—Rinpoche made a broad dismissive gesture—" 'You're insane! There's no apocalypse here! What are you talking about?' "

Hill couldn't help smiling. "They did say that at first. I know *I* did."

"At first, yes!" Rinpoche tapped his head. "But not at *last*." He tapped his heart. "Because when it reached *here*, people believed. They believed for the same reason we believe many myths and . . . what do you call them? . . . urban legends. Because we think they *could* be true. Maybe we even think they *should* be true."

"I think I know what you mean . . . pollution, poverty, genocide, terrorism . . . You think at first all of this prophecy stuff is bunk, and then when something like the sores happens, it really scares you. You think, 'Well, I suppose if *I* were God, *I'd* be pretty pissed off, too.' "

"Yes! You see, that is Karma," said Rinpoche. "You never get away with anything. Isn't that right, Mr. Catholic Priest?"

"Don't look at me," Deauchez said dryly. "We have confessionals."

Hill looked at the priest and the monk expectantly, but they were both off in their own thoughts again. "So . . . come on, guys! If this thing has gotten away even from the Red Scepter— if we're plummeting downhill like some . . . some 'Karmic snowball' into absolute destruction, I mean . . ."

Everyone looked at him.

"How do we *stop* it? *Can* we stop it?"

"Not to mention *should* we stop it?" said Rinpoche, poising his slim brown finger in the air. "Ah, Mr. Hill, you have put your tongue on precisely the question! Maybe our new visitor will help us find the answers."

"New visitor?" Deauchez asked.

"Oh, yes!" said Rinpoche. "And I think we should make some lunch before he gets here. Shall we?"

The new visitor arrived just as lunch was being put on the table. Lamba Rinpoche went to answer the door and they heard his typically enthusiastic greeting. He returned leading a tall, black-haired man into the kitchen.

"It's Will Cougar," Hill said, dumbfounded.

"You see him, too?" Deauchez could have sworn he was

imagining it. He had not seen Cougar since the day after Santa Pelagia—it felt like years ago now.

Will Cougar came to the table and looked carefully first at Hill, then Deauchez. He nodded once, as if to himself, then sat down and dug into a proffered plate of food.

Deauchez looked at Hill to see if he had any ideas, but the reporter only shrugged as if to say that it beat the hell out of him.

"How did you get here?" Deauchez asked Will Cougar.

"I followed the signs." The shaman didn't seem inclined to get more specific.

"What happened to your mission? Your message from Santa Pelagia?"

Will Cougar looked up from his plate with steady black eyes. "It took time, but I finally saw that I was mistaken."

"Oh." Deauchez would have liked to know more, to know every detail of such an awakening. But Cougar was like a mysterious book in a forgotten tongue. Even if you could find a way to crack it open, you probably could not read what was written there.

"You have been traveling with him?" Will Cougar asked Deauchez, jerking his thumb toward Hill.

"Yes."

Will Cougar studied Hill, perhaps judging his merits as a traveling companion. Hill cocked an eyebrow and stared back. Will Cougar grunted. "I know what *he* has to do with it," he said to Deauchez. "But what do *you* have to do with it?"

"I . . ." The priest blushed guiltily. "I was one of the prophets. I completely denied the message."

Will Cougar seemed surprised at this. At least, his eyebrows rose a notch. He chewed a bite of food. "What about him?" He tilted his head toward the monk.

Deauchez looked at Lamba Rinpoche, not wanting to speak for him. But the monk just sat there and smiled.

"He's one of the prophets, too. He knew the message was an illusion from the start. He did not tell anyone."

"You must be very wise," Will Cougar said to Rinpoche.

"Goodness! Everything is relative."

"I'm . . . uh . . . glad you showed up, Will Cougar," Hill said, still looking mystified. "We've been trying to figure things out."

"I, too."

"Yeah? Whaddya think?"

"You first," said Will Cougar. He motioned his fork at Hill a few times, as if giving him the floor.

By the time Deauchez and Hill had finished their story, Will Cougar had finished his meal. He suggested the next move. Deauchez fought the idea determinedly, but eventually his resistance was worn down.

Will Cougar wanted to lead a spirit walk for the three prophets. He had led such group walks many times at his camp, he said. He wanted to try to take the three of them back to Santa Pelagia, to that voice. Because there were things he was seeing in his visions, things he didn't understand, and one of them might. Because that might be the reason he was led to them.

Rinpoche thought it sounded like fun. Hill, like Deauchez, hated it. Deauchez was touched by his protectiveness, but Will Cougar only looked at the reporter with those steady black eyes that made one feel like an idiot.

In the end it was those eyes, and Rinpoche's frankly expectant ones, staring at him, that made Deauchez give in. He had blocked his vision. If it could give them any information at all, he had to try to face it.

So the lights were dimmed in the community room and they settled into a small circle. Rinpoche sat in a relaxed pose and fell into a meditative state at once. Will Cougar took Deauchez through a series of exercises to put him in a semiconscious state. For a while Deauchez fought the experience, sitting uncomfortably on the floor. This was a door he had worked long and hard to bolt shut. Now he was being asked to open it. He was terrified.

But the thing that made that door so frightening was that it *wanted* to fly open; there were things *pressing on it* from the other side. Will Cougar had only to calm Deauchez, convince him to put his hand on the latch . . .

. . . and the priest was gone.

He was walking through Maria Sanchez's field. It was nearly dusk. On every side of him bodies pressed. He fought to get through.

Excuse me, he said, please excuse me.

He could smell pungent sweat and the reek of onions. Somewhere in the distance an old woman was singing "Ave Maria" in a tremulous voice, the Latin swollen with Hispanic roundness.

A heavy, dark-haired mother with a one-year-old on one hip and a three-year-old clutching her thigh called out to him. Padre, *bless us. Bless my poor doomed children.*

He made the sign of a cross hurriedly and pushed on.

The people were praying, moaning, swaying, and the fear and anticipation were thick. Some were striking their chests with their fists in self-mortification. Others mumbled through rosaries, eyes rolled up to heaven. He'd heard the rumors in the streets earlier: that this was the last night, that perhaps the world would be granted a pardon, perhaps she would say it was just a warning, and oh the fear, fear, fear that she would not.

In his hand he clutched a small Mary statuette. He had brought her from Rome to make sure she was not altered, was not fixed. He clutched her tightly and pushed past the poor and the stinking, the meek, and the sweating. A child with big dark eyes stared up at him as he went by . . .

There, at the front of the crowd, was what he sought. There, some more palely Caucasian and more darkly exotic faces in the crowd up ahead. They were the ones he wanted to watch, but he could not focus on them as he should, note them, note who, note why, note what, because his attention was distracted by the cypress, the tree, the branches. For some reason it fascinated, pulled his eye.

He realized he was standing still, staring, had been for some time.

No! Something inside him bolted. This was not supposed to happen. Something was wrong. Why did he feel so flushed, so sick, was it the crowd, fear, hysteria? It was the crowd, must be, it was too tight, no air.

People were kneeling, crying, and someone behind him tugged at his coat to make him get down. His knees struck the dry brown dirt grass with the slow-motion thundering of Goliath falling. His brain was not functioning. He was sick, drugged, claustrophobic, and now he wanted only to get out, but he could barely stay erect on his knees, much less fight his way through the crowd. He moaned and trembled, pale and clammy like a woman about to faint.

Sick. I'm so sick so sick so sick so sick.

The crowd gasped as one. He managed to lift his weighted head and saw in the branches of the tree there was a light, a light, a light in the tree in the branches.

Then the field was gone, the earth was gone, the dirt beneath his knees was gone, and he was plummeting down, down, down into darkness; down, down, and the air was biting cold, cold as the grave. Terror consumed him, his brain, his reason, eating him alive, and below in the darkness were fire and flames and a city—hell, it was hell—he was falling into hell, screaming and . . .

The tree was there in front of him and above its branches such a sight—a being, a woman, her; it was the Virgin; it was the Blessed Womb, she of the divine seed, the Queen of Heaven, of Sorrows, of Tender Mercy. Black flowed around her, her face was white and thin and dewy, her hands folded neatly out of the dark, the dark, the black of her robe, and her eyes were light streaming, like holes with light streaming. She was God, divine, holy angel, sweet mother.

Mother, ah, ah! he wept. He tried to hide his eyes, but his lids had vanished. There was no turning from her presence. His heart was bursting in the unbearable terror and joy and ecstasy of her presence—mother!

Ah!

Her mouth opened, that jeweled mouth, and light streamed forth from her tongue. The light was burning, burning, burning his soul.

BEHOLD.

The words shook him; the voice was made of glass that cut through his defenses, his fear.

BEHOLD THOU CHOSEN PROPHET. CHOSEN OF GOD, CHOSEN AMONG MEN. THOU SEED, THOU WITNESS OF THE WORD OF GOD GIVEN UNTO MEN THIS DAY THROUGH HIS INTERCESSOR THE BLESSED MOTHER OF GOD, THE BLESSED VIRGIN, THE FEMALE ESSENCE DIVINE, THE COREDEMPTRIX, IMMACULATE CONCEPTION.

Her hands unfolded like a row of petals unfurling, long gleaming fingers to polished ivory palms. Deauchez felt something hot and wet; had he soiled himself? He looked down at his palms upturned just like hers where blood gushed. The statuette rolled to the ground slick with blood.

He wept, laughed, his heart broken open.

BECAUSE THOU HAST NOT TURNED THY HEART FROM WAR AND HATE IN FIVE THOUSAND YEARS, OH MAN, BE-

*CAUSE THOU HAS NOT LEARNED TO LOVE THE CRE-
ATIONS OF THY GOD, NEITHER THE EARTH NOR THE LIV-
ING THINGS UPON IT, NOR DOST THOU LOVE EVEN THY
FELLOW MAN, SO SHALL THE DIVINE EXPERIMENT END.*

*REVELATION 16:2. THE FIRST PLAGUE OF THE END-
TIMES, THE PLAGUE OF SORES, IS COMING. PROPHESY
IT TO THY FELLOW MEN THAT THEY SHOULDST KNOW
THY WITNESS IS TRUE. MAKE THY VOICE HEARD WITHIN
FOUR DAYS, THOU SEED, THOU WITNESS, OR THOU SHALT
FAIL IN THY DIVINE MISSION. OH MAN, REPENT, FOR THE
JUDGE IS COMING TO JUDGE THE PEOPLE. IT IS THE BE-
GINNING OF THE END AND NOTHING MAY STOP IT.*

*IN PREPARATION FOR JUDGMENT TAKE THYSELF,
MICHELE DEAUCHEZ, TO ROME AND GATHER THERE
THOSE OF LIKE FAITH, YEA ALL WHO WILL HEED THEE.
THERE AWAIT CHRIST'S RETURN AND THEE AND THY
FLOCK WILL BE BLESSED IN HIS SIGHT. FOR THY FAITH
THOU SHALT BE SPARED THE BITTER CUP, THE DREAD-
FUL FIRE, THE PAIN AND DARKNESS OF THE END-TIMES.
THIS IS THE MERCY OF OUR LORD.*

*Blood spilled down his face. It was in his eyes. His left side
ached and his shirt was heavy. He cried at the terrible, blank
wrath of the presence before him; the terrible, blank female
wrath; the apparition, the wrath of mother, grandmother, women,
and even then his mind was splitting and forgetting, seeking a
way out, tunneling through the cerebral maze of walls he had
built in his childhood, going to that black box where he hid just
such terrors.*

No, no, no, no, no, no, no, no.

*The blood, blood, blood, focus on the blood: bright red, real.
Below him somewhere on the dirt, grass, the statuette of Mary
was bleeding, gushing, like an artery severed, and whose blood
was that—where was it coming from?*

*THIS IS THE END OF THE WORD OF GOD. THOU SHALT
SOON BE NUMBERED AMONG THE SAINTS IN GLORY
WITH GOD AND ALL HIS ANGELS. HAVE COURAGE AND
FULFILL THY APPOINTED TASK, AMEN.*

*But the voice was already fading. He'd almost escaped it.
He'd go down, yes, into the darkness, down to hell if that was
what it took to escape the voice, the eyes, the mouth, the . . .*

* * *

He heard a familiar voice in his ear. Warm hand on his brow. He opened his eyes and did not know where or who he was. Something slick was on his hands and clothes, on the blanket beneath him. The floor was hard. The room was cold.

Where am I?

For a moment, he could not make sense of his surroundings, did not know the people hovering over him. There was a stabbing pain in his temple as his mind slipped into gear, and a dark face about him took on meaning, like a photograph coming into focus.

Simon, his friend, eyes filled with tears and compassion. "I think the bleeding's stopped. *Man!* He's lost a ton of blood. Can you see me? Do you know me? Father, *please!*"

And then someone else stuck their head in, a wizened little brown head, and it grinned at him. Deauchez felt his current reality jelling, not by any magic that the monk had, but because of the absurdity of that grin that could belong nowhere else but here and now.

"My goodness!" Rinpoche said excitedly. "Did you see it?"

"W-what?" Deauchez asked, finding his tongue. Hill groaned and squeezed his arm with relief.

"The rainbows," said Will Cougar. He pulled one of Deauchez's hands toward him gently and used the tail of his shirt to wipe at it. "It's stopped. The holes are closed."

Deauchez looked down at himself. "Oh," he said. He was covered with blood.

Rinpoche's monks arrived with a basin and cloths and began gently but persistently pushing their way in to clean Deauchez. Will Cougar held his ground. "Did you see the rainbows?" he asked.

Deauchez shook his head. Gentle hands wiped the blood from his face and hairline, opened his shirt. "No. Just . . . just the apparition, the Virgin, and some horrible place. Someplace like hell."

Will Cougar nodded knowingly. "Yes. I know this place." He turned to look at Rinpoche. "Did *you* see them?"

"Yes." Rinpoche nodded soberly. "I saw the rainbows."

Deauchez bore the monks' ministrations impatiently, trying to sit up. "What are you two talking about? *What* rainbows?"

"Yeah, what rainbows?" Hill asked. But he seemed to be having a hard time following the conversation. He kept staring at

Deauchez's hands. Deauchez looked down at them, too. As Will Cougar said, there were no wounds anywhere on him now. It was as if the blood had simply put itself on the wrong side of his skin.

Rinpoche held a finger up in the air. "Before we begin, I have a thought. You told me about the . . . what do they call them? Earthweb huts? Yes, and how they were used to distribute the poisons. There is one of these things that we pass by every day on our walk, okay? It's about a mile from here. Perhaps, Simon, you might lead an expedition to examine the hut while Michele is resting a bit? You have not done that yet, have you?"

"No," said Hill, pulling his eyes from Deauchez. "It's a good idea."

"Thank you." Rinpoche bowed. "Then I will send with you two monks and some tools, okay? All right?"

Hill looked torn. "Are you sure you're okay?" he asked Deauchez.

Deauchez took his hand and smiled. "Yes, Simon. Go ahead."

Deauchez's faithful Hawaiian shirt was finally gone—stained beyond recovery. The monks brought him pants and a warm sweater, and he slipped into the bathroom to put them on. When he emerged, Rinpoche and Will Cougar were in the kitchen talking.

"People are the Earth's soul," Will Cougar was saying. "If the soul is sick, the body becomes sick. For a long time, the Earth has been sick because of the people, but this is something new. This sickness is not just a weakness or a heartsickness. It is a *death*-sickness."

"Yes," sighed Rinpoche. "Very true."

"So how do we stop it?" Deauchez asked, slipping onto a stool.

"As in all medicine, to cure the sickness we first have to cure the soul," Will Cougar said. "And the soul must *want* to be cured."

"I'm sure people don't *want* to die. If we can make them understand that they don't *have* to."

"Michele," Rinpoche said gently, "we must tell not their *ears*, but their *hearts*. Then, if they still have the will to live, they will listen."

"Very well. How do we do that?"

Will Cougar looked at the monk.

"The rainbows," Rinpoche said.

The Earthweb hut was very much as the diagram on the web pictured it; a small, rounded, Fiberglas shell with a satellite receiver on top. The door fit snugly into the frame, and next to it was a keypad and keycard lock. Hill studied the situation for several minutes, then took a crowbar and began working at the tight seam around the door. It took a great deal of banging and prying just to insert the flat end. When Hill tired, the monks took turns. By the time they'd busted the door, Hill's muscles were shaking with fatigue.

Inside, the hut was clean, if slightly dusty. Equipment racks lined the walls, leaving only a five-foot path between them. Wires were stapled to the Fiberglas behind the racks. Some of them led to boxes farther along the racks, and others led to the hut's peak. At that pinnacle a large metal cover—about three feet by three feet—was attached to the ceiling.

Hill examined the racks, but the electrical components were unfathomable for the most part. There was what looked like a main computer controller with no monitor or keyboard attached. Servicemen probably brought portables, Hill thought. There were several radio and transmitting devices.

He reached the conclusion that the central box on the ceiling was where the "big stuff " was kept. He surveyed it from below; then, with the monks' help, he stepped on the wire racks to boost himself closer to it. The metal plate was attached with a number of oddly shaped screws. He called down for a hammer and screwdriver and began, gently, banging and prying at the casing.

Ten minutes later, the box cover lay bent and twisted on the floor. Hill's muscles were trembling as he perched on the wire rack. Sweat covered his brow. He swiped at it with a sleeve. "Okay, there's a five-inch round metal disk up here, right at the top. It's probably some kind of outlet because there's a tube coming into it, a one-inch tube that runs down . . ." He stooped. "Down along the wall to—yeah, see that large storage box over there?"

One of the monks went obediently to stand by it. He put a hand on it.

"No—don't touch it! I think the toxic spores were housed in there. And they come up this tube to be projected out."

The monk jerked away his hand.

"Um . . . let's see. There's also a smaller unit attached to the ceiling up here. It's a black metal box that looks really heavy. It has a silver plate on it . . . says 'Lasercorp.' "

The name sounded familiar. Hill began to let himself down and the monks helped him. He sat on a bare wedge of shelving to rest and wiped his brow again. "Lasercorp . . ."

Then he remembered where he'd seen something like it. Five years earlier he'd covered a laser light show in New York and was shown around the equipment. The guy in charge had proudly demonstrated a box similar to this one. A computer program told the box what patterns and colors to display, and the computer program had a front end not unlike a graphics program in which the light show could be designed.

"Must have used one like this in Santa Pelagia to cause the light in the trees," Hill muttered. "But why have one here?"

"What is it?" one of the monks asked.

"Lemme see if I can show you." Hill followed a cable from the box with his eyes, down, down. It entered a small device with a built-in monitor and keyboard. More cables ran out of it and went into what was obviously the main computer. But the laser light controller *was* on—its dull green screen said "RUN-NING," and *it* had a little keypad.

"What does it do?" the monk asked curiously.

"Just a minute," Hill said, typing with one finger.

"I listened again to the voice of the woman," Will Cougar was saying. "And afterward she disappeared and I saw the darkness and the Earth spinning out of its place in the heavens. Then a light appeared. That's when I saw the rainbows."

Deauchez looked at Rinpoche. "You saw the same thing?"

"Something similar. But rainbows, of course! Beautiful rainbows."

Deauchez frowned, upset. "I don't understand why I did not see it. Was it part of the message?"

Will Cougar shook his head firmly. "*No*. The rainbows are of true spirit."

"How did you both see it if it was not part of the programming?"

"Anyone can go to the spirit world. If they know how to open themselves to it," Will Cougar said.

"And if they know the way," the monk added. He tilted his head graciously at the shaman.

Deauchez was beginning to wonder about the value of his own theological training. "But how do the rainbows *help*? What do they *mean*?"

Lamba Rinpoche and Will Cougar looked at each other expectantly.

"Do *you* know?" Rinpoche asked.

Will Cougar's brow knit in a frown. "I was led here to find the answer."

"Well, my goodness, then we shall have to think very hard!"

The three of them thought.

"To our people, the rainbow is a symbol of hope," offered Will Cougar, "a new beginning. It is this way in your Bible, is it not?"

"*Oui.* God produced a rainbow after the great flood. He told Noah it was a promise that he would never destroy the Earth again."

"You see? Many people know this story, or one like it."

"But how could we get rainbows to appear?"

No one had an answer.

Deauchez sighed. "Perhaps we should discuss the message we are trying to convey. I have been thinking: What if we made a television broadcast? We could present our stories, uncover the conspiracy, and give our theory about the earthquakes. It may cause enough doubt to stop the activity for a time. And if it *does* stop, it will reinforce their belief that it's over, and there will be fewer quakes and so on—a *reverse* snowball."

"What proof do we have?" Rinpoche asked politely.

"Nothing physical," Deauchez admitted.

"Many people would not believe your ideas about the earthquakes. White men do not think like this—about the power of the mind and the spirit," Will Cougar said. "And I do not think they will believe in a conspiracy, either. Once people's minds are on a track, it takes something blinding to get them off of it. They are on this track now, as you have said. I believe your story, but I am already off the track. It echoes what I know in my heart. Your story will not convince anyone still on the track, not without proof."

Deauchez was frustrated by the blunt truth of it, but he assented with a sharp nod.

"While you and Simon were out investigating, I was keeping

a close eye on everything from our monastery here," Rinpoche said. "Although I did not choose to participate in my part of the message, I knew something was happening. You see what I mean?"

"Of course," Deauchez said.

"Well, I was just thinking about the way Mal Abbas announced himself. Do you remember?"

"I did not see the broadcast itself, but I know it came later on. I was in New York by then."

"Oh, goodness! Well, he came forward on the TV. He said God told him especially to wait until day thirteen."

Deauchez thought about it, his hands working silently on the table.

"The world knows there are still two prophets missing, thanks to the good efforts of Simon and those like him. They have been told there are Twenty-Four and, so far, they only have twenty-two!" Rinpoche smiled. "You and I, Michele, we are the two who are missing."

It was so obvious yet so completely unforeseen: That his being a prophet might in some way be fortuitous instead of simply horrifying came as a revelation. "*Oui!* But . . . if they would not believe us about the conspiracy, why would they believe that we are prophets?"

"Why did they believe Mal Abbas?" asked the monk, raising his shoulders. "Because they were *expecting* more prophets to appear. Yes? You see? They are not *expecting* someone to uncover a conspiracy. And also, they believed because he had an acknowledged prophet, the Sufi master, to say that he was telling the truth!" Rinpoche looked meaningfully at the shaman. "And *we* have Will Cougar!"

Will Cougar frowned a little. "I have not made myself public."

"Not as public, perhaps, as that Baptist person. But your likeness and name have been in all the papers. I have seen it myself. They *will* believe you. And therefore they will believe *us*, as long as we stay . . . how did you put it, my friend? . . . *on the track*."

"But what do we say?" Deauchez asked excitedly. For the first time in a long time, he had a spark of hope. "We can't simply tell them: 'Stop believing the apocalypse is here and the earthquakes will stop.' "

"No. We cannot explain it to their *conscious* minds. We must reach their *subconscious* minds." Rinpoche rose and walked over to the window. He stood looking out for a moment, toward the hut. "But perhaps we should talk about *how* to reach the people. How would we get this broadcast out?"

"It would have to be aired on all stations, all around the world," Will Cougar said. "You would need a lot of power to do something like that."

"Simon must have connections," Deauchez said. "If he can get it on WWN, the other stations would pick it up."

Will Cougar shook his head. "Things are very bad out there. Even on the radio, many stations are no longer on the air. I do not think we can count on news moving as fast as it once did."

"I think you are underestimating the difficulties, dear one," Rinpoche said regretfully. "Yes, I am quite sure we will not be able to do anything like this on our own."

Deauchez winced as pain lanced his temple, the by-now familiar stress alarm. The monk was right, of course. How long had he and Hill struggled to get *their* message out, even to a newspaper, to no avail? His sense of hope evaporated.

"*You* know who could help us, Michele. Do you not?"

Deauchez looked blankly at the back of the monk's robe for a moment, trying to figure out what he meant. He looked at the Native American, who was also rising and stretching. Will Cougar did not look confused at all.

"*Who?* " Deauchez demanded.

Rinpoche turned. "Who can get us on all stations at once, perhaps even around the world?"

Deauchez shrugged helplessly. If he and Hill had known that, this would all have ended long ago.

The monk smiled and walked over to him. He placed a hand on the priest's chest. "Do not think with your *prejudices*; think beyond them. It is a simple question."

Deauchez looked up at the monk, his brows knit in bewilderment. He tried to do as the monk suggested and gasped. "No!"

"Yes, Michele. The president of the United States is the only one holding this authority at the moment."

Deauchez gawked at his companions, amazed that they could be so calm. He realized that they had no idea. Despite listening to his story they obviously did not *begin* to comprehend. "Anthony Cole? He would kill us in a heartbeat if he even knew where we were!"

"You think of him as the enemy." Rinpoche sighed. "That is useless. Do you know what Buddhists say? They say 'my enemy is my teacher.' "

Deauchez got up, shaking his head doggedly. "Anthony Cole is a *mass murderer*! Compared with him, Hitler was an altar boy!"

Rinpoche frowned sadly. "That may be true, but it will not help us to think about this. We must think about our purpose. You understand? Is our purpose to stop the earthquakes? Because, I can assure you, right now that is *President Cole's* highest purpose. Do you know what I'm saying?"

Deauchez looked from Rinpoche's expectant face to Will Cougar's placid one. He was surprised that the shaman did not protest. As if reading his mind, Will Cougar said matter-of-factly, "Without opening the channels, we cannot reach the people."

Deauchez shook his head adamantly, his face hot.

"You are afraid," Rinpoche said, placing a wiry arm around his shoulder. "I understand. But I think, perhaps, we should take a walk now, yes? Okay? It is time for us to go see what our good friend Simon has discovered at the hut."

Will Cougar was already heading for the door. Deauchez followed numbly, his mind in turmoil.

They had walked a half mile or so up the mountain path when a certain realization struck Deauchez. He'd been dazed from the hypnosis when the suggestion was made to go check out the hut, and he'd been busy with other thoughts ever since. Now something—perhaps it was the distant sound of a helicopter—reawakened what Hill always referred to as Deauchez's paranoia.

The priest stopped dead in his tracks. "They broke into the hut!"

"Yes, dear one," Rinpoche said over his shoulder, not bothering to stop.

"But that is—it—it must be *filled* with silent alarms!"

Deauchez pushed past Will Cougar and Rinpoche roughly, staring up into the sky. Yes, the helicopters were louder now. There had to be half a dozen of them. Deauchez saw the first set of blades rising over a distant peak.

"Ah!" said Rinpoche, "more visitors!"

"Mother of God!" Deauchez cried. He began to run.

As he rounded the bend he got his first glimpse of the hut and of the rainbow, glowing from mountain to mountain in a huge arc of fire.

CHAPTER 28

Anthony Cole answered the Prime One link on his desk. "Peter?"

"It's me. Listen, we had an alarm go off at an EWH in Texas. We just picked up the intruders." There was a pause. "You'll never believe who it was."

The agitation in his brother's voice told him everything the location did not. "Lamba Rinpoche."

"Right! But *with* him . . ."

"Deauchez and Hill."

"Yes!" Peter sounded amazed at his brother's guesswork. "Will Cougar was with them, too."

"My, my." Cole settled back in his chair. The sense of relief he would have felt days before was not there. No, Deauchez and Hill's capture was moot at this point. But he was curious about the three of them being together—Deauchez, Rinpoche, and Cougar. Despite everything, he was still interested enough in the plan's psychology to be curious about that. "They're in custody?"

"We have them all right—at our ranch near Amarillo. My first response was to clean them immediately."

Cole picked up a pen and tapped the desk. "No. We'll want to examine them—particularly Deauchez."

"I know. Louise suggested the same thing. But, Anthony, there's something else. I mean, this—this is complete bullshit, I know, but . . ." There was a heavy pause. "They insist that they need to see *you* right away. They claim they can explain . . . Anthony, they're *claiming* . . ."

But Cole suddenly knew. "I'm on my way."

AMARILLO, TEXAS

Amarillo was chokingly dry and cursedly barren, giving new insight into the phrase "great American dustbowl" for those who were seeing it for the first time. The huge ranch was on a wasteland stretch that sustained only a scrub brush dressing on phyllo-like layers of dusty soil. The location was miles away from prying eyes. And although this was undoubtedly the grounds for its engagement, its blasted fruitlessness seemed to Deauchez like a perfect setting for their first official meeting with the Red Scepter.

They had landed on helicopter pads, but the ranch supported a runway as well. From the small window in their cement cell, Deauchez could see the staff at full military-style bustle out there, at the airstrip.

He turned from the window, his face stricken. *"He's coming."*

They were searched again and taken across the courtyard to the big house, an enormous log cabin decorated with elk horns and Indian relics. They were put in a room where a circle of tan leather chairs awaited—one each for Rinpoche, Deauchez, Cougar, and Hill. Three stood poignantly empty. Armed guards were stationed at the doors.

No one had spoken to them this time—a relief after the relentless questioning they'd experienced on arrival. Nor did any of them speak; the circumstances were too serious for that. So they sat in the room in silence. The silence was deep enough for Deauchez to hear the clock ticking down the hall. It was deep enough for him to hear his pounding pulse. He caught Hill's eye and understood intimately the mix of panic and disbelief he saw there. They were in the lion's maw.

From outside came the low sounds of an airplane's approach.

Long, painful minutes later the double doors opened and Anthony Cole entered the room. He was followed by a younger man and—to Deauchez's surprise—Dr. Janovich. Cole was in charge of the situation at once. He assessed his guests with cool hazel eyes as he crossed the room and entered the circle. He approached the monk and held out a fine-boned hand.

"Good afternoon, Lamba Rinpoche. I'm Anthony Cole."

Rinpoche rose and shook his hand, offering a smile and a bow. "Thank you for seeing us, Mr. President."

Will Cougar shook Cole's hand, too. His face, as usual, was impassive, but his black eyes were wary, appraising.

Then Cole was standing in front of Deauchez. "Father Deauchez. Your bravery and ingenuity have intrigued me. I'm glad to have the chance to meet you." Cole's eyes were surprisingly animated and not at all spiteful. Yet underneath Deauchez sensed the cold—sensed it ran deep. He flushed, tongue-tied, and managed only a sharp nod. But he did shake Cole's hand—smooth, cool, soft. It was like touching the hand of Satan himself.

Cole moved on. "Simon Hill. You're probably the most tenacious reporter in the United States, Mr. Hill."

"Yes, sir, I am," Hill said. His tone held a trace of a threat. He shook Cole's hand quickly and sat back down.

Cole introduced Janovich and his brother, Peter. Janovich glared at Deauchez and Hill with barely masked hatred. Cole motioned for the doors to be closed, and the Secret Service agents and guards filed out. The only ones left were those who looked in from the veranda doors and the windows.

"The room is soundproof," Cole said, "which is appropriate, because this discussion is extremely sensitive. I trust you will respect this opportunity, and I *hope* you have something meaningful to say, as you claim."

He walked behind his own chair and stood, hands resting lightly on its back. It might have been construed as a power gesture—that he alone would be left standing—if he were not so obviously in control already.

Hill spoke first. "If this discussion is so sensitive, what happens when the doors *open*?"

"That depends entirely on the results of the discussion, Mr. Hill," Cole said, with no trace of malice.

Hill glanced at Deauchez with an "oh, shit" expression. Deauchez tried to reassure him with a smile.

"Gentlemen," Cole said, leaning forward, "let me be brutally honest. The world is in a profound crisis. Either you are part of the solution, or you mean nothing to us whatsoever." He looked at each of them with solemn intent. "Some of you hate me . . . us. It doesn't matter. I have no interest in threatening or cajoling you. My only concern has been—and is most emphatically at the moment—to save humankind from extinction."

Deauchez wanted to laugh out loud at the audacity of that

statement. But Lamba Rinpoche said, "We, too, have this goal. Therefore our interests are united."

"I *hope* that is your goal."

"It is," Deauchez said bitterly. "Even if we have to make a deal with the devil to do it."

"My sentiments exactly. You say you have information about the earthquakes and volcanoes. I'd like to hear it."

"First tell me this," Deauchez said, sitting forward on the edge of his chair. "At Santa Pelagia there were over a dozen stigmatic events and instances of statues and icons bleeding in the town. You didn't plan that—did you?"

Janovich looked at Cole and he nodded at her. She responded icily. "*Three* stigmatics were planted: Sanchez, Daunsey, and you, Father Deauchez. It is, after all, a *Catholic* phenomenon."

"And the statues were not your doing?"

Janovich shook her head. She answered dismissively. "Such things have manifested before around stigmatics, usually faked, if my perusal of the literature is any indication."

"Usually," Deauchez agreed. "But not at Santa Pelagia. The 'unplanted' cases of stigmata were not faked either. The fact is, more phenomena appeared than you planned for. Did it not occur to you that a similar overreaction might continue—might *escalate* with the appearance of the signs?"

"Please continue, Father Deauchez," Cole said, his face betraying nothing.

Deauchez and Lamba Rinpoche explained what they believed the mass hysteria was now doing: fulfilling the countdown, anticipating and subconsciously producing the seventh sign. Throughout their argument Janovich rolled her eyes, looking at Cole as if to conspire with him in her ridicule. But the president ignored her. He left the circle and went to the window.

"It's absurd to suggest that thought processes—subconscious or otherwise—could in any way affect the movements of the Earth's tectonic plates," Janovich said with skin-mottled belligerence. "There's not a single shred of evidence that man has anything remotely *like* a capacity to—"

"No?" Deauchez mocked. "Yet in your representation to the World Psychiatric Conference in 1990 you yourself demonstrated that power! Flesh burned when ice was placed on it—skin unfazed by hot coals! You yourself implanted the suggestion of stigmata in the prophets and saw it appear at your whim. How can you say that the mind is incapable of affecting physical reality?"

"Well . . . yes, but affecting your own body through some kind of biochemical feedback is quite a different matter than—"

"What about the statues?" Hill broke in impatiently. "They couldn't have been caused by 'biochemical feedback.' "

Janovich glared at the reporter with murder in her eyes. There were still traces of bruises on her face, Deauchez saw; shadows across her cheek. He remembered, with a start, that they had killed her husband. It was no use trying to convince Janovich of anything.

"*Mr.* Cole," Deauchez said, trying to sound calm, "you're a businessman. You know that panic on Wall Street can cause a feared event to become reality—if everyone thinks the market will go down and they pull out, then it *does* go down. There have been philosophers who argued that reality is only that which we all *agree* that it is. Perhaps they are right. Perhaps our minds and our world are linked in ways we don't understand."

"Superstitious poppycock," Janovich sneered.

"Doctor, Father Deauchez—*please,*" Cole said. "I think I understand the argument." He stared out the window and they waited. The clock down the hall ticked on and on.

"I'm afraid I agree with our guests, Doctor," Cole said. "There is a connection. We had unanticipated phenomena appear at Santa Pelagia. Now we have this new problem—a 'sign' that we did not stage appearing."

"It isn't a *sign*," Peter said, shaking his head.

" 'And the seventh angel poured out his vial into the air,' " quoted Deauchez, " 'and there was a great earthquake, such as was not since men were upon the earth, so mighty an earthquake, and so great.' "

" 'And every island fled away, and the mountains were not found,' " the president finished. "Haven't you been reading your Bible, Peter?"

"It's coincidence!"

Cole spun from the window and walked toward them with a resolved expression. "So you keep telling me. But I've yet to hear any better theories about what's going on. In fact, I haven't heard any other theories at all."

He stopped near Deauchez and Hill, looked at them coldly. "I suppose you want me to announce that the apocalypse is a sham?"

"Not necessarily," Rinpoche offered with a tentative smile. "Another option would be to suggest that there has been a reprieve. Yes? You see?"

"We know you would never agree to anything outside your own best interests," Deauchez said, with some contempt, "however twisted those interests might be. Therefore it *is* possible that we can stop the panic without uncovering your . . . your plot."

"We need you to set up the global emergency alert system," Hill said.

"So *you* want to go on the air?" Cole seemed taken aback. "Why would I let you do that? We can compose a 'reprieve' message well enough ourselves."

"Uh, no, you can't," Hill pointed out with obvious relish. "You've done too good a job of hiding your involvement. 'President Cole' doesn't know God's will. The prophets do."

"Excuse me," said Rinpoche, "but it is a matter of convincing not only the mind but the *soul*. Remember, you have the benefit of having the two final unannounced prophets sitting right here in this room."

Cole's eyes narrowed in surprised appreciation.

"Yes," Rinpoche said, smiling. "It is time for Father Deauchez and myself to make our debuts."

"And we will need to use the rainbows," Will Cougar added.

Janovich took a sharp breath.

"How did you know about that?" Cole asked, his face guarded.

"They triggered the Lasercorp box in the hut," Peter explained. "The rainbow was up when we got there."

Janovich uttered a smug, spiteful laugh. "Well, forget it! We dropped it from the prophets' programming before we even began."

"Was it s'posed to be one of the signs?" Hill asked.

"Originally, the rainbows were to be a termination fail-safe," Cole said bluntly. "A way to call off the prophets if we had to. We decided not to use it, but the Lasercorp hardware was already installed."

"Why did you decide not to use it?" Deauchez asked, studying Cole intently.

"Why?" Cole smiled with an air of tragic bemusement. "First, because the lasers work only if there's cloud cover for the light to bounce off of, so there were technological issues we never resolved."

"And?" Deauchez probed.

Across the circle, Janovich coughed nervously.

"Yes, *and,*" Cole said, with a breath of a sigh. "You think we're monsters. You're wrong. We dropped it from the plan because I feared that if we *had* a panic button, we would be tempted to use it." He walked back to the window. "Things were going to get ugly. No matter how much we'd prepared ourselves for it . . . we *are* only human."

Deauchez couldn't see Cole's face, for the president had turned away quite deliberately. But he thought he knew what Cole meant. Cole meant that the *other* members of the Red Scepter were only human. They might go a little green once the massive deaths were right before their eyes. Cole couldn't take that chance, so he'd made sure there was no way to stop it once it had begun.

"Gee, plenty of cloud cover, as it turns out," Hill said dryly.

"Why—I believe you're right, Mr. Hill. The volcanic ash." Cole seemed to find this touch of irony amusing.

"It doesn't matter," Janovich insisted, pushing back her hair with a shaking hand. "If we'd programmed the rainbows we could use them, but the simple fact is that we didn't. The rainbows' appearance wouldn't mean a thing to the prophets."

"It does not have to," Will Cougar said. "It will mean something to the people."

Cole leaned back against the window frame. "Mmmm. I think I have a clear picture of what you're suggesting."

"*No,* Anthony!" Peter protested.

Cole merely glanced at him and continued. "I don't know that I buy into your theory about the seismic activity. But . . . to be honest . . . I can't see how your plan could hurt either. Very well. We'll prepare a script. But I warn you: If any of you deviate from the program *at all*—the broadcast, and your lives, will be brought to an abrupt end."

Cole straightened up and glanced at his watch. "We must meet with our people before we can set a time. Perhaps early next week . . ."

Deauchez rose, his fists clenched at his side. "*No.* We will broadcast *now,* today. And the Santarém antidote, this too goes out, *with* the broadcast. No more deaths, Mr. Cole. It ends here."

Cole turned his head slowly and looked at Deauchez with a kind of hostile amusement at his hubris. Peter Cole was not amused. He stood up, sputtering. "Who do you think you are? Who are you to tell the president what to do?"

"Sit down, Peter," Cole said quietly. Peter glanced at him imploringly but sat.

"You have no idea what we're trying to accomplish," Cole said to Deauchez.

"Yeah? Well, *I'd* like to know. What exactly are you trying to accomplish?" Hill asked, frowning angrily.

Cole sucked in his cheeks and considered the reporter. "Mmmm. I suppose since you've read about Project Apocalypse on our host, you might as well understand the motivation behind it. The media—I'm sorry, Mr. Hill, but it's true—reports on everything but what's real. The majority of the people on this planet have no idea what kind of crisis we've been in—how close we've been to the brink."

Deauchez knew what was coming. Like a teenager being sat down for a stern talking-to, he felt anger and resentment in advance at anything Cole might have to say. He glanced at Hill to share this emotion, but Hill was watching Cole with interest. He wasn't exactly his old, information-sucking self, but he was listening.

"Well, the Red Scepter knew," Cole said. "Since the 1920s we've been tracking the population explosion, the depletion of the world's finite resources, the political and financial tides. Without action, we were facing complete meltdown by 2050. Few politicians would admit it because it's bad for business, but the greenhouse effect—unchecked—would cause global climate change. We were looking at worldwide crop failure. In fact, we had already begun to see it, as you know perfectly well. With the overpopulation of the Earth, the only possible outcome was complete anarchy—global war as people fought for food, violent revolutions. And with the nuclear arsenal of the cold war on the market for any revolutionary or terrorist with an agenda, what do you think would be the end result?"

"Why, that's absurd!" Deauchez jeered. "You fear massive death and destruction, so you *cause* massive death and destruction?"

"Exactly our choice," Cole said. He turned his eyes to Deauchez in a challenge. "Massive population reduction *was* inevitable. If we did nothing, it would happen. At least with Project Apocalypse we had the chance to *control* the destruction, to use it as an opportunity to change the world for the better, to put people and policies in key positions so that we could take our world into a new golden age."

"*Golden age?* Is that what you call this?" Deauchez mocked.

Cole smiled grimly. "Of course not. This is only the necessary price for what comes next. Can you imagine a world where there are no national boundaries? No more war—*ever?* Do you think there's any other way we'll survive as a technologically oriented species? And what about quality of life? You were in India a few weeks ago, Father Deauchez. The standard of living for most people on this planet is unrelenting poverty. In the new world every single human being will be clothed, housed, educated, and well fed. Or doesn't that matter to you? Are such concerns just lip service for you religious? A decent standard of living for all is simply not possible with six billion people on the planet—not to mention where we were *headed* with population. And it's certainly not possible with the world's old partisan leadership. In most countries bribery and corruption are rampant. In the West, politicians are stonewalled to death by special-interest groups. It's a joke!" Cole's words—and his face—were dark with passion.

"Whatever your interests are," Deauchez said carefully, "there are other ways to—"

"Oh, yes! There are ways to do things nicely, *politely*—and we've tried them all! Over the centuries the R.S. has supported all kinds of efforts. In the last century alone there was Planned Parenthood, Greenpeace, even the U.N. And what has been the result?"

Deauchez glowered and folded his arms.

"No answer, Father? Well, I'll tell you—next to nothing. People think this world is moving forward—that we're progressing as rational beings! But for every move we try to take forward—legalized abortion, for example—there's a conservative movement poised to sweep us back into superstition and ignorance!"

Cole was speaking fervently, and it was so odd to see him like that. Every picture or news clip Deauchez had ever seen of him matched the Cole that had walked into this room—cool and white as marble.

Deauchez looked down at his hands, which were twisting in his lap. He forced them to be still. "So you tried to kill all the conservatives? Well, I'm afraid it will do you little good. They *will* be back. You cannot change human nature."

"No." Cole ran a hand through his dark hair, making an effort to regain composure. "But then, they will not be given much voice in the new world."

Deauchez glanced at his friends. Hill's lips were pursed in a frown, his eyes distant and withdrawn. Rinpoche was looking down at his lap. Will Cougar, as usual, was unreadable.

Deauchez spoke softly, his anger like a steadfast flame inside him that would not be moved but didn't require any shouting either. "I don't know what the future would have held. Upheaval? Perhaps. But you had no right to try to impose *your* ideals on the rest of humanity. You had no right to take even a single human life."

"No right?" Cole gave a huff of a laugh. "No, I had a *duty*. I wish I could afford your idealism, Father Deauchez, but idealists haven't saved this world. The Red Scepter believes that we are in charge of our *own* destiny. We won't stick our heads in the sand and wait for gods or aliens to save us. Sometimes what needs to be done is not easy. Sometimes a man like myself is necessary."

"Yes, well, you have clearly done so much for mankind already," Deauchez said with quiet brutality.

The president sucked in his cheeks. There was a flush of outrage on his pale skin, a burning clarity in his gaze. Cole and Deauchez glared at each other like that, across a chasm that neither one of them could or would ever cross.

Lamba Rinpoche stood up and bowed. "Perhaps we can get back to the broadcast? Yes?"

Cole turned his eyes to the monk.

"I'm afraid, Mr. President, that Father Deauchez does have a point. We can stop this only if those who are left have the will . . . yes, *the will* to live. And so you see, the dead, too, have something to say about it! The dead tug at the living. The force of their pull is already great. The time will come when it will be irresistible, if it is not already. We must act as soon as possible. Yes, right away."

Cole did not answer at once. He turned back to the window and just stood there, gazing out. The six men and women in the room watched the lines of his back and waited. Peter was shaking his head vigorously. Janovich appeared frozen with indecision. From the faces of his companions, Deauchez knew they were feeling what he felt: that the very fate of the world depended on how well they had argued their case.

When Cole faced them again, surrender was too strong a word for what was in those eyes, but recognition of his vulnerability was there.

"Very well," he said. "So be it."

EMERGENCY SYSTEM BULLETIN
8:00 P.M. AMARILLO, 2:00 A.M. GREENWICH, 9 P.M. EAST COAST

They began running the announcement of a coming emergency alert an hour before it aired. In Sedona, Santa Pelagia, Harlem, and many of the other prophet centers, they gathered around portable TVs and radios. In New York City the emergency alert symbol was posted in Times Square waiting for transmission. WWN was still doggedly on the air these days, which proved that ratings could solve just about anything. They played the announcement immediately and spent the hour waiting for it by discussing theories about what the announcement could be with anyone and everyone they could get on the phone—a digital clock ticking down in the corner. Stations that had been off-line for days sprang to life with the emergency alert banner and tone. In homes around the country and around the world, those who were still huddled inside sat around the TV as their ancestors had once sat around the fire on cold, windy nights.

When the countdown finished, the banner flickered.

This is the emergency broadcasting system.

This is not a test. Please stand by.

TEN
NINE
EIGHT
SEVEN
SIX
FIVE
FOUR
THREE
TWO
ONE

Video of Anthony Cole. He looked handsome, as always, and intensely serious.

"This is Anthony Cole, president of the United States. I have an important message for you. It's good news at last. Early this

morning there was a breakthrough at the Health Aid International laboratory. We have tested a new formula on several patients in stage three of Santarém and their immediate improvement was nothing short of miraculous. What I'm telling you is that we believe we have a cure. It will be disseminated as quickly as we can manufacture it."

The president paused to let that sink in.

"That's not the only reason for this broadcast. A well-respected reporter came to me today, and I agreed that what he had to say deserved to reach you as quickly as possible. Please listen, my fellow citizens, and have hope."

Cole lowered his head dramatically, and the picture cut to four men seated at a newsroom counter. Around the counter sat a dark-haired Caucasian priest in clerical garb, an Asian monk in a saffron robe, and a Native American and an African-American, both in jeans and casual shirts. Behind them were the call letters KFOX 8.

The African-American spoke, reading from a paper in front of him. *"This is Simon Hill. Many of you know my work as lead reporter for the* New York Times *on the Santa Pelagia story. You may recall that there were twenty-four prophets anticipated by prophecy. Two have never declared themselves. I've spent the past few weeks tracking them down."*

The reporter paused and wiped at his forehead nervously. He was visibly sweating under the lights.

"They are Father Michele Deauchez, a priest who was sent to Santa Pelagia by the Vatican, and Lamba Rinpoche, a respected Tibetan Buddhist monk and teacher. I have here with me also the prophet Will Cougar of Washington."

"I am Will Cougar," said the Native American. *"I have agreed to speak to the public in order to fulfill my task. These two men were with me in Santa Pelagia. They received the vision. They are the last two prophets."*

"I am Father Michele Deauchez," said the priest, his face white, his pupils so dilated they appeared black. *"I was told by the Virgin Mary not to come forward with my story until day twenty-six."*

"And I, too," said the monk in a breathy voice, *"was to wait until day twenty-six."*

"The president helped us arrange this broadcast so we could

reach all of you as quickly as possible," Simon Hill said. *"Listen now to the message of the last two prophets of Santa Pelagia."*

The television audience, as one, leaned forward. The silence was absolute in each home and across entire chrome-and-canvas communities where people were gathered. People stopped breathing to listen, as if their lives hung on the words. Their eyes were locked on the men on the screen.

The camera cut to a close-up of the monk.

"I was told that many would have died by day twenty-six, and it has come to pass. My brothers and sisters, God sent us warning that we would be facing an apocalypse of destruction, and we have faced it." The monk smiled sadly. *"It was not his will that caused this. In the past twenty-six days God simply turned his back and left us to reap what we have sown."*

"On day twenty-six," the priest added in a dazed voice, *"the cup of God's sorrow will overflow and he will intercede to save his people."*

"The night has ended," Rinpoche said. *"The dawn has come."*

"He will give us a sign of this promise," said the priest, *"in the skies around the globe."*

He held up his hands, palms together in a prayerful gesture. He seemed to be looking off-camera, his eyes remote.

"Go and look," said Will Cougar. *"The sign will appear everywhere. A sign of cleansing. The world is broken, purified, and reborn. This is his promise."*

"The Earth will recover from her death throes," said the monk. *"She will regain her harmony and balance. This is his promise."*

On the priest's hands, something dark appeared. The camera panned in for a better look. A thick line of blood was erupting through the flesh on the back of his hand, running down his wrist, down into his sleeve.

The camera moved up to his face, where crimson globs were oozing from the pores of his pale forehead. His eyes were focused on some distant sight and he was crying soundlessly, his face transformed by something wonderful and horrible, something his eyes beheld that they did not want to see. Words came from him in a broken stream.

"He has not . . . abandoned us. This is his promise. Blessed . . . blessed is God, our heavenly father, creator of the Universe."

In Sedona, an image broke upon the ash-enshrouded dusk in

bright colors, arcing across the heavens. The light was brilliant
and improbable, dancing on the air. The people rose from their
television screens or put down their radios and stood, staring upward. For a heartbeat, everyone only looked at the image, wanting to be sure. And when they were sure, strangers clutched at
each other and wept out loud.

In New York, rainbows rose above the night skyline like jewel-
encrusted moons. Over Washington, and Alabama, Florida and
Texas, the lights blossomed like opening lotuses. In Tokyo and
Munich they spread out over the shrouded, gray daytime sky like
translucent parachutes. People went to their doors, some opening them for the first time in weeks, and wandered into the
streets to see them. There were high places where three or four
could be seen, and low places where just the tops of them peeked
out over yellow trees, mountains, or suburbs. They shimmered
on lakes and crested cityscapes light and dark. They shone in remote areas where only hermits and coyotes were there to see
them. Over rural highways packed with cars bound for nowhere,
they emerged from the darkness like glowing ghosts.

And everywhere they were greeted with joy and wonder.

When the broadcast was over, the four of them went outside
onto a second-floor balcony and watched the fire glowing in the
sky. Down below, in the parking lot, the men who had escorted
them to the station stood mute, their wards forgotten, their bodies leached of menace as they stared upward, weapons and intent
slack.

The balcony was small and Deauchez, weak. He leaned
against the warm bulk of Hill, still feeling a little dazed. On his
right, Rinpoche grasped his elbow with surprising strength.

"It's over," Deauchez whispered.

Hill exhaled a shaky breath. "Yeah. Thank God. I hate being
on TV."

"That's not what I meant, Simon. You know what I meant."
Deauchez pulled himself up a bit straighter and looked at Hill.
The reporter's forehead smoothed out for the first time in days.

"Yeah. I guess I do," Hill said softly. "It's been a long haul,
Father."

"It's not exactly how we pictured it, is it?"

The reporter did not seem to share Deauchez's disappointment.
He gazed out at the sky, his eyes moist, his face peaceful. "You
know what, Father? If it'll end it, that's good enough for me."

The priest turned to follow his gaze. Perhaps it was only that the fog was finally lifting from his self-induced trance, or perhaps his wounded pride had been in the way, but for the first time he really saw the rainbows—not as objects, not as tactics of Cole or Janovich, but as something more, luminescent with a fire that was more than human, that was magical. Hill was right. He, Deauchez, had spent so much of the past few weeks railing at God in his mind, so furious that God was not going to step in and do something, furious that he could have believed in a God that would not step in and do something. But the four of them had found each other, and they'd somehow convinced Cole to end it. If that wasn't miraculous, then nothing was. Those fingertip traces of lights against the indigo hue of sky—they were God's answer.

He was flooded with a jumble of emotions: tremendous relief, quaking gratitude, love for Hill who had fought with him for so long, and for Rinpoche and Will Cougar, too, for their strength and wisdom. Those disparate emotions merged with the individual colors in the air, until his being was a palette of surging hues. The intensity of the moment was almost unbearable. Rocked by the tides within, he felt the peaks of first one emotion then the next until he found the bottom of that palette. There, anchoring and defining all else, was a deep, bruised mourning for what had been lost, for the price that had been paid.

Tears rose up in his eyes.

Rinpoche squeezed his elbow gently. "There, there. You see, dear Michele? God has not forgotten us."

"But why did he wait so long?" Deauchez asked, his words choked. "Why did he let them go so far?"

Rinpoche cocked his head to one side and considered it. "Sometimes . . . sometimes our greatest flaws are our only salvation."

The words were low, thoughtful. Deauchez wiped at his eyes. "I do not understand you."

"No. It is very difficult to understand, is it not?"

Deauchez looked past the monk's small, round head at the Native American and saw on Will Cougar's sober face an implacable knowing. The shaman nodded once in agreement.

"But . . ." Deauchez began.

Hill slipped his arm around Deauchez's shoulder. "It's okay, Father."

To his surprise, Deauchez found that it *was* okay. He didn't have to understand. Perhaps, just this once, he could take it on faith. He didn't know what the future would bring. Yet, he felt a distinct impression of renewal about it, a sense that the tide had turned against Cole, that the future would not be what Cole had anticipated any more than he had anticipated this. And somewhere along the way, Deauchez had learned to trust his instincts.

He smiled gratefully at his friend. The hand on his shoulder was warm and passive; Hill's mouth smiled back, but not his eyes. Something had gone out of him. Deauchez had known it for some time. If Cole allowed them to walk away from this, Hill would not write about it; maybe not for a long while, maybe not ever. Simon Hill was not a reporter anymore. He had found a truth deeper than the world was ready to hear, and that left him with little to say.

And was he, Deauchez, still a priest? Yes. He found that he wanted very much to be.

He spoke shyly: "Does anyone mind if we pray?"

DEL REY® ONLINE!

The Del Rey Internet Newsletter...

A monthly electronic publication e-mailed to subscribers and posted on the rec.arts.sf.written Usenet newsgroup and on our Del Rey Books Web site (www.randomhouse.com/delrey/). It features hype-free descriptions of books that are new in the stores, a list of our upcoming books, special promotional programs and offers, announcements and news, a signing/reading/convention-attendance calendar for Del Rey authors and editors, "In Depth" essays in which professionals in the field (authors, artists, cover designers, salespeople, etc.) talk about their jobs in science fiction, a question-and-answer section, and more!

Subscribe to the DRIN: send a blank message to
join-drin-dist@list.randomhouse.com

The Del Rey Books Web Site!

We make a lot of information available on our Web site at
www.randomhouse.com/delrey/

- all back issues and the current issue of the Del Rey Internet Newsletter
- sample chapters of almost every new book
- detailed interactive features for some of our books
- special features on various authors and SF/F worlds
- reader reviews of some upcoming books
- news and announcements
- our Works in Progress report, detailing the doings of our most popular authors
- and more!

If You're Not on the Web...

You can subscribe to the DRIN via e-mail (send a blank message to join-drin-dist@list.randomhouse.com) or read it on the rec.arts.sf.written Usenet newsgroup the first few days of every month. We also have editors and other representatives who participate in America Online and CompuServe SF/F forums and rec.arts.sf.written, making contact and sharing information with SF/F readers.

Questions? E-mail us...

at delrey@randomhouse.com (though it sometimes takes us a little while to answer).